BETTY ZANE

and

TO THE LAST MAN

FORGE BOOKS BY ZANE GREY

Betty Zane
Desert Gold
The Desert of Wheat
George Washington, Frontiersman
The Heritage of the Desert
Ken Ward in the Jungle
The Last of the Plainsmen
The Last Trail
The Lone Star Ranger
The Man of the Forest
The Mysterious Rider
The Rainbow Trail
The Redheaded Outfield
Riders of the Purple Sage
Roping Lions in the Grand Canyon
The Short-Stop
The Spirit of the Border
To the Last Man
Western Colors (omnibus)
Western Legends (omnibus)
Wildfire
The Zane Grey Frontier Trilogy (omnibus)

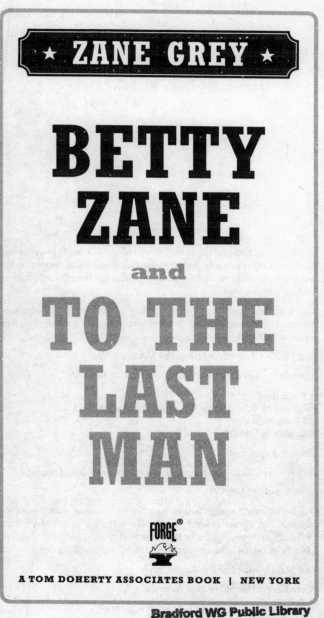

★ ZANE GREY ★

BETTY ZANE

and

TO THE LAST MAN

FORGE®

A TOM DOHERTY ASSOCIATES BOOK | NEW YORK

This is a work of fiction. All of the characters, organizations, and events portrayed in these novels are either products of the author's imagination or are used fictitiously.

BETTY ZANE AND TO THE LAST MAN

A Forge Book
Published by Tom Doherty Associates
175 Fifth Avenue
New York, NY 10010

www.tor-forge.com

Forge® is a registered trademark of Macmillan Publishing Group, LLC.

ISBN 978-0-7653-9351-7

Our books may be purchased in bulk for promotional, educational, or business use. Please contact your local bookseller or the Macmillan Corporate and Premium Sales Department at 1-800-221-7945, extension 5442, or by e-mail at MacmillanSpecialMarkets@macmillan.com.

First Mass Market Edition: August 2017

Printed in the United States of America

0 9 8 7 6 5 4 3 2 1

CONTENTS

BETTY ZANE

To the Betty Zane chapter of
The Daughters of the Revolution,
this book is respectfully
dedicated by the author.

NOTE

In a quiet corner of the stately little city of Wheeling, West Virginia, stands a monument on which is inscribed:

"By authority of the State of West Virginia, to commemorate the siege of Fort Henry, Sept. 11, 1782, the last battle of the American Revolution, this tablet is here placed."

Had it not been for the heroism of a girl the foregoing inscription would never have been written, and the city of Wheeling would never have existed.

From time to time I have read short stories and magazine articles which have been published about Elizabeth Zane and her famous exploit; but they are unreliable in some particulars, which is owing, no doubt, to the singularly meager details available in histories of our western border.

For a hundred years the stories of Betty and Isaac Zane have been familiar, oft-repeated tales in my family—tales told with that pardonable ancestral pride which seems inherent in every one. My grandmother loved to cluster the children round her and tell them that when she was a little girl she had knelt at the feet of Betty Zane, and listened to the old lady as she told of her brother's capture by the Indian Princess, of the burning of the Fort, and of her own race for life. I knew these stories by heart when a child.

Two years ago my mother came to me with an old notebook which had been discovered in some rubbish that had been placed in the yard to burn. The book had probably been hidden in an old picture frame for many years. It had belonged to my great-grandfather, Colonel Ebenezer Zane. From its faded and time-worn pages I have taken the main facts of my story. My regret is that a worthier pen than mine has not had this wealth of material.

In this busy progressive age there are no heroes of the kind so dear to all lovers of chivalry and romance. There are heroes, perhaps, but they are the patient sad-faced kind, of whom few take cognizance as they hurry onward. But cannot we all remember some one who suffered greatly, who accomplished great deeds, who died on the battlefield—some one around whose name lingers a halo of glory? Few of us are so unfortunate that we cannot look backward on kith or kin and thrill with love and reverence as we dream of an act of heroism or martyrdom which rings down the annals of time like the melody of the huntsman's horn, as it peals out on a frosty October morn purer and sweeter with each succeeding note.

If to any of those who have such remembrances, as well as those who have not, my story gives an hour of pleasure I shall be rewarded.

PROLOGUE

On June 16, 1716, Alexander Spotswood, Governor of the Colony of Virginia, and a gallant soldier who had served under Marlborough in the English wars, rode, at the head of a dauntless band of cavaliers, down the quiet street of quaint old Williamsburg.

The adventurous spirits of this party of men urged them toward the land of the setting sun, that unknown west far beyond the blue crested mountains rising so grandly before them.

Months afterward they stood on the western range of the Great North mountains towering above the picturesque Shenandoah Valley, and from the summit of one of the loftiest peaks, where, until then, the foot of a white man had never trod, they viewed the vast expanse of plain and forest with glistening eyes. Returning to Williamsburg they told of the wonderful richness of the newly discovered country and thus opened the way for the venturesome pioneer who was destined to overcome all difficulties and make a home in the western world.

But fifty years and more passed before a white man penetrated far beyond the purple spires of those majestic mountains.

One bright morning in June 1769, the figure of a stalwart, broad shouldered man could have been seen standing on the wild and rugged promontory which rears its rocky bluff high above the Ohio River, at a point near the mouth of Wheeling Creek. He was alone save for the companionship of a deerhound that crouched at his feet. As he leaned on a long rifle, contemplating the glorious scene that stretched before him, a smile flashed across his bronzed cheek, and his heart bounded as he forecast the future of that spot. In the river below him lay an island so round and green that it resembled a huge lily pad floating placidly on the water. The fresh green foliage of the trees sparkled with glittering dewdrops. Back of him rose the high ridges, and, in front, as far as eye could reach, extended an unbroken forest.

Beneath him to the left and across a deep ravine he saw a wide level clearing. The few scattered and blackened tree stumps showed the ravages made by a forest fire in the years gone by. The field was now overgrown with hazel and laurel bushes, and intermingling with them were the trailing arbutus, the honeysuckle, and the wild rose. A fragrant perfume was wafted upward to him. A rushing creek bordered one edge of the clearing. After a long quiet reach of water, which could be seen winding back in the hills, the stream tumbled madly over a rocky ledge, and white with foam, it hurried onward as if impatient of long restraint, and lost its individuality in the broad Ohio.

This solitary hunter was Colonel Ebenezer Zane. He was one of those daring men, who, as the tide of emigration started westward, had left his friends and family and had struck out alone into the wilderness. Departing from his home in Eastern Virginia he had plunged into the woods, and after many days of hunting and exploring, he reached the then far Western Ohio valley.

The scene so impressed Colonel Zane that he concluded to found a settlement there. Taking "tomahawk possession" of the locality (which consisted of blazing a few trees with his tomahawk), he built himself a rude shack and remained that summer on the Ohio.

In the autumn he set out for Berkeley County, Virginia, to tell his people of the magnificent country he had discovered. The following spring he persuaded a number of settlers, of a like spirit with himself, to accompany him to the wilderness. Believing it unsafe to take their families with them at once, they left them at Red Stone on the Monongahela river, while the men, including Colonel Zane, his brothers Silas, Andrew, Jonathan and Isaac, the Wetzels, McCollochs, Bennets, Metzars and others, pushed on ahead.

The country through which they passed was one tangled, almost impenetrable forest; the axe of the pioneer had never sounded in this region, where every rod of the way might harbor some unknown danger.

These reckless bordermen knew not the meaning of fear; to all, daring adventure was welcome, and the screech of a redskin and the ping of a bullet were familiar sounds; to the Wetzels, McCollochs and Jonathan Zane the hunting of Indians was the most thrilling passion of their lives; indeed, the Wetzels, particularly, knew no other occupation. They had attained a wonderful skill with the rifle; long practice had rendered their senses as acute as those of the fox. Skilled in every variety of woodcraft, with lynx eyes ever on the alert for detecting a trail, or the curling smoke of some campfire, or the minutest sign of an enemy, these men stole onward through the forest with the cautious but dogged and persistent determination that was characteristic of the settler.

They at length climbed the commanding bluff overlooking the majestic river, and as they gazed out on the undulating and uninterrupted area of green, their hearts beat high with hope.

The keen axe, wielded by strong arms, soon opened the

clearing and reared stout log cabins on the river bluff. Then Ebenezer Zane and his followers moved their families and soon the settlement began to grow and flourish. As the little village commenced to prosper the redmen became troublesome. Settlers were shot while plowing the fields or gathering the harvests. Bands of hostile Indians prowled around and made it dangerous for anyone to leave the clearing. Frequently the first person to appear in the early morning would be shot at by an Indian concealed in the woods.

General George Rodgers Clark, commandant of the Western Military Department, arrived at the village in 1774. As an attack from the savages was apprehended during the year the settlers determined to erect a fort as a defense for the infant settlement. It was planned by General Clark and built by the people themselves. At first they called it Fort Fincastle, in honor of Lord Dunmore, who, at the time of its erection, was Governor of the Colony of Virginia. In 1776 its name was changed to Fort Henry, in honor of Patrick Henry.

For many years it remained the most famous fort on the frontier, having withstood numberless Indian attacks and two memorable sieges, one in 1777, which year is called the year of the "Bloody Sevens," and again in 1782. In this last siege the British Rangers under Hamilton took part with the Indians, making the attack practically the last battle of the Revolution.

CHAPTER 1

The Zane family was a remarkable one in early days, and most of its members are historical characters.

The first Zane of whom any trace can be found was a Dane of aristocratic lineage, who was exiled from his country and came to America with William Penn. He was prominent for several years in the new settlement founded by Penn, and Zane street, Philadelphia, bears his name. Being a proud and arrogant man, he soon became obnoxious to his Quaker brethren. He therefore cut loose from them and emigrated to Virginia, settling on the Potomac river, in what was then known as Berkeley county. There his five sons, and one daughter, the heroine of this story, were born.

Ebenezer Zane, the eldest, was born October 7, 1747, and grew to manhood in the Potomac valley. There he married Elizabeth McColloch, a sister of the famous McColloch brothers so well known in frontier history.

Ebenezer was fortunate in having such a wife and no pioneer could have been better blessed. She was not only a handsome woman, but one of remarkable force of character as well as kindness of heart. She was particularly noted for a rare skill in the treatment of illness, and her deftness in handling the surgeon's knife and extracting a poisoned bullet or arrow from a wound had restored to health many a settler when all had despaired.

The Zane brothers were best known on the border for their athletic prowess, and for their knowledge of Indian warfare and cunning. They were all powerful men, exceedingly active and as fleet as deer. In appearance they were singularly pleasing and bore a marked resemblance to one another, all having smooth faces, clear cut, regular features, dark eyes and long black hair.

When they were as yet boys they had been captured by Indians, soon after their arrival on the Virginia border, and had been taken far into the interior, and held as captives for two years. Ebenezer, Silas, and Jonathan Zane were then taken to Detroit and ransomed. While attempting to swim the Scioto river in an effort to escape, Andrew Zane had been shot and killed by his pursuers.

But the bonds that held Isaac Zane, the remaining and youngest brother, were stronger than those of interest or revenge such as had caused the captivity of his brothers. He was loved by an Indian princess, the daughter of Tarhe, the chief of the puissant Huron race. Isaac had escaped on various occasions, but had always been retaken, and at the time of the opening of our story nothing had been heard of him for several years, and it was believed he had been killed.

At the period of the settling of the little colony in the wilderness, Elizabeth Zane, the only sister, was living with an aunt in Philadelphia, where she was being educated.

Colonel Zane's house, a two story structure built of rough hewn logs, was the most comfortable one in the settlement, and occupied a prominent site on the hillside about one hundred yards from the fort. It was constructed of heavy timber and presented rather a forbidding appearance with its square corners, its ominous looking portholes, and strongly barred doors and windows. There were three rooms on the ground floor, a kitchen, a magazine room for military supplies, and a large room for general use. The several sleeping rooms were on the second floor, which was reached by a steep stairway.

The interior of a pioneer's rude dwelling did not reveal, as a rule, more than bare walls, a bed or two, a table and a few chairs—in fact, no more than the necessities of life. But Colonel Zane's house proved an exception to this. Most interesting was the large room. The chinks between the logs had been plastered up with clay and then the walls covered with white birch bark; trophies of the chase, Indian bows and arrows, pipes and tomahawks hung upon them; the wide spreading antlers of a noble buck adorned the space above the mantelpiece; buffalo robes covered the couches; bearskin rugs lay scattered about on the hardwood floor. The wall on the western side had been built over a huge stone, into which had been cut an open fireplace.

This blackened recess, which had seen two houses burned over it, when full of blazing logs had cheered many noted men with its warmth. Lord Dunmore, General Clark, Simon Kenton, and Daniel Boone had sat beside that fire. There Cornplanter, the Seneca chief, had made his famous deal with Colonel Zane, trading the island in the river opposite the settlement for a barrel of whiskey. Logan, the Mingo chief and friend of the whites, had smoked many pipes of peace there with Colonel Zane. At a later period, when King Louis Phillippe, who had been exiled from France by Napoleon, had come to America, during the course of his melancholy wanderings he had stopped at Fort Henry a few days. His stay there was marked by a fierce blizzard and the royal guest passed most of his time at Colonel Zane's fireside. Musing by those roaring logs perhaps he saw the radiant star of the Man of Destiny rise to its magnificent zenith.

One cold, raw night in early spring the Colonel had just returned from one of his hunting trips and the tramping of horses mingled with the rough voices of the negro slaves sounded without. When Colonel Zane entered the house he was greeted affectionately by his wife and sister. The latter, at the death of her aunt in Philadelphia, had come west to live with her brother, and had been there since late in the preceding autumn. It was a welcome sight for the eyes of a tired and weary hunter. The tender kiss of his comely wife, the cries of the delighted children, and the crackling of the fire warmed his heart and made him feel how good it was to be home again after a three days' march in the woods. Placing his rifle in a corner and throwing aside his wet hunting coat, he turned and stood with his back to the bright blaze. Still young and vigorous, Colonel Zane was a handsome man. Tall, though not heavy, his frame denoted great strength and endurance. His face was smooth; his heavy eyebrows met in a straight line; his eyes were dark and now beamed with a kindly light; his jaw was square and massive; his mouth resolute; in fact, his whole face was strikingly expressive of courage and geniality. A great wolf dog had followed him in and, tired from travel, had stretched himself out before the fireplace, laying his noble head on the paws he had extended toward the warm blaze.

"Well! Well! I am nearly starved and mighty glad to get back," said the Colonel, with a smile of satisfaction at the steaming dishes a negro servant was bringing from the kitchen.

"We are glad you have returned," answered his wife, whose glowing face testified to the pleasure she felt. "Supper is ready—Annie, bring in some cream—yes, indeed, I am happy that you are home. I never have a moment's peace when you are away, especially when you are accompanied by Lewis Wetzel."

"Our hunt was a failure," said the Colonel, after he had helped himself to a plate full of roast wild turkey. "The bears have just come out of their winter's sleep and are unusually wary at this time. We saw many signs of their work, tearing rotten logs to pieces in search of grubs and bees' nests. Wetzel killed a deer and we baited a likely place where we had discovered many bear tracks. We stayed up all night in a drizzling rain, hoping to get a shot. I am tired out. So is Tige. Wetzel did not mind the weather or the ill luck, and when we ran across some Indian sign he went off on one of his lonely tramps, leaving me to come home alone."

"He is such a reckless man," remarked Mrs. Zane.

"Wetzel is reckless, or rather, daring. His incomparable nerve carries him safely through many dangers, where an ordinary man would have no show whatever. Well, Betty, how are you?"

"Quite well," said the slender, dark-eyed girl who had just taken the seat opposite the Colonel.

"Bessie, has my sister indulged in any shocking escapade in my absence? I think that last trick of hers, when she gave a bucket of hard cider to that poor tame bear, should last her a spell."

"No, for a wonder Elizabeth has been very good. However, I do not attribute it to any unusual change of temperament; simply the cold, wet weather. I anticipate a catastrophe very shortly if she is kept indoors much longer."

"I have not had much opportunity to be anything but well behaved. If it rains a few days more I shall become desperate. I want to ride my pony, roam the woods, paddle my canoe, and enjoy myself," said Elizabeth.

"Well! Well! Betts, I knew it would be dull here for you,

but you must not get discouraged. You know you got here late last fall, and have not had any pleasant weather yet. It is perfectly delightful in May and June. I can take you to fields of wild white honeysuckle and May flowers and wild roses. I know you love the woods, so be patient a little longer."

Elizabeth had been spoiled by her brothers—what girl would not have been by five great big worshippers?—and any trivial thing gone wrong with her was a serious matter to them. They were proud of her, and of her beauty and accomplishments were never tired of talking. She had the dark hair and eyes so characteristic of the Zanes; the same oval face and fine features; and added to this was a certain softness of contour and a sweetness of expression which made her face bewitching. But, in spite of that demure and innocent face, she possessed a decided will of her own, and one very apt to be asserted; she was mischievous; inclined to coquettishness, and more terrible than all she had a fiery temper which could be aroused with the most surprising ease.

Colonel Zane was wont to say that his sister's accomplishments were innumerable. After only a few months on the border she could prepare the flax and weave a linsey dress-cloth with admirable skill. Sometimes to humor Betty the Colonel's wife would allow her to get the dinner, and she would do it in a manner that pleased her brothers, and called forth golden praises from the cook, old Sam's wife, who had been with the family twenty years. Betty sang in the little church on Sundays; she organized and taught a Sunday school class; she often beat Colonel Zane and Major McColloch at their favorite game of checkers, which they had played together since they were knee high; in fact, Betty did nearly everything well, from baking pies to painting the birch bark walls of her room. But these things were insignificant in Colonel

Zane's eyes. If the Colonel were ever guilty of bragging it was about his sister's ability in those acquirements demanding a true eye, a fleet foot, a strong arm and a daring spirit. He had told all the people in the settlement, to many of whom Betty was unknown, that she could ride like an Indian and shoot with undoubted skill; that she had a generous share of the Zanes' fleetness of foot, and that she would send a canoe over as bad a place as she could find. The boasts of the Colonel remained as yet unproven, but, be that as it may, Betty had, notwithstanding her many faults, endeared herself to all. She made sunshine and happiness everywhere; the old people loved her; the children adored her; and the broad shouldered, heavy footed young settlers were shy and silent, yet blissfully happy in her presence.

"Betty, will you fill my pipe?" asked the Colonel, when he had finished his supper and had pulled his big chair nearer the fire. His oldest child, Noah, a sturdy lad of six, climbed upon his knee and plied him with questions.

"Did you see any bars and bufflers?" he asked, his eyes large and round.

"No, my lad, not one."

"How long will it be until I am big enough to go?"

"Not for a very long time, Noah."

"But I am not afraid of Betty's bar. He growls at me when I throw sticks at him, and snaps his teeth. Can I go with you next time?"

"My brother came over from Short Creek to-day. He has been to Fort Pitt," interposed Mrs. Zane. As she was speaking a tap sounded on the door, which, being opened by Betty, disclosed Captain Boggs, his daughter Lydia, and Major Samuel McColloch, the brother of Mrs. Zane.

"Ah, Colonel! I expected to find you at home to-night. The weather has been miserable for hunting and it is not getting any better. The wind is blowing from the northwest and a storm is coming," said Captain Boggs, a fine, soldierly looking man.

"Hello, Captain! How are you? Sam, I have not had the pleasure of seeing you for a long time," replied Colonel Zane, as he shook hands with his guests.

Major McColloch was the eldest of the brothers of that name. As an Indian killer he ranked next to the intrepid Wetzel; but while Wetzel preferred to take his chances alone and track the Indians through the untrodden wilds, McColloch was a leader of expeditions against the savages. A giant in stature, massive in build, bronzed and bearded, he looked the typical frontiersman. His blue eyes were like those of his sister and his voice had the same pleasant ring.

"Major McColloch, do you remember me?" asked Betty.

"Indeed I do," he answered, with a smile. "You were a little girl, running wild, on the Potomac when I last saw you!"

"Do you remember when you used to lift me on your horse and give me lessons in riding?"

"I remember better than you. How you used to stick on the back of that horse was a mystery to me."

"Well, I shall be ready soon to go on with those lessons in riding. I have heard of your wonderful leap over the hill and I should like to have you tell me all about it. Of all the stories I have heard since I arrived at Fort Henry, the one of your ride and leap for life is the most wonderful."

"Yes, Sam, she will bother you to death about that ride, and will try to give you lessons in leaping down precipices. I should not be at all surprised to find her trying to duplicate your feat. You know the Indian pony I got from that fur trader last summer. Well, he is as wild as a deer and she has been riding him without his being broken," said Colonel Zane.

"Some other time I shall tell you about my jump over the hill. Just now I have important matters to discuss," answered the Major to Betty.

It was evident that something unusual had occurred, for after chatting a few moments the three men withdrew into the magazine room and conversed in low, earnest tones.

Lydia Boggs was eighteen, fair haired and blue eyed. Like Betty she had received a good education, and, in that respect, was superior to the border girls, who seldom knew more than to keep house and to make linen. At the outbreak of the Indian wars General Clark had stationed Captain Boggs at Fort Henry and Lydia had lived there with him two years. After Betty's arrival, which she hailed with delight, the girls had become fast friends.

Lydia slipped her arm affectionately around Betty's neck and said, "Why did you not come over to the Fort to-day?"

"It has been such an ugly day, so disagreeable altogether, that I have remained indoors."

"You missed something," said Lydia, knowingly.

"What do you mean? What did I miss?"

"Oh, perhaps, after all, it will not interest you."

"How provoking! Of course it will. Anything or anybody would interest me to-night. Do tell me, please."

"It isn't much. Only a young soldier came over with Major McColloch."

"A soldier? From Fort Pitt? Do I know him? I have met most of the officers."

"No, you have never seen him. He is a stranger to all of us."

"There does not seem to be so much in your news," said Betty, in a disappointed tone. "To be sure, strangers are a rarity in our little village, but, judging from the strangers who have visited us in the past, I imagine this one cannot be much different."

"Wait until you see him," said Lydia, with a serious little nod of her head.

"Come, tell me all about him," said Betty, now much interested.

"Major McColloch brought him in to see papa, and he was introduced to me. He is a southerner and from one of those old families. I could tell by his cool, easy, almost reckless air. He is handsome, tall and fair, and his face is frank and open. He has such beautiful manners. He bowed low to me and really I felt so embarrassed that I hardly spoke. You know I am used to these big hunters seizing your hand and giving it a squeeze which makes you want to scream. Well, this young man is different. He is a cavalier. All the girls are in love with him already. So will you be."

"I? Indeed not. But how refreshing. You must have been strongly impressed to see and remember all you have told me."

"Betty Zane, I remember so well because he is just the man you described one day when we were building castles and telling each other what kind of a hero we wanted."

"Girls, do not talk such nonsense," interrupted the Colonel's wife, who was perturbed by the colloquy in the other room. She had seen those ominous signs before. "Can you find nothing better to talk about?"

Meanwhile Colonel Zane and his companions were earnestly discussing certain information which had arrived that day. A friendly Indian runner had brought news to Short Creek, a settlement on the river between Fort Henry and Fort Pitt, of an intended raid by the Indians all along the Ohio valley. Major McColloch, who had been warned by Wetzel of the fever of unrest among the Indians—a fever which broke out every spring—had gone to Fort Pitt with the hope of bringing back reinforcements, but, excepting the young soldier, who had volunteered to return with him, no help could he enlist, so he journeyed back post-haste to Fort Henry.

The information he brought disturbed Captain Boggs, who commanded the garrison, as a number of men were away on a logging expedition up the river, and were not expected to raft down to the Fort for two weeks.

Jonathan Zane, who had been sent for, joined the trio at this moment, and was acquainted with the particulars. The Zane Brothers were always consulted where any question concerning Indian craft and cunning was to be decided. Colonel Zane had a strong friendly influence with certain tribes, and his advice was invaluable. Jonathan Zane hated the sight of an Indian and except for his knowledge as a scout, or Indian tracker or fighter, he was of little use in a council. Colonel Zane informed the men of the fact that Wetzel and he had discovered Indian tracks within ten miles of the Fort, and he dwelt particularly on the disappearance of Wetzel.

"Now, you can depend on what I say. There are Wyandots in force on the war path. Wetzel told me to dig for the Fort and he left me in a hurry. We were near that cranberry bog over at the foot of Bald mountain. I do not believe we shall be attacked. In my opinion the Indians would come up from the west and keep to the high ridges along Yellow creek. They always come that way. But, of course, it is best to know surely, and I daresay Lew will come in to-night or to-morrow with the facts. In the meantime put out some scouts back in the woods and let Jonathan and the Major watch the river."

"I hope Wetzel will come in," said the Major. "We can trust him to know more about the Indians than any one. It was a week before you and he went hunting that I saw him. I went to Fort Pitt and tried to bring over some men, but the garrison is short and they need men as much as we do. A young soldier named Clarke volunteered to come and I brought him along with me. He has not seen any Indian fighting, but he is a likely looking chap, and I guess will do. Captain Boggs will give him a place in the block house if you say so."

"By all means. We shall be glad to have him," said Colonel Zane.

"It would not be so serious if I had not sent the men up the river," said Captain Boggs, in anxious tones. "Do you think it possible they might have fallen in with the Indians?"

"It is possible, of course, but not probable," answered Colonel Zane. "The Indians are all across the Ohio. Wetzel is over there and he will get here long before they do."

"I hope it may be as you say. I have much confidence in your judgment," returned Captain Boggs. "I shall put out scouts and take all the precaution possible. We must return now. Come, Lydia."

"Whew! What an awful night this is going to be," said Colonel Zane, when he had closed the door after his guests' departure. "I should not care to sleep out to-night."

"Eb, what will Lew Wetzel do on a night like this?" asked Betty, curiously.

"Oh, Lew will be as snug as a rabbit in his burrow," said Colonel Zane, laughing. "In a few moments he can build a birch bark shack, start a fire inside and go to sleep comfortably."

"Ebenezer, what is all this confab about? What did my brother tell you?" asked Mrs. Zane, anxiously.

"We are in for more trouble from the Wyandots and Shawnees. But, Bessie, I don't believe it will come soon. We are too well protected here for anything but a protracted siege."

Colonel Zane's light and rather evasive answer did not deceive his wife. She knew her brother and her husband would not wear anxious faces for nothing. Her usually bright face clouded with a look of distress. She had seen enough of Indian warfare to make her shudder with horror at the mere thought. Betty seemed unconcerned. She sat down beside the dog and patted him on the head.

"Tige, Indians! Indians!" she said.

The dog growled and showed his teeth. It was only necessary to mention Indians to arouse his ire.

"The dog has been uneasy of late," continued Colonel Zane. "He found the Indian tracks before Wetzel did. You know how Tige hates Indians. Ever since he came home with Isaac four years ago he has been of great service to the scouts, as he possesses so much intelligence and sagacity. Tige followed Isaac home the last time he escaped from the Wyandots. When Isaac was in captivity he nursed and cared for the dog after he had been brutally beaten by the redskins. Have you ever heard that long mournful howl Tige gives out sometimes in the dead of night?"

"Yes I have, and it makes me cover up my head," said Betty.

"Well, it is Tige mourning for Isaac," said Colonel Zane.

"Poor Isaac," murmured Betty.

"Do you remember him? It has been nine years since you saw him," said Mrs. Zane.

"Remember Isaac? Indeed I do. I shall never forget him. I wonder if he is still living?"

"Probably not. It is now four years since he was recaptured. I think it would have been impossible to keep him that length of time, unless, of course, he has married that Indian girl. The simplicity of the Indian nature is remarkable. He could easily have deceived them and made them believe he was content in captivity. Probably, in attempting to escape again, he has been killed as was poor Andrew."

Brother and sister gazed with dark, sad eyes into the fire, now burned down to a glowing bed of coals. The silence remained unbroken save for the moan of the rising wind outside, the rattle of hail, and the patter of raindrops on the roof.

CHAPTER 2

ort Henry stood on a bluff overlooking the river and commanded a fine view of the surrounding country. In shape it was a parallelogram, being about three hundred and fifty-six feet in length, and one hundred and fifty in width. Surrounded by a stockade fence twelve feet high, with a yard wide walk running around the inside, and with bastions at each corner large enough to contain six defenders, the fort presented an almost impregnable defense. The blockhouse was two stories in height, the second story projecting out several feet over the first. The thick white oak walls bristled with portholes. Besides the blockhouse, there were a number of cabins located within the stockade. Wells had been sunk inside the inclosure, so that if the spring happened to go dry, an abundance of good water could be had at all times.

In all the histories of frontier life mention is made of the forts and the protection they offered in time of savage warfare. These forts were used as homes for the settlers, who often lived for weeks inside the walls.

Forts constructed entirely of wood without the aid of a nail or spike (for the good reason that these things could not be had) may seem insignificant in these days of great naval and military garrisons. However, they answered the purpose at that time and served to protect many an infant settlement from the savage attacks of Indian tribes. During a siege of Fort Henry, which had occurred about a year previous, the settlers would have lost scarcely a man had they kept to the fort. But Captain Ogle, at that time in charge of the garrison, had led a company out in search of the Indians. Nearly all of his men were killed, several only making their way to the fort.

On the day following Major McColloch's arrival at Fort Henry, the settlers had been called in from their spring plowing and other labors, and were now busily engaged in moving their stock and the things they wished to save from the destructive torch of the redskin. The women had their hands full with the children, the cleaning of rifles and moulding of bullets, and the thousand and one things the sterner tasks of their husbands had left them. Major McColloch, Jonathan and Silas Zane, early in the day, had taken different directions along the river to keep a sharp lookout for signs of the enemy. Colonel Zane intended to stay in his own house and defend it, so he had not moved anything to the fort excepting his horses and cattle. Old Sam, the negro, was hauling loads of hay inside the stockade. Captain Boggs had detailed several scouts to watch the roads and one of these was the young man, Clarke, who had accompanied the Major from Fort Pitt.

The appearance of Alfred Clarke, despite the fact that he wore the regulation hunting garb, indicated a young man to whom the hard work and privation of the settler were unaccustomed things. So thought the pioneers who noticed his graceful walk, his fair skin and smooth hands. Yet those who carefully studied his clearcut features were favorably impressed; the women, by the direct, honest gaze of his blue eyes and the absence of ungentle lines in his face; the men, by the good nature, and that indefinable something by which a man marks another as true steel.

He brought nothing with him from Fort Pitt except his horse, a black-coated, fine limbed thoroughbred, which he frankly confessed was all he could call his own. When asking Colonel Zane to give him a position in the garrison he said he was a Virginian and had been educated in Philadelphia; that after his father died his mother married again, and this, together with a natural love of adventure, had induced him to run away and seek his fortune with the hardy pioneer and the cunning savage of the border. Beyond a few months' service under General Clark he knew nothing of frontier life; but he was tired of idleness; he was strong and not afraid of work, and he could learn. Colonel Zane, who prided himself on his judgment of character, took a liking to the young man at once, and giving him a rifle and accoutrements, told him the border needed young men of pluck and fire, and that if he brought a strong hand and a willing heart he could surely find fortune. Possibly if Alfred Clarke could have been told of the fate in store for him he might have mounted his black steed and have placed miles between him and the frontier village, but, as there were none to tell, he went cheerfully out to meet that fate.

On this bright spring morning he patrolled the road leading along the edge of the clearing, which was distant a quarter of a mile from the fort. He kept a keen eye on the opposite side of the river, as he had been directed. From the upper end of the island, almost straight across from where he stood, the river took a broad turn, which could not be observed from the fort windows. The river was high from the recent rains and brush heaps and logs and debris of all descriptions were floating down with the swift current. Rabbits and other small animals, which had probably been surrounded on some island and compelled to take to the brush or drown, crouched on floating logs and piles of driftwood. Happening to glance down the road, Clarke saw a horse galloping in his direction. At first he thought it was a messenger for himself, but as it neared him he saw that the horse was an Indian pony and the rider a young girl, whose long, black hair was flying in the wind.

"Hello! I wonder what the deuce this is? Looks like an Indian girl," said Clarke to himself. "She rides well, whoever she may be."

He stepped behind a clump of laurel bushes near the roadside and waited. Rapidly the horse and rider approached him. When they were but a few paces distant he sprang out and, as the pony shied and reared at sight of him, he clutched the bridle and pulled the pony's head down. Looking up he encountered the astonished and bewildered gaze from a pair of the prettiest dark eyes it had ever been his fortune, or misfortune, to look into.

Betty, for it was she, looked at the young man in amazement, while Alfred was even more surprised and disconcerted. For a moment they looked at each other in silence. But Betty, who was scarcely ever at a loss for words, presently found her voice.

"Well, sir! What does this mean?" she asked indignantly.

"It means that you must turn around and go back to the fort," answered Alfred, also recovering himself.

Now Betty's favorite ride happened to be along this road. It lay along the top of the bluff a mile or more and afforded a fine unobstructed view of the river. Betty had either not heard of the Captain's order, that no one was to leave the fort, or she had disregarded it altogether; probably the latter, as she generally did what suited her fancy.

"Release my pony's head!" she cried, her face flushing,

as she gave a jerk to the reins. "How dare you? What right have you to detain me?"

The expression Betty saw on Clarke's face was not new to her, for she remembered having seen it on the faces of young gentlemen whom she had met at her aunt's house in Philadelphia. It was the slight, provoking smile of the man familiar with the various moods of young women, the expression of an amused contempt for their imperiousness. But it was not that which angered Betty. It was the coolness with which he still held her pony regardless of her commands.

"Pray do not get excited," he said. "I am sorry I cannot allow such a pretty little girl to have her own way. I shall hold your pony until you say you will go back to the fort."

"Sir!" exclaimed Betty, blushing a bright red. "You—you are impertinent!"

"Not at all," answered Alfred, with a pleasant laugh. "I am sure I do not intend to be. Captain Boggs did not acquaint me with full particulars or I might have declined my present occupation; not, however, that it is not agreeable just at this moment. He should have mentioned the danger of my being run down by Indian ponies and imperious young ladies."

"Will you let go of that bridle, or shall I get off and walk back for assistance?" said Betty, getting angrier every moment.

"Go back to the fort at once," ordered Alfred, authoritatively. "Captain Boggs' orders are that no one shall be allowed to leave the clearing."

"Oh! Why did you not say so? I thought you were Simon Girty, or a highwayman. Was it necessary to keep me here all this time to explain that you were on duty?"

"You know sometimes it is difficult to explain," said Alfred, "besides, the situation had its charm. No, I am not a robber, and I don't believe you thought so. I have only thwarted a young lady's whim, which I am aware is a great crime. I am very sorry. Goodbye."

Betty gave him a withering glance from her black eyes, wheeled her pony and galloped away. A mellow laugh was borne to her ears before she got out of hearing, and again the red blood mantled her cheeks.

"Heavens! What a little beauty," said Alfred to himself, as he watched the graceful rider disappear. "What spirit! Now, I wonder who she can be. She had on moccasins and buckskin gloves and her hair tumbled like a tomboy's, but she is no backwoods girl, I'll bet on that. I'm afraid I was a little rude, but after taking such a stand I could not weaken, especially before such a haughty and disdainful little vixen. It was too great a temptation. What eyes she had! Contrary to what I expected, this little frontier settlement bids fair to become interesting."

The afternoon wore slowly away, and until late in the day nothing further happened to disturb Alfred's meditations, which consisted chiefly of different mental views and pictures of red lips and black eyes. Just as he decided to return to the fort for his supper he heard the barking of a dog that he had seen running along the road some moments before. The sound came from some distance down the riverbank and nearer the fort. Walking a few paces up the bluff Alfred caught sight of a large black dog running along the edge of the water. He would run into the water a few paces and then come out and dash along the shore. He barked furiously all the while. Alfred concluded he must have been excited by a fox or perhaps a wolf; so he climbed down the steep bank and spoke to the dog. Thereupon the dog barked louder and more fiercely than ever, ran to the water, looked out into the river and then up at the man with almost human intelligence.

Alfred understood. He glanced out over the muddy water, at first making out nothing but driftwood. Then suddenly he saw a log with an object clinging to it which he took to be a man, and an Indian at that. Alfred raised his rifle to his shoulder and was in the act of pressing the trigger when he thought he heard a faint halloo. Looking closer, he found he was not covering the smooth polished head adorned with the small tuft of hair, peculiar to a redskin on the warpath, but a head from which streamed long black hair.

Alfred lowered his rifle and studied intently the log with its human burden. Drifting with the current it gradually approached the bank, and as it came nearer he saw that it bore a white man, who was holding to the log with one hand and with the other was making feeble strokes. He concluded the man was either wounded or nearly drowned, for his movements were becoming slower and weaker every moment. His white face lay against the log and barely above water. Alfred shouted encouraging words to him.

At the bend of the river a little rocky point jutted out a few yards into the water. As the current carried the log toward this point, Alfred, after divesting himself of some of his clothing, plunged in and pulled it to the shore. The pallid face of the man clinging to the log showed that he was nearly exhausted, and that he had been rescued in the nick of time. When Alfred reached shoal water he slipped his arm around the man, who was unable to stand, and carried him ashore.

The rescued man wore a buckskin hunting shirt and leggins and moccasins of the same material, all very much the worse for wear. The leggins were torn into tatters and the moccasins worn through. His face was pinched with suffering and one arm was bleeding from a gunshot wound near the shoulder.

"Can you not speak? Who are you?" asked Clarke, supporting the limp figure.

The man made several efforts to answer, and finally said something that to Alfred sounded like "Zane," then he fell to the ground unconscious.

All this time the dog had acted in a most peculiar manner, and if Alfred had not been so intent on the man he would have noticed the animal's odd maneuvers. He ran to and fro on the sandy beach; he scratched up the sand and pebbles, sending them flying in the air; he made short, furious dashes; he jumped, whirled, and, at last, crawled close to the motionless figure and licked its hand.

Clarke realized that he would not be able to carry the inanimate figure, so he hurriedly put on his clothes and set out on a run for Colonel Zane's house. The first person whom he saw was the old negro slave, who was brushing one of the Colonel's horses.

Sam was deliberate and took his time about everything. He slowly looked up and surveyed Clarke with his rolling eyes. He did not recognize in him any one he had ever seen before, and being of a sullen and taciturn nature, especially with strangers, he seemed in no hurry to give the desired information as to Colonel Zane's whereabouts.

"Don't stare at me that way," said Clarke. "Quick, where is the Colonel?"

At that moment Colonel Zane came out of the barn and started to speak, when Clarke interrupted him.

"Colonel, I have just pulled a man out of the river who says his name is Zane, or if he did not mean that, he knows you, for he surely said 'Zane.' "

"What!" exclaimed the Colonel, letting his pipe fall from his mouth.

Clarke related the circumstances in a few hurried words. Calling Sam they ran quickly down to the river, where they found the prostrate figure as Clarke had left him, the dog still crouched close by.

"My God! It is Isaac!" exclaimed Colonel Zane, when

he saw the white face. "Poor boy, he looks as if he were dead. Are you sure he spoke? Of course he must have spoken for you could not have known. Yes, his heart is still beating."

Colonel Zane raised his head from the unconscious man's breast, where he had laid it to listen for the beating heart.

"Clarke, God bless you for saving him," said he fervently. "It shall never be forgotten. He is alive, and, I believe, only exhausted, for that wound amounts to little. Let us hurry."

"I did not save him. It was the dog." Alfred made haste to answer.

They carried the dripping form to the house, where the door was opened by Mrs. Zane.

"Oh, dear, another poor man," she said, pityingly. Then, as she saw his face. "Great Heavens, it is Isaac! Oh! don't say he is dead!"

"Yes, it is Isaac, and he is worth any number of dead men yet," said Colonel Zane, as they laid the insensible man on the couch. "Bessie, there is work here for you. He has been shot."

"Is there any other wound beside this one in his arm?" asked Mrs. Zane, examining it.

"I do not think so, and that injury is not serious. It is loss of blood, exposure and starvation. Clarke, will you please run over to Captain Boggs and tell Betty to hurry home. Sam, you get a blanket and warm it by the fire. That's right, Bessie, bring the whiskey." And Colonel Zane went on giving orders.

Alfred did not know in the least who Betty was, but, as he thought that unimportant, he started off on a run for the fort. He had a vague idea that Betty was the servant, possibly Sam's wife, or some one of the Colonel's several slaves.

Let us return to Betty. As she wheeled her pony and rode away from the scene of her adventure on the river bluff, her state of mind can be more readily imagined than described. Betty hated opposition of any kind, whether justifiable or not; she wanted her own way, and when prevented from doing as she pleased she invariably got angry. To be ordered and compelled to give up her ride, and that by a stranger, was intolerable. To make it all the worse this stranger had been decidedly flippant. He had familiarly spoken to her as "a pretty little girl." Not only that, which was a great offense, but he had stared at her, and she had a confused recollection of a gaze in which admiration had been ill disguised. Of course, it was that soldier Lydia had been telling her about. Strangers were of so rare an occurrence in the little village that it was not probable there could be more than one.

Approaching the house she met her brother who told her she had better go indoors and let Sam put up the pony. Accordingly, Betty called Sam, and then went into the house. Bessie had gone to the fort with the children. Betty found no one to talk to, so she tried to read. Finding she could not become interested she threw the book aside and took up her embroidery. This also turned out a useless effort; she got the linen hopelessly twisted and tangled, and presently she tossed this upon the table. Throwing her shawl over her shoulders, for it was now late in the afternoon and growing chilly, she walked downstairs and out into the yard. She strolled aimlessly to and fro awhile, and then went over to the fort and into Captain Bogg's house, which adjoined the blockhouse. Here she found Lydia preparing flax.

"I saw you racing by on your pony. Goodness, how you can ride! I should be afraid of breaking my neck," exclaimed Lydia, as Betty entered.

"My ride was spoiled," said Betty, petulantly.

"Spoiled? By what—whom?"

"By a man, of course," retorted Betty, whose temper still was high. "It is always a man that spoils everything."

"Why, Betty, what in the world do you mean? I never heard you talk that way," said Lydia, opening her blue eyes in astonishment.

"Well, Lyde, I'll tell you. I was riding down the river road and just as I came to the end of the clearing a man jumped out from behind some bushes and grasped Madcap's bridle. Imagine! For a moment I was frightened out of my wits. I instantly thought of the Girtys, who, I have heard, have evinced a fondness for kidnapping little girls. Then the fellow said he was on guard and ordered me, actually commanded me to go home."

"Oh, is that all?" said Lydia, laughing.

"No, that is not all. He—he said I was a pretty little girl and that he was sorry I could not have my own way; that his present occupation was pleasant, and that the situation had its charm. The very idea. He was most impertinent." And Betty's telltale cheeks reddened again at the recollection.

"Betty, I do not think your experience was so dreadful, certainly nothing to put you out as it has," said Lydia, laughing merrily. "Be serious. You know we are out in the backwoods now and must not expect so much of the men. These rough border men know little of refinement like that with which you have been familiar. Some of them are quiet and never speak unless addressed; their simplicity is remarkable; Lew Wetzel and your brother Jonathan, when they are not fighting Indians, are examples. On the other hand, some of them are boisterous and if they get anything to drink they will make trouble for you. Why, I went to a party one night after I had been here only a few weeks and they played a game in which every man in the place kissed me."

"Gracious! Please tell me when any such games are likely to be proposed and I'll stay home," said Betty.

"I have learned to get along very well by simply making the best of it," continued Lydia. "And to tell the truth, I have learned to respect these rugged fellows. They are uncouth; they have no manners, but their hearts are honest and true, and that is of much greater importance in frontiersmen than the little attentions and courtesies upon which women are apt to lay too much stress."

"I think you speak sensibly and I shall try and be more reasonable hereafter. But, to return to the man who spoiled my ride. He, at least, is no frontiersman, notwithstanding his gun and his buckskin suit. He is an educated man. His manner and accent showed that. Then he looked at me so differently. I know it was that soldier from Fort Pitt."

"Mr. Clarke? Why, of course!" exclaimed Lydia, clapping her hands in glee. "How stupid of me!"

"You seem to be amused," said Betty, frowning.

"Oh, Betty, it is such a good joke."

"Is it? I fail to see it."

"But I can. I am very much amused. You see, I heard Mr. Clarke say, after papa told him there were lots of pretty girls here, that he usually succeeded in finding those things out and without any assistance. And the very first day he has met you and made you angry. It is delightful."

"Lyde, I never knew you could be so horrid."

"It is evident that Mr. Clarke is not only discerning, but not backward in expressing his thoughts. Betty, I see a romance."

"Don't be ridiculous," retorted Betty, with an angry blush. "Of course, he had a right to stop me, and perhaps he did me a good turn by keeping me inside the clearing, though I cannot imagine why he hid behind the bushes. But he might have been polite. He made me angry. He was so cool and—and—"

"I see," interrupted Lydia, teasingly. "He failed to recognize your importance."

"Nonsense, Lydia. I hope you do not think I am a silly little fool. It is only that I have not been accustomed to that kind of treatment, and I will not have it."

Lydia was rather pleased that some one had appeared on the scene who did not at once bow down before Betty, and therefore she took the young man's side of the argument.

"Do not be hard on poor Mr. Clarke. Maybe he mistook you for an Indian girl. He is handsome. I am sure you saw that."

"Oh, I don't remember how he looked," said Betty. She did remember, but would not admit it.

The conversation drifted into other channels after this, and soon twilight came stealing down on them. As Betty rose to go there came a hurried tap on the door.

"I wonder who would knock like that," said Lydia, rising. "Betty, wait a moment while I open the door."

On doing this she discovered Clarke standing on the step with his cap in his hand.

"Why, Mr. Clarke! Will you come in?" exclaimed Lydia.

"Thank you, only for a moment," said Alfred. "I cannot stay. I came to find Betty. Is she here?"

He had not observed Betty, who had stepped back into the shadow of the darkening room. At his question Lydia became so embarrassed she did not know what to say or do, and stood looking helplessly at him.

But Betty was equal to the occasion. At the mention of her first name in such a familiar manner by this stranger, who had already grievously offended her once before that day, Betty stood perfectly still a moment, speechless with surprise, then she stepped quickly out of the shadow.

Clarke turned as he heard her step and looked straight

into a pair of dark, scornful eyes and a face pale with anger.

"If it be necessary that you use my name, and I do not see how that can be possible, will you please have courtesy enough to say Miss Zane?" she cried haughtily.

Lydia recovered her composure sufficiently to falter out:

"Betty, allow me to introduce—"

"Do not trouble yourself, Lydia. I have met this person once before to-day, and I do not care for an introduction."

When Alfred found himself gazing into the face that had haunted him all the afternoon, he forgot for the moment all about his errand. He was finally brought to a realization of the true state of affairs by Lydia's words.

"Mr. Clarke, you are all wet. What has happened?" she exclaimed, noticing the water dripping from his garments.

Suddenly a light broke in on Alfred. So the girl he had accosted on the road and "Betty" were one and the same person. His face flushed. He felt that his rudeness on that occasion may have merited censure, but that it had not justified the humiliation she had put upon him.

These two persons, so strangely brought together, and on whom Fate had made her inscrutable designs, looked steadily into each other's eyes. What mysterious force thrilled through Alfred Clarke and made Betty Zane tremble?

"Miss Boggs, I am twice unfortunate," said Alfred, turning to Lydia, and there was an earnest ring in his deep voice. "This time I am indeed blameless. I have just left Colonel Zane's house, where there has been an accident, and I was dispatched to find 'Betty,' being entirely ignorant as to who she might be. Colonel Zane did not stop to explain. Miss Zane is needed at the house, that is all."

And without so much as a glance at Betty he bowed low to Lydia and then strode out of the open door.

"What did he say?" asked Betty, in a small trembling voice, all her anger and resentment vanished.

"There has been an accident. He did not say what or to whom. You must hurry home. Oh, Betty, I hope no one has been hurt! And you were very unkind to Mr. Clarke. I am sure he is a gentleman, and you might have waited a moment to learn what he meant."

Betty did not answer, but flew out of the door and down the path to the gate of the fort. She was almost breathless when she reached Colonel Zane's house, and hesitated on the step before entering. Summoning her courage she pushed open the door. The first thing that struck her after the bright light was the pungent odor of strong liniment. She saw several women neighbors whispering together. Major McColloch and Jonathan Zane were standing by a couch over which Mrs. Zane was bending. Colonel Zane sat at the foot of the couch. Betty saw this in the first rapid glance, and then, as the Colonel's wife moved aside, she saw a prostrate figure, a white face and dark eyes that smiled at her.

"Betty," came in a low voice from those pale lips.

Her heart leaped and then seemed to cease beating. Many long years had passed since she had heard that voice, but it had never been forgotten. It was the best beloved voice of her childhood, and with it came the sweet memories of her brother and playmate. With a cry of joy she fell on her knees beside him and threw her arms around his neck.

"Oh, Isaac, brother, brother!" she cried, as she kissed him again and again. "Can it really be you? Oh, it is too good to be true! Thank God! I have prayed and prayed that you would be restored to us."

Then she began to cry and laugh at the same time in that strange way in which a woman relieves a heart too full of joy.

"Yes, Betty. It is all that is left of me," he said, running his hand caressingly over the dark head that lay on his breast.

"Betty, you must not excite him," said Colonel Zane.

"So you have not forgotten me?" whispered Isaac.

"No, indeed, Isaac. I have never forgotten," answered Betty, softly. "Only last night I spoke of you and wondered if you were living. And now you are here. Oh, I am so happy!" The quivering lips and the dark eyes bright with tears spoke eloquently of her joy.

"Major, will you tell Captain Boggs to come over after supper? Isaac will be able to talk a little by then, and he has some news of the Indians," said Colonel Zane.

"And ask the young man who saved my life to come that I may thank him," said Isaac.

"Saved your life?" exclaimed Betty, turning to her brother, in surprise, while a dark red flush spread over her face. A humiliating thought had flashed into her mind.

"Saved his life, of course," said Colonel Zane, answering for Isaac. "Young Clarke pulled him out of the river. Didn't he tell you?"

"No," said Betty, rather faintly.

"Well, he is a modest young fellow. He saved Isaac's life, there is no doubt of that. You will hear all about it after supper. Don't make Isaac talk any more at present."

Betty hid her face on Isaac's shoulder and remained quiet a few moments; then, rising, she kissed his cheek and went quietly to her room. Once there she threw herself on the bed and tried to think. The events of the day, coming after a long string of monotonous, wearying days, had been confusing; they had succeeded one another in such rapid order as to leave no time for reflection. The meeting by the river with the rude but interesting stranger; the shock to her dignity; Lydia's kindly advice; the stranger again, this time emerging from the dark depths of disgrace into the luminous light as the hero of her brother's rescue—all these thoughts jumbled in her mind making it difficult for her to think clearly. But after a time one thing forced itself upon her. She could not help being conscious that she had wronged some one to whom she would be forever indebted. Nothing could alter that. She was under an eternal obligation to the man who had saved the life she loved best on earth. She had unjustly scorned and insulted the man to whom she owed the life of her brother.

Betty was passionate and quick-tempered, but she was generous and tenderhearted as well, and when she realized how unkind and cruel she had been she felt very miserable. Her position admitted of no retreat. No matter how much pride rebelled; no matter how much she disliked to retract anything she had said, she knew no other course lay open to her. She would have to apologize to Mr. Clarke. How could she? What would she say? She remembered how cold and stern his face had been as he turned from her to Lydia. Perplexed and unhappy, Betty did what any girl in her position would have done: she resorted to the consoling and unfailing privilege of her sex—a good cry.

When she became composed again she got up and bathed her hot cheeks, brushed her hair, and changed her gown for a becoming one of white. She tied a red ribbon about her throat and put a rosette in her hair. She had forgotten all about the Indians. By the time Mrs. Zane called her for supper she had her mind made up to ask Mr. Clarke's pardon, tell him she was sorry, and that she hoped they might be friends.

Isaac Zane's fame had spread from the Potomac to Detroit and Louisville. Many an anxious mother on the border used the story of his captivity as a means to frighten truant youngsters who had evinced a love for running wild in the woods. The evening of Isaac's return every one in the settlement called to welcome home the wanderer. In spite of the troubled times and the dark cloud hanging over them they made the occasion one of rejoicing.

Old John Bennet, the biggest and merriest man in the colony, came in and roared his appreciation of Isaac's return. He was a huge man, and when he stalked into the room he made the floor shake with his heavy tread. His honest face expressed his pleasure as he stood over Isaac and nearly crushed his hand.

"Glad to see you, Isaac. Always knew you would come back. Always said so. There are not enough damn redskins on the river to keep you prisoner."

"I think they managed to keep him long enough," remarked Silas Zane.

"Well, here comes the hero," said Colonel Zane, as Clarke entered, accompanied by Captain Boggs, Major McColloch and Jonathan. "Any sign of Wetzel or the Indians?"

Jonathan had not yet seen his brother, and he went over and seized Isaac's hand and wrung it without speaking.

"There are no Indians on this side of the river," said Major McColloch, in answer to the Colonel's question.

"Mr. Clarke, you do not seem impressed with your importance," said Colonel Zane. "My sister said you did not tell her what part you took in Isaac's rescue."

"I hardly deserve all the credit," answered Alfred. "Your big black dog merits a great deal of it."

"Well, I consider your first day at the fort a very satisfactory one, and an augury of that fortune you came west to find."

"How are you?" said Alfred, going up to the couch where Isaac lay.

"I am doing well, thanks to you," said Isaac, warmly shaking Alfred's hand.

"It is good to see you pulling out all right," answered Alfred. "I tell you, I feared you were in a bad way when I got you out of the water."

Isaac reclined on the couch with his head and shoulder propped up by pillows. He was the handsomest of the brothers. His face would have been but for the marks of privation, singularly like Betty's; the same low, level brows and dark eyes; the same mouth, though the lips were stronger and without the soft curves which made his sister's mouth so sweet.

Betty appeared at the door, and seeing the room filled with men she hesitated a moment before coming forward. In her white dress she made such a dainty picture that she seemed out of place among those surroundings. Alfred Clarke, for one, thought such a charming vision was wasted on the rough settlers, every one of whom wore a faded and dirty buckskin suit and a belt containing a knife and a tomahawk. Colonel Zane stepped up to Betty and placing his arm around her turned toward Clarke with pride in his eyes.

"Betty, I want to make you acquainted with the hero of the hour, Mr. Alfred Clarke. This is my sister."

Betty bowed to Alfred, but lowered her eyes instantly on encountering the young man's gaze.

"I have had the pleasure of meeting Miss Zane twice to-day," said Alfred.

"Twice?" asked Colonel Zane, turning to Betty. She did not answer, but disengaged herself from his arm and sat down by Isaac.

"It was on the river road that I first met Miss Zane, although I did not know her then," answered Alfred. "I had some difficulty in stopping her pony from going to Fort Pitt, or some other place down the river."

"Ha! Ha! Well, I know she rides that pony pretty hard," said Colonel Zane, with his hearty laugh. "I'll tell you,

Clarke, we have some riders here in the settlement. Have you heard of Major McColloch's leap over the hill?"

"I have heard it mentioned, and I would like to hear the story," responded Alfred. "I am fond of horses, and think I can ride a little myself. I am afraid I shall be compelled to change my mind."

"That is a fine animal you rode from Fort Pitt," remarked the Major. "I would like to own him."

"Come, draw your chairs up and we'll listen to Isaac's story," said Colonel Zane.

"I have not much of a story to tell," said Isaac, in a voice still weak and low. "I have some bad news, I am sorry to say, but I shall leave that for the last. This year, if it had been completed, would have made my tenth year as a captive of the Wyandots. This last period of captivity, which has been nearly four years, I have not been ill-treated and have enjoyed more comfort than any of you can imagine. Probably you are all familiar with the reason for my long captivity. Because of the interest of Myeerah, the Indian Princess, they have importuned me for years to be adopted into the tribe, marry the White Crane, as they call Myeerah, and become a Wyandot chief. To this I would never consent, though I have been careful not to provoke the Indians. I was allowed the freedom of the camp, but have always been closely watched. I should still be with the Indians had I not suspected that Hamilton, the British Governor, had formed a plan with the Hurons, Shawnees, Delawares, and other tribes, to strike a terrible blow at the whites along the river. For months I have watched the Indians preparing for an expedition, the extent of which they had never before undertaken. I finally learned from Myeerah that my suspicions were well founded. A favorable chance to escape presented and I took it and got away. I outran all the braves, even Arrowswift, the Wyandot runner, who shot me through the arm. I have had a hard time of it these last three or four days, living on herbs and roots, and when I reached the river I was ready to drop. I pushed a log into the water and started to drift over. When the old dog saw me I knew I was safe if I could hold on. Once, when the young man pointed his gun at me, I thought it was all over. I could not shout very loud."

"Were you going to shoot?" asked Colonel Zane of Clarke.

"I took him for an Indian, but fortunately I discovered my mistake in time," answered Alfred.

"Are the Indians on the way here?" asked Jonathan.

"That I cannot say. At present the Wyandots are at home. But I know that the British and the Indians will make a combined attack on the settlements. It may be a month, or a year, but it is coming."

"And Hamilton, the hair buyer, the scalp buyer, is behind the plan," said Colonel Zane, in disgust.

"The Indians have their wrongs. I sympathize with them in many ways. We have robbed them, broken faith with them, and have not lived up to the treaties. Pipe and Wingenund are particularly bitter toward the whites. I understand Cornplanter is also. He would give anything for Jonathan's scalp, and I believe any of the tribes would give a hundred of their best warriors for 'Black Wind,' as they call Lew Wetzel."

"Have you ever seen Red Fox?" asked Jonathan, who was sitting near the fire and as usual saying but little. He was the wildest and most untamable of all the Zanes. Most of the time he spent in the woods, not so much to fight Indians, as Wetzel did, but for pure love of outdoor life. At home he was thoughtful and silent.

"Yes, I have seen him," answered Isaac. "He is a Shawnee chief and one of the fiercest warriors in that tribe of fighters. He was at Indian-head, which is the name of one of the Wyandot villages, when I visited there last, and he had two hundred of his best braves with him."

"He is a bad Indian. Wetzel and I know him. He swore he would hang our scalps up in his wigwam," said Jonathan.

"What has he in particular against you?" asked Colonel Zane. "Of course, Wetzel is the enemy of all Indians."

"Several years ago Wetzel and I were on a hunt down the river at the place called Girty's Point, where we fell in with the tracks of five Shawnees. I was for coming home, but Wetzel would not hear of it. We trailed the Indians and, coming up on them after dark, we tomahawked them. One of them got away crippled, but we could not follow him because we discovered that they had a white girl as captive, and one of the red devils, thinking we were a rescuing party, had tomahawked her. She was not quite dead. We did all we could to save her life. She died and we buried her on the spot. They were Red Fox's braves and were on their way to his camp with the prisoner. A year or so afterwards I learned from a friendly Indian that the Shawnee chief had sworn to kill us. No doubt he will be a leader in the coming attack."

"We are living in the midst of terrible times," remarked Colonel Zane. "Indeed, these are the times that try men's souls, but I firmly believe the day is not far distant when the redmen will be driven far over the border."

"Is the Indian Princess pretty?" asked Betty of Isaac.

"Indeed she is, Betty, almost as beautiful as you are," said Isaac. "She is tall and very fair for an Indian. But I have something to tell about her more interesting than that. Since I have been with the Wyandots this last time I have discovered a little of the jealously guarded secret of Myeerah's mother. When Tarhe and his band of Hurons lived in Canada their home was in the Muskoka Lakes region on the Moon river. The old warriors tell wonderful stories of the beauty of that country. Tarhe took captive some French travellers, among them a woman named La Durante. She had a beautiful little girl. The prisoners, except this little girl, were released. When she grew up Tarhe married her. Myeerah is her child. Once Tarhe took his wife to Detroit and she was seen there by an old Frenchman who went crazy over her and said she was his child. Tarhe never went to the white settlements again. So you see, Myeerah is from a great French family on her mother's side, as this old Frenchman was probably Chevalier La Durante, and Myeerah's grandfather."

"I would love to see her, and yet I hate her. What an odd name she has," said Betty.

"It is the Indian name for the white crane, a rare and beautiful bird. I never saw one. The name has been celebrated among the Hurons as long as any one of them can remember. The Indians call her the White Crane, or Walk-in-the-Water, because of her love for wading in the stream."

"I think we have made Isaac talk enough for one night," said Colonel Zane. "He is tired out. Major, tell Isaac and Betty, and Mr. Clarke, too, of your jump over the cliff."

"I have heard of that leap from the Indians," said Isaac.

"Major, from what hill did you jump your horse?" asked Alfred.

"You know the bare rocky bluff that stands out prominently on the hill across the creek. From that spot Colonel Zane first saw the valley, and from there I leaped my horse. I can never convince myself that it really happened. Often I look up at that cliff in doubt. But the Indians and Colonel Zane, Jonathan, Wetzel and others say they actually saw the deed done, so I must accept it," said Major McColloch.

"It seems incredible!" said Alfred. "I cannot understand how a man or horse could go over that precipice and live."

"That is what we all say," responded the Colonel. "I suppose I shall have to tell the story. We have fighters and makers of history here, but few talkers."

"I am anxious to hear it," answered Clarke, "and I am curious to see this man Wetzel, whose fame has reached as far as my home, way down in Virginia."

"You will have your wish gratified soon, I have no doubt," resumed the Colonel. "Well, now for the story of McColloch's mad ride for life and his wonderful leap down Wheeling hill. A year ago, when the fort was besieged by the Indians, the Major got through the lines and made off for Short Creek. He returned next morning with forty mounted men. They marched boldly up to the gate, and all succeeded in getting inside save the gallant Major, who had waited to be the last man to go in. Finding it impossible to make the short distance without going under the fire of the Indians, who had rushed up to prevent the relief party from entering the fort, he wheeled his big stallion, and, followed by the yelling band of savages, he took the road leading around back of the fort to the top of the bluff. The road lay along the edge of the cliff and I saw the Major turn and wave his rifle at us, evidently with the desire of assuring us that he was safe. Suddenly, on the very summit of the hill, he reined in his horse as if undecided. I knew in an instant what had happened. The Major had run right into the returning party of Indians, which had been sent out to intercept our reinforcements. In a moment more we heard the exultant yells of the savages, and saw them gliding from tree to tree, slowly lengthening out their line and surrounding the unfortunate Major. They did not fire a shot. We in the fort were stupefied with horror, and stood helplessly with our useless guns, watching and waiting for the seemingly inevitable doom of our comrade. Not so with the Major! Knowing that he was a marked man by the Indians and feeling that any death was preferable to the gauntlet, the knife, the stake and torch of the merciless savage, he had grasped at a desperate chance. He saw his enemies stealthily darting from rock to tree, and tree to bush, creeping through the brush, and slipping closer and closer every moment. On three sides were his hated foes and on the remaining side—the abyss. Without a moment's hesitation the intrepid Major spurred his horse at the precipice. Never shall I forget that thrilling moment. The three hundred savages were silent as they realized the Major's intention. Those in the fort watched with staring eyes. A few bounds and the noble steed reared high on his hind legs. Outlined by the clear blue sky the magnificent animal stood for one brief instant, his black mane flying in the wind, his head thrown up and his front hoofs pawing the air like Marcus Curtius' mailed steed of old, and then down with a crash, a cloud of dust, and the crackling of pine limbs. A long yell went up from the Indians below, while those above ran to the edge of the cliff. With cries of wonder and baffled vengeance they gesticulated toward the dark ravine into which horse and rider had plunged rather than wait to meet a more cruel death. The precipice at this point is over three hundred feet in height, and in places is almost perpendicular. We believed the Major to be lying crushed and mangled on the rocks. Imagine our frenzy of joy when we saw the daring soldier and his horse dash out of the bushes that skirt the base of the cliff, cross the creek, and come galloping to the fort in safety."

"It was wonderful! Wonderful!" exclaimed Isaac, his eyes glistening. "No wonder the Indians call you the 'Flying chief.'"

"Had the Major not jumped into the clump of pine trees which grow thickly some thirty feet below the summit he would not now be alive," said Colonel Zane. "I am certain of that. Nevertheless that does not detract from the courage of his deed. He had no time to pick out the best place to jump. He simply took his one chance, and came out all right. That leap will live in the minds of men as long as yonder bluff stands as a monument to McColloch's ride for life."

Alfred had listened with intense interest to the Colonel's recital. When it ended, although his pulses quickened and his soul expanded with awe and reverence for the hero of that ride, he sat silent. Alfred honored courage in a man more than any other quality. He marvelled at the simplicity of these bordermen who, he thought, took the most wonderful adventures and daring escapes as a matter of course, a compulsory part of their daily lives. He had already, in one day, had more excitement than had ever befallen him; and was beginning to believe his thirst for a free life of stirring action would be quenched long before he had learned to become useful in his new sphere. During the remaining half hour of his call on his lately acquired friends, he took little part in the conversation, but sat quietly watching the changeful expressions on Betty's face, and listening to Colonel Zane's jokes. When he rose to go he bade his host good-night, and expressed a wish that Isaac, who had fallen asleep, might have a speedy recovery. He turned toward the door to find that Betty had intercepted him.

"Mr. Clarke," she said, extending a little hand that trembled slightly. "I wish to say—that—I want to say that my feelings have changed. I am sorry for what I said over at Lydia's. I spoke hastily and rudely. You have saved my brother's life. I will be forever grateful to you. It is useless to try to thank you. I—I hope we may be friends."

Alfred found it desperately hard to resist that low voice, and those dark eyes which were raised shyly, yet bravely, to his. But he had been deeply hurt. He pretended not to see the friendly hand held out to him, and his voice was cold when he answered her.

"I am glad to have been of some service," he said, "but I think you overrate my action. Your brother would not have drowned, I am sure. You owe me nothing. Good-night."

Betty stood still one moment staring at the door through which he had gone before she realized that her overtures of friendship had been politely, but coldly, ignored. She had actually been snubbed. The impossible had happened to Elizabeth Zane. Her first sensation after she recovered from her momentary bewilderment was one of amusement, and she laughed in a constrained manner; but, presently, two bright red spots appeared in her cheeks, and she looked quickly around to see if any of the others had noticed the incident. None of them had been paying any attention to her and she breathed a sigh of relief. It was bad enough to be snubbed without having others see it. That would have been too humiliating. Her eyes flashed fire as she remembered the disdain in Clarke's face, and that she had not been clever enough to see it in time.

"Tige, come here!" called Colonel Zane. "What ails the dog?"

The dog had jumped to his feet and ran to the door, where he sniffed at the crack over the threshold. His aspect was fierce and threatening. He uttered low growls and then two short barks. Those in the room heard a soft moccasined footfall outside. The next instant the door opened wide and a tall figure stood disclosed.

"Wetzel!" exclaimed Colonel Zane. A hush fell on the little company after that exclamation, and all eyes were fastened on the new comer.

Well did the stranger merit close attention. He stalked into the room, leaned his long rifle against the mantelpiece and spread out his hands to the fire. He was clad from head to foot in fringed and beaded buckskin, which showed evidence of a long and arduous tramp. It was torn and wet and covered with mud. He was a magnificently made man, six feet in height, and stood straight as an arrow. His wide shoulders, and his muscular, though not heavy, limbs denoted wonderful strength and activity. His long hair, black as a raven's wing, hung far down his shoulders. Presently he turned and the light shone on a remarkable face. So calm and cold and stern it was that it seemed chiselled out of marble. The most striking features were its unusual pallor, and the eyes, which were coal black, and piercing as the dagger's point.

"If you have any bad news out with it," cried Colonel Zane, impatiently.

"No need fer alarm," said Wetzel. He smiled slightly as he saw Betty's apprehensive face. "Don't look scared, Betty. The redskins are miles away and goin' fer the Kanawha settlement."

CHAPTER 3

Many weeks of quiet followed the events of the last chapter. The settlers planted their corn, harvested their wheat and labored in the fields during the whole of one spring and summer without hearing the dreaded war cry of the Indians. Colonel Zane, who had been a disbursing officer in the army of Lord Dunmore, where he had attained the rank of Colonel, visited Fort Pitt during the summer in the hope of increasing the number of soldiers in his garrison. His efforts proved fruitless. He returned to Fort Henry by way of the river with several pioneers, who with their families were bound for Fort Henry. One of these pioneers was a minister who worked in the fields every weekday and on Sundays preached the Gospel to those who gathered in the meeting house.

Alfred Clarke had taken up his permanent abode at the fort, where he had been installed as one of the regular garrison. His duties, as well as those of the nine other members of the garrison, were light. For two hours out of the twenty-four he was on guard. Thus, he had ample time to acquaint himself with the settlers and their families.

Alfred and Isaac had now become firm friends. They spent many hours fishing in the river, and roaming the woods in the vicinity, as Colonel Zane would not allow Isaac to stray far from the fort. Alfred became a regular visitor at Colonel Zane's house. He saw Betty every day, but as yet, nothing had mended the breach between them. They were civil to each other when chance threw them together, but Betty usually left the room on some pretext soon after he entered. Alfred regretted his hasty exhibition of resentment and would have been glad to establish friendly relations with her. But she would not give him an opportunity. She avoided him on all possible occasions. Though Alfred was fast succumbing to the charm of Betty's beautiful face, though his desire to be near her had grown well nigh resistless, his pride had not yet broken down. Many of the summer evenings found him on the Colonel's doorstep, smoking a pipe, or playing with the children. He was that rare and best company—a good listener. Although he laughed at Colonel Zane's stories, and never tired of hearing of Isaac's experiences among the Indians, it is probable he would not have partaken of the Colonel's hospitality nearly so often had it not been that he usually saw Betty, and if he got only a glimpse of her he went away satisfied. On Sundays he attended the services at the little church, and listened to Betty's sweet voice as she led the singing.

There were a number of girls at the fort near Betty's age. With all of these girls Alfred was popular. He appeared so entirely different from the usual young man on the frontier that he was more than welcome everywhere. Girls in the backwoods are much the same as girls in thickly populated and civilized districts. They liked his manly ways; his frank and pleasant manners; and when to these virtues he added a certain deferential regard, a courtliness to which they were unaccustomed, they were all the better pleased. He paid the young women little attentions, such as calling on them, taking them to parties and out driving, but there was not one of them who could think that she, in particular, interested him.

The girls noticed, however, that he never approached Betty after service, or on any occasion, and while it caused some wonder and gossip among them, for Betty enjoyed the distinction of being the belle of the border, they were secretly pleased. Little hints and knowing smiles, with which girls are so skillful, made known to Betty all of this, and, although she was apparently indifferent, it hurt her sensitive feelings. It had the effect of making her believe she hated the cause of it more than ever.

What would have happened had things gone on in this way, I am not prepared to say; probably had not a meddling Fate decided to take a hand in the game, Betty would have continued to think she hated Alfred, and I would never have had occasion to write his story; but Fate did interfere, and, one day in the early fall, brought about an incident which changed the whole world for the two young people.

It was the afternoon of an Indian summer day—in that most beautiful time of all the year—and Betty, accompanied by her dog, had wandered up the hillside into the woods. From the hilltop the broad river could be seen winding away in the distance, and a soft, bluish, smoky haze hung over the water. The forest seemed to be on fire. The yellow leaves of the poplars, the brown of the white and black oaks, the red and purple of the maples, and the green of the pines and hemlocks flamed in a glorious blaze of color. A stillness, which was only broken now and then by the twittering of birds uttering the plaintive notes peculiar to them in the autumn as they band together before their pilgrimage to the far south, pervaded the forest.

Betty loved the woods, and she knew all the trees. She could tell their names by the bark or the shape of the leaves. The giant black oak, with its smooth shiny bark and sturdy limbs, the chestnut with its rugged, seamed sides and bristling burrs, the hickory with its lofty height and curled shelling bark, were all well known and well loved by Betty. Many times had she wondered at the trembling, quivering leaves of the aspen, and the foliage of the silver-leaf as it glinted in the sun. To-day, especially, as she walked through the woods, did their beauty appeal to her. In the little sunny patches of clearing which were scattered here and there in the grove, great clusters of goldenrod grew profusely. The golden heads swayed gracefully on the long stems. Betty gathered a few sprigs and added to them a bunch of warmly tinted maple leaves.

The chestnut burrs were opening. As Betty mounted a little rocky eminence and reached out for a limb of a chestnut tree, she lost her footing and fell. Her right foot had twisted under her as she went down, and when a sharp pain shot through it she was unable to repress a cry. She got up, tenderly placed the foot on the ground and tried her weight on it, which caused acute pain. She unlaced and removed her moccasin to find that her ankle had commenced to swell. Assured that she had sprained it, and aware of the serious consequences of an injury of that nature, she felt greatly distressed. Another effort to place her foot on the ground and bear her weight on it caused such severe pain that she was compelled to give up the attempt. Sinking down by the trunk of the tree and leaning her head against it she tried to think of a way out of her difficulty.

The fort, which she could plainly see, seemed a long distance off, although it was only a little way down the grassy slope. She looked and looked, but not a person was to be seen. She called to Tige. She remembered that he had been chasing a squirrel a short while ago, but now there was no sign of him. He did not come at her call. How annoying! If Tige were only there she could have sent him for help. She shouted several times, but the distance was too great for her voice to carry to the fort. The mocking echo of her call came back from the bluff that rose to her left. Betty now began to be alarmed in earnest, and the tears started to roll down her cheeks. The throbbing pain in her ankle, the dread of having to remain out in that lonesome forest after dark, and the fear that she might not be found for hours, caused Betty's usually brave spirit to falter; she was weeping unreservedly.

In reality she had been there only a few minutes— although they seemed hours to her—when she heard the light tread of moccasined feet on the moss behind her. Starting up with a cry of joy she turned and looked up into the astonished face of Alfred Clarke.

Returning from a hunt back in the woods he had walked up to her before being aware of her presence. In a single glance he saw the wildflowers scattered beside her, the little moccasin turned inside out, the woebegone, tearstained face, and he knew Betty had come to grief.

Confused and vexed, Betty sank back at the foot of the tree. It is probable she would have encountered Girty or a member of his band of redmen, rather than have this young man find her in this predicament. It provoked her to think that of all the people at the fort it should be the only one she could not welcome who should find her in such a sad plight.

"Why, Miss Zane!" he exclaimed, after a moment of hesitation. "What in the world has happened? Have you been hurt? May I help you?"

"It is nothing," said Betty, bravely, as she gathered up her flowers and the moccasin and rose slowly to her feet. "Thank you, but you need not wait."

The cold words nettled Alfred and he was in the act of turning away from her when he caught, for the fleetest part of a second, the full gaze of her eyes. He stopped short. A closer scrutiny of her face convinced him that she was suffering and endeavoring with all her strength to conceal it.

"But I will wait. I think you have hurt yourself. Lean upon my arm," he said, quietly.

"Please let me help you," he continued, going nearer to her.

But Betty refused his assistance. She would not even allow him to take the goldenrod from her arms. After a few hesitating steps she paused and lifted her foot from the ground.

"Here, you must not try to walk a step farther," he said, resolutely, noting how white she had suddenly become. "You have sprained your ankle and are needlessly torturing yourself. Please let me carry you?"

"Oh, no, no, no!" cried Betty, in evident distress. "I will manage. It is not so—very—far."

She resumed the slow and painful walking, but she had taken only a few steps when she stopped again and this time a low moan issued from her lips. She swayed slightly backward and if Alfred had not dropped his rifle and caught her she would have fallen.

"Will you—please—go—for some one?" she whispered faintly, at the same time pushing him away.

"How absurd!" burst out Alfred, indignantly. "Am I, then, so distasteful to you that you would rather wait here and suffer a half hour longer while I go for assistance? It is only common courtesy on my part. I do not want to carry you. I think you would be quite heavy."

He said this in a hard, bitter tone, deeply hurt that she would not accept even a little kindness from him. He looked away from her and waited. Presently a soft, half-smothered sob came from Betty and it expressed such utter wretchedness that his heart melted. After all she was only a child. He turned to see the tears running down her cheeks, and with a suppressed imprecation upon the willfulness of young women in general, and this one in particular, he stepped forward and before she could offer any resistance, he had taken her up in his arms, goldenrod and all, and had started off at a rapid walk toward the fort.

Betty cried out in angry surprise, struggled violently for a moment, and then, as suddenly, lay quietly in his arms. His anger changed to self-reproach as he realized what a light burden she made. He looked down at the dark head lying on his shoulder. Her face was hidden by the dusky rippling hair, which tumbled over his breast, brushed against his cheek, and blew across his lips. The touch of those fragrant tresses was a soft caress. Almost unconsciously he pressed her closer to his heart. And as a sweet mad longing grew upon him he was blind to all save that he held her in his arms, that uncertainty was gone forever, and that he loved her. With these thoughts running riot in his brain he carried her down the hill to Colonel Zane's house.

Sam came out of the kitchen, dropped the bucket he had in his hand and ran into the house when he saw them. When Alfred reached the gate Colonel Zane and Isaac were hurrying out to meet him.

"For Heaven's sake! What has happened? Is she badly hurt? I have always looked for this," said the Colonel, excitedly.

"You need not look so alarmed," answered Alfred. "She has only sprained her ankle, and trying to walk afterward hurt her so badly that she became faint and I had to carry her."

"Dear me, is that all?" said Mrs. Zane, who had also come out. "We were terribly frightened. Sam came running into the house saying something had happened to Betty."

"How ridiculous! Colonel Zane, that servant of yours never fails to say something against me," said Alfred, as he carried Betty into the house.

"For some reason, Sam just doesn't like you. But you need not mind Sam. We are certainly indebted to you," returned the Colonel.

Betty was laid on the couch and consigned to the skillful hands of Mrs. Zane, who pronounced the injury a bad sprain.

"Well, Betty, this will keep you quiet for a few days," said she, with a touch of humor, as she gently felt the swollen ankle.

"Alfred, you have been our good angel so often that I don't see how we shall ever reward you," said Isaac to Alfred.

"Oh, that time will come. Don't worry about that," said Alfred, jestingly, and then, turning to the others he continued, earnestly. "I will apologize for the manner in which I disregarded Miss Zane's wish not to help her. I am sure I could do no less. I believe my rudeness has spared her considerable suffering."

"What did he mean, Betts?" asked Isaac, going back to his sister after he had closed the door. "Didn't you want him to help you?"

Betty did not answer. She sat on the couch while Mrs. Zane held the little bare foot and slowly poured the hot water over the swollen and discolored ankle. Betty's lips were pale. She winced every time Mrs. Zane touched her foot, but as yet she had not uttered even a sigh.

"Betty, does it hurt much?" asked Isaac.

"Hurt? Do you think I am made of wood? Of course it hurts," retorted Betty. "That water is so hot. Bessie, will not cold water do as well?"

"I am sorry. I won't tease any more," said Isaac, taking his sister's hand. "I'll tell you what, Betty, we owe Alfred

Clarke a great deal, you and I. I am going to tell you something so you will know how much more you owe him. Do you remember last month when that red heifer of yours got away. Well, Clarke chased her all day and finally caught her in the woods. He asked me to say I had caught her. Somehow or other he seems to be afraid of you. I wish you and he would be good friends. He is a mighty fine fellow."

In spite of the pain Betty was suffering, a bright blush suffused her face at the words of her brother, who, blind as brothers are in regard to their own sisters, went on praising his friend.

Betty was confined to the house for a week or more and during this enforced idleness she had ample time for reflection and opportunity to inquire into the perplexed state of her mind.

The small room, which Betty called her own, faced the river and fort. Most of the day she lay by the window trying to read her favorite books, but often she gazed out on the quiet scene, the rolling river, the everchanging trees and the pastures in which the red and white cows grazed peacefully; or she would watch with idle, dreamy eyes the flight of the crows over the hills, and the graceful motion of the hawk as he sailed around and around in the azure sky, looking like a white sail far out on a summer sea.

But Betty's mind was at variance with this peaceful scene. The consciousness of a change, which she could not readily define, in her feelings toward Alfred Clarke, vexed and irritated her. Why did she think of him so often? True, he had saved her brother's life. Still she was compelled to admit to herself that this was not the reason. Try as she would, she could not banish the thought of him. Over and over again, a thousand times, came the recollection of that moment when he had taken her up in his arms as though she were a child. Some vague feeling stirred in her heart as she remembered the strong yet gentle clasp of his arms.

Several times from her window she had seen him coming across the square between the fort and her brother's house, and womanlike, unseen herself, she had watched him. How erect was his carriage. How pleasant his deep voice sounded as she heard him talking to her brother. Day by day, as her ankle grew stronger and she knew she could not remain much longer in her room, she dreaded more and more the thought of meeting him. She could not understand herself; she had strange dreams; she cried seemingly without the slightest cause; and she was restless and unhappy. Finally she grew angry and scolded herself. She said she was silly and sentimental. This had the effect of making her bolder, but it did not quiet her unrest. Betty did not know that the little blind God, who steals unawares on his victim, had marked her for his own, and that all this sweet perplexity was the unconscious awakening of the heart.

One afternoon, near the end of Betty's siege indoors, two of her friends, Lydia Boggs and Alice Reynolds, called to see her.

Alice had bright blue eyes, and her nut brown hair hung in rebellious curls around her demure and pretty face. An adorable dimple lay hidden in her rosy cheek and flashed into light with her smiles.

"Betty, you are a lazy thing!" exclaimed Lydia. "Lying here all day long doing nothing but gaze out of the window."

"Girls, I am glad you came over," said Betty. "I am blue. Perhaps you will cheer me up."

"Betty needs some one of the sterner sex to cheer her," said Alice, mischievously, her eyes twinkling. "Don't you think so, Lydia?"

"Of course," answered Lydia. "When I get blue—"

"Please spare me," interrupted Betty, holding up her hands in protest. "I have not a single doubt that your masculine remedies are sufficient for all your ills. Girls who have lost their interest in the old pleasures, who spend their spare time making linen and quilts, and who have sunk their very personalities in a great big tyrant of a man, are not liable to get blue. They are afraid he may see a tear or a frown. But, thank goodness, I have not yet reached that stage."

"Oh, Betty Zane! Just you wait! Wait!" exclaimed Lydia, shaking her finger at Betty. "Your turn is coming. When it does do not expect any mercy from us, for you shall never get it."

"Unfortunately, you and Alice have monopolized the attentions of the only two eligible young men at the fort," said Betty, with a laugh.

"Nonsense. There are plenty of young men all eager for your favor, you little coquette," answered Lydia. "Harry Martin, Will Metzer, Captain Swearengen, of Short Creek, and others too numerous to count. Look at Lew Wetzel and Billy Bennet."

"Lew cares for nothing except hunting Indians and Billy is only a boy," said Betty.

"Well, have it your own way," said Lydia. "Only this, I know Billy adores you, for he told me so, and a better lad never lived."

"Lyde, you forget to include one other among those prostrate before Betty's charms," said Alice.

"Oh, yes, you mean Mr. Clarke. To be sure, I had forgotten him," answered Lydia. "How odd that he should be the one to find you the day you hurt your foot. Was it an accident?"

"Of course. I slipped off the bank," said Betty.

"No, no. I don't mean that. Was his finding you an accident?"

"Do you imagine I waylaid Mr. Clarke, and then sprained my ankle on purpose?" said Betty, who began to look dangerous.

"Certainly not that; only it seems so odd that he should be the one to rescue all the damsels in distress. Day before yesterday he stopped a runaway horse, and saved Nell Metzer, who was in the wagon, a severe shaking up, if not something more serious. She is desperately in love with him. She told me Mr. Clarke—"

"I really do not care to hear about it," interrupted Betty.

"But, Betty, tell us. Wasn't it dreadful, his carrying you?" asked Alice, with a sly glance at Betty. "You know you are so—so prudish, one may say. Did he take you in his arms? It must have been very embarrassing for you, considering your dislike of Mr. Clarke, and he so much in love with—"

"You hateful girls," cried Betty, throwing a pillow at Alice, who just managed to dodge it. "I wish you would go home."

"Never mind, Betty. We will not tease anymore," said Lydia, putting her arm around Betty. "Come, Alice, we will tell Betty you have named the day for your wedding. See. She is all eyes now."

The young people of the frontier settlements were usually married before they were twenty. This was owing to the fact that there was little distinction of rank and family pride. The object of the pioneers in moving West was, of course, to better their condition; but, the realization of their dependence on one another, the common cause of their labors, and the terrible dangers to which they were continually exposed, brought them together as one large family.

Therefore, early love affairs were encouraged, not

frowned upon as they are to-day—and they usually resulted in early marriages.

However, do not let it be imagined that the path of the
youthful swain was strewn with flowers. Courting or
"sparking" his sweetheart had a painful as well as a joyous side. Many and varied were the tricks played on the
fortunate lover by the gallants who had vied with him for
the favor of the maid. Brave, indeed, he who won her. If
he marched up to her home in the early evening he was
made the object of innumerable jests, even the young
lady's family indulging in and enjoying the banter. Later,
when he came out of the door, it was more than likely
that, if it were winter, he would be met by a volley of water-
soaked snowballs, or big buckets of icewater, or a mountain of snow shoved off the roof by some trickster, who
had waited patiently for such an opportunity. On summer
nights his horse would be stolen, led far into the woods
and tied, or the wheels of his wagon would be taken off
and hidden, leaving him to walk home. Usually the successful lover, and especially if he lived at a distance,
would make his way only once a week and then late at
night to the home of his betrothed. Silently, like a thief in
the dark, he would crawl through the grass and shrubs until beneath her window. At a low signal, prearranged between them, she would slip to the door and let him in
without disturbing her parents. Fearing to make a light,
and perhaps welcoming that excuse to enjoy the darkness
beloved by sweethearts, they would sit quietly, whispering low, until the brightening in the east betokened the
break of day, and then he was off, happy and lighthearted,
to his labors.

A wedding was looked forward to with much pleasure
by old and young. Practically, it meant the only gathering
of the settlers which was not accompanied by the work
of reaping the harvest, building a cabin, planning an

expedition to relieve some distant settlement, or a defense for themselves. For all, it meant a rollicking good time; to the old people a feast, and the looking on at the merriment of their children—to the young folk, a pleasing break in the monotony of their busy lives, a day given up to fun and gossip, a day of romance, a wedding, and best of all, a dance. Therefore, Alice Reynold's wedding proved a great event to the inhabitants of Fort Henry.

The day dawned bright and clear. The sun, rising like a ball of red gold, cast its yellow beams over the bare, brown hills, shining on the cabin roofs white with frost, and making the delicate weblike coat of ice on the river sparkle as if it had been sprinkled with powdered diamonds. William Martin, the groom, and his attendants, met at an appointed time to celebrate an old time-honored custom which always took place before the party started for the house of the bride. This performance was called "the race for the bottle."

A number of young men, selected by the groom, were asked to take part in this race, which was to be run over as rough and dangerous a track as could be found. The worse the road, the more ditches, bogs, trees, stumps, brush, in fact, the more obstacles of every kind, the better, as all these afforded opportunity for daring and expert horsemanship. The English fox race, now famous on three continents, while it involves risk and is sometimes dangerous, cannot, in the sense of hazard to life and limb, be compared to this race for the bottle.

On this day the run was not less exciting than usual. The horses were placed as nearly abreast as possible and the starter gave an Indian yell. Then followed the cracking of whips, the furious pounding of heavy hoofs, the commands of the contestants, and the yells of the onlookers. Away they went at a mad pace down the road.

The course extended a mile straightaway down the creek bottom. The first hundred yards the horses were bunched. At the ditch beyond the creek bridge a beautiful, clean-limbed animal darted from among the furiously gallop-ing horses and sailed over the deep furrow like a bird. All recognized the rider as Alfred Clarke on his black thor-oughbred. Close behind was George Martin mounted on a large roan of powerful frame and long stride. Through the willows they dashed, over logs and brush heaps, up the little ridges of rising ground, and down the shallow gullies, unheeding the stinging branches and the splash-ing water. Half the distance covered and Alfred turned, to find the roan close behind. On a level road he would have laughed at the attempt of that horse to keep up with his racer, but he was beginning to fear that the strong-limbed stallion deserved his reputation. Directly before them rose a pile of logs and matted brush, placed there by the daredevil settlers who had mapped out the route. It was too high for any horse to be put at. With pale cheek and clinched teeth Alfred touched the spurs to Roger and then threw himself forward. The gallant beast responded nobly. Up, up, up he rose, clearing all but the topmost branches. Alfred turned again and saw the giant roan make the leap without touching a twig. The next instant Roger went splash into a swamp. He sank to his knees in the soft black soil. He could move but one foot at a time, and Alfred saw at a glance he had won the race. The great weight of the roan handicapped him here. When Alfred reached the other side of the bog, where the bottle was swinging from a branch of a tree, his rival's horse was floundering hopelessly in the middle of the treacher-ous mire. The remaining three horsemen, who had come up by this time, seeing that it would be useless to attempt further efforts, had drawn up on the bank. With friendly shouts to Clarke, they acknowledged themselves beaten.

There were no judges required for this race, because the man who reached the bottle first won it.

The five men returned to the starting point, where the victor was greeted by loud whoops. The groom got the first drink from the bottle, then came the attendants, and others in order, after which the bottle was put away to be kept as a memento of the occasion.

The party now repaired to the village and marched to the home of the bride. The hour for the observance of the marriage rites was just before the midday meal. When the groom reached the bride's home he found her in readiness. Sweet and pretty Alice looked in her gray linsey gown, perfectly plain and simple though it was, without an ornament or a ribbon. Proud indeed looked her lover as he took her hand and led her up to the waiting minister. When the whisperings had ceased the minister asked who gave this woman to be married. Alice's father answered.

"Will you take this woman to be your wedded wife, to love, cherish and protect her all the days of her life?" asked the minister.

"I will," answered a deep bass voice.

"Will you take this man to be your wedded husband, to love, honor and obey him all the days of your life?"

"I will," said Alice, in a low tone.

"I pronounce you man and wife. Those whom God has joined together let no man put asunder."

There was a brief prayer and the ceremony ended. Then followed the congratulations of relatives and friends. The felicitations were apt to be trying to the nerves of even the best-tempered groom. The hand shakes, the heavy slaps on the back, and the pommeling he received at the hands of his intimate friends were as nothing compared to the anguish of mind he endured while they were kissing his wife. The young bucks would not have considered it a real wedding had they been prevented from kissing the bride, and for that matter, every girl within reach. So fast as the burly young settlers could push themselves through the densely packed rooms they kissed the bride, and then the first girl they came to.

Betty and Lydia had been Alice's maids of honor. This being Betty's first experience at a frontier wedding, it developed that she was much in need of Lydia's advice, which she had previously disdained. She had rested secure in her dignity. Poor Betty! The first man to kiss Alice was George Martin, a big, strong fellow, who gathered his brother's bride into his arms and gave her a bearish hug and a resounding kiss. Releasing her he turned toward Lydia and Betty. Lydia eluded him, but one of his great hands clasped around Betty's wrist. She tried to look haughty, but with everyone laughing, and the young man's face expressive of honest fun and happiness she found it impossible. She stood still and only turned her face a little to one side while George kissed her. The young men now made a rush for her. With blushing cheeks Betty, unable to stand her ground any longer, ran to her brother, the Colonel. He pushed her away with a laugh. She turned to Major McColloch, who held out his arms to her. With an exclamation she wrenched herself free from a young man, who had caught her hand, and flew to the Major. But alas for Betty! The Major was not proof against the temptation and he kissed her himself.

"Traitor!" cried Betty, breaking away from him.

Poor Betty was in despair. She had just made up her mind to submit when she caught sight of Wetzel's familiar figure. She ran to him and the hunter put one of his long arms around her.

"I reckon I kin take care of you, Betty," he said, a smile playing over his usually stern face. "See here, you young bucks. Betty don't want to be kissed, and if you keep on pesterin' her I'll have to scalp a few of you."

The merriment grew as the day progressed. During the wedding feast great hilarity prevailed. It culminated in the dance which followed the dinner. The long room of the blockhouse had been decorated with evergreens, autumn leaves and goldenrod, which were scattered profusely about, hiding the blackened walls and bare rafters. Numerous blazing pine knots, fastened on sticks which were stuck into the walls, lighted up a scene, which for color and animation could not have been surpassed.

Colonel Zane's old slave, Sam, who furnished the music, sat on a raised platform at the upper end of the hall, and the way he sawed away on his fiddle, accompanying the movements of his arm with a swaying of his body and a stamping of his heavy foot, showed he had a hearty appreciation of his own music.

Prominent among the men and women standing and sitting near the platform could be distinguished the tall forms of Jonathan Zane, Major McColloch and Wetzel, all, as usual, dressed in their hunting costumes and carrying long rifles. The other men had made more or less effort to improve their appearance. Bright homespun shirts and scarfs had replaced the everyday buckskin garments. Major McColloch was talking to Colonel Zane. The genial faces of both reflected the pleasure they felt in the enjoyment of the younger people. Jonathan Zane stood near the door. Moody and silent he watched the dance. Wetzel leaned against the wall. The black barrel of his rifle lay in the hollow of his arm. The hunter was gravely contemplating the members of the bridal party who were dancing in front of him. When the dance ended Lydia and Betty stopped before Wetzel and Betty said: "Lew, aren't you going to ask us to dance?"

The hunter looked down into the happy, gleaming faces, and smiling in his half-sad way, answered: "Every man to his gifts."

"But you can dance. I want you to put aside your gun long enough to dance with me. If I waited for you to ask me, I fear I should have to wait a long time. Come, Lew, here I am asking you, and I know the other men are dying to dance with me," said Betty, coaxingly, in a roguish voice.

Wetzel never refused a request of Betty's, and so, laying aside his weapons, he danced with her, to the wonder and admiration of all. Colonel Zane clapped his hands, and everyone stared in amazement at the unprecedented sight. Wetzel danced not ungracefully. He was wonderfully light on his feet. His striking figure, the long black hair, and the fancifully embroidered costume he wore contrasted strangely with Betty's slender, graceful form and pretty gray dress.

"Well, well, Lewis, I would not have believed anything but the evidence of my own eyes," said Colonel Zane, with a laugh, as Betty and Wetzel approached him.

"If all the men could dance as well as Lew, the girls would be thankful, I can assure you," said Betty.

"Betty, I declare you grow prettier every day," said old John Bennet, who was standing with the Colonel and the Major. "If I were only a young man once more I should try my chances with you, and I wouldn't give up very easily."

"I do not know, Uncle John, but I am inclined to think that if you were a young man and should come a-wooing you would not get a rebuff from me," answered Betty, smiling on the old man, of whom she was very fond.

"Miss Zane, will you dance with me?"

The voice sounded close by Betty's side. She recognized it, and an unaccountable sensation of shyness suddenly came over her. She had firmly made up her mind, should Mr. Clarke ask her to dance, that she would tell him she was tired, or engaged for that number—anything so that she could avoid dancing with him. But, now that the moment had come she either forgot her resolution or lacked the courage to keep it, for as the music commenced, she turned and without saying a word or looking at him, she placed her hand on his arm. He whirled her away. She gave a start of surprise and delight at the familiar step and then gave herself up to the charm of the dance. Supported by his strong arm she floated around the room in a sort of dream. Dancing as they did was new to the young people at the Fort—it was a style then in vogue in the east—and everyone looked on with great interest and curiosity. But all too soon the dance ended and before Betty had recovered her composure she found that her partner had led her to a secluded seat in the lower end of the hall. The bench was partly obscured from the dancers by masses of autumn leaves.

"That was a very pleasant dance," said Alfred. "Miss Boggs told me you danced the round dance."

"I was much surprised and pleased," said Betty, who had indeed enjoyed it.

"It has been a delightful day," went on Alfred, seeing that Betty was still confused. "I almost killed myself in that race for the bottle this morning. I never saw such logs and brush heaps and ditches in my life. I am sure that if the fever of recklessness which seemed in the air had not suddenly seized me I would never have put my horse at such leaps."

"I heard my brother say your horse was one of the best he had ever seen, and that you rode superbly," murmured Betty.

"Well, to be honest, I would not care to take that ride again. It certainly was not fair to the horse."

"How do you like the fort by this time?"

"Miss Zane, I am learning to love this free, wild life. I really think I was made for the frontier. The odd customs and manners which seemed strange at first have become very acceptable to me now. I find everyone so honest and simple and brave. Here one must work to live, which is right. Do you know, I never worked in my life until I came to Fort Henry. My life was all uselessness, idleness."

"I can hardly believe that," answered Betty. "You have learned to dance and ride and—"

"What?" asked Alfred, as Betty hesitated.

"Never mind. It was an accomplishment with which the girls credited you," said Betty, with a little laugh.

"I suppose I did not deserve it. I heard I had a singular aptitude for discovering young ladies in distress."

"Have you become well acquainted with the boys?" asked Betty, hastening to change the subject.

"Oh, yes, particularly with your Indianized brother, Isaac. He is the finest fellow, as well as the most interesting, I ever knew. I like Colonel Zane immensely too. The dark, quiet fellow, Jack, or John, they call him, is not like your other brothers. The hunter, Wetzel, inspires me with awe. Everyone has been most kind to me and I have almost forgotten that I was a wanderer."

"I am glad to hear that," said Betty.

"Miss Zane," continued Alfred, "doubtless you have heard that I came West because I was compelled to leave my home. Please do not believe everything you hear of me. Some day I may tell you my story if you care to hear it. Suffice it to say now that I left my home of my own free will and I could go back to-morrow."

"I did not mean to imply—" began Betty, coloring.

"Of course not. But tell me about yourself. Is it not rather dull and lonesome here for you?"

"It was last winter. But I have been contented and happy this summer. Of course, it is not Philadelphia life, and I miss the excitement and gayety of my uncle's house. I knew my place was with my brothers. My aunt pleaded with me to live with her and not go to the wilderness. I had everything I wanted there—luxury, society, parties, balls, dances, friends, all that the heart of a girl could desire, but I preferred to come to this little frontier settlement. Strange choice for a girl, was it not?"

"Unusual, yes," answered Alfred, gravely. "And I cannot but wonder what motives actuated our coming to Fort Henry. I came to seek my fortune. You came to bring sunshine into the home of your brother, and left your fortune behind you. Well, your motive has the element of nobility. Mine has nothing but that of recklessness. I would like to read the future."

"I do not think it is right to have such a wish. With the veil rolled away could you work as hard, accomplish as much? I do not want to know the future. Perhaps some of it will be unhappy. I have made my choice and will cheerfully abide by it. I rather envy your being a man. You have the world to conquer. A woman—what can she do? She can knead the dough, ply the distaff, and sit by the lattice and watch and wait."

"Let us postpone such melancholy thoughts until some future day. I have not as yet said anything that I intended. I wish to tell you how sorry I am that I acted in such a rude way the night your brother came home. I do not know what made me do so, but I know I have regretted it ever since. Will you forgive me and may we not be friends?"

"I—I do not know," said Betty, surprised and vaguely troubled by the earnest light in his eyes.

"But why? Surely you will make some little allowance for a naturally quick temper, and you know you did not— that you were—"

"Yes, I remember I was hasty and unkind. But I made amends, or at least, I tried to do so."

"Try to overlook my stupidity. I will not give up until you forgive me. Consider how much you can avoid by being generous."

"Very well, then, I will forgive you," said Betty, who

had arrived at the conclusion that this young man was one of determination.

"Thank you. I promise you shall never regret it. And the sprained ankle? It must be well, as I noticed you danced beautifully."

"I am compelled to believe what the girls say—that you are inclined to the language of compliment. My ankle is nearly well, thank you. It hurts a little now and then."

"Speaking of your accident reminds me of the day it happened," said Alfred, watching her closely. He desired to tease her a little, but he was not sure of his ground. "I had been all day in the woods with nothing but my thoughts—mostly unhappy ones—for company. When I met you I pretended to be surprised. As a matter of fact I was not, for I had followed your dog. He took a liking to me and I was extremely pleased, I assure you. Well, I saw your face a moment before you knew I was near you. When you heard my footsteps you turned with a relieved and joyous cry. When you saw whom it was your glad expression changed, and if I had been a hostile Wyandot you could not have looked more unfriendly. Such a woeful, tearstained face I never saw."

"Mr. Clarke, please do not speak any more of that," said Betty, with dignity. "I desire that you forget it."

"I will forget all except that it was I who had the happiness of finding you and of helping you. I cannot forget that. I am sure we should never have been friends but for that accident."

"There is Isaac. He is looking for me," answered Betty, rising.

"Wait a moment longer—please. He will find you," said Alfred, detaining her. "Since you have been so kind I have grown bolder. May I come over to see you to-morrow?"

He looked straight down into the dark eyes which wavered and fell before he had completed his question.

"There is Isaac. He cannot see me here. I must go."

"But not before telling me. What is the good of your forgiving me if I may not see you. Please say yes."

"You may come," answered Betty, half amused and half provoked at his persistence. "I should think you would know that such permission invariably goes with a young woman's forgiveness."

"Hello, here you are. What a time I have had in finding you," said Isaac, coming up with flushed face and eyes bright with excitement. "Alfred, what do you mean by hiding the belle of the dance away like this? I want to dance with you, Betts. I am having a fine time. I have not danced anything but Indian dances for ages. Sorry to take her away, Alfred. I can see she doesn't want to go. Ha! Ha!" And with a mischievous look at both of them he led Betty away.

Alfred kept his seat awhile lost in thought. Suddenly he remembered that it would look strange if he did not make himself agreeable, so he got up and found a partner. He danced with Alice, Lydia, and the other young ladies. After an hour he slipped away to his room. He wished to be alone. He wanted to think; to decide whether it would be best for him to stay at the fort, or ride away in the darkness and never return. With the friendly touch of Betty's hand the madness with which he had been battling for weeks rushed over him stronger than ever. The thrill of that soft little palm remained with him, and he pressed the hand it had touched to his lips.

For a long hour he sat by his window. He could dimly see the broad winding river, with its curtain of pale gray mist, and beyond, the dark outline of the forest. A cool breeze from the water fanned his heated brow, and the quiet and solitude soothed him.

CHAPTER 4

"Good morning, Harry. Where are you going so early?" called Betty from the doorway.

A lad was passing down the path in front of Colonel Zane's house as Betty hailed him. He carried a rifle almost as long as himself.

"Mornin', Betty. I am goin' 'cross the crick fer that turkey I hear gobblin'," he answered, stopping at the gate and smiling brightly at Betty.

"Hello, Harry Bennet. Going after that turkey? I have heard him several mornings and he must be a big, healthy gobbler," said Colonel Zane, stepping to the door. "You are going to have company. Here comes Wetzel."

"Good morning, Lew. Are you too off on a turkey hunt?" said Betty.

"Listen," said the hunter, as he stopped and leaned against the gate. They listened. All was quiet save for the tinkle of a cowbell in the pasture adjoining the Colonel's barn. Presently the silence was broken by a long, shrill, peculiar cry.

"Chug-a-lug, chug-a-lug, chug-a-lug-chug."

"Well, it's a turkey, all right, and I'll bet a big gobbler," remarked Colonel Zane, as the cry ceased.

"Has Jonathan heard it?" asked Wetzel.

"Not that I know of. Why do you ask?" said the Colonel, in a low tone. "Look here, Lew, is that not a genuine call?"

"Goodbye, Harry, be sure and bring me a turkey," called Betty, as she disappeared.

"I calkilate it's a red turkey," answered the hunter, and motioning the lad to stay behind, he shouldered his rifle and passed swiftly down the path.

Of all the Wetzel family—a family noted from one end of the frontier to the other—Lewis was the most famous. The early history of West Virginia and Ohio is replete with the daring deeds of this wilderness roamer, this lone hunter and insatiable Nemesis, justly called the greatest Indian slayer known to men.

When Lewis was about twenty years old, and his brothers John and Martin little older, they left their Virginia home for a protracted hunt. On their return they found the smoking ruins of the home, the mangled remains of father and mother, the naked and violated bodies of their sisters, and the scalped and bleeding corpse of a baby brother.

Lewis Wetzel swore sleepless and eternal vengeance on the whole Indian race. Terribly did he carry out that resolution. From that time forward he lived most of the time in the woods, and an Indian who crossed his trail was a doomed man. The various Indian tribes gave him different names. The Shawnees called him "Long Knife"; the Hurons, "Destroyer"; the Delawares, "Death Wind," and any one of these names would chill the heart of the stoutest warrior.

To most of the famed pioneer hunters of the border, Indian fighting was only a side issue—generally a necessary one—but with Wetzel it was the business of his life. He lived solely to kill Indians. He plunged recklessly into the strife, and was never content unless roaming the wilderness solitudes, trailing the savages to their very homes and ambushing the village bridlepath like a panther waiting for his prey. Often in the gray of the morning the Indians, sleeping around their campfire, were awakened by a horrible, screeching yell. They started up in terror only to fall victims to the tomahawk of their merciless foe, or to hear a rifle shot and get a glimpse of a form with flying black hair disappearing with wonderful quickness in the forest. Wetzel always left death behind him, and he was gone before his demoniac yell ceased to echo throughout the woods. Although often pursued, he invariably eluded the Indians, for he was the fleetest runner on the border.

For many years he was considered the right hand of the defense of the fort. The Indians held him in superstitious dread, and the fact that he was known to be in the settlement had averted more than one attack by the Indians.

Many regarded Wetzel as a savage, a man who was mad for the blood of the red men, and without one redeeming quality. But this was an unjust opinion. When that restless fever for revenge left him—it was not always with him—he was quiet and peaceable. To those few who knew him well he was even amiable. But Wetzel, although known to everyone, cared for few. He spent little time in the settlements and rarely spoke except when addressed.

Nature had singularly fitted him for his preeminent position among scouts and hunters. He was tall and broad across the shoulders; his strength, agility and endurance were marvelous; he had an eagle eye, the sagacity of the bloodhound, and that intuitive knowledge which plays such an important part in a hunter's life. He knew not fear. He was daring where daring was the wiser part. Crafty, tireless and implacable, Wetzel was incomparable in his vocation.

His long raven-black hair, of which he was vain, when combed out reached to within a foot of the ground. He had a rare scalp, one for which the Indians would have bartered anything.

A favorite Indian decoy, and the most fatal one, was the imitation of the call of the wild turkey. It had often happened that men from the settlements who had gone out for a turkey which had been gobbling, had not returned.

For several mornings Wetzel had heard a turkey call, and becoming suspicious of it, had determined to satisfy himself. On the east side of the creek hill there was a cavern some fifty or sixty yards above the water. The entrance to this cavern was concealed by vines and foliage. Wetzel knew of it, and, crossing the stream some distance above, he made a wide circuit and came up back of the cave. Here he concealed himself in a clump of bushes and waited. He had not been there long when directly below him sounded the cry, "Chug-a-lug, Chug-a-lug, Chug-a-lug." At the same time the polished head and brawny shoulders of an Indian warrior rose out of the cavern. Peering cautiously around, the savage again gave the peculiar cry, and then sank back out of sight. Wetzel screened himself safely in his position and watched the savage repeat the action at least ten times before he made up his mind that the Indian was alone in the cave. When he had satisfied himself of this he took a quick aim at the twisted tuft of hair and fired. Without waiting to see the result of his shot—so well did he trust his unerring aim—he climbed down the steep bank and brushing aside the vines entered the cave. A stalwart Indian lay in the entrance with his face pressed down on the vines. He still clutched in his sinewy fingers the buckhorn mouthpiece with which he had made the calls that had resulted in his death.

"Huron," muttered the hunter to himself as he ran the

keen edge of his knife around the twisted tuft of hair and tore off the scalp-lock.

The cave showed evidence of having been inhabited for some time. There was a cunningly contrived fireplace made of stones, against which pieces of birch bark were placed in such a position that not a ray of light could get out of the cavern. The bed of black coals between the stones still smoked; a quantity of parched corn lay on a little rocky shelf which jutted out from the wall; a piece of jerked meat and a buckskin pouch hung from a peg.

Suddenly Wetzel dropped on his knees and began examining the footprints in the sandy floor of the cavern. He measured the length and width of the dead warrior's foot. He closely scrutinized every moccasin print. He crawled to the opening of the cavern and carefully surveyed the moss.

Then he rose to his feet. A remarkable transformation had come over him during the last few moments. His face had changed; the calm expression was replaced by one sullen and fierce; his lips were set in a thin, cruel line, and a strange light glittered in his eyes.

He slowly pursued a course leading gradually down to the creek. At intervals he would stop and listen. The strange voices of the woods were not mysteries to him. They were more familiar to him than the voices of men.

He recalled that, while on his circuit over the ridge to get behind the cavern, he had heard the report of a rifle far off in the direction of the chestnut grove, but, as that was a favorite place of the settlers for shooting squirrels, he had not thought anything of it at the time. Now it had a peculiar significance. He turned abruptly from the trail he had been following and plunged down the steep hill. Crossing the creek he took to the cover of the willows, which grew profusely along the banks, and striking a sort of bridle path he started on a run. He ran easily, as though accustomed to that mode of travel, and his long strides covered a couple of miles in short order. Coming to the rugged bluff, which marked the end of the ridge, he stopped and walked slowly along the edge of the water. He struck the trail of the Indians where it crossed the creek, just where he expected. There were several moccasin tracks in the wet sand and, in some of the depressions made by the heels the rounded edges of the imprints were still smooth and intact. The little pools of muddy water, which still lay in these hollows, were other indications to his keen eyes that the Indians had passed this point early that morning.

The trail led up the hill and far into the woods. Never in doubt the hunter kept on his course; like a shadow he passed from tree to tree and from bush to bush; silently, cautiously, but rapidly he followed the tracks of the Indians. When he had penetrated the dark backwoods of the Black Forest, tangled underbrush, windfalls and gullies crossed his path and rendered fast trailing impossible. Before these almost impassible barriers he stopped and peered on all sides, studying the lay of the land, the deadfalls, the gorges, and all the time keeping in mind the probable route of the redskins. Then he turned aside to avoid the roughest travelling. Sometimes these detours were only a few hundred feet long; often they were miles; but nearly always he struck the trail again. This almost superhuman knowledge of the Indian's ways of traversing the forest, which probably no man could have possessed without giving his life to the hunting of Indians, was the one feature of Wetzel's woodcraft which placed him so far above other hunters, and made him so dreaded by the savages.

Descending a knoll he entered a glade where the trees grew farther apart and the underbrush was only knee high. The black soil showed that the tract of land had been burned over. On the banks of a babbling brook which wound its way through this open space, the hunter found tracks which brought an exclamation from him. Clearly defined in the soft earth was the impress of a white man's moccasin. The footprints of an Indian toe inward. Those of a white man are just the opposite. A little farther on Wetzel came to a slight crushing of the moss, where he concluded some heavy body had fallen. As he had seen the tracks of a buck and doe all the way down the brook he thought it probable one of them had been shot by the white hunter. He found a pool of blood surrounded by moccasin prints; and from that spot the trail led straight toward the west, showing that for some reason the Indians had changed their direction.

This new move puzzled the hunter, and he leaned against the trunk of a tree, while he revolved in his mind the reasons for this abrupt departure—for such he believed it. The trail he had followed for miles was the devious trail of hunting Indians, stealing slowly and stealthily along watching for their prey, whether it be man or beast. The trail toward the west was straight as the crow flies; the moccasin prints that indented the soil were wide apart, and to an inexperienced eye looked like the track of one Indian. To Wetzel this indicated that the Indians had all stepped in the tracks of a leader.

As was usually his way, Wetzel decided quickly. He had calculated that there were eight Indians in all, not counting the chief whom he had shot. This party of Indians had either killed or captured the white man who had been hunting. Wetzel believed that a part of the Indians would push on with all possible speed, leaving some of their number to ambush the trail or double back on it to see if they were pursued.

An hour of patient waiting, in which he never moved from his position, proved the wisdom of his judgment.

Suddenly, away at the other end of the grove, he caught a flash of brown, of a living, moving something, like the flitting of a bird behind a tree. Was it a bird or a squirrel? Then again he saw it, almost lost in the shade of the forest. Several minutes passed, in which Wetzel never moved and hardly breathed. The shadow had disappeared behind a tree. He fixed his keen eyes on that tree and presently a dark object glided from it and darted stealthily forward to another tree. One, two, three dark forms followed the first one. They were Indian warriors, and they moved so quickly that only the eyes of a woodsman like Wetzel could have discerned their movement at that distance.

Probably most hunters would have taken to their heels while there was yet time. The thought did not occur to Wetzel. He slowly raised the hammer of his rifle. As the Indians came into plain view he saw they did not suspect his presence, but were returning on the trail in their customary cautious manner.

When the first warrior reached a big oak tree some two hundred yards distant, the long, black barrel of the hunter's rifle began slowly, almost imperceptibly, to rise, and as it reached a level the savage stepped forward from the tree. With the sharp report of the weapon he staggered and fell.

Wetzel sprang up and knowing that his only escape was in rapid flight, with his well known yell, he bounded off at the top of his speed. The remaining Indians discharged their guns at the fleeing, dodging figure, but without effect. So rapidly did he dart in and out among the trees that an effectual aim was impossible. Then, with loud yells, the Indians, drawing their tomahawks, started in pursuit, expecting soon to overtake their victim.

In the early years of his Indian hunting, Wetzel had perfected himself in a practice which had saved his life many times, and had added much to his fame. He could reload his rifle while running at topmost speed. His extraordinary fleetness enabled him to keep ahead of his pursuers until his rifle was reloaded. This trick he now employed. Keeping up his uneven pace until his gun was ready, he turned quickly and shot the nearest Indian dead in his tracks. The next Indian had by this time nearly come up with him and close enough to throw his tomahawk, which whizzed dangerously near Wetzel's head. But he leaped forward again and soon his rifle was reloaded. Every time he looked around the Indians treed, afraid to face his unerring weapon. After running a mile or more in this manner, he reached an open space in the woods where he wheeled suddenly on his pursuers. The foremost Indian jumped behind a tree, but, as it did not entirely screen his body, he, too, fell a victim to the hunter's aim. The Indian must have been desperately wounded, for his companion now abandoned the chase and went to his assistance. Together they disappeared in the forest.

Wetzel, seeing that he was no longer pursued, slackened his pace and proceeded thoughtfully toward the settlement.

That same day, several hours after Wetzel's departure in quest of the turkey, Alfred Clarke strolled over from the fort and found Colonel Zane in the yard. The Colonel was industriously stirring the contents of a huge copper kettle which swung over a brisk wood fire. The honeyed fragrance of apple-butter mingled with the pungent odor of burning hickory.

"Morning, Alfred, you see they have me at it," was the Colonel's salute.

"So I observe," answered Alfred, as he seated himself

on the wood-pile. "What is it you are churning so vigorously?"

"Apple-butter, my boy, apple-butter. I don't allow even Bessie to help when I am making apple-butter."

"Colonel Zane, I have come over to ask a favor. Ever since you notified us that you intended sending an expedition up the river I have been worried about my horse Roger. He is too light for a packhorse, and I cannot take two horses."

"I'll let you have the bay. He is big and strong enough. That black horse of yours is a beauty. You leave Roger with me and if you never come back I'll be in a fine horse. Ha! Ha! But, seriously, Clarke, this proposed trip is a hazardous undertaking, and if you would rather stay—"

"You misunderstand me," quickly replied Alfred, who had flushed. "I do not care about myself. I'll go and take my medicine. But I do mind about my horse."

"That's right. Always think of your horses. I'll have Sam take the best of care of Roger."

"What is the nature of this excursion, and how long shall we be gone?"

"Jonathan will guide the party. He says it will take six weeks if you have pleasant weather. You are to go by way of Short Creek, where you will help put up a blockhouse. Then you go to Fort Pitt. There you will embark on a raft with the supplies I need and make the return journey by water. You will probably smell gunpowder before you get back."

"What shall we do with the horses?"

"Bring them along with you on the raft, of course."

"That is a new way to travel with horses," said Alfred, looking dubiously at the swift river. "Will there be any way to get news from Fort Henry while we are away?"

"Yes, there will be several runners."

"Mr. Clarke, I am going to feed my pets. Would you like to see them?" asked a voice which brought Alfred to his feet. He turned and saw Betty. Her dog followed her, carrying a basket.

"I shall be delighted," answered Alfred. "Have you more pets than Tige and Madcap?"

"Oh, yes, indeed. I have a bear, six squirrels, one of them white, and some pigeons."

Betty led the way to an enclosure adjoining Colonel Zane's barn. It was about twenty feet square, made of pine saplings which had been split and driven firmly into the ground. As Betty took down a bar and opened the small gate a number of white pigeons fluttered down from the roof of the barn, several of them alighting on her shoulders. A half-grown black bear came out of a kennel and shuffled toward her. He was unmistakably glad to see her, but he avoided going near Tige, and looked doubtfully at the young man. But after Alfred had stroked his head and had spoken to him he seemed disposed to be friendly, for he sniffed around Alfred's knees and then stood up and put his paws against the young man's shoulders.

"Here, Cæsar, get down," said Betty. "He always wants to wrestle, especially with anyone of whom he is not suspicious. He is very tame and will do almost anything. Indeed, you would marvel at his intelligence. He never forgets an injury. If anyone plays a trick on him you may be sure that person will not get a second opportunity. The night we caught him Tige chased him up a tree and Jonathan climbed the tree and lassoed him. Ever since he has evinced a hatred of Jonathan, and if I should leave Tige alone with him there would be a terrible fight. But for that I could allow Cæsar to run free about the yard."

"He looks bright and sagacious," remarked Alfred.

"He is, but sometimes he gets into mischief. I nearly died laughing one day. Bessie, my brother's wife, you know, had the big kettle on the fire, just as you saw it a moment ago, only this time she was boiling down maple syrup. Tige was out with some of the men and I let Cæsar loose awhile. If there is anything he loves it is maple sugar, so when he smelled the syrup he pulled down the kettle and the hot syrup went all over his nose. Oh, his howls were dreadful to hear. The funniest part about it was he seemed to think it was intentional, for he remained sulky and cross with me for two weeks."

"I can understand your love for animals," said Alfred. "I think there are many interesting things about wild creatures. There are comparatively few animals down in Virginia where I used to live, and my opportunities to study them have been limited."

"Here are my squirrels," said Betty, unfastening the door of a cage. A number of squirrels ran out. Several jumped to the ground. One perched on top of the box. Another sprang on Betty's shoulder. "I fasten them up every night, for I'm afraid the weasels and foxes will get them. The white squirrel is the only albino we have seen around here. It took Jonathan weeks to trap him, but once captured he soon grew tame. Is he not pretty?"

"He certainly is. I never saw one before; in fact, I did not know such a beautiful little animal existed," answered Alfred, looking in admiration at the graceful creature, as he leaped from the shelf to Betty's arm and ate from her hand, his great, bushy white tail arching over his back and his small pink eyes shining.

"There! Listen," said Betty. "Look at the fox squirrel, the big brownish red one. I call him the Captain, because he always wants to boss the others. I had another fox squirrel, older than this fellow, and he ran things to suit himself, until one day the grays united their forces and routed him. I think they would have killed him had I not freed him. Well, this one is commencing the same way. Do you hear that odd clicking noise? That comes from the Captain's teeth, and he is angry and jealous because I show so much attention to this one. He always does that, and he would fight too if I were not careful. It is a singular fact, though, that the white squirrel has not even a little pugnacity. He either cannot fight, or he is too well behaved. Here, Mr. Clarke, show Snowball this nut, and then hide it in your pocket, and see him find it."

Alfred did as he was told, except that while he pretended to put the nut in his pocket he really kept it concealed in his hand.

The pet squirrel leaped lightly on Alfred's shoulder, ran over his breast, peeped in all his pockets, and even pushed his cap to one side of his head. Then he ran down Alfred's arm, sniffed in his coat sleeve, and finally wedged a cold little nose between his closed fingers.

"There, he has found it, even though you did not play fair," said Betty, laughing gaily.

Alfred never forgot the picture Betty made standing there with the red cap on her dusky hair, and the loving smile upon her face as she talked to her pets. A white fantail pigeon had alighted on her shoulder and was picking daintily at the piece of cracker she held between her lips. The squirrels were all sitting up, each with a nut in his little paws, and each with an alert and cunning look in the corner of his eye, to prevent, no doubt, being surprised out of a portion of his nut. Cæsar was lying on all fours, growling and tearing at his breakfast, while the dog looked on with a superior air, as if he knew they would not have had any breakfast but for him.

"Are you fond of canoeing and fishing?" asked Betty, as they returned to the house.

"Indeed I am. Isaac has taken me out on the river

often. Canoeing may be pleasant for a girl, but I never knew one who cared for fishing."

"Now you behold one. I love dear old Izaak Walton. Of course, you have read his books?"

"I am ashamed to say I have not."

"And you say you are a fisherman? Well, you have a great pleasure in store, as well as an opportunity to learn something of the 'contemplative man's recreation.' I shall lend you the books."

"I have not seen a book since I came to Fort Henry."

"I have a fine little library, and you are welcome to any of my books. But to return to fishing. I love it, and yet I nearly always allow the fish to go free. Sometimes I bring home a pretty sunfish, place him in a tub of water, watch him and try to tame him. But I must admit failure. It is the association which makes fishing so delightful. The canoe gliding down a swift stream, the open air, the blue sky, the birds and trees and flowers—these are what I love. Come and see my canoe."

Thus, Betty rattled on as she led the way through the sitting-room and kitchen to Colonel Zane's magazine and store-house which opened into the kitchen. This little low-roofed hut contained a variety of things. Boxes, barrels and farming implements filled one corner; packs of dried skins were piled against the wall; some otter and fox pelts were stretched on the wall, and a number of powder kegs lined a shelf. A slender canoe swung from ropes thrown over the rafters. Alfred slipped it out of the loops and carried it outside.

The canoe was a superb specimen of Indian handiwork. It had a length of fourteen feet and was made of birch bark, stretched over a light framework of basswood. The bow curved gracefully upward, ending in a carved image representing a warrior's head. The sides were beautifully ornamented and decorated in fanciful Indian designs.

"My brother's Indian guide, Tomepomehala, a Shawnee chief, made it for me. You see this design on the bow. The arrow and the arm mean in Indian language, 'The race is to the swift and the strong.' The canoe is very light. See, I can easily carry it," said Betty, lifting it from the grass.

She ran into the house and presently came out with two rods, a book and a basket.

"These are Jack's rods. He cut them out of the heart of ten-year-old basswood trees, so he says. We must be careful of them."

Alfred examined the rods with the eye of a connoisseur and pronounced them perfect.

"These rods have been made by a lover of the art. Anyone with half an eye could see that. What shall we use for bait?" he said.

"Sam got me some this morning."

"Did you expect to go?" asked Alfred, looking up in surprise.

"Yes, I intended going, and as you said you were coming over, I meant to ask you to accompany me."

"That was kind of you."

"Where are you young people going?" called Colonel Zane, stopping in his task.

"We are going down to the sycamore," answered Betty.

"Very well. But be certain and stay on this side of the creek and do not go out on the river," said the Colonel.

"Why, Eb, what do you mean? One might think Mr. Clarke and I were children," exclaimed Betty.

"You certainly aren't much more. But that is not my reason. Never mind the reason. Do as I say or do not go," said Colonel Zane.

"All right, brother. I shall not forget," said Betty, soberly, looking at the Colonel. He had not spoken in his usual teasing way, and she was at a loss to understand him. "Come, Mr. Clarke, you carry the canoe and follow me down this path and look sharp for roots and stones or you may trip."

"Where is Isaac?" asked Alfred, as he lightly swung the canoe over his shoulder.

"He took his rifle and went up to the chestnut grove an hour or more ago."

A few minutes' walk down the willow-skirted path and they reached the creek. Here it was a narrow stream, hardly fifty feet wide, shallow, and full of stones over which the clear brown water rushed noisily.

"Is it not rather risky going down there?" asked Alfred, as he noticed the swift current and the numerous boulders poking treacherous heads just above the water.

"Of course. That is the great pleasure in canoeing," said Betty, calmly. "If you would rather walk—"

"No, I'll go if I drown. I was thinking of you."

"It is safe enough if you can handle a paddle," said Betty, with a smile at his hesitation. "And, of course, if your partner in the canoe sits trim."

"Perhaps you had better allow me to use the paddle. Where did you learn to steer a canoe?"

"I believe you are actually afraid. Why, I was born on the Potomac, and have used a paddle since I was old enough to lift one. Come, place the canoe in here and we will keep to the near shore until we reach the bend. There is a little fall just below this and I love to shoot it."

He steadied the canoe with one hand while he held out the other to help her, but she stepped nimbly aboard without his assistance.

"Wait a moment while I catch some crickets and grasshoppers."

"Gracious! What a fisherman. Don't you know we have had frost?"

"That's so," said Alfred, abashed by her simple remark.

"But you might find some crickets under those logs," said Betty. She laughed merrily at the awkward spectacle made by Alfred crawling over the ground, improvising a sort of trap out of his hat, and pouncing down on a poor little insect.

"Now, get in carefully, and give the canoe a push. There, we are off," she said, taking up the paddle.

The little bark glided slowly down stream, at first hugging the bank as though reluctant to trust itself to the deeper water, and then gathering headway as a few gentle strokes of the paddle swerved it into the current. Betty knelt on one knee and skillfully plied the paddle, using the Indian stroke in which the paddle was not removed from the water.

"This is great!" exclaimed Alfred, as he leaned back in the bow facing her. "There is nothing more to be desired. This beautiful clear stream, the air so fresh, the gold lined banks, the autumn leaves, a guide who—"

"Look," said Betty. "There is the fall over which we must pass."

He looked ahead and saw that they were swiftly approaching two huge stones that reared themselves high out of the water. They were only a few yards apart and surrounded by smaller rocks, about which the water rushed white with foam.

"Please do not move!" cried Betty, her eyes shining bright with excitement.

Indeed, the situation was too novel for Alfred to do anything but feel a keen enjoyment. He had made up his mind that he was sure to get a ducking, but, as he watched Betty's easy, yet vigorous sweeps with the paddle, and her smiling, yet resolute lips, he felt reassured. He could see that the fall was not a great one, only a few feet, but one of those glancing sheets of water like a mill race, and he well knew that if they struck a stone disaster would be theirs.

Twenty feet above the white-capped wave which marked the fall, Betty gave a strong forward pull on the paddle, a deep stroke which momentarily retarded their progress even in that swift current, and then, a short backward stroke, far under the stern of the canoe, and the little vessel turned straight, almost in the middle of the course between the two rocks. As she raised her paddle, into the canoe and smiled at the fascinated young man, the bow dipped, and with that peculiar downward movement, that swift, exhilarating rush so dearly loved by canoeists, they shot down the smooth incline of water, were lost for a moment in a white cloud of mist, and in another they floated into a placid pool.

"Was not that delightful?" she asked, with just a little conscious pride glowing in her dark eyes.

"Miss Zane, it was more than that. I apologize for my suspicions. You have admirable skill. I only wish that on my voyage down the River of Life I could have such a sure eye and hand to guide me through the dangerous reefs and rapids."

"You are poetical," said Betty, who laughed, and at the same time blushed slightly. "But you are right about the guide. Jonathan says 'always get a good guide,' and as guiding is his work he ought to know. But this has nothing in common with fishing, and here is my favorite place under the old sycamore."

With a long sweep of the paddle she ran the canoe alongside a stone beneath a great tree which spread its long branches over the creek and shaded the pool. It was a grand old tree and must have guarded that sylvan spot for centuries. The gnarled and knotted trunk was scarred and seamed with the ravages of time. The upper part was dead. Long limbs extended skyward, gaunt and bare, like the masts of a storm-beaten vessel. The lower branches were white and shining, relieved here and there by brown patches of bark which curled up like old parchment as they shelled away from the inner bark. The ground beneath the tree was carpeted with a velvety moss with little plots of grass and clusters of maidenhair fern growing on it. From under an overhanging rock on the bank a spring of crystal water bubbled forth.

Alfred rigged up the rods, and baiting a hook directed Betty to throw her line well out into the current and let it float down into the eddy. She complied, and hardly had the line reached the circle of the eddy, where bits of white foam floated round and round, when there was a slight splash, a scream from Betty and she was standing up in the canoe holding tightly to her rod.

"Be careful!" exclaimed Alfred. "Sit down. You will have the canoe upset in a moment. Hold your rod steady and keep the line taut. That's right. Now lead him round toward me. There." And grasping the line he lifted a fine rock bass over the side of the canoe.

"Oh! I always get so intensely excited," breathlessly cried Betty. "I can't help it. Jonathan always declares he will never take me fishing again. Let me see the fish. It's a goggle-eye. Isn't he pretty? Look how funny he bats his eyes." And she laughed gleefully as she gingerly picked up the fish by the tail and dropped him into the water. "Now, Mr. Goggle-eye, if you are wise, in future you will beware of tempting looking bugs."

For an hour they had splendid sport. The pool teemed with sunfish. The bait would scarcely touch the water when the little orange-colored fellows would rush for it. Now and then a black bass darted wickedly through the school of sunfish and stole the morsel from them. Or a sharp-nosed fiery-eyed pickerel—vulture of the water—rising to the surface and, supreme in his indifference to man or fish, would swim lazily round until he had discovered the cause of all this commotion among the smaller fishes, and then, opening wide his jaws would take the bait with one voracious snap.

Presently something took hold of Betty's line and moved out toward the middle of the pool. She struck and the next instant her rod was bent double and the tip under water.

"Pull your rod up!" shouted Alfred. "Here, hand it to me."

But it was too late. A surge right and left, a vicious tug and Betty's line floated on the surface of the water.

"Now, isn't that too bad? He has broken my line. Goodness, I never before felt such a strong fish. What shall I do?"

"You should be thankful you were not pulled in. I have been in a state of fear ever since we commenced fishing. You move round in this canoe as though it were a raft. Let me paddle out to that little ripple and try once there; then we will stop. I know you are tired."

Near the center of the pool a half-submerged rock checked the current and caused a little ripple of the water. Several times Alfred had seen the dark shadow of a large fish followed by a swirl of the water, and the frantic leaping of little bright-sided minnows in all directions. As his hook, baited with a lively shiner, floated over the spot, a long, yellow object shot from out that shaded lair. There was a splash, not unlike that made by the sharp edge of a paddle impelled by a short, powerful stroke, the minnow disappeared, and the broad tail of the fish flapped on the water. The instant Alfred struck, the water boiled and the big fish leaped clear into the air, shaking himself convulsively to get rid of the hook. He made mad rushes up and down the pool, under the canoe, into the swift current and against the rocks, but all to no avail. Steadily Alfred increased the strain on the line and gradually it began to tell, for the plunges of the fish became shorter and less frequent. Once again, in a last magnificent effort, he leaped straight into the air, and failing to get loose, gave up the struggle and was drawn gasping and exhausted to the side of the canoe.

"Are you afraid to touch him?" asked Alfred.

"Indeed I am not," answered Betty.

"Then run your hand gently down the line, slip your fingers in under his gills and lift him over the side carefully."

"Five pounds," exclaimed Alfred, when the fish lay at his feet. "This is the largest black bass I ever caught. It is a pity to take such a beautiful fish out of his element."

"Let him go, then. May I?" said Betty.

"No, you have allowed them all to go, even the pickerel, which I think ought to be killed. We will keep this fellow alive, and place him in that nice clear pool over in the fort-yard."

"I like to watch you play a fish," said Betty. "Jonathan always hauls them right out. You are so skillful. You let this fish run so far and then you checked him. Then you gave him a line to go the other way, and no doubt he felt free once more when you stopped him again."

"You are expressing a sentiment which has been, is, and always will be particularly pleasing to the fair sex, I believe," observed Alfred, smiling rather grimly as he wound up his line.

"Would you mind being explicit?" she questioned.

Alfred had laughed and was about to answer when the whip-like crack of a rifle came from the hillside. The echoes of the shot reverberated from hill to hill and were finally lost far down the valley.

"What can that be?" exclaimed Alfred anxiously, recalling Colonel Zane's odd manner when they were about to leave the house.

"I am not sure, but I think that is my turkey, unless Lew

Wetzel happened to miss his aim," said Betty, laughing. "And that is such an unprecedented thing that it can hardly be considered. Turkeys are scarce this season. Jonathan says the foxes and wolves ate up the broods. Lew heard this turkey calling and he made little Harry Bennet, who had started out with his gun, stay at home and went after Mr. Gobbler himself."

"Is that all? Well, that is nothing to get alarmed about, is it? I actually had a feeling of fear, or a presentiment, we might say."

They beached the canoe and spread out the lunch in the shade near the spring. Alfred threw himself at length upon the grass and Betty sat leaning against the tree. She took a biscuit in one hand, a pickle in the other, and began to chat volubly to Alfred of her school life, and of Philadelphia, and the friends she had made there. At length, remarking his abstraction, she said, "You are not listening to me."

"I beg your pardon. My thoughts did wander. I was thinking of my mother. Something about you reminds me of her. I do not know what, unless it is that little mannerism you have of pursing up your lips when you hesitate or stop to think."

"Tell me of her," said Betty, seeing his softened mood.

"My mother was very beautiful, and as good as she was lovely. I never had a care until my father died. Then she married again, and as I did not get on with my step-father I ran away from home. I have not been in Virginia for four years."

"Do you get homesick?"

"Indeed I do. While at Fort Pitt I used to have spells of the blues which lasted for days. For a time I felt more contented here. But I fear the old fever of restlessness will come over me again. I can speak freely to you because I know you will understand, and I feel sure of your sympathy. My father wanted me to be a minister. He sent me to the theological seminary at Princeton, where for two years I tried to study. Then my father died. I went home and looked after things until my mother married again. That changed everything for me. I ran away and have since been a wanderer. I feel that I am not lazy, that I am not afraid of work, but four years have drifted by and I have nothing to show for it. I am discouraged. Perhaps that is wrong, but tell me how I can help it. I have not the stoicism of the hunter, Wetzel, nor have I the philosophy of your brother. I could not be content to sit on my doorstep and smoke my pipe and watch the wheat and corn grown. And then, this life of the borderman, environed as it is by untold dangers, leads me, fascinates me, and yet appalls me with the fear that here I shall fall a victim to an Indian's bullet or spear, and find a nameless grave."

A long silence ensued. Alfred had spoken quietly, but with an undercurrent of bitterness that saddened Betty. For the first time she saw a shadow of pain in his eyes. She looked away down the valley, not seeing the brown and gold hills boldly defined against the blue sky, nor the beauty of the river as the setting sun cast a ruddy glow on the water. Her companion's words had touched an unknown chord in her heart. When finally she turned to answer him a beautiful light shone in her eyes, a light that shines not on land or sea—the light of woman's hope.

"Mr. Clarke," she said, and her voice was soft and low, "I am only a girl, but I can understand. You are unhappy. Try to rise above it. Who knows what will befall this little settlement? It may be swept away by the savages, and it may grow to be a mighty city. It must take that chance. So must you, so must we all take chances. You are here. Find your work and do it cheerfully, honestly, and let the future take care of itself. And let me say—do not be offended—beware of idleness and drink. They are as great a danger—nay, greater than the Indians."

"Miss Zane, if you were to ask me not to drink I would never touch a drop again," said Alfred, earnestly.

"I did not ask that," answered Betty, flushing slightly. "But I shall remember it as a promise and some day I may ask it of you."

He looked wonderingly at the girl beside him. He had spent most of his life among educated and cultured people. He had passed several years in the backwoods. But with all his experience with people he had to confess that this young woman was a revelation to him. She could ride like an Indian and shoot like a hunter. He had heard that she could run almost as swiftly as her brothers. Evidently she feared nothing, for he had just seen an example of her courage in a deed that had tried even his own nerve, and, withal, she was a bright, happy girl, earnest and true, possessing all the softer graces of his sisters, and that exquisite touch of feminine delicacy and refinement which appeals more to men than any other virtue.

"Have you not met Mr. Miller before he came here from Fort Pitt?" asked Betty.

"Why do you ask?"

"I think he mentioned something of the kind."

"What else did he say?"

"Why—Mr. Clarke, I hardly remember."

"I see," said Alfred, his face darkening. "He has talked about me. I do not care what he said. I knew him at Fort Pitt, and we had trouble there. I venture to say he has told no one about it. He certainly would not shine in the story. But I am not a tattler."

"It is not very difficult to see that you do not like him. Jonathan does not, either. He says Mr. Miller was friendly with McKee, and the notorious Simon Girty, the soldiers who deserted from Fort Pitt and went to the Indians. The girls like him, however."

"Usually if a man is good looking and pleasant that is enough for the girls. I noticed that he paid you a great deal of attention at the dance. He danced three times with you."

"Did he? How observing you are," said Betty, giving him a little sidelong glance. "Well, he is very agreeable, and he dances better than many of the young men."

"I wonder if Wetzel got the turkey. I have heard no more shots," said Alfred, showing plainly that he wished to change the subject.

"Oh, look there! Quick!" exclaimed Betty, pointing toward the hillside.

He looked in the direction indicated and saw a doe and a spotted fawn wading into the shallow water. The mother stood motionless a moment, with head erect and long ears extended. Then she drooped her graceful head and drank thirstily of the cool water. The fawn splashed playfully round while its mother was drinking. It would dash a few paces into the stream and then look back to see if its mother approved. Evidently she did not, for she would stop her drinking and call the fawn back to her side with a soft, crooning noise. Suddenly she raised her head, the long ears shot up, and she seemed to sniff the air. She waded through the deeper water to get round a rocky bluff which ran out into the creek. Then she turned and called the little one. The fawn waded until the water reached its knees, then stopped and uttered piteous little bleats. Encouraged by the soft crooning it plunged into the deep water and with great splashing and floundering managed to swim the short distance. Its slender legs shook as it staggered up the bank. Exhausted or frightened, it shrank close to its mother. Together they disappeared in the willows which fringed the side of the hill.

"Was not that little fellow cute? I have had several fawns, but have never had the heart to keep them," said Betty. Then, as Alfred made no motion to speak, she continued:

"You do not seem very talkative."

"I have nothing to say. You will think me dull. The fact is when I feel deepest I am least able to express myself."

"I will read to you," said Betty, taking up the book. He lay back against the grassy bank and gazed dreamily at the many hued trees on the little hillside; at the bare rugged sides of McColloch's Rock which frowned down upon them. A silver-breasted eagle sailed slowly round and round in the blue sky, far above the bluff. Alfred wondered what mysterious power sustained that solitary bird as he floated high in the air without perceptible movement of his broad wings. He envied the king of birds his reign over that illimitable space, his far-reaching vision, and his freedom. Round and round the eagle soared, higher and higher, with each perfect circle, and at last, for an instant poising as lightly as if he were about to perch on his lonely crag, he arched his wings and swooped down through the air with the swiftness of a falling arrow.

Betty's low voice, the water rushing so musically over the falls, the great yellow leaves falling into the pool, the gentle breeze stirring the clusters of goldenrod—all came softly to Alfred as he lay there with half-closed eyes.

The time slipped swiftly by as only such time can.

"I fear the melancholy spirit of the day has prevailed upon you," said Betty, half wistfully. "You did not know I had stopped reading, and I do not believe you heard my favorite poem. I have tried to give you a pleasant afternoon and have failed."

"No, no," said Alfred, looking at her with a blue flame in his eyes. "The afternoon has been perfect. I have forgotten my role, and have allowed you to see my real self, something I have tried to hide from all."

"And are you always sad when you are sincere?"

"Not always. But I am often sad. Is it any wonder? Is not all nature sad? Listen! There is the song of the oriole. Breaking in on the stillness it is mournful. The breeze is sad, the brook is sad, this dying Indian summer day is sad. Life itself is sad."

"Oh, no. Life is beautiful."

"You are a child," said he, with a thrill in his deep voice. "I hope you may always be as you are to-day, in heart, at least."

"It grows late. See, the shadows are falling. We must go."

"You know I am going away to-morrow. I don't want to go. Perhaps that is why I have been such poor company to-day. I have a presentiment of evil. I am afraid I may never come back."

"I am sorry you must go."

"Do you really mean that?" asked Alfred, earnestly, bending toward her. "You know it is a very dangerous undertaking. Would you care if I never returned?"

She looked up and their eyes met. She had raised her head haughtily, as if questioning his right to speak to her in that manner, but as she saw the unspoken appeal in his eyes her own wavered and fell while a warm color crept into her cheek.

"Yes, I would be sorry," she said, gravely. Then, after a moment: "You must portage the canoe round the falls, and from there we can paddle back to the path."

The return trip made, they approached the house. As they turned the corner they saw Colonel Zane standing at the door talking to Wetzel. They saw that the Colonel looked pale and distressed, and the face of the hunter was dark and gloomy.

"Lew, did you get my turkey?" said Betty, after a moment of hesitation. A nameless fear filled her breast.

For answer Wetzel threw back the flaps of his coat and there at his belt hung a small tuft of black hair. Betty knew at once it was the scalp-lock of an Indian. Her face turned white and she placed a hand on the hunter's arm.

"What do you mean? That is an Indian's scalp. Lew, you look so strange. Tell me, is it because we went off in the canoe and have been in danger?"

"Betty, Isaac has been captured again," said the Colonel.

"Oh, no, no, no," cried Betty in agonized tones, and wringing her hands. Then, excitedly, "Something can be done. You must pursue them. Oh, Lew, Mr. Clarke, cannot you rescue him? They have not had time to go far."

"Isaac went to the chestnut grove this morning. If he had stayed there he would not have been captured. But he went far into the Black Forest. The turkey call we heard across the creek was made by a Wyandot concealed in the cave. Lewis tells me that a number of Indians have camped there for days. He shot the one who was calling and followed the others until he found where they had taken Isaac's trail."

Betty turned to the younger man with tearful eyes, and with beseeching voice implored them to save her brother.

"I am ready to follow you," said Clarke to Wetzel.

The hunter shook his head, but did not answer.

"It is that hateful White Crane," passionately burst out Betty, as the Colonel's wife led her weeping into the house.

"Did you get more than one shot at them?" asked Clarke.

The hunter nodded, and the slight, inscrutable smile flitted across his stern features. He never spoke of his deeds. For this reason many of the thrilling adventures which he must have had will forever remain unrevealed. That evening there was sadness at Colonel Zane's supper table. They felt the absence of the Colonel's usual spirits, his teasing of Betty, and his cheerful conversation. He had nothing to say. Betty sat at the table a little while, and then got up and left the room saying she could not eat. Jonathan, on hearing of his brother's recapture, did not speak, but retired in gloomy silence. Silas was the only one of the family who was not utterly depressed. He said it could have been a great deal worse; that they must make the best of it, and that the sooner Isaac married his Indian Princess the better for his scalp and for the happiness of all concerned.

"I remember Myeerah very well," he said. "It was eight years ago, and she was only a child. Even then she was very proud and willful, and the loveliest girl I ever laid eyes on."

Alfred Clarke stayed late at Colonel Zane's that night. Before going away for so many weeks he wished to have a few more moments alone with Betty. But a favorable opportunity did not present itself during the evening, so when he had bade them all goodbye and goodnight, except Betty, who opened the door for him, he said softly to her:

"It is bright moonlight outside. Come, please, and walk to the gate with me."

A full moon shone serenely down on hill and dale, flooding the valley with its pure white light, and bathing the pastures in its glory; at the foot of the bluff the waves of the river gleamed like myriads of stars all twinkling and dancing on a bed of snowy clouds. Thus illumined, the river wound down the valley, its brilliance growing fainter and fainter until at last, resembling the shimmering of a silver thread which joined the earth to heaven, it disappeared in the horizon.

"I must say goodbye," said Alfred, as they reached the gate.

"Friends must part. I am sorry you must go, Mr. Clarke, and I trust you may return safe. It seems only yesterday that you saved my brother's life, and I was so grateful and happy. Now he is gone."

"You should not think about it so much nor brood over it," answered the young man. "Grieving will not bring him back nor do you any good. It is not nearly so bad as if he had been captured by some other tribe. Wetzel assures us that Isaac was taken alive. Please do not grieve."

"I have cried until I cannot cry anymore. I am so unhappy. We were children together, and I have always loved him better than any one since my mother died. To have him back again and then to lose him! Oh! I cannot bear it."

She covered her face with her hands and a low sob escaped her.

"Don't, don't grieve," he said in an unsteady voice, as he took the little hands in his and pulled them away from her face.

Betty trembled. Something in his voice, a tone she had never heard before startled her. She looked up at him half unconscious that he still held her hands in his. Never had she appeared so lovely.

"You cannot understand my feelings."

"I loved my mother."

"But you have not lost her. That makes all the difference."

"I want to comfort you and I am powerless. I am unable to say what—-I—"

He stopped short. As he stood gazing down into her sweet face, burning, passionate words came to his lips; but he was dumb; he could not speak. All day long he had been living in a dream. Now he realized that but a moment remained for him to be near the girl he loved so well. He was leaving her, perhaps never to see her again, or to return to find her another's. A fierce pain tore his heart.

"You—you are holding my hands," faltered Betty, in a doubtful, troubled voice. She looked up into his face and saw that it was pale with suppressed emotion.

Alfred was mad indeed. He forgot everything. In that moment the world held nothing for him save that fair face. Her eyes, uplifted to his in the moonlight, beamed with a soft radiance. They were honest eyes, just now filled with innocent sadness and regret, but they drew him with irresistible power. Without realizing in the least what he was doing he yielded to the impulse. Bending his head he kissed the tremulous lips.

"Oh," whispered Betty, standing still as a statue and looking at him with wonderful eyes. Then, as reason returned, a hot flush dyed her face, and wrenching her hands free she struck him across the cheek.

"For God's sake, Betty, I did not mean to do that! Wait. I have something to tell you. For pity's sake, let me explain," he cried, as the full enormity of his offence dawned upon him.

Betty was deaf to the imploring voice, for she ran into the house and slammed the door.

He called to her, but received no answer. He knocked on the door, but it remained closed. He stood still awhile, trying to collect his thoughts, and to find a way to undo the mischief he had wrought. When the real significance of his act came to him he groaned in spirit. What a fool he had been! Only a few short hours and he must start on a perilous journey, leaving the girl he loved in ignorance of his real intentions. Who was to tell her that he loved her? Who was to tell her that it was because his whole heart and soul had gone to her that he had kissed her?

With bowed head he slowly walked away toward the fort, totally oblivious of the fact that a young girl, with hands pressed tightly over her breast to try to still a madly beating heart, watched him from her window until he disappeared into the shadow of the blockhouse.

Alfred paced up and down his room the four remaining hours of that eventful day. When the light was breaking in at the east and dawn near at hand he heard the rough voices of men and the tramping of iron-shod hoofs. The hour of his departure was at hand.

He sat down at his table and by the aid of the dim light from a pine knot he wrote a hurried letter to Betty. A little hope revived in his heart as he thought that perhaps all might yet be well. Surely some one would be up to whom he could intrust the letter, and if no one he would run over and slip it under the door of Colonel Zane's house.

In the gray of the early morning Alfred rode out with the daring band of heavily armed men, all grim and stern, each silent with the thought of the man who knows he may never return. Soon the settlement was left far behind.

CHAPTER 5

During the last few days, in which the frost had cracked open the hickory nuts, and in which the squirrels had been busily collecting and storing away their supply of nuts for winter use, it had been Isaac's wont to shoulder his rifle, walk up the hill, and spend the morning in the grove.

On this crisp autumn morning he had started off as usual, and had been called back by Colonel Zane, who advised him not to wander far from the settlement. This admonition, kind and brotherly though it was, annoyed Isaac. Like all the Zanes he had born in him an intense love for the solitude of the wilderness. There were times when nothing could satisfy him but the calm of the deep woods.

One of these moods possessed him now. Courageous to a fault and daring where daring was not always the wiser part, Isaac lacked the practical sense of the Colonel and the cool judgment of Jonathan. Impatient of restraint, independent in spirit, and it must be admitted, in his persistence in doing as he liked instead of what he ought to do, he resembled Betty more than he did his brothers.

Feeling secure in his ability to take care of himself, for he knew he was an experienced hunter and woodsman, he resolved to take a long tramp in the forest. This resolution was strengthened by the fact that he did not believe what the Colonel and Jonathan had told him—that it was not improbable some of the Wyandot braves were lurking in the vicinity, bent on killing or recapturing him. At any rate he did not fear it.

Once in the shade of the great trees the fever of discontent left him, and, forgetting all except the happiness of being surrounded by the silent oaks, he penetrated deeper and deeper into the forest. The brushing of a branch against a tree, the thud of a falling nut, the dart of a squirrel, and the sight of a bushy tail disappearing round a limb—all these things which indicated that the little gray fellows were working in the treetops, and which would usually have brought Isaac to a standstill, now did not seem to interest him. At times he stooped to examine the tender shoots growing at the foot of a sassafras tree. Then, again, he closely examined marks he found in the soft banks of the streams.

He went on and on. Two hours of this still-hunting found him on the bank of a shallow gully through which a brook went rippling and babbling over the mossy green stones. The forest was dense here; rugged oaks and tall poplars grew high over the tops of the first growth of white oaks and beeches; the wild grapevines which coiled round the trees like gigantic serpents, spread out in the upper branches and obscured the sun; witch-hopples and laurel bushes grew thickly; monarchs of the forest, felled by some bygone storm, lay rotting on the ground; and in places the windfalls were so thick and high as to be impenetrable.

Isaac hesitated. He realized that he had plunged far into the Black Forest. Here it was gloomy; a dreamy quiet prevailed, that deep calm of the wilderness, unbroken save for the distant note of the hermit-thrush, the strange bird whose lonely cry, given at long intervals, pierced the stillness. Although Isaac had never seen one of these birds, he was familiar with that cry which was never heard except in the deepest woods, far from the haunts of man.

A black squirrel ran down a tree and seeing the hunter scampered away in alarm. Isaac knew the habits of the black squirrel, that it was a denizen of the wildest woods and frequented only places remote from civilization. The song of the hermit and the sight of the black squirrel caused Isaac to stop and reflect, with the result that he concluded he had gone much farther from the fort than he had intended. He turned to retrace his steps when a faint sound from down the ravine came to his sharp ears.

There was no instinct to warn him that a hideously painted face was raised a moment over the clump of laurel bushes to his left, and that a pair of keen eyes watched every move he made.

Unconscious of impending evil Isaac stopped and looked around him. Suddenly above the musical babble of the brook and the rustle of the leaves by the breeze came a repetition of the sound. He crouched close by the trunk of a tree and strained his ears. All was quiet for some moments. Then he heard the patter, patter of little hoofs coming down the stream. Nearer and nearer they came. Sometimes they were almost inaudible and again he heard them clearly and distinctly. Then there came a splashing and the faint hollow sound caused by hard hoofs striking the stones in shallow water. Finally the sounds ceased.

Cautiously peering from behind the tree Isaac saw a doe standing on the bank fifty yards down the brook. Trembling she had stopped as if in doubt or uncertainty. Her ears pointed straight upward, and she lifted one front foot from the ground like a thoroughbred pointer. Isaac knew a doe always led the way through the woods and if there were other deer they would come up unless warned by the doe. Presently the willows parted and a magnificent buck with wide spreading antlers stepped out and stood motionless on the bank. Although they were down the wind Isaac knew the deer suspected some hidden danger. They looked steadily at the clump of laurels at Isaac's left, a circumstance he remarked at the time, but did not understand the real significance of until long afterward.

Following the ringing report of Isaac's rifle the buck sprang almost across the stream, leaped convulsively up the bank, reached the top, and then his strength failing, slid down into the stream, where, in his dying struggles, his hoofs beat the water into white foam. The doe had disappeared like a brown flash.

Isaac, congratulating himself on such a fortunate shot—for rarely indeed does a deer fall dead in his tracks even when shot through the heart—rose from his crouching position and commenced to reload his rifle. With great care he poured the powder into the palm of his hand, measuring the quantity with his eye—for it was an evidence of a hunter's skill to be able to get the proper quantity for the ball. Then he put the charge into the barrel. Placing a little greased linsey rag, about half an inch square, over the muzzle, he laid a small lead bullet on it, and with the ramrod began to push the ball into the barrel.

A slight rustle behind him, which sounded to him like the gliding of a rattlesnake over the leaves, caused him to start and turn around. But he was too late. A crushing blow on the head from a club in the hand of a brawny Indian laid him senseless on the ground.

When Isaac regained his senses he felt a throbbing pain in his head, and when he opened his eyes he was so dizzy that he was unable to discern objects clearly. After a few moments his sight returned. When he had struggled to a sitting posture he discovered that his hands were bound with buckskin thongs. By his side he saw two long poles of basswood, with some strips of green bark and pieces of grapevine laced across and tied fast to the poles. Evidently this had served as a litter on which he had been carried. From his wet clothes and the position of the sun, now low in the west, he concluded he had been brought across the river and was now miles from the fort. In front of him he saw three Indians sitting before a fire. One of them was cutting slices from a haunch of deer meat, another was drinking from a gourd, and the third was roasting a piece of venison which he held on a sharpened stick. Isaac knew at once the Indians were Wyandots, and he saw they were in full war paint. They were not young braves, but middle-aged warriors. One of them Isaac recognized as Crow, a chief of one of the Wyandot tribes, and a warrior renowned for his daring and for his ability to make his way in a straight line through the wilderness. Crow was a short, heavy Indian and his frame denoted great strength. He had a broad forehead, high cheekbones, prominent nose, and his face would have been handsome and intelligent but for the scar which ran across his cheek, giving him a sinister look.

"Hugh!" said Crow, as he looked up and saw Isaac staring at him. The other Indians immediately gave vent to a like exclamation.

"Crow, you have caught me again," said Isaac, in the Wyandot tongue, which he spoke fluently.

"The white chief is sure of eye and swift of foot, but he cannot escape the Huron. Crow has been five times on his trail since the moon was bright. The white chief's eyes were shut and his ears were deaf," answered the Indian loftily.

"How long have you been near the fort?"

"Two moons have the warriors of Myeerah hunted the paleface."

"Have you any more Indians with you?"

The chief nodded and said a party of nine Wyandots had been in the vicinity of Wheeling for a month. He named some of the warriors.

Isaac was surprised to learn of the renowned chiefs who had been sent to recapture him. Not to mention Crow, the Delaware chiefs Son-of-Wingenund and Wapatomeka were among the most cunning and sagacious Indians of the west. Isaac reflected that this year's absence from Myeerah had not caused her to forget him.

Crow untied Isaac's hands and gave him water and venison. Then he picked up his rifle and with a word to the Indians he stepped into the underbrush that skirted the little dale, and was lost to view.

Isaac's head ached and throbbed so that after he had satisfied his thirst and hunger he was glad to close his eyes and lean back against the tree. Engrossed in thoughts of the home he might never see again, he had lain there an hour without moving, when he was aroused from his meditations by low guttural exclamations from the Indians. Opening his eyes he saw Crow and another Indian enter the glade, leading and half supporting a third savage.

They helped this Indian to the log, where he sat down slowly and wearily, holding one hand over his breast. He was a magnificent specimen of Indian manhood, almost a giant in stature, with broad shoulders in proportion to his height. His headdress and the gold rings which encircled his bare muscular arms indicated that he was a chief high in power. The seven eagle plumes in his scalp-lock represented seven warriors that he had killed in battle. Little sticks of wood plaited in his coal black hair and painted different colors showed to an Indian eye how many times the chief had been wounded by bullet, knife, or tomahawk.

His face was calm. If he suffered he allowed no sign of it to escape him. He gazed thoughtfully into the fire, slowly the while untying the belt which contained his knife and tomahawk. The weapons were raised and held before him, one in each hand, and then waved on high. The action was repeated three times. Then slowly and reluctantly the Indian lowered them as if he knew their work on earth was done.

It was growing dark and the bright blaze from the campfire lighted up the glade, thus enabling Isaac to see the drooping figure on the log, and in the background Crow, holding a whispered consultation with the other Indians. Isaac heard enough of the colloquy to guess the facts. The chief had been desperately wounded; the pale-faces were on their trail, and a march must be commenced at once.

Isaac knew the wounded chief. He was the Delaware Son-of-Wingenund. He married a Wyandot squaw, had spent much of his time in the Wyandot village and on warring expeditions which the two friendly nations made on other tribes. Isaac had hunted with him, slept under the same blanket with him, and had grown to like him.

As Isaac moved slightly in his position the chief saw him. He straightened up, threw back the hunting shirt and pointed to a small hole in his broad chest. A slender stream of blood issued from the wound and flowed down his chest.

"Wind-of-Death is a great white chief. His gun is always loaded," he said calmly, and a look of pride gleamed across his dark face, as though he gloried in the wound made by such a warrior.

"Deathwind" was one of the many names given to Wetzel by the savages, and a thrill of hope shot through

Isaac's heart when he saw the Indians feared Wetzel was on their track. This hope was short lived, however, for when he considered the probabilities of the thing he knew that pursuit would only result in his death before the settlers could come up with the Indians, and he concluded that Wetzel, familiar with every trick of the redmen would be the first to think of the hopelessness of rescuing him and so would not attempt it.

The four Indians now returned to the fire and stood beside the chief. It was evident to them that his end was imminent. He sang in a low, not unmusical tone the death-chant of the Hurons. His companions silently bowed their heads. When he had finished singing he slowly rose to his great height, showing a commanding figure. Slowly his features lost their stern pride, his face softened, and his dark eyes, gazing straight into the gloom of the forest, bespoke a superhuman vision.

"Wingenund has been a great chief. He has crossed his last trail. The deeds of Wingenund will be told in the wigwams of the Lenape," said the chief in a loud voice, and then sank back into the arms of his comrades. They laid him gently down.

A convulsive shudder shook the stricken warrior's frame. Then, starting up he straightened out his long arm and clutched wildly at the air with his sinewy fingers as if to grasp and hold the life that was escaping him.

Isaac could see the fixed, somber light in the eyes, and the pallor of death stealing over the face of the chief. He turned his eyes away from the sad spectacle, and when he looked again the majestic figure lay still.

The moon sailed out from behind a cloud and shed its mellow light down on the little glade. It showed the four Indians digging a grave beneath the oak tree. No word was spoken. They worked with their tomahawks on the soft duff and soon their task was completed. A bed of moss and ferns lined the last resting place of the chief. His weapons were placed beside him, to go with him to the Happy Hunting Ground, the eternal home of the redmen, where the redmen believe the sun will always shine, and where they will be free from their cruel white foes.

When the grave had been filled and the log rolled on it the Indians stood by it a moment, each speaking a few words in a low tone, while the night wind moaned the dead chief's requiem through the treetops.

Accustomed as Isaac was to the bloody conflicts common to the Indians, and to the tragedy that surrounded the life of a borderman, the ghastly sight had unnerved him. The last glimpse of that stern, dark face, of that powerful form, as the moon brightened up the spot in seeming pity, he felt he could never forget. His thoughts were interrupted by the harsh voice of Crow bidding him get up. He was told that the slightest inclination on his part to lag behind on the march before them, or in any way to make their trail plainer, would be the signal for his death. With that Crow cut the thongs which bound Isaac's legs and placing him between two of the Indians, led the way into the forest.

Moving like spectres in the moonlight they marched on and on for hours. Crow was well named. He led them up the stony ridges where their footsteps left no mark, and where even a dog could not find their trail; down into the valleys and into the shallow streams where the running water would soon wash away all trace of their tracks; then out on the open plain, where the soft, springy grass retained little impress of their moccasins.

Single file they marched in the leader's tracks as he led them onward through the dark forests, out under the shining moon, never slacking his rapid pace, ever in a straight line, and yet avoiding the roughest going with that unerring instinct which was this Indian's gift. Toward dawn the moon went down, leaving them in darkness, but this made no difference, for, guided by the stars, Crow kept straight on his course. Not till break of day did he come to a halt.

Then, on the banks of a narrow stream, the Indians kindled a fire and broiled some of the venison. Crow told Isaac he could rest, so he made haste to avail himself of the permission, and almost instantly was wrapped in the deep slumber of exhaustion. Three of the Indians followed suit, and Crow stood guard. Sleepless, tireless, he paced to and fro on the bank, his keen eyes vigilant for signs of pursuers.

The sun was high when the party resumed their flight toward the west. Crow plunged into the brook and waded several miles before he took to the woods on the other shore. Isaac suffered severely from the sharp and slippery stones, which in no wise bothered the Indians. His feet were cut and bruised; still he struggled on without complaining. They rested part of the night, and the next day the Indians, now deeming themselves practically safe from pursuit, did not exercise unusual care to conceal their trail.

That evening about dusk they came to a rapidly flowing stream which ran northwest. Crow and one of the other Indians parted the willows on the bank at this point and dragged forth a long birch-bark canoe which they ran into the stream. Isaac recognized the spot. It was near the head of Mad River, the river which ran through the Wyandot settlements.

Two of the Indians took the bow, the third Indian and Isaac sat in the middle, back to back, and Crow knelt in the stern. Once launched on that wild ride Isaac forgot his weariness and his bruises. The night was beautiful; he loved the water, and was not lacking in sentiment. He gave himself up to the charm of the silver moonlight, of the changing scenery, and the musical gurgle of the water. Had it not been for the cruel face of Crow, he could have imagined himself on one of those enchanted canoes in fairyland, of which he had read when a boy. Ever varying pictures presented themselves as the canoe, impelled by vigorous arms, flew over the shining bosom of the stream. Here, in a sharp bend, was a narrow place where the trees on each bank interlaced their branches and hid the moon, making a dark and dim retreat. Then came a short series of ripples, with merry, bouncing waves and foamy currents; below lay a long, smooth reach of water, deep and placid, mirroring the moon and the countless stars. Noiseless as a shadow the canoe glided down this stretch, the paddle dipping regularly, flashing brightly, and scattering diamond drops in the clear moonlight.

Another turn in the stream and a sound like the roar of an approaching storm as it is borne on a rising wind, broke the silence. It was the roar of rapids or falls. The stream narrowed; the water ran swifter; rocky ledges rose on both sides, gradually getting higher and higher. Crow rose to his feet and looked ahead. Then he dropped to his knees and turned the head of the canoe into the middle of the stream. The roar became deafening. Looking forward Isaac saw that they were entering a dark gorge. In another moment the canoe pitched over a fall and shot between two high, rocky bluffs. These walls ran up almost perpendicularly two hundred feet; the space between was scarcely twenty feet wide, and the water fairly screamed as it rushed madly through its narrow passage. In the center it was like a glancing sheet of glass, weird and dark, and was bordered on the sides by white, seething foam-capped waves which tore and dashed and leaped at their stony confines.

Though the danger was great, though Death lurked in those jagged stones and in those black walls Isaac felt no fear; he knew the strength of that arm, now rigid and again moving with lightning swiftness; he knew the power of the eye which guided them.

Once more out under the starry sky; rifts, shallows, narrows, and lake-like basins were passed swiftly. At length as the sky was becoming gray in the east, they passed into the shadow of what was called the Standing Stone. This was a peculiarly shaped stone-faced bluff, standing high over the river, and taking its name from Tarhe, or Standing Stone, chief of all the Hurons.

At the first sight of that well-known landmark, which stood by the Wyandot village, there mingled with Isaac's despondency and resentment some other feeling that was akin to pleasure; with a quickening of the pulse came a confusion of expectancy and bitter memories as he thought of the dark-eyed maiden from whom he had fled a year ago.

"Co-wee-Co-wee," called out one of the Indians in the bow of the canoe. The signal was heard, for immediately an answering shout came from the shore.

When a few moments later the canoe grated softly upon a pebbly beach, Isaac saw, indistinctly in the morning mist, the faint outlines of tepees and wigwams, and he knew he was once more in the encampment of the Wyandots.

Late in the afternoon of that day Isaac was awakened from his heavy slumber and told that the chief had summoned him. He got up from the buffalo robes upon which he had flung himself that morning, stretched his aching limbs, and walked to the door of the lodge.

The view before him was so familiar that it seemed as if he had suddenly come home after being absent a long time. The last rays of the setting sun shone ruddy and bright over the top of the Standing Stone; they touched the scores of lodges and wigwams which dotted the little valley; they crimsoned the swift, narrow river, rushing noisily over its rocky bed. The banks of the stream were lined with rows of canoes; here and there a bridge made of a single tree spanned the stream. From the campfires long, thin columns of blue smoke curled lazily upward; giant maple trees, in their garb of purple and gold, rose high above the wigwams, adding a further beauty to this peaceful scene.

As Isaac was led down a lane between two long lines of tepees the watching Indians did not make the demonstration that usually marked the capture of a paleface. Some of the old squaws looked up from their work round the campfires and steaming kettles and grinned as the prisoner passed. The braves who were sitting upon their blankets and smoking their long pipes, or lounging before the warm blaze, maintained a stolid indifference; the dusky maidens smiled shyly, and the little Indian boys, with whom Isaac had always been a great favorite, manifested their joy by yelling and running after him. One youngster grasped Isaac round the leg and held on until he was pulled away.

In the center of the village were several lodges connected with one another and larger and more imposing than the surrounding tepees. These were the wigwams of the chief, and thither Isaac was conducted. The guards led him to a large and circular apartment and left him there alone. This room was the council-room. It contained nothing but a low seat and a knotted war-club.

Isaac heard the rattle of beads and bear claws, and as he turned a tall and majestic Indian entered the room. It was Tarhe, the chief of all the Wyandots. Though Tarhe was over seventy, he walked erect; his calm face, dark as a bronze mask, showed no trace of his advanced age. Every line and feature of his face had race in it; the high forehead, the square, protruding jaw, the stern mouth, the falcon eyes—all denoted the price and unbending will of the last of the Tarhes.

"The White Eagle is again in the power of Tarhe," said the chief in his native tongue. "Though he had the swiftness of the bounding deer or the flight of the eagle it would avail him not. The wild geese as they fly northward are not swifter than the warriors of Tarhe. Swifter than all is the vengeance of the Huron. The young paleface has cost the lives of some great warriors. What has he to say?"

"It was not my fault," answered Isaac quickly. "I was struck down from behind and had no chance to use a weapon. I have never raised my hand against a Wyandot. Crow will tell you that. If my people and friends kill your braves I am not to blame. Yet I have had good cause to shed Huron blood. Your warriors have taken me from my home and have wounded me many times."

"The White Chief speaks well. Tarhe believes his words," answered Tarhe in his sonorous voice. "The Lenape seek the death of the paleface. Wingenund grieves for his son. He is Tarhe's friend. Tarhe is old and wise and he is king here. He can save the White Chief from Wingenund and Cornplanter. Listen. Tarhe is old and he has no son. He will make you a great chief and give you lands and braves and honors. He shall not ask you to raise your hand against your people, but help to bring peace. Tarhe does not love this war. He wants only justice. He wants only to keep his lands, his horses, and his people. The White Chief is known to be brave; his step is light, his eye is keen, and his bullet is true. For many long moons Tarhe's daughter has been like the singing bird without its mate. She sings no more. She shall be the White Chief's wife. She has the blood of her mother and not that of the last of the Tarhes. Thus, the mistakes of Tarhe's youth come to disappoint his old age. He is the friend of the young paleface. Tarhe has said. Now go and make your peace with Myeerah."

The chief motioned toward the back of the lodge. Isaac stepped forward and went through another large room, evidently the chief's, as it was fitted up with a wild and barbaric splendor. Isaac hesitated before a bearskin curtain at the farther end of the chief's lodge. He had been there many times before, but never with such conflicting emotions. What was it that made his heart beat faster? With a quick movement he lifted the curtain and passed under it.

The room which he entered was circular in shape and furnished with all the bright colors and luxuriance known to the Indian. Buffalo robes covered the smooth, hard-packed clay floor; animals, allegorical pictures, and fanciful Indian designs had been painted on the wall; bows and arrows, shields, strings of bright-colored beads and Indian scarfs hung round the room. The wall was made of dried deerskins sewed together and fastened over long poles which were planted in the ground and bent until the ends met overhead. An oval-shaped opening let in the light. Through a narrow aperture, which served as a door leading to a smaller apartment, could be seen a low couch covered with red blankets, and a glimpse of many hued garments hanging on the wall.

As Isaac entered the room a slender maiden ran impulsively to him and throwing her arms round his neck hid her face on his breast. A few broken, incoherent words escaped her lips. Isaac disengaged himself from the clinging arms and put her from him. The face raised to his was strikingly beautiful. Oval in shape, it was as white as his own, with a broad, low brow and regular features. The eyes were large and dark and they dilated and quickened with a thousand shadows of thought.

"Myeerah, I am taken again. This time there has been

blood shed. The Delaware chief was killed, and I do not know how many more Indians. The chiefs are all for putting me to death. I am in great danger. Why could you not leave me in peace?"

At his first words the maiden sighed and turned sorrowfully and proudly away from the angry face of the young man. A short silence ensued.

"Then you are not glad to see Myeerah?" she said, in English. Her voice was music. It rang low, sweet, clear-toned as a bell.

"What has that to do with it? Under some circumstances I would be glad to see you. But to be dragged back here and perhaps murdered—no, I don't welcome it. Look at this mark where Crow hit me," said Isaac, passionately, bowing his head to enable her to see the bruise where the club had struck him.

"I am sorry," said Myeerah, gently.

"I know that I am in great danger from the Delawares."

"The daughter of Tarhe has saved your life before and will save it again."

"They may kill me in spite of you."

"They will not dare. Do not forget that I saved you from the Shawnees. What did my father say to you?"

"He assured me that he was my friend and that he would protect me from Wingenund. But I must marry you and become one of the tribe. I cannot do that. And that is why I am sure they will kill me."

"You are angry now. I will tell you. Myeerah tried hard to win your love, and when you ran away from her she was proud for a long time. But there was no singing of birds, no music of the waters, no beauty in anything after you left her. Life became unbearable without you. Then Myeerah remembered that she was a daughter of kings. She summoned the bravest and greatest warriors of two tribes and said to them, 'Go and bring to me the paleface,

White Eagle. Bring him to me alive or dead. If alive, Myeerah will smile once more upon her warriors. If dead, she will look once upon his face and die.' Ever since Myeerah was old enough to remember she has thought of you. Would you wish her to be inconstant, like the moon?"

"It is not what I wish you to be. It is that I cannot live always without seeing my people. I told you that a year ago."

"You told me other things in that past time before you ran away. They were tender words that were sweet to the ear of the Indian maiden. Have you forgotten them?"

"I have not forgotten them. I am not without feeling. You do not understand. Since I have been home this last time I have realized more than ever that I could not live away from my home."

"Is there any maiden in your old home whom you have learned to love more than Myeerah?"

He did not reply, but looked gloomily out of the opening in the wall. Myeerah had placed her hand upon his arm, and as he did not answer the hand tightened its grasp.

"She shall never have you."

The low tones vibrated with intense feeling, with a deathless resolve. Isaac laughed bitterly and looked up at her. Myeerah's face was pale and her eyes burned like fire.

"I should not be surprised if you gave me up to the Delawares," said Isaac, coldly. "I am prepared for it, and I would not care very much. I have despaired of your ever becoming civilized enough to understand the misery of my sister and family. Why not let the Indians kill me?"

He knew how to wound her. A quick, shuddering cry broke from her lips. She stood before him with bowed head and wept. When she spoke again her voice was broken and pleading.

"You are cruel and unjust. Though Myeerah has Indian blood she is a white woman. She can feel as your people do. In your anger and bitterness you forget that Myeerah saved you from the knife of the Shawnees. You forget her tenderness; you forget that she nursed you when you were wounded. Myeerah has a heart to break. Has she not suffered? Is she not laughed at, scorned, called a 'paleface' by the other tribes? She thanks the Great Spirit for the Indian blood that keeps her true. The white man changes his loves and his wives. That is not an Indian gift."

"No, Myeerah, I did not say so. There is no other woman. It is that I am wretched and sick at heart. Do you not see that this will end in a tragedy some day? Can you not realize that we would be happier if you would let me go? If you love me you would not want to see me dead. If I do not marry you they will kill me; if I try to escape again they will kill me. Let me go free."

"I cannot! I cannot!" she cried. "You have taught me many of the ways of your people, but you cannot change my nature."

"Why cannot you free me?"

"I love you, and I will not live without you."

"Then come and go to my home and live there with me," said Isaac, taking the weeping maiden in his arms. "I know that my people will welcome you."

"Myeerah would be pitied and scorned," she said, sadly, shaking her head.

Isaac tried hard to steel his heart against her, but he was only mortal and he failed. The charm of her presence influenced him; her love wrung tenderness from him. Those dark eyes, so proud to all others, but which gazed wistfully and yearningly into his, stirred his heart to its depths. He kissed the tear-wet cheeks and smiled upon her.

"Well, since I am a prisoner once more, I must make the best of it. Do not look so sad. We shall talk of this another day. Come, let us go and find my little friend, Captain Jack. He remembered me, for he ran out and grasped my knee and they pulled him away."

CHAPTER 6

When the first French explorers invaded the northwest, about the year 1615, the Wyandot Indians occupied the territory between Georgian Bay and the Muskoka Lakes in Ontario. These Frenchmen named the tribe Huron because of the manner in which they wore their hair.

At this period the Hurons were at war with the Iroquois, and the two tribes kept up a bitter fight until in 1649, when the Hurons suffered a decisive defeat. They then abandoned their villages and sought other hunting grounds. They travelled south and settled in Ohio along the south and west shores of Lake Erie. The present site of Zanesfield, named from Isaac Zane, marks the spot where the largest tribe of Hurons once lived.

In a grove of maples on the banks of a swift little river named Mad River, the Hurons built their lodges and their wigwams. The stately elk and graceful deer abounded in this fertile valley, and countless herds of bison browsed upon the uplands.

There for many years the Hurons lived a peaceful and contented life. The long war cry was not heard. They were at peace with the neighboring tribes. Tarhe, the Huron chief, attained great influence with the Delawares. He became a friend of Logan, the Mingo chief.

With the invasion of the valley of the Ohio by the whites, with the march into the wilderness of that wild-turkey breed of heroes of which Boone, Kenton, the Zanes, and the Wetzels were the first, the Indian's nature gradually changed until he became a fierce and relentless foe.

The Hurons had sided with the French in Pontiac's war, and in the Revolution they aided the British. They allied themselves with the Mingoes, Delawares and Shawnees and made a fierce war on the Virginian pioneers. Some powerful influence must have engineered this implacable hatred in these tribes, particularly in the Mingo and the Wyandot.

The war between the Indians and the settlers along the Pennsylvania and West Virginia borders was known as "Dunmore's War." The Hurons, Mingoes, and Delawares living in the "hunter's paradise" west of the Ohio River, seeing their land sold by the Iroquois and the occupation of their possessions by a daring band of white men naturally were filled with fierce anger and hate. But remembering the past bloody war and British punishment they slowly moved backward toward the setting sun and kept the peace. In 1774 a canoe filled with friendly Wyandots was attacked by white men below Yellow Creek and the Indians were killed. Later the same year a party of men under Colonel Cresop made an unprovoked and dastardly massacre of the family and relatives of Logan. This attack reflected the deepest dishonor upon all the white men concerned, and was the principal cause of the long and bloody war which followed. The settlers on the border sent messengers to Governor Dunmore at Williamsburg for immediate relief parties. Knowing well that the Indians would not allow this massacre to go unavenged the frontiersmen erected forts and blockhouses.

Logan, the famous Mingo chief, had been a noted friend of the white men. After the murder of his people he made ceaseless war upon them. He incited the wrath of the Hurons and the Delawares. He went on the warpath, and when his lust for vengeance had been satisfied he sent the following remarkable address to Lord Dunmore:

"I appeal to any white man to say if ever he entered Logan's cabin and he gave him not meat; if ever he came cold and naked and he clothed him not. During the course of the last long and bloody war Logan remained idle in his cabin, an advocate of peace. Such was my love for the whites that my countrymen pointed as they passed and said: 'Logan is the friend of the white man.' I had even thought to have lived with you but for the injuries of one man, Colonel Cresop, who, last spring, in cold blood and unprovoked, murdered all the relatives of Logan, not even sparing my women and children. There runs not a drop of my blood in the veins of any living creature. This called upon me for vengeance. I have sought it; I have killed many; I have glutted my vengeance. For my country I will rejoice at the beams of peace. But do not harbor a thought that mine is the joy of fear. Logan never felt fear; he would not turn upon his heel to save his life. Who is there to mourn for Logan? Not one." The war between the Indians and the pioneers was waged for years. The settlers pushed farther and farther into the wilderness. The Indians, who at first sought only to save their farms and their stock, now fought for revenge. That is why every ambitious pioneer who went out upon those borders carried his life in his hands; why there was always the danger of being shot or tomahawked from behind every tree; why wife and children were constantly in fear of the terrible enemy.

To creep unawares upon a foe and strike him in the dark was Indian warfare; to an Indian it was not dishonorable;

it was not cowardly. He was taught to hide in the long grass like a snake, to shoot from coverts, to worm his way stealthily through the dense woods and to ambush the paleface's trail. Horrible cruelties, such as torturing white prisoners and burning them at the stake were never heard of before the war made upon the Indians by the whites.

Comparatively little is known of the real character of the Indian of that time. We ourselves sit before our warm fires and talk of the deeds of the redman. We while away an hour by reading Pontiac's siege of Detroit, of the battle of Braddock's fields, and of Custer's last charge. We lay the book down with a fervent expression of thankfulness that the day of the horrible redman is past. Because little has been written on the subject, no thought is given to the long years of deceit and treachery practiced upon Pontiac; we are ignorant of the causes which led to the slaughter of Braddock's army; and we know little of the life of bitterness suffered by Sitting Bull.

Many intelligent white men, who were acquainted with the true life of the Indian before he was harrassed and driven to desperation by the pioneers, said that he had been cruelly wronged. Many white men in those days loved the Indian life so well that they left the settlements and lived with the Indians. Boone, who knew the Indian nature, said the honesty and the simplicity of the Indian were remarkable. Kenton said he had been happy among the Indians. Colonel Zane had many Indian friends. Isaac Zane, who lived most of his life with the Wyandots, said the American redman had been wrongfully judged a bloodthirsty savage, an ignorant, thieving wretch, capable of not one virtue. He said the free picturesque life of the Indians would have appealed to any white man; that it had a wonderful charm; and that before the war with the whites the Indians were kind to their prisoners, and sought only to make Indians of them. He told tales of how easily white boys become Indianized, so attached to the wild life and freedom of the redmen that it was impossible to get the captives to return to civilized life. The boys had been permitted to grow wild with the Indian lads; to fish and shoot and swim with them; to play the Indian games—to live idle, joyous lives. He said these white boys had been ransomed and taken from captivity and returned to their homes and, although a close watch was kept on them, they contrived to escape and return to the Indians, and that while they were back among civilized people it was difficult to keep the boys dressed. In summer time it was useless to attempt it. The strongest hemp-linen shirts, made with the strongest collar and wrist-band, would directly be torn off and the little rascals found swimming in the river or rolling on the sand.

If we may believe what these men have said—and there seems no good reason why we may not—the Indian was very different from the impression given of him. There can be little doubt that the redman once lived a noble and blameless life; that he was simple, honest and brave; that he had a regard for honor and a respect for a promise far exceeding that of most white men. Think of the beautiful poetry and legends left by these silent men; men who were a part of the woods; men whose music was the sighing of the wind, the rustling of the leaf, the murmur of the brook; men whose simple joys were the chase of the stag, and the light in the dark eye of a maiden.

If we wish to find the highest type of the American Indian we must look for him before he was driven west by the land-seeking pioneer and before he was degraded by the rum-selling French trader.

The French claimed all the land watered by the Mississippi River and its tributaries. The French Canadian was a restless, roaming adventurer and he found his vocation in the fur-trade. This fur-trade engendered a strange class of men—bush-rangers they were called—whose work was to paddle the canoe along the lakes and streams and exchange their cheap rum for the valuable furs of the Indians. To these men the Indians of the west owe their degradation. These bush-rangers or *coureurs-des-bois*, perverted the Indians and sank into barbarism with them.

The few travellers there in those days were often surprised to find in the wigwams of the Indians men who acknowledged the blood of France, yet who had lost all semblance to the white man. They lived in their tepee with their Indian squaws and lolled on their blankets while the squaws cooked their venison and did all the work. They let their hair grow long and wore feathers in it; they painted their faces hideously with ochre and vermilion.

These were the worthless traders and adventurers who, from the year 1748 to 1783, encroached on the hunting grounds of the Indians and explored the wilderness, seeking out the remote tribes and trading the villainous rum for the rare pelts. In 1784 the French authorities, realizing that these vagrants were demoralizing the Indians, warned them to get off the soil. Finding this course ineffectual they arrested those that could be apprehended and sent them to Canada. But it was too late: the harm had been done; the poor, ignorant savage had tasted of the terrible "fire-water," as he called the rum, and his ruin was inevitable.

It was a singular fact that almost every Indian who had once tasted strong drink, was unable to resist the desire for more. When a trader came to one of the Indian hamlets the braves purchased a keg of rum and then they held a council to see who was to get drunk and who was to keep sober. It was necessary to have some sober Indians in camp, otherwise the drunken braves would kill one another. The weapons would have to be concealed. When the Indians had finished one keg of rum they would buy another, and so on until not a beaver-skin was left. Then the trader would move on. When the Indians sobered up they would be much dejected, for invariably they would find that some had been wounded, others crippled, and often several had been killed.

Logan, using all his eloquence, travelled from village to village visiting the different tribes and making speeches. He urged the Indians to shun the dreaded "fire-water." He exclaimed against the whites for introducing liquor to the Indians and thus debasing them. At the same time Logan admitted his own fondness for rum. This intelligent and noble Indian was murdered in a drunken fight shortly after sending his address to Lord Dunmore.

Thus it was that the poor Indians had no chance to avert their downfall; the steadily increasing tide of land-stealing settlers rolling westward, and the insidious, debasing, soul-destroying liquor were the noble redman's doom.

Isaac Zane dropped back not altogether unhappily into his old place in the wigwam, in the hunting parties, and in the Indian games.

When the braves were in camp, the greater part of the day was spent in shooting and running matches, in canoe races, in wrestling, and in the game of ball. The chiefs and the older braves who had won their laurels and the maidens of the tribe looked on and applauded.

Isaac entered into all these pastimes, partly because he had a natural love for them, and partly because he wished to win the regard of the Indians. In wrestling, and in those sports which required weight and endurance, he usually suffered defeat. In a foot race there was not a brave in the entire tribe who could keep even with him. But it was with the rifle that Isaac won his greatest distinction. The Indians never learned the finer shooting with the rifle. Some few of them could shoot well, but for the most part they were poor marksmen.

Accordingly, Isaac was always taken on the fall hunt. Every autumn there were three parties sent out to bring in the supply of meat for the winter. Because of Isaac's fine marksmanship he was always taken with the bear hunters. Bear hunting was exciting and dangerous work. Before the weather got very cold and winter actually set in the bears crawled into a hole in a tree or a cave in the rocks, where they hibernated. A favorite place for them was in hollow trees. When the Indians found a tree with the scratches of a bear on it and a hole large enough to admit the body of a bear, an Indian climbed up the tree and with a long pole tried to punch Bruin out of his den. Often this was a hazardous undertaking, for the bear would get angry on being disturbed in his winter sleep and would rush out before the Indian could reach a place of safety. At times there were even two or three bears in one den. Sometimes the bears would refuse to come out, and on these occasions, which were rare, the hunters would resort to fire. A piece of dry, rotten wood was fastened to a long pole and was set on fire. When this was pushed in on the bear he would give a sniff and a growl and come out in a hurry.

The buffalo and elk were hunted with the bow and arrow. This effective weapon did not make a noise and frighten the game. The wary Indian crawled through the high grass until within easy range and sometimes killed several buffalo or elk before the herd became alarmed. The meat was then jerked. This consisted in cutting it into thin strips and drying it in the sun. Afterwards it was hung up in the lodges. The skins were stretched on poles to dry, and when cured they served as robes, clothing and wigwam-coverings.

The Indians were fond of honey and maple sugar. The finding of a hive of bees, or a good run of maple syrup was an occasion for general rejoicing. They found the honey in hollow trees, and they obtained the maple sugar in two ways. When the sap came up in the maple trees a hole was bored in the trees about a foot from the ground and a small tube, usually made from a piece of alder, was inserted in the hole. Through this the sap was carried into a vessel which was placed under the tree. This sap was boiled down in kettles. If the Indians had no kettles they made the frost take the place of heat in preparing the sugar. They used shallow vessels made of bark, and these were filled with water and the maple sap. It was left to freeze overnight and in the morning the ice was broken and thrown away. The sugar did not freeze. When this process had been repeated several times the residue was very good maple sugar.

Isaac did more than his share toward the work of provisioning the village for the winter. But he enjoyed it. He was particularly fond of fishing by moonlight. Early November was the best season for this sport, and the Indians caught large numbers of fish. They placed a torch in the bow of a canoe and paddled noiselessly over the stream. In the clear water a bright light would so attract and fascinate the fish that they would lie motionless near the bottom of the shallow stream.

One cold night Isaac was in the bow of the canoe. Seeing a large fish he whispered to the Indians with him to exercise caution. His guides paddled noiselessly through the water. Isaac stood up and raised the spear, ready to strike. In another second Isaac had cast the iron, but in his eagerness he overbalanced himself and plunged head first into the icy current, making a great splash and spoiling any further fishing. Incidents like this were a source of infinite amusement to the Indians.

Before the autumn evenings grew too cold the Indian held their courting dances. All unmarried maidens and braves were expected to take part in these dances. In the bright light of huge fires, and watched by the chiefs, the old men, the squaws, and the children, the maidens and the braves, arrayed in their gaudiest apparel, marched into the circle. They formed two lines a few paces apart. Each held in the right hand a dry gourd which contained pebbles. Advancing toward one another they sang the courting song, keeping time to the tune with the rattling of the pebbles. When they met in the center the braves bent forward and whispered a word to the maidens. At a center point in the song, which was indicated by a louder note, the maidens would change their positions, and this was continued until every brave had whispered to every maiden, when the dance ended.

Isaac took part in all these pleasures; he entered into every phase of the Indian's life; he hunted, worked, played, danced, and sang with faithfulness. But when the long, dreary winter days came with their ice-laden breezes, enforcing idleness on the Indians, he became restless. Sometimes for days he would be morose and gloomy, keeping beside his own tent and not mingling with the Indians. At such times Myeerah did not question him.

Even in his happier hours his diversions were not many. He never tired of watching and studying the Indian children. When he had an opportunity without being observed, which was seldom, he amused himself with the papooses. The Indian baby was strapped to a flat piece of wood and covered with a broad flap of buckskin. The squaws hung these primitive baby carriages up on the pole of a tepee, on a branch of a tree, or threw them round anywhere. Isaac never heard a papoose cry. He often pulled down the flap of buckskin and looked at the solemn little fellow, who would stare up at him with big, wondering eyes.

Isaac's most intimate friend was a six-year-old Indian boy, whom he called Captain Jack. He was the son of Thundercloud, the war-chief of the Hurons. Jack made a brave picture in his buckskin hunting suit and his war bonnet. Already he could stick tenaciously on the back of a racing mustang, and with his little bow he could place arrow after arrow in the center of the target. Knowing Captain Jack would some day be a mighty chief, Isaac taught him to speak English. He endeavored to make Jack love him, so that when the lad should grow to be a man he would remember his white brother and show mercy to the prisoners who fell into his power.

Another of Isaac's favorites was a half-breed Ottawa Indian, a distant relative of Tarhe's. This Indian was very old; no one knew how old; his face was seamed and scarred and wrinkled. Bent and shrunken was his form. He slept most of the time, but at long intervals he would brighten up and tell of his prowess when a warrior.

One of his favorite stories was the part he had taken in the events of that fatal and memorable July 2, 1755, when General Braddock and his English army were massacred by the French and Indians near Fort Duquesne.

The old chief told how Beaujeu with his Frenchmen and his five hundred Indians ambushed Braddock's army, surrounded the soldiers, fired from the ravines, the trees, the long grass, poured a pitiless hail of bullets on the bewildered British soldiers, who, unaccustomed to this deadly and unseen foe, huddled under the trees like herds of frightened sheep, and were shot down with hardly an effort to defend themselves.

The old chief related that fifteen years after that battle he went to the Kanawha settlement to see the Big Chief,

General George Washington, who was travelling on the Kanawha. He told General Washington how he had fought in the battle of Braddock's Fields; how he had shot and killed General Braddock; how he had fired repeatedly at Washington, and had killed two horses under him, and how at last he came to the conclusion that Washington was protected by the Great Spirit who destined him for a great future.

Myeerah was the Indian name for a rare and beautiful bird—the white crane—commonly called by the Indians, Walk-in-the-Water. It had been the name of Tarhe's mother and grandmother. The present Myeerah was the daughter of a French woman, who had been taken captive at a very early age, adopted into the Huron tribe, and married to Tarhe. The only child of this union was Myeerah. She grew to be a beautiful woman and was known in Detroit and the Canadian forts as Tarhe's white daughter. The old chief often visited the towns along the lake shore, and so proud was he of Myeerah that he always had her accompany him. White men travelled far to look at the Indian beauty. Many French soldiers wooed her in vain. Once, while Tarhe was in Detroit, a noted French family tried in every way to get possession of Myeerah.

The head of this family believed he saw in Myeerah the child of his long lost daughter. Tarhe hurried away from the city and never returned to the white settlement.

Myeerah was only five years old at the time of the capture of the Zane brothers and it was at this early age that she formed the attachment for Isaac Zane which clung to her all her life. She was seven when the men came from Detroit to ransom the brothers, and she showed such grief when she learned that Isaac was to be returned to his people that Tarhe refused to accept any ransom for Isaac. As Myeerah grew older her childish fancy for the white boy deepened into an intense love.

But while this love rendered her inexorable to Isaac on the question of giving him his freedom, it undoubtedly saved his life as well as the lives of other white prisoners, on more than one occasion.

To the white captives who fell into the hands of the Hurons, she was kind and merciful; many of the wounded she had tended with her own hands, and many poor wretched she had saved from the gauntlet and the stake. When her efforts to persuade her father to save any one were unavailing she would retire in sorrow to her lodge and remain there.

Her infatuation for the White Eagle, the Huron name for Isaac, was an old story; it was known to all the tribes and had long ceased to be questioned. At first some of the Delawares and the Shawnee braves, who had failed to win Myeerah's love, had openly scorned her for her love for the paleface. The Wyandot warriors to a man worshipped her; they would have marched straight into the jaws of death at her command; they resented the insults which had been cast on their princess, and they had wiped them out in blood: now none dared taunt her.

In the spring following Isaac's recapture a very serious accident befell him. He had become expert in the Indian game of ball, which is a game resembling the Canadian lacrosse, and from which, in fact, it had been adopted. Goals were placed at both ends of a level plain. Each party of Indians chose a goal which they endeavored to defend and at the same time would try to carry the ball over their opponent's line.

A well-contested game of Indian ball presented a scene of wonderful effort and excitement. Hundreds of strong and supple braves could be seen running over the plain, darting this way and that, or struggling in a yelling, kicking, fighting mass, all in a mad scramble to get the ball.

As Isaac had his share of the Zane swiftness of foot, at times his really remarkable fleetness enabled him to get control of the ball. In front of the band of yelling savages he would carry it down the field, and evading the guards at the goal would throw it between the posts. This was a feat of which any brave could be proud.

During one of these games Red Fox, a Wyandot brave, who had long been hopelessly in love with Myeerah, and who cordially hated Isaac, used this opportunity for revenge. Red Fox, who was a swift runner, had vied with Isaac for the honors, but being defeated in the end, he had yielded to his jealous frenzy and had struck Isaac a terrible blow on the head with his bat.

It happened to be a glancing blow or Isaac's life would have been ended then and there. As it was he had a deep gash in his head. The Indians carried him to his lodge and the medicine men of the tribe were summoned.

When Isaac recovered consciousness he asked for Myeerah and entreated her not to punish Red Fox. He knew that such a course would only increase his difficulties, and, on the other hand, if he saved the life of the Indian who had struck him in such a cowardly manner such an act would appeal favorably to the Indians. His entreaties had no effect on Myeerah, who was furious, and who said that if Red Fox, who had escaped, ever returned he would pay for his unprovoked assault with his life, even if she had to kill him herself. Isaac knew that Myeerah would keep her word. He dreaded every morning that the old squaw who prepared his meals would bring him the news that his assailant had been slain. Red Fox was a popular brave, and there were many Indians who believed the blow he had struck Isaac was not intentional. Isaac worried needlessly, however, for Red Fox never came back, and nothing could be learned as to his whereabouts.

It was during his convalescence that Isaac learned really to love the Indian maiden. She showed such distress in the first days after his injury, and such happiness when he was out of danger and on the road to recovery that Isaac wondered at her. She attended him with anxious solicitude; when she bathed and bandaged his wound her every touch was a tender caress; she sat by him for hours; her low voice made soft melody as she sang the Huron love songs. The moments were sweet to Isaac when in the gathering twilight she leaned her head on his shoulder while they listened to the evening carol of the whip-poor-will. Days passed and at length Isaac was entirely well. One day when the air was laden with the warm breath of summer Myeerah and Isaac walked by the river.

"You are sad again," said Myeerah.

"I am homesick. I want to see my people. Myeerah, you have named me rightly. The Eagle can never be happy unless he is free."

"The Eagle can be happy with his mate. And what life could be freer than a Huron's? I hope always that you will grow content."

"It has been a long time now, Myeerah, since I have spoken with you of my freedom. Will you ever free me? Or must I take again those awful chances of escape? I cannot always live here in this way. Some day I shall be killed while trying to get away, and then, if you truly love me, you will never forgive yourself."

"Does not Myeerah truly love you?" she asked, gazing straight into his eyes, her own misty and sad.

"I do not doubt that, but I think sometimes that it is not the right kind of love. It is too savage. No man should be made a prisoner for no other reason than that he is loved by a woman. I have tried to teach you many things; the language of my people, their ways and thoughts, but I have failed to civilize you. I cannot make you understand that it is unwomanly—do not turn away. I am not indifferent. I have learned to care for you. Your beauty and tenderness have made anything else impossible."

"Myeerah is proud of her beauty, if it pleases the Eagle. Her beauty and her love are his. Yet the Eagle's words make Myeerah sad. She cannot tell what she feels. The paleface's words flow swiftly and smoothly like rippling waters, but Myeerah's heart is full and her lips are dumb."

Myeerah and Isaac stopped under a spreading elm tree the branches of which drooped over and shaded the river. The action of the high water had worn away the earth round the roots of the old elm, leaving them bare and dry when the stream was low. As though Nature had been jealous in the interest of lovers, she had twisted and curled the roots into a curiously shaped bench just above the water, which was secluded enough to escape all eyes except those of the beaver and the muskrat. The bank above was carpeted with fresh, dewy grass; blue bells and violets hid modestly under their dark green leaves; delicate ferns, like wonderful fairy lace, lifted their dainty heads to sway in the summer breeze. In this quiet nook the lovers passed many hours.

"Then, if my White Chief has learned to care for me, he must not try to escape," whispered Myeerah, tenderly, as she crept into Isaac's arms and laid her head on his breast. "I love you. I love you. What will become of Myeerah if you leave her? Could she ever be happy? Could she ever forget? No, no, I will keep my captive."

"I cannot persuade you to let me go?"

"If I free you I will come and lie here," cried Myeerah, pointing to the dark pool.

"Then come with me to my home and live there."

"Go with you to the village of the palefaces, where

Myeerah would be scorned, pointed at as your captor, laughed at and pitied? No! No!"

"But you would not be," said Isaac, eagerly. "You would be my wife. My sister and people will love you. Come, Myeerah, save me from this bondage; come home with me and I will make you happy."

"It can never be," she said, sadly, after a long pause. "How would we ever reach the fort by the big river? Tarhe loves his daughter and will not give her up. If we tried to get away the braves would overtake us and then even Myeerah could not save your life. You would be killed. I dare not try. No, no, Myeerah loves too well for that."

"You might make the attempt," said Isaac, turning away in bitter disappointment. "If you loved me you could not see me suffer."

"Never say that again," cried Myeerah, pain and scorn in her dark eyes. "Can an Indian Princess who has the blood of great chiefs in her veins prove her love in any way that she has not? Some day you will know that you wrong me. I am Tarhe's daughter. A Huron does not lie."

They slowly wended their way back to the camp, both miserable at heart; Isaac longing to see his home and friends, and yet with tenderness in his heart for the Indian maiden who would not free him; Myeerah with pity and love for him, and a fear that her long-cherished dream could never be realized.

One dark, stormy night, when the rain beat down in torrents and the swollen river raged almost to its banks, Isaac slipped out of his lodge unobserved and under cover of the pitchy darkness he got safely between the lines of tepees to the river. He had just the opportunity for which he had been praying. He plunged into the water and floating down with the swift current he soon got out of sight of the flickering campfires. Half a mile below he left the water and ran along the bank until he came to a large tree, a landmark he remembered, when he turned abruptly to the east and struck out through the dense woods. He travelled due east all that night and the next day without resting, and with nothing to eat except a small piece of jerked buffalo meat which he had taken the precaution to hide in his hunting shirt. He rested part of the second night and next morning pushed on toward the east. He had expected to reach Ohio that day, but he did not and he noticed that the ground seemed to be gradually rising. He did not come across any swampy lands or saw grass or vegetation characteristic of the lowlands. He stopped and tried to get his bearings. The country was unknown to him, but he believed he knew the general lay of the ridges and the watercourses.

The fourth day found Isaac hopelessly lost in the woods. He was famished, having eaten but a few herbs and berries in the last two days; his buckskin garments were torn in tatters; his moccasins were worn out and his feet lacerated by the sharp thorns.

Darkness was fast approaching when he first realized that he was lost. He waited hopefully for the appearance of the north star—that most faithful of hunter's guides—but the sky clouded over and no stars appeared. Tired out and hopeless he dragged his weary body into a dense laurel thicket and lay down to wait for dawn. The dismal hoot of an owl nearby, the stealthy steps of some soft-footed animal prowling round the thicket, and the mournful sough of the wind in the treetops kept him awake for hours, but at last he fell asleep.

CHAPTER 7

The chilling rains of November and December's flurry of snow had passed and mid-winter with its icy blasts had set in. The Black Forest had changed autumn's gay crimson and yellow to the sombre hue of winter and now looked indescribably dreary. An icy gorge had formed in the bend of the river at the head of the island and from bank to bank logs, driftwood, broken ice and giant floes were packed and jammed so tightly as to resist the action of the mighty current. This natural bridge would remain solid until spring had loosened the frozen grip of old winter. The hills surrounding Fort Henry were white with snow. The huge drifts were on a level with Colonel Zane's fence and in some places the top rail had disappeared. The pine trees in the yard were weighted down and drooped helplessly with their white burden.

On this frosty January morning the only signs of life round the settlement were a man and a dog walking up Wheeling hill. The man carried a rifle, an axe, and several steel traps. His snowshoes sank into the drifts as he labored up the steep hill. All at once he stopped. The big black dog had put his nose high in the air and had sniffed at the cold wind.

"Well, Tige, old fellow, what is it?" said Jonathan Zane, for this was he.

The dog answered with a low whine. Jonathan looked up and down the creek valley and along the hillside, but he saw no living thing. Snow, snow everywhere, its white monotony relieved here and there by a black tree trunk. Tige sniffed again and then growled. Turning his ear to the breeze Jonathan heard faint yelps from far over the hilltop. He dropped his axe and the traps and ran the remaining short distance up the hill. When he reached the summit the clear baying of hunting wolves was borne to his ears.

The hill sloped gradually on the other side, ending in a white, unbroken plain which extended to the edge of the laurel thicket a quarter mile distant. Jonathan could not see the wolves, but he heard distinctly their peculiar, broken howls. They were in pursuit of something, whether quadruped or man he could not decide. Another moment and he was no longer in doubt, for a deer dashed out of the thicket. Jonathan saw that it was a buck and that he was well nigh exhausted; his head swung low from side to side; he sank slowly to his knees, and showed every indication of distress.

The next instant the baying of the wolves, which had ceased for a moment, sounded close at hand. The buck staggered to his feet; he turned this way and that. When he saw the man and the dog he started toward them without a moment's hesitation.

At a warning word from Jonathan the dog sank on the snow. Jonathan stepped behind a tree, which, however, was not large enough to screen his body. He thought the buck would pass close by him and he determined to shoot at the most favorable moment.

The buck, however, showed no intention of passing by; in his abject terror he saw in the man and the dog foes less terrible than those which were yelping on his trail.

He came on in a lame uneven trot, making straight for the tree. When he reached the tree he crouched, or rather fell, on the ground within a yard of Jonathan and his dog. He quivered and twitched; his nostrils flared; at every pant drops of blood flecked the snow; his great dark eyes had a strained and awful look, almost human in its agony.

Another yelp from the thicket and Jonathan looked up in time to see five timber wolves, gaunt, hungry looking beasts, burst from the bushes. With their noses close to the snow they followed the trail. When they came to the spot where the deer had fallen a chorus of angry, thirsty howls filled the air.

"Well, if this doesn't beat me! I thought I knew a little about deer," said Jonathan. "Tige, we will save this buck from those gray devils if it costs a leg. Steady now, old fellow, wait."

When the wolves were within fifty yards of the tree and coming swiftly Jonathan threw his rifle forward and yelled with all the power of his strong lungs:

"Hi! Hi! Hi! Take 'em, Tige!"

In trying to stop quickly on the slippery snowcrust the wolves fell all over themselves. One dropped dead and another fell wounded at the report of Jonathan's rifle. The others turned tail and loped swiftly off into the thicket. Tige made short work of the wounded one.

"Old White Tail, if you were the last buck in the valley, I would not harm you," said Jonathan, looking at the panting deer. "You need have no farther fear of that pack of cowards."

So saying Jonathan called to Tige and wended his way down the hill toward the settlement.

An hour afterward he was sitting in Colonel Zane's comfortable cabin, where all was warmth and cheerfulness. Blazing hickory logs roared and crackled in the stone fireplace.

"Hello, Jack, where did you come from?" said Colonel Zane, who had just come in. "Haven't seen you since we were snowed up. Come over to see about the horses? If I were you I would not undertake that trip to Fort Pitt until the weather breaks. You could go in the sled, of course, but if you care anything for my advice you will stay home. This weather will hold on for some time. Let Lord Dunmore wait."

"I guess we are in for some stiff weather."

"Haven't a doubt of it. I told Bessie last fall we might expect a hard winter. Everything indicated it. Look at the thick corn-husks. The hulls of the nuts from the shell-bark here in the yard were larger and tougher than I ever saw them. Last October Tige killed a raccoon that had the wooliest kind of a fur. I could have given you a dozen signs of a hard winter. We shall still have a month or six weeks of it. In a week will be ground-hog day and you had better wait and decide after that."

"I tell you, Eb, I get tired of chopping wood and hanging round the house."

"Aha! Another moody spell," said Colonel Zane, glancing kindly at his brother. "Jack, if you were married you would outgrow those 'blue-devils.' I used to have them. It runs in the family to be moody. I have known our father to take his gun and go into the woods and stay there until he had fought out the spell. I have done that myself, but since I married Bessie I have had no return of the old feeling. Get married, Jack, and then you will settle down and work. You will not have time to roam around alone in the woods."

"I prefer the spells, as you call them, any day," answered Jonathan, with a short laugh. "A man with my disposition has no right to get married. This weather is trying, for it keeps me indoors. I cannot hunt because we do not need the meat. And even if I did want to hunt I should not have to go out of sight of the fort. There were three deer in front of the barn this morning. They were nearly starved. They ran off a little at sight of me, but in a few moments came back for the hay I pitched out of the loft. This afternoon Tige and I saved a big buck from a pack of wolves. The buck came right up to me. I could have touched him. This storm is sending the deer down from the hills."

"You are right. It is too bad. Severe weather like this will kill more deer than an army could. Have you been doing anything with your traps?"

"Yes, I have thirty traps out."

"If you are going, tell Sam to fetch down another load of fodder before he unhitches."

"Eb, I have no patience with your brothers," said Colonel Zane's wife to him after he had closed the door. "They are all alike; forever wanting to be on the go. If it isn't Indians it is something else. The very idea of going up the river in this weather. If Jonathan doesn't care for himself he should think of the horses."

"My dear, I was just as wild and discontented as Jack before I met you," remarked Colonel Zane. "You may not think so, but a home and pretty little woman will do wonders for any man. My brothers have nothing to keep them steady."

"Perhaps. I do not believe that Jonathan ever will get married. Silas may; he certainly has been keeping company long enough with Mary Bennet. You are the only Zane who has conquered that adventurous spirit and the desire to be always roaming the woods in search of something to kill. Your old boy, Noah, is growing up like all the Zanes. He fights with all the children in the settlement. I cannot break him of it. He is not a bully, for I have never known him to do anything mean or cruel. It is just sheer love of fighting."

"Ha! Ha! I fear you will not break him of that," answered Colonel Zane. "It is a good joke to say he gets it all from the Zanes. How about the McCollochs? What have you to say of your father and the Major and John McColloch? They are not anything if not the fighting kind. It's the best trait the youngster could have, out here on the border. He'll need it all. Don't worry about him. Where is Betty?"

"I told her to take the children out for a sled ride. Betty needs exercise. She stays indoors too much, and of late she looks pale."

"What! Betty not looking well! She was never ill in her life. I have noticed no change in her."

"No, I daresay you have not. You men can't see anything. But I can, and I tell you, Betty is very different from the girl she used to be. Most of the time she sits and gazes out of her window. She used to be so bright, and when she was not romping with the children she busied herself with her needle. Yesterday as I entered her room she hurriedly picked up a book, and, I think, intentionally hid her face behind it. I saw she had been crying."

"Come to think of it, I believe I have missed Betty," said Colonel Zane, gravely. "She seems more quiet. Is she unhappy? When did you first see this change?"

"I think it was a little while after Mr. Clarke left here last fall."

"Clarke! What has he to do with Betty? What are you driving at?" exclaimed the Colonel, stopping in front of his wife. His face had paled slightly. "I had forgotten Clarke. Bess, you can't mean—"

"Now, Eb, do not get that look on your face. You always frighten me," answered his wife, as she quietly placed her hand on his arm. "I do not mean anything much, certainly nothing against Mr. Clarke. He was a true gentleman. I really liked him."

"So did I," interrupted the Colonel.

"I believe Betty cared for Mr. Clarke. She was always different with him. He has gone away and has forgotten her. That is strange to us, because we cannot imagine any one indifferent to our beautiful Betty. Nevertheless, no matter how attractive a woman may be men sometimes love and ride away. I hear the children coming now. Do not let Betty see that we have been talking about her. She is as quick as a steel trap."

A peal of childish laughter came from without. The door opened and Betty ran in, followed by the sturdy, rosy-cheeked youngsters. All three were white with snow.

"We have had great fun," said Betty. "We went over the bank once and tumbled off the sled into the snow. Then we had a snow-balling contest, and the boys compelled me to strike my colors and fly for the house."

Colonel Zane looked closely at his sister. Her cheeks were glowing with health; her eyes were sparkling with pleasure. Failing to observe any indication of the change in Betty of which his wife had spoken, he concluded that women were better qualified to judge their own sex than were men. He had to confess to himself that the only change he could see in his sister was that she grew prettier every day of her life.

"Oh, papa. I hit Sam right in the head with a big snowball, and I made Betty run into the house, and I slid down the hill all by myself. Sam was afraid," said Noah to his father.

"Noah, if Sammy saw the danger in sliding down the hill he was braver than you. Now both of you run to Annie and have these wet things taken off."

"I must go get on dry clothes myself," said Betty. "I am nearly frozen. It is growing colder. I saw Jack come in. Is he going to Fort Pitt?"

"No. He has decided to wait until good weather. I met

Mr. Miller over at the garrison this afternoon and he wants you to go on the sled-ride to-night. There is to be a dance down at Watkins' place. All the young people are going. It is a long ride, but I guess it will be perfectly safe. Silas and Wetzel are going. Dress yourself warmly and go with them. You have never seen old Grandma Watkins."

"I shall be pleased to go," said Betty.

Betty's room was very cozy, considering that it was in a pioneer's cabin. It had two windows, the larger of which opened on the side toward the river. The walls had been smoothly plastered and covered with white birch-bark. They were adorned with a few pictures and Indian ornaments. A bright homespun carpet covered the floor. A small bookcase stood in the corner. The other furniture consisted of two chairs, a small table, a bureau with a mirror, and a large wardrobe. It was in this last that Betty kept the gowns which she had brought from Philadelphia, and which were the wonder of all the girls in the village.

"I wonder why Eb looked so closely at me," mused Betty, as she slipped on her little moccasins. "Usually he is not anxious to have me go so far from the fort; and now he seemed to think I would enjoy this dance to-night. I wonder what Bessie has been telling him."

Betty threw some wood on the smouldering fire in the little stone grate and sat down to think. Like every one who has a humiliating secret, Betty was eternally suspicious and feared the very walls would guess it. Swift as light came the thought that her brother and his wife had suspected her secret and had been talking about her, perhaps pitying her. With this thought came the fear that if she had betrayed herself to the Colonel's wife she might have done so to others. The consciousness that this might well be true and that even now the girls might be talking and laughing at her caused her exceeding shame and bitterness.

Many weeks had passed since that last night that Betty and Alfred Clarke had been together.

In due time Colonel Zane's men returned and Betty learned from Jonathan that Alfred had left them at Fort Pitt, saying he was going south to his old home. At first she had expected some word from Alfred, a letter, or if not that, surely an apology for his conduct on that last evening they had been together. But Jonathan brought her no word, and after hoping against hope and wearing away the long days looking for a letter that never came, she ceased to hope and plunged into despair.

The last few months had changed her life; changed it as only constant thinking, and suffering that must be hidden from the world, can change the life of a young girl. She had been so intent on her own thoughts, so deep in her dreams that she had taken no heed of other people. She did not know that those who loved her were always thinking of her welfare and would naturally see even a slight change in her. With a sudden shock of surprise and pain she realized that to-day for the first time in a month she had played with the boys. Sammy had asked her why she did not laugh any more. Now she understood the mad antics of Tige that morning; Madcap's whinney of delight; the chattering of the squirrels, and Cæsar's pranks in the snow. She had neglected her pets. She had neglected her work, her friends, the boys' lessons, and her brother. For what? What would her girl friends say? That she was pining for a lover who had forgotten her. They would say that and it would be true. She did think of him constantly.

With bitter pain she recalled the first days of the acquaintance which now seemed so long past; how much she had disliked Alfred; how angry she had been with him and how contemptuously she had spurned his first proffer of friendship; how, little by little, her pride had been subdued; then the struggle with her heart. And, at last, after he had gone, came the realization that the moments spent with him had been the sweetest of her life. She thought of him as she used to see him stand before her; so good to look at; so strong and masterful, and yet so gentle.

"Oh, I cannot bear it," whispered Betty with a half sob, giving up to a rush of tender feeling. "I love him. I love him, and I cannot forget him. Oh, I am so ashamed."

Betty bowed her head on her knees. Her slight form quivered a while and then grew still. When a half hour later she raised her head her face was pale and cold. It bore the look of a girl who had suddenly become a woman; a woman who saw the battle of life before her and who was ready to fight. Stern resolve gleamed from her flashing eyes; there was no faltering in those set lips.

Betty was a Zane and the Zanes came of a fighting race. Their blood had ever been hot and passionate; the blood of men quick to love and quick to hate. It had flowed in the veins of daring, reckless men who had fought and died for their country; men who had won their sweethearts with the sword; men who had had unconquerable spirits. It was this fighting instinct that now rose in Betty; it gave her strength and pride to defend her secret; the resolve to fight against the longing in her heart.

"I will forget him! I will tear him out of my heart!" she exclaimed passionately. "He never deserved my love. He did not care. I was a little fool to let him amuse himself with me. He went away and forgot. I hate him."

At length Betty subdued her excitement, and when she went down to supper a few minutes later she tried to maintain a cheerful composure of manner and to chat with her old-time vivacity.

"Bessie, I am sure you have exaggerated things," remarked Colonel Zane after Betty had gone upstairs to dress for the dance. "Perhaps it is only that Betty grows a little tired of this howling wilderness. Small wonder if she does. You know she has always been used to comfort and many young people, places to go and all that. This is her first winter on the frontier. She'll come round all right."

"Have it your way, Ebenezer," answered his wife with a look of amused contempt on her face. "I am sure I hope you are right. By the way what do you think of this Ralfe Milier? He has been much with Betty of late."

"I do not know the fellow, Bessie. He seems agreeable. He is a good-looking young man. Why do you ask?"

"The Major told me that Miller had a bad name at Pitt, and that he had been a friend of Simon Girty before Girty became a renegade."

"Humph! I'll have to speak to Sam. As for knowing Girty, there is nothing terrible in that. All the women seem to think that Simon is the very prince of devils. I have known all the Girtys for years. Simon was not a bad fellow before he went over to the Indians. It is his brother James who has committed most of those deeds which have made the name of Girty so infamous."

"I don't like Miller," continued Mrs. Zane in a hesitating way. "I must admit that I have no sensible reason for my dislike. He is pleasant and agreeable, yes, but behind it there is a certain intensity. That man has something on his mind."

"If he is in love with Betty, as you seem to think, he has enough on his mind. I'll vouch for that," said Colonel Zane. "Betty is inclined to be a coquette. If she liked Clarke pretty well, it may be a lesson to her."

"I wish she were married and settled down. It may have been no great harm for Betty to have had many admirers while in Philadelphia, but out here on the border it will never do. These men will not have it. There will be trouble come of Betty's coquettishness."

"Why, Bessie, she is only a child. What would you have her do? Marry the first man who asked her?"

"The clod-hoppers are coming," said Mrs. Zane as the jingling of sleigh bells broke the stillness.

Colonel Zane sprang up and opened the door. A broad stream of light flashed from the room and lighted up the road. Three powerful teams stood before the door. They were hitched to sleds, or clod-hoppers, which were nothing more than wagon-beds fastened on wooden runners. A chorus of merry shouts greeted Colonel Zane as he appeared in the doorway.

"All right! All right! Here she is," he cried, as Betty ran down the steps.

The Colonel bundled her in a buffalo robe in a corner of the foremost sled. At her feet he placed a buckskin bag containing a hot stone Mrs. Zane thoughtfully had provided.

"All ready here. Let them go," called the Colonel. "You will have clear weather. Coming back look well to the traces and keep a watch for the wolves."

The long whips cracked, the bells jingled, the impatient horses plunged forward and away they went over the glistening snow. The night was clear and cold; countless stars blinked in the black vault overhead; the pale moon cast its wintry light down on a white and frozen world. As the runners glided swiftly and smoothly onward showers of dry snow like fine powder flew from under the horses' hoofs and soon whitened the black-robed figures in the sleds. The way led down the hill past the Fort, over the creek bridge and along the road that skirted the Black Forest. The ride was long; it led up and down hills, and through a lengthy stretch of gloomy forest. Sometimes the drivers walked the horses up a steep climb and again raced them along a level bottom. Making a turn in the road they saw a bright light in the distance which marked their destination. In five minutes the horses dashed into a wide clearing. An immense log fire burned in front of a two-story structure. Streams of light poured from the small windows; the squeaking of fiddles, the shuffling of many feet, and gay laughter came through the open door.

The steaming horses were unhitched, covered carefully with robes and led into sheltered places, while the merry party disappeared into the house.

The occasion was the celebration of the birthday of old Dan Watkins' daughter. Dan was one of the oldest settlers along the river; in fact, he had located his farm several years after Colonel Zane had founded the settlement. He was noted for his openhanded dealing and kindness of heart. He had loaned many a head of cattle which had never been returned, and many a sack of flour had left his mill unpaid for in grain. He was a good shot, he would lay a tree on the ground as quickly as any man who ever swung an axe, and he could drink more whiskey than any man in the valley.

Dan stood at the door with a smile of welcome upon his rugged features and a handshake and a pleasant word for everyone. His daughter Susan greeted the men with a little curtsy and kissed the girls upon the cheek. Susan was not pretty, though she was strong and healthy; her laughing blue eyes assured a sunny disposition, and she numbered her suitors by the score.

The young people lost no time. Soon the floor was covered with their whirling forms.

In one corner of the room sat a little dried-up old woman with white hair and bright dark eyes. This was Grandma Watkins. She was very old, so old that no one knew her age, but she was still vigorous enough to do her day's work with more pleasure than many a younger woman. Just now she was talking to Wetzel, who leaned upon his inseparable rifle and listened to her chatter. The hunter liked the old lady and would often stop at her cabin while on his way to the settlement and leave at her door a fat turkey or a haunch of venison.

"Lew Wetzel, I am ashamed of you," Grandmother Watkins was saying. "Put that gun in the corner and get out there and dance. Enjoy yourself. You are only a boy yet."

"I'd better look on, mother," answered the hunter.

"Pshaw! You can hop and skip around like any of them and laugh too if you want. I hope that pretty sister of Eb Zane has caught your fancy."

"She is not for the like of me," he said gently. "I haven't the gifts."

"Don't talk about gifts. Not to an old woman who has lived three times and more your age," she said impatiently. "It is not gifts a woman wants out here in the West. If she does 'twill do her no good. She needs a strong arm to build cabins, a quick eye with a rifle, and a fearless heart. What border-women want are houses and children. They must bring up men, men to drive the redskins back, men to till the soil, or else what is the good of our suffering here."

"You are right," said Wetzel thoughtfully. "But I'd hate to see a flower like Betty Zane in a rude hunter's cabin."

"I have known the Zanes for forty year' and I never saw one yet that was afraid of work. And you might win her if you would give up running mad after Indians. I'll allow no woman would put up with that. You have killed many Indians. You ought to be satisfied."

"Fightin' redskins is somethin' I can't help," said the hunter, slowly shaking his head. "If I got married the fever would come on and I'd leave home. No, I'm no good for a woman. Fightin' is all I'm good for."

"Why not fight for her, then? Don't let one of these boys walk off with her. Look at her. She likes fun and admiration. I believe you do care for her. Why not try to win her?

"Who is that tall man with her?" continued the old lady as Wetzel did not answer. "There, they have gone into the other room. Who is he?"

"His name is Miller."

"Lewis, I don't like him. I have been watching him all evening. I'm a contrary old woman, I know, but I have seen a good many men in my time, and his face is not honest. He is in love with her. Does she care for him?"

"No, Betty doesn't care for Miller. She's just full of life and fun."

"You may be mistaken. All the Zanes are fire and brimstone and this girl is a Zane clear through. Go and fetch her to me, Lewis. I'll tell you if there's a chance for you."

"Dear mother, perhaps there's a wife in Heaven for me. There's none on earth," said the hunter, a sad smile flitting over his calm face.

Ralfe Miller, whose actions had occasioned the remarks of the old lady, would have been conspicuous in any assembly of men. There was something in his dark face that compelled interest and yet left the observer in doubt. His square chin, deep-set eyes and firm mouth denoted a strong and indomitable will. He looked a man whom it would be dangerous to cross.

Little was known of Miller's history. He hailed from Fort Pitt, where he had a reputation as a good soldier, but a man of morose and quarrelsome disposition. It was whispered that he drank, and that he had been friendly with the renegades McKee, Elliott, and Girty. He had passed the fall and winter at Fort Henry, serving on garrison duty. Since he had made the acquaintance of Betty he had shown her all the attention possible.

On this night a close observer would have seen that Miller was laboring under some strong feeling. A half-subdued fire gleamed from his dark eyes. A peculiar nervous twitching of his nostrils betrayed a poorly suppressed excitement.

All evening he followed Betty like a shadow. Her kindness may have encouraged him. She danced often with him and showed a certain preference for his society. Alice and Lydia were puzzled by Betty's manner. As they were intimate friends they believed they knew something of her likes and dislikes. Had not Betty told them she did not care for Mr. Miller? What was the meaning of the arch glances she bestowed upon him, if she did not care for him? To be sure, it was nothing wonderful for Betty to smile—she was always prodigal of her smiles—but she had never been known to encourage any man. The truth was that Betty had put her new resolution into effect; to be as merry and charming as any fancy-free maiden could possibly be, and the farthest removed from a young lady pining for an absent and indifferent sweetheart. To her sorrow Betty played her part too well.

Except to Wetzel, whose keen eyes little escaped, there was no significance in Miller's hilarity one moment and sudden thoughtfulness the next. And if there had been, it would have excited no comment. Most of the young men had sampled some of old Dan's best rye and their flushed faces and unusual spirits did not result altogether from the exercise of the dance.

After one of the reels Miller led Betty, with whom he had been dancing, into one of the side rooms. Round the dimly lighted rooms were benches upon which were seated some of the dancers. Betty was uneasy in mind and now wished that she had remained at home. They had exchanged several commonplace remarks when the music struck up and Betty rose quickly to her feet.

"See, the others have gone. Let us return," she said.

"Wait," said Miller hurriedly. "Do not go just yet. I

wish to speak to you. I have asked you many times if you will marry me. Now I ask you again."

"Mr. Miller, I thanked you and begged you not to cause us both pain by again referring to that subject," answered Betty with dignity. "If you will persist in bringing it up we cannot be friends any longer."

"Wait, please wait. I have told you that I will not take 'No' for an answer. I love you with all my heart and soul and I cannot give you up."

His voice was low and hoarse and thrilled with a strong man's passion. Betty looked up into his face and tears of compassion filled her eyes. Her heart softened to this man, and her conscience gave her a little twinge of remorse. Could she not have averted all this? No doubt she had been much to blame, and this thought made her voice very low and sweet as she answered him.

"I like you as a friend, Mr. Miller, but we can never be more than friends. I am very sorry for you, and angry with myself that I did not try to help you instead of making it worse. Please do not speak of this again. Come, let us join the others."

They were quite alone in the room. As Betty finished speaking and started for the door Miller intercepted her. She recoiled in alarm from his white face.

"No, you don't go yet. I won't give you up so easily. No woman can play fast and loose with me. Do you understand? What have you meant all this winter? You encouraged me. You know you did," he cried passionately.

"I thought you were a gentleman. I have really taken the trouble to defend you against persons who evidently were not misled as to your real nature. I will not listen to you," said Betty coldly. She turned away from him, all her softened feelings changed to scorn.

"You *shall* listen to me," he whispered as he grasped

her wrist and pulled her backward. All the man's brutal passion had been aroused. The fierce border blood boiled within his heart. Unmasked he showed himself in his true colors—a frontier desperado. His eyes gleamed dark and lurid beneath his bent brows and a short, desperate laugh passed his lips.

"I will make you love me, my proud beauty. I shall have you yet, one way or another."

"Let me go. How dare you touch me!" cried Betty, the hot blood coloring her face. She struck him a stinging blow with her free hand and struggled with all her might to free herself; but she was powerless in his iron grasp. Closer he drew her.

"If it costs me my life I will kiss you for that blow," he muttered hoarsely.

"Oh, you coward! you ruffian! Release me or I will scream."

She had opened her lips to call for help when she saw a dark figure cross the threshold. She recognized the tall form of Wetzel. The hunter stood in the doorway for a second and then with the swiftness of light he sprang forward. The single straightening of his arm sent Miller backward over a bench to the floor with a crashing sound. Miller rose with some difficulty and stood with one hand to his head.

"Lew, don't draw your knife," cried Betty as she saw Wetzel's hand go inside his hunting shirt. She had thrown herself in front of him as Miller got to his feet. With both little hands she clung to the brawny arm of the hunter, but she could not stay it. Wetzel's hand slipped to his belt.

"For God's sake, Lew, do not kill him," implored Betty, gazing horror-stricken at the glittering eyes of the hunter. "You have punished him enough. He only tried to kiss me. I was partly to blame. Put your knife away. Do not shed blood. For my sake, Lew, for my sake!"

When Betty found that she could not hold Wetzel's arm she threw her arms round his neck and clung to him with all her young strength. No doubt her action averted a tragedy. If Miller had been inclined to draw a weapon then he might have had a good opportunity to use it. He had the reputation of being quick with his knife, and many of his past fights testified that he was not a coward. But he made no effort to attack Wetzel. It was certain that he measured with his eye the distance to the door. Wetzel was not like other men. Irrespective of his wonderful strength and agility there was something about the Indian hunter that terrified all men. Miller shrank before those eyes. He knew that never in all his life of adventure had he been as near death as at that moment. There was nothing between him and eternity but the delicate arms of this frail girl. At a slight wave of the hunter's hand towards the door he turned and passed out.

"Oh, how dreadful!" cried Betty, dropping upon a bench with a sob of relief. "I am glad you came when you did even though you frightened me more than he did. Promise me that you will not do Miller any further harm. If you had fought it would all have been on my account; one or both of you might have been killed. Don't look at me so. I do not care for him. I never did. Now that I know him I despise him. He lost his senses and tried to kiss me. I could have killed him myself."

Wetzel did not answer. Betty had been holding his hand in both her own while she spoke impulsively.

"I understand how difficult it is for you to overlook an insult to me," she continued earnestly. "But I ask it of you. You are my best friend, almost my brother, and I promise you that if he ever speaks a word to me again that is not what it should be I will tell you."

"I reckon I'll let him go, considerin' how set on it you are."

"But remember, Lew, that he is revengeful and you must be on the lookout," said Betty gravely as she recalled the malignant gleam in Miller's eyes.

"He's dangerous only like a moccasin snake that hides in the grass."

"Am I all right? Do I look mussed or—or excited—or anything?" asked Betty.

Lewis smiled as she turned round for his benefit. Her hair was a little awry and the lace at her neck disarranged. The natural bloom had not quite returned to her cheeks. With a look in his eyes that would have mystified Betty for many a day had she but seen it he ran his gaze over the dainty figure. Then reassuring her that she looked as well as ever, he led her into the dance-room.

"So this is Betty Zane. Dear child, kiss me," said Grand-mother Watkins when Wetzel had brought Betty up to her. "Now, let me get a good look at you. Well, well, you are a true Zane. Black hair and eyes; all fire and pride. Child, I knew your father and mother long before you were born. Your father was a fine man but a proud one. And how do you like the frontier? Are you enjoying yourself?"

"Oh, yes, indeed," said Betty, smiling brightly at the old lady.

"Well, dearie, have a good time while you can. Life is hard in a pioneer's cabin. You will not always have the Colonel to look after you. They tell me you have been to some grand school in Philadelphia. Learning is very well, but it will not help you in the cabin of one of these rough men."

"There is a great need of education in all the pioneers' homes. I have persuaded brother Eb to have a school-teacher at the Fort next spring."

"First teach the boys to plow and the girls to make Johnny-cake. How much you favor your brother Isaac. He used to come and see me often. So must you in summertime. Poor lad, I suppose he is dead by this time. I have seen so many brave and good lads go. There now, I did not mean to make you sad." And the old lady patted Betty's hand and sighed.

"He often spoke of you and said that I must come with him to see you. Now he is gone," said Betty.

"Yes, he is gone, Betty, but you must not be sad while you are so young. Wait until you are old like I am. How long have you known Lew Wetzel?"

"All my life. He used to carry me in his arms when I was a baby. Of course I do not remember that, but as far back as I can go in memory I can see Lew. Oh, the many times he has saved me from disaster! But why do you ask?"

"I think Lew Wetzel cares more for you than for all the world. He is as silent as an Indian, but I am an old woman and I can read men's hearts. If he could be made to give up his wandering life he would be the best man on the border."

"Oh, indeed I think you are wrong. Lew does not care for me in that way," said Betty, surprised and troubled by the old lady's vehemence.

A loud blast from a hunting-horn directed the attention of all to the platform at the upper end of the hall, where Dan Watkins stood. The fiddlers ceased playing, the dancers stopped, and all looked expectantly. The scene was simple, strong, and earnest. The light in the eyes of these maidens shone like the light from the pinecones on the walls. It beamed soft and warm. These fearless sons of the wilderness, these sturdy sons of progress, standing there clasping the hands of their partners and with faces glowing with happiness, forgetful of all save the enjoyment of the moment, were ready to go out on the morrow and battle unto the death for the homes and the lives of their loved ones.

"Friends," said Dan when the hum of voices had ceased,

"I never thought as how I'd have to get up here and make a speech to-night or I might have taken to the woods. Howsomever, mother and Susan says as it's gettin' late it's about time we had some supper. Somewhere in the big cake is hid a gold ring. If one of the girls gets it she can keep it as a gift from Susan, and should one of the boys find it he may make a present to his best girl. And in the bargain he gets to kiss Susan. She made some objection about this and said that part of the game didn't go, but I reckon the lucky young man will decide that for hisself. And now to the festal board."

Ample justice was done to the turkey, the venison, and the bear meat. Grandmother Watkins' delicious apple and pumpkin pies, for which she was renowned, disappeared as by magic. Likewise the cakes and the sweet cider and the apple butter vanished.

When the big cake had been cut and divided among the guests, Wetzel discovered the gold ring within his share. He presented the ring to Betty, and gave his privilege of kissing Susan to George Reynolds, with the remark: "George, I calkilate Susan would like it better if you do the kissin' part." Now it was known to all that George had long been an ardent admirer of Susan's, and it was suspected that she was not indifferent to him. Nevertheless, she protested that it was not fair. George acted like a man who had the opportunity of his life. Amid uproarious laughter he ran Susan all over the room, and when he caught her he pulled her hands away from her blushing face and bestowed a right hearty kiss on her cheek. To everyone's surprise and to Wetzel's discomfiture, Susan walked up to him and saying that as he had taken such an easy way out of it she intended to punish him by kissing him. And so she did. Poor Lewis's face looked the picture of dismay. Probably he had never been kissed before in his life.

Happy hours speed away on the wings of the wind. The feasting over, the good-byes were spoken, the girls were wrapped in the warm robes, for it was now intensely cold, and soon the horses, eager to start on the long homeward journey, were pulling hard on their bits. On the party's return trip there was an absence of the hilarity which had prevailed on their coming. The bells were taken off before the sleds left the blockhouse, and the traces and the harness examined and tightened with the caution of men who were apprehensive of danger and who would take no chances.

In winter time the foes most feared by the settlers were the timber wolves. Thousands of these savage beasts infested the wild forest regions which bounded the lonely roads, and their wonderful power of scent and swift and tireless pursuit made a long night ride a thing to be dreaded. While the horses moved swiftly danger from wolves was not imminent; but carelessness or some mishap to a trace or a wheel had been the cause of more than one tragedy.

Therefore it was not remarkable that the drivers of our party breathed a sigh of relief when the top of the last steep hill had been reached. The girls were quiet, and tired out and cold they pressed close to one another; the men were silent and watchful.

When they were half way home and had just reached the outskirts of the Black Forest the keen ear of Wetzel caught the cry of a wolf. It came from the south and sounded so faint that Wetzel believed at first that he had been mistaken. A few moments passed in which the hunter turned his ear to the south. He had about made up his mind that he had only imagined he had heard something when the unmistakable yelp of a wolf came down on the wind. Then another, this time clear and distinct, caused the driver to turn and whisper to Wetzel. The hunter spoke in a low tone and the driver whipped up his horses. From out the depths of the dark woods along which they were riding came a long and mournful howl. It was a wolf answering the call of his mate. This time the horses heard it, for they threw back their ears and increased their speed. The girls heard it, for they shrank closer to the men.

There is that which is frightful in the cry of a wolf. When one is safe in camp before a roaring fire the short, sharp bark of a wolf is startling, and the long howl will make one shudder. It is so lonely and dismal. It makes no difference whether it be given while the wolf is sitting on his haunches near some cabin waiting for the remains of the settler's dinner, or while he is in full chase after his prey—the cry is equally wild, savage, and bloodcurdling.

Betty had never heard it and though she was brave, when the howl from the forest had its answer in another howl from the creek thicket, she slipped her little mittened hand under Wetzel's arm and looked up at him with frightened eyes.

In half an hour the full chorus of yelps, barks and howls swelled hideously on the air, and the ever increasing pack of wolves could be seen scarcely a hundred yards behind the sleds. The patter of their swiftly flying feet on the snow could be distinctly heard. The slender, dark forms came nearer and nearer every moment. Presently the wolves had approached close enough for the occupants of the sleds to see their shining eyes looking like little balls of green fire. A gaunt beast bolder than the others, and evidently the leader of the pack, bounded forward until he was only a few yards from the last sled. At every jump he opened his great jaws and uttered a quick bark as if to embolden his followers.

Almost simultaneously with the red flame that burst from Wetzel's rifle came a sharp yelp of agony from the leader. He rolled over and over. Instantly followed a horrible mingling of snarls and barks, and snapping of jaws as the band fought over the body of their luckless comrade.

This short delay gave the advantage to the horses. When the wolves again appeared they were a long way behind. The distance to the fort was now short and the horses were urged to their utmost. The wolves kept up the chase until they reached the creek bridge and the mill. Then they slowed up, the howling became desultory, and finally the dark forms disappeared in the thickets.

CHAPTER 8

Winter dragged by uneventfully for Betty. Unlike the other pioneer girls, who were kept busy all the time with their mending, and linsey weaving, and household duties, Betty had nothing to divert her but her embroidery and her reading. These she found very tiresome. Her maid was devoted to her and never left a thing undone. Annie was old Sam's daughter, and she had waited on Betty since she had been a baby. The cleaning or mending or darning—anything in the shape of work that would have helped pass away the monotonous hours for Betty, was always done before she could lift her hand.

During the day she passed hours in her little room and most of them were dreamed away by her window. Lydia and Alice came over sometimes and whiled away the tedious moments with their bright chatter and merry laughter, their castle-building, and their romancing on heroes and love and marriage as girls always will until the end of time. They had not forgotten Mr. Clarke, but as Betty had rebuked them with a dignity which forbade any further teasing on that score, they had transferred their fun-making to the use of Mr. Miller's name.

Fearing her brothers' wrath Betty had not told them of

the scene with Miller at the dance. She had learned enough of rough border justice to dread the consequence of such a disclosure. She permitted Miller to come to the house, although she never saw him alone. Miller had accepted this favor gratefully. He said that on the night of the dance he had been a little the worse for Dan Watkins' strong liquor, and that, together with his bitter disappointment, made him act in the mad way which had so grievously offended her. He exerted himself to win her forgiveness. Betty was always tender-hearted, and though she did not trust him, she said they might still be friends, but that that depended on his respect for her forbearance. Miller had promised he would never refer to the old subject and he had kept his word.

Indeed Betty welcomed any diversion for the long winter evenings. Occasionally some of the young people visited her, and they sang and danced, roasted apples, popped chestnuts, and played games. Often Wetzel and Major McColloch came in after supper. Betty would come down and sing for them, and afterward would coax Indian lore and woodcraft from Wetzel, or she would play checkers with the Major. If she succeeded in winning from him, which in truth was not often, she teased him unmercifully. When Colonel Zane and the Major had settled down to their series of games, from which nothing short of Indians could have diverted them, Betty sat by Wetzel. The silent man of the woods, an appellation the hunter had earned by his reticence, talked for Betty as he would for no one else.

One night while Colonel Zane, his wife and Betty were entertaining Captain Boggs and Major McColloch and several of Betty's girl friends, after the usual music and singing, storytelling became the order of the evening. Little Noah told of the time he had climbed the apple-tree in the yard after a raccoon and got severely bitten.

"One day," said Noah, "I heard Tige barking out in the orchard and I ran out there and saw a funny little fur ball up in the tree with a black tail and white rings around it. It looked like a pretty cat with a sharp nose. Every time Tige barked the little animal showed his teeth and swelled up his back. I wanted him for a pet. I got Sam to give me a sack and I climbed the tree and the nearer I got to him the farther he backed down the limb. I followed him and put out the sack to put it over his head and he bit me. I fell from the limb, but he fell too and Tige killed him and Sam stuffed him for me."

"Noah, you are quite a valiant hunter," said Betty. "Now, Jonathan, remember that you promised to tell me of your meeting with Daniel Boone."

"It was over on the Muskingong near the mouth of the Sandusky. I was hunting in the open woods along the bank when I saw an Indian. He saw me at the same time and we both treed. There we stood a long time each afraid to change position. Finally I began to get tired and resorted to an old ruse. I put my coonskin cap on my ramrod and cautiously poked it from behind the tree, expecting every second to hear the whistle of the redskin's bullet. Instead I heard a jolly voice yell: 'Hey, young feller, you'll have to try something better'n that.' I looked and saw a white man standing out in the open and shaking all over with laughter. I went up to him and found him to be a big strong fellow with an honest, merry face. He said: 'I'm Boone.' I was considerably taken aback, especially when I saw he knew I was a white man all the time. We camped and hunted along the river a week and at the Falls of the Muskingong he struck out for his Kentucky home."

"Here is Wetzel," said Colonel Zane, who had risen and gone to the door. "Now, Betty, try and get Lew to tell us something."

"Come, Lewis, here is a seat by me," said Betty. "We

have been pleasantly passing the time. We have had bear stories, snake stories, ghost stories—all kinds of tales. Will you tell us one?"

"Lewis, did you ever have a chance to kill a hostile Indian and not take it?" asked Colonel Zane.

"Never but once," answered Lewis.

"Tell us about it. I imagine it will be interesting."

"Well, I ain't good at tellin' things," began Lewis. "I reckon I've seen some strange sights. I kin tell you about the only redskin I ever let off. Three years ago I was takin' a fall hunt over on the Big Sandy, and I run into a party of Shawnees. I plugged a chief and started to run. There was some good runners and I couldn't shake 'em in the open country. Comin' to the Ohio I jumped in and swum across, keepin' my rifle and powder dry by holdin' 'em up. I hid in some bulrushes and waited. Pretty soon along comes three Injuns, and when they saw where I had taken to the water they stopped and held a short powwow. Then they all took to the water. This was what I was waitin' for. When they got nearly acrosst I shot the first redskin, and loadin' quick I got a bullet into the others. The last Injun did not sink. I watched him go floatin' down stream expectin' every minute to see him go under as he was hurt so bad he could hardly keep his head above water. He floated down a long ways and the current carried him to a pile of driftwood which had lodged against a little island. I saw the Injun crawl up on the drift. I went down stream and by keepin' the island between me and him I got out to where he was. I pulled my tomahawk and went around the head of the island and found the redskin leanin' against a big log. He was a young brave and a fine lookin' strong feller. He was tryin' to stop the blood from my bullet-hole in his side. When he saw me he tried to get up, but he was too weak. He smiled, pointed to the wound and said: 'Deathwind not heap times bad shot.'

Then he bowed his head and waited for the tomahawk. Well, I picked him up and carried him ashore and made a shack by a spring. I stayed there with him. When he got well enough to stand a few days' travel I got him across the river and givin' him a hunk of deer meat I told him to go, and if I ever saw him again I'd make a better shot.

"A year afterwards I trailed two Shawnees into Wingenund's camp and got surrounded and captured. The Delaware chief is my great enemy. They beat me, shot salt into my legs, made me run the gauntlet, tied me on the back of a wild mustang. Then they got ready to burn me at the stake. That night they painted my face black and held the usual death dances. Some of the braves got drunk and worked themselves into a frenzy. I allowed I'd never see daylight. I seen that one of the braves left to guard me was the young feller I had wounded the year before. He never took no notice of me. In the gray of the early mornin' when all were asleep and the other watch dozin' I felt cold steel between my wrists and my buckskin thongs dropped off. Then my feet were cut loose. I looked round and in the dim light I seen my young brave. He handed me my own rifle, knife and tomahawk, put his finger on his lips and with a bright smile, as if to say he was square with me, he pointed to the east. I was out of sight in a minute."

"How noble of him!" exclaimed Betty, her eyes all aglow. "He paid his debt to you, perhaps at the price of his life."

"I have never known an Indian to forget a promise, or a kind action, or an injury," observed Colonel Zane.

"Are the Indians half as bad as they are called?" asked Betty. "I have heard as many stories of their nobility as of their cruelty."

"The Indians consider that they have been robbed and driven from their homes. What we think hideously inhuman is war to them," answered Colonel Zane.

"When I came here from Fort Pitt I expected to see and fight Indians every day," said Captain Boggs. "I have been here at Wheeling for nearly two years and have never seen a hostile Indian. There have been some Indians in the vicinity during that time, but not one has shown himself to me. I'm not up to Indian tricks, I know, but I think the last siege must have been enough for them. I don't believe we shall have any more trouble from them."

"Captain," called out Colonel Zane, banging his hand on the table. "I'll bet you my best horse to a keg of gunpowder that you see enough Indians before you are a year older to make you wish you had never seen or heard of the western border."

"And I'll go you the same bet," said Major McColloch.

"You see, Captain, you must understand a little of the nature of the Indian," continued Colonel Zane. "We have had proof that the Delawares and the Shawnees have been preparing for an expedition for months. We shall have another siege some day and to my thinking it will be a longer and harder one than the last. What say you, Wetzel?"

"I ain't sayin' much, but I don't calkilate on goin' on any long hunts this summer," answered the hunter.

"And do you think Tarhe, Wingenund, Pipe, Cornplanter, and all those chiefs will unite their forces and attack us?" asked Betty of Wetzel.

"Cornplanter won't. He has been paid for most of his land and he ain't so bitter. Tarhe is not likely to bother us. But Pipe and Wingenund and Red Fox—they all want blood."

"Have you seen these chiefs?" said Betty.

"Yes, I know 'em all and they all know me," answered the hunter. "I've watched over many a trail waitin' for one of 'em. If I can ever get a shot at any of 'em I'll give up Injuns and go farmin'. Good night, Betty."

"What a strange man is Wetzel," mused Betty, after the

visitors had gone. "Do you know, Eb, he is not at all like anyone else. I have seen the girls shudder at the mention of his name and I have heard them say they could not look in his eyes. He does not affect me that way. It is not often I can get him to talk, but sometimes he tells me beautiful things about the woods; how he lives in the wilderness, his home under the great trees; how every leaf on the trees and every blade of grass has its joy for him as well as its knowledge; how he curls up in his little bark shack and is lulled to sleep by the sighing of the wind through the pine tops. He told me he has often watched the stars for hours at a time. I know there is a waterfall back in the Black Forest somewhere that Lewis goes to, simply to sit and watch the water tumble over the precipice."

"Wetzel is a wonderful character, even to those who know him only as an Indian slayer and a man who wants no other occupation. Some day he will go off on one of these long jaunts and will never return. That is certain. The day is fast approaching when a man like Wetzel will be of no use in life. Now, he is a necessity. Like Tige he can smell Indians. Betty, I believe Lewis tells you so much and is so kind and gentle toward you because he cares for you."

"Of course Lew likes me. I know he does and I want him to," said Betty. "But he does not care as you seem to think. Grandmother Watkins said the same. I am sure both of you are wrong."

"Did Dan's mother tell you that? Well, she's pretty shrewd. It's quite likely, Betty, quite likely. It seems to me you are not so quick-witted as you used to be."

"Why so?" asked Betty, quickly.

"Well, you used to be different somehow," said her brother, as he patted her hand.

"Do you mean I am more thoughtful?"

"Yes, and sometimes you seem sad."

"I have tried to be brave and—and happy," said Betty, her voice trembling slightly.

"Yes, yes, I know you have, Betty. You have done wonderfully well here in this dead place. But tell me, don't be angry, don't you think too much of some one?"

"You have no right to ask me that," said Betty, flushing and turning away toward the stairway.

"Well, well, child, don't mind me. I did not mean anything. There, good night, Betty."

Long after she had gone upstairs Colonel Zane sat by his fireside. From time to time he sighed. He thought of the old Virginia home and of the smile of his mother. It seemed only a few short years since he had promised her that he would take care of the baby sister. How had he kept that promise, made when Betty was a little thing bouncing on his knee? It seemed only yesterday. How swift the flight of time! Already Betty was a woman; her sweet, gay girlhood had passed; already a shadow had fallen on her face, the shadow of a secret sorrow.

March with its blustering winds had departed, and now April's showers and sunshine were gladdening the hearts of the settlers. Patches of green freshened the slopes of the hills; the lilac bushes showed tiny leaves, and the maple-buds were bursting. Yesterday a bluebird—surest harbinger of spring—had alighted on the fence-post and had sung his plaintive song. A few more days and the blossoms were out mingling their pink and white with the green; the redbud, the hawthorne, and the dog-wood were in bloom, checkering the hillsides.

"Bessie, spring is here," said Colonel Zane, as he stood in the doorway. "The air is fresh, the sun shines warm, the birds are singing; it makes me feel good."

"Yes, it is pleasant to have spring with us again," answered his wife. "I think, though, that in winter I am happier. In summer I am always worried. I am afraid for the children to be out of my sight, and when you are away on a hunt I am distraught until you are home safe."

"Well, if the redskins let us alone this summer it will be something new," he said, laughing. "By the way, Bess, some new people came to the fort last night. They rafted down from the Monongahela settlements. Some of the women suffered considerably. I intend to offer them the cabin on the hill until they can cut the timber and run up a house. Sam said the cabin roof leaked and the chimney smoked, but with a little work I think they can be made more comfortable there than at the blockhouse."

"It is the only vacant cabin in the settlement. I can accommodate the women folks here."

"Well, we'll see about it. I don't want you and Betty inconvenienced. I'll send Sam up to the cabin and have him fix things up a bit and make it more habitable."

The door opened, admitting Colonel Zane's elder boy. The lad's face was dirty, his nose was all bloody, and a big bruise showed over his right eye.

"For the land's sake!" exclaimed his mother. "Look at the boy. Noah, come here. What have you been doing?"

Noah crept close to his mother and grasping her apron with both hands hid his face. Mrs. Zane turned the boy around and wiped his discolored features with a wet towel. She gave him a little shake and said: "Noah, have you been fighting again?"

"Let him go and I'll tell you about it," said the Colonel, and when the youngster had disappeared he continued: "Right after breakfast Noah went with me down to the mill. I noticed several children playing in front of Reihart's blacksmith shop. I went in, leaving Noah outside. I got the plow-share which I had left with Reihart to be repaired. He came to the door with me and all at once he said: 'Look at the kids.' I looked and saw Noah walk up to a boy and say something to him. The lad was a stranger, and I have no doubt belongs to these new people I told you about. He was bigger than Noah. At first the older boy appeared very friendly and evidently wanted to join the others in their game. I guess Noah did not approve of this, for after he had looked the stranger over he hauled away and punched the lad soundly. To make it short the strange boy gave Noah the worst beating he ever got in his life. I told Noah to come straight to you and confess."

"Well, did you ever!" exclaimed Mrs. Zane. "Noah is a bad boy. And you stood and watched him fight. You are laughing about it now. Ebenezer Zane, I would not put it beneath you to set Noah to fighting. Anyway, it serves Noah right and I hope it will be a lesson to him."

"I'll make you a bet, Bessie," said the Colonel, with another laugh. "I'll bet you that unless we lock him up, Noah will fight that boy every day or every time he meets him."

"I won't bet," said Mrs. Zane, with a smile of resignation.

"Where's Betts? I haven't seen her this morning. I am going over to Short Creek to-morrow or next day, and think I'll take her with me. You know I am to get a commission to lay out several settlements along the river and I want to get some work finished at Short Creek this spring. Mrs. Raymer will be delighted to have Betty. Shall I take her?"

"By all means. A visit there will brighten her up and do her good."

"Well, what on earth have you been doing?" cried the Colonel. His remark had been called forth by a charming vision that had entered by the open door. Betty—for it was she—wore a little red cap set jauntily on her black hair. Her linsey dress was crumpled and covered with hayseed.

"I've been in the haymow," said Betty, waving a small

basket. "For a week that old black hen has circumvented me, but at last I have conquered. I found the nest in the farthest corner under the hay."

"How did you get up in the loft?" inquired Mrs. Zane.

"Bessie, I climbed up the ladder of course. I acknowledge being unusually lighthearted and happy this morning, but I have not as yet grown wings. Sam said I could not climb up that straight ladder, but I found it easy enough."

"You should not climb up into the loft," said Mrs. Zane, in a severe tone. "Only last fall Hugh Bennet's little boy slid off the hay down into one of the stalls and the horse kicked him nearly to death."

"Oh, fiddlesticks, Bessie, I am not a baby," said Betty, with vehemence. "There is not a horse in the barn but would stand on his hind legs before he would step on me, let alone kick me."

"I don't know, Betty, but I think that black horse Mr. Clarke left here would kick any one," remarked the Colonel.

"Oh, no, he would not hurt me."

"Betty, we have had pleasant weather for about three days," said the Colonel, gravely. "In that time you have let out that crazy bear of yours to turn everything topsy-turvy. Only yesterday I got my hands in the paint you have put on your canoe. If you had asked my advice I would have told you that painting your canoe should not have been done for a month yet. Silas told me you fell down the creek hill; Sam said you tried to drive his team over the bluff, and so on. We are happy to see you get back your old time spirits, but could you not be a little more careful? Your versatility is bewildering. We do not know what to look for next. I fully expect to see you brought to the house some day maimed for life, or all that beautiful black hair gone to decorate some Huron's lodge."

"I tell you I am perfectly delighted that the weather is again so I can go out. I am tired to death of staying indoors. This morning I could have cried for very joy. Bessie will soon be lecturing me about Madcap. I must not ride farther than the fort. Well, I don't care. I intend to ride all over."

"Betty, I do not wish you to think I am lecturing you," said the Colonel's wife. "But you are as wild as a March hare, and some one must tell you things. Now listen. My brother, the Major, told me that Simon Girty, the renegade, had been heard to say that he had seen Eb Zane's little sister and that if he ever got his hands on her he would make a squaw of her. I am not teasing you. I am telling you the truth. Girty saw you when you were at Fort Pitt two years ago. Now what would you do if he caught you on one of your lonely rides and carried you off to his wigwam? He has done things like that before. James Girty carried off one of the Johnson girls. Her brothers tried to rescue her and lost their lives. It is a common trick of the Indians."

"What would I do if Mr. Simon Girty tried to make a squaw of me?" exclaimed Betty, her eyes flashing fire. "Why, I'd kill him!"

"I believe it, Betts, on my word I do," spoke up the Colonel. "But let us hope you may never see Girty. All I ask is that you be careful. I am going over to Short Creek to-morrow. Will you go with me? I know Mrs. Raymer will be pleased to see you."

"Oh, Eb, that will be delightful!"

"Very well, get ready and we shall start early in the morning."

Two weeks later Betty returned from Short Creek and seemed to have profited much by her short visit. Colonel Zane remarked with satisfaction to his wife that Betty had regained all her former cheerfulness.

The morning after Betty's return was a perfect spring morning—the first in that month of May-days. The sun shone bright and warm; the mayflowers blossomed; the trailing arbutus scented the air; everywhere the grass and the leaves looked fresh and green; swallows flitted in and out of the barn door; the bluebirds twittered; a meadow-lark caroled forth his pure melody, and the busy hum of bees came from the fragrant apple-blossoms.

"Mis' Betty, Madcap 'pears powerfo' skittenish," said old Sam, when he had led the pony to where Betty stood on the hitching block. "Whoa, dar, you rascal."

Betty laughed as she leaped lightly into the saddle, and soon she was flying over the old familiar road, down across the creek bridge, past the old gristmill, around the fort and then out on the river bluff. The Indian pony was fiery and mettlesome. He pranced and sidestepped, galloped and trotted by turns. He seemed as glad to get out again into the warm sunshine as was Betty herself. He tore down the road a mile at his best speed. Coming back Betty pulled him into a walk. Presently her musings were interrupted by a sharp switch in the face from a twig of a tree. She stopped the pony and broke off the offending branch. As she looked around the recollection of what had happened to her in that very spot flashed into her mind. It was here that she had been stopped by the man who had passed almost as swiftly out of her life as he had crossed her path that memorable afternoon. She fell to musing on the old perplexing question. After all could there not have been some mistake? Perhaps she might have misjudged him? And then the old spirit, which resented her thinking of him in that softened mood, rose and fought the old battle over again. But as often happened the mood conquered, and Betty permitted herself to sink for the moment into the sad thoughts which returned like a mournful strain of music once sung by beloved voices, now forever silent.

She could not resist the desire to ride down to the old sycamore. The pony turned into the bridle path that led down the bluff and the sure-footed beast picked his way carefully over the roots and stones. Betty's heart beat quicker when she saw the noble tree under whose spreading branches she had spent the happiest day of her life. The old monarch of the forest was not one whit changed by the wild winds of winter. The dew sparkled on the nearly full grown leaves; the little sycamore balls were already as large as marbles.

Betty drew rein at the top of the bank and looked absently at the tree and into the foam-covered pool beneath. At that moment her eyes saw nothing physical. They held the faraway light of the dreamer, the look that sees so much of the past and nothing of the present.

Presently her reflections were broken by the actions of the pony. Madcap had thrown up her head, laid back her ears, and commenced to paw the ground with her forefeet. Betty looked round to see the cause of Madcap's excitement. What was that! She saw a tall figure clad in brown leaning against the stone. She saw a long fishing-rod. What was there so familiar in the poise of that figure? Madcap dislodged a stone from the path and it went rattling down the rocky slope and fell with a splash into the water. The man heard it, turned and faced the hillside. Betty recognized Alfred Clarke. For a moment she believed she must be dreaming. She had had many dreams of the old sycamore. She looked again. Yes, it was he. Pale, worn, and older he undoubtedly looked, but the features were surely those of Alfred Clarke. Her heart gave a great bound and then seemed to stop beating while a very agony of joy surged over her and made her faint. So he still lived. That was her first thought, glad and joyous, and then memory returning, her face went white as with clenched teeth she wheeled Madcap and struck her with the switch. Once on the level bluff she urged her toward the house at a furious pace.

Colonel Zane had just stepped out of the barn door and his face took on an expression of amazement when he saw the pony come tearing up the road, Betty's hair flying in the wind and with a face as white as if she were pursued by a thousand yelling Indians.

"Say, Betts, what the dawn is wrong?" cried the Colonel, when Betty reached the fence.

"Why did you not tell me that man was here again?" she demanded in intense excitement.

"That man! What man?" asked Colonel Zane, considerably taken back by this angry apparition.

"Mr. Clarke, of course. Just as if you did not know. I suppose you thought it a fine opportunity for one of your jokes."

"Oh, Clarke. Well, the fact is I just found it out myself. Haven't I been away as well as you? I certainly cannot imagine how any man could create such evident excitement in your mind. Poor Clarke, what has he done now?"

"You might have told me. Somebody could have told me and saved me from making a fool of myself," retorted Betty, who was plainly on the verge of tears. "I rode down to the old sycamore tree and he saw me in, of all the places in the world, the one place where I would not want him to see me."

"Huh!" said the Colonel, who often gave vent to the Indian exclamation. "Is that all? I thought something had happened."

"All! Is it not enough? I would rather have died. He is a man and he will think I followed him down there, that I was thinking of—that—Oh!" cried Betty, passionately, and then she strode into the house, slammed the door, and left the Colonel, lost in wonder.

"Humph! These women beat me. I can't make them

out, and the older I grow the worse I get," he said, as he led the pony into the stable.

Betty ran upstairs to her room, her head in a whirl. Stronger than the surprise of Alfred's unexpected appearance in Fort Henry and stronger than the mortification in having been discovered going to a spot she should have been too proud to remember was the bittersweet consciousness that his mere presence had thrilled her through and through. It hurt her and made her hate herself in that moment. She hid her face in shame at the thought that she could not help being glad to see the man who had only trifled with her, the man who had considered the acquaintance of so little consequence that he had never taken the trouble to write her a line or send her a message. She wrung her trembling hands. She endeavored to still that throbbing heart and to conquer that sweet vague feeling which had crept over her and made her weak. The tears began to come and with a sob she threw herself on the bed and buried her head in the pillow.

An hour after, when Betty had quieted herself and had seated herself by the window a light knock sounded on the door and Colonel Zane entered. He hesitated and came in rather timidly, for Betty was not to be taken liberties with, and seeing her by the window he crossed the room and sat down by her side.

Betty did not remember her father or her mother. Long ago when she was a child she had gone to her brother, laid her head on his shoulder and told him all her troubles. The desire grew strong within her now. There was comfort in the strong clasp of his hand. She was not proof against it, and her dark head fell on his shoulder.

Alfred Clarke had indeed made his reappearance in Fort Henry. The preceding October when he left the settlement to go on the expedition up the Monongahela

River his intention had been to return to the fort as soon as he had finished his work, but what he did do was only another illustration of that fatality which affects everything. Man hopefully makes his plans and an inexorable destiny works out what it has in store for him.

The men of the expedition returned to Fort Henry in due time, but Alfred had been unable to accompany them. He had sustained a painful injury and had been compelled to go to Fort Pitt for medical assistance. While there he had received word that his mother was lying very ill at his old home in Southern Virginia and if he wished to see her alive he must not delay in reaching her bedside. He left Fort Pitt at once and went to his home, where he remained until his mother's death. She had been the only tie that bound him to the old home, and now that she was gone he determined to leave the scene of his boyhood forever.

Alfred was the rightful heir to all of the property, but an unjust and selfish stepfather stood between him and any contentment he might have found there. He decided he would be a soldier of fortune. He loved the daring life of a ranger, and preferred to take his chances with the hardy settlers on the border rather than live the idle life of a gentleman farmer. He declared his intention to his stepfather, who ill-concealed his satisfaction at the turn affairs had taken. Then Alfred packed his belongings, secured his mother's jewels, and with one sad, backward glance rode away from the stately old mansion.

It was Sunday morning and Clarke had been two days in Fort Henry. From his little room in the blockhouse he surveyed the well-remembered scene. The rolling hills, the broad river, the green forests seemed like old friends.

"Here I am again," he mused. "What a fool a man can be. I have left a fine old plantation, slaves, horses, a country noted for its pretty women—for what? Here there can be nothing for me but Indians, hard work, privation, and trouble. Yet I could not get here quickly enough. Pshaw! What use to speak of the possibilities of a new country. I cannot deceive myself. It is *she*. I would walk a thousand miles and starve myself for months just for one glimpse of her sweet face. Knowing this what care I for all the rest. How strange she should ride down to the old sycamore tree yesterday at the moment I was there and thinking of her. Evidently she had just returned from her visit. I wonder if she ever cared. I wonder if she ever thinks of me. Shall I accept that incident as a happy augury? Well, I am here to find out and find out I will. Aha! There goes the church bell."

Laughing a little at his eagerness he brushed his coat, put on his cap and went downstairs. The settlers with their families were going into the meeting house. As Alfred started up the steps he met Lydia Boggs.

"Why, Mr. Clarke, I heard you had returned," she said, smiling pleasantly and extending her hand. "Welcome to the fort. I am very glad to see you."

While they were chatting her father and Colonel Zane came up and both greeted the young man warmly.

"Well, well, back on the frontier," said the Colonel, in his hearty way. "Glad to see you at the fort again. I tell you, Clarke, I have taken a fancy to that black horse you left me last fall. I did not know what to think when Jonathan brought back my horse. To tell you the truth I always looked for you to come back. What have you been doing all winter?"

"I have been at home. My mother was ill all winter and she died in April."

"My lad, that's bad news. I am sorry," said Colonel Zane, putting his hand kindly on the young man's shoulder. "I was wondering what gave you that older and graver look. It's hard, lad, but it's the way of life."

"I have come back to get my old place with you, Colonel Zane, if you will give it to me."

"I will, and can promise you more in the future. I am going to open a road through to Maysville, Kentucky, and start several new settlements along the river. I will need young men, and am more than glad you have returned."

"Thank you, Colonel Zane. That is more than I could have hoped for."

Alfred caught sight of a trim figure in a gray linsey gown coming down the road. There were several young people approaching, but he saw only Betty. By some evil chance Betty walked with Ralfe Miller, and for some mysterious reason, which women always keep to themselves, she smiled and looked up into his face at a time of all times she should not have done so. Alfred's heart turned to lead.

When the young people reached the steps the eyes of the rivals met for one brief second, but that was long enough for them to understand each other. They did not speak. Lydia hesitated and looked toward Betty.

"Betty, here is—" began Colonel Zane, but Betty passed them with flaming cheeks and with not so much as a glance at Alfred. It was an awkward moment for him.

"Let us go in," he said composedly, and they all filed into the church.

As long as he lived Alfred Clarke never forgot that hour. His pride kept him chained in his seat. Outwardly he maintained his composure, but inwardly his brain seemed throbbing, whirling, bursting. What an idiot he had been! He understood now why his letter had never been answered. Betty loved Miller, a man who hated him, a man who would leave no stone unturned to destroy even a little liking which she might have felt for him. Once again Miller had crossed his path and worsted him. With a sudden sickening sense of despair he realized that all his fond hopes had been but dreams, a fool's dreams. The dream of that moment when he would give her his mother's jewels, the dream of that charming face uplifted to his, the dream of the little cottage to which he would hurry after his day's work and find her waiting at the gate—these dreams must be dispelled forever. He could barely wait until the end of the service. He wanted to be alone; to fight it out with himself; to crush out of his heart that fair image. At length the hour ended and he got out before the congregation and hurried to his room.

Betty had company all that afternoon and it was late in the day when Colonel Zane ascended the stairs and entered her room to find her alone.

"Betty, I wish to know why you ignored Mr. Clarke this morning?" said Colonel Zane, looking down on his sister. There was a gleam in his eye and an expression about his mouth seldom seen in the Colonel's features.

"I do not know that it concerns any one but myself," answered Betty quickly, as her head went higher and her eyes flashed with a gleam not unlike that in her brother's.

"I beg your pardon. I do not agree with you," replied Colonel Zane. "It does concern others. You cannot do things like that in this little place where every one knows all about you and expect it to pass unnoticed. Martin's wife saw you cut Clarke and you know what a gossip she is. Already every one is talking about you and Clarke."

"To that I am indifferent."

"But I care. I won't have people talking about you," replied the Colonel, who began to lose patience. Usually he had the best temper imaginable. "Last fall you allowed Clarke to pay you a good deal of attention and apparently you were on good terms when he went away. Now that he has returned you won't even speak to him. You let this fellow Miller run after you. In my estimation Miller is not to be compared to Clarke, and judging from the warm greetings I saw Clarke receive this morning, there are a number of folk who agree with me. Not that I am praising Clarke. I simply say this because to Bessie, to Jack, to everyone, your act is incomprehensible. People are calling you a flirt and saying that they would prefer some country manners."

"I have not allowed Mr. Miller to run after me, as you are pleased to term it," retorted Betty with indignation. "I do not like him. I never see him any more unless you or Bessie or some one else is present. You know that. I cannot prevent him from walking to church with me."

"No, I suppose not, but are you entirely innocent of those sweet glances which you gave him this morning?"

"I did not," cried Betty with an angry flush. "I won't be called a flirt by you or by anyone else. The moment I am civil to some man all these old maids and old women say I am flirting. It is outrageous."

"Now, Betty, don't get excited. We are getting from the question. Why are you not civil to Clarke?" asked Colonel Zane. She did not answer and after a moment he continued. "If there is anything about Clarke that I do not know and that I should know I want you to tell me. Personally I like the fellow. I am not saying that to make you think you ought to like him because I do. You might not care for him at all, but that would be no good reason for your actions. Betty, in these frontier settlements a man is soon known for his real worth. Every one at the Fort liked Clarke. The youngsters adored him. Bessie liked him very much. You know he and Isaac became good friends. I think he acted like a man to-day. I saw the look Miller gave him. I don't like this fellow Miller, anyway. Now, I am taking the trouble to tell you my side of the argument. It is not a question of your liking Clarke—that is none of my affair. It is simply that either he is not the man we all

think him or you are acting in a way unbecoming a Zane.
I do not purpose to have this state of affairs continue.
Now, enough of this beating about the bush."

Betty had seen the Colonel angry more than once, but
never with her. It was quite certain she had angered him
and she forgot her own resentment. Her heart had warmed
with her brother's praise of Clarke. Then as she remembered the past she felt a scorn for her weakness and such
a revulsion of feeling that she cried out passionately:

"He is a trifler. He never cared for me. He insulted me."

Colonel Zane reached for his hat, got up without saying another word and went downstairs.

Betty had not intended to say quite what she had and
instantly regretted her hasty words. She called to the Colonel, but he did not answer her, nor return.

"Betty, what in the world could you have said to my
husband?" said Mrs. Zane as she entered the room. She
was breathless from running up the stairs and her comely
face wore a look of concern. "He was as white as that
sheet and he stalked off toward the Fort without a word
to me."

"I simply told him Mr. Clarke had insulted me,"
answered Betty calmly.

"Great Heavens! Betty, what have you done?" exclaimed Mrs. Zane. "You don't know Eb when he is
angry. He is a big fool over you, anyway. He is liable to
kill Clarke."

Betty's blood was up now and she said that would not
be a matter of much importance.

"When did he insult you?" asked the elder woman,
yielding to her natural curiosity.

"It was last October."

"Pooh! It took you a long time to tell it. I don't believe
it amounted to much. Mr. Clarke did not appear to be the

sort of a man to insult anyone. All the girls were crazy about him last year. If he was not all right they would not have been."

"I do not care if they were. The girls can have him and welcome. I don't want him. I never did. I am tired of hearing everyone eulogize him. I hate him. Do you hear? I hate him! And I wish you would go away and leave me alone."

"Well, Betty, all I will say is that you are a remarkable young woman," answered Mrs. Zane, who saw plainly that Betty's violent outburst was a prelude to a storm of weeping. "I don't believe a word you have said. I don't believe you hate him. There!"

Colonel Zane walked straight to the Fort, entered the blockhouse and knocked on the door of Clarke's room. A voice bade him come in. He shoved open the door and went into the room. Clarke had evidently just returned from a tramp in the hills, for his garments were covered with burrs and his boots were dusty. He looked tired, but his face was calm.

"Why, Colonel Zane! Have a seat. What can I do for you?"

"I have come to ask you to explain a remark of my sister's."

"Very well, I am at your service," answered Alfred slowly, lighting his pipe, after which he looked straight into Colonel Zane's face.

"My sister informs me that you insulted her last fall before you left the Fort. I am sure you are neither a liar nor a coward, and I expect you to answer as a man."

"Colonel Zane, I am not a liar, and I hope I am not a coward," said Alfred coolly. He took a long pull on his pipe and blew a puff of white smoke toward the ceiling.

"I believe you, but I must have an explanation. There is something wrong somewhere. I saw Betty pass you without speaking this morning. I did not like it and I took her to task about it. She then said you had insulted her. Betty is prone to exaggerate, especially when angry, but she never told me a lie in her life. Ever since you pulled Isaac out of the river I have taken an interest in you. That's why I'd like to avoid any trouble. But this thing has gone far enough. Now be sensible, swallow your pride and let me hear your side of the story."

Alfred had turned pale at his visitor's first words. There was no mistaking Colonel Zane's manner. Alfred well knew that the Colonel, if he found Betty had really been insulted, would call him out and kill him. Colonel Zane spoke quietly, even kindly, but there was an undercurrent of intense feeling in his voice, a certain deadly intent which boded ill to anyone who might cross him at that moment. Alfred's first impulse was a reckless desire to tell Colonel Zane he had nothing to explain and that he stood ready to give any satisfaction in his power. But he wisely thought better of this. It struck him that this would not be fair, for no matter what the girl had done the Colonel had always been his friend. So Alfred pulled himself together and resolved to make a clean breast of the whole affair.

"Colonel Zane, I do not feel that I owe your sister anything, and what I am going to tell you is simply because you have always been my friend, and I do not want you to have any wrong ideas about me. I'll tell you the truth and you can be the judge as to whether or not I insulted your sister. I fell in love with her, almost at first sight. The night after the Indians recaptured your brother, Betty and I stood out in the moonlight and she looked so bewitching and I felt so sorry for her and so carried away by my love for her that I yielded to a momentary impulse and kissed her. I simply could not help it. There is no excuse for me. She struck me across the face and ran into the house. I had intended that night to tell her of my love and place my fate in her hands, but, of course, the unfortunate occurrence made that impossible. As I was to leave at dawn next day, I remained up all night, thinking what I ought to do. Finally I decided to write. I wrote her a letter, telling her all and begging her to become my wife. I gave the letter to your slave, Sam, and told him it was a matter of life and death, and not to lose the letter nor fail to give it to Betty. I have had no answer to that letter. To-day she coldly ignored me. That is my story, Colonel Zane."

"Well, I don't believe she got the letter," said Colonel Zane. "She has not acted like a young lady who has had the privilege of saying 'yes' or 'no' to you. And Sam never had any use for you. He disliked you from the first, and never failed to say something against you."

"I'll kill him if he did not deliver that letter," said Clarke, jumping up in his excitement. "I never thought of that. Good Heaven! What could she have thought of me? She would think I had gone away without a word. If she knew I really loved her she could not think so terribly of me."

"There is more to be explained, but I am satisfied with your side of it," said Colonel Zane. "Now I'll go to Sam and see what has become of that letter. I am glad I am justified in thinking of you as I have. I imagine this thing has hurt you and I don't wonder at it. Maybe we can untangle the problem yet. My advice would be—but never mind that now. Anyway, I'm your friend in this matter. I'll let you know the result of my talk with Sam."

"I thought that young fellow was a gentleman," mused Colonel Zane as he crossed the green square and started up the hill toward the cabins. He found Sam seated on his doorstep.

"Sam, what did you do with a letter Mr. Clarke gave you last October and instructed you to deliver to Betty?"

"I dun recollec' no lettah, sah," replied Sam.

"Now, Sam, don't lie about it. Clarke has just told me that he gave you the letter. What did you do with it?"

"Massa Zane, I ain dun seen no lettah," answered the old man, taking a dingy pipe from his mouth and rolling his eyes at his master.

"If you lie again I will punish you," said Colonel Zane sternly. "You are getting old, Sam, so you find that letter now."

Sam grumbled, and shuffled inside the cabin. Colonel Zane heard him rummaging around. Presently he came back to the door and handed a very badly soiled paper to the Colonel.

"What possessed you to do this, Sam? You have always been honest. Your act has caused great misunderstanding and it might have led to worse."

"He's one of dem no good Southern white trash; he's good fer nuttin'," said Sam. "I saw yo' sistah, Mis' Betty, wif him, and I seen she was gittin' fond of him, and I says I ain't gwinter have Mis' Betty runnin' off wif him. And I'se never gibbin de lettah to her."

That was all the explanation Sam would vouchsafe, and Colonel Zane, knowing it would be useless to say more to the well-meaning but ignorant and superstitious old man, turned and wended his way back to the house. He looked at the paper and saw that it was addressed to Elizabeth Zane, and that the ink was faded until the letters were scarcely visible.

"What have you there?" asked his wife, who had watched him go up the hill to Sam's cabin. She breathed a sigh of relief when she saw that her husband's face had recovered its usual placid expression.

"It is a little letter for that young firebrand upstairs, and I believe it will clear up the mystery. Clarke gave it to Sam last fall and Sam never gave it to Betty."

"I hope with all my heart it may settle Betty. She worries me to death with her love affairs."

Colonel Zane went upstairs and found the young lady exactly as he had left her. She gave an impatient toss of her head as he entered.

"Well, Madam, I have here something that may excite even your interest," he said cheerily.

"What?" asked Betty with a start. She flushed crimson when she saw the letter and at first refused to take it from her brother. She was at a loss to understand his cheerful demeanor. He had been anything but pleasant a few moments since.

"Here, take it. It is a letter from Mr. Clarke which you should have received last fall. That last morning he gave his letter to Sam to deliver to you, and the crazy old man kept it. However, it is too late to talk of that, only it does seem a great pity. I feel sorry for both of you. Clarke never will forgive you, even if you want him to, which I am sure you do not. I don't know exactly what is in this letter, but I know it will make you ashamed to think you did not trust him."

With this parting reproof the Colonel walked out, leaving Betty completely bewildered. The words "too late," "never forgive," and "a great pity" rang through her head. What did he mean? She tore the letter open with trembling hands and holding it up to the now fast-waning light, she read:

"Dear Betty:

"If you had waited only a moment longer I know you would not have been so angry with me. The words I wanted so much to say choked me and I could not speak them. I love you. I have loved you from the very first moment, that blessed moment when I looked up over your pony's head to see the sweetest face the

sun ever shone on. I'll be the happiest man on earth if you will say you care a little for me and promise to be my wife.

"It was wrong to kiss you and I beg your forgiveness. Could you but see your face as I saw it last night in the moonlight, I would not need to plead: you would know that the impulse which swayed me was irresistible. In that kiss I gave you my hope, my love, my life, my all. Let it plead for me.

"I expect to return from Ft. Pitt in about six or eight weeks, but I cannot wait until then for your answer.

"With hope I sign myself,

"Yours until death,
"ALFRED."

Betty read the letter through. The page blurred before her eyes; a sensation of oppression and giddiness made her reach out helplessly with both hands. Then she slipped forward and fell on the floor. For the first time in all her young life Betty had fainted. Colonel Zane found her lying pale and quiet under the window.

CHAPTER 9

Gyantwaia, or, as he was more commonly called, Cornplanter, was originally a Seneca chief, but when the five war tribes consolidated, forming the historical "Five Nations," he became their leader. An old historian said of this renowned chieftain: "Tradition says that the blood of a famous white man coursed through the veins of Cornplanter. The tribe he led was originally ruled by an Indian queen of singular power and beauty. She was born to govern her people by the force of her character. Many a great chief importuned her to become his wife, but she preferred to cling to her power and dignity. When this white man, then a very young man, came to the Ohio valley the queen fell in love with him, and Cornplanter was their son."

Cornplanter lived to a great age. He was a wise counsellor, a great leader, and he died when he was one hundred years old, having had more conceded to him by the white men than any other chieftain. General Washington wrote of him: "The merits of Cornplanter and his friendship for the United States are well known and shall not be forgotten."

But Cornplanter had not always been a friend to the

palefaces. During Dunmore's war and for years after, he was one of the most vindictive of the savage leaders against the invading pioneers.

It was during this period of Cornplanter's activity against the whites that Isaac Zane had the misfortune to fall into the great chief's power.

We remember Isaac last when, lost in the woods, weak from hunger and exposure, he had crawled into a thicket and had gone to sleep. He was awakened by a dog licking his face. He heard Indian voices. He got up and ran as fast as he could, but exhausted as he was he proved no match for his pursuers. They came up with him and seeing that he was unable to defend himself they grasped him by the arms and led him down a well-worn bridle path.

"Damn poor run. No good legs," said one of his captors, and at this the other two Indians laughed. Then they whooped and yelled, at which signal other Indians joined them. Isaac saw that they were leading him into a large encampment. He asked the big savage who led him what camp it was, and learned that he had fallen into the hands of Cornplanter.

While being marched through the large Indian village Isaac saw unmistakable indications of war. There was a busy hum on all sides; the squaws were preparing large quantities of buffalo meat, cutting it in long, thin strips, and were parching corn in stone vessels. The braves were cleaning rifles, sharpening tomahawks, and mixing war paints. All these things Isaac knew to be preparations for long marches and for battle. That night he heard speech after speech in the lodge next to the one in which he lay, but they were in an unknown tongue. Later he heard the yelling of the Indians and the dull thud of their feet as they stamped on the ground. He heard the ring of the tomahawks as they were struck into hard wood. The Indians were dancing the war-dance round the war-post. This continued with some little intermission all the four days that Isaac lay in the lodge rapidly recovering his strength. The fifth day a man came into the lodge. He was tall and powerful, his hair fell over his shoulders and he wore the scanty buckskin dress of the Indian. But Isaac knew at once he was a white man, perhaps one of the many French traders who passed through the Indian village.

"Your name is Zane," said the man in English, looking sharply at Isaac.

"That is my name. Who are you?" asked Isaac in great surprise.

"I am Girty. I've never seen you, but I knew Colonel Zane and Jonathan well. I've seen your sister; you all favor one another."

"Are you Simon Girty?"

"Yes."

"I have heard of your influence with the Indians. Can you do anything to get me out of this?"

"How did you happen to git over here? You are not many miles from Wingenund's Camp," said Girty, giving Isaac another sharp look from his small black eyes.

"Girty, I assure you I am not a spy. I escaped from the Wyandot village on Mad River and after traveling three days lost my way. I went to sleep in a thicket and when I awoke an Indian dog had found me. I heard voices and saw three Indians. I got up and ran, but they easily caught me."

"I know about you. Old Tarhe has a daughter who kept you from bein' ransomed."

"Yes, and I wish I were back there. I don't like the look of things."

"You are right, Zane. You got ketched at a bad time. The Indians are mad. I suppose you don't know that Colonel Crawford massacred a lot of Indians a few days ago. It'll go hard with any white man that gits captured. I'm afraid I can't do nothin' for you."

A few words concerning Simon Girty, the White Savage. He had two brothers, James and George, who had been desperadoes before they were adopted by the Delawares, and who eventually became fierce and relentless savages. Simon had been captured at the same time as his brothers, but he did not at once fall under the influence of the unsettled, free-and-easy life of the Indians. It is probable that while in captivity he acquired the power of commanding the Indians' interest and learned the secret of ruling them—two capabilities few white men ever possessed. It is certain that he, like the noted French-Canadian Joucaire, delighted to sit round the campfires and to go into the council-lodge and talk to the assembled Indians.

At the outbreak of the revolution Girty was a commissioned officer of militia at Fort Pitt. He deserted from the fort, taking with him the Tories McKee and Elliott, and twelve soldiers, and these traitors spread as much terror among the Delaware Indians as they did among the whites. The Delawares had been one of the few peacefully disposed tribes. In order to get them to join their forces with Governor Hamilton, the British commander, Girty declared that General Washington had been killed, that Congress had been dispersed, and that the British were winning all the battles.

Girty spoke most of the Indian languages, and Hamilton employed him to go among the different Indian tribes and incite them to greater hatred of the pioneers. This proved to be just the life that suited him. He soon rose to have a great and bad influence on all the tribes. He became noted for his assisting the Indians in marauds, for his midnight forays, for his scalpings, and his efforts to capture white women, and for his devilish cunning and cruelty.

For many years Girty was the Deathshead of the frontier. The mention of his name alone created terror in any household; in every pioneer's cabin it made the children cry out in fear and paled the cheeks of the stoutest-hearted wife.

It is difficult to conceive of a white man's being such a fiend in human guise. The only explanation that can be given is that renegades rage against the cause of their own blood with the fury of insanity rather than with the malignity of a naturally ferocious temper. In justice to Simon Girty it must be said that facts not known until his death showed he was not so cruel and base as believed; that some deeds of kindness were attributed to him; that he risked his life to save Kenton from the stake, and that many of the terrible crimes laid at his door were really committed by his savage brothers.

Isaac Zane suffered no annoyance at the hands of Cornplanter's braves until the seventh day of his imprisonment. He saw no one except the squaw who brought him corn and meat. On that day two savages came for him and led him into the immense council-lodge of the Five Nations. Cornplanter sat between his right-hand chiefs, Big Tree and Half Town, and surrounded by the other chiefs of the tribes. An aged Indian stood in the center of the lodge and addressed the others. The listening savages sat immovable, their faces as cold and stern as stone masks. Apparently they did not heed the entrance of the prisoner.

"Zane, they're havin' a council," whispered a voice in Isaac's ear. Isaac turned and recognized Girty. "I want to prepare you for the worst."

"Is there, then, no hope for me?" asked Isaac.

"I'm afraid not," continued the renegade, speaking in a low whisper. "They wouldn't let me speak at the coun-

cil. I told Cornplanter that killin' you might bring the
Hurons down on him, but he wouldn't listen. Yesterday, in
the camp of the Delawares, I saw Colonel Crawford burnt
at the stake. He was a friend of mine at Pitt, and I didn't
dare to say one word to the frenzied Indians. I had to
watch the torture. Pipe and Wingenund, both old friends
of Crawford, stood by and watched him walk round the
stake on the red-hot coals for five hours."

Isaac shuddered at the words of the renegade, but did
not answer. He had felt from the first that his case was
hopeless, and that no opportunity for escape could possibly present itself in such a large encampment. He set his
teeth hard and resolved to show the red devils how a white
man could die.

Several speeches were made by different chiefs and
then an impressive oration by Big Tree. At the conclusion
of the speeches, which were in an unknown tongue to
Isaac, Cornplanter handed a war-club to Half Town. This
chief got up, walked to the end of the circle, and there
brought the club down on the ground with a resounding
thud. Then he passed the club to Big Tree. In a solemn
and dignified manner every chief duplicated Half Town's
performance with the club.

Isaac watched the ceremony as if fascinated. He had
seen a war-club used in the councils of the Hurons and
knew that striking it on the ground signified war and death.

"White man, you are a killer of Indians," said Cornplanter in good English. "When the sun shines again you
die."

A brave came forward and painted Isaac's face black.
This Isaac knew to indicate that death awaited him on the
morrow. On his way back to his prison-lodge he saw that
a war-dance was in progress.

A hundred braves with tomahawks, knives, and mal-
lets in their hands were circling round a post and keeping

time to the low music of a muffled drum. Close together, with heads bowed, they marched. At certain moments, which they led up to with a dancing on rigid legs and a stamping with their feet, they wheeled, and uttering hideous yells, started to march in the other direction. When this had been repeated three times a brave stepped from the line, advanced, and struck his knife or tomahawk into the post. Then with a loud voice he proclaimed his past exploits and great deeds in war. The other Indians greeted this with loud yells of applause and a flourishing of weapons. Then the whole ceremony was gone through again.

That afternoon many of the Indians visited Isaac in his lodge and shook their fists at him and pointed their knives at him. They hissed and groaned at him. Their vindictive faces expressed the malignant joy they felt at the expectation of putting him to the torture.

When night came Isaac's guards laced up the lodge-door and shut him from the sight of the maddened Indians. The darkness that gradually enveloped him was a relief. By and by all was silent except for the occasional yell of a drunken savage. To Isaac it sounded like a long, rolling death-cry echoing throughout the encampment and murdering his sleep. Its horrible meaning made him shiver and his flesh creep. At length even that yell ceased. The watchdogs quieted down and the perfect stillness which ensued could almost be felt. Through Isaac's mind ran over and over again the same words. His last night to live! His last night to live! He forced himself to think of other things. He lay there in the darkness of his tent, but he was faraway in thought, faraway in the past with his mother and brothers before they had come to this bloodthirsty country. His thoughts wandered to the days of his boyhood when he used to drive the cows to the pasture on the hillside, and in his dreamy, disordered fancy he was once more letting down the bars of the gate. Then he was wading in the brook and whacking the green frogs with his stick. Old playmates' faces, forgotten for years, were there looking at him from the dark wall of his wigwam. There was Andrew's face; the faces of his other brothers; the laughing face of his sister; the serene face of his mother. As he lay there with the shadow of death over him sweet was the thought that soon he would be reunited with that mother. The images faded slowly away, swallowed up in the gloom. Suddenly a vision appeared to him. A radiant white light illumined the lodge and shone full on the beautiful face of the Indian maiden who had loved him so well. Myeerah's dark eyes were bright with an undying love and her lips smiled hope.

A rude kick dispelled Isaac's dreams. A brawny savage pulled him to his feet and pushed him outside of the lodge.

It was early morning. The sun had just cleared the low hills in the east and its red beams crimsoned the edges of the clouds of fog which hung over the river like a great white curtain. Though the air was warm, Isaac shivered a little as the breeze blew softly against his cheek. He took one long look toward the rising sun, toward that east he had hoped to see, and then resolutely turned his face away forever.

Early though it was the Indians were astir and their whooping rang throughout the valley. Down the main street of the village the guards led the prisoner, followed by a screaming mob of squaws and young braves and children who threw sticks and stones at the hated Long Knife.

Soon the inhabitants of the camp congregated on the green oval in the midst of the lodges. When the prisoner appeared they formed in two long lines facing each other, and several feet apart. Isaac was to run the gauntlet—one of the severest of Indian tortures. With the exception of Cornplanter and several of his chiefs, every Indian in the village was in line. Little Indian boys hardly large enough to sling a stone; maidens and squaws with switches or spears; athletic young braves with flashing tomahawks; grim, matured warriors swinging knotted war clubs—all were there in line, yelling and brandishing their weapons in a manner frightful to behold.

The word was given, and stripped to the waist, Isaac bounded forward fleet as a deer. He knew the Indian way of running the gauntlet. The head of that long lane contained the warriors and older braves and it was here that the great danger lay. Between these lines he sped like a flash, dodging this way and that, running close in under the raised weapons, taking what blows he could on his uplifted arms, knocking this warrior over and doubling that one up with a lightning blow in the stomach, never slacking his speed for one stride, so that it was extremely difficult for the Indians to strike him effectually. Once past that formidable array, Isaac's gauntlet was run, for the squaws and children scattered screaming before the sweep of his powerful arms.

The old chiefs grunted their approval. There was a bruise on Isaac's forehead and a few drops of blood mingled with beads of perspiration. Several lumps and scratches showed on his bare shoulders and arms, but he had escaped any serious injury. This was a feat almost without a parallel in gauntlet running.

When he had been tied with wet buckskin thongs to the post in the center of the oval, the youths, the younger braves, and the squaws began circling round him, yelling like so many demons. The old squaws thrust sharpened sticks, which had been soaked in salt water, into his flesh. The maidens struck him with willows which left red welts on his white shoulders. The braves buried the blades of their tomahawks in the post as near as possible to his head without actually hitting him.

Isaac knew the Indian nature well. To command the respect of the savages was the only way to lessen his torture. He knew that a cry for mercy would only increase his sufferings and not hasten his death—indeed it would prolong both. He had resolved to die without a moan. He had determined to show absolute indifference to his torture, which was the only way to appeal to the savage nature, and if anything could, make the Indians show mercy. Or, if he could taunt them into killing him at once he would be spared all the terrible agony which they were in the habit of inflicting on their victims.

One handsome young brave twirled a glittering tomahawk which he threw from a distance of ten, fifteen, and twenty feet and every time the sharp blade of the hatchet sank deep into the stake within an inch of Isaac's head. With a proud and disdainful look Isaac gazed straight before him and paid no heed to his tormentor.

"Does the Indian boy think he can frighten a white warrior?" said Isaac scornfully at length. "Let him go and earn his eagle plumes. The paleface laughs at him."

The young brave understood the Huron language, for he gave a frightful yell and cast his tomahawk again, this time shaving a lock of hair from Isaac's head.

This was what Isaac had prayed for. He hoped that one of these glittering hatchets would be propelled less skilfully than its predecessors and would kill him instantly. But the enraged brave had no other opportunity to cast his weapon, for the Indians jeered at him and pushed him from the line.

Other braves tried their proficiency in the art of throwing knives and tomahawks, but their efforts called forth only words of derision from Isaac. They left the weapons sticking in the post until round Isaac's head and shoulders there was scarcely room for another.

"The White Eagle is tired of boys," cried Isaac to a chief standing near. "What has he done that he be made the plaything of children? Let him die the death of a chief."

The maidens had long since desisted in their efforts to torment the prisoner. Even the hardened old squaws had withdrawn. The prisoner's proud, handsome face, his upright bearing, his scorn for his enemies, his indifference to the cuts and bruises, and red welts upon his clear white skin had won their hearts.

Not so with the braves. Seeing that the paleface scorned all efforts to make him flinch, the young brave turned to Big Tree. At a command from this chief the Indians stopped their maneuvering round the post and formed a large circle. In another moment a tall warrior appeared carrying an armful of bundled sticks.

In spite of his iron nerve Isaac shuddered with horror. He had anticipated running the gauntlet, having his nails pulled out, powder and salt shot into his flesh, being scalped alive, and a host of other Indian tortures, but as he had killed no members of this tribe he had not thought of being burned alive. God, it was too horrible!

The Indians were now quiet. Their songs and dances would break out soon enough. They piled the wood round Isaac's feet. The Indian warrior knelt on the ground; the steel clicked on the flint; a little shower of sparks dropped on the pieces of punk and then—a tiny flame shot up, and a slender little column of blue smoke floated on the air.

Isaac shut his teeth hard and prayed with all his soul for a speedy death.

Simon Girty came hurriedly through the lines of waiting, watching Indians. He had obtained permission to speak to the man of his own color.

"Zane, you made a brave stand. Any other time but this it might have saved you. If you want I'll get word to your people." And then bending and placing his mouth close to Isaac's ear, he whispered, "I did all I could for you, but it must have been too late."

"Try and tell them at Fort Henry," Isaac said simply.

There was a little cracking of dried wood and then a narrow tongue of red flame darted up from the pile of wood and licked at the buckskin fringe on the prisoner's leggins. At this supreme moment when the attention of all centered on that motionless figure lashed to the stake, and when only the low chanting of the death-song broke the stillness, a long, piercing yell rang out on the quiet morning air. So strong, so sudden, so startling was the break in that almost perfect calm that for a moment afterward there was a silence as of death. All eyes turned to the ridge of rising ground whence that sound had come. Now came the unmistakable thunder of horses' hoofs pounding furiously on the rocky ground. A moment of paralyzed inaction ensued. The Indians stood bewildered, petrified. Then on that ridge of rising ground stood, silhouetted against the blue sky, a great black horse with arching neck and flying mane. Astride him sat a plumed warrior, who waved his rifle high in the air. Again that shrill screeching yell came floating to the ears of the astonished Indians.

The prisoner had seen that horse and rider before; he had heard that long yell; his heart bounded with hope. The Indians knew that yell; it was the terrible war-cry of the Hurons.

A horse followed closely after the leader, and then another appeared on the crest of the hill. Then came two abreast, and then four abreast, and now the hill was black with plunging horses. They galloped swiftly down the slope and into the narrow street of the village. When the black horse entered the oval the train of racing horses extended to the top of the ridge. The plumes of the riders streamed gracefully on the breeze; their feathers shone; their weapons glittered in the bright sunlight.

Never was there more complete surprise. In the early morning the Hurons had crept up to within a rifle shot of the encampment, and at an opportune moment when all the scouts and runners were round the torture-stake, they had reached the hillside from which they rode into the village before the inhabitants knew what had happened. Not an Indian raised a weapon. There were screams from the women and children, a shouted command from Big Tree, and then all stood still and waited.

Thundercloud, the war chief of the Wyandots, pulled his black stallion back on his haunches not twenty feet from the prisoner at the stake. His band of painted devils closed in behind him. Full two hundred strong were they and all picked warriors tried and true. They were naked to the waist. Across their brawny chests ran a broad bar of flaming red paint; hideous designs in black and white covered their faces. Every head had been clean-shaven except where the scalp lock bristled like a porcupine's quills. Each warrior carried a plumed spear, a tomahawk, and a rifle. The shining heads, with the little tufts of hair tied tightly close to the scalp, were enough to show that these Indians were on the war-path.

From the back of one of the foremost horses a slender figure dropped and darted toward the prisoner at the stake. Surely that wildly flying hair proved this was not a warrior. Swift as a flash of light this figure reached the stake; the blazing wood sticks scattered right and left; a naked blade gleamed; the thongs fell from the prisoner's wrists; and the front ranks of the Hurons opened and closed on the freed man. The deliverer turned to the gaping Indians, disclosing to their gaze the pale and beautiful face of Myeerah, the Wyandot Princess.

"Summon your chief," she commanded.

The tall form of the Seneca chief moved from among the warriors and with slow and measured tread approached the maiden. His bearing fitted the leader of five nations of Indians. It was of one who knew that he was the wisest of chiefs, the hero of a hundred battles. Who dared beard him in his den? Who dared defy the greatest power in all Indian tribes? When he stood before the maiden he folded his arms and waited for her to speak.

"Myeerah claims the White Eagle," she said.

Cornplanter did not answer at once. He had never seen Myeerah, though he had heard many stories of her loveliness. Now he was face to face with the Indian Princess whose fame had been the theme of many an Indian romance, and whose beauty had been sung of in many an Indian song. The beautiful girl stood erect and fearless. Her disordered garments, torn and bedraggled and stained from the long ride, ill-concealed the grace of her form. Her hair rippled from the uncovered head and fell in dusky splendor over her shoulders; her dark eyes shone with a stern and steady fire; her bosom swelled with each deep breath. She was the daughter of great chiefs; she looked the embodiment of savage love.

"The Huron squaw is brave," said Cornplanter. "By what right does she come to free my captive?"

"He is an adopted Wyandot."

"Why does the paleface hide like a fox near the camp of Cornplanter?"

"He ran away. He lost the trail to the Fort on the river."

"Cornplanter takes prisoners to kill; not to free."

"If you will not give him up Myeerah will take him," she answered, pointing to the long line of mounted warriors. "And should harm befall Tarhe's daughter it will be avenged."

Cornplanter looked at Thundercloud. Well he knew that chief's prowess in the field. He ran his eyes over the silent, watching Hurons, and then back to the sombre face of their leader. Thundercloud sat rigid upon his stallion; his head held high; every muscle tense and strong for instant action. He was ready and eager for the fray. He, and every one of his warriors, would fight like a thousand tigers for their Princess—the pride of the proud race of Wyandots. Cornplanter saw this and he felt that on the eve of important marches he dared not sacrifice one of his braves for any reason, much less a worthless paleface; and yet to let the prisoner go galled the haughty spirit of the Seneca chief.

"The Long Knife is not worth the life of one of my dogs," he said, with scorn in his deep voice. "If Cornplanter willed he could drive the Hurons before him like leaves before the storm. Let Myeerah take the paleface back to her wigwam and there feed him and make a squaw of him. When he stings like a snake in the grass remember the chief's words. Cornplanter turns on his heel from the Huron maiden who forgets her blood."

When the sun reached its zenith it shone down upon a long line of mounted Indians riding single file along the narrow trail and like a huge serpent winding through the forest and over the plain.

They were Wyandot Indians, and Isaac Zane rode among them. Freed from the terrible fate which had menaced him, and knowing that he was once more on his way to the Huron encampment, he had accepted his destiny and quarreled no more with fate. He was thankful beyond all words for his rescue from the stake.

Coming to a clear, rapid stream, the warriors dismounted and rested while their horses drank thirstily of the cool water. An Indian touched Isaac on the arm and silently pointed toward the huge maple tree under which Thundercloud and Myeerah were sitting. Isaac turned his horse and rode the short distance intervening. When he got near he saw that Myeerah stood with one arm over her pony's neck. She raised eyes that were weary and sad, which yet held a lofty and noble resolve.

"White Eagle, this stream leads straight to the Fort on the river," she said briefly, almost coldly. "Follow it, and when the sun reaches the top of yonder hill you will be with your people. Go, you are free."

She turned her face away. Isaac's head whirled in his amazement. He could not believe his ears. He looked closely at her and saw that though her face was calm her throat swelled, and the hand which lay over the neck of her pony clenched the bridle in a fierce grasp. Isaac glanced at Thundercloud and the other Indians nearby. They sat unconcerned with the invariable unreadable expression.

"Myeerah, what do you mean?" asked Isaac.

"The words of Cornplanter cut deep into the heart of Myeerah," she answered bitterly. "They were true. The Eagle does not care for Myeerah. She shall no longer keep him in a cage. He is free to fly away."

"The Eagle does not want his freedom. I love you, Myeerah. You have saved me and I am yours. If you will go home with me and marry me there as my people are married I will go back to the Wyandot village."

Myeerah's eyes softened with unutterable love. With a quick cry she was in his arms. After a few moments of forgetfulness Myeerah spoke to Thundercloud and waved her hand toward the west. The chief swung himself over his horse, shouted a single command, and rode down the bank into the water. His warriors followed him, wading their horses into the shallow creek, with never a backward look. When the last rider had disappeared in the willows the lovers turned their horses eastward.

CHAPTER 10

It was near the close of a day in early summer. A small group of persons surrounded Colonel Zane where he sat on his doorstep. From time to time he took the long Indian pipe from his mouth and blew great clouds of smoke over his head. Major McColloch and Captain Boggs were there. Silas Zane half reclined on the grass. The Colonel's wife stood in the doorway, and Betty sat on the lower step with her head leaning against her brother's knee. They all had grave faces. Jonathan Zane had returned that day after an absence of three weeks, and was now answering the many questions with which he was plied.

"Don't ask me any more and I'll tell you the whole thing," he had just said, while wiping the perspiration from his brow. His face was worn; his beard ragged and unkempt; his appearance suggestive of extreme fatigue. "It was this way: Colonel Crawford had four hundred and eighty men under him, with Slover and me acting as guides. This was a large force of men and comprised soldiers from Pitt and the other forts and settlers from all along the river. You see, Crawford wanted to crush the Shawnees at one blow. When we reached the Sandusky

River, which we did after an arduous march, not one Indian did we see. You know Crawford expected to surprise the Shawnee camp, and when he found it deserted he didn't know what to do. Slover and I both advised an immediate retreat. Crawford would not listen to us. I tried to explain to him that ever since the Guadenhutten massacre keen-eyed Indian scouts had been watching the border. The news of the present expedition had been carried by fleet runners to the different Indian tribes and they were working like hives of angry bees. The deserted Shawnee village meant to me that the alarm had been sounded in the towns of the Shawnees and the Delawares; perhaps also in the Wyandot towns to the north. Colonel Crawford was obdurate and insisted on resuming the march into the Indian country. The next day we met the Indians coming directly toward us. It was the combined force of the Delaware chiefs, Pipe and Wingenund. The battle had hardly commenced when the redskins were reinforced by four hundred warriors under Shanshota, the Huron chief. The enemy skulked behind trees and rocks, hid in ravines, and crawled through the long grass. They could be picked off only by Indian hunters, of whom Crawford had but few—probably fifty all told. All that day we managed to keep our position, though we lost sixty men. That night we lay down to rest by great fires which we built, to prevent night surprises.

"Early next morning we resumed the fight. I saw Simon Girty on his white horse. He was urging and cheering the Indians on to desperate fighting. Their fire became so deadly that we were forced to retreat. In the afternoon Slover, who had been out scouting, returned with the information that a mounted force was approaching, and that he believed they were the reinforcements which Colonel Crawford expected. The reinforcements came up and proved to be Butler's British Rangers from Detroit. This stunned Crawford's soldiers. The fire of the enemy became hotter and hotter. Our men were falling like leaves around us. They threw aside their rifles and ran, many of them right into the hands of the savages. I believe some of the experienced bordermen escaped, but most of Crawford's force met death on the field. I hid in a hollow log. Next day when I felt that it could be done safely I crawled out. I saw scalped and mutilated bodies everywhere, but did not find Colonel Crawford's body. The Indians had taken all the clothing, weapons, blankets, and everything of value. The Wyandots took a northwest trail and the Delawares and the Shawnees traveled east. I followed the latter because their trail led toward home. Three days later I stood on the high bluff above Wingenund's camp. From there I saw Colonel Crawford tied to a stake and a fire started at his feet. I was not five hundred yards from the camp. I saw the war chiefs, Pipe and Wingenund; I saw Simon Girty and a British officer in uniform. The chiefs and Girty were once Crawford's friends. They stood calmly by and watched the poor victim slowly burn to death. The Indians yelled and danced round the stake; they devised every kind of hellish torture. When at last an Indian ran in and tore off the scalp of the still living man I could bear to see no more, and I turned and ran. I have been in some tough places, but this last was the worst."

"My God! It is awful—and to think that man Girty was once a white man," cried Colonel Zane.

"He came very near being a dead man," said Jonathan, with grim humor. "I got a long shot at him and killed his big white horse."

"It's a pity you missed him," said Silas Zane.

"Here comes Wetzel. What will he say about the massacre?" remarked Major McColloch.

Wetzel joined the group at that moment and shook

hands with Jonathan. When interrogated about the failure of Colonel Crawford's expedition Wetzel said that Slover had just made his appearance at the cabin of Hugh Bennet, and that he was without clothing and almost dead from exposure.

"I'm glad Slover got out alive. He was against the march all along. If Crawford had listened to us he would have averted this terrible affair and saved his own life. Lew, did Slover know how many men got out?" asked Jonathan.

"He said not many. The redskins killed all the prisoners exceptin' Crawford and Knight."

"I saw Colonel Crawford burned at the stake. I did not see Dr. Knight. Maybe they murdered him before I reached the camp of the Delawares," said Jonathan.

"Wetzel, in your judgment, what effect will this massacre and Crawford's death have on the border?" inquired Colonel Zane.

"It means another bloody year like 1777," answered Wetzel.

"We are liable to have trouble with the Indians any day. You mean that."

"There'll be war all along the river. Hamilton is hatchin' some new devil's trick with Girty. Colonel Zane, I calkilate that Girty has a spy in the river settlements and knows as much about the forts and defense as you do."

"You can't mean a white spy."

"Yes, just that."

"That is a strong assertion, Lewis, but coming from you it means something. Step aside here and explain yourself," said Colonel Zane, getting up and walking out to the fence.

"I don't like the looks of things," said the hunter. "A month ago I ketched this man Miller pokin' his nose round the blockhouse where he hadn't ought to be. And I kep' watchin' him. If my suspicions is correct he's playin' some deep game. I ain't got any proof, but things looks bad."

"That's strange, Lewis," said Colonel Zane soberly. "Now that you mention it I remember Jonathan said he met Miller near the Kanawha three weeks ago. That was when Crawford's expedition was on the way to the Shawnee villages. The Colonel tried to enlist Miller, but Miller said he was in a hurry to get back to the Fort. And he hasn't come back yet."

"I ain't surprised. Now, Colonel Zane, you are in command here. I'm not a soldier and for that reason I'm all the better to watch Miller. He won't suspect me. You give me authority and I'll round up his little game."

"By all means, Lewis. Go about it your own way, and report anything to me. Remember you may be mistaken and give Miller the benefit of the doubt. I don't like the fellow. He has a way of appearing and disappearing, and for no apparent reason, that makes me distrust him. But for Heaven's sake, Lew, how would he profit by betraying us?"

"I don't know. All I know is he'll bear watchin'."

"My gracious, Lew Wetzel!" exclaimed Betty as her brother and the hunter rejoined the others. "Have you come all the way over here without a gun? And you have on a new suit of buckskin."

Lewis stood a moment by Betty, gazing down at her with his slight smile. He looked exceedingly well. His face was not yet bronzed by summer suns. His long black hair, of which he was as proud as a woman could have been, and of which he took as much care as he did of his rifle, waved over his shoulders.

"Betty, this is my birthday, but that ain't the reason I've got my fine feathers on. I'm goin' to try and make an impression on you," replied Lewis, smiling.

"I declare, this is very sudden. But you have succeeded.

Who made the suit? And where did you get all that pretty fringe and those beautiful beads?"

"That stuff I picked up round an Injun camp. The suit I made myself."

"I think, Lewis, I must get you to help me make my new gown," said Betty, roguishly.

"Well, I must be gettin' back," said Wetzel, rising.

"Oh, don't go yet. You have not talked to me at all," said Betty petulantly. She walked to the gate with him.

"What can an Injun hunter say to amuse the belle of the border?"

"I don't want to be amused exactly. I mean I'm not used to being unnoticed, especially by you." And then in a lower tone she continued: "What did you mean about Mr. Miller? I heard his name and Eb looked worried. What did you tell him?"

"Never mind now, Betty. Maybe I'll tell you some day. It's enough for you to know the Colonel don't like Miller and that I think he is a bad man. You don't care nothin' for Miller, do you Betty?"

"Not in the least."

"Don't see him any more, Betty. Good-night, now, I must be goin' to supper."

"Lew, stop! or I shall run after you."

"And what good would your runnin' do?" said Lewis. "You'd never ketch me. Why, I could give you twenty paces start and beat you to yon tree."

"You can't. Come, try it," retorted Betty, catching hold of her skirt. She could never have allowed a challenge like that to pass.

"Ha! ha! We are in for a race. Betty, if you beat him, start or no start, you will have accomplished something never done before," said Colonel Zane.

"Come, Silas, step off twenty paces and make them long ones," said Betty, who was in earnest.

"We'll make it forty paces," said Silas, as he commenced taking immense strides.

"What is Lewis looking at?" remarked Colonel Zane's wife.

Wetzel, in taking his position for the race, had faced the river. Mrs. Zane had seen him start suddenly, straighten up and for a moment stand like a statue. Her exclamation drew the attention of the others to the hunter.

"Look!" he cried, waving his hand toward the river.

"I declare, Wetzel, you are always seeing something. Where shall I look? Ah, yes, there is a dark form moving along the bank. By jove! I believe it's an Indian," said Colonel Zane.

Jonathan darted into the house. When he reappeared a second later he had three rifles.

"I see horses, Lew. What do you make out?" said Jonathan. "It's a bold manœuvre for Indians unless they have a strong force."

"Hostile Injuns wouldn't show themselves like that. Maybe they ain't redskins at all. We'll go down to the bluff."

"Oh, yes, let us go," cried Betty, walking down the path toward Wetzel.

Colonel Zane followed her, and presently the whole party were on their way to the river. When they reached the bluff they saw two horses come down the opposite bank and enter the water. Then they seemed to fade from view. The tall trees cast a dark shadow over the water and the horses had become lost in this obscurity. Colonel Zane and Jonathan walked up and down the bank seeking to find a place which afforded a clearer view of the river.

"There they come," shouted Silas.

"Yes, I see them just swimming out of the shadow," said Colonel Zane. "Both horses have riders. Lewis, what can you make out?"

"It's Isaac and an Indian girl," answered Wetzel.

This startling announcement created a commotion in the little group. It was followed by a chorus of exclamations.

"Heavens! Wetzel, you have wonderful eyes. I hope to God you are right. There, I see the foremost rider waving his hand," cried Colonel Zane.

"Oh, Bessie, Bessie! I believe Lew is right. Look at Tige," said Betty excitedly.

Everybody had forgotten the dog. He had come down the path with Betty and had pressed close to her. First he trembled, then whined, then with a loud bark he ran down the bank and dashed into the water.

"Hel-lo, Betts," came the cry across the water. There was no mistaking that clear voice. It was Isaac's.

Although the sun had long gone down behind the hills daylight lingered. It was bright enough for the watchers to recognize Isaac Zane. He sat high on his horse and in his hand he held the bridle of a pony that was swimming beside him. The pony bore the slender figure of a girl. She was bending forward and her hands were twisted in the pony's mane.

By this time the Colonel and Jonathan were standing in the shallow water waiting to grasp the reins and lead the horses up the steep bank. Attracted by the unusual sight of a wildly gesticulating group on the river bluff, the settlers from the Fort hurried down to the scene of action. Captain Boggs and Alfred Clarke joined the crowd. Old Sam came running down from the barn. All were intensely excited as Colonel Zane and Jonathan reached for the bridles and led the horses up the slippery incline.

"Eb, Jack, Silas, here I am alive and well," cried Isaac as he leaped from his horse. "Betty, you darling, it's Isaac. Don't stand staring as if I were a ghost."

Whereupon Betty ran to him, flung her arms around his neck and clung to him. Isaac kissed her tenderly and disengaged himself from her arms.

"You'll get all wet. Glad to see me? Well, I never had such a happy moment in my life. Betty, I have brought you some one whom you must love. This is Myeerah, your sister. She is wet and cold. Take her home and make her warm and comfortable. You must forget all the past, for Myeerah has saved me from the stake."

Betty had forgotten the other. At her brother's words she turned and saw a slender form. Even the wet, mudstained and ragged Indian costume failed to hide the grace of that figure. She saw a beautiful face, as white as her own, and dark eyes full of unshed tears.

"The Eagle is free," said the Indian girl in her low, musical voice.

"You have brought him home to us. Come," said Betty, taking the hand of the trembling maiden.

The settlers crowded round Isaac and greeted him warmly, while they plied him with innumerable questions. Was he free? Who was the Indian girl? Had he run off with her? Were the Indians preparing for war?

On the way to the Colonel's house Isaac told briefly of his escape from the Wyandots, of his capture by Cornplanter, and of his rescue. He also mentioned the preparations for war he had seen in Cornplanter's camp, and Girty's story of Colonel Crawford's death.

"How does it come that you have the Indian girl with you?" asked Colonel Zane as they left the curious settlers and entered the house.

"I am going to marry Myeerah and I brought her with me for that purpose. When we are married I will go back to the Wyandots and live with them until peace is declared."

"Humph! Will it be declared?"

"Myeerah has promised it, and I believe she can bring it about, especially if I marry her. Peace with the Hurons may help to bring about peace with the Shawnees. I shall never cease to work for that end; but even if peace cannot be secured, my duty still is to Myeerah. She saved me from a most horrible death."

"If your marriage with this Indian girl will secure the friendly offices of that grim old warrior Tarhe, it is far more than fighting will ever do. I do not want you to go back. Would we ever see you again?"

"Oh, yes, often I hope. You see, if I marry Myeerah the Hurons will allow me every liberty."

"Well, that puts a different light on the subject."

"Oh, how I wish you and Jonathan could have seen Thundercloud and his two hundred warriors ride into Cornplanter's camp. It was magnificent! The braves were all crowded near the stake where I was bound. The fire had been lighted. Suddenly the silence was shattered by an awful yell. It was Thundercloud's yell. I knew it because I had heard it before, and anyone who had once heard that yell could never forget it. In what seemed an incredibly short time Thundercloud's warriors were lined up in the middle of the camp. The surprise was so complete that, had it been necessary, they could have ridden Cornplanter's braves down, killed many, routed the others, and burned the village. Cornplanter will not get over that surprise in many a moon."

Betty had always hated the very mention of the Indian girl who had been the cause of her brother's long absence from home. But she was so happy in the knowledge of his return that she felt that it was in her power to forgive much; more-over, the white, weary face of the Indian maiden touched Betty's warm heart. With her quick intuition she had divined that this was even a greater trial for Myeerah. Undoubtedly the Indian girl feared the scorn of her lover's people. She showed it in her trembling hands, in her fearful glances.

Finding that Myeerah could speak and understand English Betty became more interested in her charge every moment. She set about to make Myeerah comfortable, and while she removed the wet and stained garments she talked all the time. She told her how happy she was that Isaac was alive and well. She said Myeerah's heroism in saving him should atone for all the past, and that Isaac's family would welcome her in his home.

Gradually Myeerah's agitation subsided under Betty's sweet graciousness, and by the time Betty had dressed her in a white gown, had brushed the dark hair and added a bright ribbon, Myeerah had so far forgotten her fears as to take a shy pleasure in the picture of herself in the mirror. As for Betty, she gave vent to a little cry of delight.

"Oh, you are perfectly lovely," cried Betty. "In that gown no one would know you as a Wyandot princess."

"Myeerah's mother was a white woman."

"I have heard your story, Myeerah, and it is wonderful. You must tell me all about your life with the Indians. You speak my language almost as well as I do. Who taught you?"

"Myeerah learned to talk with the White Eagle. She can speak French with the *Coureurs-des-bois*."

"That's more than I can do, Myeerah. And I had a French teacher," said Betty, laughing.

"Hello, up there," came Isaac's voice from below.

"Come up, Isaac," called Betty.

"Is this my Indian sweetheart?" exclaimed Isaac, stopping at the door. "Betty, isn't she—"

"Yes," answered Betty, "she is simply beautiful."

"Come, Myeerah, we must go down to supper," said Isaac, taking her in his arms and kissing her. "Now you must not be afraid, nor mind being looked at."

"Everyone will be kind to you," said Betty, taking her hand. Myeerah had slipped from Isaac's arm and hesitated and hung back. "Come," continued Betty, "I will stay with you, and you need not talk if you do not wish."

Thus reassured Myeerah allowed Betty to lead her downstairs. Isaac had gone ahead and was waiting at the door.

The big room was brilliantly lighted with pine knots. Mrs. Zane was arranging the dishes on the table. Old Sam and Annie were hurrying to and fro from the kitchen. Colonel Zane had just come up the cellar stairs carrying a moldy looking cask. From its appearance it might have been a powder keg, but the merry twinkle in the Colonel's eyes showed that the cask contained something as precious, perhaps, as powder, but not quite so dangerous. It was a cask of wine over thirty years old. With Colonel Zane's other effects it had stood the test of the long wagon-train journey over the Virginia mountains, and of the raft-ride down the Ohio. Colonel Zane thought the feast he had arranged for Isaac would be a fitting occasion for the breaking of the cask.

Major McColloch, Captain Boggs and Hugh Bennet had been invited. Wetzel had been persuaded to come. Betty's friends Lydia and Alice were there.

As Isaac, with an air of pride, led the two girls into the room Old Sam saw them and he exclaimed, "For de Lawd's sakes, Marsh Zane, dar's two pippins, sure can't tell 'em from one anudder."

Betty and Myeerah did resemble each other. They were of about the same size, tall and slender. Betty was rosy, bright-eyed and smiling; Myeerah was pale one moment and red the next.

"Friends, this is Myeerah, the daughter of Tarhe," said Isaac simply. "We are to be married to-morrow."

"Oh, why did you not tell me?" asked Betty in great surprise. "She said nothing about it."

"You see Myeerah has that most excellent trait in a woman—knowing when to keep silent," answered Isaac with a smile.

The door opened at this moment, admitting Will Martin and Alfred Clarke.

"Everybody is here now, Bessie, and I guess we may as well sit down to supper," said Colonel Zane. "And, good friends, let me say that this is an occasion for rejoicing. It is not so much a marriage that I mean. That we might have any day if Lydia or Betty would show some of the alacrity which got a good husband for Alice. Isaac is a free man and we expect his marriage will bring about peace with a powerful tribe of Indians. To us, and particularly to you, young people, that is a matter of great importance. The friendship of the Hurons cannot but exert an influence on other tribes. I, myself, may live to see the day that my dream shall be realized—peaceful and friendly relations with the Indians, the freedom of the soil, well-tilled farms and growing settlements, and at last, the opening of this glorious country to the world. Therefore, let us rejoice; let every one be happy; let your gayest laugh ring out, and tell your best story."

Betty had blushed painfully at the entrance of Alfred and again at the Colonel's remark. To add to her embarrassment she found herself seated opposite Alfred at the table. This was the first time he had been near her since the Sunday at the meeting-house, and the incident had a singular effect on Betty. She found herself possessed, all at once, of an unaccountable shyness, and she could not lift her eyes from her plate. But at length she managed to steal a glance at Alfred. She failed to see any signs in his beaming face of the broken spirit of which her brother had hinted. He looked very well indeed. He was eating his dinner like any other healthy man, and talking and laughing with Lydia. This developed another unaccountable feeling in Betty, but this time it was resentment. Who ever heard of a man, who was as much in love as his letter said, looking well and enjoying himself with any other than the object of his affections? He had got over it, that was all. Just then Alfred turned and gazed full into Betty's eyes. She lowered them instantly, but not so quickly that she failed to see in his a reproach.

"You are going to stay with us a while, are you not?" asked Betty of Isaac.

"No, Betts, not more than a day or so. Now, do not look so distressed. I do not go back as a prisoner. Myeerah and I can often come and visit you. But just now I want to get back and try to prevent the Delawares from urging Tarhe to war."

"Isaac, I believe you are doing the wisest thing possible," said Captain Boggs. "And when I look at your bride-to-be I confess I do not see how you remained single so long."

"That's so, Captain," answered Isaac. "But you see, I have never been satisfied or contented in captivity. I wanted nothing but to be free."

"In other words, you were blind," remarked Alfred, smiling at Isaac.

"Yes, Alfred, I was. And I imagine had you been in my place you would have discovered the beauty and virtue of my Princess long before I did. Nevertheless, please do not favor Myeerah with so many admiring glances. She is not used to it. And that reminds me that I must expect trouble tomorrow. All you fellows will want to kiss her."

"And Betty is going to be maid of honor. She, too, will have her troubles," remarked Colonel Zane.

"Think of that, Alfred," said Isaac. "A chance to kiss the two prettiest girls on the border—a chance of a lifetime."

"It is customary, is it not?" said Alfred coolly.

"Yes, it's a custom, if you can catch the girl," answered Colonel Zane.

Betty's face flushed at Alfred's cool assumption. How dare he? In spite of her will she could not resist the power that compelled her to look at him. As plainly as if it were written there, she saw in his steady blue eyes the light of a memory—the memory of a kiss. And Betty dropped her head, her face burning, her heart on fire with shame, and love, and regret.

"It'll be a good chance for me, too," said Wetzel. His remark instantly turned attention to himself.

"The idea is absurd," said Isaac. "Why, Lew Wetzel, you could not be made to kiss any girl."

"I would not be backward about it," said Colonel Zane.

"You have forgotten the fuss you made when the boys were kissing me," said Mrs. Zane with a fine scorn.

"My dear," said Colonel Zane, in an aggrieved tone, "I did not make so much of a fuss, as you call it, until they had kissed you a great many times more than was reasonable."

"Isaac, tell us one thing more," said Captain Boggs. "How did Myeerah learn of your capture by Cornplanter? Surely she could not have trailed you?"

"Will you tell us?" said Isaac to Myeerah.

"A bird sang it to me," answered Myeerah.

"She will never tell, that is certain," said Isaac. "And for that reason I believe Simon Girty got word to her that I was in the hands of Cornplanter. At the last moment when the Indians were lashing me to the stake Girty came to me and said he must have been too late."

"Yes, Girty might have done that," said Colonel Zane.

"I suppose, though, he dared not interfere in behalf of poor Crawford."

"Isaac, can you get Myeerah to talk? I love to hear her speak," said Betty, in an aside.

"Myeerah, will you sing a Huron love-song?" said Isaac. "Or, if you do not wish to sing, tell a story. I want them to know how well you can speak our language."

"What shall Myeerah say?" she said, shyly.

"Tell them the legend of the Standing Stone."

"A beautiful Indian girl once dwelt in the pine forests," began Myeerah, with her eyes cast down and her hand seeking Isaac's. "Her voice was like rippling waters, her beauty like the rising sun. From near and from far came warriors to see the fair face of this maiden. She smiled on them all and they called her Smiling Moon. Now there lived on the Great Lake a Wyandot chief. He was young and bold. No warrior was as great as Tarhe. Smiling Moon cast a spell on his heart. He came many times to woo her and make her his wife. But Smiling Moon said: 'Go, do great deeds, and come again.'

"Tarhe searched the east and the west. He brought her strange gifts from strange lands. She said: 'Go and slay my enemies.' Tarhe went forth in his war paint and killed the braves who named her Smiling Moon. He came again to her and she said: 'Run swifter than the deer, be more cunning than the beaver, dive deeper than the loon.'

"Tarhe passed once more to the island where dwelt Smiling Moon. The ice was thick, the snow was deep. Smiling Moon turned not from her warm fire as she said: 'The chief is a great warrior, but Smiling Moon is not easily won. It is cold. Change winter into summer and then Smiling Moon will love him.'

"Tarhe cried in a loud voice to the Great Spirit: 'Make me a master.'

"A voice out of the forest answered: 'Tarhe, great war-

rior, wise chief, waste not thy time, go back to thy wigwam.'

"Tarhe unheeding cried, 'Tarhe wins or dies. Make him
a master so that he may drive the ice northward.'

"Stormed the wild tempest; thundered the rivers of ice;
chill blew the north wind, the cold northwest wind, against
the mild south wind; snow-spirits and hail-spirits fled before the warm raindrops; the white mountains melted,
and lo! it was summer.

"On the mountain top Tarhe waited for his bride. Never
wearying, ever faithful he watched many years. There he
turned to stone. There he stands to-day, the Standing
Stone of ages. And Smiling Moon, changed by the Great
Spirit into the Night Wind, forever wails her lament at
dusk through the forest trees, and moans over the mountain tops."

Myeerah's story elicited cheers and praises from all.
She was entreated to tell another, but smilingly shook her
head. Now that her shyness had worn off to some extent
she took great interest in the jest and the general conversation.

Colonel Zane's fine old wine flowed like water. The
custom was to fill a guest's cup as soon as it was empty.
Drinking much was rather encouraged than otherwise.
But Colonel Zane never allowed this custom to go too far
in his house.

"Friends, the hour grows late," he said. "To-morrow,
after the great event, we shall have games, shooting
matches, running races, and contests of all kinds. Captain Boggs and I have arranged to give prizes, and I expect the girls can give something to lend a zest to the
competition."

"Will the girls have a chance in these races?" asked
Isaac. "If so, I should like to see Betty and Myeerah run."

"Betty can outrun any woman, red or white, on the

border," said Wetzel. "And she could make some of the men run their level best."

"Well, perhaps we shall give her one opportunity tomorrow," observed the Colonel. "She used to be good at running, but it seems to me that of late she has taken to books and—"

"Oh, Eb! that is untrue," interrupted Betty.

Colonel Zane laughed and patted his sister's cheek. "Never mind, Betty," and then, rising, he continued, "Now let us drink to the bride and groom-to-be. Captain Boggs, I call on you."

"We drink to the bride's fair beauty; we drink to the groom's good luck," said Captain Boggs, raising his cup.

"Do not forget the maid-of-honor," said Isaac.

"Yes, and the maid-of-honor. Mr. Clarke, will you say something appropriate?" asked Colonel Zane.

Rising, Clarke said: "I would be glad to speak fittingly on this occasion, but I do not think I can do it justice. I believe as Colonel Zane does, that this Indian Princess is the first link in that chain of peace which will some day unite the red men and the white men. Instead of the White Crane she should be called the White Dove. Gentlemen, rise and drink to her long life and happiness."

The toast was drunk. Then Clarke refilled his cup and holding it high over his head he looked at Betty.

"Gentlemen, to the maid-of-honor. Miss Zane, your health, your happiness, in this good old wine."

"I thank you," murmured Betty with downcast eyes. "I bid you all good-night. Come, Myeerah."

Once more alone with Betty, the Indian girl turned to her with eyes like twin stars.

"My sister has made me very happy," whispered Myeerah, in her soft, low voice. "Myeerah's heart is full."

"I believe you are happy, for I know you love Isaac dearly."

"Myeerah has always loved him. She will love his sister."

"And I will love you," said Betty. "I will love you because you have saved him. Ah! Myeerah, yours has been a wonderful, wonderful love."

"My sister is loved," whispered Myeerah. "Myeerah saw the look in the eyes of the great hunter. It was the sad light of the moon on the water. He loves you. And the other looked at my sister with eyes like the blue of northern skies. He, too, loves you."

"Hush!" whispered Betty, trembling and hiding her face. "Hush! Myeerah, do not speak of him."

CHAPTER 11

The following afternoon the sun shone fair and warm; the sweet smell of the tan-bark pervaded the air; and the birds sang their gladsome songs. The scene before the grim, battle-scarred old fort was not without its picturesqueness. The low vine-covered cabins on the hillside looked more like picture houses than like real habitations of men; the mill with its burned-out roof—a reminder of the Indians—and its great wheel, now silent and still, might have been from its lonely and dilapidated appearance a hundred years old.

On a little knoll carpeted with velvety grass sat Isaac and his Indian bride. He had selected this vantage point because it afforded a fine view of the green square where the races and the matches were to take place. Admiring women stood around him and gazed at his wife. They gossiped in whispers about her white skin, her little hands, her beauty. The girls stared with wide open and wondering eyes. The youngsters ran round and round the little group; they pushed each other over, and rolled in the long grass, and screamed with delight.

It was to be a gala occasion and every man, woman and child in the settlement had assembled on the green. Col-

onel Zane and Sam were planting a post in the center of
the square. It was to be used in the shooting matches. Captain Boggs and Major McColloch were arranging the
contestants in order. Jonathan Zane, Will Martin, Alfred
Clarke—all the young men were carefully charging and
priming their rifles. Betty was sitting on the black stallion which Colonel Zane had generously offered as first
prize. She was in the gayest of moods and had just coaxed
Isaac to lift her on the tall horse, from which height she
purposed watching the sports. Wetzel alone did not seem
infected by the spirit of gladsomeness which pervaded.
He stood apart leaning on his long rifle and taking no interest in the proceedings behind him. He was absorbed
in contemplating the forest on the opposite shore of the
river.

"Well, boys, I guess we are ready for the fun," called
Colonel Zane, cheerily. "Only one shot apiece, mind you,
except in case of a tie. Now, everybody shoot his best."

The first contest was a shooting match known as "driving the nail." It was as the name indicated, nothing less
than shooting at the head of a nail. In the absence of a
nail—for nails were scarce—one was usually fashioned
from a knife blade, or an old file, or even a piece of silver. The nail was driven lightly into the stake, the contestants shot at it from a distance as great as the eyesight
permitted. To drive the nail hard and fast into the wood
at one hundred yards was a feat seldom accomplished. By
many hunters it was deemed more difficult than "snuff-
ing the candle," another border pastime, which consisted
of placing in the dark at any distance a lighted candle, and
then putting out the flame with a single rifle ball. Many
settlers, particularly those who handled the plow more
than the rifle, sighted from a rest, and placed a piece of
moss under the rifle-barrel to prevent its spring at the
discharge.

The match began. Of the first six shooters Jonathan Zane and Alfred Clarke scored the best shots. Each placed a bullet in the half-inch circle round the nail.

"Alfred, very good, indeed," said Colonel Zane. "You have made a decided improvement since the last shooting match."

Six other settlers took their turns. All were unsuccessful in getting a shot inside the little circle. Thus a tie between Alfred and Jonathan had to be decided.

"Shoot close, Alfred," yelled Isaac. "I hope you beat him. He always won from me and then crowed over it."

Alfred's second shot went wide of the mark, and as Jonathan placed another bullet in the circle, this time nearer the center, Alfred had to acknowledge defeat.

"Here comes Miller," said Silas Zane. "Perhaps he will want a try."

Colonel Zane looked round. Miller had joined the party. He carried his rifle and accoutrements, and evidently had just returned to the settlement. He nodded pleasantly to all.

"Miller, will you take a shot for the first prize, which I was about to award to Jonathan?" said Colonel Zane.

"No. I am a little late, and not entitled to a shot. I will take a try for the others," answered Miller.

At the arrival of Miller on the scene Wetzel had changed his position to one nearer the crowd. The dog, Tige, trotted closely at his heels. No one heard Tige's low growl or Wetzel's stern word to silence him. Throwing his arm over Betty's pony, Wetzel apparently watched the shooters. In reality he studied intently Miller's every movement.

"I expect some good shooting for this prize," said Colonel Zane, waving a beautifully embroidered buckskin bullet pouch, which was one of Betty's donations.

Jonathan having won his prize was out of the lists and

could compete no more. This entitled Alfred to the first shot for second prize. He felt he would give anything he possessed to win the dainty trifle which the Colonel had waved aloft. Twice he raised his rifle in his exceeding earnestness to score a good shot and each time lowered the barrel. When finally he did shoot the bullet embedded itself in the second circle. It was a good shot, but he knew it would never win that prize.

"A little nervous, eh?" remarked Miller, with a half sneer on his swarthy face.

Several young settlers followed in succession, but their aims were poor. Then little Harry Bennet took his stand. Harry had won many prizes in former matches, and many of the pioneers considered him one of the best shots in the country.

"Only a few more after you, Harry," said Colonel Zane. "You have a good chance."

"All right, Colonel. That's Betty's prize and somebody'll have to do some mighty tall shootin' to beat me," said the lad, his blue eyes flashing as he toed the mark.

Shouts and cheers of approval greeted his attempt. The bullet had passed into the wood so close to the nail that a knife blade could not have been inserted between.

Miller's turn came next. He was a fine marksman and he knew it. With the confidence born of long experience and knowledge of his weapons, he took a careful though quick aim and fired. He turned away satisfied that he would carry off the coveted prize. He had nicked the nail.

But Miller reckoned without his host. Betty had seen the result of his shot and the self-satisfied smile on his face. She watched several of the settlers make poor attempts at the nail, and then, convinced that not one of the other contestants could do so well as Miller, she slipped off the horse and ran around to where Wetzel was standing by her pony.

"Lew, I believe Miller will win my prize," she whispered, placing her hand on the hunter's arm. "He has scratched the nail, and I am sure no one except you can do better. I do not want Miller to have anything of mine."

"And, little girl, you want me to shoot fer you," said Lewis.

"Yes, Lew, please come and shoot for me."

It was said of Wetzel that he never wasted powder. He never entered into the races and shooting-matches of the settlers, yet it was well known that he was the fleetest runner and the most unerring shot on the frontier. Therefore, it was with surprise and pleasure that Colonel Zane heard the hunter say he guessed he would like one shot anyway.

Miller looked on with a grim smile. He knew that, Wetzel or no Wetzel, it would take a remarkably clever shot to beat his.

"This shot's fer Betty," said Wetzel as he stepped to the mark. He fastened his keen eyes on the stake. At that distance the head of the nail looked like a tiny black speck. Wetzel took one of the locks of hair that waved over his broad shoulders and held it up in front of his eyes a moment. He thus ascertained that there was not any perceptible breeze. The long black barrel started slowly to rise—it seemed to the interested onlookers that it would never reach a level—and when, at last, it became rigid, there was a single second in which man and rifle appeared as if carved out of stone. Then followed a burst of red flame, a puff of white smoke, a clear ringing report.

Many thought the hunter had missed altogether. It seemed that the nail had not changed its position; there was no bullet hole in the white lime wash that had been smeared round the nail. But on close inspection the nail was found to have been driven to its head in the wood.

"A wonderful shot!" exclaimed Colonel Zane. "Lewis, I don't remember having seen the like more than once or twice in my life."

Wetzel made no answer. He moved away to his former position and commenced to reload his rifle. Betty came running up to him, holding in her hand the prize bullet pouch.

"Oh, Lew, if I dared I would kiss you. It pleases me more for you to have won my prize than if any one else had won it. And it was the finest, straightest shot ever made."

"Betty, it's a little fancy for redskins, but it'll be a keepsake," answered Lewis, his eyes reflecting the bright smile on her face.

Friendly rivalry in feats that called for strength, speed and daring was the diversion of the youth of that period, and the pioneers conducted this good-natured but spirited sport strictly on its merits. Each contestant strove his utmost to outdo his opponent. It was hardly to be expected that Alfred would carry off any of the laurels. Used as he had been to comparative idleness he was no match for the hardy lads who had been brought up and trained to a life of action, wherein a ten-mile walk behind a plow, or a cord of wood chopped in a day, were trifles. Alfred lost in the foot-race and the sack-race, but by dint of exerting himself to the limit of his strength, he did manage to take one fall out of the best wrestler. He was content to stop here, and, throwing himself on the grass, endeavored to recover his breath. He felt happier today than for some time past. Twice during the afternoon he had met Betty's eyes and the look he encountered there made his heart stir with a strange feeling of fear and hope. While he was ruminating on what had happened between Betty and himself he allowed his eyes to wander from one person to another. When his gaze alighted on Wetzel it became riveted there. The hunter's attitude struck him as singular. Wetzel had his face half turned toward the boys romping near him and he leaned carelessly against a white oak tree. But a close observer would have seen, as Alfred did, that there was a certain alertness in that rigid and motionless figure. Wetzel's eyes were fixed on the western end of the island. Almost involuntarily Alfred's eyes sought the same direction. The western end of the island ran out into a long low point covered with briars, rushes and saw grass. As Alfred directed his gaze along the water line of this point he distinctly saw a dark form flit from one bush to another. He was positive he had not been mistaken. He got up slowly and unconcernedly, and strolled over to Wetzel.

"Wetzel, I saw an object just now," he said in a low tone. "It was moving behind those bushes at the head of the island. I am not sure whether it was an animal or an Indian."

"Injuns. Go back and be natur'l like. Don't say nothin' and watch Miller," whispered Wetzel.

Much perturbed by the developments of the last few moments, and wondering what was going to happen, Alfred turned away. He had scarcely reached the others when he heard Betty's voice raised in indignant protest.

"I tell you I did swim my pony across the river," cried Betty. "It was just even with that point and the river was higher than it is now."

"You probably overestimated your feat," said Miller, with his disagreeable, doubtful smile. "I have seen the river so low that it could be waded, and then it would be a very easy matter to cross. But now your pony could not swim half the distance."

"I'll show you," answered Betty, her black eyes flashing. She put her foot in the stirrup and leaped on Madcap.

"Now, Betty, don't try that foolish ride again," implored Mrs. Zane. "What do you care whether strangers believe it or not? Eb, make her come back."

Colonel Zane only laughed and made no attempt to detain Betty. He rather indulged her caprices.

"Stop her!" cried Clarke.

"Betty, where are you goin'?" said Wetzel, grabbing at Madcap's bridle. But Betty was too quick for him. She avoided the hunter, and with a saucy laugh she wheeled the fiery little pony and urged her over the bank. Almost before any one could divine her purpose she had Madcap in the water up to her knees.

"Betty, stop!" cried Wetzel.

She paid no attention to his call. In another moment the pony would be off the shoal and swimming.

"Stop! Turn back, Betty, or I'll shoot the pony," shouted Wetzel, and this time there was a ring of deadly earnestness in his voice. With the words he had cocked and thrown forward the long rifle.

Betty heard, and in alarm she turned her pony. She looked up with great surprise and concern, for she knew Wetzel was not one to trifle.

"For God's sake!" exclaimed Colonel Zane, looking in amazement at the hunter's face, which was now white and stern.

"Why, Lew, you do not mean you would shoot Madcap?" said Betty, reproachfully, as she reached the shore.

All present in that watching crowd were silent, awaiting the hunter's answer. They felt that mysterious power which portends the revelation of strange events. Colonel Zane and Jonathan knew the instant they saw Wetzel that something extraordinary was coming. His face had grown cold and gray; his lips were tightly compressed; his eyes dilated and shone with a peculiar lustre.

"Where were you headin' your pony?" asked Wetzel.

"I wanted to reach that point where the water is shallow," answered Betty.

"That's what I thought. Well, Betty, hostile Injuns are hidin' and waitin' fer you in them high rushes right where you were makin' fer," said Wetzel. Then he shouldered his rifle and walked rapidly away.

"Oh, he cannot be serious!" cried Betty. "Oh, how foolish I am."

"Get back up from the river, everybody," commanded Colonel Zane.

"Colonel Zane," said Clarke, walking beside the Colonel up the bank, "I saw Wetzel watching the island in a manner that I thought odd, under the circumstances, and I watched too. Presently I saw a dark form dart behind a bush. I went over and told Wetzel, and he said there were Indians on the island."

"This is most damn strange," said Colonel Zane, frowning heavily. "Wetzel's suspicions, Miller turns up, teases Betty attempting that foolhardy trick, and then—Indians! It may be a coincidence, but it looks bad."

"Colonel Zane, don't you think Wetzel may be mistaken?" said Miller, coming up. "I came over from the other side this morning and I did not see any Indian sign. Probably Wetzel has caused needless excitement."

"It does not follow that because you came from over the river there are no Indians there," answered Colonel Zane, sharply. "Do you presume to criticise Wetzel's judgment?"

"I saw an Indian!" cried Clarke, facing Miller with blazing eyes. "And if you say I did not, you lie! What is more, I believe you know more than any one else about it. I watched you. I saw you were uneasy and that you looked across the river from time to time. Perhaps you had better explain to Colonel Zane the reason you taunted his sister into attempting that ride."

With a snarl more like that of a tiger than of a human being, Miller sprang at Clarke. His face was dark with malignant hatred as he reached for and drew an ugly knife. There were cries of fright from the children and screams from the women. Alfred stepped aside with the wonderful quickness of the trained boxer and shot out his right arm. His fist caught Miller a hard blow on the head, knocking him down and sending the knife flying in the air.

It had all happened so quickly that everyone was as if paralyzed. The settlers stood still and watched Miller rise slowly to his feet.

"Give me my knife!" he cried hoarsely. The knife had fallen at the feet of Major McColloch, who had concealed it with his foot.

"Let this end right here," ordered Colonel Zane. "Clarke, you have made a very strong statement. Have you anything to substantiate your words?"

"I think I have," said Clarke. He was standing erect, his face white and his eyes like blue steel. "I knew him at Fort Pitt. He was a liar and a drunkard there. He was a friend of the Indians and of the British. What he was there he must be here. It was Wetzel who told me to watch him. Wetzel and I both think he knew the Indians were on the island."

"Colonel Zane, it is false," said Miller, huskily. "He is trying to put you against me. He hates me because your sister————"

"You cur!" cried Clarke, striking at Miller. Colonel Zane struck up the infuriated young man's arm.

"Give us knives, or anything," panted Clarke.

"Yes, let us fight it out now," said Miller.

"Captain Boggs, take Clarke to the blockhouse. Make him stay there if you have to lock him up," commanded Colonel Zane. "Miller, as for you, I cannot condemn you without proof. If I knew positively that there were Indians on the island and that you were aware of it, you would be a dead man in less time than it takes to say it. I will give you the benefit of the doubt and twenty-four hours to leave the Fort."

The villagers dispersed and went to their homes. They were inclined to take Clarke's side. Miller had become disliked. His drinking habits and his arrogant and bold manner had slowly undermined the friendships he had made during the early part of his stay at Fort Henry; while Clarke's good humor and willingness to help any one, his gentleness with the children, and his several acts of heroism had strengthened their regard.

"Jonathan, this looks like some of Girty's work. I wish I knew the truth," said Colonel Zane, as he, his brothers and Betty and Myeerah entered the house. "Confound it! We can't have even one afternoon of enjoyment. I must see Lewis. I cannot be sure of Clarke. He is evidently bitter against Miller. That would have been a terrible fight. Those fellows have had trouble before, and I am afraid we have not seen the last of their quarrel."

"If they meet again—but how can you keep them apart?" said Silas. "If Miller leaves the Fort without killing Clarke he'll hide around in the woods and wait for a chance to shoot him."

"Not with Wetzel here," answered Colonel Zane. "Betty, do you see what your——" he began, turning to his sister, but when he saw her white and miserable face he said no more.

"Don't mind, Betts. It wasn't any fault of yours," said Isaac, putting his arm tenderly round the trembling girl. "I for another believe Clarke was right when he said Miller knew there were Indians over the river. It looks like a plot to abduct you. Have no fear for Alfred. He can take care of himself. He showed that pretty well."

An hour later Clarke had finished his supper and was sitting by his window smoking his pipe. His anger had cooled somewhat and his reflections were not of the pleasantest kind. He regretted that he lowered himself so far as to fight with a man little better than an outlaw. Still there was a grim satisfaction in the thought of the blow he had given Miller. He remembered he had asked for a knife and that his enemy and he be permitted to fight to the death. After all to have ended, then and there, the feud between them would have been the better course; for he well knew Miller's desperate character, that he had killed more than one white man, and that now a fair fight might not be possible. Well, he thought, what did it matter? He was not going to worry himself. He did not care much, one way or another. He had no home; he could not make one without the woman he loved. He was a Soldier of Fortune; he was at the mercy of Fate, and he would drift along and let what came be welcome. A soft footfall on the stairs and a knock on the door interrupted his thoughts.

"Come in," he said.

The door opened and Wetzel strode into the room.

"I came over to say somethin' to you," said the hunter, taking the chair by the window and placing his rifle over his knee.

"I will be pleased to listen or talk, as you desire," said Alfred.

"I don't mind tellin' you that the punch you give Miller was what he deserved. If he and Girty didn't hatch up that trick to ketch Betty, I don't know nothin'. But we can't prove nothin' on him yet. Mebbe he knew about the redskins; mebbe he didn't. Personally, I think he did. But I can't kill a white man because I think somethin'. I'd have to know fer sure. What I want to say is to put you on your guard against the baddest man on the river."

"I am aware of that," answered Alfred. "I knew his record at Fort Pitt. What would you have me do?"

"Keep close till he's gone."

"That would be cowardly."

"No, it wouldn't. He'd shoot you from behind some tree or cabin."

"Well, I'm much obliged to you for your kind advice, but for all that I won't stay in the house," said Alfred, beginning to wonder at the hunter's earnest manner.

"You're in love with Betty, ain't you?"

The question came with Wetzel's usual bluntness and it staggered Alfred. He could not be angry, and he did not know what to say. The hunter went on:

"You needn't say so, because I know it. And I know she loves you and that's why I want you to look out fer Miller."

"My God! man, you're crazy," said Alfred, laughing scornfully. "She cares nothing for me."

"That's your great failin', young feller. You fly off'en the handle too easy. And so does Betty. You both care fer each other and are unhappy about it. Now, you don't know Betty, and she keeps misunderstandin' you."

"For Heaven's sake! Wetzel, if you know anything tell me. Love her? Why, the words are weak! I love her so well that an hour ago I would have welcomed death at Miller's hands only to fall and die at her feet defending her. Your words set me on fire. What right have you to say that? How do you know?"

The hunter leaned forward and put his hand on Alfred's shoulder. On his pale face was that sublime light which comes to great souls when they give up a life long secret, or when they sacrifice what is best loved. His broad chest heaved: his deep voice trembled.

"Listen. I'm not a man fer words, and it's hard to tell. Betty loves you. I've carried her in my arms when she was a baby. I've made her toys and played with her when she was a little girl. I know all her moods. I can read her like I do the moss, and the leaves, and the bark of the forest. I've loved her all my life. That's why I know she loves you. I can feel it. Her happiness is the only dear thing left on earth fer me. And that's why I'm your friend."

In the silence that followed his words the door opened and closed and he was gone.

Betty awoke with a start. She was wide awake in a second. The moonbeams came through the leaves of the maple tree near her window and cast fantastic shadows on the wall of her room. Betty lay quiet, watching the fairy-like figures on the wall and listening intently. What had awakened her? The night was still; the crow of a cock in the distance proclaimed that the hour of dawn was near at hand. She waited for Tige's bark under her window, or Sam's voice, or the kicking and trampling of horses in the barn—sounds that usually broke her slumbers in the morning. But no such noises were forthcoming. Suddenly she heard a light, quick tap, tap, and then a rattling in the corner. It was like no sound but that made by a pebble striking the floor, bounding and rolling across the room. There it was again. Some one was tossing stones in at her window. She slipped out of bed, ran, and leaned on the windowsill and looked out. The moon was going down behind the hill, but there was light enough for her to distinguish objects. She saw a dark figure crouching by the fence.

"Who is it?" said Betty, a little frightened, but more curious.

"Sh-h-h, it's Miller," came the answer, spoken in a low voice.

The bent form straightened and stood erect. It stepped forward under Betty's window. The light was dim, but

Betty recognized the dark face of Miller. He carried a rifle in his hand and a pack on his shoulder.

"Go away, or I'll call my brother. I will not listen to you," said Betty, making a move to leave the window.

"Sh-h-h, not so loud," said Miller, in a quick, hoarse whisper. "You'd better listen. I am going across the border to join Girty. He is going to bring the Indians and the British here to burn the settlement. If you will go away with me I'll save the lives of your brothers and their families. I have aided Girty and I have influence with him. If you won't go you'll be taken captive and you'll see all your friends and relatives scalped and burned. Quick, your answer."

"Never, traitor! Monster! I'd be burned at the stake before I'd go a step with you!" cried Betty.

"Then remember that you've crossed a desperate man. If you escape the massacre you will beg on your knees to me. This settlement is doomed. Now, go to your white-faced lover. You'll find him cold. Ha! Ha! Ha!" and with a taunting laugh he leaped the fence and disappeared in the gloom.

Betty sank to the floor stunned, horrified. She shuddered at the malignity expressed in Miller's words. How had she ever been deceived in him? He was in league with Girty. At heart he was a savage, a renegade. Betty went over his words, one by one.

"Your white-faced lover. You will find him cold," whispered Betty. "What did he mean?"

Then came the thought. Miller had murdered Clarke. Betty gave one agonized quiver, as if a knife had been thrust into her side, and then her paralyzed limbs recovered the power of action. She flew out into the passageway and pounded on her brother's door.

"Eb! Eb! Get up! Quickly, for God's sake!" she cried. A smothered exclamation, a woman's quick voice, the heavy thud of feet striking the floor followed Betty's alarm. Then the door opened.

"Hello, Betts, what's up!" said Colonel Zane, in his rapid voice.

At the same moment the door at the end of the hall opened and Isaac came out.

"Eb, Betty, I heard voices outdoors and in the house. What's the row?"

"Oh, Isaac! Oh, Eb! Something terrible has happened!" cried Betty, breathlessly.

"Then it is no time to get excited," said the Colonel, calmly. He placed his arm round Betty and drew her into the room. "Isaac, get down the rifles. Now, Betty, time is precious. Tell me quickly, briefly."

"I was awakened by a stone rolling on the floor. I ran to the window and saw a man by the fence. He came under my window and I saw it was Miller. He said he was going to join Girty. He said if I would go with him he would save the lives of all my relatives. If I would not they would all be killed, massacred, burned alive, and I would be taken away as his captive. I told him I'd rather die before I'd go with him. Then he said we were all doomed, and that my white-faced lover was already cold. With that he gave a laugh which made my flesh creep and ran off toward the river. Oh! he has murdered Mr. Clarke."

"Hell! What a fiend!" cried Colonel Zane, hurriedly getting into his clothes. "Betts, you had a gun in there. Why didn't you shoot him? Why didn't I pay more attention to Wetzel's advice?"

"You should have allowed Clarke to kill him yesterday," said Isaac. "Like as not he'll have Girty here with a lot of howling devils. What's to be done?"

"I'll send Wetzel after him and that'll soon wind up his ball of yarn," answered Colonel Zane.

"Please—go—and find—if Mr. Clarke——"

"Yes, Betty, I'll go at once. You must not lose courage, Betty. It's quite possible that Miller has killed Alfred and there's worse to follow."

"I'll come, Eb, as soon as I have told Myeerah. She is scared half to death," said Isaac, starting for the door.

"All right, only hurry," said Colonel Zane, grabbing his rifle. Without wasting more words, and lacing up his hunting shirt as he went he ran out of the room.

The first rays of dawn came streaking in at the window. The chill gray light brought no cheer with its herald of the birth of another day. For what might the morning sun disclose? It might shine on a long line of painted Indians. The fresh breeze from over the river might bring the long war-whoop of the savage.

No wonder Noah and his brother, awakened by the voices of their father, sat up in their little bed and looked about with frightened eyes. No wonder Mrs. Zane's face blanched. How many times she had seen her husband grasp his rifle and run out to meet danger!

"Bessie," said Betty. "If it's true I will not be able to bear it. It's all my fault."

"Nonsense! You heard Eb say Miller and Clarke had quarreled before. They hated each other before they ever saw you."

A door banged, quick footsteps sounded on the stairs, and Isaac came rushing into the room. Betty, deathly pale, stood with her hands pressed to her bosom, and looked at Isaac with a question in her eyes that her tongue could not speak.

"Betty, Alfred's badly hurt, but he's alive. I can tell you no more now," said Isaac. "Bessie, bring your needle, silk linen, liniment—everything you need for a bad knife wound, and come quickly."

Betty's haggard face changed as if some warm light had

been reflected on it; her lips moved, and with a sob of thankfulness she fled to her room.

Two hours later, while Annie was serving breakfast to Betty and Myeerah, Colonel Zane strode into the room.

"Well, one has to eat whatever happens," he said, his clouded face brightening somewhat. "Betty, there's been bad work, bad work. When I got to Clarke's room, I found him lying on the bed with a knife sticking in him. As it is we are doubtful about pulling him through."

"May I see him?" whispered Betty, with pale lips.

"If the worst comes to the worst I'll take you over. But it would do no good now and would surely unnerve you. He still has a fighting chance."

"Did they fight, or was Mr. Clarke stabbed in his sleep?"

"Miller climbed into Clarke's window and knifed him in the dark. As I came over I met Wetzel and told him I wanted him to trail Miller and find if there is any truth in his threat about Girty and the Indians. Sam just now found Tige tied fast in the fence corner back of the barn. That explains the mystery of Miller's getting so near the house. You know he always took pains to make friends with Tige. The poor dog was helpless; his legs were tied and his jaw bound fast. Oh, Miller is as cunning as an Indian! He has had this all planned out, and he has had more than one arrow to his bow. But, if I mistake not he has shot his last one."

"Miller must be safe from pursuit by this time," said Betty.

"Safe for the present, yes," answered Colonel Zane, "but while Jonathan and Wetzel live I would not give a snap of my fingers for Miller's chances. Hello, I hear some one talking. I sent for Jack and the Major."

The Colonel threw open the door. Wetzel, Major

McColloch, Jonathan and Silas Zane were approaching. They were all heavily armed. Wetzel was equipped for a long chase. Double leggins were laced round his legs. A buckskin knapsack was strapped to his shoulders.

"Major, I want you and Jonathan to watch the river," said Colonel Zane. "Silas, you are to go to the mouth of Yellow Creek and reconnoiter. We are in for a siege. It may be twenty-four hours and it may be ten days. In the meantime I will get the Fort in shape to meet the attack. Lewis, you have your orders. Have you anything to suggest?"

"I'll take the dog," answered Wetzel. "He'll save time for me. I'll stick to Miller's trail and find Girty's forces. I've believed all along that Miller was helpin' Girty, and I'm thinkin' that where Miller goes there I'll find Girty and his redskins. If it's night when I get back I'll give the call of the hoot-owl three times, quick, so Jack and the Major will know I want to get back acrost the river."

"All right, Lewis, we'll be expecting you any time," said Colonel Zane.

"Betty, I'm goin' now and I want to tell you somethin'," said Wetzel, as Betty appeared in the door. "Come as far as the end of the path with me."

"I'm sorry you must go. But Tige seems delighted," said Betty, walking beside Wetzel, while the dog ran on before.

"Betty, I wanted to tell you to stay close like to the house, fer this feller Miller has been layin' traps fer you, and the Injuns is on the war-path. Don't ride your pony, and stay home now."

"Indeed, I shall never again do anything as foolish as I did yesterday. I have learned my lesson. And Oh! Lew, I am so grateful to you for saving me. When will you return to the Fort?"

"Mebbe never, Betty."

"Oh, no. Don't say that. I know all this Indian talk will blow over, as it always does, and you will come back and everything will be all right again."

"I hope it'll be as you say, Betty, but there's no tellin', there's no tellin'."

"You are going to see if the Indians are making preparations to besiege the Fort?"

"Yes, I am goin' fer that. And if I happen to find Miller on my way I'll give him Betty's regards."

Betty shivered at his covert meaning. Long ago in a moment of playfulness, Betty had scratched her name on the hunter's rifle. Ever after that Wetzel called his fatal weapon by her name.

"If you were going simply to avenge me I would not let you go. That wretch will get his just due some day, never fear for that."

"Betty, 'taint likely he'll get away from me, and if he does there's Jonathan. This mornin' when we trailed Miller down to the riverbank Jonathan points acrost the river and says: 'You or me,' and I says: 'Me,' so it's all settled."

"Will Mr. Clarke live?" said Betty, in an altered tone, asking the question which was uppermost in her mind.

"I think so, I hope so. He's a husky young chap and the cut wasn't bad. He lost so much blood. That's why he's so weak. If he gets well he'll have somethin' to tell you."

"Lew, what do you mean?" demanded Betty, quickly.

"Me and him had a long talk last night and——"

"You did not go to him and talk of me, did you?" said Betty, reproachfully.

They had now reached the end of the path. Wetzel stopped and dropped the butt of his rifle on the ground. Tige looked on and wagged his tail. Presently the hunter spoke.

"Yes, we talked about you."

"Oh! Lewis. What did—could you have said?" faltered Betty.

"You think I hadn't ought to speak to him of you?"

"I do not see why you should. Of course you are my good friend, but he—it is not like you to speak of me."

"Fer once I don't agree with you. I knew how it was with him so I told him. I knew how it was with you so I told him, and I know how it is with me, so I told him that too."

"With you?" whispered Betty.

"Yes, with me. That kind of gives me a right, don't it, considerin' it's all fer your happiness?"

"With you?" echoed Betty in a low tone. She was beginning to realize that she had not known this man. She looked up at him. His eyes were misty with an unutterable sadness.

"Oh, no! No! Lew. Say it is not true," she cried, piteously. All in a moment Betty's burdens became too heavy for her. She wrung her little hands. Her brother's kindly advice, Bessie's warnings, and old Grandmother Watkins's words came back to her. For the first time she believed what they said—that Wetzel loved her. All at once the scales fell from her eyes and she saw this man as he really was. All the thousand and one things he had done for her, his simple teaching, his thoughtfulness, his faithfulness, and his watchful protection—all came crowding on her as debts that she could never pay. For now what could she give this man to whom she owed more than her life? Nothing. It was too late. Her love could have reclaimed him, could have put an end to that solitary wandering, and have made him a good, happy man.

"Yes, Betty, it's time to tell it. I've loved you always," he said softly.

She covered her face and sobbed. Wetzel put his arm round her and drew her to him until the dark head rested on his shoulder. Thus they stood a moment.

"Don't cry, little one," he said, tenderly. "Don't grieve fer me. My love fer you has been the only good in my life. It's been happiness to love you. Don't think of me. I can see you and Alfred in a happy home, surrounded by bright-eyed children. There'll be a brave lad named fer me, and when I come, if I ever do, I'll tell him stories, and learn him the secrets of the woods, and how to shoot, and things I know so well."

"I am so wretched—so miserable. To think I have been so—so blind, and I have teased you—and—it might have been—only now it's too late," said Betty, between her sobs.

"Yes, I know, and it's better so. This man you love rings true. He has learnin' and edication. I have nothin' but muscle and a quick eye. And that'll serve you and Alfred when you are in danger. I'm goin' now. Stand here till I'm out of sight."

"Kiss me goodbye," whispered Betty.

The hunter bent his head and kissed her on the brow. Then he turned and with a rapid step went along the bluff toward the west. When he reached the laurel bushes which fringed the edge of the forest he looked back. He saw the slender gray clad figure standing motionless in the narrow path. He waved his hand and then turned and plunged into the forest. The dog looked back, raised his head and gave a long, mournful howl. Then, he too disappeared.

A mile west of the settlement Wetzel abandoned the forest and picked his way down the steep bluff to the river. Here he prepared to swim to the western shore. He took off his buckskin garments, spread them out on the ground, placed his knapsack in the middle, and rolling all into a small bundle tied it round his rifle. Grasping the rifle just above the hammer he waded into the water up to his waist and then, turning easily on his back he held the rifle straight up, allowing the butt to rest on his breast. This left his right arm unhampered. With a powerful back-arm stroke he rapidly swam the river, which was deep and narrow at this point. In a quarter of an hour he was once more in his dry suit.

He was now two miles below the island, where yesterday the Indians had been concealed, and where this morning Miller had crossed. Wetzel knew Miller expected to be trailed, and that he would use every art and cunning of woodcraft to elude his pursuers, or to lead them into a death trap. Wetzel believed Miller had joined the Indians, who had undoubtedly been waiting for him, or for a signal from him, and that he would use them to ambush the trail.

Therefore Wetzel decided he would try to strike Miller's tracks far west of the river. He risked a great deal in attempting this because it was possible he might fail to find any trace of the spy. But Wetzel wasted not one second. His course was chosen. With all possible speed, which meant with him walking only when he could not run, he traveled northwest. If Miller had taken the direction Wetzel suspected, the trails of the two men would cross about ten miles from the Ohio. But the hunter had not traversed more than a mile of the forest when the dog put his nose high in the air and growled. Wetzel slowed down into a walk and moved cautiously onward, peering through the green aisles of the woods. A few rods farther on Tige uttered another growl and put his nose to the ground. He found a trail. On examination Wetzel discovered in the moss two moccasin tracks. Two Indians had passed that point that morning. They were going northwest directly toward the camp of Wingenund. Wetzel stuck close to the trail all that day and an hour before dusk he heard the sharp crack of a rifle. A moment afterward a doe came crashing through the thicket to Wetzel's right and bounding across a little brook she disappeared.

A tree with a bushy, leafy top had been uprooted by a storm and had fallen across the stream at this point. Wetzel crawled among the branches. The dog followed and lay down beside him. Before darkness set in Wetzel saw that the clear water of the brook had been roiled; therefore, he concluded that somewhere upstream Indians had waded into the brook. Probably they had killed a deer and were getting their evening meal.

Hours passed. Twilight deepened into darkness. One by one the stars appeared; then the crescent moon rose over the wooded hill in the west, and the hunter never moved. With his head leaning against the log he sat quiet and patient. At midnight he whispered to the dog, and crawling from his hiding place glided stealthily up the stream. Far ahead from the dark depths of the forest peeped the flickering light of a campfire. Wetzel consumed a half hour in approaching within one hundred feet of this light. Then he got down on his hands and knees and crawled behind a tree on top of the little ridge which had obstructed a view of the camp scene.

From this vantage point Wetzel saw a clear space surrounded by pines and hemlocks. In the center of this glade a fire burned briskly. Two Indians lay wrapped in their blankets, sound asleep. Wetzel pressed the dog close to the ground, laid aside his rifle, drew his tomahawk, and lying flat on his breast commenced to work his way, inch by inch, toward the sleeping savages. The tall ferns trembled as the hunter wormed his way among them, but there was no sound, not a snapping of a twig nor a rustling of a leaf. The night-wind sighed softly through the pines; it blew the bright sparks from the burning logs, and fanned the embers into a red glow; it swept caressingly over the sleeping savages, but it could not warn them that another wind, the Wind-of-Death, was near at hand.

A quarter of an hour elapsed. Nearer and nearer; slowly but surely drew the hunter. With what wonderful patience and self-control did this cold-blooded Nemesis approach his victims! Probably any other Indian slayer would have fired his rifle and then rushed to combat with a knife or a tomahawk. Not so Wetzel. He scorned to use powder. He crept forward like a snake gliding upon its prey. He slid one hand in front of him and pressed it down on the moss, at first gently, then firmly, and when he had secured a good hold he slowly dragged his body forward the length of his arm. At last his dark form rose and stood over the unconscious Indians, like a minister of Doom. The tomahawk flashed once, twice in the firelight, and the Indians, without a moan, and with a convulsive quivering and straightening of their bodies, passed from the tired sleep of nature to the eternal sleep of death.

Foregoing his usual custom of taking the scalps, Wetzel hurriedly left the glade. He had found that the Indians were Shawnees and he had expected they were Delawares. He knew Miller's red comrades belonged to the latter tribe. The presence of Shawnees so near the settlement confirmed his belief that a concerted movement was to be made on the whites in the near future. He would not have been surprised to find the woods full of redskins. He spent the remainder of that night close under the side of a log with the dog curled up beside him.

Next morning Wetzel ran across the trail of a white man and six Indians. He tracked them all that day and half of the night before he again rested. By noon of the following day he came in sight of the cliff from which Jonathan Zane had watched the sufferings of Colonel Crawford. Wetzel now made his favorite move, a wide detour, and came up on the other side of the encampment.

From the top of the bluff he saw down into the village of the Delawares. The valley was alive with Indians; they were working like beavers; some with weapons, some painting themselves, and others dancing war-dances. Packs were being strapped on the backs of ponies. Everywhere was the hurry and bustle of the preparation for war. The dancing and the singing were kept up half the night.

At daybreak Wetzel was at his post. A little after sunrise he heard a long yell which he believed announced the arrival of an important party. And so it turned out. Amid shrill yelling and whooping, the like of which Wetzel had never before heard, Simon Girty rode into Wingenund's camp at the head of one hundred Shawnee warriors and two hundred British Rangers from Detroit. Wetzel recoiled when he saw the red uniforms of the Britishers and their bayonets. Including Pipe's and Wingenund's braves the total force which was going to march against the Fort exceeded six hundred. An impotent frenzy possessed Wetzel as he watched the orderly marching of the Rangers and the proud bearing of the Indian warriors. Miller had spoken the truth. Fort Henry was doomed.

"Tige, there's one of them struttin' turkey cocks as won't see the Ohio," said Wetzel to the dog.

Hurriedly slipping from round his neck the bullet-pouch that Betty had given him, he shook out a bullet and with the point of his knife he scratched deep in the soft lead the letter W. Then he cut the bullet half through. This done he detached the pouch from the cord and running the cord through the cut in the bullet he bit the lead. He tied the string round the neck of the dog and pointing eastward he said: "Home."

The intelligent animal understood perfectly. His duty was to get that warning home. His clear brown eyes as much as said: "I will not fail." He wagged his tail, licked the hunter's hand, bounded away and disappeared in the forest.

Wetzel rested easier in mind. He knew the dog would stop for nothing, and that he stood a far better chance of reaching the Fort in safety than did he himself.

With a lurid light in his eyes Wetzel now turned to the Indians. He would never leave that spot without sending a leaden messenger into the heart of some-one in that camp. Glancing on all sides he at length selected a place where it was possible he might approach near enough to the camp to get a shot. He carefully studied the lay of the ground, the trees, rocks, bushes, grass—everything that could help screen him from the keen eye of savage scouts. When he had marked his course he commenced his perilous descent. In an hour he had reached the bottom of the cliff. Dropping flat on the ground, he once more started his snail-like crawl. A stretch of swampy ground, luxuriant with rushes and saw grass, made a part of the way easy for him, though it led through mud, and slime, and stagnant water. Frogs and turtles warming their backs in the sunshine scampered in alarm from their logs. Lizards blinked at him. Moccasin snakes darted wicked forked tongues at him and then glided out of reach of his tomahawk. The frogs had stopped their deep bass notes. A swamp-blackbird rose in fright from her nest in the saw grass, and twittering plaintively fluttered round and round over the pond. The flight of the bird worried Wetzel. Such little things as these might attract the attention of some Indian scout. But he hoped that in the excitement of the war preparations these unusual disturbances would escape notice. At last he gained the other side of the swamp. At the end of the cornfield before him was the clump of laurel which he had marked from the cliff as his objective point. The Indian corn was now about five feet high. Wetzel passed through this field unseen. He reached the laurel bushes, where he dropped to the ground and lay quiet a few minutes. In the dash which he would soon make to the forest he needed all his breath and all his fleetness. He looked to the right to see how far the woods were from where he lay. Not more than one hundred feet. He was safe. Once in the dark shade of those trees, and with his foes behind him, he could defy the whole race of Delawares. He looked to his rifle, freshened the powder in the pan, carefully adjusted the flint, and then rose quietly to his feet.

Wetzel's keen gaze, as he swept it from left to right, took in every detail of the camp. He was almost in the village. A tepee stood not twenty feet from his hiding-place. He could have tossed a stone in the midst of squaws, and braves, and chiefs. The main body of Indians was in the center of the camp. The British were lined up further on. Both Indians and soldiers were resting on their arms and waiting. Suddenly Wetzel started and his heart leaped. Under a maple tree not one hundred and fifty yards distant stood four men in earnest consultation. One was an Indian. Wetzel recognized the fierce, stern face, the haughty, erect figure. He knew that long, trailing war-bonnet. It could have adorned the head of but one chief—Wingenund, the sachem of the Delawares. A British officer, girdled and epauletted, stood next to Wingenund. Simon Girty, the renegade, and Miller, the traitor, completed the group.

Wetzel sank to his knees. The perspiration poured from his face. The mighty hunter trembled, but it was from eagerness. Was not Girty, the white savage, the bane of the poor settlers, within range of a weapon that never failed? Was not the murderous chieftain, who had once whipped and tortured him, who had burned Crawford alive, there in plain sight? Wetzel revelled a moment in fiendish glee. He passed his hands tenderly over the long barrel of his rifle. In that moment as never before he gloried in his power—a power which enabled him to put a bullet in the eye of a squirrel at the distance these men were from him. But only for an instant did the hunter yield to this feeling. He knew too well the value of time and opportunity.

He rose again to his feet and peered out from under the shading laurel branches. As he did so the dark face of Miller turned full toward him. A tremor, like the intense thrill of a tiger when he is about to spring, ran over Wetzel's frame. In his mad gladness at being within rifle-shot of his great Indian foe, Wetzel had forgotten the man he had trailed for two days. He had forgotten Miller. He had only one shot—and Betty was to be avenged. He gritted his teeth. The Delaware chief was as safe as though he were a thousand miles away. This opportunity for which Wetzel had waited so many years, and the successful issue of which would have gone so far toward the fulfillment of a life's purpose, was worse than useless. A great temptation assailed the hunter.

Wetzel's face was white when he raised the rifle; his dark eye, gleaming vengefully, ran along the barrel. The little bead on the front sight first covered the British officer, and then the broad breast of Girty. It moved reluctantly and searched out the heart of Wingenund, where it lingered for a fleeting instant. At last it rested upon the swarthy face of Miller.

"Fer Betty," muttered the hunter, between his clenched teeth as he pressed the trigger.

The spiteful report awoke a thousand echoes. When the shot broke the stillness Miller was talking and gesticulating. His hand dropped inertly; he stood upright for a second, his head slowly bowing and his body swaying perceptibly. Then he plunged forward like a log, his face striking the sand. He never moved again. He was dead even before he struck the ground.

Blank silence followed this tragic denouement. Wing-enund, a cruel and relentless Indian, but never a traitor, pointed to the small bloody hole in the middle of Miller's forehead, and then nodded his head solemnly. The wondering Indians stood aghast. Then with loud yells the braves ran to the cornfield; they searched the laurel bushes. But they only discovered several moccasin prints in the sand, and a puff of white smoke wafting away upon the summer breeze.

CHAPTER 12

Alfred Clarke lay between life and death. Miller's knife-thrust, although it had made a deep and dangerous wound, had not pierced any vital part; the amount of blood lost made Alfred's condition precarious. Indeed, he would not have lived through that first day but for a wonderful vitality. Colonel Zane's wife, to whom had been consigned the delicate task of dressing the wound, shook her head when she first saw the direction of the cut. She found on a closer examination that the knife-blade had been deflected by a rib, and had just missed the lungs. The wound was bathed, sewed up, and bandaged, and the greatest precaution taken to prevent the sufferer from loosening the linen. Every day when Mrs. Zane returned from the bedside of the young man she would be met at the door by Betty, who, in that time of suspense, had lost her bloom, and whose pale face showed the effects of sleepless nights.

"Betty, would you mind going over to the Fort and relieving Mrs. Martin an hour or two?" said Mrs. Zane one day as she came home, looking worn and weary. "We are both tired to death, and Nell Metzar was unable to come. Clarke is unconscious, and will not know you, besides he is sleeping now."

Betty hurried over to Captain Boggs' cabin, next the blockhouse, where Alfred lay, and with a palpitating heart and a trepidation wholly out of keeping with the brave front she managed to assume, she knocked gently on the door.

"Ah, Betty, 'tis you, bless your heart," said a matronly little woman who opened the door. "Come right in. He is sleeping now, poor fellow, and it's the first real sleep he has had. He has been raving crazy forty-eight hours."

"Mrs. Martin, what shall I do?" whispered Betty.

"Oh, just watch him, my dear," answered the elder woman. "If you need me send one of the lads up to the house for me. I shall return as soon as I can. Keep the flies away—they are bothersome—and bathe his head every little while. If he wakes and tried to sit up, as he does sometimes, hold him back. He is weak as a cat. If he raves, soothe him by talking to him. I must go now, dearie."

Betty was left alone in the little room. Though she had taken a seat near the bed where Alfred lay, she had not dared to look at him. Presently conquering her emotion, Betty turned her gaze on the bed. Alfred was lying easily on his back, and notwithstanding the warmth of the day he was covered with a quilt. The light from the window shone on his face. How deathly white it was! There was not a vestige of color in it; the brow looked like chiseled marble; dark shadows underlined the eyes, and the whole face was expressive of weariness and pain.

There are times when a woman's love is all motherliness. All at once this man seemed to Betty like a helpless child. She felt her heart go out to the poor sufferer with a feeling before unknown. She forgot her pride and her fears and her disappointments. She remembered only that this strong man lay there at death's door because he had resented an insult to her. The past with all its bitterness rolled away and was lost, and in its place welled up a tide of forgiveness strong and sweet and hopeful. Her love, like a fire that had been choked and smothered, smouldering but never extinct, and which blazes up with the first breeze, warmed and quickened to life with the touch of her hand on his forehead.

An hour passed. Betty was now at her ease and happier than she had been for months. Her patient continued to sleep peacefully and dreamlessly. With a feeling of womanly curiosity Betty looked around the room. Over the rude mantelpiece were hung a sword, a brace of pistols, and two pictures. These last interested Betty very much. They were portraits; one of them was a likeness of a sweet-faced woman who Betty instinctively knew was his mother. Her eyes lingered tenderly on that face, so like the one lying on the pillow. The other portrait was of a beautiful girl whose dark, magnetic eyes challenged Betty. Was this his sister or—someone else? She could not restrain a jealous twinge, and she felt annoyed to find herself comparing that face with her own. She looked no longer at that portrait, but recommenced her survey of the room. Upon the door hung a broad-brimmed hat with eagle plumes stuck in the band. A pair of high-topped riding-boots, a saddle, and a bridle lay on the floor in the corner. The table was covered with Indian pipes, tobacco pouches, spurs, silk stocks, and other articles.

Suddenly Betty felt that some one was watching her. She turned timidly toward the bed and became much frightened when she encountered the intense gaze from a pair of steel-blue eyes. She almost fell from the chair; but presently she recollected that Alfred had been unconscious for days, and that he would not know who was watching by his bedside.

"Mother, is that you?" asked Alfred, in a weak, low voice.

"Yes, I am here," answered Betty, remembering the old woman's words about soothing the sufferer.

"But I thought you were ill."

"I was, but I am better now, and it is you who are ill."

"My head hurts so."

"Let me bathe it for you."

"How long have I been home?"

Betty bathed and cooled his heated brow. He caught and held her hands, looking wonderingly at her the while.

"Mother, somehow I thought you had died. I must have dreamed it. I am very happy; but tell me, did a message come for me to-day?"

Betty shook her head, for she could not speak. She saw he was living in the past, and he was praying for the letter which she would gladly have written had she but known.

"No message, and it is now so long."

"It will come to-morrow," whispered Betty.

"Now, mother, that is what you always say," said the invalid, as he began to toss his head wearily to and fro. "Will she never tell me? It is not like her to keep me in suspense. She was the sweetest, truest, loveliest girl in all the world. When I get well, mother, I am going to find out if she loves me."

"I am sure she does. I know she loves you," answered Betty softly.

"It is very good of you to say that." He went on in his rambling talk. "Some day I'll bring her to you and we'll make her a queen here in the old home. I'll be a better son now and not run away from home again. I've given the dear old mother many a heartache, but that's all past now. The wanderer has come home. Kiss me good-night, mother."

Betty looked down with tear-blurred eyes on the haggard face. Unconsciously she had been running her fingers through the fair hair that lay so damp over his brow. Her pity and tenderness had carried her far beyond herself, and at the last words she bent her head and kissed him on the lips.

"Who are you? You are not my mother. She is dead," he cried, starting up wildly, and looking at her with brilliant eyes.

Betty dropped the fan and rose quickly to her feet. What had she done? A terrible thought had flashed into her mind. Suppose he were not delirious, and had been deceiving her. Oh! for a hiding-place, or that the floor would swallow her. Oh! if some one would only come.

Footsteps sounded on the stairs and Betty ran to the door. To her great relief Mrs. Martin was coming up.

"You can run home now, there's a dear," said the old lady. "We have several watchers for to-night. It will not be long now when he will commence to mend, or else he will die. Poor boy, please God that he gets well. Has he been good? Did he call for any particular young lady? Never fear, Betty, I'll keep the secret. He'll never know you were here unless you tell him yourself."

Meanwhile the days had been busy ones for Colonel Zane. In anticipation of an attack from the Indians, the settlers had been fortifying their refuge and making the blockhouse as nearly impregnable as possible. Everything that was movable and was of value they put inside the stockade fence, out of reach of the destructive redskins. All the horses and cattle were driven into the inclosure. Wagon-loads of hay, grain and food were stored away in the blockhouse.

Never before had there been such excitement on the frontier. Runners from Fort Pitt, Short Creek, and other settlements confirmed the rumor that all the towns along the Ohio were preparing for war. Not since the outbreak of the Revolution had there been so much confusion and alarm among the pioneers. To be sure, those on the very verge of the frontier, as at Fort Henry, had heretofore little to fear from the British. During most of this time there had been comparative peace on the western border, excepting those occasional murders, raids, and massacres perpetrated by the different Indian tribes, and instigated no doubt by Girty and the British at Detroit. Now all kinds of rumors were afloat: Washington was defeated; a close alliance between England and the confederated western tribes had been formed; Girty had British power and wealth back of him. These and many more alarming reports travelled from settlement to settlement.

The death of Colonel Crawford had been a terrible shock to the whole country. On the border spread a universal gloom, and the low, sullen mutterings of revengeful wrath. Crawford had been so prominent a man, so popular, and, except in his last and fatal expedition, such an efficient leader that his sudden taking off was almost a national calamity. In fact no one felt it more keenly than did Washington himself, for Crawford was his esteemed friend.

Colonel Zane believed Fort Henry had been marked by the British and the Indians. The last runner from Fort Pitt had informed him that the description of Miller tallied with that of one of the ten men who had deserted from Fort Pitt in 1778 with the tories Girty, McKee, and Elliott. Colonel Zane was now satisfied that Miller was an agent of Girty and therefore of the British. So since all the weaknesses of the Fort, the number of the garrison, and the favorable conditions for a siege were known to Girty, there was nothing left for Colonel Zane and his men but to make a brave stand.

Jonathan Zane and Major McColloch watched the river. Wetzel had disappeared as if the earth had swallowed him. Some pioneers said he would never return. But Colonel

Zane believed Wetzel would walk into the Fort, as he had done many times in the last ten years, with full information concerning the doings of the Indians. However, the days passed and nothing happened. Their work completed, the settlers waited for the first sign of an enemy. But as none came, gradually their fears were dispelled and they began to think the alarm had been a false one.

All this time Alfred Clarke was recovering his health and strength. The day came when he was able to leave his bed and sit by the window. How glad it made him feel to look out on the green woods and the broad, winding river; how sweet to his ears were the songs of the birds; how soothing was the drowsy hum of the bees in the fragrant honeysuckle by his window. His hold on life had been slight and life was good. He smiled in pitying derision as he remembered his recklessness. He had not been in love with life. In his gloomy moods he had often thought life was hardly worth the living. What sickly sentiment! He had been on the brink of the grave, but he had been snatched back from the dark river of Death. It needed but this to show him the joy of breathing, the glory of loving, the sweetness of living. He resolved that for him there would be no more drifting, no more purposelessness. If what Wetzel had told him was true, if he really had not loved in vain, then his cup of happiness was overflowing. Like a far-off and almost forgotten strain of music some memory struggled to take definite shape in his mind; but it was so hazy, so vague, so impalpable, that he could remember nothing clearly.

Isaac Zane and his Indian bride called on Alfred that afternoon.

"Alfred, I can't tell you how glad I am to see you up again," said Isaac, earnestly, as he wrung Alfred's hand. "Say, but it was a tight squeeze! It has been a bad time for you."

Nothing could have been more pleasing than Myeerah's shy yet eloquent greeting. She gave Alfred her little hand and said in her figurative style of speaking, "Myeerah is happy for you and for others. You are strong like the West Wind that never dies."

"Myeerah and I are going this afternoon, and we came over to say good-bye to you. We intend riding down the river fifteen miles and then crossing, to avoid running into any band of Indians."

"And how does Myeerah like the settlement by this time?"

"Oh, she is getting on famously. Betty and she have fallen in love with each other. It is amusing to hear Betty try to talk in the Wyandot tongue, and to see Myeerah's consternation when Betty gives her a lesson in deportment."

"I rather fancy it would be interesting too. Are you not going back to the Wyandots at a dangerous time?"

"As to that I can't say. I believe, though, it is better that I get back to Tarhe's camp before we have any trouble with the Indians. I am anxious to get there before Girty or some of his agents."

"Well, if you must go, good luck to you, and may we meet again."

"It will not be long, I am sure. And, old man," he continued, with a bright smile, "when Myeerah and I come again to Fort Henry we expect to find all well with you. Cheer up, and good-bye."

All the preparations had been made for the departure of Isaac and Myeerah to their far-off Indian home. They were to ride the Indian ponies on which they had arrived at the Fort. Colonel Zane had given Isaac one of his pack-horses. This animal carried blankets, clothing, and food which insured comparative comfort in the long ride through the wilderness.

"We will follow the old trail until we reach the hickory swale," Isaac was saying to the Colonel, "and then we will turn off and make for the river. Once across the Ohio we can make the trip in two days."

"I think you'll make it all right," said Colonel Zane.

"Even if I do meet Indians I shall have no fear, for I have a protector here," answered Isaac as he led Myeerah's pony up to the step.

"Good-bye, Myeerah; he is yours, but do not forget he is dear to us," said Betty, embracing and kissing the Indian girl.

"My sister does not know Myeerah. The White Eagle will return."

"Good-bye, Betts, don't cry. I shall come home again. And when I do I hope I shall be in time to celebrate another event, this time with you as the heroine. Good-bye. Good-bye."

The ponies cantered down the road. At the bend Isaac and Myeerah turned and waved their hands until the foliage of the trees hid them from view.

"Well, these things happen naturally enough. I suppose they must be. But I should much have preferred Isaac staying here. Hello! What is that? By Lord! It's Tige!"

The exclamation following Colonel Zane's remarks had been called forth by Betty's dog. He came limping painfully up the road from the direction of the river. When he saw Colonel Zane he whined and crawled to the Colonel's feet. The dog was wet and covered with burrs, and his beautiful glossy coat, which had been Betty's pride, was dripping with blood.

"Silas, Jonathan, come here," cried Colonel Zane. "Here's Tige, back without Wetzel, and the poor dog has been shot almost to pieces. What does it mean?"

"Indians," said Jonathan, coming out of the house with

Silas, and Mrs. Zane and Betty, who had heard the Colonel's call.

"He has come a long way. Look at his feet. They are torn and bruised," continued Jonathan. "And he has been near Wingenund's camp. You see that red clay on his paws. There is no red clay that I know of round here, and there are miles of it this side of the Delaware camp."

"What is the matter with Tige?" asked Betty.

"He is done for. Shot through, poor fellow. How did he ever reach home?" said Silas.

"Oh, I hope not! Dear old Tige," said Betty as she knelt and tenderly placed the head of the dog in her lap. "Why, what is this? I never put that there. Eb, Jack, look here. There is a string around his neck," and Betty pointed excitedly to a thin cord which was almost concealed in the thick curly hair.

"Good gracious! Eb, look! It is the string off the prize bullet pouch I made, and that Wetzel won on Isaac's wedding-day. It is a message from Lew," said Betty.

"Well, by Heavens! This is strange. So it is. I remember that string. Cut it off, Jack," said Colonel Zane.

When Jonathan had cut the string and held it up they all saw the lead bullet. Colonel Zane examined it and showed them what had been rudely scratched on it.

"A letter W. Does that mean Wetzel?" asked the Colonel.

"It means war. It's a warning from Wetzel—not the slightest doubt of that," said Jonathan. "Wetzel sends this because he knows we are to be attacked, and because there must have been great doubt of his getting back to tell us. And Tige has been shot on his way home."

This called the attention to the dog, which had been momentarily forgotten. His head rolled from Betty's knee; a quiver shook his frame; he struggled to rise to his feet, but his strength was too far spent; he crawled close to Betty's feet; his eyes looked up at her with almost human affection; then they closed, and he lay still. Tige was dead.

"It is all over, Betty. Tige will romp no more. He will never be forgotten, for he was faithful to the end. Jonathan, tell the Major of Wetzel's warning, and both of you go back to your posts on the river. Silas, send Captain Boggs to me."

An hour after the death of Tige the settlers were waiting for the ring of the meeting-house bell to summon them to the Fort.

Supper at Colonel Zane's that night was not the occasion of good-humored jest and pleasant conversation. Mrs. Zane's face wore a distressed and troubled look; Betty was pale and quiet; even the Colonel was gloomy; and the children, missing the usual cheerfulness of the evening meal, shrank close to their mother.

Darkness slowly settled down; and with it came a feeling of relief, at least for the night, for the Indians rarely attacked the settlements after dark. Captain Boggs came over and he and Colonel Zane conversed in low tones.

"The first thing in the morning I want you to ride over to Short Creek for reinforcements. I'll send the Major also and by a different route. I expect to hear tonight from Wetzel. Twelve times has he crossed that threshold with the information which made an Indian surprise impossible. And I feel sure he will come again."

"What was that?" said Betty, who was sitting on the doorstep.

"Sh-h!" whispered Colonel Zane, holding up his finger.

The night was warm and still. In the perfect quiet which followed the Colonel's whispered exclamation the listeners heard the beating of their hearts. Then from the river-bank came the cry of an owl; low but clear it came floating to their ears, its single melancholy note thrilling them. Faint and far off in the direction of the island sounded the answer.

"I knew it. I told you. We shall know all presently," said Colonel Zane. "The first call was Jonathan's, and it was answered."

The moments dragged away. The children had fallen asleep on the bearskin rug. Mrs. Zane and Betty had heard the Colonel's voice, and sat with white faces, waiting, waiting for they knew not what.

A familiar, light-moccasined tread sounded on the path, a tall figure loomed up from the darkness; it came up the path, passed up the steps, and crossed the threshold.

"Wetzel!" exclaimed Colonel Zane and Captain Boggs. It was indeed the hunter. How startling was his appearance! The buckskin hunting coat and leggins were wet, torn and bespattered with mud; the water ran and dripped from him to form little muddy pools on the floor; only his rifle and powder horn were dry. His face was ghastly white except where a bullet wound appeared on his temple, from which the blood had oozed down over his cheek. An unearthly light gleamed from his eyes. In that moment Wetzel was an appalling sight.

"Colonel Zane, I'd been here days before, but I run into some Shawnees, and they gave me a hard chase. I have to report that Girty, with four hundred Injuns and two hundred Britishers, are on the way to Fort Henry."

"My God!" exclaimed Colonel Zane. Strong man as he was the hunter's words had unnerved him.

The loud and clear tone of the church-bell rang out on the still night air. Only once it sounded, but it reverberated among the hills, and its single deep-toned ring was like a knell. The listeners almost expected to hear it followed by the fearful war-cry, that cry which betokened for many desolation and death.

CHAPTER 13

Morning found the settlers, with the exception of Colonel Zane, his brother Jonathan, the black man Sam, and Martin Wetzel, all within the Fort. Colonel Zane had determined, long before, that in the event of another siege, he would use his house as an outpost. Twice it had been destroyed by fire at the hands of the Indians. Therefore, surrounding himself by these men, who were all expert marksmen, Colonel Zane resolved to protect his property and at the same time render valuable aid to the Fort.

Early that morning a pirogue loaded with cannon balls, from Fort Pitt and bound for Louisville, had arrived and Captain Sullivan, with his crew of three men, had demanded admittance. In the absence of Captain Boggs and Major McColloch, both of whom had been dispatched for reinforcements, Colonel Zane had placed his brother Silas in command of the Fort. Sullivan informed Silas that he and his men had been fired on by Indians and that they sought the protection of the Fort. The services of himself and men, which he volunteered, were gratefully accepted.

All told, the little force in the blockhouse did not exceed forty-two, and that counting the boys and the women who could handle rifles. The few preparations had been completed and now the settlers were awaiting the appearance of the enemy. Few words were spoken. The children were secured where they would be out of the way of flying bullets. They were huddled together silent and frightened; pale-faced but resolute women passed up and down the length of the blockhouse; some carried buckets of water and baskets of food; others were tearing bandages; grim-faced men peered from the portholes; all were listening for the war-cry.

They had not long to wait. Before noon the well-known whoop came from the wooded shore of the river, and it was soon followed by the appearance of hundreds of Indians. The river, which was low, at once became a scene of great animation. From a placid, smoothly flowing stream it was turned into a muddy, splashing, turbulent torrent. The mounted warriors urged their steeds down the bank and into the water; the unmounted improvised rafts and placed their weapons and ammunition upon them; then they swam and pushed, kicked and yelled their way across; other Indians swam, holding the bridles of the packhorses. A detachment of British soldiers followed the Indians. In an hour the entire army appeared on the river bluff not three hundred yards from the Fort. They were in no hurry to begin the attack. Especially did the Indians seem to enjoy the lull before the storm, and as they stalked to and fro in plain sight of the garrison, or stood in groups watching the Fort, they were seen in all their hideous war-paint and formidable battle-array. They were exultant. Their plumes and eagle feathers waved proudly in the morning breeze. Now and then the long, peculiarly broken yell of the Shawnees rang out clear and strong. The soldiers were drawn off to one side and well out of range of the settlers' guns. Their red coats and flashing bayonets were new to most of the little band of men in the block-house.

"Ho, the Fort!"

It was a strong, authoritative voice and came from a man mounted on a black horse.

"Well, Girty, what is it?" shouted Silas Zane.

"We demand unconditional surrender," was the answer.

"You will never get it," replied Silas.

"Take more time to think it over. You see we have a force here large enough to take the Fort in an hour."

"That remains to be seen," shouted some one through a porthole.

An hour passed. The soldiers and the Indians lounged around on the grass and walked to and fro on the bluff. At intervals a taunting Indian yell, horrible in its suggestiveness, came floating on the air. When the hour was up three mounted men rode out in advance of the waiting Indians. One was clad in buckskin, another in the uniform of a British officer, and the third was an Indian chief whose powerful form was naked except for his buckskin belt and leggins.

"Will you surrender?" came in the harsh and arrogant voice of the renegade.

"Never! Go back to your squaws!" yelled Sullivan.

"I am Captain Pratt of the Queen's Rangers. If you surrender I will give you the best protection King George affords," shouted the officer.

"To hell with King George! Go back to your hair-buying Hamilton and tell him the whole British army could not make us surrender," roared Hugh Bennet.

"If you do not give up, the Fort will be attacked and burned. Your men will be massacred and your women given to the Indians," said Girty.

"You will never take a man, woman or child alive," yelled Silas. "We remember Crawford, you white traitor, and we are not going to give up to be butchered. Come on with your red-jackets and your red-devils. We are ready."

"We have captured and killed the messenger you sent out, and now all hope of succor must be abandoned. Your doom is sealed."

"What kind of a man was he?" shouted Sullivan.

"A fine, active young fellow," answered the outlaw.

"That's a lie," snapped Sullivan, "he was an old, gray-haired man."

As the officer and the outlaw chief turned, apparently to consult their companion, a small puff of white smoke shot forth from one of the portholes of the blockhouse. It was followed by the ringing report of a rifle. The Indian chief clutched wildly at his breast, fell forward on his horse, and after vainly trying to keep his seat, slipped to the ground. He raised himself once, then fell backward and lay still. Full two hundred yards was not proof against Wetzel's deadly small-bore, and Red Fox, the foremost war chieftain of the Shawnees, lay dead, a victim to the hunter's vengeance. It was characteristic of Wetzel that he picked the chief, for he could have shot either the British officer or the renegade. They retreated out of range, leaving the body of the chief where it had fallen, while the horse, giving a frightened snort, galloped toward the woods. Wetzel's yell coming quickly after his shot, excited the Indians to a very frenzy, and they started on a run for the Fort, discharging their rifles and screeching like so many demons.

In the cloud of smoke which at once enveloped the scene the Indians spread out and surrounded the Fort. A tremendous rush by a large party of Indians was made for the gate of the Fort. They attacked it fiercely with their tomahawks, and a log which they used as a battering-ram. But the stout gate withstood their united efforts, and the galling fire from the portholes soon forced them to fall back and seek cover behind the trees and the rocks. From these points of vantage they kept up an uninterrupted fire.

The soldiers had made a dash at the stockade-fence, yelling derision at the small French cannon which was mounted on top of the block-house. They thought it a "dummy" because they had learned that in the 1777 siege the garrison had no real cannon, but had tried to utilize a wooden one. They yelled and hooted and mocked at this piece and dared the garrison to fire it. Sullivan, who was in charge of the cannon, bided his time. When the soldiers were massed closely together and making another rush for the stockade-fence Sullivan turned loose the little "bulldog," spreading consternation and destruction in the British ranks.

"Stand back! Stand back!" Captain Pratt was heard to yell. "By God! There's no wood about that gun."

After this the besiegers withdrew for a breathing spell. At this early stage of the siege the Indians were seen to board Sullivan's pirogue, and it was soon discovered they were carrying the cannon balls from the boat to the top of the bluff. In their simple minds they had conceived a happy thought. They procured a white-oak log probably a foot in diameter, split it through the middle and hollowed out the inside with their tomahawks. Then with iron chains and bars, which they took from Reihart's blacksmith shop, they bound and securely fastened the sides together. They dragged the improvised cannon nearer to the Fort, placed it on two logs and weighted it down with stones. A heavy charge of powder and ball was then rammed into the wooden gun. The soldiers, though much interested in the manœuvre, moved back to a safe distance, while many of the Indians crowded round the new weapon. The torch was applied; there was a red flash——boom! The hillside was shaken by the tremendous explosion, and when the smoke lifted from the scene the naked forms of the Indians could be seen writhing in agony on the ground. Not a vestige of the wooden gun remained. The iron chains had proved terrible death-dealing missiles to the Indians near the gun. The Indians now took to their natural methods of warfare. They hid in the long grass, in the deserted cabins, behind the trees and up in the branches. Not an Indian was visible, but the rain of bullets pattered steadily against the block-house. Every bush and every tree spouted little puffs of white smoke, and the leaden messengers of Death whistled through the air.

After another unsuccessful effort to destroy a section of the stockade-fence the soldiers had retired. Their red jackets made them a conspicuous mark for the sharp-eyed settlers. Captain Pratt had been shot through the thigh. He suffered great pain, and was deeply chagrined by the surprising and formidable defense of the garrison which he had been led to believe would fall an easy prey to the King's soldiers. He had lost one-third of his men. Those who were left refused to run straight in the face of certain death. They had not been drilled to fight an unseen enemy. Captain Pratt was compelled to order a retreat to the river bluff, where he conferred with Girty.

Inside the blockhouse was great activity, but no confusion. That little band of fighters might have been drilled for a king's bodyguard. Kneeling before each porthole on the river side of the Fort was a man who would fight while there was breath left in him. He did not discharge his weapon aimlessly as the Indians did, but waited until he saw the outline of an Indian form, or a red coat, or a puff of white smoke; then he would thrust the rifle-barrel forward, take a quick aim and fire. By the side of every man stood a heroic woman whose face was blanched, but who spoke never a word as she put the muzzle of the hot rifle into a bucket of water, cooled the barrel, wiped it dry and passed it back to the man beside her.

Silas Zane had been wounded at the first fire. A glancing ball had struck him on the head, inflicting a painful scalp wound. It was now being dressed by Colonel Zane's wife, whose skilled fingers were already tired with the washing and the bandaging of the injuries received by the defenders. In all that horrible din of battle; the shrill yells of the savages, the hoarse shouts of the settlers, the boom of the cannon overhead, the cracking of rifles and the whistling of bullets; in all that din of appalling noise, and amid the stifling smoke, the smell of burned powder, the sickening sight of the desperately wounded and the already dead, the Colonel's brave wife had never faltered. She was here and there; binding the wounds, helping Lydia and Betty mold bullets, encouraging the men, and by her example, enabling those women to whom border war was new to bear up under the awful strain.

Sullivan, who had been on top of the blockhouse, came down the ladder almost without touching it. Blood was running down his bare arm and dripping from the ends of his fingers.

"Zane, Martin has been shot," he said hoarsely. "The same Indian who shot away these fingers did it. The bullets seem to come from some elevation. Send some scout up there and find out where that damned Indian is hiding."

"Martin shot? God, his poor wife! Is he dead?" said Silas.

"Not yet. Bennet is bringing him down. Here, I want this hand tied up, so that my gun won't be so slippery."

Wetzel was seen stalking from one porthole to another. His fearful yell sounded above all the others. He seemed to bear a charmed life, for not a bullet had so much as scratched him. Silas communicated to him what Sullivan had said. The hunter mounted the ladder and went up on the roof. Soon he reappeared, descended into the room and ran into the west end of the blockhouse. He kneeled before a porthole through which he pushed the long black barrel of his rifle. Silas and Sullivan followed him and looked in the direction indicated by his weapon. It pointed toward the bushy top of a tall poplar tree which stood on the hill west of the Fort. Presently a little cloud of white smoke issued from the leafy branches, and it was no sooner seen than Wetzel's rifle was discharged. There was a great commotion among the leaves, the branches swayed and thrashed, and then a dark body plunged downward to strike on the rocky slope of the bluff and roll swiftly out of sight. The hunter's unnatural yell pealed out.

"Great God! The man's crazy," cried Sullivan, staring at Wetzel's demon-like face.

"No, no. It's his way," answered Silas.

At that moment the huge frame of Bennet filled up the opening in the roof and started down the ladder. In one arm he carried the limp body of a young man. When he reached the floor he laid the body down and beckoned to Mrs. Zane. Those watching saw that the young man was Will Martin, and that he was still alive. But it was evident that he had not long to live. His face had a leaden hue and his eyes were bright and glassy. Alice, his wife, flung herself on her knees beside him and tenderly raised the drooping head. No words could express the agony in her face as she raised it to Mrs. Zane. In it was a mute appeal, an unutterable prayer for hope. Mrs. Zane turned sorrowfully to her task. There was no need of her skill here. Alfred Clarke, who had been ordered to take Martin's place on top of the blockhouse, paused a moment in silent sympathy. When he saw that little hole in the bared chest, from which the blood welled up in an awful stream, he shuddered and passed on. Betty looked up from her work and then turned away sick and faint. Her mute lips moved as if in prayer.

Alice was left alone with her dying husband. She tenderly supported his head on her bosom, leaned her face against his and kissed the cold, numb lips. She murmured into his already deaf ear the old tender names. He knew her, for he made a feeble effort to pass his arm round her neck. A smile illumined his face. Then death claimed him. With wild, distended eyes and with hands pressed tightly to her temples Alice rose slowly to her feet.

"Oh, God! Oh, God!" she cried.

Her prayer was answered. In a momentary lull in the battle was heard the deadly hiss of a bullet as it sped through one of the portholes. It ended with a slight sickening spat as the lead struck the flesh. Then Alice, without a cry, fell on the husband's breast. Silas Zane found her lying dead with the body of her husband clasped closely in her arms. He threw a blanket over them and went on his wearying round of the bastions.

The besiegers had been greatly harassed and hampered by the continual fire from Colonel Zane's house. It was exceedingly difficult for the Indians, and impossible for the British, to approach near enough to the Colonel's house to get an effective shot. Colonel Zane and his men had the advantage of being on higher ground. Also they had four rifles to a man, and they used every spare moment for reloading. Thus they were enabled to pour a deadly fire into the ranks of the enemy, and to give the impression of being much stronger in force than they really were.

About dusk the firing ceased and the Indians repaired to the river bluff. Shortly afterward their campfires were extinguished and all became dark and quiet. Two hours passed. Fortunately the clouds, which had at first obscured the moon, cleared away somewhat, and enough light was shed on the scene to enable the watchers to discern objects near by.

Colonel Zane had just called together his men for a conference. He suspected some cunning deviltry on part of the Indians.

"Sam, take what stuff to eat you can lay your hands on and go up to the loft. Keep a sharp lookout and report anything to Jonathan or me," said the Colonel.

All afternoon Jonathan Zane had loaded and fired his rifles in sullen and dogged determination. He had burst one rifle and disabled another. The other men were fine marksmen, but it was undoubtedly Jonathan's unerring aim that made the house so unapproachable. He used an extremely heavy, large bore rifle. In the hands of a man strong enough to stand its fierce recoil it was a veritable cannon. The Indians had soon learned to respect the range of that rifle, and they gave the cabin a wide berth.

But now that darkness had enveloped the valley the advantage lay with the savages. Colonel Zane glanced apprehensively at the blackened face of his brother.

"Do you think the Fort can hold out?" he asked in a husky voice. He was a bold man, but he thought now of his wife and children.

"I don't know," answered Jonathan. "I saw that big Shawnee chief today. His name is Fire. He is well named. He is a fiend. Girty has a picked band."

"The Fort has held out surprisingly well against such combined and fierce attacks. The Indians are desperate. You can easily see that in the way in which they almost threw their lives away. The green square is covered with dead Indians."

"If help does not come in twenty-four hours not one man will escape alive. Even Wetzel could not break through that line of Indians. But if we can hold the Indians off a day longer they will get tired and discouraged. Girty will not be able to hold them much longer. The British don't count. It's not their kind of war. They can't shoot, and so far as I can see they haven't done much damage."

"To your posts, men, and every man think of the women and children in the blockhouse."

For a long time, which seemed hours to the waiting and watching settlers, not a sound could be heard, nor any sign of the enemy seen. Thin clouds had again drifted over the moon, allowing only a pale, wan light to shine down on the valley. Time dragged on and the clouds grew thicker and denser until the moon and the stars were totally obscured. Still no sign or sound of the Indians.

"What was that?" suddenly whispered Colonel Zane.

"It was a low whistle from Sam. We'd better go up," said Jonathan.

They went up the stairs to the second floor from which they ascended to the loft by means of a ladder. The loft was as black as pitch. In that Egyptian darkness it was no use to look for anything, so they crawled on their hands and knees over the piles of hides and leather which lay on the floor. When they reached the small window they made out the form of the black man.

"What is it, Sam?" whispered Jonathan.

"Look, see thar, Massa Zane," came the answer in a hoarse whisper from Sam and at the same time he pointed down toward the ground.

Colonel Zane put his head alongside Jonathan's and all three men peered out into the darkness.

"Jack, can you see anything?" said Colonel Zane.

"No, but wait a minute until the moon throws a light."

A breeze had sprung up. The clouds were passing rapidly over the moon, and at long intervals a rift between the clouds let enough light through to brighten the square for an instant.

"Now, Massa Zane, thar!" exclaimed the slave.

"I can't see a thing. Can you, Jack?"

"I am not sure yet. I can see something, but whether it is a log or not I don't know."

Just then there was a faint light like the brightening of a firefly, or like the blowing of a tiny spark from a stick of burning wood. Jonathan uttered a low curse.

"Damn 'em! At their old tricks with fire. I thought all this quiet meant something. The grass out there is full of Indians, and they are carrying lighted arrows under them so as to cover the light. But we'll fool the red devils this time."

"I can see 'em, Massa Zane."

"Sh-h-h! no more talk," whispered Colonel Zane.

The men waited with cocked rifles. Another spark rose seemingly out of the earth. This time it was nearer the house. No sooner had its feeble light disappeared than the report of Sam's rifle awoke the sleeping echoes. It was succeeded by a yell which seemed to come from under the window. Several dark forms rose so suddenly that they appeared to spring out of the ground. Then came the peculiar twang of Indian bows. There were showers of sparks and little streaks of fire with long tails like comets winged their parabolic flight toward the cabin. Falling short they hissed and sputtered in the grass. Jonathan's rifle spoke and one of the fleeing forms tumbled to the earth. A series of long yells from all around the Fort greeted this last shot, but not an Indian fired a rifle.

Fire-tipped arrows were now shot at the blockhouse, but not one took effect, although a few struck the stockade-fence. Colonel Zane had taken the precaution to have the high grass and the clusters of goldenrod cut down all round the Fort. The wisdom of this course now became evident, for the wily savages could not crawl near enough to send their fiery arrows on the roof of the blockhouse. This attempt failing, the Indians drew back to hatch up some other plot to burn the Fort.

"Look!" suddenly exclaimed Jonathan.

Far down the road, perhaps five hundred yards from the Fort, a point of light had appeared. At first it was still, and then it took an odd jerky motion, to this side and to that, up and down like a jack-o-lantern.

"What the hell?" muttered Colonel Zane, sorely puzzled. "Jack, by all that's strange it's getting bigger."

Sure enough the spark of fire, or whatever it was, grew larger and larger. Colonel Zane thought it might be a light carried by a man on horseback. But if this were true where was the clatter of the horse's hoofs? On that rocky bluff no horse could run noiselessly. It could not be a horse. Fascinated and troubled by this new mystery which seemed to presage evil to them the watchers waited with that patience known only to those accustomed to danger. They knew that whatever it was, it was some satanic stratagem of the savages, and that it would come all too soon.

The light was now zigzagging back and forth across the road, and approaching the Fort with marvelous rapidity. Now its motion was like the wide swinging of a lighted lantern on a dark night. A moment more of breathless suspense and the lithe form of an Indian brave could be seen behind the light. He was running with almost incredible swiftness down the road in the direction of the Fort. Passing at full speed within seventy-five yards of the stockade-fence the Indian shot his arrow. Like a fiery serpent flying through the air the missile sped onward in its graceful flight, going clear over the blockhouse, and striking with a spiteful thud the roof of one of the cabins beyond. Unhurt by the volley that was fired at him, the daring brave passed swiftly out of sight.

Deeds like this were dear to the hearts of the savages. They were deeds which made a warrior of a brave, and for which honor any Indian would risk his life over and over again. The exultant yells which greeted this performance proclaimed its success.

The breeze had already fanned the smouldering arrow into a blaze and the dry roof of the cabin had caught fire and was burning fiercely.

"That infernal redskin is going to do that again," exclaimed Jonathan.

It was indeed true. That same small bright light could be seen coming down the road gathering headway with every second. No doubt the same Indian, emboldened by his success, and maddened with that thirst for glory so often fatal to his kind, was again making the effort to fire the blockhouse.

The eyes of Colonel Zane and his companions were fastened on the light as it came nearer and nearer with its changing motion. The burning cabin brightened the square before the Fort. The slender, shadowy figure of the Indian could be plainly seen emerging from the gloom. So swiftly did he run that he seemed to have wings. Now he was in the full glare of the light. What a magnificent nerve, what a terrible assurance there was in his action! It seemed to paralyze all. The red arrow emitted a shower of sparks as it was discharged. This time it winged its way straight and true and imbedded itself in the roof of the blockhouse.

Almost at the same instant a solitary rifle shot rang out and the daring warrior plunged headlong, sliding face downward in the dust of the road, while from the Fort came that demoniac yell now grown so familiar.

"Wetzel's compliments," muttered Jonathan. "But the mischief is done. Look at that damned burning arrow. If it doesn't blow out the Fort will go."

The arrow was visible, but it seemed a mere spark. It alternately paled and glowed. One moment it almost went out, and the next it gleamed brightly. To the men, compelled to look on and powerless to prevent the burning of the now apparently doomed blockhouse, that spark was like the eye of Hell.

"Ho, the Fort," yelled Colonel Zane with all the power of his strong lungs. "Ho, Silas, the roof is on fire!"

Pandemonium had now broken out among the Indians. They could be plainly seen in the red glare thrown by the burning cabin. It had been a very dry season, the rough shingles were like tinder, and the inflammable material burst quickly into great flames, lighting up the valley as far as the edge of the forest. It was an awe-inspiring and a horrible spectacle. Columns of yellow and black smoke rolled heavenward; every object seemed dyed a deep crimson; the trees assumed fantastic shapes; the river veiled itself under a red glow. Above the roaring and crackling of the flames rose the inhuman yelling of the savages. Like demons of the inferno they ran to and fro, their naked painted bodies shining in the glare. One group of savages formed a circle and danced hands-around a stump as gayly as a band of schoolgirls at a May party. They wrestled with and hugged one another; they hopped, skipped and jumped, and in every possible way manifested their fiendish joy.

The British took no part in this revelry. To their credit it must be said they kept in the background as though ashamed of this horrible fire-war on people of their own blood.

"Why don't they fire the cannon?" impatiently said Colonel Zane. "Why don't they do something?"

"Perhaps it is disabled, or maybe they are short of ammunition," suggested Jonathan.

"The blockhouse will burn down before our eyes.

Look! The hell-hounds have set fire to the fence. I see men running and throwing water."

"I see something on the roof of the blockhouse," cried Jonathan. "There, down towards the east end of the roof, and in the shadow of the chimney. And as I'm a living sinner it's a man crawling towards that blazing arrow. The Indians have not discovered him yet. He is still in the shadow. But they'll see him. God! What a nervy thing to do in the face of all those redskins. It is almost certain death."

"Yes, and they see him," said the Colonel.

With shrill yells the Indians bounded forward and aimed and fired their rifles at the crouching figure of the man. Some hid behind the logs they had rolled toward the Fort; others boldly faced the steady fire now pouring from the portholes. The savages saw in the movement of that man an attempt to defeat their long-cherished hope of burning the Fort. Seeing he was discovered, the man did not hesitate, nor did he lose a second. Swiftly he jumped and ran toward the end of the roof where the burning arrow, now surrounded by blazing shingles, was sticking in the roof. How he ever ran along that slanting roof and with a pail in his hand was incomprehensible. In moments like that men become superhuman. It all happened in an instant. He reached the arrow, kicked it over the wall, and then dashed the bucket of water on the blazing shingles. In that single instant, wherein his tall form was outlined against the bright light behind him, he presented the fairest kind of a mark for the Indians. Scores of rifles were leveled and discharged at him. The bullets pattered like hail on the roof of the blockhouse, but apparently none found their mark, for the man ran back and disappeared.

"It was Clarke!" exclaimed Colonel Zane. "No one but Clarke has such light hair. Wasn't that a plucky thing?"

"It has saved the blockhouse for to-night," answered Jonathan. "See, the Indians are falling back. They can't stand in the face of that shooting. Hurrah! Look at them fall! It could not have happened better. The light from the cabin will prevent any more close attacks for an hour and daylight is near."

CHAPTER 14

The sun rose red. Its ruddy rays peeped over the eastern hills, kissed the treetops, glinted along the stony bluffs, and chased away the gloom of night from the valley. Its warm gleams penetrated the portholes of the Fort and cast long bright shadows on the walls; but it brought little cheer to the sleepless and almost exhausted defenders. It brought to many of the settlers the familiar old sailor's maxim: "Redness 'a the morning, sailor's warning." Rising in its crimson glory the sun flooded the valley, dyeing the river, the leaves, the grass, the stones, tingeing everything with that awful color which stained the stairs, the benches, the floor, even the portholes of the blockhouse.

Historians call this the time that tried men's souls. If it tried the men think what it must have been to those grand, heroic women. Though they had helped the men load and fire nearly forty-eight hours; though they had worked without a moment's rest and were now ready to succumb to exhaustion; though the long room was full of stifling smoke and the sickening odor of burned wood and powder, and though the row of silent, covered bodies had steadily lengthened, the thought of giving up never occurred to the women. Death there would be sweet compared to what it would be at the hands of the redmen.

At sunrise Silas Zane, bare-chested, his face dark and fierce, strode into the bastion which was connected with the blockhouse. It was a small shedlike room, and with portholes opening to the river and the forest. This bastion had seen the severest fighting. Five men had been killed here. As Silas entered four haggard and powder-begrimed men, who were kneeling before the portholes, looked up at him. A dead man lay in one corner.

"Smith's dead. That makes fifteen," said Silas. "Fifteen out of forty-two, that leaves twenty-seven. We must hold out. Men, don't expose yourselves recklessly. How goes it at the south bastion?"

"All right. There's been firin' over there all night," answered one of the men. "I guess it's been kinder warm over that way. But I ain't heard any shootin' for some time."

"Young Bennet is over there, and if the men needed anything they would send him for it," answered Silas. "I'll send some food and water. Anything else?"

"Powder. We're nigh out of powder," replied the man addressed. "And we might jes as well make ready fer a high old time. The red devils hain't been quiet all this last hour fer nothin'."

Silas passed along the narrow hallway which led from the bastion into the main room of the blockhouse. As he turned the corner at the head of the stairway he encountered a boy who was dragging himself up the steps.

"Hello! Who's this? Why, Harry!" exclaimed Silas, grasping the boy and drawing him into the room. Once in the light Silas saw that the lad was so weak he could hardly stand. He was covered with blood. It dripped from a bandage wound tightly about his arm; it oozed through a hole in his hunting shirt, and it flowed from a wound over his temple. The shadow of death was already stealing over the pallid face, but from the gray eyes shone an indomitable spirit, a spirit which nothing but death could quench.

"Quick!" the lad panted. "Send men to the south wall. The redskins are breakin' in where the water from the spring runs under the fence."

"Where are Metzar and the other men?"

"Dead! Killed last night. I've been there alone all night. I kept on shootin'. Then I gets plugged here under the chin. Knowin' it's all up with me I deserted my post when I heard the Injuns choppin' on the fence where it was on fire last night. But I only—run—because—they're gettin' in."

"Wetzel, Bennet, Clarke!" yelled Silas, as he laid the boy on the bench.

Almost as Silas spoke the tall form of the hunter confronted him. Clarke and the other men were almost as prompt.

"Wetzel, run to the south wall. The Indians are cutting a hole through the fence."

Wetzel turned, grabbed his rifle and an axe and was gone like a flash.

"Sullivan, you handle the men here. Bessie, do what you can for this brave lad. Come, Bennet, Clarke, we must follow Wetzel," commanded Silas.

Mrs. Zane hastened to the side of the fainting lad. She washed away the blood from the wound over his temple. She saw that a bullet had glanced on the bone and that the wound was not deep or dangerous. She unlaced the hunting shirt at the neck and pulled the flaps apart. There on the right breast, on a line with the apex of the lung, was a horrible gaping wound. A murderous British slug had passed through the lad. From the hole at every heartbeat poured the dark, crimson life-tide. Mrs. Zane turned her white face away for a second; then she folded a small piece of linen, pressed it tightly over the wound, and wrapped a towel round the lad's breast.

"Don't waste time on me. It's all over," he whispered. "Will you call Betty here a minute?"

Betty came, white-faced and horror-stricken. For forty hours she had been living in a maze of terror. Her movements had almost become mechanical. She had almost ceased to hear and feel. But the light in the eyes of this dying boy brought her back to the horrible reality of the present.

"Oh, Harry! Harry! Harry!" was all Betty could whisper.

"I'm goin', Betty. And I wanted—you to say a little prayer for me—and say good-bye to me," he panted.

Betty knelt by the bench and tried to pray.

"I hated to run, Betty, but I waited and waited and nobody came, and the Injuns was gettin' in. They'll find dead Injuns in piles out there. I was shootin' fer you, Betty, and every time I aimed I thought of you."

The lad rambled on, his voice growing weaker and weaker and finally ceasing. The hand which had clasped Betty's so closely loosened its hold. His eyes closed. Betty thought he was dead, but no! he still breathed. Suddenly his eyes opened. The shadow of pain was gone. In its place shone a beautiful radiance.

"Betty, I've cared a lot for you—and I'm dyin'—happy because I've fought fer you—and somethin' tells me—you'll—be saved. Good-bye." A smile transformed his face and his gray eyes gazed steadily into hers. Then his head fell back. With a sigh his brave spirit fled.

Hugh Bennet looked once at the pale face of his son, then he ran down the stairs after Silas and Clarke. When the three men emerged from behind Captain Boggs' cabin, which was adjacent to the blockhouse, and which hid the south wall from their view, they were two hundred feet from Wetzel. They heard the heavy thump of a log being rammed against the fence; then a splitting and splintering of one of the six-inch oak planks. Another and another smashing blow and the lower half of one of the planks fell inwards, leaving an aperture large enough to admit an Indian. The men dashed forward to the assistance of Wetzel, who stood by the hole with uplaised axe. At the same moment a shot rang out. Bennet stumbled and fell headlong. An Indian had shot through the hole in the fence. Silas and Alfred sheered off toward the fence, out of line. When within twenty yards of Wetzel they saw a swarthy-faced and athletic savage squeeze through the narrow crevice. He had not straightened up before the axe, wielded by the giant hunter, descended on his head, cracking his skull as if it were an eggshell. The savage sank to the earth without even a moan. Another savage, naked and powerful, slipped in. He had to stoop to get through. He raised himself, and seeing Wetzel, he tried to dodge the lightning sweep of the axe. It missed his head, at which it had been aimed, but struck over the shoulders, and buried itself in flesh and bone. The Indian uttered an agonizing yell which ended in a choking, gurgling sound as the blood spurted from his throat. Wetzel pulled the weapon from the body of his victim, and with the same motion he swung it around. This time the blunt end met the next Indian's head with a thud like that made by the butcher when he strikes the bullock to the ground. The Indian's rifle dropped, his tomahawk flew into the air, while his body rolled down the little embankment into the spring. Another and another Indian met the same fate. Then two Indians endeavored to get through the aperture. The awful axe swung by those steel arms, dispatched both of them in the twinkling of an eye. Their bodies stuck in the hole.

Silas and Alfred stood riveted to the spot. Just then Wetzel in all his horrible glory was a sight to freeze the marrow of any man. He had cast aside his hunting shirt in that run to the fence and was now stripped to the waist. He was covered with blood. The muscles of his broad back and his brawny arms swelled and rippled under the brown skin. At every swing of the gory axe he let out a yell the like of which had never before been heard by the white men. It was the hunter's mad yell of revenge. In his thirst for vengeance he had forgotten that he was defending the Fort with its women and its children; he was fighting because he loved to kill.

Silas Zane heard the increasing clamor outside and knew that hundreds of Indians were being drawn to the spot. Something must be done at once. He looked around and his eyes fell on a pile of white-oak logs that had been hauled inside the Fort. They had been placed there by Colonel Zane, with wise forethought. Silas grabbed Clarke and pulled him toward the pile of logs, at the same time communicating his plan. Together they carried a log to the fence and dropped it in front of the hole. Wetzel immediately stepped on it and took a vicious swing at an Indian who was trying to poke his rifle sideways through the hole. This Indian had discharged his weapon twice. While Wetzel held the Indian at bay, Silas and Clarke piled the logs one upon another, until the hole was closed. This effectually fortified and barricaded the weak place in the stockade fence. The settlers in the bastions were now pouring such a hot fire into the ranks of the savages that they were compelled to retreat out of range.

While Wetzel washed the blood from his arms and his shoulders Silas and Alfred hurried back to where Bennet had fallen. They expected to find him dead, and were overjoyed to see the big settler calmly sitting by the brook binding up a wound in his shoulder.

"It's nothin' much. Jest a scratch, but it tumbled me over," he said. "I was comin' to help you. That was the wust Injun scrap I ever saw. Why didn't you keep on lettin' 'em come in? The red varmints would 'a kept on comin' and Wetzel was good fer the whole tribe. All you'd had to do was to drag the dead Injuns aside and give him elbow room."

Wetzel joined them at this moment, and they hurried back to the blockhouse. The firing had ceased on the bluff. They met Sullivan at the steps of the Fort. He was evidently coming in search of them.

"Zane, the Indians and the Britishers are getting ready for a more determined and persistent effort than any that has yet been made," said Sullivan.

"How so?" asked Silas.

"They have got hammers from the blacksmith's shop, and they boarded my boat and found a keg of nails. Now they are making a number of ladders. If they make a rush all at once and place ladders against the fence we'll have the Fort full of Indians in ten minutes. They can't stand in the face of a cannon charge. We *must* use the cannon."

"Clarke, go into Captain Boggs' cabin and fetch out two kegs of powder," said Silas.

The young man turned in the direction of the cabin, while Silas and the others ascended the stairs.

"The firing seems to be all on the south side," said Silas, "and is not so heavy as it was."

"Yes, as I said, the Indians on the riverfront are busy with their new plans," answered Sullivan.

"Why does not Clarke return?" said Silas, after waiting a few moments at the door of the long room. "We have no time to lose. I want to divide one keg of that powder among the men."

Clarke appeared at the moment. He was breathing

heavily as though he had run up the stairs, or was laboring under a powerful emotion. His face was gray.

"I could not find any powder!" he exclaimed. "I searched every nook and corner in Captain Boggs' house. There is no powder there."

A brief silence ensued. Everyone in the blockhouse heard the young man's voice. No one moved. They all seemed waiting for someone to speak. Finally Silas Zane burst out:

"Not find it? You surely could not have looked well. Captain Boggs himself told me there were three kegs of powder in the storeroom. I will go and find it myself."

Alfred did not answer, but sat down on a bench, with an odd numb feeling round his heart. He knew what was coming. He had been in the Captain's house and had seen those kegs of powder. He knew exactly where they had been. Now they were not on the accustomed shelf, nor at any other place in the storeroom. While he sat there waiting for the awful truth to dawn on the garrison, his eyes roved from one end of the room to the other. At last they found what they were seeking. A young woman knelt before a charcoal fire which she was blowing with a bellows. It was Betty. Her face was pale and weary, her hair dishevelled, her shapely arms blackened with charcoal, but notwithstanding she looked calm, resolute, self-contained. Lydia was kneeling by her side holding a bullet-mold on a block of wood. Betty lifted the ladle from the red coals and poured the hot metal with a steady hand and an admirable precision. Too much or too little lead would make an imperfect ball. The little missile had to be just so for those soft-metal, smooth-bore rifles. Then Lydia dipped the mold in a bucket of water, removed it and knocked it on the floor. A small, shiny lead bullet rolled out. She rubbed it with a greasy rag and then dropped it in a jar. For nearly forty hours, without sleep or rest, almost without food, those brave girls had been at their post.

Silas Zane came running into the room. His face was ghastly, even his lips were white and drawn.

"Sullivan, in God's name, what can we do? The powder is gone!" he cried in a strident voice.

"Gone?" repeated several voices.

"Gone?" echoed Sullivan. "Where?"

"God knows. I know where the kegs stood a few days ago. There were marks in the dust. They have been moved."

"Perhaps Boggs put them here somewhere," said Sullivan. "We will look."

"No use. No use. We were always careful to keep the powder out of here on account of fire. The kegs are gone, gone."

"Miller stole them," said Wetzel in his calm voice.

"What difference does that make now?" burst out Silas, turning passionately on the hunter, whose quiet voice in that moment seemed so unfeeling. "They're gone!"

In the silence which ensued after these words the men looked at each other with slowly whitening faces. There was no need of words. Their eyes told one another what was coming. The fate which had overtaken so many border forts was to be theirs. They were lost! And every man thought not of himself, cared not for himself, but for those innocent children, those brave young girls and heroic women.

A man can die. He is glorious when he calmly accepts death; but when he fights like a tiger, when he stands at bay his back to the wall, a broken weapon in his hand, bloody, defiant, game to the end, then he is sublime. Then he wrings respect from the souls of even his bitterest foes. Then he is avenged even in his death.

But what can women do in times of war? They help,

they cheer, they inspire, and if their cause is lost they must accept death or worse. Few women have the courage for self-destruction. "To the victor belong the spoils," and women have ever been the spoils of war.

No wonder Silas Zane and his men weakened in that moment. With only a few charges for their rifles and none for the cannon how could they hope to hold out against the savages? Alone they could have drawn their tomahawks and have made a dash through the lines of Indians, but with the women and children that was impossible.

"Wetzel, what can we do? For God's sake, advise us!" said Silas hoarsely. "We cannot hold the Fort without powder. We cannot leave the women here. We had better tomahawk every woman in the blockhouse than let her fall into the hands of Girty."

"Send some one fer powder," answered Wetzel.

"Do you think it possible," said Silas quickly, a ray of hope lighting up his haggard features. "There's plenty of powder in Eb's cabin. Whom shall we send? Who will volunteer?"

Three men stepped forward, and others made a movement.

"They'd plug a man full of lead afore he'd get ten foot from the gate," said Wetzel. "I'd go myself, but it wouldn't do no good. Send a boy, and one as can run like a streak."

"There are no lads big enough to carry a keg of powder. Harry Bennet might go," said Silas. "How is he, Bessie?"

"He is dead," answered Mrs. Zane.

Wetzel made a motion with his hands and turned away. A short, intense silence followed this indication of hopelessness from him. The women understood, for some of them covered their faces, while others sobbed.

"I will go."

It was Betty's voice, and it rang clear and vibrant throughout the room. The miserable women raised their drooping heads, thrilled by that fresh young voice. The men looked stupefied. Clarke seemed turned to stone. Wetzel came quickly toward her.

"Impossible!" said Sullivan.

Silas Zane shook his head as if the idea were absurd.

"Let me go, brother, let me go?" pleaded Betty as she placed her little hands softly, caressingly on her brother's bare arm. "I know it is only a forlorn chance, but still it is a chance. Let me take it. I would rather die that way than remain here and wait for death."

"Silas, it ain't a bad plan," broke in Wetzel. "Betty can run like a deer. And bein' a woman they may let her get to the cabin without shootin'."

Silas stood with arms folded across his broad chest. As he gazed at his sister great tears coursed down his dark cheeks and splashed on the hands which so tenderly clasped his own. Betty stood before him transformed; all signs of weariness had vanished; her eyes shone with a fateful resolve; her white and eager face was surpassingly beautiful with its light of hope, of prayer, of heroism.

"Let me go, brother. You know I can run, and oh! I will fly today. Every moment is precious. Who knows? Perhaps Captain Boggs is already near at hand with help. You cannot *spare* a man. Let me go."

"Betty, Heaven bless and save you, you shall go," said Silas.

"No! No! Do not let her go!" cried Clarke, throwing himself before them. He was trembling, his eyes were wild, and he had the appearance of a man suddenly gone mad.

"She shall not go," he cried.

"What authority have you here?" demanded Silas Zane, sternly. "What right have you to speak?"

"None, unless it is that I love her and I will go for her," answered Alfred desperately.

"Stand back!" cried Wetzel, placing his powerful hand on Clarke's breast and pushing him backward. "If you love her you don't want to have her wait here for them red devils." And he waved his hand toward the river. "If she gets back she'll save the Fort. If she fails she'll at least escape Girty."

Betty gazed into the hunter's eyes and then into Alfred's. She understood both men. One was sending her out to her death because he knew it would be a thousand times more merciful than the fate which awaited her at the hands of the Indians. The other had not the strength to watch her go to her death. He had offered himself rather than see her take such fearful chances.

"I know. If it were possible you would both save me," said Betty, simply. "Now you can do nothing but pray that God may spare my life long enough to reach the gate. Silas, I am ready."

Downstairs a little group of white-faced men were standing before the gateway. Silas Zane had withdrawn the iron bar. Sullivan stood ready to swing in the ponderous gate. Wetzel was speaking with a clearness and a rapidity which were wonderful under the circumstances.

"When we let you out you'll have a clear path. Run, but not very fast. Save your speed. Tell the Colonel to empty a keg of powder in a table cloth. Throw it over your shoulder and start back. Run like you was racin' with me, and keep on comin' if you do get hit. Now go!"

The huge gate creaked and swung in. Betty ran out, looking straight before her. She had covered half the distance between the Fort and the Colonel's house when long taunting yells filled the air.

"Squaw! Waugh! Squaw! Waugh!" yelled the Indians in contempt.

Not a shot did they fire. The yells ran all along the riverfront, showing that hundreds of Indians had seen the slight figure running up the gentle slope toward the cabin.

Betty obeyed Wetzel's instructions to the letter. She ran easily and not at all hurriedly, and was as cool as if there had not been an Indian within miles.

Colonel Zane had seen the gate open and Betty come forth. When she bounded up the steps he flung open the door and she ran into his arms.

"Betts, for God's sake! What's this?" he cried.

"We are out of powder. Empty a keg of powder into a table cloth. Quick! I've not a second to lose," she answered, at the same time slipping off her outer skirt. She wanted nothing to hinder that run for the blockhouse.

Jonathan Zane heard Betty's first words and disappeared into the magazine-room. He came out with a keg in his arms. With one blow of an axe he smashed in the top of the keg. In a twinkling a long black stream of the precious stuff was piling up in a little hill in the center of the table. Then the corners of the table cloth were caught up, turned and twisted, and the bag of powder was thrown over Betty's shoulder.

"Brave girl, so help me God, you are going to do it!" cried Colonel Zane, throwing open the door. "I know you can. Run as you never ran in all your life."

Like an arrow sprung from a bow Betty flashed past the Colonel and out on the green. Scarcely ten of the long hundred yards had been covered by her flying feet when a roar of angry shouts and yells warned Betty that the keen-eyed savages saw the bag of powder and now knew they had been deceived by a girl. The cracking of rifles began at a point on the bluff nearest Colonel Zane's house, and extended in a half circle to the eastern end of the clearing. The leaden messengers of Death whistled past Betty. They sped before her and behind her, scattering pebbles in her path, striking up the dust, and ploughing little furrows in the ground. A quarter of the distance covered! Betty had passed the top of the knoll now and she was going down the gentle slope like the wind. None but a fine marksman could have hit that small, flitting figure. The yelling and screeching had become deafening. The reports of the rifles blended in a roar. Yet above it all Betty heard Wetzel's stentorian yell. It lent wings to her feet. Half the distance covered! A hot, stinging pain shot through Betty's arm, but she heeded it not. The bullets were raining about her. They sang over her head; hissed close to her ears, and cut the grass in front of her; they pattered like hail on the stockade-fence, but still untouched, unharmed, the slender brown figure sped toward the gate. Three-fourths of the distance covered! A tug at the flying hair, and a long, black tress cut off by a bullet, floated away on the breeze. Betty saw the big gate swing; she saw the tall figure of the hunter; she saw her brother. Only a few more yards! On! On! On! A blinding red mist obscured her sight. She lost the opening in the fence, but unheeding she rushed on. Another second and she stumbled; she felt herself grasped by eager arms; she heard the gate slam and the iron bar shoot into place; then she felt and heard no more.

Silas Zane bounded up the stairs with a doubly precious burden in his arms. A mighty cheer greeted his entrance. It aroused Alfred Clarke, who had bowed his head on the bench and had lost all sense of time and place. What were the women sobbing and crying over? To whom belonged that white face? Of course, it was the face of the girl he loved. The face of the girl who had gone to her death. And he writhed in his agony.

Then something wonderful happened. A warm, living flush swept over that pale face. The eyelids fluttered; they opened, and the dark eyes, radiant, beautiful, gazed straight into Alfred's.

Still Alfred could not believe his eyes. That pale face and the wonderful eyes belonged to the ghost of his sweetheart. They had come back to haunt him. Then he heard a voice.

"O-h! but that brown place burns!"

Alfred saw a bare and shapely arm. Its beauty was marred by a cruel red welt. He heard that same sweet voice laugh and cry together. Then he came back to life and hope. With one bound he sprang to a porthole.

"God, what a woman!" he said between his teeth, as he thrust the rifle forward.

It was indeed not a time for inaction. The Indians, realizing they had been tricked and had lost a golden opportunity, rushed at the Fort with renewed energy. They attacked from all sides and with the persistent fury of savages long disappointed in their hopes. They were received with a scathing, deadly fire. Bang! roared the cannon, and the detachment of savages dropped their ladders and fled. The little "bull dog" was turned on its swivel and directed at another rush of Indians. Bang! and the bullets, chainlinks, and bits of iron ploughed through the ranks of the enemy. The Indians never lived who could stand in the face of well-aimed cannon-shot. They fell back. The settlers, inspired, carried beyond themselves by the heroism of a girl, fought as they had never fought before. Every shot went to a redskin's heart. Impelled by the powder for which a brave girl had offered her life, guided by hands and arms of iron, and aimed by eyes as fixed and stern as Fate, every bullet shed the life-blood of a warrior.

Slowly and sullenly the red men gave way before that fire. Foot by foot they retired. Girty was seen no more.

Fire, the Shawnee chief, lay dead in the road almost in the same spot where two days before his brother chief, Red Fox, had bit the dust. The British had long since retreated.

When night came the exhausted and almost famished besiegers sought rest and food.

The moon came out clear and beautiful, as if ashamed of her traitor's part of the night before, and brightened up the valley, bathing the Fort, the river, and the forest in her silver light.

Shortly after daybreak the next morning the Indians, despairing of success, held a powwow. While they were grouped in plain view of the garrison, and probably conferring over the question of raising the siege, the long, peculiar whoop of an Indian spy, who had been sent out to watch for the approach of a relief party, rang out. This seemed a signal for retreat. Scarcely had the shrill cry ceased to echo in the hills when the Indians and the British, abandoning their dead, moved rapidly across the river.

After a short interval a mounted force was seen galloping up the creek road. It proved to be Captain Boggs, Swearengen, and Williamson with seventy men. Great was the rejoicing! Captain Boggs had expected to find only the ashes of the Fort. And the gallant little garrison, although saddened by the loss of half its original number, rejoiced that it had repulsed the united forces of braves and British.

CHAPTER 15

Peace and quiet reigned once more at Fort Henry. Before the glorious autumn days had waned the settlers had repaired the damage done to their cabins, and many of them were now occupied with the fall plowing. Never had the Fort experienced such busy days. Many new faces were seen in the little meeting-house. Pioneers from Virginia, from Fort Pitt, and eastward had learned that Fort Henry had repulsed the biggest force of Indians and soldiers that Governor Hamilton and his minions could muster. Settlers from all points along the river were flocking to Colonel Zane's settlement. New cabins dotted the hillside; cabins and barns in all stages of construction could be seen. The sounds of hammers, the ringing stroke of the axe, and the crashing down of mighty pines or poplars were heard all day long.

Colonel Zane sat oftener and longer than ever before in his favorite seat on his doorstep. On this evening he had just returned from a hard day in the fields, and sat down to rest a moment before going to supper. A few days previous Isaac Zane and Myeerah had come to the settlement. Myeerah brought a treaty of peace signed by Tarhe and the other Wyandot chieftains. The once implacable Huron was now ready to be friendly with the white people. Colonel Zane and his brothers signed the treaty, and Betty, by dint of much persuasion, prevailed on Wetzel to bury the hatchet with the Hurons. So Myeerah's love, like the love of many other women, accomplished more than years of war and bloodshed.

The genial and happy smile never left Colonel Zane's face, and as he saw the well-laden rafts coming down the river, and the air of liveliness and animation about the growing settlement, his smile broadened into one of pride and satisfaction. The prophecy that he had made twelve years before was fulfilled. His dream was realized. The wild, beautiful spot where he had once built a bark shack and camped half a year without seeing a white man was now the scene of a bustling settlement; and he believed he would live to see that settlement grow into a prosperous city. He did not think of the thousands of acres which would one day make him a wealthy man. He was a pioneer at heart; he had opened up that rich new country; he had conquered all obstacles, and that was enough to make him content.

"Papa, when shall I be big enough to fight bars and bufflers and Injuns?" asked Noah, stopping in his play and straddling his father's knee.

"My boy, did you not have Indians enough a short time ago?"

"But, papa, I did not get to see any. I heard the shooting and yelling. Sammy was afraid, but I wasn't. I wanted to look out of the little holes, but they locked us up in the dark room."

"If that boy ever grows up to be like Jonathan or Wetzel it will be the death of me," said the Colonel's wife, who had heard the lad's chatter.

"Don't worry, Bessie. When Noah grows to be a man the Indians will be gone."

Colonel Zane heard the galloping of a horse and looking up saw Clarke coming down the road on his black thoroughbred. The Colonel rose and walked out to the hitching-block, where Clarke had reined in his fiery steed.

"Ah, Alfred. Been out for a ride?"

"Yes, I have been giving Roger a little exercise."

"That's a magnificent animal. I never get tired watching him move. He's the best bit of horseflesh on the river. By the way, we have not seen much of you since the siege. Of course you have been busy. Getting ready to put on the harness, eh? Well, that's what we want the young men to do. Come over and see us."

"I have been trying to come. You know how it is with me—about Betty, I mean. Colonel Zane, I—I love her. That's all."

"Yes, I know, Alfred, and I don't wonder at your fears. But I have always liked you, and now I guess it's about time for me to put a spoke in your wheel of fortune. If Betty cares for you—and I have a sneaking idea she does—I will give her to you."

"I have nothing. I gave up everything when I left home."

"My lad, never mind about that," said the Colonel, laying his hand on Clarke's knee. "We don't need riches. I have so often said that we need nothing out here on the border but honest hearts and strong, willing hands. These you have. That is enough for me and for my people, and as for land, why, I have enough for an army of young men. I got my land cheap. That whole island there I bought from Cornplanter. You can have that island or any tract of land along the river. Some day I shall put you at the head of my men. It will take you years to cut that road through to Maysville. Oh, I have plenty of work for you."

"Colonel Zane, I cannot thank you," answered Alfred, with emotion. "I shall try to merit your friendship and esteem. Will you please tell your sister I shall come over in the morning and beg to see her alone."

"That I will, Alfred. Good-night."

Colonel Zane strode across his threshold with a happy smile on his face. He loved to joke and tease, and never lost an opportunity.

"Things seem to be working out all right. Now for some fun with Her Highness," he said to himself.

As the Colonel surveyed the pleasant home scene he felt he had nothing more to wish for. The youngsters were playing with a shaggy little pup which had already taken Tige's place in their fickle affections. His wife was crooning a lullaby as she gently rocked the cradle to and fro. A wonderful mite of humanity peacefully slumbered in that old cradle. Annie was beginning to set the table for the evening meal. Isaac lay with a contented smile on his face, fast asleep on the couch, where, only a short time before, he had been laid bleeding and almost dead. Betty was reading to Myeerah, whose eyes were rapturously bright as she leaned her head against her sister and listened to the low voice.

"Well, Betty, what do you think?" said Colonel Zane, stopping before the girls.

"What do I think?" retorted Betty. "Why, I think you are very rude to interrupt me. I am reading to Myeerah her first novel."

"I have a very important message for you."

"For me? What! From whom?"

"Guess."

Betty ran through a list of most of her acquaintances, but after each name her brother shook his head.

"Oh, well, I don't care," she finally said. The color in her cheeks had heightened noticeably.

"Very well. If you do not care, I will say nothing more," said Colonel Zane.

At this juncture Annie called them to supper. Later, when Colonel Zane sat on the doorstep smoking, Betty came and sat beside him with her head resting against his shoulder. The Colonel smoked on in silence. Presently the dusky head moved restlessly.

"Eb, tell me the message," whispered Betty.

"Message? What message?" asked Colonel Zane. "What are you talking about?"

"Do not tease—not now. Tell me." There was an undercurrent of wistfulness in Betty's voice which touched the kindhearted brother.

"Well, to-day a certain young man asked me if he could relieve me of the responsibility of looking after a certain young lady."

"Oh——"

"Wait a moment. I told him I would be delighted."

"Eb, that was unkind."

"Then he asked me to tell her he was coming over to-morrow morning to fix it up with her."

"Oh, horrible!" cried Betty. "Were those the words he used?"

"Betts, to tell the honest truth, he did not say much of anything. He just said: 'I love her,' and his eyes blazed."

Betty uttered a half articulate cry and ran to her room. Her heart was throbbing. What could she do? She felt that if she looked once into her lover's eyes she would have no strength. How dared she allow herself to be so weak! Yet she knew this was the end. She could deceive him no longer. For she felt a stir in her heart, stronger than all, beyond all resistance, an exquisite agony, the sweet, blind, tumultuous exultation of the woman who loves and is loved.

ess, what do you think?" said Colonel Zane, going into the kitchen next morning, after he had returned from the pasture. "Clarke just came over and asked for

Betty. I called her. She came down looking as sweet and cool as one of the lilies out by the spring. She said: 'Why, Mr. Clarke, you are almost a stranger. I am pleased to see you. Indeed, we are all very glad to know you have recovered from your severe burns.' She went on talking like that for all the world like a girl who didn't care a snap for him. And she knows as well as I do. Not only that, she has been actually breaking her heart over him all these months. How did she do it? Oh, you women beat me all hollow!"

"Would you expect Betty to fall into his arms?" asked the Colonel's worthy spouse, indignantly.

"Not exactly. But she was too cool, too friendly. Poor Alfred looked as if he hadn't slept. He was nervous and scared to death. When Betty ran up stairs I put a bug in Alfred's ear. He'll be all right now, if he follows my advice."

"Humph! What did Colonel Ebenezer Zane tell him?" asked Bessie, in disgust.

"Oh, not much. I simply told him not to lose his nerve; that a woman never meant 'no'; that she often says it only to be made to say 'yes.' And I ended up with telling him if she got a little skittish, as thoroughbreds do sometimes, to try a strong arm. That was my way."

"Colonel Zane, if my memory does not fail me, you were as humble and beseeching as the proudest girl could desire."

"I beseeching? Never!"

"I hope Alfred's wooing may go well. I like him very much. But I'm afraid. Betty has such a spirit that it is quite likely she will refuse him for no other reason than that he built his cabin before he asked her."

"Nonsense. He asked her long ago. Never fear, Bess, my sister will come back as meek as a lamb."

Meanwhile Betty and Alfred were strolling down the

familiar path toward the river. The October air was fresh with a suspicion of frost. The clear notes of a hunter's horn came floating down from the hills. A flock of wild geese had alighted on the marshy ground at the end of the island where they kept up a continual honk! honk! The brown hills, the red forest, and the yellow fields were now at the height of their autumnal beauty. Soon the November north wind would thrash the trees bare, and bow the proud heads of the daisies and the goldenrod; but just now they flashed in the sun, and swayed back and forth in all their glory.

"I see you limp. Are you not entirely well?" Betty was saying.

"Oh, I am getting along famously, thank you," said Alfred. "This one foot was quite severely burned and is still tender."

"You have had your share of injuries. I heard my brother say you had been wounded three times within a year."

"Four times."

"Jonathan told of the axe wound; then the wound Miller gave you, and finally the burns. These make three, do they not?"

"Yes, but you see, all three could not be compared to the one you forgot to mention."

"Let us hurry past here," said Betty, hastening to change the subject. "This is where you had the dreadful fight with Miller."

"As Miller did go to meet Girty, and as he did not return to the Fort with the renegade, we must believe he is dead. Of course, we do not know this to be actually a fact. But something makes me think so. Jonathan and Wetzel have not said anything; I can't get any satisfaction on that score from either; but I am sure neither of them would rest until Miller was dead."

"I think you are right. But we may never know. All I

can tell you is that Wetzel and Jack trailed Miller to the river, and then they both came back. I was the last to see Lewis that night before he left on Miller's trail. It isn't likely I shall forget what Lewis said and how he looked. Miller was a wicked man; yes, a traitor."

"He was a bad man, and he nearly succeeded in every one of his plans. I have not the slightest doubt that had he refrained from taking part in the shooting match he would have succeeded in abducting you, in killing me, and in leading Girty here long before he was expected."

"There are many things that may never be explained, but one thing Miller did always mystified us. How did he succeed in binding Tige?"

"To my way of thinking that was not so difficult as climbing into my room and almost killing me, or stealing the powder from Captain Boggs' room."

"The last, at least, gave me a chance to help," said Betty, with a touch of her old roguishness.

"That was the grandest thing a woman ever did," said Alfred, in a low tone.

"Oh, no, I only ran fast."

"I would have given the world to have seen you, but I was lying on the bench wishing I were dead. I did not have strength to look out of a porthole. Oh! that horrible time! I can never forget it. I lie awake at night and hear the yelling and shooting. Then I dream of running over the burning roofs and it all comes back so vividly I can almost feel the flames and smell the burnt wood. Then I wake up and think of that awful moment when you were carried into the blockhouse white, and, as I thought, dead."

"But I wasn't. And I think it best for us to forget that horrible siege. It is past. It is a miracle that any one was spared. Ebenezer says we should not grieve for those who are gone; they were heroic; they saved the Fort. He says, too, that we shall never again be troubled by Indians. Therefore let us forget and be happy. I have forgotten Miller. You can afford to do the same."

"Yes, I forgive him." Then, after a long silence, Alfred continued, "Will you go down to the old sycamore?"

Down the winding path they went. Coming to a steep place in the rocky bank Alfred jumped down and then turned to help Betty. But she avoided his gaze, pretended to not see his outstretched hands, and leaped lightly down beside him. He looked at her with perplexity and anxiety in his eyes. Before he could speak she ran on ahead of him and climbed down the bank to the pool. He followed slowly, thoughtfully. The supreme moment had come. He knew it, and somehow he did not feel the confidence the Colonel had inspired in him. It had been easy for him to think of subduing this imperious young lady; but when the time came to assert his will he found he could not remember what he had intended to say, and his feelings were divided between his love for her and the horrible fear that he should lose her.

When he reached the sycamore tree he found her sitting behind it with a cluster of yellow daisies in her lap. Alfred gazed at her, conscious that all his hopes of happiness were dependent on the next few words that would issue from her smiling lips. The little brown hands, which were now rather nervously arranging the flowers, held more than his life.

"Are they not sweet?" asked Betty, giving him a fleeting glance. "We call them 'black-eyed Susans.' Could anything be lovelier than that soft, dark brown?"

"Yes," answered Alfred, looking into her eyes.

"But––but you are not looking at my daisies at all," said Betty, lowering her eyes.

"No, I am not," said Alfred. Then suddenly: "A year ago this very day we were here."

"Here? Oh, yes, I believe I do remember. It was the day we came in my canoe and had such fine fishing."

"Is that all you remember?"

"I can recollect nothing in particular. It was so long ago."

"I suppose you will say you had no idea why I wanted you to come to this spot in particular."

"I supposed you simply wanted to take a walk, and it is very pleasant here."

"Then Colonel Zane did not tell you?" demanded Alfred. Receiving no reply he went on.

"Did you read my letter?"

"What letter?"

"The letter old Sam should have given you last fall. Did you read it?"

"Yes," answered Betty, faintly.

"Did your brother tell you I wanted to see you this morning?"

"Yes, he told me, and it made me very angry," said Betty, raising her head. There was a bright red spot in each cheek. "You—you seemed to think you—that I—well—I did not like it."

"I think I understand; but you are entirely wrong. I have never thought you cared for me. My wildest dreams never left me any confidence. Colonel Zane and Wetzel both had some deluded notion that you cared——"

"But they had no right to say that or to think it," said Betty, passionately. She sprang to her feet, scattering the daisies over the grass. "For them to presume that I cared for you is absurd. I never gave them any reason to think so, for—for I—I don't."

"Very well, then, there is nothing more to be said," answered Alfred, in a voice that was calm and slightly cold. "I am sorry if you have been annoyed. I have been mad, of course, but I promise you that you need fear no further annoyance from me. Come, I think we should return to the house."

And he turned and walked slowly up the path. He had taken perhaps a dozen steps when she called him.

"Mr. Clarke, come back."

Alfred retraced his steps and stood before her again. Then he saw a different Betty. The haughty poise had disappeared. Her head was bowed. Her little hands were tightly pressed over a throbbing bosom.

"Well," said Alfred, after a moment.

"Why—why are you in such a hurry to go?"

"I have learned what I wanted to know. And after that I do not imagine I would be very agreeable. I am going back. Are you coming?"

"I did not mean quite—quite what I said," whispered Betty.

"Then what did you mean?" asked Alfred, in a stern voice.

"I don't know. Please don't speak so."

"Betty, forgive my harshness. Can you expect a man to feel as I do and remain calm? You know I love you. You must not trifle any longer. You must not fight any longer."

"But I can't help fighting."

"Look at me," said Alfred, taking her hands. "Let me see your eyes. I believe you care a little for me, or else you wouldn't have called me back. I love you. Can you understand that?"

"Yes, I can; and I think you should love me a great deal to make up for what you made me suffer."

"Betty, look at me."

Slowly she raised her head and lifted the downcast eyes. Those telltale traitors no longer hid her secret. With a glad cry Alfred caught her in his arms. She tried to hide her face, but he got his hand under her chin and held it firmly so that the sweet crimson lips were very near his own. Then he slowly bent his head.

Betty saw his intention, closed her eyes and whispered:

"Alfred, please don't—it's not fair—I beg of you—Oh!"

That kiss was Betty's undoing. She uttered a strange little cry. Then her dark head found a hiding place over his heart, and her slender form, which a moment before had resisted so fiercely, sank yielding into his embrace.

"Betty, do you dare tell me now that you do not care for me?" Alfred whispered into the dusky hair which rippled over his breast.

Betty was brave even in her surrender. Her hands moved slowly upward along his arms, slipped over his shoulders, and clasped round his neck. Then she lifted a flushed and tearstained face with tremulous lips and wonderful shining eyes.

"Alfred, I do love you—with my whole heart I love you. I never knew until now."

The hours flew apace. The prolonged ringing of the dinner bell brought the lovers back to earth, and to the realization that the world held others than themselves. Slowly they climbed the familiar path, but this time as never before. They walked hand in hand. From the bluff they looked back. They wanted to make sure they were not dreaming. The water rushed over the fall more musically than ever before; the white patches of foam floated round and round the shady pool; the leaves of the sycamore rustled cheerily in the breeze. On a dead branch a woodpecker hammered industriously.

"Before we get out of sight of that dear old tree I want to make a confession," said Betty, as she stood before Alfred. She was pulling at the fringe on his hunting-coat.

"You need not make confessions to me."

"But this was dreadful; it preys on my conscience."

"Very well, I will be your judge. Your punishment shall be slight."

"One day when you were lying unconscious from your wound, Bessie sent me to watch you. I nursed you for hours, and—and—do not think badly of me—I—I kissed you."

"My darling," cried the enraptured young man.

When they at last reached the house they found Colonel Zane on the doorstep.

"Where on earth have you been?" he said. "Wetzel was here. He said he would not wait to see you. There he goes up the hill. He is behind that laurel."

They looked and presently saw the tall figure of the hunter emerge from the bushes. He stopped and leaned on his rifle. For a minute he remained motionless. Then he waved his hand and plunged into the thicket. Betty sighed and Alfred said:

"Poor Wetzel! ever restless, ever roaming."

"Hello, there!" exclaimed a voice. The lovers turned to see the smiling face of Isaac, and over his shoulder Myeerah's happy face beaming on them. "Alfred, you are a lucky dog. You can thank Myeerah and me for this; because if I had not taken to the river and nearly drowned myself to give you that opportunity you would not wear that happy face to-day. Blush away, Betts, it becomes you mightily."

"Bessie, here they are!" cried Colonel Zane, in his hearty voice. "She is tamed at last. No excuses, Alfred, in to dinner you go."

Colonel Zane pushed the young people up the steps before him, and stopping on the threshold while he knocked the ashes from his pipe, he smiled contentedly.

AFTERWORD

Betty lived all her after life on the scene of her famous exploit. She became a happy wife and mother. When she grew to be an old lady, with her grandchildren about her knee, she delighted to tell them that when a girl she had run the gauntlet of the Indians.

Colonel Zane became the friend of all redmen. He maintained a trading-post for many years, and his dealings were ever kind and honorable. After the country got settled he received from time to time various marks of distinction from the State, Colonial, and National governments. His most noted achievement was completed about 1796. President Washington, desiring to open a National road from Fort Henry to Maysville, Kentucky, paid a great tribute to Colonel Zane's ability by employing him to undertake the arduous task. His brother Jonathan and the Indian guide, Tomepomehala, rendered valuable aid in blazing out the path through the wilderness. This road, famous for many years as Zane's Trace, opened the beautiful Ohio valley to the ambitious pioneer. For this service Congress granted Colonel Zane the privilege of locating military warrants upon three sections of land, each a square mile in extent, which property the government eventually presented to him. Colonel Zane was the founder of Wheeling, Zanesville, Martin's Ferry, and Bridgeport. He died in 1811.

Isaac Zane received from the government a patent of ten thousand acres of land on Mad River. He established his home in the center of this tract, where he lived with the Wyandots until his death. A white settlement sprang up, prospered, and grew, and today it is the thriving city of Zanesfield.

Jonathan Zane settled down after peace was declared with the Indians, found himself a wife, and eventually became an influential citizen. However, he never lost his love for the wild woods. At times he would take down the old rifle and disappear for two or three days. He always returned cheerful and happy from these lonely hunts.

Wetzel alone did not take kindly to the march of civilization; but then he was a hunter, not a pioneer. He kept his word of peace with his old enemies, the Hurons, though he never abandoned his wandering and vengeful quests after the Delawares.

As the years passed Wetzel grew more silent and taciturn. From time to time he visited Fort Henry, and on these visits he spent hours playing with Betty's children. But he was restless in the settlement, and his sojourns grew briefer and more infrequent as time rolled on. True to his conviction that no wife existed on earth for him, he never married. His home was the trackless wilds, where he was true to his calling—a foe to the redman.

Wonderful to relate his long, black hair never adorned the walls of an Indian's lodge, where a warrior might point with grim pride and say: "No more does the Death-wind blow over the hills and vales." We could tell of how his keen eye once again saw Wingenund over the sights of his fatal rifle, and how he was once again a prisoner in the camp of that lifelong foe, but that's another story, which, perhaps, we may tell some day.

To-day the beautiful city of Wheeling rises on the

banks of the Ohio, where the yells of the Indians once blanched the cheeks of the pioneers. The broad, winding river rolls on as of yore; it alone remains unchanged. What were Indians and pioneers, forts and cities to it? Eons of time before human beings lived it flowed slowly toward the sea, and ages after men and their works are dust, it will roll on placidly with its eternal scheme of nature.

Upon the island still stand noble beeches, oaks, and chestnuts—trees that long ago have covered up their bullet-scars, but they could tell, had they the power to speak, many a wild thrilling tale. Beautiful parks and stately mansions grace the island; and polished equipages roll over the ground that once knew naught save the soft tread of the deer and the moccasin.

McColloch's Rock still juts boldly out over the river as steep and rugged as when the brave Major leaped to everlasting fame. Wetzel's Cave, so named to this day, remains on the side of the bluff overlooking the creek. The grapevines and wild rosebushes still cluster round the cavern-entrance, where, long ago, the wily savage was wont to lie in wait for the settler, lured there by the false turkey-call. The boys visit the cave on Saturday afternoons and play "Injuns."

Not long since the writer spent a quiet afternoon there, listening to the musical flow of the brook, and dreaming of those who had lived and loved, fought and died by that stream one hundred and twenty years ago. The city with its long blocks of buildings, its spires and bridges, faded away, leaving the scene as it was in the days of Fort Henry—unobscured by smoke, the river undotted by puffing boats, and everywhere the green and verdant forest.

Nothing was wanting in that dream picture: Betty tearing along on her pony; the pioneer plowing in the field; the stealthy approach of the savage; Wetzel and

Jonathan watching the river; the deer browsing with the cows in the pasture, and the old fort, grim and menacing on the bluff—all were there as natural as in those times which tried men's souls.

And as the writer awoke to the realities of life, that his dreams were of long ago, he was saddened by the thought that the labor of the pioneer is ended; his faithful, heroic wife's work is done. That beautiful country, which their sacrifices made ours, will ever be a monument to them.

Sad, too, is the thought that the poor Indian is un-mourned. He is almost forgotten; he is in the shadow; his songs are sung; no more will he sing to his dusky bride; his deeds are done; no more will he boast of his all-conquering arm or of his speed like the Northwind; no more will his heart bound at the whistle of the stag, for he sleeps in the shade of the oaks, under the moss and the ferns.

TO THE
LAST
MAN

FOREWORD

It was inevitable that in my efforts to write romantic history of the great West I should at length come to the story of a feud. For long I have steered clear of this rock. But at last I have reached it and must go over it, driven by my desire to chronicle the stirring events of pioneer days.

Even to-day it is not possible to travel into the remote corners of the West without seeing the lives of people still affected by a fighting past. How can the truth be told about the pioneering of the West if the struggle, the fight, the blood be left out? It cannot be done. How can a novel be stirring and thrilling, as were those times, unless it be full of sensation? My long labors have been devoted to making stories resemble the times they depict. I have loved the West for its vastness, its contrast, its beauty and color and life, for its wildness and violence, and for the fact that I have seen how it developed great men and women who died unknown and unsung.

In this materialistic age, this hard, practical, swift, greedy age of realism, it seems there is no place for writers of romance, no place for romance itself. For many years all the events leading up to the great war were realistic, and the war itself was horribly realistic, and the aftermath is likewise. Romance is only another name for idealism; and I contend that life without ideals is not worth living. Never in the history of the world were ideals needed so terribly as now. Walter Scott wrote romance; so did Victor Hugo; and likewise Kipling, Hawthorne, Stevenson. It was Stevenson, particularly, who wielded a bludgeon against the realists. People live for the dream in their hearts. And I have yet to know anyone who has not some secret dream, some hope, however dim, some storied wall to look at in the dusk, some painted window leading to the soul. How strange indeed to find that the realists have ideals and dreams! To read them one would think their lives held nothing significant. But they love, they hope, they dream, they sacrifice, they struggle on with that dream in their hearts just the same as others. We all are dreamers, if not in the heavy-lidded wasting of time, then in the meaning of life that makes us work on.

It was Wordsworth who wrote, "The world is too much with us"; and if I could give the secret of my ambition as a novelist in a few words it would be contained in that quotation. My inspiration to write has always come from nature. Character and action are subordinated to setting. In all that I have done I have tried to make people see how the world is too much with them. Getting and spending they lay waste their powers, with never a breath of the free and wonderful life of the open!

So I come back to the main point of this foreword, in which I am trying to tell why and how I came to write the story of a feud notorious in Arizona as the Pleasant Valley War.

Some years ago Mr. Harry Adams, a cattleman of Vermajo Park, New Mexico, told me he had been in the Tonto Basin of Arizona and thought I might find interesting material there concerning this Pleasant Valley War. His version of the war between cattlemen and sheepmen certainly determined me to look over the ground. My old guide, Al Doyle of Flagstaff, had led me over half of Arizona, but never down into that wonderful wild and rugged basin between the Mogollon Mesa and the Mazatzal Mountains. Doyle had long lived on the frontier and his version of the Pleasant Valley War differed markedly from that of Mr. Adams. I asked other old timers about it, and their remarks further excited my curiosity.

Once down there, Doyle and I found the wildest, most rugged, roughest, and most remarkable country either of us had visited; and the few inhabitants were like the country. I went in ostensibly to hunt bear and lion and turkey, but what I really was hunting for was the story of that Pleasant Valley War. I engaged the services of a bear hunter who had three strapping sons as reserved and strange and aloof as he was. No wheel tracks of any kind had ever come within miles of their cabin. I spent two wonderful months hunting game and reveling in the beauty and grandeur of that Rim Rock country, but I came out knowing no more about the Pleasant Valley War. These Texans and their few neighbors, likewise from Texas, did not talk. But all I saw and felt only inspired me the more. This trip was in the fall of 1918.

The next year I went again with the best horses, outfit, and men the Doyles could provide. And this time I did not ask any questions. But I rode horses—some of them too wild for me—and packed a rifle many a hundred miles, riding sometimes thirty and forty miles a day, and I climbed in and out of the deep cañons, desperately staying at the heels of one of those long-legged Texans. I learned the life of those backwoodsmen, but I did not get the story of the Pleasant Valley War. I had, however, won the friendship of that hardy people.

In 1920 I went back with a still larger outfit, equipped to stay as long as I liked. And this time, without my asking it, different natives of the Tonto came to tell me about the Pleasant Valley War. No two of them agreed on anything concerning it, except that only one of the active participants survived the fighting. Whence comes my title, *To the Last Man*. Thus I was swamped in a mass of material out of which I could only flounder to my own conclusion. Some of the stories told me are singularly tempting to a novelist. But, though I believe them myself, I cannot risk their improbability to those who have no idea of the wildness of wild men at a wild time. There really was a terrible and bloody feud, perhaps the most deadly and least known in all the annals of the West. I saw the ground, the cabins, the graves, all so darkly suggestive of what must have happened.

I never learned the truth of the cause of the Pleasant Valley War, or if I did hear it I had no means of recognizing it. All the given causes were plausible and convincing. Strange to state, there is still secrecy and reticence all over the Tonto Basin as to the facts of this feud. Many descendents of those killed are living there now. But no one likes to talk about it. Assuredly many of the incidents told me really occurred, as, for example, the terrible one of the two women, in the face of relentless enemies, saving the bodies of their dead husbands from being devoured by wild hogs. Suffice it to say that this romance is true to my conception of the war, and I base it upon the setting I learned to know and love so well, upon the strange passions of primitive people, and upon my instinctive reaction to the facts and rumors that I gathered.

ZANE GREY

AVALON, CALIFORNIA

April, 1921

CHAPTER 1

At the end of a dry, uphill ride over barren country Jean Isbel unpacked to camp at the edge of the cedars where a little rocky cañon, green with willow and cottonwood, promised water and grass.

His animals were tired, especially the pack mule that had carried a heavy load; and with slow heave of relief they knelt and rolled in the dust. Jean experienced something of relief himself as he threw off his chaps. He had not been used to hot, dusty, glaring days on the barren lands. Stretching his long length beside a tiny rill of clear water that tinkled over the red stones, he drank thirstily. The water was cool, but it had an acrid taste—an alkali bite that he did not like. Not since he had left Oregon had he tasted clear, sweet, cold water; and he missed it just as he longed for the stately shady forests he had loved. This wild, endless Arizona land bade fair to earn his hatred.

By the time he had leisurely completed his tasks twilight had fallen and coyotes had begun their barking. Jean listened to the yelps and to the moan of the cool wind in the cedars with a sense of satisfaction that these lonely sounds were familiar. This cedar wood burned into a pretty fire and the smell of its smoke was newly pleasant.

"Reckon maybe I'll learn to like Arizona," he mused, half aloud. "But I've a hankerin' for waterfalls an' dark-green forests. Must be the Indian in me. . . . Anyway, dad needs me bad, an' I reckon I'm here for keeps."

Jean threw some cedar branches on the fire, in the light of which he opened his father's letter, hoping by repeated reading to grasp more of its strange portent. It had been two months in reaching him, coming by traveler, by stage and train, and then by boat, and finally by stage again. Written in lead pencil on a leaf torn from an old ledger, it would have been hard to read even if the writing had been more legible.

"Dad's writin' was always bad, but I never saw it so shaky," said Jean, thinking aloud.

GRASS VALLY, ARIZONA.

SON JEAN,—Come home. Here is your home and here your needed. When we left Oregon we all reckoned you would not be long behind. But its years now. I am growing old, son, and you was always my steadiest boy. Not that you ever was so dam steady. Only your wildness seemed more for the woods. You take after mother, and your brothers Bill and Guy take after me. That is the red and white of it. Your part Indian, Jean, and that Indian I reckon I am going to need bad. I am rich in cattle and horses. And my range here is the best I ever seen. Lately we have been losing stock. But that is not all nor so bad. Sheepmen have moved into the Tonto and are grazing down on Grass Vally. Cattlemen and sheepmen can never bide in this country. We have bad times ahead. Reckon I have more reasons to worry and need you, but you must wait to hear that by word of mouth. Whatever your doing, chuck it and rustle for Grass Vally so to make here by spring. I am asking you to take pains to pack in some guns and a lot of shells. And hide them in your outfit. If you meet any-one when your coming down into the Tonto, listen more than you talk. And last, son, dont let anything keep you in Oregon. Reckon you have a sweetheart, and if so fetch her along. With love from your dad,

GASTON ISBEL.

Jean pondered over this letter. Judged by memory of his father, who had always been self-sufficient, it had been a surprise and somewhat of a shock. Weeks of travel and reflection had not helped him to grasp the meaning between the lines.

"Yes, dad's growin' old," mused Jean, feeling a warmth and a sadness stir in him. "He must be 'way over sixty. But he never looked old. . . . So he's rich now an' losin' stock, an' goin' to be sheeped off his range. Dad could stand a lot of rustlin', but not much from sheepmen."

The softness that stirred in Jean merged into a cold, thoughtful earnestness which had followed every perusal of his father's letter. A dark, full current seemed flowing in his veins, and at times he felt it swell and heat. It trou-bled him, making him conscious of a deeper, stronger self, opposed to his careless, free, and dreamy nature. No ties had bound him in Oregon, except love for the great, still forests and the thundering rivers; and this love came from his softer side. It had cost him a wrench to leave. And all the way by ship down the coast to San Diego and across the Sierra Madres by stage, and so on to this last overland travel by horseback, he had felt a retreating of the self that was tranquil and happy and a dominating of this unknown somber self, with its menacing possibilities. Yet despite a nameless regret and a loyalty to Oregon, when he lay in his blankets he had to confess a keen interest in his adventurous future, a keen enjoyment of this stark, wild Arizona. It appeared to be a different

sky stretching in dark, star-spangled dome over him—
closer, vaster, bluer. The strong fragrance of sage and
cedar floated over him with the camp-fire smoke, and all
seemed drowsily to subdue his thoughts.

At dawn he rolled out of his blankets and, pulling on
his boots, began the day with a zest for the work that must
bring closer his calling future. White, crackling frost
and cold, nipping air were the same keen spurs to action
that he had known in the uplands of Oregon, yet they were
not wholly the same. He sensed an exhilaration similar
to the effect of a strong, sweet wine. His horse and mule
had fared well during the night, having been much re-
freshed by the grass and water of the little cañon. Jean
mounted and rode into the cedars with gladness that at
last he had put the endless leagues of barren land behind
him.

The trail he followed appeared to be seldom traveled.
It led, according to the meager information obtainable at
the last settlement, directly to what was called the Rim,
and from there Grass Valley could be seen down in the
Basin. The ascent of the ground was so gradual that only
in long, open stretches could it be seen. But the nature
of the vegetation showed Jean how he was climbing.
Scant, low, scraggy cedars gave place to more numerous,
darker, greener, bushier ones, and these to high, full-
foliaged, green-berried trees. Sage and grass in the open
flats grew more luxuriously. Then came the piñons, and
presently among them the checker-barked junipers. Jean
hailed the first pine tree with a hearty slap on the brown,
rugged bark. It was a small dwarf pine struggling to live.
The next one was larger, and after that came several, and
beyond them pines stood up everywhere above the lower
trees. Odor of pine needles mingled with the other dry
smells that made the wind pleasant to Jean. In an hour

from the first line of pines he had ridden beyond the cedars and piñons into a slowly thickening and deepening forest. Underbrush appeared scarce except in ravines, and the ground in open patches held a bleached grass. Jean's eye roved for sight of squirrels, birds, deer, or any moving creature. It appeared to be a dry, uninhabited forest. About midday Jean halted at a pond of surface water, evidently melted snow, and gave his animals a drink. He saw a few old deer tracks in the mud and several huge bird tracks new to him which he concluded must have been made by wild turkeys.

The trail divided at this pond. Jean had no idea which branch he ought to take. "Reckon it doesn't matter," he muttered, as he was about to remount. His horse was standing with ears up, looking back along the trail. Then Jean heard a clip-clop of trotting hoofs, and presently espied a horseman.

Jean made a pretense of tightening his saddle girths while he peered over his horse at the approaching rider. All men in this country were going to be of exceeding interest to Jean Isbel. This man at a distance rode and looked like all the Arizonians Jean had seen, he had a superb seat in the saddle, and he was long and lean. He wore a huge black sombrero and a soiled red scarf. His vest was open and he was without a coat.

The rider came trotting up and halted several paces from Jean.

"Hullo, stranger!" he said, gruffly.

"Howdy yourself!" replied Jean. He felt an instinctive importance in the meeting with the man. Never had sharper eyes flashed over Jean and his outfit. He had a dust-colored, sun-burned face, long, lean, and hard, a huge sandy mustache that hid his mouth, and eyes of piercing light intensity. Not very much hard Western experience had passed by this man, yet he was not old, measured by years. When he dismounted Jean saw he was tall, even for an Arizonian.

"Seen your tracks back a ways," he said, as he slipped the bit to let his horse drink. "Where bound?"

"Reckon I'm lost, all right," replied Jean. "New country for me."

"Shore. I seen thet from your tracks an' your last camp. Wal, where was you headin' for before you got lost?"

The query was deliberately cool, with a dry, crisp ring. Jean felt the lack of friendliness or kindliness in it.

"Grass Valley. My name's Isbel," he replied, shortly.

The rider attended to his drinking horse and presently rebridled him; then with long swing of leg he appeared to step into the saddle.

"Shore I knowed you was Jean Isbel," he said. "Everybody in the Tonto has heerd old Gass Isbel sent fer his boy."

"Well then, why did you ask?" inquired Jean, bluntly.

"Reckon I wanted to see what you'd say."

"So? All right. But I'm not carin' very much for what *you* say."

Their glances locked steadily then and each measured the other by the intangible conflict of spirit.

"Shore thet's natural," replied the rider. His speech was slow, and the motions of his long, brown hands, as he took a cigarette from his vest, kept time with his words. "But seein' you're one of the Isbels, I'll hev my say whether you want it or not. My name's Colter an' I'm one of the sheepmen Gass Isbel's riled with."

"Colter. Glad to meet you," replied Jean. "An' I reckon who riled my father is goin' to rile me."

"Shore. If thet wasn't so you'd not be an Isbel," returned Colter, with a grim little laugh. "It's easy to see you ain't run into any Tonto Basin fellers yet. Wal, I'm goin' to tell you thet your old man gabbed like a woman down at

Greaves's store. Bragged aboot you an' how you could fight an' how you could shoot an' how you could track a hoss or a man! Bragged how you'd chase every sheep herder back up on the Rim. . . . I'm tellin' you because we want you to git our stand right. We're goin' to run sheep down in Grass Valley."

"Ahuh! Well, who's we?" queried Jean, curtly.

"Wha-at? . . . We—I mean the sheepmen rangin' this Rim from Black Butte to the Apache country."

"Colter, I'm a stranger in Arizona," said Jean, slowly. "I know little about ranchers or sheepmen. It's true my father sent for me. It's true, I dare say, that he bragged, for he was given to bluster an' blow. An' he's old now. I can't help it if he bragged about me. But if he has, an' if he's justified in his stand against you sheepmen, I'm goin' to do my best to live up to his brag."

"I get your hunch. Shore we understand each other, an' thet's a powerful help. You take my hunch to your old man," replied Colter, as he turned his horse away toward the left. "Thet trail leadin' south is yours. When you come to the Rim you'll see a bare spot down in the Basin. Thet'll be Grass Valley."

He rode away out of sight into the woods. Jean leaned against his horse and pondered. It seemed difficult to be just to this Colter, not because of his claims, but because of a subtle hostility that emanated from him. Colter had the hard face, the masked intent, the turn of speech that Jean had come to associate with dishonest men. Even if Jean had not been prejudiced, if he had known nothing of his father's trouble with these sheepmen, and if Colter had met him only to exchange glances and greetings, still Jean would never have had a favorable impression. Colter grated upon him, roused an antagonism seldom felt.

"Heigho!" sighed the young man. "Good-by to huntin' an' fishin'! Dad's given me a man's job."

340 ★ ZANE GREY

With that he mounted his horse and started the pack mule into the right-hand trail. Walking and trotting, he traveled all afternoon, toward sunset getting into heavy forest of pine. More than one snow bank showed white through the green, sheltered on the north slopes of shady ravines. And it was upon entering this zone of richer, deeper forestland that Jean sloughed off his gloomy forebodings. These stately pines were not the giant firs of Oregon, but any lover of the woods could be happy under them. Higher still he climbed until the forest spread before and around him like a level park, with thicketed ravines here and there on each side. And presently that deceitful level led to a higher bench upon which the pines towered, and were matched by beautiful trees he took for spruce. Heavily barked, with regular spreading branches, these conifers rose in symmetrical shape to spear the sky with silver plumes. A graceful gray-green moss, waved like veils from the branches. The air was not so dry and it was colder, with a scent and touch of snow. Jean made camp at the first likely site; taking the precaution to unroll his bed some little distance from his fire. Under the softly moaning pines he felt comfortable, having lost the sense of an immeasurable open space falling away from all around him.

The gobbling of wild turkeys awakened Jean, "Chug-a-lug, chug-a-lug, chug-a-lug-chug." There was not a great difference between the gobble of a wild turkey and that of a tame one. Jean got up, and taking his rifle went out into the gray obscurity of dawn to try to locate the turkeys. But it was too dark, and finally when daylight came they appeared to be gone. The mule had strayed, and, what with finding it and cooking breakfast and packing, Jean did not make a very early start. On this last lap of his long journey he had slowed down. He was weary of hurrying; the change from weeks in the glaring sun and dust-laden wind to this sweet cool darkly green and brown forest was very welcome; he wanted to linger along the shaded trail. This day he made sure would see him reach the Rim. By and by he lost the trail. It had just worn out from lack of use. Every now and then Jean would cross an old trail, and as he penetrated deeper into the forest every damp or dusty spot showed tracks of turkey, deer, and bear. The amount of bear sign surprised him. Presently his keen nostrils were assailed by a smell of sheep, and soon he rode into a broad sheep trail. From the tracks Jean calculated that the sheep had passed there the day before.

An unreasonable antipathy seemed born in him. To be sure he had been prepared to dislike sheep, and that was why he was unreasonable. But on the other hand this band of sheep had left a broad bare swath, weedless, grassless, flowerless, in their wake. Where sheep grazed they destroyed. That was what Jean had against them.

An hour later he rode to the crest of a long parklike slope, where new green grass was sprouting and flowers peeped everywhere. The pines appeared far apart; gnarled oak trees showed rugged and gray against the green wall of woods. A white strip of snow gleamed like a moving stream away down in the woods.

Jean heard the musical tinkle of bells and the baa-baa of sheep and the faint, sweet bleating of lambs. As he rode toward these sounds a dog ran out from an oak thicket and barked at him. Next Jean smelled a camp-fire and soon he caught sight of a curling blue column of smoke, and then a small peaked tent. Beyond the clump of oaks Jean encountered a Mexican lad carrying a carbine. The boy had a swarthy, pleasant face, and to Jean's greeting he replied, *"Buenos dias."* Jean understood little Spanish, and about all he gathered by his simple queries was that the lad was not alone—and that it was "lambing time."

This latter circumstance grew noisily manifest. The forest seemed shrilly full of incessant baas and plaintive bleats. All about the camp, on the slope, in the glades, and everywhere, were sheep. A few were grazing; many were lying down; most of them were ewes suckling white fleecy little lambs that staggered on their feet. Everywhere Jean saw tiny lambs just born. Their pin-pointed bleats pierced the heavier baa-baa of their mothers.

Jean dismounted and led his horse down toward the camp, where he rather expected to see another and older Mexican, from whom he might get information. The lad walked with him. Down this way the plaintive uproar made by the sheep was not so loud.

"Hello there!" called Jean, cheerfully, as he approached the tent. No answer was forthcoming. Dropping his bridle, he went on, rather slowly, looking for some one to appear. Then a voice from one side startled him.

"Mawnin', stranger."

A girl stepped out from beside a pine. She carried a rifle. Her face flashed richly brown, but she was not Mexican. This fact, and the sudden conviction that she had been watching him, somewhat disconcerted Jean.

"Beg pardon—miss," he floundered. "Didn't expect to see a—girl. . . . I'm sort of lost—lookin' for the Rim—an' thought I'd find a sheep herder who'd show me. I can't savvy this boy's lingo."

While he spoke it seemed to him an intentness of expression, a strain relaxed from her face. A faint suggestion of hostility likewise disappeared. Jean was not even sure that he had caught it, but there had been something that now was gone.

"Shore I'll be glad to show y'u," she said.

"Thanks, miss. Reckon I can breathe easy now," he replied. "It's a long ride from San Diego. Hot an' dusty!

I'm pretty tired. An' maybe this woods isn't good medicine to achin' eyes!"

"San Diego! Y'u're from the coast?"

"Yes."

Jean had doffed his sombrero at sight of her and he still held it, rather deferentially, perhaps. It seemed to attract her attention.

"Put on y'ur hat, stranger. . . . Shore I can't recollect when any man bared his haid to me." She uttered a little laugh in which surprise and frankness mingled with a tint of bitterness.

Jean sat down with his back to a pine, and, laying the sombrero by his side, he looked full at her, conscious of a singular eagerness, as if he wanted to verify by close scrutiny a first hasty impression. If there had been an instinct in his meeting with Colter, there was more in this. The girl half sat, half leaned against a log, with the shiny little carbine across her knees. She had a level, curious gaze upon him, and Jean had never met one just like it. Her eyes were rather a wide oval in shape, clear and steady, with shadows of thought in their amber-brown depths. They seemed to look through Jean, and his gaze dropped first. Then it was he saw her ragged homespun skirt and a few inches of brown, bare ankles, strong and round, and crude worn-out moccasins that failed to hide the shapeliness of her feet. Suddenly she drew back her stockingless ankles and ill-shod little feet. When Jean lifted his gaze again he found her face half averted and a stain of red in the gold tan of her cheek. That touch of embarrassment somehow removed her from this strong, raw, wild woodland setting. It changed her poise. It detracted from the curious, unabashed, almost bold, look that he had encountered in her eyes.

"Reckon you're from Texas," said Jean, presently.

"Shore am," she drawled. She had a lazy Southern voice, pleasant to hear. "How'd y'u-all guess that?"

"Anybody can tell a Texan. Where I came from there were a good many pioneers an' ranchers from the old Lone Star State. I've worked for several. An', come to think of it, I'd rather hear a Texas girl talk than anybody."

"Did y'u know many Texas girls?" she inquired, turning again to face him.

"Reckon I did—quite a good many."

"Did y'u go with them?"

"Go with them? Reckon you mean keep company. Why, yes, I guess I did—a little," laughed Jean. "Sometimes on a Sunday or a dance once in a blue moon, an' occasionally a ride."

"Shore that accounts," said the girl, wistfully.

"For what?" asked Jean.

"Y'ur bein' a gentleman," she replied, with force. "Oh, I've not forgotten. I had friends when we lived in Texas. . . . Three years ago. Shore it seems longer. Three miserable years in this damned country!"

Then she bit her lip, evidently to keep back further unwitting utterance to a total stranger. And it was that biting of her lip that drew Jean's attention to her mouth. It held beauty of curve and fullness and color that could not hide a certain sadness and bitterness. Then the whole flashing brown face changed for Jean. He saw that it was young, full of passion and restraint, possessing a power which grew on him. This, with her shame and pathos and the fact that she craved respect, gave a leap to Jean's interest.

"Well, I reckon you flatter me," he said, hoping to put her at her ease again. "I'm only a rough hunter an' fisherman—woodchopper an' horse tracker. Never had all the school I needed—nor near enough company of nice girls like you."

"Am I nice?" she asked, quickly.

"You sure are," he replied, smiling.

"In these rags," she demanded, with a sudden flash of passion that thrilled him. "Look at the holes." She showed rips and worn-out places in the sleeves of her buckskin blouse, through which gleamed a round, brown arm. "I sew when I have anythin' to sew with. . . . Look at my skirt—a dirty rag. An' I have only one other to my name. . . . Look!" Again a color tinged her cheeks, most becoming, and giving the lie to her action. But shame could not check her violence now. A dammed-up resentment seemed to have broken out in flood. She lifted the ragged skirt almost to her knees. "No stockings! No shoes! . . . How can a girl be nice when she has no clean, decent woman's clothes to wear?"

"How—how can a girl . . ." began Jean. "See here, miss, I'm beggin' your pardon for—sort of stirrin' you to forget yourself a little. Reckon I understand. You don't meet many stranger an' I sort of hit you wrong—makin' you feel too much—an' talk too much. Who an' what you are is none of my business. But we met. . . . An' I reckon somethin' has happened—perhaps more to me than to you. . . . Now let me put you straight about clothes an' women. Reckon I know most women love nice things to wear an' think because clothes make them look pretty that they're nicer or better. But they're wrong. You're wrong. Maybe it 'd be too much for a girl like you to be happy without clothes. But you can be—you are just as nice, an'—an' fine—an', for all you know, a good deal more appealin' to some men."

"Stranger, y'u shore must excuse my temper an' the show I made of myself," replied the girl, with composure. "That, to say the least, was not nice. An' I don't want anyone thinkin' better of me than I deserve. My mother died in Texas, an' I've lived out heah in this wild country—a girl alone among rough men. Meetin' y'u to-day makes me see what a hard lot they are—an' what it's done to me."

Jean smothered his curiosity and tried to put out of his mind a growing sense that he pitied her, liked her.

"Are you a sheep herder?" he asked.

"Shore I am now an' then. My father lives back heah in a cañon. He's a sheepman. Lately there's been herders shot at. Just now we're short an' I have to fill in. But I like shepherdin' an' I love the woods, and the Rim Rock an' all the Tonto. If they were all, I'd shore be happy."

"Herders shot at!" exclaimed Jean, thoughtfully. "By whom? An' what for?"

"Trouble brewin' between the cattlemen down in the Basin an' the sheepmen up on the Rim. Dad says there'll shore be hell to pay. I tell him I hope the cattlemen chase him back to Texas."

"Then—Are you on the ranchers' side?" queried Jean, trying to pretend casual interest.

"No. I'll always be on my father's side," she replied, with spirit. "But I'm bound to admit I think the cattlemen have the fair side of the argument."

"How so?"

"Because there's grass everywhere. I see no sense in a sheepman goin' out of his way to surround a cattleman an' sheep off his range. That started the row. Lord knows how it 'll end. For most all of them heah are from Texas."

"So I was told," replied Jean. "An' I heard 'most all these Texans got run out of Texas. Any truth in that?"

"Shore I reckon there is," she replied, seriously. "But, stranger, it might not be healthy for y'u to say that anywhere. My dad, for one, was not run out of Texas. Shore I never can see why he came heah. He's accumulated stock, but he's not rich nor so well off as he was back home."

"Are you goin' to stay here always?" queried Jean, suddenly.

"If I do so it 'll be in my grave," she answered, darkly. "But what's the use of thinkin'? People stay places until they drift away. Y'u can never tell. . . . Well, stranger, this talk is keepin' y'u."

She seemed moody now, and a note of detachment crept into her voice. Jean rose at once and went for his horse. If this girl did not desire to talk further he certainly had no wish to annoy her. His mule had strayed off among the bleating sheep. Jean drove it back and then led his horse up to where the girl stood. She appeared taller and, though not of robust build, she was vigorous and lithe, with something about her that fitted the place. Jean was loath to bid her good-by.

"Which way is the Rim?" he asked, turning to his saddle girths.

"South," she replied, pointing. "It's only a mile or so. I'll walk down with y'u. . . . Suppose y'u're on the way to Grass Valley?"

"Yes; I've relatives there," he returned. He dreaded her next question, which he suspected would concern his name. But she did not ask. Taking up her rifle she turned away. Jean strode ahead to her side. "Reckon if you walk I won't ride."

So he found himself beside a girl with the free step of a mountaineer. Her bare, brown head came up nearly to his shoulder. It was a small, pretty head, graceful, well held, and the thick hair on it was a shiny, soft brown. She wore it in a braid, rather untidily and tangled, he thought, and it was tied with a string of buckskin. Altogether her apparel proclaimed poverty.

Jean let the conversation languish for a little. He wanted to think what to say presently, and then he felt a rather vague pleasure in stalking beside her. Her profile was straight cut and exquisite in line. From this side view the soft curve of lips could not be seen.

She made several attempts to start conversation, all of which Jean ignored, manifestly to her growing constraint. Presently Jean, having decided what he wanted to say, suddenly began: "I like this adventure. Do you?"

"Adventure! Meetin' me in the woods?" And she laughed the laugh of youth. "Shore you must be hard up for adventure, stranger."

"Do you like it?" he persisted, and his eyes searched the half-averted face.

"I might like it," she answered, frankly, "if—if my temper had not made a fool of me. I never meet any one I care to talk to. Why should it not be pleasant to run across some one new—some one strange in this heah wild country?"

"We are as we are," said Jean, simply. "I didn't think you made a fool of yourself. If I thought so, would I want to see you again?"

"Do y'u?" The brown face flashed on him with surprise, with a light he took for gladness. And because he wanted to appear calm and friendly, not too eager, he had to deny himself the thrill of meeting those changing eyes.

"Sure I do. Reckon I'm overbold on such short acquaintance. But I might not have another chance to tell you, so please don't hold it against me."

This declaration over, Jean felt relief and something of exultation. He had been afraid he might not have the courage to make it. She walked on as before, only with her head bowed a little and her eyes downcast. No color but the gold-brown tan and the blue tracery of veins showed in her cheeks. He noticed then a slight swelling quiver of her throat; and he became alive to its graceful contour, and to how full and pulsating it was, how nobly it set into the curve of her shoulder. Here in her quivering throat was

the weakness of her, the evidence of her sex, the woman-
liness that belied the mountaineer stride and the grasp of
strong brown hands on a rifle. It had an effect on Jean totally inexplicable to him, both in the strange warmth that
stole over him and in the utterance he could not hold back.

"Girl, we're strangers, but what of that? We've met, an'
I tell you it means somethin' to me. I've known girls for
months an' never felt this way. I don't know who you are
an' I don't care. You betrayed a good deal to me. You're
not happy. You're lonely. An' if I didn't want to see you
again for my own sake, I would for yours. Some things
you said I'll not forget soon. I've got a sister, an' I know
you have no brother. An' I reckon . . ."

At this juncture Jean in his earnestness and quite without thought grasped her hand. The contact checked the
flow of his speech and suddenly made him aghast at his
temerity. But the girl did not make any effort to withdraw
it. So Jean, inhaling a deep breath and trying to see
through his bewilderment, held on bravely. He imagined
he felt a faint, warm, returning pressure. She was young,
she was friendless, she was human. By this hand in his
Jean felt more than ever the loneliness of her. Then, just
as he was about to speak again, she pulled her hand free.

"Heah's the Rim," she said, in her quaint Southern
drawl. "An' there's y'ur Tonto Basin."

Jean had been intent only upon the girl. He had kept
step beside her without taking note of what was ahead of
him. At her words he looked up expectantly, to be struck
mute.

He felt a sheer force, a downward drawing of an immense abyss beneath him. As he looked afar he saw a
black basin of timbered country, the darkest and wildest
he had ever gazed upon, a hundred miles of blue distance
across to an unflung mountain range, hazy purple against
the sky. It seemed to be a stupendous gulf surrounded on

three sides by bold, undulating lines of peaks, and on his side by a wall so high that he felt lifted aloft on the rim of the sky.

"Southeast y'u see the Sierra Anchas," said the girl, pointing. "That notch in the range is the pass where sheep are driven to Phoenix an' Maricopa. Those big rough mountains to the south are the Mazatzals. Round to the west is the Four Peaks Range. An' y'u're standin' on the Rim."

Jean could not see at first just what the Rim was, but by shifting his gaze westward he grasped this remarkable phenomenon of nature. For leagues and leagues a colossal red and yellow wall, a rampart, a mountain-faced cliff, seemed to zigzag westward. Grand and bold were the promontories reaching out over the void. They ran toward the westering sun. Sweeping and impressive were the long lines slanting away from them, sloping darkly spotted down to merge into the black timber. Jean had never seen such a wild and rugged manifestation of nature's depths and upheavals. He was held mute.

"Stranger, look down," said the girl.

Jean's sight was educated to judge heights and depths and distances. This wall upon which he stood sheered precipitously down, so far that it made him dizzy to look, and then the craggy broken cliffs merged into red-slided, cedar-greened slopes running down and down into gorges choked with forests, and from which soared up a roar of rushing waters. Slope after slope, ridge beyond ridge, cañon merging into cañon—so the tremendous bowl sunk away to its black, deceiving depths, a wilderness across which travel seemed impossible.

"Wonderful!" exclaimed Jean.

"Indeed it is!" murmured the girl. "Shore that is Arizona. I reckon I love *this*. The heights an' depths—the awfulness of its wilderness!"

"An' you want to leave it?"

"Yes an' no. I don't deny the peace that comes to me heah. But not often do I see the Basin, an' for that matter, one doesn't live on grand scenery."

"Child, even once in a while—this sight would cure any misery, if you only see. I'm glad I came. I'm glad you showed it to me first."

She too seemed under the spell of a vastness and loneliness and beauty and grandeur that could not but strike the heart.

Jean took her hand again. "Girl, say you will meet me here," he said, his voice ringing deep in his ears.

"Shore I will," she replied, softly, and turned to him. It seemed then that Jean saw her face for the first time. She was beautiful as he had never known beauty. Limned against that scene, she gave it life—wild, sweet, young life—the poignant meaning of which haunted yet eluded him. But she belonged there. Her eyes were again searching his, as if for some lost part of herself, unrealized, never known before. Wondering, wistful, hopeful, glad— they were eyes that seemed surprised, to reveal part of her soul.

Then her red lips parted. Their tremulous movement was a magnet to Jean. An invisible and mighty force pulled him down to kiss them. Whatever the spell had been, that rude, unconscious action broke it.

He jerked away, as if he expected to be struck. "Girl— I—I"—he gasped in amaze and sudden-dawning contrition—"I kissed you—but I swear it wasn't intentional—I never thought. . . ."

The anger that Jean anticipated failed to materialize. He stood, breathing hard, with a hand held out in unconscious appeal. By the same magic, perhaps, that had transfigured her a moment past, she was now invested again by the older character.

"Shore I reckon my callin' y'u a gentleman was a little previous," she said, with a rather dry bitterness. "But, stranger, y'u're sudden."

"You're not insulted?" asked Jean, hurriedly.

"Oh, I've been kissed before. Shore men are all alike."

"They're not," he replied, hotly, with a subtle rush of disillusion, a dulling of enchantment. "Don't you class me with other men who've kissed you. I wasn't myself when I did it an' I'd have gone on my knees to ask your forgiveness. . . . But now I wouldn't—an' I wouldn't kiss you again, either—even if you—you wanted it."

Jean read in her strange gaze what seemed to him a vague doubt, as if she was questioning him.

"Miss, I take that back," added Jean, shortly. "I'm sorry. I didn't mean to be rude. It was a mean trick for me to kiss you. A girl alone in the woods who's gone out of her way to be kind to me! I don't know why I forgot my manners. An' I ask your pardon."

She looked away then, and presently pointed far out and down into the Basin.

"There's Grass Valley. That long gray spot in the black. It's about fifteen miles. Ride along the Rim that way till y'u cross a trail. Shore y'u can't miss it. Then go down."

"I'm much obliged to you," replied Jean, reluctantly accepting what he regarded as his dismissal. Turning his horse, he put his foot in the stirrup, then, hesitating, he looked across the saddle at the girl. Her abstraction, as she gazed away over the purple depths, suggested loneliness and wistfulness. She was not thinking of that scene spread so wondrously before her. It struck Jean she might be pondering a subtle change in his feeling and attitude, something he was conscious of, yet could not define.

"Reckon this is good-by," he said, with hesitation.

"*Adios, señor,*" she replied, facing him again. She lifted

the little carbine to the hollow of her elbow and, half turning, appeared ready to depart.

"Adios means good-by?" he queried.

"Yes, good-by till to-morrow or good-by forever. Take it as y'u like."

"Then you'll meet me here day after to-morrow?" How eagerly he spoke, on impulse, without a consideration of the intangible thing that had changed him!

"Did I say I wouldn't?"

"No. But I reckoned you'd not care to after——" he replied, breaking off in some confusion.

"Shore I'll be glad to meet y'u. Day after to-morrow about mid-afternoon. Right heah. Fetch all the news from Grass Valley."

"All right. Thanks. That 'll be—fine," replied Jean, and as he spoke he experienced a buoyant thrill, a pleasant lightness of enthusiasm, such as always stirred boyishly in him at a prospect of adventure. Before it passed he wondered at it and felt unsure of himself. He needed to think.

"Stranger, shore I'm not recollectin' that y'u told me who y'u are," she said.

"No, reckon I didn't tell," he returned. "What difference does that make? I said I didn't care who or what you are. Can't you feel the same about me?"

"Shore—I felt that way," she replied, somewhat nonplussed, with the level brown gaze steadily on his face. "But now y'u make me think."

"Let's meet without knowin' any more about each other than we do now."

"Shore. I'd like that. In this big wild Arizona a girl—an' I reckon a man—feels so insignificant. What's a name, anyhow? Still, people an' things have to be distinguished. I'll call y'u 'Stranger' an' be satisfied—if y'u say it's fair for y'u not to tell who y'u are."

"Fair! No, it's not," declared Jean, forced to confession. "My name's Jean—Jean Isbel."

"*Isbel!*" she exclaimed, with a violent start. "Shore y'u can't be son of old Gass Isbel. . . . I've seen both his sons."

"He has three," replied Jean, with relief, now the secret was out. "I'm the youngest. I'm twenty-four. Never been out of Oregon till now. On my way—"

The brown color slowly faded out of her face, leaving her quite pale, with eyes that began to blaze. The suppleness of her seemed to stiffen.

"My name's Ellen Jorth," she burst out, passionately. "Does it mean anythin' to y'u?"

"Never heard it in my life," protested Jean. "Sure I reckoned you belonged to the sheep raisers who 're on the outs with my father. That's why I had to tell you I'm Jean Isbel. . . . Ellen Jorth. It's strange an' pretty. . . . Reckon I can be just as good a—a friend to you—"

"No Isbel can ever be a friend to me," she said, with bitter coldness. Stripped of her ease and her soft wistfulness, she stood before him one instant, entirely another girl, a hostile enemy. Then she wheeled and strode off into the woods.

Jean, in amaze, in consternation, watched her swiftly draw away with her lithe, free step, wanting to follow her, wanting to call to her; but the resentment roused by her suddenly avowed hostility held him mute in his tracks. He watched her disappear, and when the brown-and-green wall of forest swallowed the slender gray form he fought against the insistent desire to follow her, and fought in vain.

CHAPTER 2

But Ellen Jorth's moccasined feet did not leave a distinguishable trail on the springy pine needle covering of the ground, and Jean could not find any trace of her.

A little futile searching to and fro cooled his impulse and called pride to his rescue. Returning to his horse, he mounted, rode out behind the pack mule to start it along, and soon felt the relief of decision and action. Clumps of small pines grew thickly in spots on the Rim, making it necessary for him to skirt them; at which times he lost sight of the purple basin. Every time he came back to an opening through which he could see the wild ruggedness and colors and distances, his appreciation of their nature grew on him. Arizona from Yuma to the Little Colorado had been to him an endless waste of wind-scoured, sun-blasted barrenness. This black-forested rock-rimmed land of untrodden ways was a world that in itself would satisfy him. Some instinct in Jean called for a lonely, wild land, into the fastnesses of which he could roam at will and be the other strange self that he had always yearned to be but had never been.

Every few moments there intruded into his flowing consciousness the flashing face of Ellen Jorth, the way she had looked at him, the things she had said. "Reckon I was a fool," he soliloquized, with an acute sense of humiliation. "She never saw how much in earnest I was." And Jean began to remember the circumstances with a vividness that disturbed and perplexed him.

The accident of running across such a girl in that lonely place might be out of the ordinary—but it had happened. Surprise had made him dull. The charm of her appearance, the appeal of her manner, must have drawn him at the very first, but he had not recognized that. Only at her words, "Oh, I've been kissed before," had his feelings been checked in their heedless progress. And the utterance of them had made a difference he now sought to analyze. Some personality in him, some voice, some idea had begun to defend her even before he was conscious that he had arraigned her before the bar of his judgment. Such defense seemed clamoring in him now and he forced himself to listen. He wanted, in his hurt pride, to justify his amazing surrender to a sweet and sentimental impulse.

He realized now that at first glance he should have recognized in her look, her poise, her voice the quality he called thoroughbred. Ragged and stained apparel did not prove her of a common sort. Jean had known a number of fine and wholesome girls of good family; and he remembered his sister. This Ellen Jorth was that kind of a girl irrespective of her present environment. Jean championed her loyally, even after he had gratified his selfish pride.

It was then—contending with an intangible and stealing glamour, unreal and fanciful, like the dream of a forbidden enchantment—that Jean arrived at the part in the little woodland drama where he had kissed Ellen Jorth and had been unrebuked. Why had she not resented his action? Dispelled was the illusion he had been dreamily and nobly constructing. "Oh, I've been kissed before!" The shock to him now exceeded his first dismay. Half bitterly she had spoken, and wholly scornful of herself, or of him, or of all men. For she had said all men were alike. Jean chafed under the smart of that, a taunt every decent man hated. Naturally every happy and healthy young man would want to kiss such red, sweet lips. But if those lips had been for others—never for him! Jean reflected that not since childish games had he kissed a girl—until this brown-faced Ellen Jorth came his way. He wondered at it. Moreover, he wondered at the significance he placed upon it. After all, was it not merely an accident? Why should he remember? Why should he ponder? What was the faint, deep, growing thrill that accompanied some of his thoughts?

Riding along with busy mind, Jean almost crossed a well-beaten trail, leading through a pine thicket and down over the Rim. Jean's pack mule led the way without being driven. And when Jean reached the edge of the bluff one look down was enough to fetch him off his horse. That trail was steep, narrow, clogged with stones, and as full of sharp corners as a crosscut saw. Once on the descent with a packed mule and a spirited horse, Jean had no time for mind wanderings and very little for occasional glimpses out over the cedar tops to the vast blue hollow asleep under a westering sun.

The stones rattled, the dust rose, the cedar twigs snapped, the little avalanches of red earth slid down, the iron-shod hoofs rang on the rocks. This slope had been narrow at the apex in the Rim where the trail led down a crack, and it widened in fan shape as Jean descended. He zigzagged down a thousand feet before the slope benched into dividing ridges. Here the cedars and junipers failed and pines once more hid the sun. Deep ravines were black with brush. From somewhere rose a roar of running water, most pleasant to Jean's ears. Fresh deer and bear tracks covered old ones made in the trail.

Those timbered ridges were but billows of that tremendous slope that now sheered above Jean, ending in a magnificent yellow wall of rock, greened in niches, stained by weather rust, carved and cracked and caverned. As Jean descended farther the hum of bees made melody, the roar of rapid water and the murmur of a rising breeze filled him with the content of the wild. Sheepmen like Colter and wild girls like Ellen Jorth and all that seemed promising or menacing in his father's letter could never change the Indian in Jean. So he thought. Hard upon that conclusion rushed another—one which troubled with its stinging revelation. Surely these influences he had defied were just the ones to bring out in him the Indian he had sensed but had never known. The eventful day had brought new and bitter food for Jean to reflect upon.

The trail landed him in the boulder-strewn bed of a wide cañon, where the huge trees stretched a canopy of foliage which denied the sunlight, and where a beautiful brook rushed and foamed. Here at last Jean tasted water that rivaled his Oregon springs. "Ah," he cried, "that sure is good!" Dark and shaded and ferny and mossy was this streamway; and everywhere were tracks of game, from the giant spread of a grizzly bear to the tiny, birdlike imprints of a squirrel. Jean heard familiar sounds of deer crackling the dead twigs; and the chatter of squirrels was incessant. This fragrant, cool retreat under the Rim brought back to him the dim recesses of Oregon forests. After all, Jean felt that he would not miss anything that he had loved in the Cascades. But what was the vague sense of all not being well with him—the essence of a faint regret—the insistence of a hovering shadow? And then flashed again, etched more vividly by the repetition in memory, a picture of eyes, of lips—of something he had to forget.

Wild and broken as this rolling Basin floor had appeared from the Rim, the reality of traveling over it made that first impression a deceit of distance. Down here all was on a big, rough, broken scale. Jean did not find even a few rods of level ground. Boulders as huge as houses obstructed the stream bed; spruce trees eight feet thick tried to lord it over the brawny pines; the ravine was a veritable cañon from which occasional glimpses through the foliage showed the Rim as a lofty red-tipped mountain peak.

Jean's pack mule became frightened at scent of a bear or lion and ran off down the rough trail, imperiling Jean's outfit. It was not an easy task to head him off nor, when that was accomplished, to keep him to a trot. But his fright and succeeding skittishness at least made for fast traveling. Jean calculated that he covered ten miles under the Rim before the character of ground and forest began to change.

The trail had turned southeast. Instead of gorge after gorge, red-walled and choked with forest, there began to be rolling ridges, some high; others were knolls; and a thick cedar growth made up for a falling off of pine. The spruce had long disappeared. Juniper thickets gave way more and more to the beautiful manzanita; and soon on the south slopes appeared cactus and a scrubby live oak. But for the well-broken trail, Jean would have fared ill through this tough brush.

Jean espied several deer, and again a coyote, and what he took to be a small herd of wild horses. No more turkey tracks showed in the dusty patches. He crossed a number of tiny brooklets, and at length came to a place where the trail ended or merged in a rough road that showed evidence of considerable travel. Horses, sheep, and cattle had passed along there that day. This road turned southward, and Jean began to have pleasurable expectations.

The road, like the trail, led down grade, but no longer at such steep angles, and was bordered by cedar and piñon, jack-pine and juniper, mescal and manzanita. Quite sharply, going around a ridge, the road led Jean's eye down to a small open flat of marshy, or at least grassy, ground. This green oasis in the wilderness of red and timbered ridges marked another change in the character of the Basin. Beyond that the country began to spread out and roll gracefully, its dark-green forest interspersed with grassy parks, until Jean headed into a long, wide gray-green valley surrounded by black-fringed hills. His pulses quickened here. He saw cattle dotting the expanse, and here and there along the edge log cabins and corrals.

As a village, Grass Valley could not boast of much, apparently, in the way of population. Cabins and houses were widely scattered, as if the inhabitants did not care to encroach upon one another. But the one store, built of stone, and stamped also with the characteristic isolation, seemed to Jean to be a rather remarkable edifice. Not exactly like a fort did it strike him, but if it had not been designed for defense it certainly gave that impression, especially from the long, low side with its dark eye-like windows about the height of a man's shoulder. Some rather fine horses were tied to a hitching rail. Otherwise dust and dirt and age and long use stamped this Grass Valley store and its immediate environment.

Jean threw his bridle, and, getting down, mounted the low porch and stepped into the wide open door. A face, gray against the background of gloom inside, passed out of sight just as Jean entered. He knew he had been seen. In front of the long, rather low-ceiled store were four men, all absorbed, apparently, in a game of checkers. Two were playing and two were looking on. One of these, a gaunt-faced man past middle age, casually looked up as Jean entered. But the moment of that casual glance afforded Jean time enough to meet eyes he instinctively distrusted. They masked their penetration. They seemed neither curious nor friendly. They saw him as if he had been merely thin air.

"Good evenin'," said Jean.

After what appeared to Jean a lapse of time sufficient to impress him with a possible deafness of these men, the gaunt-faced one said, "Howdy, Isbel!"

The tone was impersonal, dry, easy, cool, laconic, and yet it could not have been more pregnant with meaning. Jean's sharp sensibilities absorbed much. None of the slouch-sombreroed, long-mustached Texans—for so Jean at once classed them—had ever seen Jean, but they knew him and knew that he was expected in Grass Valley. All but the one who had spoken happened to have their faces in shadow under the wide-brimmed black hats. Motley-garbed, gun-belted, dusty-booted, they gave Jean the same impression of latent force that he had encountered in Colter.

"Will somebody please tell me where to find my father, Gaston Isbel?" inquired Jean, with as civil a tongue as he could command.

Nobody paid the slightest attention. It was the same as if Jean had not spoken. Waiting, half amused, half irritated, Jean shot a rapid glance around the store. The place had felt bare; and Jean, peering back through gloomy space, saw that it did not contain much. Dry goods and sacks littered a long rude counter; long rough shelves divided their length into stacks of canned foods and empty sections; a low shelf back of the counter held a generous burden of cartridge boxes, and next to it stood a rack of rifles. On the counter lay open cases of plug tobacco, the odor of which was second in strength only to that of rum.

Jean's swift-roving eye reverted to the men, three of

whom were absorbed in the greasy checkerboard. The fourth man was the one who had spoken and he now deigned to look at Jean. Not much flesh was there stretched over his bony, powerful physiognomy. He stroked a lean chin with a big mobile hand that suggested more of bridle holding than familiarity with a bucksaw and plow handle. It was a lazy hand. The man looked lazy. If he spoke at all it would be with lazy speech. Yet Jean had not encountered many men to whom he would have accorded more potency to stir in him the instinct of self-preservation.

"Shore," drawled this gaunt-faced Texan, "old Gass lives aboot a mile down heah." With slow sweep of the big hand he indicated a general direction to the south; then, appearing to forget his questioner, he turned his attention to the game.

Jean muttered his thanks and, striding out, he mounted again, and drove the pack mule down the road. "Reckon I've run into the wrong folds to-day," he said. "If I remember dad right he was a man to make an' keep friends. Somehow I'll bet there's goin' to be hell." Beyond the store were some rather pretty and comfortable homes, little ranch houses back in the coves of the hills. The road turned west and Jean saw his first sunset in the Tonto Basin. It was a pageant of purple clouds with silver edges, and background of deep rich gold. Presently Jean met a lad driving a cow. "Hello, Johnny!" he said, genially, and with a double purpose. "My name's Jean Isbel. By Golly! I'm lost in Grass Valley. Will you tell me where my dad lives?"

"Yep. Keep right on, an' y'u cain't miss him," replied the lad, with a bright smile. "He's lookin' fer y'u."

"How do you know, boy?" queried Jean, warmed by that smile.

"Aw, I know. It's all over the valley thet y'u'd ride in

ter-day. Shore I wus the one thet tole yer dad an' he give me a dollar."

"Was he glad to hear it?" asked Jean, with a queer sensation in his throat.

"Wal, he plumb was."

"An' who told you I was goin' to ride in to-day?"

"I heerd it at the store," replied the lad, with an air of confidence. "Some sheepmen was talkin' to Greaves. He's the storekeeper. I was settin' outside, but I heerd. A Mexican come down off the Rim ter-day an' he fetched the news." Here the lad looked furtively around, then whispered. "An' thet greaser was sent by somebody. I never heerd no more, but them sheepmen looked pretty plumb sour. An' one of them, comin' out, give me a kick, darn him. It shore is the luckedest day fer us cowmen."

"How's that, Johnny?"

"Wal, that's shore a big fight comin' to Grass Valley. My dad says so an' he rides fer yer dad. An' if it comes now y'u'll be heah."

"Ahuh!" laughed Jean. "An' what then, boy?"

The lad turned bright eyes upward. "Aw, now, y'u-all cain't come thet on me. Ain't y'u an Injun, Jean Isbel? Ain't y'u a hoss tracker thet rustlers cain't fool? Ain't y'u a plumb dead shot? Ain't y'u wuss'ern a grizzly bear in a rough-an'-tumble? . . . Now ain't y'u, shore?"

Jean bade the flattering lad a rather sober good day and rode on his way. Manifestly a reputation somewhat difficult to live up to had preceded his entry into Grass Valley.

Jean's first sight of his future home thrilled him through. It was a big, low, rambling log structure standing well out from a wooded knoll at the edge of the valley. Corrals and barns and sheds lay off at the back. To the fore stretched broad pastures where numberless cattle and horses grazed. At sunset the scene was one of rich color. Prosperity and abundance and peace seemed attendant upon that ranch; lusty voices of burros braying and cows bawling seemed welcoming Jean. A hound bayed. The first cool touch of wind fanned Jean's cheek and brought a fragrance of wood smoke and frying ham.

Horses in the pasture romped to the fence and whistled at these newcomers. Jean espied a white-faced black horse that gladdened his sight. "Hello, Whiteface! I'll sure straddle you," called Jean. Then up the gentle slope he saw the tall figure of his father—the same as he had seen him thousands of times, bareheaded, shirt sleeved, striding with long step. Jean waved and called to him.

"Hi, you prodigal!" came the answer. Yes, the voice of his father—and Jean's boyhood memories flashed. He hurried his horse those last few rods. No—dad was not the same. His hair shone gray.

"Here I am, dad," called Jean, and then he was dismounting. A deep, quiet emotion settled over him, stilling the hurry, the eagerness, the pang in his breast.

"Son, I shore am glad to see you," said his father, and wrung his hand. "Wal, wal, the size of you! Shore you've grown, an' how you favor your mother."

Jean felt in the iron clasp of hand, in the uplifting of the handsome head, in the strong, fine light of piercing eyes that there was no difference in the spirit of his father. But the old smile could not hide lines and shades strange to Jean.

"Dad, I'm as glad as you," replied Jean, heartily. "It seems long we've been parted, now I see you. Are you well, dad, an' all right?"

"Not complainin', son. I can ride all day same as ever," he said. "Come. Never mind your hosses. They'll be looked after. Come meet the folks. . . . Wal, wal, you got heah at last."

On the porch of the house a group awaited Jean's coming, rather silently, he thought. Wide-eyed children were there, very shy and watchful. The dark face of his sister corresponded with the image of her in his memory. She appeared taller, more womanly, as she embraced him. "Oh, Jean, Jean, I'm glad you've come!" she cried, and pressed him close. Jean felt in her a woman's anxiety for the present as well as affection for the past. He remembered his aunt Mary, though he had not seen her for years. His half brothers, Bill and Guy, had changed but little except perhaps to grow lean and rangy. Bill resembled his father, though his aspect was jocular rather than serious. Guy was smaller, wiry, and hard as rock, with snapping eyes in a brown, still face, and he had the bow-legs of a cattleman. Both had married in Arizona. Bill's wife, Kate, was a stout, comely little woman, mother of three of the children. The other wife was young, a strapping girl, redheaded and freckled, with wonderful lines of pain and strength in her face. Jean remembered, as he looked at her, that some one had written him about the tragedy in her life. When she was only a child the Apaches had murdered all her family. Then next to greet Jean were the little children, all shy, yet all manifestly impressed by the occasion. A warmth and intimacy of forgotten home emotions flooded over Jean. Sweet it was to get home to these relatives who loved him and welcomed him with quiet gladness. But there seemed more. Jean was quick to see the shadow in the eyes of the women in that household and to sense a strange reliance which his presence brought.

"Son, this heah Tonto is a land of milk an' honey," said his father, as Jean gazed spellbound at the bounteous supper.

Jean certainly performed gastronomic feats on this occasion, to the delight of Aunt Mary and the wonder of the children. "Oh, he's starv-ved to death," whispered one of the little boys to his sister. They had begun to warm to this stranger uncle. Jean had no chance to talk, even had he been able to, for the meal-time showed a relaxation of restraint and they all tried to tell him things at once. In the bright lamplight his father looked easier and happier as he beamed upon Jean.

After supper the men went into an adjoining room that appeared most comfortable and attractive. It was long, and the width of the house, with a huge stone fireplace, low ceiling of hewn timbers and walls of the same, small windows with inside shutters of wood, and home-made table and chairs and rugs.

"Wal, Jean, do you recollect them shootin'-irons?" inquired the rancher, pointing above the fireplace. Two guns hung on the spreading deer antlers there. One was a musket Jean's father had used in the war of the rebellion and the other was a long, heavy, muzzle-loading flintlock Kentucky rifle with which Jean had learned to shoot.

"Reckon I do, dad," replied Jean, and with reverent hands and a rush of memory he took the old gun down.

"Jean, you shore handle thet old arm some clumsy," said Guy Isbel, dryly. And Bill added a remark to the effect that perhaps Jean had been leading a luxurious and tame life back there in Oregon, and then added, "But I reckon he's packin' that six-shooter like a Texan."

"Say, I fetched a gun or two along with me," replied Jean, jocularly. "Reckon I near broke my poor mule's back with the load of shells an' guns. Dad, what was the idea askin' me to pack out an arsenal?"

"Son, shore all shootin' arms an' such are at a premium in the Tonto," replied his father. "An' I was givin' you a hunch to come loaded."

His cool, drawling voice seemed to put a damper upon the pleasantries. Right there Jean sensed the charged atmosphere. His brothers were bursting with utterance about to break forth, and his father suddenly wore a look that recalled to Jean critical times of days long past. But the entrance of the children and the womenfolk put an end to confidences. Evidently the youngsters were laboring under subdued excitement. They preceded their mother, the smallest boy in the lead. For him this must have been both a dreadful and a wonderful experience, for he seemed to be pushed forward by his sister and brother and mother, and driven by yearnings of his own. "There now, Lee. Say, 'Uncle Jean, what did you fetch us?'" The lad hesitated for a shy, frightened look at Jean, and then, gaining something from his scrutiny of his uncle, he toddled forward and bravely delivered the question of tremendous importance.

"What did I fetch you, hey?" cried Jean, in delight, as he took the lad up on his knee. "Wouldn't you like to know? I didn't forget, Lee. I remembered you all. Oh! the job I had packin' your bundle of presents. . . . Now, Lee, make a guess."

"I dess you fetched a dun," replied Lee.

"A dun!—I'll bet you mean a gun," laughed Jean. "Well, you four-year-old Texas gunman! Make another guess."

That appeared too momentous and entrancing for the other two youngsters, and, adding their shrill and joyous voices to Lee's, they besieged Jean.

"Dad, where's my pack?" cried Jean. "These young Apaches are after my scalp."

"Reckon the boys fetched it onto the porch," replied the rancher.

Guy Isbel opened the door and went out. "By golly! heah's three packs," he called. "Which one do you want, Jean?"

"It's a long, heavy bundle all tied up," replied Jean.

Guy came staggering in under a burden that brought a whoop from the youngsters and bright gleams to the eyes of the women. Jean lost nothing of this. How glad he was that he had tarried in San Francisco because of a mental picture of this very reception in far-off wild Arizona.

When Guy deposited the bundle on the floor it jarred the room. It gave forth metallic and rattling and crackling sounds.

"Everybody stand back an' give me elbow room," ordered Jean, majestically. "My good folks, I want you all to know this is somethin' that doesn't happen often. The bundle you see here weighed about a hundred pounds when I packed it on my shoulder down Market Street in Frisco. It was stolen from me on shipboard. I got it back in San Diego an' licked the thief. It rode on a burro from San Diego to Yuma an' once I thought the burro was lost for keeps. It came up the Colorado River from Yuma to Ehrenberg an' there went on top of a stage. We got chased by bandits an' once when the horses were gallopin' hard it near rolled off. Then it went on the back of a pack horse an' helped wear him out. An' I reckon it would be somewhere else now if I hadn't fallen in with a freighter goin' north from Phoenix to the Santa Fe Trail. The last lap when it sagged the back of a mule was the riskiest an' full of the narrowest escapes. Twice my mule bucked off his pack an' left my outfit scattered. Worst of all, my precious bundle made the mule top heavy comin' down that place back here where the trail seems to drop off the earth. There I was hard put to keep sight of my pack. Sometimes it was on top an' other times the mule. But it got here at last. . . . An' now I'll open it."

After this long and impressive harangue, which at least augmented the suspense of the women and worked the children into a frenzy, Jean leisurely untied the many knots round the bundle and unrolled it. He had packed that bundle for just such travel as it had sustained. Three clothbound rifles he laid aside, and with them a long, very heavy package tied between two thin wide boards. From this came the metallic clink. "Oo, I know what dem is!" cried Lee, breaking the silence of suspense. Then Jean, tearing open a long flat parcel, spread before the mute, rapt-eyed youngsters such magnificent things as they had never dreamed of—picture books, mouthharps, dolls, a toy gun and a toy pistol, a wonderful whistle and a fox horn, and last of all a box of candy. Before these treasures on the floor, too magical to be touched at first, the two little boys and their sister simply knelt. That was a sweet, full moment for Jean; yet even that was clouded by the something which shadowed these innocent children fatefully born in a wild place at a wild time. Next Jean gave to his sister the presents he had brought her— beautiful cloth for a dress, ribbons and a bit of lace, handkerchiefs and buttons and yards of linen, a sewing case and a whole box of spools of thread, a comb and brush and mirror, and lastly a Spanish brooch inlaid with garnets. "There, Ann," said Jean, "I confess I asked a girl friend in Oregon to tell me some things my sister might like." Manifestly there was not much difference in girls. Ann seemed stunned by this munificence, and then awakening, she hugged Jean in a way that took his breath. She was not a child any more, that was certain. Aunt Mary turned knowing eyes upon Jean. "Reckon you couldn't have pleased Ann more. She's engaged, Jean, an' where girls are in that state these things mean a heap. . . . Ann, you'll be married in that!" And she pointed to the beautiful folds of material that Ann had spread out.

"What's this?" demanded Jean. His sister's blushes were enough to convict her, and they were mightily becoming, too.

"Here, Aunt Mary," went on Jean, "here's yours, an' here's somethin' for each of my new sisters." This distribution left the women as happy and occupied, almost, as the children. It left also another package, the last one in the bundle. Jean laid hold of it and, lifting it, he was about to speak when he sustained a little shock of memory. Quite distinctly he saw two little feet, with bare toes peeping out of worn-out moccasins, and then round, bare, symmetrical ankles that had been scratched by brush. Next he saw Ellen Jorth's passionate face as she looked when she had made the violent action so disconcerting to him. In this happy moment the memory seemed farther off than a few hours. It had crystallized. It annoyed while it drew him. As a result he slowly laid this package aside and did not speak as he had intended to.

"Dad, I reckon I didn't fetch a lot for you an' the boys," continued Jean. "Some knives, some pipes an' tobacco. An' sure the guns."

"Shore, you're a regular Santa Claus, Jean," replied his father. "Wal, wal, look at the kids. An' look at Mary. An' for the land's sake look at Ann! Wal, wal, I'm gettin' old. I'd forgotten the pretty stuff an' gimcracks that mean so much to women. We're out of the world heah. It's just as well you've lived apart from us, Jean, for comin' back this way, with all that stuff, does us a lot of good. I cain't say, son, how obliged I am. My mind has been set on the hard side of life. An' it's shore good to forget—to see the smiles of the women an' the joy of the kids."

At this juncture a tall young man entered the open door. He looked a rider. All about him, even his face, except his eyes, seemed old, but his eyes were young, fine, soft, and dark.

"How do, y'u-all!" he said, evenly.

Ann rose from her knees. Then Jean did not need to be told who this newcomer was.

"Jean, this is my friend, Andrew Colmor."

Jean knew when he met Colmor's grip and the keen flash of his eyes that he was glad Ann had set her heart upon one of their kind. And his second impression was something akin to the one given him in the road by the admiring lad. Colmor's estimate of him must have been a monument built of Ann's eulogies. Jean's heart suffered misgivings. Could he live up to the character that somehow had forestalled his advent in Grass Valley? Surely life was measured differently here in the Tonto Basin.

The children, bundling their treasures to their bosoms, were dragged off to bed in some remote part of the house, from which their laughter and voices came back with happy significance. Jean forthwith had an interested audience. How eagerly these lonely pioneer people listened to news of the outside world! Jean talked until he was hoarse. In their turn his hearers told him much that had never found place in the few and short letters he had received since he had been left in Oregon. Not a word about sheepmen or any hint of rustlers! Jean marked the omission and thought all the more seriously of probabilities because nothing was said. Altogether the evening was a happy reunion of a family of which all living members were there present. Jean grasped that this fact was one of significant satisfaction to his father.

"Shore we're all goin' to live together heah," he declared. "I started this range. I call most of this valley mine. We'll run up a cabin for Ann soon as she says the word. An' you, Jean, where's your girl? I shore told you to fetch her."

"Dad, I didn't have one," replied Jean.

"Wal, I wish you had," returned the rancher. "You'll go courtin' one of these Tonto hussies that I might object to."

"Why, father, there's not a girl in the valley Jean would look twice at," interposed Ann Isbel, with spirit.

Jean laughed the matter aside, but he had an uneasy memory. Aunt Mary averred, after the manner of relatives, that Jean would play havoc among the women of the settlement. And Jean retorted that at least one member of the Isbels should hold out against folly and fight and love and marriage, the agents which had reduced the family to these few present. "I'll be the last Isbel to go under," he concluded.

"Son, you're talkin' wisdom," said his father. "An' shore that reminds me of the uncle you're named after. Jean Isbel! . . . Wal, he was my youngest brother an' shore a fire-eater. Our mother was a French creole from Louisiana, an' Jean must have inherited some of his fightin' nature from her. When the war of the rebellion started Jean an' I enlisted. I was crippled before we ever got to the front. But Jean went through three years before he was killed. His company had orders to fight to the last man. An' Jean fought an' lived long enough just to be that last man."

At length Jean was left alone with his father.

"Reckon you're used to bunkin' outdoors?" queried the rancher, rather abruptly.

"Most of the time," replied Jean.

"Wal, there's room in the house, but I want you to sleep out. Come get your beddin' an' gun. I'll show you."

They went outside on the porch, where Jean shouldered his roll of tarpaulin and blankets. His rifle, in its saddle sheath, leaned against the door. His father took it up and, half pulling it out, looked at it by the starlight. "Forty-four, eh? Wal, wal, there's shore no better, if a man can hold straight." At the moment a big gray dog trotted up to sniff at Jean. "An' heah's your bunkmate, Shepp. He's part lofer, Jean. His mother was a favorite shepherd dog of mine. His father was a big timber wolf that took us two years to kill. Some bad wolf packs runnin' this Basin."

The night was cold and still, darkly bright under moon and stars; the smell of hay seemed to mingle with that of cedar. Jean followed his father round the house and up a gentle slope of grass to the edge of the cedar line. Here several trees with low-sweeping thick branches formed a dense, impenetrable shade.

"Son, your uncle Jean was scout for Liggett, one of the greatest rebels the South had," said the rancher. "An' you're goin' to be scout for the Isbels of Tonto. Reckon you'll find it 'most as hot as your uncle did. . . . Spread your bed inside. You can see out, but no one can see you. Reckon there's been some queer happenin's 'round heah lately. If Shepp could talk he'd shore have lots to tell us. Bill an' Guy have been sleepin' out, trailin' strange hoss tracks, an' all that. But shore whoever's been prowlin' around heah was too sharp for them. Some bad, crafty, light-steppin' woodsmen 'round heah, Jean. . . . Three mawnin's ago, just after daylight, I stepped out the back door an' some one of these sneaks I'm talkin' aboot took a shot at me. Missed my head a quarter of an inch! To-morrow I'll show you the bullet hole in the doorpost. An' some of my gray hairs that're stickin' in it!"

"Dad!" ejaculated Jean, with a hand outstretched. "That's awful! You frighten me."

"No time to be scared," replied his father, calmly. "They're shore goin' to kill me. That's why I wanted you home. . . . In there with you, now! Go to sleep. You shore can trust Shepp to wake you if he gets scent or sound. . . . An' good night, my son. I'm sayin' that I'll rest easy tonight."

Jean mumbled a good night and stood watching his father's shining white head move away under the starlight. Then the tall, dark form vanished, a door closed, and all was still. The dog Shepp licked Jean's hand. Jean felt grateful for that warm touch. For a moment he sat on his roll of bedding, his thought still locked on the shuddering revelation of his father's words, "They're shore goin' to kill me." The shock of inaction passed. Jean pushed his

pack in the dark opening and, crawling inside, he unrolled
it and made his bed.

When at length he was comfortably settled for the night
he breathed a long sigh of relief. What bliss to relax! A
throbbing and burning of his muscles seemed to begin
with his rest. The cool starlit night, the smell of cedar, the
moan of wind, the silence—all were real to his senses.
After long weeks of long, arduous travel he was home.
The warmth of the welcome still lingered but it seemed
to have been pierced by an icy thrust. What lay before
him? The shadow in the eyes of his aunt, in the younger,
fresher eyes of his sister—Jean connected that with the
meaning of his father's tragic words. Far past was the
morning that had been so keen, the breaking of camp in
the sunlit forest, the riding down the brown aisles under
the pines, the music of bleating lambs that had called him
not to pass by. Thought of Ellen Jorth recurred. Had he
met her only that morning? She was up there in the forest, asleep under the starlit pines. Who was she? What was
her story? That savage fling of her skirt, her bitter speech
and passionate flaming face—they haunted Jean. They
were crystallizing into simpler memories, growing away
from his bewilderment, and therefore at once sweeter and
more doubtful. "Maybe she meant differently from what
I thought," Jean soliloquized. "Anyway, she was honest."
Both shame and thrill possessed him at the recall of an
insidious idea—dare he go back and find her and give her
the last package of gifts he had brought from the city?
What might they mean to poor, ragged, untidy, beautiful
Ellen Jorth? The idea grew on Jean. It could not be dispelled. He resisted stubbornly. It was bound to go to its
fruition. Deep into his mind had sunk an impression of
her need—a material need that brought spirit and pride
to abasement. From one picture to another his memory
wandered, from one speech and act of hers to another,

choosing, selecting, casting aside, until clear and sharp as
the stars shone the words, "Oh, I've been kissed before!"
That stung him now. By whom? Not by one man, but by
several, by many, she had meant. Pshaw! he had only been
sympathetic and drawn by a strange girl in the woods.
To-morrow he would forget. Work there was for him in
Grass Valley. And he reverted uneasily to the remarks of
his father until at last sleep claimed him.

A cold nose against his cheek, a low whine, awakened
Jean. The big dog Shepp was beside him, keen, wary, intense. The night appeared far advanced toward dawn.
Far away a cock crowed; the near-at-hand one answered
in clarion voice. "What is it, Shepp?" whispered Jean, and
he sat up. The dog smelled or heard something suspicious
to his nature, but whether man or animal Jean could not
tell.

CHAPTER 3

The morning star, large, intensely blue-white, magnificent in its dominance of the clear night sky, hung over the dim, dark valley ramparts. The moon had gone down and all the other stars were wan, pale ghosts.

Presently the strained vacuum of Jean's ears vibrated to a low roar of many hoofs. It came from the open valley, along the slope to the south. Shepp acted as if he wanted the word to run. Jean laid a hand on the dog. "Hold on, Shepp," he whispered. Then hauling on his boots and slipping into his coat, Jean took his rifle and stole out into the open. Shepp appeared to be well trained, for it was evident that he had a strong natural tendency to run off and hunt for whatever had roused him. Jean thought it more than likely that the dog scented an animal of some kind. If there were men prowling around the ranch Shepp might have been just as vigilant, but it seemed to Jean that the dog would have shown less eagerness to leave him, or none at all.

In the stillness of the morning it took Jean a moment to locate the direction of the wind, which was very light and coming from the south. In fact that little breeze had borne the low roar of trampling hoofs. Jean circled the ranch house to the right and kept along the slope at the edge of the cedars. It struck him suddenly how well fitted he was for work of this sort. All the work he had ever done, except for his few years in school, had been in the open. All the leisure he had ever been able to obtain had been given to his ruling passion for hunting and fishing. Love of the wild had been born in Jean. At this moment he experienced a grim assurance of what his instinct and his training might accomplish if directed to a stern and daring end. Perhaps his father understood this; perhaps the old Texan had some little reason for his confidence.

Every few paces Jean halted to listen. All objects, of course, were indistinguishable in the dark-gray obscurity, except when he came close upon them. Shepp showed an increasing eagerness to bolt out into the void. When Jean had traveled half a mile from the house he heard a scattered trampling of cattle on the run, and farther out a low strangled bawl of a calf. "Ahuh!" muttered Jean. "Cougar or some varmint pulled down that calf." Then he discharged his rifle in the air and yelled with all his might. It was necessary then to yell again to hold Shepp back.

Thereupon Jean set forth down the valley, and tramped out and across and around, as much to scare away whatever had been after the stock as to look for the wounded calf. More than once he heard cattle moving away ahead of him, but he could not see them. Jean let Shepp go, hoping the dog would strike a trail. But Shepp neither gave tongue nor came back. Dawn began to break, and in the growing light Jean searched around until at last he stumbled over a dead calf, lying in a little bare wash where water ran in wet seasons. Big wolf tracks showed in the soft earth. "Lofers," said Jean, as he knelt and just covered one track with his spread hand. "We had wolves in Oregon, but not as big as these. . . . Wonder where that half-wolf dog, Shepp, went. Wonder if he can be trusted where wolves are concerned. I'll bet not, if there's a she-wolf runnin' around."

Jean found tracks of two wolves, and he trailed them out of the wash, then lost them in the grass. But, guided by their direction, he went on and climbed a slope to the cedar line, where in the dusty patches he found the tracks again. "Not scared much," he muttered, as he noted the slow trotting tracks. "Well, you old gray lofers, we're goin' to clash." Jean knew from many a futile hunt that wolves were the wariest and most intelligent of wild animals in the quest. From the top of a low foothill he watched the sun rise; and then no longer wondered why his father waxed eloquent over the beauty and location and luxuriance of this grassy valley. But it was large enough to make rich a good many ranchers. Jean tried to restrain any curiosity as to his father's dealings in Grass Valley until the situation had been made clear.

Moreover, Jean wanted to love this wonderful country. He wanted to be free to ride and hunt and roam to his heart's content; and therefore he dreaded hearing his father's claims. But Jean threw off forebodings. Nothing ever turned out so badly as it presaged. He would think the best until certain of the worst. The morning was gloriously bright, and already the frost was glistening wet on the stones. Grass Valley shone like burnished silver dotted with innumerable black spots. Burros were braying their discordant messages to one another; the colts were romping in the fields; stallions were whistling; cows were bawling. A cloud of blue smoke hung low over the ranch house, slowly wafting away on the wind. Far out in the valley a dark group of horsemen were riding toward the village. Jean glanced thoughtfully at them and reflected that he seemed destined to harbor suspicion of all men new and strange to him. Above the distant village stood the darkly green foothills leading up to the craggy slopes, and these ending in the Rim, a red, black-fringed mountain front, beautiful in the morning sunlight, lonely, serene, and mysterious against the level skyline. Mountains, ranges, distances unknown to Jean, always called to him—to come, to seek, to explore, to find, but no wild horizon ever before beckoned to him as this one. And the subtle vague emotion that had gone to sleep with him last night awoke now hauntingly. It took effort to dispel the desire to think, to wonder.

Upon his return to the house, he went around on the valley side, so as to see the place by light of day. His father had built for permanence; and evidently there had been three constructive periods in the history of that long, substantial, picturesque log house. But few nails and little sawed lumber and no glass had been used. Strong and skillful hands, axes and a crosscut saw, had been the prime factors in erecting this habitation of the Isbels.

"Good mawnin', son," called a cheery voice from the porch. "Shore we-all heard you shoot; an' the crack of that forty-four was as welcome as May flowers."

Bill Isbel looked up from a task over a saddle girth and inquired pleasantly if Jean ever slept of nights. Guy Isbel laughed and there was warm regard in the gaze he bent on Jean.

"You old Indian!" he drawled, slowly. "Did you get a bead on anythin'?"

"No. I shot to scare away what I found to be some of your lofers," replied Jean. "I heard them pullin' down a calf. An' I found tracks of two whoppin' big wolves. I found the dead calf, too. Reckon the meat can be saved. Dad, you must lose a lot of stock here."

"Wal, son, you shore hit the nail on the haid," replied the rancher. "What with lions an' bears an' lofers—an' two-footed lofers of another breed—I've lost five thousand dollars in stock this last year."

"Dad! You don't mean it!" exclaimed Jean, in astonishment. To him that sum represented a small fortune.

"I shore do," answered his father.

Jean shook his head as if he could not understand such an enormous loss where there were keen able-bodied men about. "But that's awful, dad. How could it happen? Where were your herders an' cowboys? An' Bill an' Guy?"

Bill Isbel shook a vehement fist at Jean and retorted in earnest, having manifestly been hit in a sore spot. "Where was me an' Guy, huh? Wal, my Oregon brother, we was heah, all year, sleepin' more or less aboot three hours out of every twenty-four—ridin' our boots off—an' we couldn't keep down that loss."

"Jean, you-all have a mighty tumble comin' to you out heah," said Guy, complacently.

"Listen, son," spoke up the rancher. "You want to have some hunches before you figure on our troubles. There's two or three packs of lofers, an' in winter time they are hell to deal with. Lions thick as bees, an' shore bad when the snow's on. Bears will kill a cow now an' then. An' whenever an' old silvertip comes mozyin' across from the Mazatzals he kills stock. I'm in with half a dozen cattlemen. We all work together, an' the whole outfit cain't keep these varmints down. Then two years ago the Hash Knife Gang come into the Tonto."

"Hash Knife Gang? What a pretty name!" replied Jean. "Who're they?"

"Rustlers, son. An' shore the real old Texas brand. The old Lone Star State got too hot for them, an' they followed the trail of a lot of other Texans who needed a healthier climate. Some two hundred Texans around heah, Jean, an' maybe a matter of three hundred inhabitants in the Tonto all told, good an' bad. Reckon it's aboot half an' half."

A cheery call from the kitchen interrupted the conversation of the men.

"You come to breakfast."

During the meal the old rancher talked to Bill and Guy about the day's order of work; and from this Jean gathered an idea of what a big cattle business his father conducted. After breakfast Jean's brothers manifested keen interest in the new rifles. These were unwrapped and cleaned and taken out for testing. The three rifles were forty-four caliber Winchesters, the kind of gun Jean had found most effective. He tried them out first, and the shots he made were satisfactory to him and amazing to the others. Bill had used an old Henry rifle. Guy did not favor any particular rifle. The rancher pinned his faith to the famous old single-shot buffalo gun, mostly called *needle* gun. "Wal, reckon I'd better stick to mine. Shore you cain't teach an old dog new tricks. But you boys may do well with the forty-fours. Pack 'em on your saddles an' practice when you see a coyote."

Jean found it difficult to convince himself that this interest in guns and marksmanship had any sinister propulsion back of it. His father and brothers had always been this way. Rifles were as important to pioneers as plows, and their skillful use was an achievement every frontiersman tried to attain. Friendly rivalry had always existed among the members of the Isbel family: even Ann Isbel was a good shot. But such proficiency in the use of firearms—and life in the open that was correlative with it—had not dominated them as it had Jean. Bill and Guy Isbel were born cattlemen—chips of the old block. Jean began to hope that his father's letter was an exaggeration, and particularly that the fatalistic speech of last night, "they are goin' to kill me," was just a moody inclination to see the worst side. Still, even as Jean tried to persuade himself of this more hopeful view, he recalled many references to the peculiar reputation of Texans for gun-throwing, for feuds, for never-ending hatreds. In Oregon the Isbels had lived among industrious and peaceful pioneers from all over the States; to be sure, the life had been rough and primitive, and there had been fights on occasions, though no Isbel had ever killed a man. But now they had become fixed in a wilder and sparsely settled country among men of their own breed. Jean was afraid his hopes had only sentiment to foster them. Nevertheless, he forced back a strange, brooding, mental state and resolutely held up the brighter side. Whatever the evil conditions existing in Grass Valley, they could be met with intelligence and courage, with an absolute certainty that it was inevitable they must pass away. Jean refused to consider the old, fatal law that at certain wild times and wild places in the West certain men had to pass away to change evil conditions.

"Wal, Jean, ride around the range with the boys," said the rancher. "Meet some of my neighbors, Jim Blaisdell, in particular. Take a look at the cattle. An' pick out some hosses for yourself."

"I've seen one already," declared Jean, quickly. "A black with white face. I'll take him."

"Shore you know a hoss. To my eye he's my pick. But the boys don't agree. Bill 'specially has degenerated into a fancier of pitchin' hosses. Ann can ride that black. You try him this mawnin'. . . . An', son, enjoy yourself."

True to his first impression. Jean named the black horse Whiteface and fell in love with him before ever he swung a leg over him. Whiteface appeared spirited, yet gentle. He had been trained instead of being broken. Of hard hits and quirts and spurs he had no experience. He liked to do what his rider wanted him to do.

A hundred or more horses grazed in the grassy meadow,

and as Jean rode on among them it was a pleasure to see stallions throw heads and ears up and whistle or snort. Whole troops of colts and two-year-olds raced with flying tails and manes.

Beyond these pastures stretched the range, and Jean saw the gray-green expanse speckled by thousands of cattle. The scene was inspiring. Jean's brothers led him all around, meeting some of the herders and riders employed on the ranch, one of whom was a burly, grizzled man with eyes reddened and narrowed by much riding in wind and sun and dust. His name was Evarts and he was father of the lad whom Jean had met near the village. Evarts was busily skinning the calf that had been killed by the wolves. "See heah, y'u Jean Isbel," said Evarts, "it shore was aboot time y'u come home. We-all heahs y'u hev an eye fer tracks. Wal, mebbe y'u can kill Old Gray, the lofer thet did this job. He's pulled down nine calves an' yearlin's this last two months thet I know of. An' we've not hed the spring round-up."

Grass Valley widened to the southeast. Jean would have been backward about estimating the square miles in it. Yet it was not vast acreage so much as rich pasture that made it such a wonderful range. Several ranches lay along the western slope of this section. Jean was informed that open parks and swales, and little valleys nestling among the foothills, wherever there was water and grass, had been settled by ranchers. Every summer a few new families ventured in.

Blaisdell struck Jean as being a lionlike type of Texan, both in his broad, bold face, his huge head with its up-standing tawny hair like a mane, and in the speech and force that betokened the nature of his heart. He was not as old as Jean's father. He had a rolling voice, with the same drawling intonation characteristic of all Texans, and blue eyes that still held the fire of youth. Quite a marked contrast he presented to the lean, rangy, hard-jawed, intent-eyed men Jean had begun to accept as Texans.

Blaisdell took time for a curious scrutiny and study of Jean, that, frank and kindly as it was, and evidently the adjustment of impressions gotten from hearsay, yet bespoke the attention of one used to judging men for himself, and in this particular case having reasons of his own for so doing.

"Wal, you're like your sister Ann," said Blaisdell. "Which you may take as a compliment, young man. Both of you favor your mother. But you're an Isbel. Back in Texas there are men who never wear a glove on their right hands, an' shore I reckon if one of them met up with you sudden he'd think some graves had opened an' he'd go for his gun."

Blaisdell's laugh pealed out with deep, pleasant roll. Thus he planted in Jean's sensitive mind a significant thought-provoking idea about the past-and-gone Isbels.

His further remarks, likewise, were exceedingly interesting to Jean. The settling of the Tonto Basin by Texans was a subject often in dispute. His own father had been in the first party of adventurous pioneers who had traveled up from the south to cross over the Reno Pass of the Mazatzals into the Basin. "Newcomers from outside get impressions of the Tonto accordin' to the first settlers they meet," declared Blaisdell. "An' shore it's my belief these first impressions never change. Just so strong they are! Wal, I've heard my father say there were men in his wagon train that got run out of Texas, but he swore he wasn't one of them. So I reckon that sort of talk held good for twenty years, an' for all the Texans who emigrated, except, of course, such notorious rustlers as Daggs an' men of his ilk. Shore we've got some bad men heah. There's no law. Possession used to mean more than it does now. Daggs an' his Hash Knife Gang have begun to hold forth with a high hand. No small rancher can keep enough stock to pay for his labor."

At the time of which Blaisdell spoke there were not many sheepmen and cattlemen in the Tonto, considering its vast area. But these, on account of the extreme wildness of the broken country, were limited to the comparatively open Grass Valley and its adjacent environs. Naturally, as the inhabitants increased and stock raising grew in proportion the grazing and water rights became matters of extreme importance. Sheepmen ran their flocks up on the Rim in summer time and down into the Basin in winter time. A sheepman could throw a few thousand sheep round a cattleman's ranch and ruin him. The range was free. It was as fair for sheepmen to graze their herds anywhere as it was for cattlemen. This of course did not apply to the few acres of cultivated ground that a rancher could call his own; but very few cattle could have been raised on such limited area. Blaisdell said that the sheepmen were unfair because they could have done just as well, though perhaps at more labor, by keeping to the ridges and leaving the open valley and little flats to the ranchers. Formerly there had been room enough for all; now the grazing ranges were being encroached upon by sheepmen newly come to the Tonto. To Blaisdell's way of thinking the rustler menace was more serious than the sheeping-off of the range, for the simple reason that no cattleman knew exactly who the rustlers were and for the more complex and significant reason that the rustlers did not steal sheep.

"Texas was overstocked with bad men an' fine steers," concluded Blaisdell. "Most of the first an' some of the last have struck the Tonto. The sheepmen have now got distributin' points for wool an' sheep at Maricopa an' Phoenix. They're shore waxin' strong an' bold."

"Ahuh! . . . An' what's likely to come of this mess?" queried Jean.

"Ask your dad," replied Blaisdell.

"I will. But I reckon I'd be obliged for your opinion."

"Wal, short an' sweet it's this: Texas cattlemen will never allow the range they stocked to be overrun by sheepmen."

"Who's this man Greaves?" went on Jean. "Never run into anyone like him."

"Greaves is hard to figure. He's a snaky customer in deals. But he seems to be good to the poor people 'round heah. Says he's from Missouri. Ha-ha! He's as much Texan as I am. He rode into the Tonto without even a pack to his name. An' presently he builds his stone house an' freights supplies in from Phoenix. Appears to buy an' sell a good deal of stock. For a while it looked like he was steerin' a middle course between cattlemen an' sheepmen. Both sides made a rendezvous of his store, where he heard the grievances of each. Laterly he's leanin' to the sheepmen. Nobody has accused him of that yet. But it's time some cattleman called his bluff."

"Of course there are honest an' square sheepmen in the Basin?" queried Jean.

"Yes, an' some of them are not unreasonable. But the new fellows that dropped in on us the last few years—they're the ones we're goin' to clash with."

"This—sheepman, Jorth?" went on Jean, in slow hesitation, as if compelled to ask what he would rather not learn.

"Jorth must be the leader of this sheep faction that's harryin' us ranchers. He doesn't make threats or roar around like some of them. But he goes on raisin' an' buyin' more an' more sheep. An' his herders have been grazin' down all around us this winter. Jorth's got to be reckoned with."

"Who is he?"

"Wal, I don't know enough to talk aboot. Your dad never said so, but I think he an' Jorth knew each other in Texas years ago. I never saw Jorth but once. That was in Greaves's barroom. Your dad an' Jorth met that day for the first time in this country. Wal, I've not known men for nothin'. They just stood stiff an' looked at each other. Your dad was aboot to draw. But Jorth made no sign to throw a gun."

Jean saw the growing and weaving and thickening threads of a tangle that had already involved him. And the sudden pang of regret he sustained was not wholly because of sympathies with his own people.

"The other day back up in the woods on the Rim I ran into a sheepman who said his name was Colter. Who is he?"

"Colter? Shore he's a new one. What'd he look like?"

Jean described Colter with a readiness that spoke volumes for the vividness of his impressions.

"I don't know him," replied Blaisdell. "But that only goes to prove my contention—any fellow runnin' wild in the woods can say he's a sheepman."

"Colter surprised me by callin' me by my name," continued Jean. "Our little talk wasn't exactly friendly. He said a lot about my bein' sent for to run sheep herders out of the country."

"Shore that's all over," replied Blaisdell, seriously. "You're a marked man already."

"What started such rumor?"

"Shore you cain't prove it by me. But it's not taken as rumor. It's got to the sheepmen as hard as bullets."

"Ahuh! That accunts for Colter's seemin' a little sore under the collar. Well, he said they were goin' to run sheep over Grass Valley, an' for me to take that hunch to my dad."

Blaisdell had his chair tilted back and his heavy boots against a post of the porch. Down he thumped. His neck corded with a sudden rush of blood and his eyes changed to blue fire.

"The hell he did!" he ejaculated, in furious amaze.

Jean gauged the brooding, rankling hurt of this old cattleman by his sudden break from the cool, easy Texan manner. Blaisdell cursed under his breath, swung his arms violently, as if to throw a last doubt or hope aside, and then relapsed to his former state. He laid a brown hand on Jean's knee.

"Two years ago I called the cards," he said, quietly. "It means a Grass Valley war."

Not until late that afternoon did Jean's father broach the subject uppermost in his mind. Then at an opportune moment he drew Jean away into the cedars out of sight.

"Son, I shore hate to make your home-comin' unhappy," he said, with evidence of agitation, "but so help me God I have to do it!"

"Dad, you called me Prodigal, an' I reckon you were right. I've shirked my duty to you. I'm ready now to make up for it," replied Jean, feelingly.

"Wal, wal, shore that's fine-spoken, my boy. . . . Let's set down heah an' have a long talk. First off, what did Jim Blaisdell tell you?"

Briefly Jean outlined the neighbor rancher's conversation. Then Jean recounted his experience with Colter and concluded with Blaisdell's reception of the sheepman's threat. If Jean expected to see his father rise up like a lion in his wrath he made a huge mistake. This news of Colter and his talk never struck even a spark from Gaston Isbel.

"Wal," he began, thoughtfully, "reckon there are only

two points in Jim's talk I need touch on. There's shore goin' to be a Grass Valley war. An' Jim's idea of the cause of it seems to be pretty much the same as that of all the other cattlemen. It 'll go down a black blot on the history page of the Tonto Basin as a war between rival sheepmen an' cattlemen. Same old fight over water an' grass! . . . Jean, my son, that is wrong. It 'll not be a war between sheepmen an' cattlemen. But a war of honest ranchers against rustlers maskin' as sheep-raisers! . . . Mind you, I don't belittle the trouble between sheepmen an' cattlemen in Arizona. It's real an' it's vital an' it's serious. It 'll take law an' order to straighten out the grazin' question. Some day the government will keep sheep off of cattle ranges. . . . So get things right in your mind, my son. You can trust your dad to tell the absolute truth. In this fight that 'll wipe out some of the Isbels—maybe all of them— you're on the side of justice an' right. Knowin' that, a man can fight a hundred times harder than he who knows he is a liar an' a thief."

The old rancher wiped his perspiring face and breathed slowly and deeply. Jean sensed in him the rise of a tremendous emotional strain. Wonderingly he watched the keen lined face. More than material worries were at the root of brooding, mounting thoughts in his father's eyes.

"Now next take what Jim said aboot your comin' to chase these sheep herders out of the valley. . . . Jean, I started that talk. I had my tricky reasons. I know these greaser sheep herders an' I know the respect Texans have for a gunman. Some say I bragged. Some say I'm an old fool in his dotage, ravin' aboot a favorite son. But they are people who hate me an' are afraid. True, son, I talked with a purpose, but shore I was mighty cold an' steady when I did it. My feelin' was that you'd do what I'd do if I were thirty years younger. No, I reckoned you'd do more. For I figured on your blood. Jean, you're Indian, an' Texas an' French, an' you've trained yourself in the Oregon woods. When you were only a boy, few marksmen I ever knew could beat you, an' I never saw your equal for eye an' ear, for trackin' a hoss, for all the gifts that make a woodsman. . . . Wal, rememberin' this an' seein' the trouble ahaid for the Isbels, I just broke out whenever I had a chance. I bragged before men I'd reason to believe would take my words deep. For instance, not long ago I missed some stock, an', happenin' into Greaves's place one Saturday night, I shore talked loud. His barroom was full of men an' some of them were in my black book. Greaves took my talk a little testy. He said. 'Wal, Gass, mebbe you're right aboot some of these cattle thieves livin' among us, but ain't they jest as liable to be some of your friends or relatives as Ted Meeker's or mine or any one around heah?' That was where Greaves an' me fell out. I yelled at him: 'No, by God, they're not! My record heah an' that of my people is open. The least I can say for you, Greaves, an' your crowd, is that your records fade away on dim trails.' Then he said, nasty-like, 'Wal, if you could work out all the dim trails in the Tonto you'd shore be surprised.' An' then I roared. Shore that was the chance I was lookin' for. I swore the trails he hinted of would be tracked to the holes of the rustlers who made them. I told him I had sent for you an' when you got heah these slippery, mysterious thieves, whoever they were, would shore have hell to pay. Greaves said he hoped so, but he was afraid I was partial to my Indian son. Then we had hot words. Blaisdell got between us. When I was leavin' I took a partin' fling at him. 'Greaves, you ought to know the Isbels, considerin' you're from Texas. Maybe you've got reasons for throwin' taunts at my claims for my son Jean. Yes, he's got Indian in him an' that 'll be the worse for the men who will have to meet him. I'm tellin' you, Greaves, Jean Isbel is the black sheep of the family. If you ride down his record you'll find he's shore in line to be another Poggin, or Reddy Kingfisher, or Hardin', or any of the Texas gunmen you ought to remember. . . . Greaves, there are men rubbin' elbows with you right heah that my Indian son is goin' to track down!' "

Jean bent his head in stunned cognizance of the notoriety with which his father had chosen to affront any and all Tonto Basin men who were under the ban of his suspicion. What a terrible reputation and trust to have saddled upon him! Thrills and strange, heated sensations seemed to rush together inside Jean, forming a hot ball of fire that threatened to explode. A retreating self made feeble protests. He saw his own pale face going away from this older, grimmer man.

"Son, if I could have looked forward to anythin' but blood spillin' I'd never have given you such a name to uphold," continued the rancher. "What I'm goin' to tell you now is my secret. My other sons an' Ann have never heard it. Jim Blaisdell suspects there's somethin' strange, but he doesn't know. I'll shore never tell anyone else but you. An' you must promise to keep my secret now an' after I am gone."

"I promise," said Jean.

"Wal, an' now to get it out," began his father, breathing hard. His face twitched and his hands clenched. "The sheepman heah I have to reckon with is Lee Jorth, a lifelong enemy of mine. We were born in the same town, played together as children, an' fought with each other as boys. We never got along together. An' we both fell in love with the same girl. It was nip an' tuck for a while. Ellen Sutton belonged to one of the old families of the South. She was a beauty, an' much courted, an' I reckon it was hard for her to choose. But I won her an' we became engaged. Then the war broke out. I enlisted with my brother Jean. He advised me to marry Ellen before I left. But I would not. That was the blunder of my life. Soon after our partin' her letters ceased to come. But I didn't distrust her. That was a terrible time an' all was confusion. Then I got crippled an' put in a hospital. An' in aboot a year I was sent back home."

At this juncture Jean refrained from further gaze at his father's face.

"Lee Jorth had gotten out of goin' to war," went on the rancher, in lower, thicker voice. "He'd married my sweetheart, Ellen. . . . I knew the story long before I got well. He had run after her like a hound after a hare. . . . An' Ellen married him. Wal, when I was able to get aboot I went to see Jorth an' Ellen. I confronted them. I had to know why she had gone back on me. Lee Jorth hadn't changed any with all his good fortune. He'd made Ellen believe in my dishonor. . . . But, I reckon, lies or no lies, Ellen Sutton was faithless. In my absence he had won her away from me. An' I saw that she loved him as she never had me. I reckon that killed all my generosity. If she'd been imposed upon an' weaned away by his lies an' had regretted me a little I'd have forgiven, perhaps. But she worshiped him. She was his slave. An' I, wal, I learned what hate was.

"The war ruined the Suttons, same as so many Southerners. Lee Jorth went in for raisin' cattle. He'd gotten the Sutton range an' after a few years he began to accumulate stock. In those days every cattleman was a little bit of a thief. Every cattleman drove in an' branded calves he couldn't swear was his. Wal, the Isbels were the strongest cattle raisers in that country. An' I laid a trap for Lee Jorth, caught him in the act of brandin' calves of mine I'd marked, an' I proved him a thief. I made him a rustler. I ruined him. We met once. But Jorth was one Texan not strong on the draw, at least against an Isbel. He left the country. He had friends an' relatives an' they started him at stock raisin' again. But he began to gamble an' he got in with a shady crowd. He went from bad to worse an' then he came back home. When I saw the change in proud, beautiful Ellen Sutton, an' how she still worshiped Jorth, it shore drove me near mad between pity an' hate. . . . Wal, I reckon in a Texan hate outlives any other feelin'. There came a strange turn of the wheel an' my fortunes changed. Like most young bloods of the day, I drank an' gambled. An' one night I run across Jorth an' a card-sharp friend. He fleeced me. We quarreled. Guns were thrown. I killed my man. . . . Aboot that period the Texas Rangers had come into existence. . . . An', son, when I said I never was run out of Texas I wasn't holdin' to strict truth. I rode out on a hoss.

"I went to Oregon. There I married soon, an' there Bill an' Guy were born. Their mother did not live long. An' next I married your mother, Jean. She had some Indian blood, which, for all I could see, made her only the finer. She was a wonderful woman an' gave me the only happiness I ever knew. You remember her, of course, an' those home days in Oregon. I reckon I made another great blunder when I moved to Arizona. But the cattle country had always called me. I had heard of this wild Tonto Basin an' how Texans were settlin' there. An' Jim Blaisdell sent me word to come—that this shore was a garden spot of the West. Wal, it is. An' your mother was gone—

"Three years ago Lee Jorth drifted into the Tonto. An', strange to me, along aboot a year or so after his comin' the Hash Knife Gang rode up from Texas. Jorth went in for raisin' sheep. Along with some other sheepmen he lives up in the Rim cañons. Somewhere back in the wild brakes is the hidin' place of the Hash Knife Gang. Nobody but me, I reckon, associates Colonel Jorth, as he's called, with Daggs an' his gang. Maybe Blaisdell an' a few others have a hunch. But that's no matter. As a sheepman Jorth has a legitimate grievance with the cattlemen. But what could be settled by a square consideration for the good of all an' the future Jorth will never settle. He'll never settle because he is now no longer an honest man. He's in with Daggs. I cain't prove this, son, but I know it. I saw it in Jorth's face when I met him that day with Greaves. I saw more. I shore saw what he is up to. He'd never meet me at an even break. He's dead set on usin' this sheep an' cattle feud to ruin my family an' me, even as I ruined him. But he means more, Jean. This will be a war between Texans, an' a bloody war. There are bad men in this Tonto—some of the worst that didn't get shot in Texas. Jorth will have some of these fellows. . . . Now, are we goin' to wait to be sheeped off our range an' to be murdered from ambush?"

"No, we are not," replied Jean, quietly.

"Wal, come down to the house," said the rancher, and led the way without speaking until he halted by the door. There he place his finger on a small hole in the wood at about the height of a man's head. Jean saw it was a bullet hole and that a few gray hairs stuck to its edges. The rancher stepped closer to the doorpost, so that his head was within an inch of the wood. Then he looked at Jean with eyes in which there glinted dancing specks of fire, like wild sparks.

"Son, this sneakin' shot at me was made three mawnin's ago. I recollect movin' my haid just when I heard the crack of a rifle. Shore was surprised. But I got inside quick."

Jean scarcely heard the latter part of this speech. He seemed doubled up inwardly, in hot and cold convulsions of changing emotion. A terrible hold upon his consciousness was about to break and let go. The first shot had been fired and he was an Isbel. Indeed, his father had made him ten times an Isbel. Blood was thick. His father did not speak to dull ears. This strife of rising tumult in him seemed the effect of years of calm, of peace in the woods, of dreamy waiting for he knew not what. It was the passionate primitive life in him that had awakened to the call of blood ties.

"That's aboot all, son," concluded the rancher. "You understand now why I feel they're goin' to kill me. I feel it heah." With solemn gesture he placed his broad hand over his heart. "An', Jean, strange whispers come to me at night. It seems like your mother was callin' or tryin' to warn me. I cain't explain these queer whispers. But I know what I know."

"Jorth has his followers. You must have yours." replied Jean, tensely.

"Shore, son, an' I can take my choice of the best men heah," replied the rancher, with pride. "But I'll not do that. I'll lay the deal before them an' let them choose. I reckon it 'll not be a long-winded fight. It 'll be short an bloody, after the way of Texans. I'm lookin' to you, Jean, to see that an Isbel is the last man!"

"My God—dad! is there no other way? Think of my sister Ann—of my brothers' wives—of—of other women! Dad, these damned Texas feuds are cruel, horrible!" burst out Jean, in passionate protest.

"Jean, would it be any easier for our women if we let these men shoot us down in cold blood?"

"Oh no—no, I see, there's no hope of—of. . . . But, dad. I wasn't thinkin' about myself. I don't care. Once started I'll—I'll be what you bragged I was. Only it's so hard to—to give in."

Jean leaned an arm against the side of the cabin and, bowing his face over it, he surrendered to the irresistible contention within his breast. And as if with a wrench that strange inward hold broke. He let down. He went back. Something that was boyish and hopeful—and in its place slowly rose the dark tide of his inheritance, the savage instinct of self-preservation bequeathed by his Indian mother, and the fierce, feudal blood lust of his Texan father.

Then as he raised himself, gripped by a sickening coldness in his breast, he remembered Ellen Jorth's face as she had gazed dreamily down off the Rim—so soft, so different, with tremulous lips, sad, musing, with far-seeing stare of dark eyes, peering into the unknown, the instinct of life still unlived. With confused vision and nameless pain Jean thought of her.

"Dad, it's hard on—the—the young folks," he said, bitterly. "The sins of the father, you know. An' the other side. How about Jorth? Has he any children?"

What a curious gleam of surprise and conjecture Jean encountered in his father's gaze!

"He has a daughter. Ellen Jorth. Named after her mother. The first time I saw Ellen Jorth I thought she was a ghost of the girl I had loved an' lost. Sight of her was like a blade in my side. But the looks of her an' what she is—they don't gibe. Old as I am, my heart—Bah! Ellen Jorth is a damned hussy!"

Jean Isbel went off alone into the cedars. Surrender and resignation to his father's creed should have ended his perplexity and worry. His instant and burning resolve to be as his father had represented him should have opened his mind to slow cunning, to the craft of the Indian, to the development of hate. But there seemed to be an obstacle. A cloud in the way of vision. A face limned on his memory.

Those damning words of his father's had been a shock—how little or great he could not tell. Was it only a day since he had met Ellen Jorth? What had made all the difference? Suddenly like a breath the fragrance of her hair came back to him. Then the sweet coolness of her lips!

Jean trembled. He looked around him as if he were pursued or surrounded by eyes, by instincts, by fears, by incomprehensible things.

"Ahuh! That must be what ails me," he muttered. "The look of her—an' that kiss—they've gone hard with me. I should never have stopped to talk. An' I'm goin' to kill her father an' leave her to God knows what."

Something was wrong somewhere. Jean absolutely forgot that within the hour he had pledged his manhood, his life to a feud which could be blotted out only in blood. If he had understood himself he would have realized that the pledge was no more thrilling and unintelligible in its possibilities than this instinct which drew him irresistibly.

"Ellen Jorth! So—my dad calls her a damned hussy! So—that explains the—the way she acted—why she never hit me when I kissed her. An' her words, so easy an' cool-like. Hussy? That means she's bad—bad! Scornful of me—maybe disappointed because my kiss was innocent! It was, I swear. An' all she said: 'Oh, I've been kissed before.'"

Jean grew furious with himself for the spreading of a new sensation in his breast that seemed now to ache. Had he become infatuated, all in a day, with this Ellen Jorth? Was he jealous of the men who had the privilege of her kisses? No! But his reply was hot with shame, with uncertainty. The thing that seemed wrong was outside of himself. A blunder was no crime. To be attracted by a pretty girl in the woods—to yield to an impulse was no disgrace, nor wrong. He had been foolish over a girl before, though not to such a rash extent. Ellen Jorth had stuck in his consciousness, and with her a sense of regret.

Then swiftly rang his father's bitter words, the revealing: "But the looks of her an' what she is—they don't gibe!" In the import of these words hid the meaning of the wrong that troubled him. Broodingly he pondered over them.

"The looks of her. Yes, she was pretty. But it didn't dawn on me at first. I—I was sort of excited. I liked to look at her, but didn't think." And now consciously her face was called up, infinitely sweet and more impelling for the deliberate memory. Flash of brown skin, smooth and clear; level gaze of dark, wide eyes, steady, bold, unseeing; red curved lips, sad and sweet; her strong, clean, fine face rose before Jean, eager and wistful one moment, softened by dreamy musing thought, and the next stormily passionate, full of hate, full of longing, but the more mysterious and beautiful.

"She looks like that, but she's bad," concluded Jean, with bitter finality. "I might have fallen in love with Ellen Jorth if—if she'd been different."

But the conviction forced upon Jean did not dispel the haunting memory of her face nor did it wholly silence the deep and stubborn voice of his consciousness. Later that afternoon he sought a moment with his sister.

"Ann, did you ever meet Ellen Jorth?" he asked.

"Yes, but not lately," replied Ann.

"Well, I met her as I was ridin' along yesterday. She was herdin' sheep," went on Jean, rapidly. "I asked her to show me the way to the Rim. An' she walked with me a mile or so. I can't say the meetin' was not interestin', at least to me. . . . Will you tell me what you know about her?"

"Sure, Jean," replied his sister, with her dark eyes fixed wonderingly and kindly on his troubled face. "I've heard a great deal, but in this Tonto Basin I don't believe all I hear. What I know I'll tell you. I first met Ellen Jorth two years ago. We didn't know each other's names then. She was the prettiest girl I ever saw. I liked her. She liked me. She seemed unhappy. The next time we met was at a round-up. There were other girls with me and they snubbed her. But I left them and went around with her. That snub cut her to the heart. She was lonely. She had no friends. She talked about herself—how she hated the people, but loved Arizona. She had nothin' fit to wear. I didn't need to be told that she'd been used to better things. Just when it looked as if we were goin' to be friends she told me who she was and asked me my name. I told her. Jean, I couldn't have hurt her more if I'd slapped her face. She turned white. She gasped. And then she ran off. The last time I saw her was about a year ago. I was ridin' a shortcut trail to the ranch where a friend lived. And I met Ellen Jorth ridin' with a man I'd never seen. The trail was overgrown and shady. They were ridin' close and didn't see me right off. The man had his arm round her. She pushed him away. I saw her laugh. Then he got hold of her again and was kissin' her when his horse shied at sight of mine. They rode by me then. Ellen Jorth held her head high and never looked at me."

"Ann, do you think she's a bad girl?" demanded Jean, bluntly.

"Bad? Oh, Jean!" exclaimed Ann, in surprise and embarrassment.

"Dad said she was a damned hussy."

"Jean, dad hates the Jorths."

"Sister, I'm askin' you what you think of Ellen Jorth. Would you be friends with her if you could?"

"Yes."

"Then you don't believe she's bad."

"No. Ellen Jorth is lonely, unhappy. She has no mother. She lives alone among rough men. Such a girl can't keep men from handlin' her and kissin' her. Maybe she's too free. Maybe she's wild. But she's honest, Jean. You can trust a woman to tell. When she rode past me that day her face was white and proud. She was a Jorth and I was an

Isbel. She hated herself—she hated me. But no bad girl could look like that. She knows what's said of her all around the valley. But she doesn't care. She'd encourage gossip."

"Thank you, Ann," replied Jean, huskily. "Please keep this—this meetin' of mine with her all to yourself, won't you?"

"Why, Jean, of course I will."

Jean wandered away again, peculiarly grateful to Ann for reviving and upholding something in him that seemed a wavering part of the best of him—a chivalry that had demanded to be killed by judgment of a righteous woman. He was conscious of an uplift, a gladdening of his spirit. Yet the ache remained. More than that, he found himself plunged deeper into conjecture, doubt. Had not the Ellen Jorth incident ended? He denied his father's indictment of her and accepted the faith of his sister. "Reckon that's aboot all, as dad says," he soliloquized. Yet was that all? He paced under the cedars. He watched the sun set. He listened to the coyotes. He lingered there after the call for supper; until out of the tumult of his conflicting emotions and ponderings there evolved the staggering consciousness that he must see Ellen Jorth again.

CHAPTER 4

Ellen Jorth hurried back into the forest, hotly resentful of the accident that had thrown her in contact with an Isbel.

Disgust filled her—disgust that she had been amiable to a member of the hated family that had ruined her father. The surprise of this meeting did not come to her while she was under the spell of stronger feeling. She walked under the trees, swiftly, with head erect, looking straight before her, and every step seemed a relief.

Upon reaching camp, her attention was distracted from herself. Pepe, the Mexican boy, with the two shepherd dogs, was trying to drive sheep into a closer bunch to save the lambs from coyotes. Ellen loved the fleecy, tottering little lambs, and at this season she hated all the prowling beast of the forest. From this time on for weeks the flock would be besieged by wolves, lions, bears, the last of which were often bold and dangerous. The old grizzlies that killed the ewes to eat only the milk-bags were particularly dreaded by Ellen. She was a good shot with a rifle, but had orders from her father to let the bears alone. Fortunately, such sheep-killing bears were but few, and were left to be hunted by men from the ranch. Mexican sheep herders could not be depended upon to protect their flocks from bears. Ellen helped Pepe drive in the stragglers, and she took several shots at coyotes skulking along the edge of the brush. The open glade in the forest was favorable for herding the sheep at night and the dogs could be depended upon to guard the flock, and in most cases to drive predatory beasts away.

After this task, which brought the time to sunset, Ellen had supper to cook and eat. Darkness came, and a cool night wind set in. Here and there a lamb bleated plaintively. With her work done for the day, Ellen sat before a ruddy camp-fire, and found her thoughts again centering around the singular adventure that had befallen her. Disdainfully she strove to think of something else. But there was nothing that could dispel the interest of her meeting with Jean Isbel. Thereupon she impatiently surrendered to it, and recalled every word and action which she could remember. And in the process of this meditation she came to an action of hers, recollection of which brought the blood tingling to her neck and cheeks, so unusually and burningly that she covered them with her hands. "What did he think of me?" she mused, doubtfully. It did not matter what he thought, but she could not help wondering. And when she came to the memory of his kiss she suffered more than the sensation of throbbing scarlet cheeks. Scornfully and bitterly she burst out, "Shore he couldn't have thought much good of me."

The half hour following this reminiscence was far from being pleasant. Proud, passionate, strong-willed Ellen Jorth found herself a victim of conflicting emotions. The event of the day was too close. She could not understand it. Disgust and disdain and scorn could not make this meeting with Jean Isbel as if it had never been. Pride could not efface it from her mind. The more she reflected, the harder she tried to forget, the stronger grew a significance of interest. And when a hint of this dawned upon her consciousness she resented it so forcibly that she lost her temper, scattered the camp fire, and went into the little teepee tent to roll in her blankets.

Thus settled snug and warm for the night, with a shepherd dog curled at the opening of her tent, she shut her eyes and confidently bade sleep end her perplexities. But sleep did not come at her invitation. She found herself wide awake, keenly sensitive to the sputtering of the camp fire, the tinkling of bells on the rams, the bleating of lambs, the sough of wind in the pines, and the hungry sharp bark of coyotes off in the distance. Darkness was no respecter of her pride. The lonesome night with its emphasis of solitude seemed to induce clamoring and strange thoughts, a confusing ensemble of all those that had annoyed her during the daytime. Not for long hours did sheer weariness bring her to slumber.

Ellen awakened late and failed of her usual alacrity. Both Pepe and the shepherd dog appeared to regard her with surprise and solicitude. Ellen's spirit was low this morning; her blood ran sluggishly; she had to fight a mournful tendency to feel sorry for herself. And at first she was not very successful. There seemed to be some kind of pleasure in reveling in melancholy which her common sense told her had no reason for existence. But states of mind persisted in spite of common sense.

"Pepe, when is Antonio comin' back?" she asked.

The boy could not give her a satisfactory answer. Ellen had willingly taken the sheep herder's place for a few days, but now she was impatient to go home. She looked down the green-and-brown aisles of the forest until she was tired. Antonio did not return. Ellen spent the day with the sheep; and in the manifold task of caring for a thousand new-born lambs she forgot herself. This day saw the end of lambing-time for that season. The forest resounded to a babel of baas and bleats. When night came she was glad to go to bed, for what with loss of sleep, and weariness she could scarcely keep her eyes open.

The following morning she awakened early, bright, eager, expectant, full of bounding life, strangely aware of the beauty and sweetness of the scented forest, strangely conscious of some nameless stimulus to her feelings.

Not long was Ellen in associating this new and delightful variety of sensations with the fact that Jean Isbel had set to-day for his ride up to the Rim to see her. Ellen's joyousness fled; her smiles faded. The spring morning lost its magic radiance.

"Shore there's no sense in my lyin' to myself," she soliloquized, thoughtfully. "It's queer of me—feelin' glad aboot him—without knowin'. Lord! I must be lonesome! To be glad of seein' an Isbel, even if he is different!"

Soberly she accepted the astounding reality. Her confidence died with her gayety; her vanity began to suffer. And she caught at her admission that Jean Isbel was different; she resented it in amaze; she ridiculed it; she laughed at her naïve confession. She could arrive at no conclusion other than that she was a weak-minded, fluctuating, inexplicable little fool.

But for all that she found her mind had been made up for her, without consent or desire, before her will had been consulted; and that inevitably and unalterably she meant to see Jean Isbel again. Long she battled with this strange decree. One moment she won a victory over this new curious self, only to lose it the next. And at last out of her conflict there emerged a few convictions that left her with some shreds of pride. She hated all Isbels, she hated any Isbel, and particularly she hated Jean Isbel. She was only curious—intensely curious to see if he would come back, and if he did come what he would do. She wanted only to watch him from some covert. She would not go near him, not let him see her or guess of her presence. Thus she assuaged her hurt vanity—thus she stifled her miserable doubts.

Long before the sun had begun to slant westward toward the mid-afternoon Jean Isbel had set as a meeting time Ellen directed her steps through the forest to the Rim. She felt ashamed of her eagerness. She had a guilty conscience that no strange thrills could silence. It would be fun to see him, to watch him, to let him wait for her, to fool him.

Like an Indian, she chose the soft pine-needle mats to tread upon, and her light-moccasined feet left no trace. Like an Indian also she made a wide detour, and reached the Rim a quarter of a mile west of the spot where she had talked with Jean Isbel; and here, turning east, she took care to step on the bare stones. This was an adventure, seemingly the first she had ever had in her life. Assuredly she had never before come directly to the Rim without halting to look, to wonder, to worship. This time she scarcely glanced into the blue abyss. All absorbed was she in hiding her tracks. Not one chance in a thousand would she risk. The Jorth pride burned even while the feminine side of her dominated her actions. She had some difficult rocky points to cross, then windfalls to round, and at length reached the covert she desired. A rugged yellow point of the Rim stood somewhat higher than the spot Ellen wanted to watch. A dense thicket of jack-pines grew to the very edge. It afforded an ambush that even the Indian eyes Jean Isbel was credited with could never penetrate. Moreover, if by accident she made a noise and excited suspicion, she could retreat unobserved and hide in the huge rocks below the Rim, where a ferret could not locate her.

With her plan decided upon, Ellen had nothing to do but wait, so she repaired to the other side of the pine thicket and to the edge of the Rim where she could watch and listen. She knew that long before she saw Isbel she would hear his horse. It was altogether unlikely that he would come on foot.

"Shore, Ellen Jorth, y'u're a queer girl," she mused. "I reckon I wasn't well acquainted with y'u."

Beneath her yawned a wonderful deep cañon, rugged and rocky with but few pines on the north slope, thick with dark green timber on the south slope. Yellow and gray crags, like turreted castles, stood up out of the sloping forest on the side opposite her. The trees were all sharp, spear pointed. Patches of light green aspens showed strikingly against the dense black. The great slope beneath Ellen was serrated with narrow, deep gorges, almost cañons in themselves. Shadows alternated with clear bright spaces. The mile-wide mouth of the cañon opened upon the Basin, down into a world of wild timbered ranges and ravines, valleys and hills, that rolled and tumbled in dark-green waves to the Sierra Anchas.

But for once Ellen seemed singularly unresponsive to this panorama of wildness and grandeur. Her ears were like those of a listening deer, and her eyes continually reverted to the open places along the Rim. At first, in her excitement, time flew by. Gradually, however, as the sun moved westward, she began to be restless. The soft thud of dropping pine cones, the rustling of squirrels up and down the shaggy-barked spruces, the cracking of weathered bits of rock, these caught her keen ears many times and brought her up erect and thrilling. Finally she heard a sound which resembled that of an unshod hoof on stone. Stealthily then she took her rifle and slipped back through the pine thicket to the spot she had chosen. The little pines were so close together that she had to crawl between their trunks. The ground was covered with a soft bed of pine needles, brown and fragrant. In her hurry she pricked her ungloved hand on a sharp pine cone and drew the blood. She sucked the tiny wound. "Shore I'm wonderin' if that's a bad omen," she muttered, darkly thoughtful. Then she resumed her sinuous approach to the edge of the thicket, and presently reached it.

Ellen lay flat a moment to recover her breath, then raised herself on her elbows. Through an opening in the fringe of buck brush she could plainly see the promontory where she had stood with Jean Isbel, and also the approaches by which he might come. Rather nervously she realized that her covert was hardly more than a hundred feet from the promontory. It was imperative that she be absolutely silent. Her eyes searched the openings along the Rim. The gray form of a deer crossed one of these, and she concluded it had made the sound she had heard. Then she lay down more comfortably and waited. Resolutely she held, as much as possible, to her sensorial perceptions. The meaning of Ellen Jorth lying in ambush just to see an Isbel was a conundrum she refused to ponder in the present. She was doing it, and the physical act had its fascination. Her ears, attuned to all the sounds of the lonely forest, caught them and arranged them according to her knowledge of woodcraft.

A long hour passed by. The sun had slanted to a point halfway between the zenith and the horizon. Suddenly a thought confronted Ellen Jorth: "He's not comin'," she whispered. The instant that idea presented itself she felt a blank sense of loss, a vague regret—something that must have been disappointment. Unprepared for this, she was held by surprise for a moment, and then she was stunned. Her spirit, swift and rebellious, had no time to rise in her defense. She was a lonely, guilty, miserable girl, too weak for pride to uphold, too fluctuating to know her real self. She stretched there, burying her face in the pine needles, digging her fingers into them, wanting nothing so much as that they might hide her. The moment was incomprehensible to Ellen, and utterly intolerable. The sharp pine needles, piercing her wrists and cheeks, and her hot heaving breast, seemed to give her exquisite relief.

The shrill snort of a horse sounded near at hand. With a shock Ellen's body stiffened. Then she quivered a little and her feelings underwent swift change. Cautiously and noiselessly she raised herself upon her elbows and peeped through the opening in the brush. She saw a man tying a horse to a bush somewhat back from the Rim. Drawing a rifle from its saddle sheath he threw it in the hollow of his arm and walked to the edge of the precipice. He gazed away across the Basin and appeared lost in contemplation or thought. Then he turned to look back into the forest, as if he expected some one.

Ellen recognized the lithe figure, the dark face so like an Indian's. It was Isbel. He had come. Somehow his coming seemed wonderful and terrible. Ellen shook as she leaned on her elbows. Jean Isbel, true to his word, in spite of her scorn, had come back to see her. The fact seemed monstrous. He was an enemy of her father. Long had range rumor been bandied from lip to lip—old Gass Isbel had sent for his Indian son to fight the Jorths. Jean Isbel—son of a Texan—unerring shot—peerless tracker—a bad and dangerous man! Then there flashed over Ellen a burning thought—if it were true, if he was an enemy of her father's, if a fight between Jorth and Isbel was inevitable, she ought to kill this Jean Isbel right there in his tracks as he boldly and confidently waited for her. Fool he was to think she would come. Ellen sank down and dropped her head until the strange tremor of her arms ceased. That dark and grim flash of thought retreated. She had not come to murder a man from ambush, but only to watch him, to try to see what he meant, what he thought, to allay a strange curiosity.

After a while she looked again. Isbel was sitting on an upheaved section of the Rim, in a comfortable position from which he could watch the openings in the forest and gaze as well across the west curve of the Basin to the Mazatzals. He had composed himself to wait. He was clad in a buckskin suit, rather new, and it certainly showed off to advantage, compared with the ragged and soiled apparel Ellen remembered. He did not look so large. Ellen was used to the long, lean, rangy Arizonians and Texans. This man was built differently. He had the widest shoulders of any man she had ever seen, and they made him appear rather short. But his lithe, powerful limbs proved he was not short. Whenever he moved the muscles rippled. His hands were clasped round a knee—brown, sinewy hands, very broad, and fitting the thick muscular wrists. His collar was open, and he did not wear a scarf, as did the men Ellen knew. Then her intense curiosity at last brought her steady gaze to Jean Isbel's head and face. He wore a cap, evidently of some thin fur. His hair was straight and short, and in color a dead raven black. His complexion was dark, clear tan, with no trace of red. He did not have the prominent cheek bones nor the high-bridged nose usual with white men who were part Indian. Still he had the Indian look. Ellen caught that in the dark, intent, piercing eyes, in the wide, level, thoughtful brows, in the stern impassiveness of his smooth face. He had a straight, sharp-cut profile.

Ellen whispered to herself: "I saw him right the other day. Only, I'd not admit it. . . . The finest-lookin' man I ever saw in my life is a damned Isbel! . . . Was that what I come out heah for?"

She lowered herself once more and, folding her arms under her breast, she reclined comfortably on them, and searched out a smaller peephole from which she could spy upon Isbel. And as she watched him the new and perplexing side of her mind waxed busier. Why had he come back? What did he want of her? Acquaintance, friendship, was impossible for them. He had been respectful, deferential toward her, in a way that had strangely pleased, until the surprising moment when he had kissed her. That had only disrupted her rather dreamy pleasure in a situation she had not experienced before. All the men she had met in this wild country were rough and bold; most of them had wanted to marry her, and, failing that, they had persisted in amorous attentions not particularly flattering or honorable. They were a bad lot. And contact with them had dulled some of her sensibilities. But this Jean Isbel had seemed a gentleman. She struggled to be fair, trying to forget her antipathy, as much to understand herself as to give him due credit. True, he had kissed her, crudely and forcibly. But that kiss had not been an insult. Ellen's finer feeling forced her to believe this. She remembered the honest amaze and shame and contrition with which he had faced her, trying awkwardly to explain his bold act. Likewise she recalled the subtle swift change in him at her words, "Oh, I've been kissed before!" She was glad she had said that. Still—was she glad, after all?

She watched him. Every little while he shifted his gaze from the blue gulf beneath him to the forest. When he turned thus the sun shone on his face and she caught the piercing gleam of his dark eyes. She saw, too, that he was listening. Watching and listening for her! Ellen had to still a tumult within her. It made her feel very young, very shy, very strange. All the while she hated him because he manifestly expected her to come. Several times he rose and walked a little way into the woods. The last time he looked at the westering sun and shook his head. His confidence had gone. Then he sat and gazed down into the void. But Ellen knew he did not see anything there.

He seemed an image carved in the stone of the Rim, and he gave Ellen a singular impression of loneliness and sadness. Was he thinking of the miserable battle his father had summoned him to lead—of what it would cost—of its useless pain and hatred? Ellen seemed to divine his thoughts. In that moment she softened toward him, and in her soul quivered and stirred an intangible something that was like pain, that was too deep for her understanding. But she felt sorry for an Isbel until the old pride resurged. What if he admired her? She remembered his interest, the wonder and admiration, the growing light in his eyes. And it had not been repugnant to her until he disclosed his name. "What's in a name?" she mused, recalling poetry learned in her girl-hood. " 'A rose by any other name would smell as sweet.' . . . He's an Isbel—yet he might be splendid—noble. . . . Bah! he's not—and I'd hate him anyhow."

All at once Ellen felt cold shivers steal over her. Isbel's piercing gaze was directed straight at her hiding place. Her heart stopped beating. If he discovered her there she felt that she would die of shame. Then she became aware that a blue jay was screeching in a pine above her, and a red squirrel somewhere near was chattering his shrill annoyance. These two denizens of the woods could be depended upon to espy the wariest hunter and make known his presence to their kind. Ellen had a moment of more than dread. This keen-eyed, keen-eared Indian might see right through her brushy covert, might hear the throbbing of her heart. It relieved her immeasurably to see him turn away and take to pacing the promontory, with his head bowed and his hands behind his back. He had stopped looking off into the forest. Presently he wheeled to the west, and by the light upon his face Ellen saw that the time was near sunset. Turkeys were beginning to gobble back on the ridge.

Isbel walked to his horse and appeared to be untying something from the back of his saddle. When he came back Ellen saw that he carried a small package apparently wrapped in paper. With this under his arm he strode off in the direction of Ellen's camp and soon disappeared in the forest.

For a little while Ellen lay there in bewilderment. If she had made conjectures before, they were now multiplied. Where was Jean Isbel going? Ellen sat up suddenly. "Well, shore this heah beats me," she said. "What did he have in that package? What was he goin' to do with it?"

It took no little will power to hold her there when she wanted to steal after him through the woods and find out what he meant. But his reputation influenced even her and she refused to pit her cunning in the forest against his. It would be better to wait until he returned to his horse. Thus decided, she lay back again in her covert and gave her mind over to pondering curiosity. Sooner than she expected she espied Isbel approaching through the forest, empty handed. He had not taken his rifle. Ellen averted her glance a moment and thrilled to see the rifle leaning against a rock. Verily Jean Isbel had been far removed from hostile intent that day. She watched him stride swiftly up to his horse, untie the halter, and mount. Ellen had an impression of his arrowlike straight figure, and sinuous grace and ease. Then he looked back at the promontory, as if to fix a picture of it in his mind, and rode away along the Rim. She watched him out of sight. What ailed her? Something was wrong with her, but she recognized only relief.

When Isbel had been gone long enough to assure Ellen that she might safely venture forth she crawled through the pine thicket to the Rim on the other side of the point. The sun was setting behind the Black Range, shedding a

golden glory over the Basin. Westward the zigzag Rim
reached like a streamer of fire into the sun. The vast promontories jutted out with blazing beacon lights upon their
stone-walled faces. Deep down, the Basin was turning
shadowy dark blue, going to sleep for the night.

Ellen bent swift steps toward her camp. Long shafts of
gold preceded her through the forest. Then they paled and
vanished. The tips of pines and spruces turned gold. A
hoarse-voiced old turkey gobbler was booming his chug-
a-lug from the highest ground, and the softer chick of hen
turkeys answered him. Ellen was almost breathless when
she arrived. Two packs and a couple of lop-eared burros
attested to the fact of Antonio's return. This was good
news for Ellen. She heard the bleat of lambs and tinkle of
bells coming nearer and nearer. And she was glad to feel
that if Isbel had visited her camp, most probably it was
during the absence of the herders.

The instant she glanced into her tent she saw the package Isbel had carried. It lay on her bed. Ellen stared
blankly. "The—the impudence of him!" she ejaculated.
Then she kicked the package out of the tent. Words and
action seemed to liberate a dammed-up hot fury. She
kicked the package again, and thought she would kick it
into the smoldering camp-fire. But somehow she stopped
short of that. She left the thing there on the ground.

Pepe and Antonio hove in sight, driving in the tumbling
woolly flock. Ellen did not want them to see the package,
so with contempt for herself, and somewhat lessening anger, she kicked it back into the tent. What was in it? She
peeped inside the tent, devoured by curiosity. Neat, well
wrapped and tied packages like that were not often seen
in the Tonto Basin. Ellen decided she would wait until after supper, and at a favorable moment lay it unopened on
the fire. What did she care what it contained? Manifestly

it was a gift. She argued that she was highly incensed with this insolent Isbel who had the effrontery to approach her with some sort of present.

It developed that the usually cheerful Antonio had returned taciturn and gloomy. All Ellen could get out of him was that the job of sheep herder had taken on hazards inimical to peace-loving Mexicans. He had heard something he would not tell. Ellen helped prepare the supper and she ate in silence. She had her own brooding troubles. Antonio presently told her that her father had said she was not to start back home after dark. After supper the herders repaired to their own tents, leaving Ellen the freedom of her camp-fire. Wherewith she secured the package and brought it forth to burn. Feminine curiosity rankled strong in her breast. Yielding so far as to shake the parcel and press it, and finally tear a corner off the paper, she saw some words written in lead pencil. Bending nearer the blaze, she read, "For my sister Ann." Ellen gazed at the big, bold hand-writing, quite legible and fairly well done. Suddenly she tore the outside wrapper completely off. From printed words on the inside she gathered that the package had come from a store in San Francisco. "Reckon he fetched home a lot of presents for his folks— the kids—and his sister," muttered Ellen. "That was nice of him. Whatever this is he shore meant it for sister Ann. . . . Ann Isbel. Why, she must be that black-eyed girl I met and liked so well before I knew she was an Isbel. . . . His sister!"

Whereupon for the second time Ellen deposited the fascinating package in her tent. She could not burn it up just then. She had other emotions besides scorn and hate. And memory of that soft-voiced, kind-hearted, beautiful Isbel girl checked her resentment. "I wonder if he is like his sister," she said, thoughtfully. It appeared to be an unfortunate thought. Jean Isbel certainly resembled his sister. "Too bad they belong to the family that ruined dad."

Ellen went to bed without opening the package or without burning it. And to her annoyance, whatever way she lay she appeared to touch this strange package. There was not much room in the little tent. First she put it at her head beside her rifle, but when she turned over her cheek came in contact with it. Then she felt as if she had been stung. She moved it again, only to touch it presently with her hand. Next she flung it to the bottom of her bed, where it fell upon her feet, and whatever way she moved them she could not escape the pressure of this undesirable and mysterious gift.

By and by she fell asleep, only to dream that the package was a caressing hand stealing about her, feeling for hers, and holding it with soft, strong clasp. When she awoke she had the strangest sensation in her right palm. It was moist, throbbing, hot, and the feel of it on her cheek was strangely thrilling and comforting. She lay awake then. The night was dark and still. Only a low moan of wind in the pines and the faint tinkle of a sheep bell broke the serenity. She felt very small and lonely lying there in the deep forest, and, try how she would, it was impossible to think the same then as she did in the clear light of day. Resentment, pride, anger—these seemed abated now. If the events of the day had not changed her, they had at least brought up softer and kinder memories and emotions than she had known for long. Nothing hurt and saddened her so much as to remember the gay, happy days of her childhood, her sweet mother, her old home. Then her thought returned to Isbel and his gift. It had been years since anyone had made her a gift. What could this one be? It did not matter. The wonder was that Jean Isbel should bring it to her and that she could be perturbed by its presence. "He meant it for his sister and so he thought well of me," she said, in finality.

Morning brought Ellen further vacillation. At length she rolled the obnoxious package inside her blankets, saying that she would wait until she got home and then consign it cheerfully to the flames. Antonio tied her pack on a burro. She did not have a horse, and therefore had to walk the several miles to her father's ranch.

She set off at a brisk pace, leading the burro and carrying her rifle. And soon she was deep in the fragrant forest. The morning was clear and cool, with just enough frost to make the sunlit grass sparkle as if with diamonds. Ellen felt fresh, buoyant, singularly full of life. Her youth would not be denied. It was pulsing, yearning. She hummed an old Southern tune and every step seemed one of pleasure in action, of advance toward some intangible future happiness. All the unknown of life before her called. Her heart beat high in her breast and she walked as one in a dream. Her thoughts were swift-changing, intimate, deep, and vague, not of yesterday or to-day, nor of reality.

The big, gray, white-tailed squirrels crossed ahead of her on the trail, scampered over the piny ground to hop on tree trunks, and there they paused to watch her pass. The vociferous little red squirrels barked and chattered at her. From every thicket sounded the gobble of turkeys. The blue jays squalled in the treetops. A deer lifted its head from browsing and stood motionless, with long ears erect, watching her go by.

Thus happily and dreamily absorbed, Ellen covered the forest miles and soon reached the trail that led down into the wild brakes of Chevelon Cañon. It was rough going and less conducive to sweet wanderings of mind. Ellen slowly lost them. And then a familiar feeling assailed her, one she never failed to have upon returning to her father's ranch—a reluctance, a bitter dissatisfaction with her home, a loyal struggle against the vague sense that all was not as it should be.

At the head of this cañon in a little, level, grassy meadow stood a rude one-room log shack, with a leaning red-stone chimney on the outside. This was the abode of a strange old man who had long lived there. His name was John Sprague and his occupation was raising burros. No sheep or cattle or horses did he own, not even a dog. Rumor had said Sprague was a prospector, one of the many who had searched that country for the Lost Dutchman gold mine. Sprague knew more about the Basin and Rim than any of the sheepmen or ranchers. From Black Butte to the Cibique and from Chevelon Butte to Reno Pass he knew every trail, cañon, ridge, and spring, and could find his way to them on the darkest night. His fame, however, depended mostly upon the fact that he did nothing but raise burros, and would raise none but black burros with white faces. These burros were the finest bred in all the Basin and were in great demand. Sprague sold a few every year. He had made a present of one to Ellen, although he hated to part with them. This old man was Ellen's one and only friend.

Upon her trip out to the Rim with the sheep, Uncle John, as Ellen called him, had been away on one of his infrequent visits to Grass Valley. It pleased her now to see a blue column of smoke lazily lifting from the old chimney and to hear the discordant bray of burros. As she entered the clearing Sprague saw her from the door of his shack.

"Hello, Uncle John!" she called.

"Wal, if it ain't Ellen!" he replied, heartily. "When I seen thet white-faced Jinny I knowed who was leadin' her. Where you been, girl?"

Sprague was a little, stoop-shouldered old man, with grizzled head and face, and shrewd gray eyes that beamed kindly on her over his ruddy cheeks. Ellen did not like the tobacco stain on his grizzled beard nor the dirty, motley, ragged, ill-smelling garb he wore, but she had ceased her useless attempts to make him more cleanly.

"I've been herdin' sheep," replied Ellen. "And where have y'u been, uncle? I missed y'u on the way over."

"Been packin' in some grub. An' I reckon I stayed longer in Grass Valley than I recollect. But thet was only natural, considerin'—"

"What?" asked Ellen, bluntly, as the old man paused.

Sprague took a black pipe out of his vest pocket and began rimming the bowl with his fingers. The glance he bent on Ellen was thoughtful and earnest, and so kind that she feared it was pity. Ellen suddenly burned for news from the village.

"Wal, come in an' set down, won't you?" he asked.

"No, thanks," replied Ellen, and she took a seat on the chopping block. "Tell me, uncle, what's goin' on down in the Valley?"

"Nothin' much yet—except talk. An' there's a heap of thet."

"Humph! There always was talk," declared Ellen, contemptuously. "A nasty, gossipy, catty hole, that Grass Valley!"

"Ellen, thar's goin' to be war—a bloody war in the ole Tonto Basin," went on Sprague, seriously.

"War! . . . Between whom?"

"The Isbels an' their enemies. I reckon most people down thar, an' sure all the cattlemen, air on old Gass's side. Blaisdell, Gordon, Fredericks, Blue—they'll all be in it."

"Who are they goin' to fight?" queried Ellen, sharply.

"Wal, the open talk is thet the sheepmen are forcin' this war. But thar's talk not so open, an' I reckon not very healthy for any man to whisper hyarbouts."

"Uncle John, y'u needn't be afraid to tell me anythin'," said Ellen. "I'd never give y'u away. Y'u've been a good friend to me."

"Reckon I want to be, Ellen," he returned, nodding his shaggy head. "It ain't easy to be fond of you as I am an' keep my mouth shet. . . . I'd like to know somethin'. Hev you any relatives away from hyar thet you could go to till this fight's over?"

"No. All I have, so far as I know, are right heah."

"How aboot friends?"

"Uncle John, I have none," she said, sadly, with bowed head.

"Wal, wal, I'm sorry. I was hopin' you might git away."

She lifted her face. "Shore y'u don't think I'd run off if my dad got in a fight?" she flashed.

"I hope you will."

"I'm a Jorth," she said, darkly, and dropped her head again.

Sprague nodded gloomily. Evidently he was perplexed and worried, and strongly swayed by affection for her.

"Would you go away with me?" he asked. "We could pack over to the Mazatzals an' live thar till this blows over."

"Thank y'u, Uncle John. Y'u're kind and good. But I'll stay with my father. His troubles are mine."

"Ahuh! . . . Wal, I might hev reckoned so. . . . Ellen, how do you stand on this hyar sheep an' cattle question?"

"I think what's fair for one is fair for another. I don't like sheep as much as I like cattle. But that's not the point. The range is free. Suppose y'u had cattle and I had sheep. I'd feel as free to run my sheep anywhere as y'u were to run your cattle."

"Right. But what if you throwed your sheep round my range an' sheeped off the grass so my cattle would hev to move or starve?"

"Shore I wouldn't throw my sheep round y'ur range," she declared, stoutly.

"Wal, you've answered half of the question. An' now supposin' a lot of my cattle was stolen by rustlers, but not a single one of your sheep. What 'd you think then?"

"I'd shore think rustlers chose to steal cattle because there was no profit in stealin' sheep."

"Egzactly. But wouldn't you hev a queer idee aboot it?"

"I don't know. Why queer? What 're y'u drivin' at, Uncle John?"

"Wal, wouldn't you git kind of a hunch thet the rustlers was—say a leetle friendly toward the sheepmen?"

Ellen felt a sudden vibrating shock. The blood rushed to her temples. Trembling all over, she rose.

"Uncle John!" she cried.

"Now, girl, you needn't fire up thet way. Set down an' don't—"

"Dare y'u insinuate my father has—"

"Ellen, I ain't insinuatin' nothin'," interrupted the old man. "I'm jest askin' you to think. Thet's all. You're 'most grown into a young woman now. An' you've got sense. Thar's bad times ahead, Ellen. An' I hate to see you mix in them."

"Oh, y'u do make me think," replied Ellen, with smarting tears in her eyes. "Y'u make me unhappy. Oh, I know my dad is not liked in this cattle country. But it's unjust. He happened to go in for sheep raising. I wish he hadn't. It was a mistake. Dad always was a cattleman till we came heah. He made enemies—who—who ruined him. And everywhere misfortune crossed his trail. . . . But, oh, Uncle John, my dad is an honest man."

"Wal, child, I—I didn't mean to—to make you cry," said the old man, feelingly, and he averted his troubled gaze. "Never mind what I said. I'm an old meddler. I reckon nothin' I could do or say would ever change what's goin' to happen. If only you wasn't a girl! . . . Thar I go ag'in. Ellen, face your future an' fight your way. All youngsters hev to do thet. An' it's the right kind of fight thet makes the right kind of man or woman. Only you must be sure to find yourself. An' by thet I mean to find the real, true, honest-to-God best in you an' stick to it an' die fightin' for it. You're a young woman, almost, an' a blamed handsome one. Which means you'll hev more trouble an' a harder fight. This country ain't easy on a woman when once slander has marked her."

"What do I care for the talk down in that Basin?" returned Ellen. "I know they think I'm a hussy. I've let them think it. I've helped them to."

"You're wrong, child," said Sprague, earnestly. "Pride an' temper! You must never let anyone think bad of you, much less help them to."

"I hate everybody down there," cried Ellen, passionately. "I hate them so I'd glory in their thinkin' me bad. . . . My mother belonged to the best blood in Texas. I am her daughter. I know *who and what I am*. That uplifts me whenever I meet the sneaky, sly suspicions of these Basin people. It shows me the difference between them and me. That's what I glory in."

"Ellen, you're a wild, headstrong child," rejoined the old man, in severe tones. "Word has been passed ag'in' your good name—your honor. . . . An' hevn't you given cause fer thet?"

Ellen felt her face blanch and all her blood rush back to her heart in sickening force. The shock of his words was like a stab from a cold blade. If their meaning and the stern, just light of the old man's glance did not kill her pride and vanity they surely killed her girlishness. She stood mute, staring at him, with her brown, trembling hands stealing up toward her bosom, as if to ward off another and a mortal blow.

"Eilen!" burst out Sprague, hoarsely. "You mistook me. Aw, I didn't mean—what you think, I swear. . . . Ellen, I'm old an' blunt. I ain't used to wimmen. But I've love for you, child, an' respect, jest the same as if you was my own. . . . An' I *know* you're good. . . . Forgive me. . . . I meant only hevn't you been, say, sort of—careless?"

"Care-less?" queried Ellen, bitterly and low.

"An' powerful thoughtless an'—an' blind—lettin' men kiss you an' fondle you—when you're really a growed-up woman now?"

"Yes—I have," whispered Ellen.

"Wal, then, why did you let them?"

"I—I don't know. . . . I didn't think. The men never let me alone—never—never! I got tired everlastingly pushin' them away. And sometimes—when they were kind—and I was lonely for something I—I didn't mind if one or another fooled round me. I never thought. It never looked as y'u have made it look. . . . Then—those few times ridin' the trail to Grass Valley—when people saw me—then I guess I encouraged such attentions. . . . Oh, I must be—I am a shameless little hussy!"

"Hush thet kind of talk," said the old man, as he took her hand. "Ellen, you're only young an' lonely an' bitter. No mother—no friends—no one but a lot of rough men! It's a wonder you hev kept yourself good. But now your eyes are open, Ellen. They're brave an' beautiful eyes, girl, an' if you stand by the light in them you will come through any trouble. An' you'll be happy. Don't ever forgit that. Life is hard enough, God knows, but it's unfailin' true in the end to the man or woman who finds the best in them an' stands by it."

"Uncle John, y'u talk so—so kindly. Y'u make me have hope. There seemed really so little for me to live for— hope for. . . . But I'll never be a coward again—nor a thoughtless fool. I'll find some good in me—or make some—and never fail it, come what will. I'll remember your words. I'll believe the future holds wonderful things for me. . . . I'm only eighteen. Shore all my life won't be lived heah. Perhaps this threatened fight over sheep and cattle will blow over. . . . Somewhere there must be some nice girl to be a friend—a sister to me. . . . And maybe some man who'd believe, in spite of all they say—that I'm not a hussy."

"Wal, Ellen, you remind me of what I was wantin' to tell you when you just got here. . . . Yestiddy I heard you called thet name in a barroom. An' thar was a fellar thar who raised hell. He near killed one man an' made another plumb eat his words. An' he scared thet crowd stiff."

Old John Sprague shook his grizzled head and laughed, beaming upon Ellen as if the memory of what he had seen had warmed his heart.

"Was it—y'u?" asked Ellen, tremulously.

"Me? Aw, I wasn't nowhere. Ellen, this fellar was quick as a cat in his actions an' his words was like lightnin'."

"Who?" she whispered.

"Wal, no one else but a stranger jest come to these parts—an Isbel, too. Jean Isbel."

"Oh!" exclaimed Ellen, faintly.

"In a barroom full of men—almost all of them in sympathy with the sheep crowd—most of them on the Jorth side—this Jean Isbel resented an insult to Ellen Jorth."

"No!" cried Ellen. Something terrible was happening to her mind or her heart.

"Wal, he sure did," replied the old man, "an' it's goin' to be good fer you to hear all about it."

CHAPTER 5

Old John Sprague launched into his narrative with evident zest.

"I hung round Greaves's store most of two days. An' I heerd a heap. Some of it was jest plain ole men's gab, but I reckon I got the drift of things concernin' Grass Valley. Yestiddy mornin' I was packin' my burros in Greaves's back yard, takin' my time carryin' out suppiies from the store. An' as last when I went in I seen a strange fellar was thar. Strappin' young man—not so young, either—an' he had on buckskin. Hair black as my burros, dark face, sharp eyes—you'd took him fer an Injun. He carried a rifle—one of them new forty-fours—an' also somethin' wrapped in paper thet he seemed partickler careful about. He wore a belt round his middle an' thar was a bowie knife in it, carried like I've seen scouts an' Injun fighters hev on the frontier in the 'seventies. That looked queer to me, an' I reckon to the rest of the crowd thar. No one overlooked the big six-shooter he packed Texas fashion. Wal, I didn't hev no idee this fellar was an Isbel until I heard Greaves call him thet.

"'Isbel,' said Greaves, 'reckon your money's counterfeit hyar. I cain't sell you anythin'.'"

" 'Counterfeit? Not much,' spoke up the young fellar, an' he flipped some gold twenties on the bar, where they rung like bells. 'Why not? Ain't this a store? I want a cinch strap.'

"Greaves looked particular sour thet mornin'. I'd been watchin' him fer two days. He hedn't hed much sleep fer I hed my bed back of the store, an' I heerd men come in the night an' hev long confabs with him. Whatever was in the wind hedn't pleased him none. An' I calkilated thet young Isbel wasn't a sight good fer Greaves's sore eyes, anyway. But he paid no more attention to Isbel. Acted jest as if he hedn't heerd Isbel say he wanted a cinch strap.

"I stayed inside the store then. Thar was a lot of fellars I'd seen, an' some I knowed. Couple of card games goin', an' drinkin', of course. I soon gathered thet the general atmosphere wasn't friendly to Jean Isbel. He seen thet quick enough, but he didn't leave. Between you an' me I sort of took a likin' to him. An' I sure watched him as close as I could, not seemin' to, you know. Reckon they all did the same, only you couldn't see it. It got jest about the same as if Isbel hedn't been in thar, only you knowed it wasn't really the same. Thet was how I got the hunch the crowd was all sheepmen or their friends. The day before I'd heerd a lot of talk about this young Isbel, an' what he'd come to Grass Valley fer, an' what a bad hombre he was. An' when I seen him I was bound to admit he looked his reputation.

"Wal, pretty soon in come two more fellars, an' I knowed both of them. You know them, too, I'm sorry to say. Fer I'm comin' to facts now thet will shake you. The first fellar was your father's Mexican foreman, Lorenzo, and the other was Simm Bruce. I reckon Bruce wasn't drunk, but he'd sure been lookin' on red licker. When he seen Isbel darn me if he didn't swell an' bustle all up like a mad ole turkey gobbler.

" 'Greaves,' he said, 'if thet fellar's Jean Isbel I ain't hankerin' fer the company y'u keep.' An' he made no bones of pointin' right at Isbel. Greaves looked up dry an' sour an' he bit out spiteful-like: 'Wal, Simm, we ain't hed a hell of a lot of choice in this heah matter. Thet's Jean Isbel shore enough. Mebbe you can persuade him thet his company an' his custom ain't wanted round heah!'

"Jean Isbel set on the counter an' took it all in, but he didn't say nothin'. The way he looked at Bruce was sure enough fer me to see thet thar might be a surprise any minnit. I've looked at a lot of men in my day, an' can sure feel events comin'. Bruce got himself a stiff drink an' then he straddles over the floor in front of Isbel.

" 'Air you Jean Isbel, son of the ole Gass Isbel?' asked Bruce, sort of lolling back an' givin' a hitch to his belt.

" 'Yes sir, you've identified me,' said Isbel, nice an' polite.

" 'My name's Bruce. I'm rangin' sheep heahabouts, an' I hev interest in Kurnel Lee Jorth's bizness.'

" 'Hod do, Mister Bruce,' replied Isbel, very civil an' cool as you please. Bruce hed an eye fer the crowd thet was now listenin' an' watchin'. He swaggered closer to Isbel.

" 'We heerd y'u come into the Tonto Basin to run us sheepmen off the range. How aboot thet?'

" 'Wal, you heerd wrong,' said Isbel, quietly. 'I came to work fer my father. Thet work depends on what happens.'

"Bruce began to git redder of face, an' he shook a husky hand in front of Isbel. 'I'll tell y'u this heah, my Nez Perce Isbel—' an' when he sort of choked fer more wind Greaves spoke up, 'Simm, I shore reckon thet Nez Perce handle will stick.' An' the crowd haw-hawed. Then Bruce got goin' ag'in. 'I'll tell y'u this heah, Nez Perce. Thar's been enough happen already to run y'u out of Arizona.'

" 'Wal, you don't say! What, fer instance?' asked Isbel, quick an' sarcastic.

"Thet made Bruce bust out puffin' an' spittin': 'Wha-tt, fer instance? Huh! Why, y'u dam half-breed, y'u'll git run out fer makin' up to Ellen Jorth. Thet won't go in this heah country. Not fer any Isbel.'

" 'You're a liar,' called Isbel, an' like a big cat he dropped off the counter. I heerd his moccasins pat soft on the floor. An' I bet to myself thet he was as dangerous as he was quick. But his voice an' his looks didn't change even a leetle.

" 'I'm not a liar,' yelled Bruce. 'I'll make y'u eat thet. I can prove what I say.... Y'u was seen with Ellen Jorth—up on the Rim—day before yestiddy. Y'u was watched. Y'u was with her. Y'u made up to her. Y'u grabbed her an' kissed her! . . . An' I'm heah to say. Nez Perce, thet y'u're a marked man on this range.'

" 'Who saw me?' asked Isbel, quiet an' cold. I seen then thet he'd turned white in the face.

" 'Yu cain't lie out of it,' hollered Bruce, wavin' his hands. 'We got y'u daid to rights. Lorenzo saw y'u—follered y'u—watched y'u.' Bruce pointed at the grinnin' greaser. 'Lorenzo is Kurnel Jorth's foreman. He seen y'u maulin' of Ellen Jorth. An' when he tells the Kurnel an' Tad Jorth an Jackson Jorth! . . . Haw! Haw! Why, hell 'd be a cooler place fer y'u then this heah Tonto.'

"Greaves an' his gang hed come round, sure tickled clean to thar gizzards at this mess. I noticed, howsomever, thet they was Texans enough to keep back to one side in case this Isbel started any action. . . . Wal, Isbel took a look at Lorenzo. Then with one swift grab he jerked the little greaser off his feet an' pulled him close. Lorenzo stopped grinnin'. He began to look a leetle sick. But it was plain he hed right on his side.

" 'You say you saw me?' demanded Isbel.

" '*Si*, señor,' replied Lorenzo.

" 'What did you see?'

" 'I see señor an' señorita. I hide by manzanita. I see señorita like grande señor ver mooch. She like señor keese. She—'

"Then Isbel hit the little greaser a back-handed crack in the mouth. Sure it was a crack! Lorenzo went over the counter backward an' landed like a pack load of wood. An' he didn't git up.

" 'Mister Bruce,' said Isbel, 'an' you fellars who heerd thet lyin' greaser, I did meet Ellen Jorth. An' I lost my head. I—I kissed her. . . . But it was an accident. I meant no insult. I apologized—I tried to explain my crazy action. . . . Thet was all. The greaser lied. Ellen Jorth was kind enough to show me the trail. We talked a little. Then—I suppose—because she was young an' pretty an' sweet—I lost my head. She was absolutely innocent. Thet damned greaser told a bare-faced lie when he said she liked me. The fact was she despised me. She said so. An' when she learned I was Jean Isbel she turned her back on me an' walked away.' "

At this point of his narrative the old man halted as if to impress Ellen not only with what just had been told, but particularly with what was to follow. The reciting of this tale had evidently given Sprague an unconscious pleasure. He glowed. He seemed to carry the burden of a secret that he yearned to divulge. As for Ellen, she was deadlocked in breathless suspense. All her emotions waited for the end. She begged Sprague to hurry.

"Wal, I wish I could skip the next chapter an' hev only the last to tell," rejoined the old man, and he put a heavy, but solicitous, hand upon hers. . . . "Simm Bruce haw-hawed loud an' loud. . . . 'Say, Nez Perce,' he calls out, most insolent-like, 'we air too good sheepmen heah to hev the wool pulled over our eyes. We shore know what y'u meant by Ellen Jorth. But y'u wasn't smart when y'u told her y'u was Jean Isbel! . . . Haw-haw!'

"Isbel flashed a strange, surprised look from the red-faced Bruce to Greaves and to the other men. I take it he was wonderin' if he'd heerd right or if they'd got the same hunch thet 'd come to him. An' I reckon he determined to make sure.

"'Why wasn't I smart?' he asked.

"'Shore y'u wasn't smart if y'u was aimin' to be one of Ellen Jorth's lovers,' said Bruce, with a leer. 'Fer if y'u hedn't give y'urself away y'u could hev been easy enough.'

"Thar was no mistakin' Bruce's meanin' an' when he got it out some of the men thar laughed. Isbel kept lookin' from one to another of them. Then facin' Greaves, he said, deliberately: 'Greaves, this drunken Bruce is excuse enough fer a show-down. I take it that you are sheepmen, an' you're goin' on Jorth's side of the fence in the matter of this sheep rangin'.'

"'Wal, Nez Perce, I reckon you hit plumb center,' said Greaves, dryly. He spread wide his big hands to the other men, as if to say they'd might as well own the jig was up.

"'All right. You're Jorth's backers. Have any of you a word to say in Ellen Jorth's defense? I tell you the Mexican lied. Believin' me or not doesn't matter. But this vile-mouthed Bruce hinted against thet girl's honor.'

"Ag'in some of the men laughed, but not so noisy, an' there was a nervous shufflin' of feet. Isbel looked sort of queer. His neck had a bulge round his collar. An' his eyes was like black coals of fire. Greaves spread his big hands again, as if to wash them of this part of the dirty argument.

"'When it comes to any wimmen I pass—much less play a hand fer a wildcat like Jorth's gurl,' said Greaves, sort of cold an' thick. 'Bruce shore ought to know her. Accordin' to talk heahaboots an' what *he* says, Ellen Jorth has been his gurl fer two years.'

"Then Isbel turned his attention to Bruce an' I fer one begun to shake in my boots.

" 'Say thet to me!' he called.

" 'Shore she's my gurl, an' thet's why I'm a-goin' to hev y'u run off this range.'

"Isbel jumped at Bruce. 'You damned drunken cur! You vile-mouthed liar! . . . I may be an Isbel, but by God you cain't slander thet girl to my face!' . . . Then he moved so quick I couldn't see what he did. But I heerd his fist hit Bruce. It sounded like an ax ag'in' a beef. Bruce fell clear across the room. An' by Jinny when he landed Isbel was thar. As Bruce staggered up, all bloody-faced, bellowin' an' spittin' out teeth Isbel eyed Greaves's crowd an' said: 'If any of y'u make a move it 'll mean gun-play.' Nobody moved, thet's sure. In fact, none of Greaves's outfit was packin' guns, at least in sight. When Bruce got all the way up—he's a tall fellar—why Isbel took a full swing at him an' knocked him back across the room ag'in' the counter. Y'u know when a fellar's hurt by the way he yells. Bruce got thet second smash right on his big red nose. . . . I never seen any one so quick as Isbel. He vaulted over that counter jest the second Bruce fell back on it, an' then with Greaves's gang in front so he could catch any moves of theirs, he jest slugged Bruce right an' left, an' banged his head on the counter. Then as Bruce sunk limp an' slipped down, lookin' like a bloody sack, Isbel let him fall to the floor. Then he vaulted back over the counter. Wipin' the blood off his hands, he throwed his kerchief down in Bruce's face. Bruce wasn't dead or bad hurt. He'd jest been beaten bad. He was moanin' an' slobberin'. Isbel kicked him, not hard, but jest sort of disgustful. Then he faced thet crowd. 'Greaves, thet's what I think of your Simm Bruce. Tell him next time he sees me to run or pull a gun.' An' then Isbel grabbed his rifle an' package off the counter an' went out. He didn't even look back. I seen him mount his horse an' ride away. . . . Now, girl, what hev you to say?"

Ellen could only say good-by and the word was so low as to be almost inaudible. She ran to her burro. She could not see very clearly through tear-blurred eyes, and her shaking fingers were all thumbs. It seemed she had to rush away—somewhere, anywhere—not to get away from old John Sprague, but from herself—this palpitating, bursting self whose feet stumbled down the trail. All—all seemed ended for her. That interminable story! It had taken so long. And every minute of it she had been helplessly torn asunder by feelings she had never known she possessed. This Ellen Jorth was an unknown creature. She sobbed now as she dragged the burro down the cañon trail. She sat down only to rise. She hurried only to stop. Driven, pursued, barred, she had no way to escape the flaying thoughts, no time or will to repudiate them. The death of her girlhood, the rending aside of a veil of maiden mystery only vaguely instinctively guessed, the barren, sordid truth of her life as seen by her enlightened eyes, the bitter realization of the vileness of men of her clan in contrast to the manliness and chivalry of an enemy, the hard facts of unalterable repute as created by slander and fostered by low minds, all these were forces in a cataclysm that had suddenly caught her heart and whirled her through changes immense and agonizing, to bring her face to face with reality, to force upon her suspicion and doubt of all she had trusted, to warn her of the dark, impending horror of a tragic bloody feud, and lastly to teach her the supreme truth at once so glorious and so terrible— that she could not escape the doom of womanhood.

About noon that day Ellen Jorth arrived at the Knoll, which was the location of her father's ranch. Three cañons met there to form a larger one. The Knoll was a

symmetrical hill situated at the mouth of the three cañons. It was covered with brush and cedars, with here
and there lichened rocks showing above the bleached
grass. Below the Knoll was a wide, grassy flat or meadow
through which a willow-bordered stream cut its rugged
boulder-strewn bed. Water flowed abundantly at this
season, and the deep washes leading down from the slopes
attested to the fact of cloudbursts and heavy storms. This
meadow valley was dotted with horses and cattle, and
meandered away between the timbered slopes to lose itself in a green curve. A singular feature of this cañon was
that a heavy growth of spruce trees covered the slope facing northwest; and the opposite slope, exposed to the sun
and therefore less snowbound in winter, held a sparse
growth of yellow pines. The ranch house of Colonel Jorth
stood round the rough corner of the largest of the three
cañons, and rather well hidden, it did not obtrude its rude
and broken-down log cabins, its squalid surroundings,
its black mud-holes of corrals upon the beautiful and serene meadow valley.

Ellen Jorth approached her home slowly, with dragging,
reluctant steps; and never before in the three unhappy
years of her existence there had the ranch seemed so bare,
so uncared for, so repugnant to her. As she had seen herself with clarified eyes, so now she saw her home. The
cabin that Ellen lived in with her father was a single-room
structure with one door and no windows. It was about
twenty feet square. The huge, ragged, stone chimney had
been built on the outside, with the wide open fireplace set
inside the logs. Smoke was rising from the chimney. As
Ellen halted at the door and began unpacking her burro
she heard the loud, lazy laughter of men. An adjoining log
cabin had been built in two sections, with a wide roofed
hall or space between them. The door in each cabin faced
the other, and there was a tall man standing in one. Ellen

recognized Daggs, a neighbor sheepman, who evidently spent more time with her father than at his own home, wherever that was. Ellen had never seen it. She heard this man drawl, "Jorth, heah's your kid come home."

Ellen carried her bed inside the cabin, and unrolled it upon a couch built of boughs in the far corner. She had forgotten Jean Isbel's package, and now it fell out under her sight. Quickly she covered it. A Mexican woman, relative of Antonio, and the only servant about the place, was squatting Indian fashion before the fireplace, stirring a pot of beans. She and Ellen did not get along well together, and few words ever passed between them. Ellen had a canvas curtain stretched upon a wire across a small triangular corner, and this afforded her a little privacy. Her possessions were limited in number. The crude square table she had constructed herself. Upon it was a little old-fashioned walnut-framed mirror, a brush and comb, and a dilapidated ebony cabinet which contained odds and ends the sight of which always brought a smile of derisive self-pity to her lips. Under the table stood an old leather trunk. It had come with her from Texas, and contained clothing and belongings of her mother's. Above the couch on pegs hung her scant wardrobe. A tiny shelf held several worn-out books.

When her father slept indoors, which was seldom except in winter, he occupied a couch in the opposite corner. A rude cupboard had been built against the logs next to the fireplace. It contained supplies and utensils. Toward the center, somewhat closer to the door, stood a crude table and two benches. The cabin was dark and smelled of smoke, of the stale odors of past cooked meals, of the mustiness of dry, rotting timber. Streaks of light showed through the roof where the rough-hewn shingles had split or weathered. A strip of bacon hung upon one side of the cupboard, and upon the other a haunch of venison. Ellen detested the Mexican woman because she was dirty. The inside of the cabin presented the same unkempt appearance usual to it after Ellen had been away for a few days. Whatever Ellen had lost during the retrogression of the Jorths, she had kept her habits of cleanliness, and straightway upon her return she set to work.

The Mexican woman sullenly slouched away to her own quarters outside and Ellen was left to the satisfaction of labor. Her mind was as busy as her hands. As she cleaned and swept and dusted she heard from time to time the voices of men, the clip-clop of shod horses, the bellow of cattle. And a considerable time elapsed before she was disturbed.

A tall shadow darkened the doorway.

"Howdy, little one!" said a lazy, drawling voice. "So y'u-all got home?"

Ellen looked up. A superbly built man leaned against the doorpost. Like most Texans, he was light haired and light eyed. His face was lined and hard. His long, sandy mustache hid his mouth and drooped with a curl. Spurred, booted, belted, packing a heavy gun low down on his hip, he gave Ellen an entirely new impression. Indeed, she was seeing everything strangely.

"Hello, Daggs!" replied Ellen. "Where's my dad?"

"He's playin' cairds with Jackson an' Colter. Shore's playin' bad, too, an' it's gone to his haid."

"Gamblin'?" queried Ellen.

"Mah child, when'd Kurnel Jorth ever play for fun?" said Daggs, with a lazy laugh. "There's a stack of gold on the table. Reckon yo' uncle Jackson will win it. Colter's shore out of luck."

Daggs stepped inside. He was graceful and slow. His long spurs clinked. He laid a rather compelling hand on Ellen's shoulder.

"Heah, mah gal, give us a kiss," he said.

"Daggs, I'm not your girl," replied Ellen as she slipped out from under his hand.

Then Daggs put his arm round her, not with violence or rudeness, but with an indolent, affectionate assurance, at once bold and self-contained. Ellen, however, had to exert herself to get free of him, and when she had placed the table between them she looked him square in the eyes.

"Daggs, y'u keep your paws off me," she said.

"Aw, now, Ellen, I ain't no bear," he remonstrated. "What's the matter, kid?"

"I'm not a kid. And there's nothin' the matter. Y'u're to keep your hands to yourself, that's all."

He tried to reach her across the table, and his movements were lazy and slow, like his smile. His tone was coaxing.

"Mah dear, shore you set on my knee just the other day, now, didn't you?"

Ellen felt the blood sting her cheeks.

"I was a child," she returned.

"Wal, listen to this heah grown-up young woman. All in a few days! . . . Doon't be in a temper, Ellen. . . . Come, give us a kiss."

She deliberately gazed into his eyes. Like the eyes of an eagle, they were clear and hard, just now warmed by the dalliance of the moment, but there was no light, no intelligence in them to prove he understood her. The instant separated Ellen immeasurably from him and from all of his ilk.

"Daggs, I was a child," she said. "I was lonely—hungry for affection—I was innocent. Then I was careless, too, and thoughtless when I should have known better. But I hardly understood y'u men. I put such thoughts out of my mind. I know now—know what y'u mean—what y'u have made people believe I am."

"Ahuh! Shore I get your hunch," he returned, with a change of tone. "But I asked you to marry me?"

"Yes y'u did. The first day y'u got heah to my dad's house. And y'u asked me to marry y'u after y'u found y'u couldn't have your way with me. To y'u the one didn't mean any more than the other."

"Shore I did more than Simm Bruce an' Colter," he retorted. "They never asked you to marry."

"No, they didn't. And if I could respect them at all I'd do it because they didn't ask me."

"Wal, I'll be doggoned!" ejaculated Daggs, thoughtfully, as he stroked his long mustache.

"I'll say to them what I've said to y'u," went on Ellen. "I'll tell dad to make y'u let me alone. I wouldn't marry one of y'u—y'u loafers to save my life. I've my suspicions about y'u. Y'u're a bad lot."

Daggs changed subtly. The whole indolent nonchalance of the man vanished in an instant.

"Wal, Miss Jorth, I reckon you mean we're a bad lot of sheepmen?" he queried, in the cool, easy speech of a Texan.

"No," flashed Ellen. "Shore I don't say sheepmen. I say y'u're a *bad lot.*"

"Oh, the hell you say!" Daggs spoke as he might have spoken to a man; then turning swiftly on his heel he left her. Outside he encountered Ellen's father. She heard Daggs speak: "Lee, your little wildcat is shore heah. An' take mah hunch. Somebody has been talkin' to her."

"Who has?" asked her father, in his husky voice. Ellen knew at once that he had been drinking.

"Lord only knows," replied Daggs. "But shore it wasn't any friends of ours."

"We cain't stop people's tongues," said Jorth, resignedly.

"Wal, I ain't so shore," continued Daggs, with his slow,

cool laugh. "Reckon I never yet heard any daid men's tongues wag."

Then the musical tinkle of his spurs sounded fainter. A moment later Ellen's father entered the cabin. His dark, moody face brightened at sight of her. Ellen knew she was the only person in the world left for him to love. And she was sure of his love. Her very presence always made him different. And through the years, the darker their misfortunes, the farther he slipped away from better days, the more she loved him.

"Hello, my Ellen!" he said, and he embraced her. When he had been drinking he never kissed her. "Shore I'm glad you're home. This heah hole is bad enough any time, but when you're gone it's black. . . . I'm hungry."

Ellen laid food and drink on the table; and for a little while she did not look directly at him. She was concerned about this new searching power of her eyes. In relation to him she vaguely dreaded it.

Lee Jorth had once been a singularly handsome man. He was tall, but did not have the figure of a horseman. His dark hair was streaked with gray, and was white over his ears. His face was sallow and thin, with deep lines. Under his round, prominent, brown eyes, like deadened furnaces, were blue swollen welts. He had a bitter mouth and weak chin, not wholly concealed by gray mustache and pointed beard. He wore a long frock coat and a wide-brimmed sombrero, both black in color, and so old and stained and frayed that along with the fashion of them they betrayed that they had come from Texas with him. Jorth always persisted in wearing a white linen shirt, likewise a relic of his Southern prosperity, and to-day it was ragged and soiled as usual.

Ellen watched her father eat and waited for him to speak. It occurred to her strangely that he never asked about the sheep or the new-born lambs. She divined with a subtle new woman's intuition that he cared nothing for his sheep.

"Ellen, what riled Daggs?" inquired her father, presently. "He shore had fire in his eye."

Long ago Ellen had betrayed an indignity she had suffered at the hands of a man. Her father had nearly killed him. Since then she had taken care to keep her troubles to herself. If her father had not been blind and absorbed in his own brooding he would have seen a thousand things sufficient to inflame his Southern pride and temper.

"Daggs asked me to marry him again and I said he belonged to a bad lot," she replied.

Jorth laughed in scorn. "Fool! . . . My God! Ellen, I must have dragged you low—that every damned ru—er—sheepman—who comes along thinks he can marry you."

At the break in his words, the incompleted meaning, Ellen dropped her eyes. Little things once never noted by her were now come to have a fascinating significance.

"Never mind, dad," she replied. "They cain't marry me."

"Daggs said somebody had been talkin' to you. How aboot that?"

"Old John Sprague has just gotten back from Grass Valley," said Ellen. "I stopped in to see him. Shore he told me all the village gossip."

"Anythin' to interest me?" he queried, darkly.

"Yes, dad, I'm afraid a good deal," she said, hesitatingly. Then in accordance with a decision Ellen had made she told him of the rumored war between sheepmen and cattlemen; that old Isbel had Blaisdell, Gordon, Fredericks, Blue, and other well-known ranchers on his side; that his son Jean Isbel had come from Oregon with a wonderful reputation as fighter and scout and tracker; that it was no secret how Colonel Lee Jorth was at the head of the sheepmen; that a bloody war was sure to come.

"Hah!" exclaimed Jorth, with a stain of red in his sallow cheek. "Reckon none of that is news to me. I knew all that."

Ellen wondered if he had heard of her meeting with Jean Isbel. If not he would hear as soon as Simm Bruce and Lorenzo came back. She decided to forestall them.

"Dad, I met Jean Isbel. He came into my camp. Asked the way to the Rim. I showed him. We—we talked a little. And shore were gettin' acquainted when—when he told me who he was. Then I left him—hurried back to camp."

"Colter met Isbel down in the woods," replied Jorth, ponderingly. "Said he looked like an Indian—a hard an' slippery customer to reckon with."

"Shore I guess I can indorse what Colter said," returned Ellen, dryly. She could have laughed aloud at her deceit. Still she had not lied.

"How'd this heah young Isbel strike you?" queried her father, suddenly glancing up at her.

Ellen felt the slow, sickening, guilty rise of blood in her face. She was helpless to stop it. But her father evidently never saw it. He was looking at her without seeing her.

"He—he struck me as different from men heah," she stammered.

"Did Sprague tell you aboot this half-Indian Isbel—aboot his reputation?"

"Yes."

"Did he look to you like a real woodsman?"

"Indeed he did. He wore buckskin. He stepped quick and soft. He acted at home in the woods. He had eyes black as night and sharp as lightnin'. They shore saw about all there was to see."

Jorth chewed at his mustache and lost himself in brooding thought.

"Dad, tell me, is there goin' to be a war?" asked Ellen, presently.

What a red, strange, rolling flash blazed in his eyes! His body jerked.

"Shore. You might as well know."

"Between sheepmen and cattlemen?"

"Yes."

"With y'u, dad, at the haid of one faction and Gaston Isbel the other?"

"Daughter, you have it correct, so far as you go."

"Oh! . . . Dad, can't this fight be avoided?"

"You forget you're from Texas," he replied.

"Cain't it be helped?" she repeated, stubbornly.

"No!" he declared, with deep, hoarse passion.

"Why not?"

"Wal, we sheepmen are goin' to run sheep anywhere we like on the range. An' cattlemen won't stand for that."

"But, dad, it's so foolish," declared Ellen, earnestly. "Y'u sheepmen do not have to run sheep over the cattle range."

"I reckon we do."

"Dad, that argument doesn't go with me. I know the country. For years to come there will be room for both sheep and cattle without overrunnin'. If some of the range is better in water and grass, then whoever got there first should have it. That shore is only fair. It's common sense, too."

"Ellen, I reckon some cattle people have been prejudicin' you," said Jorth, bitterly.

"Dad!" she cried, hotly.

This had grown to be an ordeal for Jorth. He seemed a victim of contending tides of feeling. Some will or struggle broke within him and the change was manifest. Haggard, shifty-eyed, with wabbling chin, he burst into speech.

"See heah, girl. You listen. There's a clique of ranchers down in the Basin, all those you named, with Isbel at their haid. They have resented sheepmen comin' down into the valley. They want it all to themselves. That's the reason. Shore there's another. All the Isbels are crooked. They're cattle an' horse thieves—have been for years. Gaston Isbel always was a maverick rustler. He's gettin' old now an' rich, so he wants to cover his tracks. He aims to blame this cattle rustlin' an' horse stealin' on to us sheepmen, an' run us out of the country."

Gravely Ellen Jorth studied her father's face, and the newly found truth-seeing power of her eyes did not fail her. In part, perhaps in all, he was telling lies. She shuddered a little, loyally battling against the insidious convictions being brought to fruition. Perhaps in his brooding over his failures and troubles he leaned toward false judgments. Ellen could not attach dishonor to her father's motives or speeches. For long, however, something about him had troubled her, perplexed her. Fearfully she believed she was coming to some revelation, and, despite her keen determination to know, she found herself shrinking.

"Dad, mother told me before she died that the Isbels had ruined you," said Ellen, very low. It hurt her so to see her father cover his face that she could hardly go on. "If they ruined you they ruined all of us. I know what we had once—what we lost again and again—and I see what we are come to now. Mother hated the Isbels. She taught me to hate the very name. But I never knew how they ruined you—or why—or when. And I want to know now."

Then it was not the face of a liar that Jorth disclosed. The present was forgotten. He lived in the past. He even seemed younger in the revivifying flash of hate that made his face radiant. The lines burned out. Hate gave him back the spirit of his youth.

."Gaston Isbel an' I were boys together in Weston, Texas," began Jorth, in swift, passionate voice. "We went to school together. We loved the same girl—your mother. When the war broke out she was engaged to Isbel. His family was rich. They influenced her people. But she loved me. When Isbel went to war she married me. He came back an' faced us. God! I'll never forget that. Your mother confessed her unfaithfulness—by Heaven! She taunted him with it. Isbel accused me of winnin' her by lies. But she took the sting out of that. . . . Isbel never forgave her an' he hounded me to ruin. He made me out a card-sharp, cheatin' my best friends. I was disgraced. Later he tangled me in the courts—he beat me out of property—an' last by convictin' me of rustlin' cattle he run me out of Texas."

Black and distorted now, Jorth's face was a spectacle to make Ellen sick with a terrible passion of despair and hate. The truth of her father's ruin and her own were enough. What mattered all else? Jorth beat the table with fluttering, nerveless hands that seemed all the more significant for their lack of physical force.

"An' so help me God, it's got to be wiped out in blood!" he hissed.

That was his answer to the wavering and nobility of Ellen. And she in her turn had no answer to make. She crept away into the corner behind the curtain, and there on her couch in the semidarkness she lay with strained heart, and a resurging, unconquerable tumult in her mind. And she lay there from the middle of that afternoon until the next morning.

When she awakened she expected to be unable to rise—she hoped she could not—but life seemed multiplied in her, and inaction was impossible. Something young and sweet and hopeful that had been in her did not greet the sun this morning. In their place was a woman's passion to learn for herself, to watch events, to meet what must come, to survive.

After breakfast, at which she sat alone, she decided to put Isbel's package out of the way, so that it would not be subjecting her to continual annoyance. The moment she picked it up the old curiosity assailed her.

"Shore I'll see what it is, anyway," she muttered, and with swift hands she opened the package. The action disclosed two pairs of fine, soft shoes, of a style she had never seen, and four pairs of stockings, two of strong, serviceable wool, and the others of a finer texture. Ellen looked at them in amaze. Of all things in the world, these would have been the last she expected to see. And, strangely, they were what she wanted and needed most. Naturally, then, Ellen made the mistake of taking them in her hands to feel their softness and warmth.

"Shore! He saw my bare legs! And he brought me these presents he'd intended for his sister. . . . He was ashamed for me—sorry for me. . . . And I thought he looked at me bold-like, as I'm used to be looked at heah! Isbel or not, he's shore . . ."

But Ellen Jorth could not utter aloud the conviction her intelligence tried to force upon her.

"It'd be a pity to burn them," she mused. "I cain't do it. Sometime I might send them to Ann Isbel."

Whereupon she wrapped them up again and hid them in the bottom of the old trunk, and slowly, as she lowered the lid, looking darkly, blankly at the wall, she whispered: "Jean Isbel! . . . I hate him!"

Later when Ellen went outdoors she carried her rifle, which was unusual for her, unless she intended to go into the woods.

The morning was sunny and warm. A group of shirt-sleeved men lounged in the hall and before the porch of the double cabin. Her father was pacing up and down, talking forcibly. Ellen heard his hoarse voice. As she approached he ceased talking and his listeners relaxed their attention. Ellen's glance ran over them swiftly—Daggs, with his superb head, like that of a hawk, uncovered to the sun; Colter with his lowered, secretive looks, his sand-gray lean face; Jackson Jorth, her uncle, huge, gaunt, hulking, with white in his black beard and hair, and the fire of a ghoul in his hollow eyes; Tad Jorth, another brother of her father's, younger, red of eye and nose, a weak-chinned drinker of rum. Three other limber-legged Texans lounged there, partners of Daggs, and they were sun-browned, light-haired, blue-eyed men singularly alike in appearance, from their dusty high-heeled boots to their broad black sombreros. They claimed to be sheepmen. All Ellen could be sure of was that Rock Wells spent most of his time there, doing nothing but look for a chance to waylay her; Springer was a gambler; and the third, who answered to the strange name of Queen, was a silent, lazy, watchful-eyed man who never wore a glove on his right hand and who never was seen without a gun within easy reach of that hand.

"Howdy, Ellen. Shore you ain't goin' to say good mawnin' to this heah bad lot?" drawled Daggs, with good-natured sarcasm.

"Why, shore! Good morning, y'u hard-working industrious *mañana* sheep-raisers," replied Ellen, coolly.

Daggs stared. The others appeared taken back by a greeting so foreign from any to which they were accustomed from her. Jackson Jorth let out a gruff haw-haw. Some of them doffed their sombreros, and Rock Wells managed a lazy, polite good morning. Ellen's father seemed most significantly struck by her greeting, and the least amused.

"Ellen, I'm not likin' your talk," he said, with a frown.

"Dad, when y'u play cards don't y'u call a spade a spade?"

"Why, shore I do."

"Well, I'm calling spades spades."

"Ahuh!" grunted Jorth, furtively dropping his eyes. "Where you goin' with your gun? I'd rather you hung round heah now."

"Reckon I might as well get used to packing my gun all the time," replied Ellen. "Reckon I'll be treated more like a man."

Then the event Ellen had been expecting all morning took place. Simm Bruce and Lorenzo rode around the slope of the Knoll and trotted toward the cabin. Interest in Ellen was relegated to the background.

"Shore they're bustin' with news," declared Daggs.

"They been ridin' some, you bet," remarked another.

"Huh!" exclaimed Jorth. "Bruce shore looks queer to me."

"Red liquor," said Tad Jorth, sententiously. "You-all know the brand Greaves hands out."

"Naw, Simm ain't drunk," said Jackson Jorth. "Look at his bloody shirt."

The cool, indolent interest of the crowd vanished at the red color pointed out by Jackson Jorth. Daggs rose in a single springy motion to his lofty height. The face Bruce turned to Jorth was swollen and bruised, with unhealed cuts. Where his right eye should have been showed a puffed dark purple bulge. His other eye, however, gleamed with hard and sullen light. He stretched a big shaking hand toward Jorth.

"Thet Nez Perce Isbel beat me half to death," he bellowed.

Jorth stared hard at the tragic, almost grotesque figure,

at the battered face. But speech failed him. It was Daggs who answered Bruce.

"Wal, Simm, I'll be damned if you don't look it."

"Beat you! What with?" burst out Jorth, explosively.

"I thought he was swingin' an ax, but Greaves swore it was his fists," bawled Bruce, in misery and fury.

"Where was your gun?" queried Jorth, sharply.

"Gun? Hell!" exclaimed Bruce, flinging wide his arms. "Ask Lorenzo. He had a gun. An' he got a biff in the jaw before my turn come. Ask him?"

Attention thus directed to the Mexican showed a heavy discolored swelling upon the side of his olive-skinned face. Lorenzo looked only serious.

"Hah! Speak up," shouted Jorth, impatiently.

"Señor Isbel heet me ver quick," replied Lorenzo, with expressive gesture. "I see thousand stars—then moocho black—all like night."

At that some of Daggs's men lolled back with dry crisp laughter. Daggs's hard face rippled with a smile. But there was no humor in anything for Colonel Jorth.

"Tell us what come off. Quick!" he ordered. "Where did it happen? Why? Who saw it? What did you do?"

Bruce lapsed into a sullen impressiveness. "Wal, I happened in Greaves's store an' run into Jean Isbel. Shore was lookin' fer him. I had my mind made up what to do, but I got to shootin' off my gab instead of my gun. I called him Nez Perce—an' I throwed all thet talk in his face about old Gass Isbel sendin' fer him—an' I told him he'd git run out of the Tonto. Reckon I was jest warmin' up. . . . But then it all happened. He slugged Lorenzo jest one. An' Lorenzo slid peaceful-like to bed behind the counter. I hadn't time to think of throwin' a gun before he whaled into me. He knocked out two of my teeth. An' I swallered one of them."

Ellen stood in the background behind three of the men and in the shadow. She did not join in the laugh that followed Bruce's remarks. She had known that he would lie. Uncertain yet of her reaction to this, but more bitter and furious as he revealed his utter baseness, she waited for more to be said.

"Wal, I'll be doggoned," drawled Daggs.

"What do you makc of this kind of fightin'?" queried Jorth.

"Darn if I know," replied Daggs in perplexity. "Shore an' sartin it's not the way of a Texan. Mebbe this young Isbel really is what old Gass swears he is. Shore Bruce ain't nothin' to give an edge to a real gun fighter. Looks to me like Isbel bluffed Greaves an' his gang an' licked your men without throwin' a gun."

"Maybe Isbel doesn't want the name of drawin' first blood," suggested Jorth.

"That 'd be like Gass," spoke up Rock Wells, quietly. "I once rode fer Gass in Texas."

"Say, Bruce," said Daggs, "was this heah palaverin' of yours an' Jean Isbel's aboot the old stock dispute? Aboot his father's range an' water? An' partickler aboot sheep?"

"Wal—I—I yelled a heap," declared Bruce, haltingly, "but I don't recollect all I said—I was riled. . . . Shore, though it was the same old argyment thet's been fetchin' us closer an' closer to trouble."

Daggs removed his keen hawklike gaze from Bruce. "Wal, Jorth, all I'll say is this. If Bruce is tellin' the truth we ain't got a hell of a lot to fear from this young Isbel. I've known a heap of gun fighters in my day. An' Jean Isbel don't run true to class. Shore there never was a gunman who'd risk cripplin' his right hand by sluggin' anybody."

"Wal," broke in Bruce, sullenly. "You-all can take it daid straight or not. I don't give a damn. But you've shore got my hunch thet Nez Perce Isbel is liable to handle any of you fellars jest as he did me, an' jest as easy. What's more, he's got Greaves figgered. An' you-all know thet Greaves is as deep in—"

"Shut up that kind of gab," demanded Jorth, stridently. "An' answer me. Was the row in Greaves's barroom aboot sheep?"

"Aw, hell! I said so, didn't I?" shouted Bruce, with a fierce uplift of his distorted face.

Ellen strode out from the shadow of the tall men who had obscured her.

"Bruce, y'u're a liar," she said, bitingly.

The surprise of her sudden appearance seemed to root Bruce to the spot. All but the discolored places on his face turned white. He held his breath a moment, then expelled it hard. His effort to recover from the shock was painfully obvious. He stammered incoherently.

"Shore y'u're more than a liar, too," cried Ellen, facing him with blazing eyes. And the rifle, gripped in both hands, seemed to declare her intent of menace. "That row was not about sheep. . . . Jean Isbel didn't beat y'u for anythin' about sheep. . . . Old John Sprague was in Greaves's store. He heard y'u. He saw Jean Isbel beat y'u as y'u deserved. . . . An' he told *me!*"

Ellen saw Bruce shrink in fear of his life; and despite her fury she was filled with disgust that he could imagine she would have his blood on her hands. Then she divined that Bruce saw more in the gathering storm in her father's eyes than he had to fear from her.

"Girl, what the hell are y'u sayin'?" hoarsely called Jorth, in dark amaze.

"Dad, y'u leave this to me," she retorted.

Daggs stepped beside Jorth, significantly on his right side. "Let her alone, Lee," he advised, coolly. "She's shore got a hunch on Bruce."

"Simm Bruce, y'u cast a dirty slur on my name," cried Ellen, passionately.

It was then that Daggs grasped Jorth's right arm and held it tight. "Jest what I thought," he said. "Stand still, Lee. Let's see the kid make him show-down."

"That's what Jean Isbel beat y'u for," went on Ellen. "For slandering a girl who wasn't there. . . . Me! Y'u rotten liar!"

"But, Ellen, it wasn't all lies," said Bruce, huskily. "I was half drunk—an' horrible jealous. . . . You know Lorenzo seen Isbel kissin' you. I can prove thet."

Ellen threw up her head and a scarlet wave of shame and wrath flooded her face.

"Yes," she cried, ringingly. "He saw Jean Isbel kiss me. Once! . . . An' it was the only decent kiss I've had in years. He meant no insult. I didn't know who he was. An' through his kiss I learned a difference between men. . . . Y'u made Lorenzo lie. An' if I had a shred of good name left in Grass Valley you dishonored it. . . . Y'u made *him* think I was your girl! Damn y'u! I ought to kill y'u. . . . Eat your words now—take them back—or I'll cripple y'u for life!"

Ellen lowered the cocked rifle toward his feet.

"Shore, Ellen, I take back—all I said," gulped Bruce. He gazed at the quivering rifle barrel and then into the face of Ellen's father. Instinct told him where his real peril lay.

Here the cool and tactful Daggs showed himself master of the situation.

"Heah, listen!" he called. "Ellen, I reckon Bruce was drunk an' out of his haid. He's shore ate his words. Now, we don't want any cripples in this camp. Let him alone. Your dad got me heah to lead the Jorths, an' that's my say to you. . . . Simm, you're shore a low-down, lyin' rascal. Keep away from Ellen after this or I'll bore you myself. . . . Jorth, it won't be a bad idee for you to forget you're a Texan till you cool off. Let Bruce stop some Isbel lead. Shore the Jorth-Isbel war is aboot on, an' I reckon we'd be smart to believe old Gass's talk aboot his Nez Perce son."

CHAPTER 6

From this hour Ellen Jorth bent all of her lately awakened intelligence and will to the only end that seemed to hold possible salvation for her. In the crisis sure to come she did not want to be blind or weak. Dreaming and indolence, habits born in her which were often a comfort to one as lonely as she, would ill fit her for the hard test she divined and dreaded. In the matter of her father's fight she must stand by him whatever the issue or the outcome; in what pertained to her own principles, her womanhood, and her soul she stood absolutely alone.

Therefore, Ellen put dreams aside, and indolence of mind and body behind her. Many tasks she found, and when these were done for a day she kept active in other ways, thus earning the poise and peace of labor.

Jorth rode off every day, sometimes with one or two of the men, often with a larger number. If he spoke of such trips to Ellen it was to give an impression of visiting the ranches of his neighbors or the various sheep camps. Often he did not return the day he left. When he did get back he smelled of rum and appeared heavy from need of sleep. His horses were always dust and sweat covered. During his absences Ellen fell victim to anxious dread until he returned. Daily he grew darker and more haggard of face, more obsessed by some impending fate. Often he stayed up late, haranguing with the men in the dim-lit cabin, where they drank and smoked, but seldom gambled any more. When the men did not gamble something immediate and perturbing was on their minds. Ellen had not yet lowered herself to the deceit and suspicion of eavesdropping, but she realized that there was a climax approaching in which she would deliberately do so.

In those closing May days Ellen learned the significance of many things that previously she had taken as a matter of course. Her father did not run a ranch. There was absolutely no ranching done, and little work. Often Ellen had to chop wood herself. Jorth did not possess a plow. Ellen was bound to confess that the evidence of this lack dumfounded her. Even old John Sprague raised some hay, beets, turnips. Jorth's cattle and horses fared ill during the winter. Ellen remembered how they used to clean up four-inch oak saplings and aspens. Many of them died in the snow. The flocks of sheep, however, were driven down into the Basin in the fall, and across the Reno Pass to Phoenix and Maricopa.

Ellen could not discover a fence post on the ranch, nor a piece of salt for the horses and cattle, nor a wagon, nor any sign of a sheep-shearing outfit. She had never seen any sheep sheared. Ellen could never keep track of the many and different horses running loose and hobbled round the ranch. There were droves of horses in the woods, and some of them wild as deer. According to her long-established understanding, her father and her uncles were keen on horse trading and buying.

Then the many trails leading away from the Jorth ranch—these grew to have a fascination for Ellen; and the time came when she rode out on them to see for herself where they led. The sheep ranch of Daggs, supposed to be only a few miles across the ridges, down in Bear Cañon, never materialized at all for Ellen. This circumstance so interested her that she went up to see her friend Sprague and got him to direct her to Bear Cañon, so that she would be sure not to miss it. And she rode from the narrow, maple-thicketed head of it near the Rim down all its length. She found no ranch, no cabin, not even a corral in Bear Cañon. Sprague said there was only one cañon by that name. Daggs had assured her of the exact location on his place, and so had her father. Had they lied? Were they mistaken in the cañon? There were many cañons, all heading up near the Rim, all running and widening down for miles through the wooded mountain, and vastly different from the deep, short, yellow-walled gorges that cut into the Rim from the Basin side. Ellen investigated the cañons within six or eight miles of her home, both to east and to west. All she discovered was a couple of old log cabins, long deserted. Still, she did not follow out all the trails to their ends. Several of them led far into the deepest, roughest, wildest brakes of gorge and thicket that she had seen. No cattle or sheep had ever been driven over these trails.

This riding around of Ellen's at length got to her father's ears. Ellen expected that a bitter quarrel would ensue, for she certainly would refuse to be confined to the camp; but her father only asked her to limit her riding to the meadow valley, and straightway forgot all about it. In fact, his abstraction one moment, his intense nervousness the next, his harder drinking and fiercer harangues with the men, grew to be distressing for Ellen. They presaged his further deterioration and the ever-present evil of the growing feud.

One day Jorth rode home in the early morning, after an absence of two nights. Ellen heard the clip-clop of horses long before she saw them.

"Hey, Ellen! Come out heah," called her father.

Ellen left her work and went outside. A stranger had ridden in with her father, a young giant whose sharp-featured face appeared marked by ferret-like eyes and a fine, light, fuzzy beard. He was long, loose jointed, not heavy of build, and he had the largest hands and feet Ellen had ever seen. Next Ellen espied a black horse they had evidently brought with them. Her father was holding a rope halter. At once the black horse struck Ellen as being a beauty and a thoroughbred.

"Ellen, heah's a horse for you," said Jorth with something of pride. "I made a trade. Reckon I wanted him myself, but he's too gentle for me an' maybe a little small for my weight."

Delight visited Ellen for the first time in many days. Seldom had she owned a good horse, and never one like this.

"Oh, dad!" she exclaimed, in her gratitude.

"Shore he's yours on one condition," said her father.

"What's that?" asked Ellen, as she laid caressing hands on the restless horse.

"You're not to ride him out of the cañon."

"Agreed. . . . All daid black, isn't he, except that white face? What's his name, dad?"

"I forgot to ask," replied Jorth, as he began unsaddling his own horse. "Slater, what's this heah black's name?"

The lanky giant grinned. "I reckon it was Spades."

"Spades?" ejaculated Ellen, blankly. "What a name! . . . Well, I guess it's as good as any. He's shore black."

"Ellen, keep him hobbled when you're not ridin' him," was her father's parting advice as he walked off with the stranger.

Spades was wet and dusty and his satiny skin quivered. He had fine, dark, intelligent eyes that watched Ellen's every move. She knew how her father and his friends dragged and jammed horses through the woods and over the rough trails. It did not take her long to discover that this horse had been a pet. Ellen cleaned his coat and brushed him and fed him. Then she fitted her bridle to suit his head and saddled him. His evident response to her kindness assured her that he was gentle, so she mounted and rode him, to discover he had the easiest gait she had ever experienced. He walked and trotted to suit her will, but when left to choose his own gait he fell into a graceful little pace that was very easy for her. He appeared quite ready to break into a run at her slightest bidding, but Ellen satisfied herself on this first ride with his slower gaits.

"Spades, y'u've shore cut out my burro Jinny," said Ellen, regretfully. "Well, I reckon women are fickle."

Next day she rode up the cañon to show Spades to her friend John Sprague. The old burro breeder was not at home. As his door was open, however, and a fire smoldering, Ellen concluded he would soon return. So she waited. Dismounting, she left Spades free to graze on the new green grass that carpeted the ground. The cabin and little level clearing accentuated the loneliness and wildness of the forest. Ellen always liked it here and had once been in the habit of visiting the old man often. But of late she had stayed away, for the reason that Sprague's talk and his news and his poorly hidden pity depressed her.

Presently she heard hoof beats on the hard, packed trail leading down the cañon in the direction from which she had come. Scarcely likely was it that Sprague should return from this direction. Ellen thought her father had sent one of the herders for her. But when she caught a glimpse of the approaching horseman, down in the aspens, she failed to recognize him. After he had passed one of the openings she heard his horse stop. Probably the man had seen her; at least she could not otherwise account for his stopping. The glimpse she had of him had given her the impression that he was bending over, peering ahead in the trail, looking for tracks. Then she heard the rider come on again, more slowly this time. At length the horse trotted out into the opening, to be hauled up short. Ellen recognized the buckskin-clad figure, the broad shoulders, the dark face of Jean Isbel.

Ellen felt prey to the strangest quaking sensation she had ever suffered. It took violence of her new-born spirit to subdue that feeling.

Isbel rode slowly across the clearing toward her. For Ellen his approach seemed singularly swift—so swift that her surprise, dismay, conjecture, and anger obstructed her will. The outwardly calm and cold Ellen Jorth was a travesty that mocked her—that she felt he would discern.

The moment Isbel drew close enough for Ellen to see his face she experienced a strong, shuddering repetition of her first shock of recognition. He was not the same. The light, the youth was gone. This, however, did not cause her emotion. Was it not a sudden transition of her nature to the dominance of hate? Ellen seemed to feel the shadow of her unknown self standing with her.

Isbel halted his horse. Ellen had been standing near the trunk of a fallen pine and she instinctively backed against it. How her legs trembled! Isbel took off his cap and crushed it nervously in his bare, brown hand.

"Good mornin', Miss Ellen!" he said.

Ellen did not return his greeting, but queried, almost breathlessly, "Did y'u come by our ranch?"

"No. I circled," he replied.

"Jean Isbel! What do y'u want heah?" she demanded.

"Don't you know?" he returned. His eyes were intensely black and piercing. They seemed to search Ellen's very soul. To meet their gaze was an ordeal that only her rousing fury sustained.

Ellen felt on her lips a scornful allusion to his half-breed Indian traits and the reputation that had preceded him. But she could not utter it.

"No" she replied.

"It's hard to call a woman a liar," he returned, bitterly. "But you must be—seein' you're a Jorth."

"Liar! Not to y'u, Jean Isbel," she retorted. "I'd not lie to y'u to save my life."

He studied her with keen, sober, moody intent. The dark fire of his eyes thrilled her.

"If that's true, I'm glad," he said.

"Shore it's true. I've no idea why y'u came heah."

Ellen did have a dawning idea that she could not force into oblivion. But if she ever admitted it to her consciousness, she must fail in the contempt and scorn and fearlessness she chose to throw in this man's face.

"Does old Sprague live here?" asked Isbel.

"Yes. I expect him back soon. . . . Did y'u come to see him?"

"No. . . . Did Sprague tell you anythin' about the row he saw me in?"

"He—did not," replied Ellen, lying with stiff lips. She who had sworn she could not lie! She felt the hot blood leaving her heart, mounting in a wave. All her conscious will seemed impelled to deceive. What had she to hide from Jean Isbel? And a still, small voice replied that she had to hide the Ellen Jorth who had waited for him that day, who had spied upon him, who had treasured a gift she could not destroy, who had hugged to her miserable heart the fact that he had fought for her name.

"I'm glad of that," Isbel was saying, thoughtfully.

"Did you come heah to see me?" interrupted Ellen. She felt that she could not endure this reiterated suggestion of fineness, of consideration in him. She would betray herself—betray what she did not even realize herself. She must force other footing—and that should be the one of strife between the Jorths and Isbels.

"No—honest. I didn't, Miss Ellen," he rejoined, humbly. "I'll tell you, presently, why I came. But it wasn't to see you. . . . I don't deny I wanted . . . but that's no matter. You didn't meet me that day on the Rim."

"Meet y'u!" she echoed, coldly. "Shore y'u never expected me?"

"Somehow I did," he replied, with those penetrating eyes on her. "I put somethin' in your tent that day. Did you find it?"

"Yes," she replied, with the same casual coldness.

"What did you do with it?"

"I kicked it out, of course," she replied.

She saw him flinch.

"And you never opened it?"

"Certainly not," she retorted, as if forced. "Doon't y'u know anythin' about—about people? . . . Shore even if y'u are an Isbel y'u never were born in Texas."

"Thank God I wasn't!" he replied. "I was born in a beautiful country of green meadows and deep forests and white rivers, not in a barren desert where men live dry and hard as the cactus. Where I come from men don't live on hate. They can forgive."

"Forgive! . . . Could y'u forgive a Jorth?"

"Yes, I could."

"Shore that's easy to say—with the wrongs all on your side," she declared, bitterly.

"Ellen Jorth, the first wrong was on your side," retorted Jean, his voice full. "Your father stole my father's sweetheart—by lies, by slander, by dishonor, by makin' terrible love to her in his absence."

"It's a lie," cried Ellen, passionately.

"It is not," he declared, solemnly.

"Jean Isbel, I say y'u lie!"

"No! *I* say you've been lied to," he thundered.

The tremendous force of his spirit seemed to fling truth at Ellen. It weakened her.

"But—mother loved dad—best."

"Yes, afterward. No wonder, poor woman! . . . But it was the action of your father and your mother that ruined all these lives. You've got to know the truth, Ellen Jorth. . . . All the years of hate have borne their fruit. God Almighty can never save us now. Blood must be spilled. The Jorths and the Isbels can't live on the same earth. . . . And you've got to know the truth because the worst of this hell falls on you and me."

The hate that he spoke of alone upheld her.

"Never, Jean Isbel!" she cried. "I'll never know truth from y'u. . . . I'll never share anythin' with y'u—not even hell."

Isbel dismounted and stood before her, still holding his bridle reins. The bay horse champed his bit and tossed his head.

"Why do you hate me so?" he asked. "I just happen to be my father's son. I never harmed you or any of your people. I met you . . . fell in love with you in a flash—though I never knew it till after. . . . Why do you hate me so terribly?"

Ellen felt a heavy, stifling pressure within her breast. "Y'u're an Isbel. . . . Doon't speak of love to me."

"I didn't intend to. But your—your hate seems unnatural. And we'll probably never meet again. . . . I can't help it. I love you. Love at first sight! Jean Isbel and Ellen Jorth! Strange, isn't it? . . . It was all so strange. My meetin' you so lonely and unhappy, my seein' you so sweet and beautiful, my thinkin' you so good in spite of—"

"Shore it was strange," interrupted Ellen, with scornful

laugh. She had found her defense. In hurting him she could hide her own hurt. "Thinking me so good in spite of—Ha-ha! And I said I'd been kissed before!"

"Yes, in spite of everything," he said.

Ellen could not look at him as he loomed over her. She felt a wild tumult in her heart. All that crowded to her lips for utterance was false.

"Yes—kissed before I met you—and since," she said, mockingly. "And I laugh at what y'u call love, Jean Isbel."

"Laugh if you want—but believe it was sweet, honorable—the best in me," he replied, in deep earnestness.

"Bah!" cried Ellen, with all the force of her pain and shame and hate.

"By Heaven, you must be different from what I thought!" exclaimed Isbel, huskily.

"Shore if I wasn't, I'd make myself. . . . Now, Mister Jean Isbel, get on your horse an' go!"

Something of composure came to Ellen with these words of dismissal, and she glanced up at him with half-veiled eyes. His changed aspect prepared her for some blow.

"That's a pretty black horse."

"Yes," replied Ellen, blankly.

"Do you like him?"

"I—I love him."

"All right, I'll give him to you then. He'll have less work and kinder treatment than if I used him. I've got some pretty hard rides ahead of me."

"Y'u—y'u give—" whispered Ellen, slowly stiffening.

"Yes. He's mine," replied Isbel. With that he turned to whistle. Spades threw up his head, snorted, and started forward at a trot. He came faster the closer he got, and if ever Ellen saw the joy of a horse at sight of a beloved master she saw it then. Isbel laid a hand on the animal's neck and caressed him, then, turning back to Ellen, he went on speaking: "I picked him from a lot of fine horses of my father's. We got along well. My sister Ann rode him a good deal. . . . He was stolen from our pasture day before yesterday. I took his trail and tracked him up here. Never lost his trail till I got to your ranch, where I had to circle till I picked it up again."

"Stolen—pasture—tracked him up heah?" echoed Ellen without any evidence of emotion whatever. Indeed, she seemed to have been turned to stone.

"Trackin' him was easy. I wish for your sake it'd been impossible," he said, bluntly.

"For my sake?" she echoed, in precisely the same tone.

Manifestly that tone irritated Isbel, beyond control. He misunderstood it. With a hand far from gentle he pushed her bent head back so he could look into her face.

"Yes, for your sake!" he declared, harshly. "Haven't you sense enough to see that? . . . What kind of a game do you think you can play with me?"

"Game! . . . Game of what?" she asked.

"Why, a—a game of ignorance—innocence—any old game to fool a man who's tryin' to be decent."

This time Ellen mutely looked her dull, blank questioning. And it inflamed Isbel.

"You know your father's a horse thief!" he thundered.

Outwardly Ellen remained the same. She had been prepared for an unknown and a terrible blow. It had fallen. And her face, her body, her hands, locked with the supreme fortitude of pride and sustained by hate, gave no betrayal of the crashing, thundering ruin within her mind and soul. Motionless she leaned there, meeting the piercing fire of Isbel's eyes, seeing in them a righteous and terrible scorn. In one flash the naked truth seemed blazed at her. The faith she had fostered died a sudden death. A thousand perplexing problems were solved in a second of whirling, revealing thought.

"Ellen Jorth, you know your father's in with this Hash Knife Gang of rustlers," thundered Isbel.

"Shore," she replied, with the cool, easy, careless defiance of a Texan.

"You know he's got this Daggs to lead his faction against the Isbels?"

"Shore."

"You know this talk of sheepmen buckin' the cattlemen is all a blind?"

"Shore," reiterated Ellen.

Isbel gazed darkly down upon her. With his anger spent for the moment, he appeared ready to end the interview. But he seemed fascinated by the strange look of her, by the incomprehensible something she emanated. Havoc gleamed in his pale, set face. He shook his dark head and his broad hand went to his breast.

"To think I fell in love with such as you!" he exclaimed, and his other hand swept out in a tragic gesture of helpless pathos and impotence.

The hell Isbel had hinted at now possessed Ellen— body, mind, and soul. Disgraced, scorned by an Isbel! Yet loved by him! In that divination there flamed up a wild, fierce passion to hurt, to rend, to flay, to fling back upon him a stinging agony. Her thought flew upon her like whips. Pride of the Jorths! Pride of the old Texan blue blood! It lay dead at her feet, killed by the scornful words of the last of that family to whom she owed her degradation. Daughter of a horse thief and rustler! Dark and evil and grim set the forces within her, accepting her fate, damning her enemies, true to the blood of the Jorths. The sins of the father must be visited upon the daughter.

"Shore y'u might have had me—that day on the Rim—if y'u hadn't told your name," she said, mockingly, and she gazed into his eyes with all the mystery of a woman's nature.

Isbel's powerful frame shook as with an ague. "Girl, what do you mean?"

"Shore, I'd have been plumb fond of havin' y'u make up to me," she drawled. It possessed her now with irresistible power, this fact of the love he could not help. Some fiendish woman's satisfaction dwelt in her consciousness of her power to kill the noble, the faithful, the good in him.

"Ellen Jorth, you lie!" he burst out, hoarsely.

"Jean, shore I'd been a toy and a rag for these rustlers long enough. I was tired of them. . . . I wanted a new lover. . . . And if y'u hadn't give yourself away—"

Isbel moved so swiftly that she did not realize his intention until his hard hand smote her mouth. Instantly she tasted the hot, salty blood from a cut lip.

"Shut up, you hussy!" he ordered, roughly. "Have you no shame? . . . My sister Ann spoke well of you. She made excuses—she pitied you."

That for Ellen seemed the culminating blow under which she almost sank. But one moment longer could she maintain this unnatural and terrible poise.

"Jean Isbel—go along with y'u," she said, impatiently. "I'm waiting heah for Simm Bruce!"

At last it was as if she struck his heart. Because of doubt of himself and a stubborn faith in her, his passion and jealousy were not proof against this last stab. Instinctive subtlety inherent in Ellen had prompted the speech that tortured Isbel. How the shock to him rebounded on her! She gasped as he lunged for her, too swift for her to move a hand. One arm crushed round her like a steel band; the other, hard across her breast and neck, forced her head back. Then she tried to wrestle away. But she was utterly powerless. His dark face bent down closer and closer. Suddenly Ellen ceased trying to struggle. She was like a stricken creature paralyzed by the piercing, hypnotic eyes of a snake. Yet in spite of her terror, if he meant death by her, she welcomed it.

"Ellen Jorth, I'm thinkin' yet—you lie!" he said, low and tense between his teeth.

"No! No!" she screamed, wildly. Her nerve broke there. She could no longer meet those terrible black eyes. Her passionate denial was not only the last of her shameful deceit; it was the woman of her, repudiating herself and him, and all this sickening, miserable situation.

Isbel took her literally. She had convinced him. And the instant held blank horror for Ellen.

"By God—then I'll have somethin'—of you anyway!" muttered Isbel, thickly.

Ellen saw the blood bulge in his powerful neck. She saw his dark, hard face, strange now, fearful to behold, come lower and lower, till it blurred and obstructed her gaze. She felt the swell and ripple and stretch—then the bind of his muscles, like huge coils of elastic rope. Then with savage rude force his mouth closed on hers. All Ellen's senses reeled, as if she were swooning. She was suffocating. The spasm passed, and a bursting spurt of blood revived her to acute and terrible consciousness. For the endless period of one moment he held her so that her breast seemed crushed. His kisses burned and bruised her lips. And then, shifting violently to her neck, they pressed so hard that she choked under them. It was as if a huge bat had fastened upon her throat.

Suddenly the remorseless binding embraces—the hot and savage kisses—fell away from her. Isbel had let go. She saw him throw up his hands, and stagger back a little, all the while with his piercing gaze on her. His face had been dark purple: now it was white.

"No—Ellen Jorth," he panted, "I don't—want any of you—that way." And suddenly he sank on the log and covered his face with his hands. "What I loved in you—was what I thought—you were."

Like a wildcat Ellen sprang upon him, beating him with her fists, tearing at his hair, scratching his face, in a blind fury. Isbel made no move to stop her, and her violence spent itself with her strength. She swayed back from him, shaking so that she could scarcely stand.

"Y'u—damned—Isbel!" she gasped, with hoarse passion. "Y'u insulted me!"

"Insulted you? . . ." laughed Isbel, in bitter scorn. "It couldn't be done."

"Oh! . . . I'll *kill* y'u!" she hissed.

Isbel stood up and wiped the red scratches on his face. "Go ahead. There's my gun," he said, pointing to his saddle sheath. "Somebody's got to begin this Jorth-Isbel feud. It'll be a dirty business. I'm sick of it already. . . . Kill me! . . . First blood for Ellen Jorth!"

Suddenly the dark grim tide that had seemed to engulf Ellen's very soul cooled and receded, leaving her without its false strength. She began to sag. She stared at Isbel's gun. "Kill him," whispered the retreating voices of her hate. But she was as powerless as if she were still held in Jean Isbel's giant embrace.

"I—I want to—kill y'u," she whispered, "but I cain't. . . . Leave me."

"You're no Jorth—the same as I'm no Isbel. We oughtn't be mixed in this deal," he said, somberly. "I'm sorrier for you than I am for myself. . . . You're a girl. . . . You once had a good mother—a decent home. And this life you've led here—mean as it's been—is nothin' to what you'll face now. Damn the men that brought you to this! I'm goin' to kill some of them."

With that he mounted and turned away. Ellen called out for him to take his horse. He did not stop nor look back.

She called again, but her voice was fainter, and Isbel was now leaving at a trot. Slowly she sagged against the tree, lower and lower. He headed into the trail leading up the cañon. How strange a relief Ellen felt! She watched him ride into the aspens and start up the slope, at last to disappear in the pines. It seemed at the moment that he took with him something which had been hers. A pain in her head dulled the thoughts that wavered to and fro. After he had gone she could not see so well. Her eyes were tired. What had happened to her? There was blood on her hands. Isbel's blood! She shuddered. Was it an omen? Low she sank against the tree and closed her eyes.

Old John Sprague did not return. Hours dragged by— dark hours for Ellen Jorth lying prostrate beside the tree, hiding the blue sky and golden sunlight from her eyes. At length the lethargy of despair, the black dull misery wore away; and she gradually returned to a condition of coherent thought.

What had she learned? Sight of the black horse grazing near seemed to prompt the trenchant replies. Spades belonged to Jean Isbel. He had been stolen by her father or by one of her father's accomplices. Isbel's vaunted cunning as a tracker had been no idle boast. Her father was a horse thief, a rustler, a sheepman only as a blind, a consort of Daggs, leader of the Hash Knife Gang. Ellen well remembered the ill repute of that gang, way back in Texas, years ago. Her father had gotten in with this famous band of rustlers to serve his own ends—the extermination of the Isbels. It was all very plain now to Ellen.

"Daughter of a horse thief an' rustler!" she muttered.

And her thoughts sped back to the days of her girlhood. Only the very early stage of that time had been happy. In the light of Isbel's revelation the many changes of residence, the sudden moves to unsettled parts of Texas, the periods of poverty and sudden prosperity, all leading to the final journey to this God-forsaken Arizona—these were now seen in their true significance. As far back as she could remember her father had been a crooked man. And her mother had known it. He had dragged her to her ruin. That degradation had killed her. Ellen realized that with poignant sorrow, with a sudden revolt against her father. Had Gaston Isbel truly and dishonestly started her father on his downhill road? Ellen wondered. She hated the Isbels with unutterable and growing hate, yet she had it in her to think, to ponder, to weigh judgments in their behalf. She owed it to something in herself to be fair. But what did it matter who was to blame for the Jorth-Isbel feud? Somehow Ellen was forced to confess that deep in her soul it mattered terribly. To be true to herself—the self that she alone knew—she must have right on her side. If the Jorths were guilty, and she clung to them and their creed, then she would be one of them.

"But I'm not," she mused, aloud. "My name's Jorth, an' I reckon I have bad blood. . . . But it never came out in me till to-day. I've been honest. I've been good—yes, *good*, as my mother taught me to be—in spite of all. . . . Shore my pride made me a fool. . . . An' now have I any choice to make? I'm a Jorth. I must stick to my father."

All this summing up, however, did not wholly account for the pang in her breast.

What had she done that day? And the answer beat in her ears like a great throbbing hammer-stroke. In an agony of shame, in the throes of hate, she had perjured herself. She had sworn away her honor. She had basely made herself vile. She had struck ruthlessly at the great heart of a man who loved her. Ah! That thrust had rebounded to leave this dreadful pang in her breast. Loved her? Yes, the strange truth, the insupportable truth! She had to contend now, not with her father and her disgrace, not with the baffling presence of Jean Isbel, but with the mysteries of her own soul. Wonder of all wonders was it that such love had been born for her. Shame worse than all other shame was it that she should kill it by a poisoned lie. By what monstrous motive had she done that? To sting Isbel as he had stung her! But that had been base. Never could she have stooped so low except in a moment of tremendous tumult. If she had done sore injury to Isbel what had she done to herself? How strange, how tenacious had been his faith in her honor! Could she ever forget? She must forget it. But she could never forget the way he had scorned those vile men in Greaves's store—the way he had beaten Bruce for defiling her name—the way he had stubbornly denied her own insinuations. She was a woman now. She had learned something of the complexity of a woman's heart. She could not change nature. And all her passionate being thrilled to the manhood of her defender. But even while she thrilled she acknowledged her hate. It was the contention between the two that caused the pang in her breast. "An' now what's left for me?" murmured Ellen. She did not analyze the significance of what had prompted that query. The most incalculable of the day's disclosures was the wrong she had done herself. "Shore I'm done for, one way or another. . . . I must stick to Dad. . . . or kill myself?"

Ellen rode Spades back to the ranch. She rode like the wind. When she swung out of the trail into the open meadow in plain sight of the ranch her appearance created a commotion among the loungers before the cabin. She rode Spades at a full run.

"Who's after you?" yelled her father, as she pulled the black to a halt. Jorth held a rifle. Daggs, Colter, the other Jorths were there, likewise armed, and all watchful, strung with expectancy.

"Shore nobody's after me," replied Ellen. "Cain't I run a horse round heah without being chased?"

Jorth appeared both incensed and relieved.

"Hah! . . . What you mean, girl, runnin' like a streak right down on us? You're actin' queer these days, an' you look queer. I'm not likin' it."

"Reckon these are queer times—for the Jorths," replied Ellen, sarcastically.

"Daggs found strange horse tracks crossin' the meadow," said her father. "An' that worried us. Some one's been snoopin' round the ranch. An' when we seen you runnin' so wild we shore thought you was bein' chased."

"No. I was only trying out Spades to see how fast he could run," returned Ellen. "Reckon when we do get chased it'll take some running to catch me."

"Haw! Haw!" roared Daggs. "It shore will, Ellen."

"Girl, it's not only your runnin' an' your looks that's queer," declared Jorth, in dark perplexity. "You talk queer."

"Shore, dad, y'u're not used to hearing spades called spades," said Ellen, as she dismounted.

"Humph!" ejaculated her father, as if convinced of the uselessness of trying to understand a woman. "Say, did you see any strange horse tracks?"

"I reckon I did. And I know who made them."

Jorth stiffened. All the men behind him showed a sudden intensity of suspense.

"Who?" demanded Jorth.

"Shore it was Jean Isbel," replied Ellen, coolly. "He came up heah tracking his black horse."

"Jean—Isbel—trackin'—his—black horse," repeated her father.

"Yes. He's not overrated as a tracker, that's shore."

Blank silence ensued. Ellen cast a slow glance over her father and the others, then she began to loosen the cinches of her saddle. Presently Jorth burst the silence with a curse, and Daggs followed with one of his sardonic laughs.

"Wal, boss, what did I tell you?" he drawled.

Jorth strode to Ellen, and, whirling her around with a strong hand, he held her facing him.

"Did y'u see Isbel?"

"Yes," replied Ellen, just as sharply as her father had asked.

"Did y'u talk to him?"

"Yes."

"What did he want up heah?"

"I told y'u. He was tracking the black horse y'u stole."

Jorth's hand and arm dropped limply. His sallow face turned a livid hue. Amaze merged into discomfiture and that gave place to rage. He raised a hand as if to strike Ellen. And suddenly Daggs's long arm shot out to clutch Jorth's wrist. Wrestling to free himself, Jorth cursed under his breath. "Let go, Daggs," he shouted, stridently. "Am I drunk that you grab me?"

"Wal, y'u ain't drunk, I reckon," replied the rustler, with sarcasm. "But y'u're shore some things I'll reserve for your private ear."

Jorth gained a semblance of composure. But it was evident that he labored under a shock.

"Ellen, did Jean Isbel see this black horse?"

"Yes. He asked me how I got Spades an' I told him."

"Did he say Spades belonged to him?"

"Shore I reckon he proved it. Y'u can always tell a horse that loves its master."

"Did y'u offer to give Spades back?"

"Yes. But Isbel wouldn't take him."

"Hah! . . . An' why not?"

"He said he'd rather I kept him. He was about to engage in a dirty, blood-spilling deal, an' he reckoned he'd not be able to care for a fine horse. . . . I didn't want

Spades. I tried to make Isbel take him. But he rode off. . . .
And that's all there is to that."

"Maybe it's not," replied Jorth, chewing his mustache
and eying Ellen with dark, intent gaze. "Y'u've met this
Isbel twice."

"It wasn't any fault of mine," retorted Ellen.

"I heah he's sweet on y'u. How aboot that?"

Ellen smarted under the blaze of blood that swept to
neck and cheek and temple. But it was only memory
which fired this shame. What her father and his crowd
might think were matters of supreme indifference. Yet she
met his suspicious gaze with truthful blazing eyes.

"I heah talk from Bruce an' Lorenzo," went on her
father. "An' Daggs heah—"

"Daggs nothin'!" interrupted that worthy. "Don't fetch
me in. I said nothin' an' I think nothin'."

"Yes, Jean Isbel *was* sweet on me, dad . . . but he will
never be again," returned Ellen, in low tones. With that
she pulled her saddle off Spades and, throwing it over her
shoulder, she walked off to her cabin.

Hardly had she gotten indoors when her father entered.

"Ellen, I didn't know that horse belonged to Isbel," he
began, in the swift, hoarse, persuasive voice so familiar
to Ellen. "I swear I didn't. I bought him—traded with
Slater for him. . . . Honest to God, I never had any idea
he was stolen! . . . Why, when y'u said 'that horse y'u
stole,' I felt as if y'u'd knifed me. . . ."

Ellen sat at the table and listened while her father paced
to and fro and, by his restless action and passionate speech,
worked himself into a frenzy. He talked incessantly, as if
her silence was condemnatory and as if eloquence alone
could convince her of his honesty. It seemed that Ellen saw
and heard with keener faculties than ever before. He had a
terrible thirst for her respect. Not so much for her love, she
divined, but that she would not see how he had fallen!

She pitied him with all her heart. She was all he had, as he was all the world to her. And so, as she gave ear to his long, illogical rigmarole of argument and defense, she slowly found that her pity and her love were making vital decisions for her. As of old, in poignant moments, her father lapsed at last into a denunciation of the Isbels and what they had brought him to. His sufferings were real, at least, in Ellen's presence. She was the only link that bound him to long-past happier times. She was her mother over again—the woman who had betrayed another man for him and gone with him to her ruin and death.

"Dad, don't go on so," said Ellen, breaking in upon her father's rant. "I will be true to y'u—as my mother was. . . . I am a Jorth. Your place is my place—your fight is my fight. . . . Never speak of the past to me again. If God spares us through this feud we will go away and begin all over again, far off where no one ever heard of a Jorth. . . . If we're not spared we'll at least have had our whack at these damned Isbels."

CHAPTER 7

During June Jean Isbel did not ride far away from Grass Valley.

Another attempt had been made upon Gaston Isbel's life. Another cowardly shot had been fired from ambush, this time from a pine thicket bordering the trail that led to Blaisdell's ranch. Blaisdell heard this shot, so near his home was it fired. No trace of the hidden foe could be found. The ground all around that vicinity bore a carpet of pine needles which showed no trace of footprints. The supposition was that this cowardly attempt had been perpetrated, or certainly instigated, by the Jorths. But there was no proof. And Gaston Isbel had other enemies in the Tonto Basin besides the sheep clan. The old man raged like a lion about this sneaking attack on him. And his friend Blaisdell urged an immediate gathering of their kin and friends. "Let's quit ranchin' till this trouble's settled," he declared. "Let's arm an' ride the trails an' meet these men half-way. . . . It won't help our side any to wait till you're shot in the back." More than one of Isbel's supporters offered the same advice.

"No; we'll wait till we know for shore," was the stubborn cattleman's reply to all these promptings.

"Know! Wal, hell! Didn't Jean find the black hoss up at Jorth's ranch?" demanded Blaisdell. "What more do we want?"

"Jean couldn't swear Jorth stole the black."

"Wal, by thunder, I can swear to it!" growled Blaisdell. "An' we're losin' cattle all the time. Who's stealin' 'em?"

"We've always lost cattle ever since we started ranchin' heah."

"Gas, I reckon y'u want Jorth to start this fight in the open."

"It'll start soon enough," was Isbel's gloomy reply.

Jean had not failed altogether in his tracking of lost or stolen cattle. Circumstances had been against him, and there was something baffling about this rustling. The summer storms set in early, and it had been his luck to have heavy rains wash out fresh tracks that he might have followed. The range was large and cattle were everywhere. Sometimes a loss was not discovered for weeks. Gaston Isbel's sons were now the only men left to ride the range. Two of his riders had quit because of the threatened war, and Isbel had let another go. So that Jean did not often learn that cattle had been stolen until their tracks were old. Added to that was the fact that this Grass Valley country was covered with horse tracks and cattle tracks. The rustlers, whoever they were, had long been at the game, and now that there was reason for them to show their cunning they did it.

Early in July the hot weather came. Down on the red ridges of the Tonto it was hot desert. The nights were cool, the early mornings were pleasant, but the day was something to endure. When the white cumulus clouds rolled up out of the southwest, growing larger and thicker and darker, here and there coalescing into a black thundercloud, Jean welcomed them. He liked to see the gray streamers of rain hanging down from a canopy of black, and the roar of rain on the trees as it approached like a trampling army was always welcome. The grassy flats, the red ridges, the rocky slopes, the thickets of manzanita and scrub oak and cactus were dusty, glaring, throat-parching places under the hot summer sun. Jean longed for the cool heights of the Rim, the shady pines, the dark sweet verdure under the silver spruces, the tinkle and murmur of the clear rills. He often had another longing, too, which he bitterly stifled.

Jean's ally, the keen-nosed shepherd dog, had disappeared one day, and had never returned. Among men at the ranch there was a difference of opinion as to what had happened to Shepp. The old rancher thought he had been poisoned or shot; Bill and Guy Isbel believed he had been stolen by sheep herders, who were always stealing dogs; and Jean inclined to the conviction that Shepp had gone off with the timber wolves. The fact was that Shepp did not return, and Jean missed him.

One morning at dawn Jean heard the cattle bellowing and trampling out in the valley; and upon hurrying to a vantage point he was amazed to see upward of five hundred steers chasing a lone wolf. Jean's father had seen such a spectacle as this, but it was a new one for Jean. The wolf was a big gray and black fellow, rangy and powerful, and until he got the steers all behind him he was rather hard put to it to keep out of their way. Probably he had dogged the herd, trying to sneak in and pull down a yearling, and finally the steers had charged him. Jean kept along the edge of the valley in the hope they would chase him within range of a rifle. But the wary wolf saw Jean and sheered off, gradually drawing away from his pursuers.

Jean returned to the house for his breakfast, and then set off across the valley. His father owned one small flock of sheep that had not yet been driven up on the Rim, where all the sheep in the country were run during the hot, dry summer down on the Tonto. Young Evarts and a Mexican boy named Bernardino had charge of this flock. The regular Mexican herder, a man of experience, had given up his job; and these boys were not equal to the task of risking the sheep up in the enemies' stronghold.

This flock was known to be grazing in a side draw, well up from Grass Valley, where the brush afforded some protection from the sun, and there was good water and a little feed. Before Jean reached his destination he heard a shot. It was not a rifle shot, which fact caused Jean a little concern. Evarts and Bernardino had rifles, but, to his knowledge, no small arms. Jean rode up on one of the black-brushed conical hills that rose on the south side of Grass Valley, and from there he took a sharp survey of the country. At first he made out only cattle, and bare meadowland, and the low encircling ridges and hills. But presently up toward the head of the valley he descried a bunch of horsemen riding toward the village. He could not tell their number. That dark moving mass seemed to Jean to be instinct with life, mystery, menace. Who were they? It was too far for him to recognize horses, let alone riders. They were moving fast, too.

Jean watched them out of sight, then turned his horse downhill again, and rode on his quest. A number of horsemen like that was a very unusual sight around Grass Valley at any time. What then did it portend now? Jean experienced a little shock of uneasy dread that was a new sensation for him. Brooding over this he proceeded on his way, at length to turn into the draw where the camp of the sheep herders was located. Upon coming in sight of it he heard a hoarse shout. Young Evarts appeared running frantically out of the brush. Jean urged his horse into a run and soon covered the distance between them. Evarts appeared beside himself with terror.

"Boy! what's the matter?" queried Jean, as he dismounted, rifle in hand, peering quickly from Evarts's white face to the camp, and all around.

"Ber-nardino! Ber-nardino!" gasped the boy, wringing his hands and pointing.

Jean ran the few remaining rods to the sheep camp. He saw the little teepee, a burned-out fire, a half-finished meal—and then the Mexican lad lying prone on the ground, dead, with a bullet hole in his ghastly face. Near him lay an old six-shooter.

"Whose gun is that?" demanded Jean, as he picked it up.

"Ber-nardino's," replied Evarts, huskily. "He—he jest got it—the other day."

"Did he shoot himself accidentally?"

"Oh no! No! He didn't do it—at all."

"Who did, then?"

"The men—they rode up—a gang—they did it," panted Evarts.

"Did you know who they were?"

"No. I couldn't tell. I saw them comin' an' I was skeered. Bernardino had gone fer water. I run an' hid in the brush. I wanted to yell, but they come too close. . . . Then I heerd them talkin'. Bernardino come back. They 'peared friendly-like. Thet made me raise up to look. An' I couldn't see good. I heerd one of them ask Bernardino to let him see his gun. An' Bernardino handed it over. He looked at the gun an' haw-hawed, an' flipped it up in the air, an' when it fell back in his hand it—it went off bang! . . . An' Bernardino dropped. . . . I hid down close. I was skeered stiff. I heerd them talk more, but not what they said. Then they rode away. . . . An' I hid there till I seen y'u comin'."

"Have you got a horse?" queried Jean, sharply.

"No. But I can ride one of Bernardino's burros."

"Get one. Hurry over to Blaisdell. Tell him to send word to Blue and Gordon and Fredericks to ride like the devil to my father's ranch. Hurry now!"

Young Evarts ran off without reply. Jean stood looking down at the limp and pathetic figure of the Mexican boy. "By Heaven!" he exclaimed, grimly, "the Jorth-Isbel war is on! . . . Deliberate, cold-blooded murder! I'll gamble Daggs did this job. He's been given the leadership. He's started it. . . . Bernardino, greaser or not, you were a faithful lad, and you won't go long unavenged."

Jean had no time to spare. Tearing a tarpaulin out of the teepee he covered the lad with it and then ran for his horse. Mounting, he galloped down the draw, over the little red ridges, out into the valley, where he put his horse to a run.

Action changed the sickening horror that sight of Bernardino had engendered. Jean even felt a strange, grim relief. The long, dragging days of waiting were over. Jorth's gang had taken the initiative. Blood had begun to flow. And it would continue to flow now till the last man of one faction stood over the dead body of the last man of the other. Would it be a Jorth or an Isbel? "My instinct was right," he muttered, aloud. "That bunch of horses gave me a queer feelin'." Jean gazed all around the grassy, cattle-dotted valley he was crossing so swiftly, and toward the village, but he did not see any sign of the dark group of riders. They had gone on to Greaves's store, there, no doubt, to drink and to add more enemies of the Isbels to their gang. Suddenly across Jean's mind flashed a thought of Ellen Jorth. "What 'll become of her? . . . What 'll become of all the women? My sister? . . . The little ones?"

No one was in sight around the ranch. Never had it appeared more peaceful and pastoral to Jean. The grazing cattle and horses in the foreground, the haystack half eaten away, the cows in the fenced pasture, the column of blue smoke lazily ascending, the cackle of hens, the solid, well-built cabins—all these seemed to repudiate Jean's haste and his darkness of mind. This place was his father's farm. There was not a cloud in the blue, summer sky.

As Jean galloped up the lane some one saw him from the door, and then Bill and Guy and their gray-headed father came out upon the porch. Jean saw how he waved the womenfolk back, and then strode out into the lane. Bill and Guy reached his side as Jean pulled his heaving horse to a halt. They all looked at Jean, swiftly and intently, with a little, hard, fiery gleam strangely identical in the eyes of each. Probably before a word was spoken they knew what to expect.

"Wal, you shore was in a hurry," remarked the father.

"What the hell's up?" queried Bill, grimly.

Guy Isbel remained silent and it was he who turned slightly pale. Jean leaped off his horse.

"Bernardino has just been killed—murdered with his own gun."

Gaston Isbel seemed to exhale a long-dammed, bursting breath that let his chest sag. A terrible deadly glint, pale and cold as sunlight on ice, grew slowly to dominate his clear eyes.

"A-huh!" ejaculated Bill Isbel, hoarsely.

Not one of the three men asked who had done the killing. They were silent a moment, motionless, locked in the secret seclusion of their own minds. Then they listened with absorption to Jean's brief story.

"Wal, that lets us in," said his father. "I wish we had more time. Reckon I'd done better to listen to you boys an' have my men close at hand. Jacobs happened to ride over. That makes five of us besides the women."

"Aw, dad, you don't reckon they'll round us up heah?" asked Guy Isbel.

"Boys, I always feared they might," replied the old man. "But I never really believed they'd have the nerve. Shore I ought to have figgered Daggs better. This heah secret bizness an' shootin' at us from ambush looked aboot Jorth's size to me. But I reckon now we'll have to fight without our friends."

"Let them come," said Jean. "I sent for Blaisdell, Blue, Gordon, and Fredericks. Maybe they'll get here in time. But if they don't it needn't worry us much. We can hold out here longer than Jorth's gang can hang around. We'll want plenty of water, wood, and meat in the house."

"Wal, I'll see to that," rejoined his father. "Jean, you go out close by, where you can see all around, an' keep watch."

"Who's goin' to tell the women?" asked Guy Isbel.

The silence that momentarily ensued was an eloquent testimony to the hardest and saddest aspect of this strife between men. The inevitableness of it in no wise detracted from its sheer uselessness. Men from time immemorial had hated, and killed one another, always to the misery and degradation of their women. Old Gaston Isbel showed this tragic realization in his lined face.

"Wal, boys, I'll tell the women," he said. "Shore you needn't worry none aboot them. They'll be game."

Jean rode away to an open knoll a short distance from the house, and here he stationed himself to watch all points. The cedared ridge back of the ranch was the one approach by which Jorth's gang might come close without being detected, but even so, Jean could see them and ride to the house in time to prevent a surprise. The moments dragged by, and at the end of an hour Jean was in hopes that Blaisdell would soon come. These hopes were well founded. Presently he heard a clatter of hoofs on hard ground to the south, and upon wheeling to look he saw the friendly neighbor coming fast along the road, riding a big white horse. Blaisdell carried a rifle in his hand, and the sight of him gave Jean a glow of warmth. He was one of the Texans who would stand by the Isbels to the last man. Jean watched him ride to the house—watched the meeting between him and his lifelong friend. There floated out to Jean old Blaisdell's roar of rage.

Then out on the green of Grass Valley, where a long, swelling plain swept away toward the village, there appeared a moving dark patch. A bunch of horses! Jean's body gave a slight start—the shock of sudden propulsion of blood through all his veins. Those horses bore riders. They were coming straight down the open valley, on the wagon road to Isbel's ranch. No subterfuge nor secrecy nor sneaking in that advance! A hot thrill ran over Jean.

"By Heaven! They mean business!" he muttered. Up to the last moment he had unconsciously hoped Jorth's gang would not come boldly like that. The verifications of all a Texan's inherited instincts left no doubts, no hopes, no illusions—only a grim certainty that this was not conjecture nor probability, but fact. For a moment longer Jean watched the slowly moving dark patch of horsemen against the green background, then he hurried back to the ranch. His father saw him coming—strode out as before.

"Dad—Jorth is comin'," said Jean, huskily. How he hated to be forced to tell his father that! The boyish love of old had flashed up.

"Whar?" demanded the old man, his eagle gaze sweeping the horizon.

"Down the road from Grass Valley. You can't see from here."

"Wal, come in an' let's get ready."

Isbel's house had not been constructed with the idea of repelling an attack from a band of Apaches. The long living room of the main cabin was the one selected for defense and protection. This room had two windows and a door facing the lane, and a door at each end, one of which opened into the kitchen and the other into an adjoining and later-built cabin. The logs of this main cabin were of large size, and the doors and window coverings were heavy, affording safer protection from bullets than the other cabins.

When Jean went in he seemed to see a host of white faces lifted to him. His sister Ann, his two sisters-in-law, the children, all mutely watched him with eyes that would haunt him.

"Wal, Blaisdell, Jean says Jorth an' his precious gang of rustlers are on the way heah," announced the rancher.

"Damn me if it's not a bad day fer Lee Jorth!" declared Blaisdell.

"Clear off that table," ordered Isbel, "an' fetch out all the guns an' shells we got."

Once laid upon the table these presented a formidable arsenal, which consisted of the three new .44 Winchesters that Jean had brought with him from the coast; the enormous buffalo, or so-called "needle" gun, that Gaston Isbel had used for years; a Henry rifle which Blaisdell had brought, and half a dozen six-shooters. Piles and packages of ammunition littered the table.

"Sort out these heah shells," said Isbel. "Everybody wants to get hold of his own."

Jacobs, the neighbor who was present, was a thick-set, bearded man, rather jovial among those lean-jawed Texans. He carried a .44 rifle of an old pattern. "Wal, boys, if I'd knowed we was in fer some fun I'd hev fetched more shells. Only got one magazine full. Mebbe them new .44's will fit my gun."

It was discovered that the ammunition Jean had brought in quantity fitted Jacobs's rifle, a fact which afforded peculiar satisfaction to all the men present.

"Wal, shore we're lucky," declared Gaston Isbel.

The women sat apart, in the corner toward the kitchen, and there seemed to be a strange fascination for them in the talk and action of the men. The wife of Jacobs was a little woman, with homely face and very bright eyes. Jean thought that she would be a help in that household during the next doubtful hours.

Every moment Jean would go to the window and peer out down the road. His companions evidently relied upon him, for no one else looked out. Now that the suspense of days and weeks was over, these Texans faced the issue with talk and act not noticeably different from those of ordinary moments.

At last Jean espied the dark mass of horsemen out in the valley road. They were close together, walking their mounts, and evidently in earnest conversation. After several ineffectual attempts Jean counted eleven horses, every one of which he was sure bore a rider.

"Dad, look out!" called Jean.

Gaston Isbel strode to the door and stood looking, without a word.

The other men crowded to the windows. Blaisdell cursed under his breath. Jacobs said: "By Golly! Come to pay us a call!" The women sat motionless, with dark, strained eyes. The children ceased their play and looked fearfully to their mother.

When just out of rifle shot of the cabins the band of horsemen halted and lined up in a half circle, all facing the ranch. They were close enough for Jean to see their gestures, but he could not recognize any of their faces. It struck him singularly that not one of them wore a mask.

"Jean, do you know any of them?" asked his father.

"No, not yet. They're too far off."

"Dad, I'll get your old telescope," said Guy Isbel, and he ran out toward the adjoining cabin.

Blaisdell shook his big, hoary head and rumbled out of

his bull-like neck, "Wal, now you're heah, you sheep fellars, what are you goin' to do aboot it?"

Guy Isbel returned with a yard-long telescope, which he passed to his father. The old man took it with shaking hands and leveled it. Suddenly it was as if he had been transfixed; then he lowered the glass, shaking violently, and his face grew gray with an exceeding bitter wrath.

"Jorth!" he swore, harshly.

Jean had only to look at his father to know that recognition had been like a mortal shock. It passed. Again the rancher leveled the glass.

"Wal, Blaisdell, there's our old Texas friend, Daggs," he drawled, dryly. "An' Greaves, our honest storekeeper of Grass Valley. An' there's Stonewall Jackson Jorth. An' Tad Jorth, with the same old red nose! . . . An', say, damn if one of that gang isn't Queen, as bad a gun fighter as Texas ever bred. Shore I thought he'd been killed in the Big Bend country. So I heard. . . . An' there's Craig, another respectable sheepman of Grass Valley. Haw-haw! . . . An', wal, I don't recognize any more of them."

Jean forthwith took the glass and moved it slowly across the faces of that group of horsemen. "Simm Bruce," he said, instantly. "I see Colter. And, yes, Greaves is there. I've seen the man next to him—face like a ham. . . ."

"Shore that is Craig," interrupted his father.

Jean knew the dark face of Lee Jorth by the resemblance it bore to Ellen's, and the recognition brought a twinge. He thought, too, that he could tell the other Jorths. He asked his father to describe Daggs and then Queen. It was not likely that Jean would fail to know these several men in the future. Then Blaisdell asked for the telescope and, when he got through looking and cursing, he passed it on to others, who, one by one, took a long look, until finally it came back to the old rancher.

"Wal, Daggs is wavin' his hand heah an' there, like a

general aboot to send out scouts. Haw-haw! . . . An' 'pears to me he's not overlookin' our hosses. Wal, that's natural for a rustler. He'd have to steal a hoss or a steer before goin' into a fight or to dinner or to a funeral."

"It 'll be his funeral if he goes to foolin' 'round them hosses," declared Guy Isbel, peering anxiously out of the door.

"Wal, son, shore it 'll be somebody's funeral," replied his father.

Jean paid but little heed to the conversation. With sharp eyes fixed upon the horsemen, he tried to grasp at their intention. Daggs pointed to the horses in the pasture lot that lay between him and the house. These animals were the best on the range and belonged mostly to Guy Isbel, who was the horse fancier and trader of the family. His horses were his passion.

"Looks like they'd do some horse stealin'," said Jean.

"Lend me that glass," demanded Guy, forcefully. He surveyed the band of men for a long moment, then he handed the glass back to Jean.

"I'm goin' out there after my hosses," he declared.

"No!" exclaimed his father.

"That gang come to steal an' not to fight. Can't you see that? If they meant to fight they'd do it. They're out there arguin' about my hosses."

Guy picked up his rifle. He looked sullenly determined and the gleam in his eye was one of fearlessness.

"Son, I know Daggs," said his father. "An' I know Jorth. They've come to kill us. It 'll be shore death for y'u to go out there."

"I'm goin', anyhow. They can't steal my hosses out from under my eyes. An' they ain't in range."

"Wal, Guy, you ain't goin' alone," spoke up Jacobs, cheerily, as he came forward.

The red-haired young wife of Guy Isbel showed no

change of her grave face. She had been reared in a stern school. She knew men in times like these. But Jacobs's wife appealed to him, "Bill, don't risk your life for a horse or two."

Jacobs laughed and answered, "Not much risk," and went out with Guy. To Jean their action seemed foolhardy. He kept a keen eye on them and saw instantly when the band became aware of Guy's and Jacob's entrance into the pasture. It took only another second then to realize that Daggs and Jorth had deadly intent. Jean saw Daggs slip out of his saddle, rifle in hand. Others of the gang did likewise, until half of them were dismounted.

"Dad, they're goin' to shoot," called out Jean, sharply. "Yell for Guy and Jacobs. Make them come back."

The old man shouted; Bill Isbel yelled; Blaisdell lifted his stentorian voice.

Jean screamed piercingly: "Guy! Run! Run!"

But Guy Isbel and his companion strode on into the pasture, as if they had not heard, as if no menacing horse thieves were within miles. They had covered about a quarter of the distance across the pasture, and were nearing the horses, when Jean saw red flashes and white puffs of smoke burst out from the front of that dark band of rustlers. Then followed the sharp, rattling crack of rifles.

Guy Isbel stopped short, and, dropping his gun, he threw up his arms and fell headlong. Jacobs acted as if he had suddenly encountered an invisible blow. He had been hit. Turning, he began to run and ran fast for a few paces. There were more quick, sharp shots. He let go of his rifle. His running broke. Walking, reeling, staggering, he kept on. A hoarse cry came from him. Then a single rifle shot pealed out. Jean heard the bullet strike. Jacobs fell to his knees, then forward on his face.

Jean Isbel felt himself turned to marble. The suddenness of this tragedy paralyzed him. His gaze remained riveted on those prostrate forms.

A hand clutched his arm—a shaking woman's hand, slim and hard and tense.

"Bill's—killed!" whispered a broken voice. "I was watchin'. . . . They're both dead!"

The wives of Jacobs and Guy Isbel had slipped up behind Jean and from behind him they had seen the tragedy.

"I asked Bill—not to—go," faltered the Jacobs woman, and, covering her face with her hands, she groped back to the corner of the cabin, where the other women, shaking and white, received her in their arms. Guy Isbel's wife stood at the window, peering over Jean's shoulder. She had the nerve of a man. She had looked out upon death before.

"Yes, they're dead," she said, bitterly. "An' how are we goin' to get their bodies?"

At this Gaston Isbel seemed to rouse from the cold spell that had transfixed him.

"God, this is hell for our women," he cried out, hoarsely. "My son—my son! . . . Murdered by the Jorths!" Then he swore a terrible oath.

Jean saw the remainder of the mounted rustlers get off, and then all of them leading their horses, they began to move around to the left.

"Dad, they're movin' round," said Jean.

"Up to some trick," declared Bill Isbel.

"Bill, you make a hole through the back wall, say aboot the fifth log up," ordered the father. "Shore we've got to look out."

The elder son grasped a tool and, scattering the children, who had been playing near the back corner, he began to work at the point designated. The little children backed away with fixed, wondering, grave eyes. The women moved their chairs, and huddled together as if waiting and listening.

Jean watched the rustlers until they passed out of his sight. They had moved toward the sloping, brushy ground to the north and west of the cabins.

"Let me know when you get a hole in the back wall," said Jean, and he went through the kitchen and cautiously out another door to slip into a low-roofed, shed-like end of the rambling cabin. This small space was used to store winter firewood. The chinks between the walls had not been filled with adobe clay, and he could see out on three sides. The rustlers were going into the juniper brush. They moved out of sight, and presently reappeared without their horses. It looked to Jean as if they intended to attack the cabins. Then they halted at the edge of the brush and held a long consultation. Jean could see them distinctly, though they were too far distant for him to recognize any particular man. One of them, however, stood and moved apart from the closely massed group. Evidently, from his strides and gestures, he was exhorting his listeners. Jean concluded this was either Daggs or Jorth. Whoever it was had a loud, coarse voice, and this and his actions impressed Jean with a suspicion that the man was under the influence of the bottle.

Presently Bill Isbel called Jean in a low voice. "Jean, I got the hole made, but we can't see any one."

"I see them," Jean replied. "They're havin' a powwow. Looks to me like either Jorth or Daggs is drunk. He's arguin' to charge us, an' the rest of the gang are holdin' back. . . . Tell dad, an' all of you keep watchin'. I'll let you know when they make a move."

Jorth's gang appeared to be in no hurry to expose their plan of battle. Gradually the group disintegrated a little; some of them sat down; others walked to and fro. Presently two of them went into the brush, probably back to the horses. In a few moments they reappeared, carrying a pack. And when this was deposited on the ground all the rustlers sat down around it. They had brought food and drink. Jean had to utter a grim laugh at their coolness; and he was reminded of many dare-devil deeds known to have been perpetrated by the Hash Knife Gang. Jean was glad of a reprieve. The longer the rustlers put off an attack the more time the allies of the Isbels would have to get here. Rather hazardous, however, would it be now for anyone to attempt to get to the Isbel cabins in the daytime. Night would be more favorable.

Twice Bill Isbel came through the kitchen to whisper to Jean. The strain in the large room, from which the rustlers could not be seen, must have been great. Jean told him all he had seen and what he thought about it. "Eatin' an' drinkin'!" ejaculated Bill. "Well, I'll be—! That 'll jar the old man. He wants to get the fight over."

"Tell him I said it 'll be over too quick—for us—unless we are mighty careful," replied Jean, sharply.

Bill went back muttering to himself. Then followed a long wait, fraught with suspense, during which Jean watched the rustlers regale themselves. The day was hot and still. And the unnatural silence of the cabin was broken now and then by the gay laughter of the children. The sound shocked and haunted Jean. Playing children! Then another sound, so faint he had to strain to hear it, disturbed and saddened him—his father's slow tread up and down the cabin floor, to and fro, to and fro. What must be in his father's heart this day!

At length the rustlers rose and, with rifles in hand, they moved as one man down the slope. They came several hundred yards closer, until Jean, grimly cocking his rifle, muttered to himself that a few more rods closer would mean the end of several of that gang. They knew the range of a rifle well enough, and once more sheered off at right angles with the cabin. When they got even with the line of corrals they stooped down and were lost to Jean's sight. This fact caused him alarm. They were, of course, crawling up on the cabins. At the end of that line of corrals ran a ditch, the bank of which was high enough to afford cover. Moreover, it ran along in front of the cabins, scarcely a hundred yards, and it was covered with grass and little clumps of brush, from behind which the rustlers could fire into the windows and through the clay chinks without any considerable risk to themselves. As they did not come into sight again, Jean concluded he had discovered their plan. Still, he waited awhile longer, until he saw faint, little clouds of dust rising from behind the far end of the embankment. That discovery made him rush out, and through the kitchen to the large cabin, where his sudden appearance startled the men.

"Get back out of sight!" he ordered, sharply, and with swift steps he reached the door and closed it. "They're behind the bank out there by the corrals. An' they're goin' to crawl down the ditch closer to us. . . . It looks bad. They'll have grass an' brush to shoot from. We've got to be mighty careful how we peep out."

"Ahuh! All right," replied his father. "You women keep the kids with you in that corner. An' you all better lay down flat."

Blaisdell, Bill Isbel, and the old man crouched at the large window, peeping through cracks in the rough edges of the logs. Jean took his post beside the small window, with his keen eyes vibrating like a compass needle. The movement of a blade of grass, the flight of a grasshopper could not escape his trained sight.

"Look sharp now!" he called to the other men. "I see dust. . . . They're workin' along almost to that bare spot on the bank. . . . I saw the tip of a rifle . . . a black hat . . . more dust. They're spreadin' along behind the bank."

Loud voices, and then thick clouds of yellow dust, coming from behind the highest and brushiest line of the embankment, attested to the truth of Jean's observation, and also to a reckless disregard of danger.

Suddenly Jean caught a glint of moving color through the fringe of brush. Instantly he was strung like a whipcord.

Then a tall, hatless and coatless man stepped up in plain sight. The sun shone on his fair, ruffled hair. Daggs!

"Hey, you —— —— Isbels!" he bawled, in magnificent derisive boldness. "Come out an' fight!"

Quick as lightning Jean threw up his rifle and fired. He saw tufts of fair hair fly from Daggs's head. He saw the squirt of red blood. Then quick shots from his comrades rang out. They all hit the swaying body of the rustler. But Jean knew with a terrible thrill that his bullet had killed Daggs before the other three struck. Daggs fell forward, his arms and half his body resting over the embankment. Then the rustlers dragged him back out of sight. Hoarse shouts rose. A cloud of yellow dust drifted away from the spot.

"Daggs!" burst out Gaston Isbel. "Jean, you knocked off the top of his haid. I seen that when I was pullin' trigger. Shore we over heah wasted our shots."

"God! he must have been crazy or drunk—to pop up there—an' brace us that way," said Blaisdell, breathing hard.

"Arizona is bad for Texans," replied Isbel, sardonically. "Shore it's been too peaceful heah. Rustlers have no practice at fightin'. An' I reckon Daggs forgot."

"Daggs made as crazy a move as that of Guy an' Jacobs," spoke up Jean. "They were overbold, an' he was drunk. Let them be a lesson to us."

Jean had smelled whisky upon his entrance to this cabin. Bill was a hard drinker, and his father was not immune. Blaisdell, too, drank heavily upon occasions. Jean made a mental note that he would not permit their chances to become impaired by liquor.

Rifles began to crack, and puffs of smoke rose all along the embankment for the space of a hundred feet. Bullets whistled through the rude window casing and spattered on the heavy door, and one split the clay between the logs before Jean, narrowly missing him. Another volley followed, then another. The rustlers had repeating rifles and they were emptying their magazines. Jean changed his position. The other men profited by his wise move. The volleys had merged into one continuous rattling roar of rifle shots. Then came a sudden cessation of reports, with silence of relief. The cabin was full of dust, mingled with the smoke from the shots of Jean and his companions. Jean heard the stifled breaths of the children. Evidently they were terror-stricken, but they did not cry out. The women uttered no sound.

A loud voice pealed from behind the embankment.

"Come out an' fight! Do you Isbels want to be killed like sheep?"

This sally gained no reply. Jean returned to his post by the window and his comrades followed his example. And they exercised extreme caution when they peeped out.

"Boys, don't shoot till you see one," said Gaston Isbel. "Maybe after a while they'll get careless. But Jorth will never show himself."

The rustlers did not again resort to volleys. One by one, from different angles, they began to shoot, and they were not firing at random. A few bullets came straight in at the windows to pat into the walls; a few others ticked and splintered the edges of the windows; and most of them broke through the clay chinks between the logs. It dawned upon Jean that these dangerous shots were not accident. They were well aimed, and most of them hit low down. The cunning rustlers had some unerring riflemen and they were picking out the vulnerable places all along the front of the cabin. If Jean had not been lying flat he would have been hit twice. Presently he conceived the idea of driving pegs between the logs, high up, and, kneeling on these, he managed to peep out from the upper edge of the window. But this position was awkward and difficult to hold for long.

He heard a bullet hit one of his comrades. Whoever had been struck never uttered a sound. Jean turned to look. Bill Isbel was holding his shoulder, where red splotches appeared on his shirt. He shook his head at Jean, evidently to make light of the wound. The women and children were lying face down and could not see what was happening. Plain it was that Bill did not want them to know. Blaisdell bound up the bloody shoulder with a scarf.

Steady firing from the rustlers went on, at the rate of one shot every few minutes. The Isbels did not return these. Jean did not fire again that afternoon. Toward sunset, when the besiegers appeared to grow restless or careless, Blaisdell fired at something moving behind the brush; and Gaston Isbel's huge buffalo gun boomed out.

"Wal, what 're they goin' to do after dark, an' what 're *we* goin' to do?" grumbled Blaisdell.

"Reckon they'll never charge us," said Gaston.

"They might set fire to the cabins," added Bill Isbel. He appeared to be the gloomiest of the Isbel faction. There was something on his mind.

"Wal, the Jorths are bad, but I reckon they'd not burn us alive," replied Blaisdell.

"Hah!" ejaculated Gaston Isbel. "Much you know aboot Lee Jorth. He would skin me alive an' throw red-hot coals on my raw flesh."

So they talked during the hour from sunset to dark.

Jean Isbel had little to say. He was revolving possibilities in his mind. Darkness brought a change in the attack of the rustlers. They stationed men at four points around the cabins; and every few minutes one of these outposts would fire. These bullets embedded themselves in the logs, causing but little anxiety to the Isbels.

"Jean, what you make of it?" asked the old rancher.

"Looks to me this way," replied Jean. "They're set for a long fight. They're shootin' just to let us know they're on the watch."

"Ahuh! Wal, what 're you goin' to do aboot it?"

"I'm goin' out there presently."

Gaston Isbel grunted his satisfaction at this intention of Jean's.

All was pitch dark inside the cabin. The women had water and food at hand. Jean kept a sharp lookout from his window while he ate his supper of meat, bread, and milk. At last the children, worn out by the long day, fell asleep. The women whispered a little in their corner.

About nine o'clock Jean signified his intention of going out to reconnoitre.

"Dad, they've got the best of us in the daytime," he said, "but not after dark."

Jean buckled on a belt that carried shells, a bowie knife, and revolver, and with rifle in hand he went out through the kitchen to the yard. The night was darker than usual, as some of the stars were hidden by clouds. He leaned against the log cabin, waiting for his eyes to become perfectly adjusted to the darkness. Like an Indian. Jean could see well at night. He knew every point around cabins and sheds and corrals, every post, log, tree, rock, adjacent to the ranch. After perhaps a quarter of an hour watching, during which time several shots were fired from behind the embankment and one each from the rustlers at the other locations. Jean slipped out on his quest.

He kept in the shadow of the cabin walls, then the line of orchard trees, then a row of currant bushes. Here, crouching low, he halted to look and listen. He was now at the edge of the open ground, with the gently rising slope before him. He could see the dark patches of cedar and juniper trees. On the north side of the cabin a streak of fire flashed in the blackness, and a shot rang out. Jean heard the bullet hit the cabin. Then silence enfolded the lonely ranch and the darkness lay like a black blanket. A low hum of insects pervaded the air. Dull sheets of lightning illumined the dark horizon to the south. Once Jean heard voices, but could not tell from which direction they came. To the west of him then flared out another rifle shot. The bullet whistled down over Jean to thud into the cabin.

Jean made a careful study of the obscure, gray-black open before him and then the background to his rear. So long as he kept the dense shadows behind him he could not be seen. He slipped from behind his covert and, gliding with absolutely noiseless footsteps, he gained the first clump of junipers. Here he waited patiently and motionlessly for another round of shots from the rustlers. After the second shot from the west side Jean sheered off to the right. Patches of brush, clumps of juniper, and isolated cedars covered this slope, affording Jean a perfect means for his purpose, which was to make a detour and come up behind the rustler who was firing from that side. Jean climbed to the top of the ridge, descended the opposite slope, made his turn to the left, and slowly worked up behind the point near where he expected to locate the rustler. Long habit in the open, by day and night, rendered his sense of direction almost as perfect as sight itself. The first flash of fire he saw from this side proved that he had come straight up toward his man. Jean's intention was to crawl up on this one of the Jorth gang and silently kill him with a knife. If the plan worked successfully, Jean meant to work round to the next rustler. Laying aside his rifle, he crawled forward on hands and knees, making no more sound than a cat. His approach was slow. He had to pick his way, be careful not to break twigs nor rattle stones. His buckskin garments made no sound against the brush. Jean located the rustler sitting on the top of the ridge in the center of an open space. He was alone. Jean saw the dull-red end of the cigarette he was smoking. The ground on the ridge top was rocky and not well adapted for Jean's purpose. He had to abandon the idea of crawling up on the rustler. Whereupon, Jean turned back, patiently and slowly, to get his rifle.

Upon securing it he began to retrace his course, this time more slowly than before, as he was hampered by the rifle. But he did not make the slightest sound, and at length he reached the edge of the open ridge top, once more to espy the dark form of the rustler silhouetted against the sky. The distance was not more than fifty yards.

As Jean rose to his knee and carefully lifted his rifle round to avoid the twigs of a juniper he suddenly experienced another emotion besides the one of grim, hard wrath at the Jorths. It was an emotion that sickened him, made him weak internally, a cold, shaking, ungovernable sensation. Suppose this man was Ellen Jorth's father. Jean lowered the rifle. He felt it shake over his knee. He was trembling all over. The astounding discovery that he did not want to kill Ellen's father—that he could not do it— awakened Jean to the despairing nature of his love for her. In this grim moment of indecision, when he knew his Indian subtlety and ability gave him a great advantage over the Jorths, he fully realized his strange, hopeless, and irresistible love for the girl. He made no attempt to deny it any longer. Like the night and the lonely wilderness around him, like the inevitableness of this Jorth-Isbel feud, this love of his was a thing, a fact, a reality.

He breathed to his own inward ear, to his soul—he could not kill Ellen Jorth's father. Feud or no feud, Isbel or not, he could not deliberately do it. And why not? There was no answer. Was he not faithless to his father? He had no hope of ever winning Ellen Jorth. He did not want the love of a girl of her character. But he loved her. And his struggle must be against the insidious and mysterious growth of that passion. It swayed him already. It made him a coward. Through his mind and heart swept the memory of Ellen Jorth, her beauty and charm, her boldness and pathos, her shame and her degradation. And the sweetness of her outweighed the boldness. And the mystery of her arrayed itself in unquenchable protest against her acknowledged shame. Jean lifted his face to the heavens, to the pitiless white stars, to the infinite depths of the dark-blue sky. He could sense the fact of his being an atom in the universe of nature. What was he, what was his revengeful father, what were hate and passion and strife in comparison to the nameless something, immense and everlasting, that he sensed in this dark moment?

But the rustlers—Daggs—the Jorths—they had killed his brother Guy—murdered him brutally and ruthlessly. Guy had been a playmate of Jean's—a favorite brother. Bill had been secretive and selfish. Jean had never loved him as he did Guy. Guy lay dead down there on the meadow. This feud had begun to run its bloody course. Jean steeled his nerve. The hot blood crept back along his veins. The dark and masterful tide of revenge waved over him. The keen edge of his mind then cut out sharp and trenchant thoughts. He must kill when and where he could. This man could hardly be Ellen Jorth's father. Jorth would be with the main crowd, directing hostilities. Jean could shoot this rustler guard and his shot would be taken by the gang as the regular one from their comrade. Then swiftly Jean leveled his rifle, covered the dark form, grew cold and set, and pressed the trigger. After the report he rose and wheeled away. He did not look nor listen for the result of his shot. A clammy sweat wet his face, the hollow of his hands, his breast. A horrible, leaden, thick sensation oppressed his heart. Nature had endowed him with Indian gifts, but the exercise of them to this end caused a revolt in his soul.

Nevertheless, it was the Isbel blood that dominated him. The wind blew cool on his face. The burden upon his shoulders seemed to lift. The clamoring whispers grew fainter in his ears. And by the time he had retraced his cautious steps back to the orchard all his physical being was strung to the task at hand. Something had come between his reflective self and this man of action.

Crossing the lane, he took to the west line of sheds, and passed beyond them into the meadow. In the grass he crawled silently away to the right, using the same precaution that had actuated him on the slope, only here he did not pause so often, nor move so slowly. Jean aimed to go far enough to the right to pass the end of the embankment behind which the rustlers had found such efficient cover. This ditch had been made to keep water, during spring thaws and summer storms, from pouring off the slope to flood the corrals.

Jean miscalculated and found he had come upon the embankment somewhat to the left of the end, which fact, however, caused him no uneasiness. He lay there awhile to listen. Again he heard voices. After a time a shot pealed out. He did not see the flash, but he calculated that it had come from the north side of the cabins.

The next quarter of an hour discovered to Jean that the nearest guard was firing from the top of the embankment, perhaps a hundred yards distant, and a second one was performing the same office from a point apparently only a few yards farther on. Two rustlers close together! Jean had not calculated upon that. For a little while he pondered on what was best to do, and at length decided to crawl round behind them, and as close as the situation made advisable.

He found the ditch behind the embankment a favorable path by which to stalk these enemies. It was dry and sandy, with borders of high weeds. The only drawback was that it was almost impossible for him to keep from brushing against the dry, invisible branches of the weeds. To offset this he wormed his way like a snail, inch by inch, taking a long time before he caught sight of the sitting figure of a man, black against the dark-blue sky. This rustler had fired his rifle three times during Jean's slow approach. Jean watched and listened a few moments, then wormed himself closer and closer, until the man was within twenty steps of him.

Jean smelled tobacco smoke, but could see no light of pipe or cigarette, because the fellow's back was turned.

"Say, Ben," said this man to his companion sitting hunched up a few yards distant, "shore it strikes me queer thet Somers ain't shootin' any over thar."

Jean recognized the dry, drawling voice of Greaves, and the shock of it seemed to contract the muscles of his whole thrilling body, like that of a panther about to spring.

CHAPTER 8

I was shore thinkin' thet same," said the other man. "An', say, didn't thet last shot sound too sharp fer Somers's forty-five?"

"Come to think of it, I reckon it did," replied Greaves.

"Wal, I'll go around over thar an' see."

The dark form of the rustler slipped out of sight over the embankment.

"Better go slow an' careful," warned Greaves. "An' only go close enough to call Somers. . . . Mebbe thet damn half-breed Isbel is comin' some Injun on us."

Jean heard the soft swish of footsteps through wet grass. Then all was still. He lay flat, with his cheek on the sand, and he had to look ahead and upward to make out the dark figure of Greaves on the bank. One way or another he meant to kill Greaves, and he had the will power to resist the strongest gust of passion that had ever stormed his breast. If he arose and shot the rustler, that act would defeat his plan of slipping on around upon the other outposts who were firing at the cabins. Jean wanted to call softly to Greaves, "You're right about the half-breed!" and then, as he wheeled aghast, to kill him as he moved. But it suited Jean to risk leaping upon the man. Jean did not

waste time in trying to understand the strange, deadly instinct that gripped him at the moment. But he realized
then he had chosen the most perilous plan to get rid of
Greaves.

Jean drew a long, deep breath and held it. He let go of
his rifle. He rose, silently as a lifting shadow. He drew the
bowie knife. Then with light, swift bounds he glided up
the bank. Greaves must have heard a rustling—a soft,
quick pad of moccasin, for he turned with a start. And that
instant Jean's left arm darted like a striking snake round
Greaves's neck and closed tight and hard. With his right
hand free, holding the knife, Jean might have ended the
deadly business in just one move. But when his bared arm
felt the hot, bulging neck something terrible burst out of
the depths of him. To kill this enemy of his father's was
not enough! Physical contact had unleashed the savage
soul of the Indian. Yet there was more, and as Jean gave
the straining body a tremendous jerk backward, he felt
the same strange thrill, the dark joy that he had known
when his fist had smashed the face of Simm Bruce.
Greaves had leered—he had corroborated Bruce's vile
insinuation about Ellen Jorth. So it was more than hate
that actuated Jean Isbel.

Greaves was heavy and powerful. He whirled himself,
feet first, over backward, in a lunge like that of a lassoed
steer. But Jean's hold held. They rolled down the bank into
the sandy ditch, and Jean landed uppermost, with his body
at right angles with that of his adversary.

"Greaves, your hunch was right," hissed Jean. "It's the
half-breed. . . . An' I'm goin' to cut you—first for Ellen
Jorth—an' then for Gaston Isbel!"

Jean gazed down into the gleaming eyes. Then his right
arm whipped the big blade. It flashed. It fell. Low down,
as far as Jean could reach, it entered Greaves's body.

All the heavy, muscular frame of Greaves seemed to

contract and burst. His spring was that of an animal in terror and agony. It was so tremendous that it broke Jean's hold. Greaves let out a strangled yell that cleared, swelling wildly, with a hideous mortal note. He wrestled free. The big knife came out. Supple and swift, he got to his knees. He had his gun out when Jean reached him again. Like a bear Jean enveloped him. Greaves shot, but he could not raise the gun, nor twist it far enough. Then Jean, letting go with his right arm, swung the bowie. Greaves's strength went out in an awful, hoarse cry. His gun boomed again, then dropped from his hand. He swayed. Jean let go. And that enemy of the Isbels sank limply in the ditch. Jean's eyes roved for his rifle and caught the starlit gleam of it. Snatching it up, he leaped over the embankment and ran straight for the cabins. From all around yells of the Jorth faction attested to their excitement and fury.

A fence loomed up gray in the obscurity. Jean vaulted it, darted across the lane into the shadow of the corral, and soon gained the first cabin. Here he leaned to regain his breath. His heart pounded high and seemed too large for his breast. The hot blood beat and surged all over his body. Sweat poured off him. His teeth were clenched tight as a vise, and it took effort on his part to open his mouth so he could breathe more freely and deeply. But these physical sensations were as nothing compared to the tumult of his mind. Then the instinct, the spell, let go its grip and he could think. He had avenged Guy, he had depleted the ranks of the Jorths, he had made good the brag of his father, all of which afforded him satisfaction. But these thoughts were not accountable for all that he felt, especially for the bittersweet sting of the fact that death to the defiler of Ellen Jorth could not efface the doubt, the regret which seemed to grow with the hours.

Groping his way into the woodshed, he entered the kitchen and, calling low, he went on into the main cabin.

"Jean! Jean!" came his father's shaking voice.

"Yes, I'm back," replied Jean.

"Are—you—all right?"

"Yes. I think I've got a bullet crease on my leg. I didn't know I had it till now. . . . It's bleedin' a little. But it's nothin'."

Jean heard soft steps and some one reached shaking hands for him. They belonged to his sister Ann. She embraced him. Jean felt the heave and throb of her breast.

"Why, Ann, I'm not hurt," he said, and held her close. "Now you lie down an' try to sleep."

In the black darkness of the cabin Jean led her back to the corner and his heart was full. Speech was difficult, because the very touch of Ann's hands had made him divine that the success of his venture in no wise changed the plight of the women.

"Wal, what happened out there?" demanded Blaisdell.

"I got two of them," replied Jean. "That fellow who was shootin' from the ridge west. An' the other was Greaves."

"Hah!" exclaimed his father.

"Shore then it was Greaves yellin'," declared Blaisdell. "By God, I never heard such yells! What'd you do, Jean?"

"I knifed him. You see, I'd planned to slip up on one after another. An' I didn't want to make noise. But I didn't get any farther than Greaves."

"Wal, I reckon that 'll end their shootin' in the dark," muttered Gaston Isbel. "We've got to be on the lookout for somethin' else—fire, most likely."

The old rancher's surmise proved to be partially correct. Jorth's faction ceased the shooting. Nothing further was seen or heard from them. But this silence and apparent break in the siege were harder to bear than deliberate hostility. The long, dark hours dragged by. The men took turns watching and resting, but none of them slept. At last the blackness paled and gray dawn stole out of the east.

The sky turned rose over the distant range and daylight came.

The children awoke hungry and noisy, having slept away their fears. The women took advantage of the quiet morning hour to get a hot breakfast.

"Maybe they've gone away," suggested Guy Isbel's wife, peering out of the window. She had done that several times since daybreak. Jean saw her somber gaze search the pasture until it rested upon the dark, prone shape of her dead husband, lying face down in the grass. Her look worried Jean.

"No, Esther, they've not gone yet," replied Jean. "I've seen some of them out there at the edge of the brush."

Blaisdell was optimistic. He said Jean's night work would have its effect and that the Jorth contingent would not renew the siege very determinedly. It turned out, however, that Blaisdell was wrong. Directly after sunrise they began to pour volleys from four sides and from closer range. During the night Jorth's gang had thrown earth banks and constructed log breastworks, from behind which they were now firing. Jean and his comrades could see the flashes of fire and streaks of smoke to such good advantage that they began to return the volleys.

In half an hour the cabin was so full of smoke that Jean could not see the womenfolk in their corner. The fierce attack then abated somewhat, and the firing became more intermittent, and therefore more carefully aimed. A glancing bullet cut a furrow in Blaisdell's hoary head, making a painful, though not serious wound. It was Esther Isbel who stopped the flow of blood and bound Blaisdell's head, a task which she performed skillfully and without a tremor. The old Texan could not sit still during this operation. Sight of the blood on his hands, which he tried to rub off, appeared to inflame him to a great degree.

"Isbel, we got to go out thar," he kept repeating, "an' kill them all."

"No, we're goin' to stay heah," replied Gaston Isbel. "Shore I'm lookin' for Blue an' Fredericks an' Gordon to open up out there. They ought to be heah, an' if they are y'u shore can bet they've got the fight sized up."

Isbel's hopes did not materialize. The shooting continued without any lull until about midday. Then the Jorth faction stopped.

"Wal, now what's up?" queried Isbel. "Boys, hold your fire an' let's wait."

Gradually the smoke wafted out of the windows and doors, until the room was once more clear. And at this juncture Esther Isbel came over to take another gaze out upon the meadows. Jean saw her suddenly start violently, then stiffen, with a trembling hand outstretched.

"Look!" she cried.

"Esther, get back," ordered the old rancher. "Keep away from that window."

"What the hell!" muttered Blaisdell. "She sees somethin', or she's gone dotty."

Esther seemed turned to stone. "Look! The hogs have broken into the pasture! . . . They'll eat Guy's body!"

Everyone was frozen with horror at Esther's statement. Jean took a swift survey of the pasture. A bunch of big black hogs had indeed appeared on the scene and were rooting around in the grass not far from where lay the bodies of Guy Isbel and Jacobs. This herd of hogs belonged to the rancher and was allowed to run wild.

"Jane, those hogs—" stammered Esther Isbel, to the wife of Jacobs. "Come! Look! . . . Do y'u know anythin' about hogs?"

The woman ran to the window and looked out. She stiffened as had Esther.

"Dad, will those hogs—eat human flesh?" queried Jean, breathlessly.

The old man stared out of the window. Surprise seemed to hold him. A completely unexpected situation had staggered him.

"Jean—can you—can you shoot that far?" he asked, huskily.

"To those hogs? No, it's out of range."

"Then, by God, we've got to stay trapped in heah an' watch an awful sight," ejaculated the old man, completely unnerved. "See that break in the fence! . . . Jorth's done that. . . . To let in the hogs!"

"Aw, Isbel, it's not so bad as all that," remonstrated Blaisdell, wagging his bloody head. "Jorth wouldn't do such a hell-bent trick."

"It's shore done."

"Wal, mebbe the hogs won't find Guy an Jacobs," returned Blaisdell, weakly. Plain it was that he only hoped for such a contingency and certainly doubted it.

"Look!" cried Esther Isbel, piercingly. "They're workin' straight up the pasture!"

Indeed, to Jean it appeared to be the fatal truth. He looked blankly, feeling a little sick. Ann Isbel came to peer out of the window and she uttered a cry. Jacobs's wife stood mute, as if dazed.

Blaisdell swore a mighty oath. "——— ———! Isbel, we cain't stand heah an' watch them hogs eat our people!"

"Wal, we'll have to. What else on earth can we do?"

Esther turned to the men. She was white and cold, except her eyes, which resembled gray flames.

"Somebody can run out there an' bury our dead men," she said.

"Why, child, it'd be shore death. Y'u saw what happened to Guy an' Jacobs. . . . We've jest got to bear it. Shore nobody needn't look out—an' see."

Jean wondered if it would be possible to keep from watching. The thing had a horrible fascination. The big hogs were rooting and tearing in the grass, some of them lazy, others nimble, and all were gradually working closer and closer to the bodies. The leader, a huge, gaunt boar, that had fared ill all his life in this barren country, was scarcely fifty feet away from where Guy Isbel lay.

"Ann, get me some of your clothes, an' a sunbonnet— quick," said Jean, forced out of his lethargy. "I'll run out there disguised. Maybe I can go through with it."

"No!" ordered his father, positively, and with dark face flaming. "Guy an' Jacobs are dead. We cain't help them now."

"But, dad—" pleaded Jean. He had been wrought to a pitch by Esther's blaze of passion, by the agony in the face of the other woman.

"I tell y'u no!" thundered Gaston Isbel, flinging his arms wide.

"*I will go!*" cried Esther, her voice ringing.

"You won't go alone!" instantly answered the wife of Jacobs, repeating unconsciously the words her husband had spoken.

"You stay right heah," shouted Gaston Isbel, hoarsely.

"I'm goin'," replied Esther. "You've no hold over me. My husband is dead. No one can stop me. I'm goin' out there to drive those hogs away an' bury him."

"Esther, for Heaven's sake, listen," replied Isbel. "If y'u show yourself outside, Jorth an' his gang will kill y'u."

"They may be mean, but no white men could be so low as that."

Then they pleaded with her to give up her purpose. But in vain! She pushed them back and ran out through the kitchen with Jacobs's wife following her. Jean turned to the window in time to see both women run out into the lane. Jean looked fearfully, and listened for shots. But only a loud, "Haw! Haw!" came from the watchers out-side. That coarse laugh relieved the tension in Jean's breast. Possibly the Jorths were not as black as his father painted them. The two women entered an open shed and came forth with a shovel and spade.

"Shore they've got to hurry," burst out Gaston Isbel.

Shifting his gaze, Jean understood the import of his fa-ther's speech. The leader of the hogs had no doubt scented the bodies. Suddenly he espied them and broke into a trot.

"Run, Esther, run!" yelled Jean, with all his might.

That urged the women to flight. Jean began to shoot. The hog reached the body of Guy. Jean's shots did not reach nor frighten the beast. All the hogs now had caught a scent and went ambling toward their leader. Esther and her companion passed swiftly out of sight behind a corral. Loud and piercingly, with some awful note, rang out their screams. The hogs appeared frightened. The leader lifted his long snout, looked, and turned away. The oth-ers had halted. Then they, too, wheeled and ran off.

All was silent then in the cabin and also outside wher-ever the Jorth faction lay concealed. All eyes manifestly were fixed upon the brave wives. They spaded up the sod and dug a grave for Guy Isbel. For a shroud Esther wrapped him in her shawl. Then they buried him. Next they hurried to the side of Jacobs, who lay some yards away. They dug a grave for him. Mrs. Jacobs took off her outer skirt to wrap round him. Then the two women la-bored hard to lift him and lower him. Jacobs was a heavy man. When he had been covered his widow knelt beside his grave. Esther went back to the other. But she remained standing and did not look as if she prayed. Her aspect was tragic—that of a woman who had lost father, mother, sis-ters, brother, and now her husband, in this bloody Arizona land.

The deed and the demeanor of these wives of the murdered men surely must have shamed Jorth and his followers. They did not fire a shot during the ordeal nor give any sign of their presence.

Inside the cabin all were silent, too. Jean's eyes blurred so that he continually had to wipe them. Old Isbel made no effort to hide his tears. Blaisdell nodded his shaggy head and swallowed hard. The women sat staring into space. The children, in round-eyed dismay, gazed from one to the other of their elders.

"Wal, they're comin' back," declared Isbel, in immense relief. "An' so help me—Jorth let them bury their daid!"

The fact seemed to have been monstrously strange to Gaston Isbel. When the women entered the old man said, brokenly: "I'm shore glad. . . . An' I reckon I was wrong to oppose you . . . an' wrong to say what I did aboot Jorth."

No one had any chance to reply to Isbel, for the Jorth gang, as if to make up for lost time and surcharged feelings of shame, renewed the attack with such a persistent and furious volleying that the defenders did not risk a return shot. They all had to lie flat next to the lowest log in order to keep from being hit. Bullets rained in through the window. And all the clay between the logs low down was shot away. This fusillade lasted for more than an hour, then gradually the fire diminished on one side and then on the other until it became desultory and finally ceased.

"Ahuh! Shore they've shot their bolt," declared Gaston Isbel.

"Wal, I doon't know aboot that," returned Blaisdell, "but they've shot a hell of a lot of shells."

"Listen," suddenly called Jean. "Somebody's yellin'."

"Hey, Isbel!" came in loud, hoarse voice. "Let your women fight for you."

Gaston Isbel sat up with a start and his face turned livid. Jean needed no more to prove that the derisive voice from outside had belonged to Jorth. The old rancher lunged up to his full height and with reckless disregard of life he rushed to the window. "Jorth," he roared, "I dare you to meet me—man to man!"

This elicited no answer. Jean dragged his father away from the window. After that a waiting silence ensued, gradually less fraught with suspense. Blaisdell started conversation by saying he believed the fight was over for that particular time. No one disputed him. Evidently Gaston Isbel was loath to believe it. Jean, however, watching at the back of the kitchen, eventually discovered that the Jorth gang had lifted the siege. Jean saw them congregate at the edge of the brush, somewhat lower down than they had been the day before. A team of mules, drawing a wagon, appeared on the road, and turned toward the slope. Saddled horses were led down out of the junipers. Jean saw bodies, evidently of dead men, lifted into the wagon, to be hauled away toward the village. Seven mounted men, leading four riderless horses, rode out into the valley and followed the wagon.

"Dad, they've gone," declared Jean. "We had the best of this fight. . . . If only Guy an' Jacobs had listened!"

The old man nodded moodily. He had aged considerably during these two trying days. His hair was grayer. Now that the blaze and glow of the fight had passed he showed a subtle change, a fixed and morbid sadness, a resignation to a fate he had accepted.

The ordinary routine of ranch life did not return for the Isbels. Blaisdell returned home to settle matters there, so that he could devote all his time to this feud. Gaston Isbel sat down to wait for the members of his clan.

The male members of the family kept guard in turn over the ranch that night. And another day dawned. It brought word from Blaisdell that Blue, Fredericks, Gordon, and

Colmor were all at his house, on the way to join the Isbels. This news appeared greatly to rejuvenate Gaston Isbel. But his enthusiasm did not last long. Impatient and moody by turns, he paced or moped around the cabin, always looking out, sometimes toward Blaisdell's ranch, but mostly toward Grass Valley.

It struck Jean as singular that neither Esther Isbel nor Mrs. Jacobs suggested a reburial of their husbands. The two bereaved women did not ask for assistance, but repaired to the pasture, and there spent several hours working over the graves. They raised mounds, which they sodded, and then placed stones at the heads and feet. Lastly, they fenced in the graves.

"I reckon I'll hitch up an' drive back home," said Mrs. Jacobs, when she returned to the cabin. "I've much to do an' plan. Probably I'll go to my mother's home. She's old an' will be glad to have me."

"If I had any place to go to I'd sure go," declared Esther Isbel, bitterly.

Gaston Isbel heard this remark. He raised his face from his hands, evidently both nettled and hurt.

"Esther, shore that's not kind," he said.

The red-haired woman—for she did not appear to be a girl any more—halted before his chair and gazed down at him, with a terrible flare of scorn in her gray eyes.

"Gaston Isbel, all I've got to say to you is this," she retorted, with the voice of a man. "Seein' that you an' Lee Jorth hate each other, why couldn't you act like men? . . . You damned Texans, with your bloody feuds, draggin' in every relation, every friend to murder each other! That's not the way of Arizona men. . . . We've all got to suffer—an' we women be ruined for life—because *you* had differences with Jorth. If you were half a man you'd go out an' kill him yourself, an' not leave a lot of widows an' orphaned children!"

Jean himself writhed under the lash of her scorn. Gaston Isbel turned a dead white. He could not answer her. He seemed stricken with merciless truth. Slowly dropping his head, he remained motionless, a pathetic and tragic figure; and he did not stir until the rapid beat of hoofs denoted the approach of horsemen. Blaisdell appeared on his white charger, leading a pack animal. And behind rode a group of men, all heavily armed, and likewise with packs.

"Get down an' come in," was Isbel's greeting. "Bill— you look after their packs. Better leave the hosses saddled."

The booted and spurred riders trooped in, and their demeanor fitted their errand. Jean was acquainted with all of them. Fredericks was a lanky Texan, the color of dust, and he had yellow, clear eyes, like those of a hawk. His mother had been an Isbel. Gordon, too, was related to Jean's family, though distantly. He resembled an industrious miner more than a prosperous cattleman. Blue was the most striking of the visitors, as he was the most noted. A little, shrunken gray-eyed man, with years of cowboy written all over him, he looked the quiet, easy, cool, and deadly Texan he was reputed to be. Blue's Texas record was shady, and was seldom alluded to, as unfavorable comment had turned out to be hazardous. He was the only one of the group who did not carry a rifle. But he packed two guns, a habit not often noted in Texans, and almost never in Arizonians.

Colmor, Ann Isbel's fiancé, was the youngest member of the clan, and the one closest to Jean. His meeting with Ann affected Jean powerfully, and brought to a climax an idea that had been developing in Jean's mind. His sister devotedly loved this lean-faced, keen-eyed Arizonian; and it took no great insight to discover that Colmor reciprocated her affection. They were young. They had long life

before them. It seemed to Jean a pity that Colmor should
be drawn into this war. Jean watched them, as they conversed apart; and he saw Ann's hands creep up to Colmor's
breast, and he saw her dark eyes, eloquent, hungry, fearful, lifted with queries her lips did not speak. Jean stepped
beside them, and laid an arm over both their shoulders.

"Colmor, for Ann's sake you'd better back out of this
Jorth-Isbel fight," he whispered.

Colmor looked insulted. "But, Jean, it's Ann's father,"
he said. "I'm almost one of the family."

"You're Ann's sweetheart, an', by Heaven, I say you
oughtn't to go with us!" whispered Jean.

"Go—with—you," faltered Ann.

"Yes. Dad is goin' straight after Jorth. Can't you tell
that? An' there'll be one hell of a fight."

Ann looked up into Colmor's face with all her soul in
her eyes, but she did not speak. Her look was noble. She
yearned to guide him right, yet her lips were sealed. And
Colmor betrayed the trouble of his soul. The code of men
held him bound, and he could not break from it, though
he divined in that moment how truly it was wrong.

"Jean, your dad started me in the cattle business," said
Colmor, earnestly. "An' I'm doin' well now. An' when I
asked him for Ann he said he'd be glad to have me in the
family. . . . Well, when this talk of fight come up, I asked
your dad to let me go in on his side. He wouldn't hear of
it. But after a while, as the time passed an' he made more
enemies, he finally consented. I reckon he needs me now.
An' I can't back out, not even for Ann."

"I would if I were you," replied Jean, and knew that he
lied.

"Jean, I'm gamblin' to come out of the fight," said Colmor, with a smile. He had no morbid fears nor presenti-
ments, such as troubled Jean.

"Why, sure—you stand as good a chance as any one,"

rejoined Jean. "It wasn't that I was worryin' about so much."

"What was it, then?" asked Ann, steadily.

"If Andrew *does* come through alive he'll have blood on his hands," returned Jean, with passion. "He can't come through without it. . . . I've begun to feel what it means to have killed my fellow men. . . . An' I'd rather your husband an' the father of your children never felt that."

Colmor did not take Jean as subtly as Ann did. She shrunk a little. Her dark eyes dilated. But Colmor showed nothing of her spiritual reaction. He was young. He had wild blood. He was loyal to the Isbels.

"Jean, never worry about my conscience," he said, with a keen look. "Nothin' would tickle me any more than to get a shot at every damn one of the Jorths."

That established Colmor's status in regard to the Jorth-Isbel feud. Jean had no more to say. He respected Ann's friend and felt poignant sorrow for Ann.

Gaston Isbel called for meat and drink to be set on the table for his guests. When his wishes had been complied with the women took the children into the adjoining cabin and shut the door.

"Hah! Wal, we can eat an' talk now."

First the newcomers wanted to hear particulars of what had happened. Blaisdell had told all he knew and had seen, but that was not sufficient. They plied Gaston Isbel with questions. Laboriously and ponderously he rehearsed the experiences of the fight at the ranch, according to his impressions. Bill Isbel was exhorted to talk, but he had of late manifested a sullen and taciturn disposition. In spite of Jean's vigilance Bill had continued to imbibe red liquor. Then Jean was called upon to relate all he had seen and done. It had been Jean's intention to keep his mouth shut, first for his own sake and, secondly, because he did not like to talk of his deeds. But when thus appealed to by these somber-faced, intent-eyed men he divined that the more carefully he described the cruelty and baseness of their enemies, and the more vividly he presented his participation in the first fight of the feud the more strongly he would bind these friends to the Isbel cause. So he talked for an hour, beginning with his meeting with Colter up on the Rim and ending with an account of his killing Greaves. His listeners sat through this long narrative with unabated interest and at the close they were leaning forward, breathless and tense.

"Ah! So Greaves got his desserts at last," exclaimed Gordon.

All the men around the table made comments, and the last, from Blue, was the one that struck Jean forcibly.

"Shore thet was a strange an' a hell of a way to kill Greaves. Why'd you do thet, Jean?"

"I told you. I wanted to avoid noise an' I hoped to get more of them."

Blue nodded his lean, eagle-like head and sat thoughtfully, as if not convinced of anything save Jean's prowess. After a moment Blue spoke again.

"Then, goin' back to Jean's tellin' aboot trackin' rustled cattle, I've got this to say. I've long suspected thet somebody livin' right heah in the valley has been drivin' off cattle an' dealin' with rustlers. An' now I'm shore of it."

This speech did not elicit the amaze from Gaston Isbel that Jean expected it would.

"You mean Greaves or some of his friends?"

"No. They wasn't none of them in the cattle business, like we are. Shore we all knowed Greaves was crooked. But what I'm figgerin' is thet some so-called honest man in our settlement has been makin' crooked deals."

Blue was a man of deeds rather than words, and so much strong speech from him, whom everybody knew to be remarkably reliable and keen, made a profound impression upon most of the Isbel faction. But, to Jean's surprise, his father did not rave. It was Blaisdell who supplied the rage and invective. Bill Isbel, also, was strangely indifferent to this new element in the condition of cattle dealing. Suddenly Jean caught a vague flash of thought, as if he had intercepted the thought of another's mind, and he wondered—could his brother Bill know anything about this crooked work alluded to by Blue? Dismissing the conjecture, Jean listened earnestly.

"An' if it's true it shore makes this difference—we cain't blame all the rustlin' on to Jorth," concluded Blue.

"Wal, it's not true," declared Gaston Isbel, roughly. "Jorth an' his Hash Knife Gang are at the bottom of all the rustlin' in the valley for years back. An' they've got to be wiped out!"

"Isbel, I reckon we'd all feel better if we talk straight," replied Blue, coolly. "I'm heah to stand by the Isbels. An' y'u know what thet means. But I'm not heah to fight Jorth because he may be a rustler. The others may have their own reasons, but mine is this—you once stood by me in Texas when I was needin' friends. Wal, I'm standin' by y'u now. Jorth is your enemy, an' so he is mine."

Gaston Isbel bowed to this ultimatum, scarcely less agitated than when Esther Isbel had denounced him. His rabid and morbid hate of Jorth had eaten into his heart to take possession there, like the parasite that battened upon the life of its victim. Blue's steely voice, his cold, gray eyes, showed the unbiased truth of the man, as well as his fidelity to his creed. Here again, but in a different manner, Gaston Isbel had the fact flung at him that other men must suffer, perhaps die, for his hate. And the very soul of the old rancher apparently rose in passionate revolt against the blind, headlong, elemental strength of his nature. So it seemed to Jean, who, in love and pity that hourly grew, saw through his father. Was it too late? Alas! Gaston Isbel could never be turned back! Yet something was altering his brooding, fixed mind.

"Wal," said Blaisdell, gruffly, "let's get down to business. . . . I'm for havin' Blue be foreman of this heah outfit, an' all of us to do as he says."

Gaston Isbel opposed this selection and indeed resented it. He intended to lead the Isbel faction.

"All right, then. Give us a hunch what we're goin' to do," replied Blaisdell.

"We're goin' to ride off on Jorth's trail—an' one way or another—kill him—*kill him!* . . . I reckon that'll end the fight."

What did old Isbel have in his mind? His listeners shook their heads.

"No," asserted Blaisdell. "Killin' Jorth might be the end of your desires, Isbel, but it'd never end *our* fight. We'll have gone too far. . . . If we take Jorth's trail from heah it means we've got to wipe out that rustler gang, or stay to the last man."

"Yes, by God!" exclaimed Fredericks.

"Let's drink to thet!" said Blue. Strangely they all turned to this Texas gunman, instinctively recognizing in him the brain and heart, and the past deeds, that fitted him for the leadership of such a clan. Blue had all in life to lose, and nothing to gain. Yet his spirit was such that he could not lean to all the possible gain of the future, and leave a debt unpaid. Then his voice, his look, his influence were those of a fighter. They all drank with him, even Jean, who hated liquor. And this act of drinking seemed the climax of the council. Preparations were at once begun for their departure on Jorth's trail.

Jean took but little time for his own needs. A horse, a blanket, a knapsack of meat and bread, a canteen, and his weapons, with all the ammunition he could pack, made up his outfit. He wore his buckskin suit, leggings, and moccasins. Very soon the cavalcade was ready to depart. Jean tried not to watch Bill Isbel say good-by to his children, but it was impossible not to. Whatever Bill was, as a man, he was father of those children, and he loved them. How strange that the little ones seemed to realize the meaning of this good-by! They were grave, somber-eyed, pale up to the last moment, then they broke down and wept. Did they sense that their father would never come back? Jean caught that dark, fatalistic presentiment. Bill Isbel's convulsed face showed that he also caught it. Jean did not see Bill say good-by to his wife. But he heard her. Old Gaston Isbel forgot to speak to the children, or else could not. He never looked at them. And his good-by to Ann was as if he were only riding to the village for a day. Jean saw woman's love, woman's intuition, woman's grief in her eyes. He could not escape her. "Oh, Jean! oh, brother!" she whispered as she enfolded him. "It's awful! It's wrong! Wrong! Wrong! . . . Good-by! . . . If killing *must* be—see that y'u kill the Jorths! . . . Good-by!"

Even in Ann, gentle and mild, the Isbel blood spoke at the last. Jean gave Ann over to the pale-faced Colmor, who took her in his arms. Then Jean fled out to his horse. This cold-blooded devastation of a home was almost more than he could bear. There was love here. What would be left?

Colmor was the last one to come out to the horses. He did not walk erect, nor as one whose sight was clear. Then, as the silent, tense, grim men mounted their horses, Bill Isbel's eldest child, the boy, appeared in the door. His little form seemed instinct with a force vastly different from grief. His face was the face of an Isbel.

"Daddy—kill 'em all!" he shouted, with a passion all the fiercer for its incongruity to the treble voice.

So the poison had spread from father to son.

CHAPTER 9

Half a mile from the Isbel ranch the cavalcade passed the log cabin of Evarts, father of the boy who had tended sheep with Bernardino.

It suited Gaston Isbel to halt here. No need to call! Evarts and his son appeared so quickly as to convince observers that they had been watching.

"Howdy, Jake!" said Isbel. "I'm wantin' a word with y'u alone."

"Shore, boss, git down an' come in," replied Evarts.

Isbel led him aside, and said something forcible that Jean divined from the very gesture which accompanied it. His father was telling Evarts that he was not to join in the Isbel-Jorth war. Evarts had worked for the Isbels a long time, and his faithfulness, along with something stronger and darker, showed in his rugged face as he stubbornly opposed Isbel. The old man raised his voice: "No, I tell you. An' that settles it."

They returned to the horses, and, before mounting, Isbel, as if he remembered something, directed his somber gaze on young Evarts.

"Son, did you bury Bernardino?"

"Dad an' me went over yestiddy," replied the lad. "I shore was glad the coyotes hadn't been round."

"How aboot the sheep?"

"I left them there. I was goin' to stay, but bein' all alone—I got skeered. . . . The sheep was doin' fine. Good water an' some grass. An' this ain't time fer varmints to hang round."

"Jake, keep your eye on that flock," returned Isbel. "An' if I shouldn't happen to come back y'u can call them sheep yours. . . . I'd like your boy to ride up to the village. Not with us, so anybody would see him. But afterward. We'll be at Abel Meeker's."

Again Jean was confronted with an uneasy premonition as to some idea or plan his father had not shared with his followers. When the cavalcade started on again Jean rode to his father's side and asked him why he had wanted the Evarts boy to come to Grass Valley. And the old man replied that, as the boy could run to and fro in the village without danger, he might be useful in reporting what was going on at Greaves's store, where undoubtedly the Jorth gang would hold forth. This appeared reasonable enough, therefore Jean smothered the objection he had meant to make.

The valley road was deserted. When, a mile farther on, the riders passed a group of cabins, just on the out-skirts of the village, Jean's quick eye caught sight of curious and evidently frightened people trying to see while they avoided being seen. No doubt the whole settlement was in a state of suspense and terror. Not likely this dark, closely grouped band of horsemen appeared to them as Jorth's gang had looked to Jean. It was an orderly, trotting march that manifested neither hurry nor excitement. But any Western eye could have caught the singular aspect of such a group, as if the intent of the riders was a visible thing.

Soon they reached the outskirts of the village. Here their approach had been watched for or had been already reported. Jean saw men, women, children peeping from behind cabins and from half-opened doors. Farther on Jean espied the dark figures of men, slipping out the back way through orchards and gardens and running north, toward the center of the village. Could these be friends of the Jorth crowd, on the way with warnings of the approach of the Isbels? Jean felt convinced of it. He was learning that his father had not been absolutely correct in his estimation of the way Jorth and his followers were regarded by their neighbors. Not improbably there were really many villagers who, being more interested in sheep raising than in cattle, had an honest leaning toward the Jorths. Some, too, no doubt, had leanings that were dishonest in deed if not in sincerity.

Gaston Isbel led his clan straight down the middle of the wide road of Grass Valley until he reached a point opposite Abel Meeker's cabin. Jean espied the same curiosity from behind Meeker's door and windows as had been shown all along the road. But presently, at Isbel's call, the door opened and a short, swarthy man appeared. He carried a rifle.

"Howdy, Gass!" he said. "What's the good word?"

"Wal, Abel, it's not good, but bad. An' it's shore started," replied Isbel. "I'm askin' y'u to let me have your cabin."

"You're welcome. I'll send the folks 'round to Jim's," returned Meeker. "An' if y'u want me, I'm with y'u, Isbel."

"Thanks, Abel, but I'm not leadin' any more kin an' friends into this heah deal."

"Wal, jest as y'u say. But I'd like damn bad to jine with y'u. . . . My brother Ted was shot last night."

"Ted! Is he daid?" ejaculated Isbel, blankly.

"We can't find out," replied Meeker. "Jim says thet Jeff Campbell said thet Ted went into Greaves's place last night. Greaves allus was friendly to Ted, but Greaves wasn't thar—"

"No, he shore wasn't," interrupted Isbel, with a dark smile, "an' he never will be there again."

Meeker nodded with slow comprehension and a shade crossed his face.

"Wal, Campbell claimed he'd heerd from some one who was thar. Anyway, the Jorths were drinkin' hard, an' they raised a row with Ted—same old sheep talk—an' somebody shot him. Campbell said Ted was thrown out back, an' he was shore he wasn't killed."

"Ahuh! Wal, I'm sorry, Abel, your family had to lose in this. Maybe Ted's not bad hurt. I shore hope so. . . . An' y'u an' Jim keep out of the fight, anyway."

"All right, Isbel. But I reckon I'll give y'u a hunch. If this heah fight lasts long the whole damn Basin will be in it, on one side or t'other."

"Abe, you're talkin' sense," broke in Blaisdell. "An' that's why we're up heah for quick action."

"I heerd y'u got Daggs," whispered Meeker, as he peered all around.

"Wal, y'u heerd correct," drawled Blaisdell.

Meeker muttered strong words into his beard. "Say, was Daggs in the Jorth outfit?"

"He *was*. But he walked right into Jean's forty-four. . . . An' I reckon his carcass would show some more."

"An' whar's Guy Isbel?" demanded Meeker.

"Daid an' buried, Abel," replied Gaston Isbel. "An' now I'd be obliged if y'u'll hurry your folks away, an' let us have your cabin an' corral. Have y'u got any hay for the hosses?"

"Shore. The barn's half full," replied Meeker, as he turned away. "Come on in."

"No. We'll wait till you've gone."

When Meeker had gone, Isbel and his men sat their horses and looked about them and spoke low. Their advent had been expected, and the little town awoke to the imminence of the impending battle. Inside Meeker's house there was the sound of indistinct voices of women and the bustle incident to a hurried vacating.

Across the wide road people were peering out on all sides, some hiding, others walking to and fro, from fence to fence, whispering in little groups. Down the wide road, at the point where it turned, stood Greaves's fort-like stone house. Low, flat, isolated, with its dark, eye-like windows, it presented a forbidding and sinister aspect. Jean distinctly saw the forms of men, some dark, others in shirt sleeves, come to the wide door and look down the road.

"Wal, I reckon only aboot five hundred good hoss steps are separatin' us from that outfit," drawled Blaisdell.

No one replied to his jocularity. Gaston Isbel's eyes narrowed to a slit in his furrowed face and he kept them fastened upon Greaves's store. Blue, likewise, had a somber cast of countenance, not, perhaps, any darker nor grimmer than those of his comrades, but more representative of intense preoccupation of mind. The look of him thrilled Jean, who could sense its deadliness, yet could not grasp any more. Altogether, the manner of the villagers and the watchful pacing to and fro of the Jorth followers and the silent, boding front of Isbel and his men summed up for Jean the menace of the moment that must very soon change to a terrible reality.

At a call from Meeker, who stood at the back of the cabin, Gaston Isbel rode into the yard, followed by the others of his party. "Somebody look after the hosses," ordered Isbel, as he dismounted and took his rifle and pack. "Better leave the saddles on, leastways till we see what's comin' off."

Jean and Bill Isbel led the horses back to the corral. While watering and feeding them, Jean somehow received the impression that Bill was trying to speak, to confide in him, to unburden himself of some load. This peculiarity of Bill's had become marked when he was perfectly sober. Yet he had never spoken or even begun anything unusual. Upon the present occasion, however, Jean believed that his brother might have gotten rid of his emotion, or whatever it was, had they not been interrupted by Colmor.

"Boys, the old man's orders are for us to sneak round on three sides of Greaves's store, keepin' out of gunshot till we find good cover, an' then crawl closer an' to pick off any of Jorth's gang who shows himself."

Bill Isbel strode off without a reply to Colmor.

"Well, I don't think so much of that," said Jean, ponderingly. "Jorth has lots of friends here. Somebody might pick us off."

"I kicked, but the old man shut me up. He's not to be bucked ag'in' now. Struck me as powerful queer. But no wonder."

"Maybe he knows best. Did he say anythin' about what he an' the rest of them are goin' to do?"

"Nope. Blue taxed him with that an' got the same as me. I reckon we'd better try it out, for a while, anyway."

"Looks like he wants us to keep out of the fight," replied Jean, thoughtfully. "Maybe, though . . . Dad's no fool. Colmor, you wait here till I get out of sight. I'll go round an' come up as close as advisable behind Greaves's store. You take the right side. An' keep hid."

With that Jean strode off, going around the barn, straight out the orchard lane to the open flat, and then climbing a fence to the north of the village. Presently he reached a line of sheds and corrals, to which he held until he arrived at the road. This point was about a quarter of a mile from Greaves's store, and around the bend. Jean

sighted no one. The road, the fields, the yards, the backs
of the cabins all looked deserted. A blight had settled
down upon the peaceful activities of Grass Valley. Crossing the road, Jean began to circle until he came close to
several cabins, around which he made a wide detour. This
took him to the edge of the slope, where brush and thickets afforded him a safe passage to a line directly back of
Greaves's store. Then he turned toward it. Soon he was
again approaching a cabin of that side, and some of its in-
mates descried him. Their actions attested to their alarm.
Jean half expected a shot from this quarter, such were his
growing doubts, but he was mistaken. A man, unknown
to Jean, closely watched his guarded movements and then
waved a hand, as if to signify to Jean that he had nothing
to fear. After this act he disappeared. Jean believed that
he had been recognized by some one not antagonistic to
the Isbels. Therefore he passed the cabin and, coming
to a thick scrub-oak tree that offered shelter, he hid there
to watch. From this spot he could see the back of Greaves's
store, at a distance probably too far for a rifle bullet to
reach. Before him, as far as the store, and on each side,
extended the village common. In front of the store ran the
road. Jean's position was such that he could not command
sight of this road down toward Meeker's house, a fact that
disturbed him. Not satisfied with this stand, he studied his
surroundings in the hope of espying a better. And he discovered what he thought would be a more favorable position, although he could not see much farther down the
road. Jean went back around the cabin and, coming out
into the open to the right, he got the corner of Greaves's
barn between him and the window of the store. Then he
boldly hurried into the open, and soon reached an old
wagon, from behind which he proposed to watch. He
could not see either window or door of the store, but if
any of the Jorth contingent came out the back way they

would be within reach of his rifle. Jean took the risk of being shot at from either side.

So sharp and roving was his sight that he soon espied Colmor slipping along behind the trees some hundred yards to the left. All his efforts to catch a glimpse of Bill, however, were fruitless. And this appeared strange to Jean, for there were several good places on the right from which Bill could have commanded the front of Greaves's store and the whole west side.

Colmor disappeared among some shrubbery, and Jean seemed left alone to watch a deserted, silent village. Watching and listening, he felt that the time dragged. Yet the shadows cast by the sun showed him that, no matter how tense he felt and how the moments seemed hours, they were really flying.

Suddenly Jean's ears rang with the vibrant shock of a rifle report. He jerked up, strung and thrilling. It came from in front of the store. It was followed by revolver shots, heavy, booming. Three he counted, and the rest were too close together to enumerate. A single hoarse yell pealed out, somehow trenchant and triumphant. Other yells, not so wild and strange, muffled the first one. Then silence clapped down on the store and the open square.

Jean was deadly certain that some of the Jorth clan would show themselves. He strained to still the trembling those sudden shots and that significant yell had caused him. No man appeared. No more sounds caught Jean's ears. The suspense, then, grew unbearable. It was not that he could not wait for an enemy to appear, but that he could not wait to learn what had happened. Every moment that he stayed there, with hands like steel on his rifle, with eyes of a falcon, but added to a dreadful, dark certainty of disaster. A rifle shot swiftly followed by revolver shots! What could they mean? Revolver shots of different caliber, surely fired by different men! What could they mean? It was not these shots that accounted for Jean's dread, but the yell which had followed. All his intelligence and all his nerve were not sufficient to fight down the feeling of calamity. And at last, yielding to it, he left his post, and ran like a deer across the open, through the cabin yard, and around the edge of the slope to the road. Here his caution brought him to a halt. Not a living thing crossed his vision. Breaking into a run, he soon reached the back of Meeker's place and entered, to hurry forward to the cabin.

Colmor was there in the yard, breathing hard, his face working, and in front of him crouched several of the men with rifles ready. The road, to Jean's flashing glance, was apparently deserted. Blue sat on the doorstep, lighting a cigarette. Then on the moment Blaisdell strode to the door of the cabin. Jean had never seen him look like that.

"Jean—look—down the road," he said, brokenly, and with big hand shaking he pointed down toward Greaves's store.

Like lightning Jean's glance shot down—down—down—until it stopped to fix upon the prostrate form of a man, lying in the middle of the road. A man of lengthy build, shirt-sleeved arms flung wide, white head in the dust—dead! Jean's recognition was as swift as his sight. His father! They had killed him! The Jorths! It was done. His father's premonition of death had not been false. And then, after these flashing thoughts, came a sense of blankness, momentarily almost oblivion, that gave place to a rending of the heart. That pain Jean had known only at the death of his mother. It passed, this agonizing pang, and its icy pressure yielded to a rushing gust of blood, fiery as hell.

"Who—did it?" whispered Jean.

"Jorth!" replied Blaisdell, huskily. "Son, we couldn't hold your dad back. . . . We couldn't. He was like a lion. . . . An' he threwed his life away! Oh, if it hadn't been for that it 'd not be so awful. Shore, we come heah to shoot an' be shot. But not like that. . . . By God, it was murder—murder!"

Jean's mute lips framed a query easily read.

"Tell him, Blue. I cain't," continued Blaisdell, and he tramped back into the cabin.

"Set down, Jean, an' take things easy," said Blue, calmly. "You know we all reckoned we'd git plugged one way or another in this deal. An' shore it doesn't matter much how a fellar gits it. All thet ought to bother us is to make shore the other outfit bites the dust—same as your dad had to."

Under this man's tranquil presence, all the more quieting because it seemed to be so deadly sure and cool, Jean felt the uplift of his dark spirit, the acceptance of fatality, the mounting control of faculties that must wait. The little gunman seemed to have about his inert presence something that suggested a rattlesnake's inherent knowledge of its destructiveness. Jean sat down and wiped his clammy face.

"Jean, your dad reckoned to square accounts with Jorth, an' save us all," began Blue, puffing out a cloud of smoke. "But he reckoned too late. Mebbe years ago—or even not long ago—if he'd called Jorth out man to man there'd never been any Jorth-Isbel war. Gaston Isbel's conscience woke too late. That's how I figger it."

"Hurry! Tell me—how it—happened," panted Jean.

"Wal, a little while after y'u left I seen your dad writin' on a leaf he tore out of a book—Meeker's Bible, as y'u can see. I thought thet was funny. An' Blaisdell gave me a hunch. Pretty soon along comes young Evarts. The old man calls him out of our hearin' an' talks to him. Then I seen him give the boy somethin' which I afterward figgered was what he wrote on the leaf out of the Bible. Me an' Blaisdell both tried to git out of him what thet meant. But not a word. I kept watchin' an' after a while I seen young Evarts slip out the back way. Mebbe half an hour I seen a bare-legged kid cross the road an' go into Greaves's store. . . . Then shore I tumbled to your dad. He'd sent a note to Jorth to come out an' meet him face to face, man to man! . . . Shore it was like readin' what your dad had wrote. But I didn't say nothin' to Blaisdell. I jest watched."

Blue drawled these last words, as if he enjoyed remembrance of his keen reasoning. A smile wreathed his thin lips. He drew twice on the cigarette and emitted another cloud of smoke. Quite suddenly then he changed. He made a rapid gesture—the whip of a hand, significant and passionate. And swift words followed:

"Colonel Lee Jorth stalked out of the store—out into the road—mebbe a hundred steps. Then he halted. He wore his long black coat an' his wide black hat, an' he stood like a stone.

" 'What the hell!' burst out Blaisdell, comin' out of his trance.

"The rest of us jest looked. I'd forgot your dad, for the minnit. So had all of us. But we remembered soon enough when we seen him stalk out. Everybody had a hunch then. I called him. Blaisdell begged him to come back. All the fellars had a say. No use! Then I shore cussed him an' told him it was plain as day thet Jorth didn't hit me like an honest man. I can sense such things. I knew Jorth had a trick up his sleeve. I've not been a gun fighter fer nothin'.

"Your dad had no rifle. He packed his gun at his hip. He jest stalked down thet road like a giant, goin' faster an' faster, holdin' his head high. It shore was fine to see him. But I was sick. I heerd Blaisdell groan, an' Fredericks thar cussed somethin' fierce. . . . When your dad halted—I reckon aboot fifty steps from Jorth—then we all went numb. I heerd your dad's voice—then Jorth's.

They cut like knives. Y'u could shore heah the hate they hed fer each other."

Blue had become a little husky. His speech had grown gradually to denote his feeling. Underneath his serenity there was a different order of man.

"I reckon both your dad an' Jorth went fer their guns at the same time—an even break. But jest as they drew, some one shot a rifle from the store. Must hev been a forty-five seventy. A big gun! The bullet must have hit your dad low down, aboot the middle. He acted thet way, sinkin' to his knees. An' he was wild in shootin'—so wild thet he must hev missed. Then he wabbled—an' Jorth run in a dozen steps, shootin' fast, till your dad fell over. . . . Jorth run closer, bent over him, an' then straightened up with an Apache yell, if I ever heerd one. . . . An' then Jorth backed slow—lookin' all the time—backed to the store, an' went in."

Blue's voice ceased. Jean seemed suddenly released from an impelling magnet that now dropped him to some numb, dizzy depth. Blue's lean face grew hazy. Then Jean bowed his head in his hands, and sat there, while a slight tremor shook all his muscles at once. He grew deathly cold and deathly sick. This paroxysm slowly wore away, and Jean grew conscious of a dull amaze at the apparent deadness of his spirit. Blaisdell placed a huge, kindly hand on his shoulder.

"Brace up, son!" he said, with voice now clear and resonant. "Shore it's what your dad expected—an' what we all must look for. . . . If y'u was goin' to kill Jorth before— think how ——— ——— shore y'u're goin' to kill him now."

"Blaisdell's talkin'," put in Blue, and his voice had a cold ring. "Lee Jorth will never see the sun rise ag'in!"

These calls to the primitive in Jean, to the Indian, were not in vain. But even so, when the dark tide rose in him, there was still a haunting consciousness of the cruelty of this singular doom imposed upon him. Strangely Ellen Jorth's face floated back in the depths of his vision, pale, fading, like the face of a spirit floating by.

"Blue," said Blaisdell, "let's get Isbel's body soon as we dare, an' bury it. Reckon we can, right after dark."

"Shore," replied Blue. "But y'u fellars figger thet out. I'm thinkin' hard. I've got somethin' on my mind."

Jean grew fascinated by the looks and speech and action of the little gunman. Blue, indeed, had something on his mind. And it boded ill to the men in that dark square stone house down the road. He paced to and fro in the yard, back and forth on the path to the gate, and then he entered the cabin to stalk up and down, faster and faster, until all at once he halted as if struck, to upfling his right arm in a singular fierce gesture.

"Jean, call the men in," he said, tersely.

They all filed in, sinister and silent, with eager faces turned to the little Texan. His dominance showed markedly.

"Gordon, y'u stand in the door an' keep your eye peeled," went on Blue. . . . "Now, boys, listen! I've thought it all out. This game of man huntin' is the same to me as cattle raisin' is to y'u. An' my life in Texas all comes back to me, I reckon, in good stead fer us now. I'm goin' to kill Lee Jorth! Him first, an' mebbe his brothers. I had to think of a good many ways before I hit on one I reckon will be shore. It's got to be *shore*. Jorth has got to die! Wal, heah's my plan. . . . Thet Jorth outfit is drinkin' some, we can gamble on it. They're not goin' to leave thet store. An' of course they'll be expectin' us to start a fight. I reckon they'll look fer some such siege as they held round Isbel's ranch. But we shore ain't goin' to do thet. I'm goin' to surprise thet outfit. There's only one man among them who is dangerous, an' thet's Queen. I know Queen. But he doesn't know me. An' I'm goin' to finish my job before he gets acquainted with me. After thet, all right!"

Blue paused a moment, his eyes narrowing down, his whole face setting in hard cast of intense preoccupation, as if he visualized a scene of extraordinary nature.

"Wal, what's your trick?" demanded Blaisdell.

"Y'u all know Greaves's store," continued Blue. "How them winders have wooden shutters thet keep a light from showin' outside? Wal, I'm gamblin' thet as soon as it's dark Jorth's gang will be celebratin'. They'll be drinkin' an' they'll have a light, an' the winders will be shut. They're not goin' to worry none aboot us. Thet store is like a fort. It won't burn. An' shore they'd never think of us chargin' them in there. Wal, as soon as it's dark, we'll go round behind the lots an' come up jest acrost the road from Greaves's. I reckon we'd better leave Isbel where he lays till this fight's over. Mebbe y'u'll have more 'n him to bury. We'll crawl behind them bushes in front of Coleman's yard. An' heah's where Jean comes in. He'll take an ax, an' his guns, of course, an' do some of his Injun sneakin' round to the back of Greaves's store. . . . An', Jean, y'u must do a slick job of this. But I reckon it 'll be easy fer you. Back there it 'll be dark as pitch, fer anyone lookin' out of the store. An' I'm figgerin' y'u can take your time an' crawl right up. Now if y'u don't remember how Greaves's back yard looks I'll tell y'u."

Here Blue dropped on one knee to the floor and with a finger he traced a map of Greaves's barn and fence, the back door and window, and especially a break in the stone foundation which led into a kind of cellar where Greaves stored wood and other things that could be left outdoors.

"Jean, I take particular pains to show y'u where this hole is," said Blue, "because if the gang runs out y'u could duck in there an' hide. An' if they run out into the yard—wal, y'u'd make it a sorry run fer them. . . . Wal, when y'u've crawled up close to Greaves's back door, an' waited long enough to see an' listen—then you're to run fast an' swing your ax smash ag'in' the winder. Take a quick peep in if y'u want to. It might help. Then jump quick an' take a swing at the door. Y'u'll be standin' to one side, so if the gang shoots through the door they won't hit y'u. Bang thet door good an' hard. . . . Wal, now's where I come in. When y'u swing thet ax I'll shore run fer the front of the store. Jorth an' his outfit will be some attentive to thet poundin' of yours on the back door. So I reckon. An' they'll be *lookin'* thet way. I'll run in—yell—an' throw my guns on Jorth."

"Humph! Is that all?" ejaculated Blaisdell.

"I reckon thet's all an' I'm figgerin' it's a hell of a lot," responded Blue, dryly. "Thet's what Jorth will think."

"Where do we come in?"

"Wal, y'u all can back me up," replied Blue, dubiously. "Y'u see, my plan goes as far as killin' Jorth—an' mebbe his brothers. Mebbe I'll get a crack at Queen. But I'll be shore of Jorth. After thet all depends. Mebbe it 'll be easy fer me to get out. An' if I do y'u fellars will know it an' can fill thet storeroom full of bullets."

"Wal, Blue, with all due respect to y'u, I shore don't like your plan," declared Blaisdell. "Success depends upon too many little things any one of which might go wrong."

"Blaisdell, I reckon I know this heah game better than y'u," replied Blue. "A gun fighter goes by instinct. This trick will work."

"But suppose that front door of Greaves's store is barred," protested Blaisdell.

"It hasn't got any bar," said Blue.

"Y'u're shore?"

"Yes, I reckon," replied Blue.

"Hell, man! Aren't y'u takin' a terrible chance?" queried Blaisdell.

Blue's answer to that was a look that brought the blood to Blaisdell's face. Only then did the rancher really comprehend how the little gunman had taken such desperate chances before, and meant to take them now, not with any hope or assurance of escaping with his life, but to live up to his peculiar code of honor.

"Blaisdell, did y'u ever heah of me in Texas?" he queried, dryly.

"Wal, no, Blue, I cain't swear I did," replied the rancher, apologetically. "An' Isbel was always sort of mysterious aboot his acquaintance with you."

"My name's not Blue."

"Ahuh! Wal, what is it, then—if I'm safe to ask?" returned Blaisdell, gruffly.

"It's King Fisher," replied Blue.

The shock that stiffened Blaisdell must have been communicated to the others. Jean certainly felt amaze, and some other emotion not fully realized, when he found himself face to face with one of the most notorious characters ever known in Texas—an outlaw long supposed to be dead.

"Men, I reckon I'd kept my secret if I'd any idee of comin' out of this Isbel-Jorth war alive," said Blue. "But I'm goin' to cash. I feel it heah. . . . Isbel was my friend. He saved me from bein' lynched in Texas. An' so I'm goin' to kill Jorth. Now I'll take it kind of y'u—if any of y'u come out of this alive—to tell who I was an' why I was on the Isbel side. Because this sheep an' cattle war—this talk of Jorth an' the Hash Knife Gang—it makes me sick. I *know* there's been crooked work on Isbel's side, too. An' I never want it on record thet I killed Jorth because he was a rustler."

"By God, Blue! it's late in the day for such talk," burst out Blaisdell, in rage and amaze. "But I reckon y'u know what y'u're talkin' aboot. . . . Wal, I shore don't want to heah it."

At this juncture Bill Isbel quietly entered the cabin, too late to hear any of Blue's statement. Jean was positive of that, for as Blue was speaking those last revealing words Bill's heavy boots had resounded on the gravel path outside. Yet something in Bill's look or in the way Blue averted his lean face or in the entrance of Bill at that particular moment, or all these together, seemed to Jean to add further mystery to the long secret causes leading up to the Jorth-Isbel war. Did Bill know what Blue knew? Jean had an inkling that he did. And on the moment, so perplexing and bitter, Jean gazed out the door, down the deserted road to where his dead father lay, white-haired and ghastly in the sunlight.

"Blue, you could have kept that to yourself, as well as your real name," interposed Jean, with bitterness. "It's too late now for either to do any good. . . . But I appreciate your friendship for dad, an' I'm ready to help carry out your plan."

That decision of Jean's appeared to put an end to protest or argument from Blaisdell or any of the others. Blue's fleeting dark smile was one of satisfaction. Then upon most of this group of men seemed to settle a grim restraint. They went out and walked and watched; they came in again, restless and somber. Jean thought that he must have bent his gaze a thousand times down the road to the tragic figure of his father. That sight roused all emotions in his breast, and the one that stirred there most was pity. The pity of it! Gaston Isbel lying face down in the dust of the village street! Patches of blood showed on the back of his vest and one white-sleeved shoulder. He had been shot through. Every time Jean saw this blood he had to stifle a gathering of wild, savage impulses.

Meanwhile the afternoon hours dragged by and the village remained as if its inhabitants had abandoned it. Not even a dog showed on the side road. Jorth and some of his men came out in front of the store and sat on the steps, in close convening groups. Every move they made seemed significant of their confidence and importance. About sunset they went back into the store, closing door and window shutters. Then Blaisdell called the Isbel faction to have food and drink. Jean felt no hunger. And Blue, who had kept apart from the others, showed no desire to eat. Neither did he smoke, though early in the day he had never been without a cigarette between his lips.

Twilight fell and darkness came. Not a light showed anywhere in the blackness.

"Wal, I reckon it's aboot time," said Blue, and he led the way out of the cabin to the back of the lot. Jean strode behind him, carrying his rifle and an ax. Silently the other men followed. Blue turned to the left and led through the field until he came within sight of a dark line of trees.

"Thet's where the road turns off," he said to Jean. "An' heah's the back of Coleman's place. . . . Wal, Jean, good luck!"

Jean felt the grip of a steel-like hand, and in the darkness he caught the gleam of Blue's eyes. Jean had no response in words for the laconic Blue, but he wrung the hard, thin hand and hurried away in the darkness.

Once alone, his part of the business at hand rushed him into eager thrilling action. This was the sort of work he was fitted to do. In this instance it was important, but it seemed to him that Blue had coolly taken the perilous part. And this cowboy with gray in his thin hair was in reality the great King Fisher! Jean marveled at the fact. And he shivered all over for Jorth. In ten minutes—fifteen, more or less, Jorth would lie gasping bloody froth and sinking down. Something in the dark, lonely, silent, oppressive summer night told Jean this. He strode on swiftly. Crossing the road at a run, he kept on over the ground he had traversed during the afternoon, and in a few moments he stood breathing hard at the edge of the common behind Greaves's store.

A pin point of light penetrated the blackness. It made Jean's heart leap. The Jorth contingent were burning the big lamp that hung in the center of Greaves's store. Jean listened. Loud voices and coarse laughter sounded discord on the melancholy silence of the night. What Blue had called his instinct had surely guided him aright. Death of Gaston Isbel was being celebrated by revel.

In a few moments Jean had regained his breath. Then all his faculties set intensely to the action at hand. He seemed to magnify his hearing and his sight. His movements made no sound. He gained the wagon, where he crouched a moment.

The ground seemed a pale, obscure medium, hardly more real than the gloom above it. Through this gloom of night, which looked thick like a cloud, but was really clear, shone the thin, bright point of light, accentuating the black square that was Greaves's store. Above this stood a gray line of tree foliage, and then the intensely dark-blue sky studded with white, cold stars.

A hound bayed lonesomely somewhere in the distance. Voices of men sounded more distinctly, some deep and low, others loud, unguarded, with the vacant note of thoughtlessness.

Jean gathered all his forces, until sense of sight and hearing were in exquisite accord with the suppleness and lightness of his movements. He glided on about ten short, swift steps before he halted. That was as far as his piercing eyes could penetrate. If there had been a guard stationed outside the store Jean would have seen him before being seen. He saw the fence, reached it, entered the yard, glided in the dense shadow of the barn until the black square began to loom gray—the color of stone at night. Jean peered through the obscurity. No dark figure of a man showed against that gray wall—only a black patch, which must be the hole in the foundation mentioned. A ray of light now streaked out from the little black window. To the right showed the wide, black door.

Farther on Jean glided silently. Then he halted. There was no guard outside. Jean heard the clink of a cup, the lazy drawl of a Texan, and then a strong, harsh voice—Jorth's. It strung Jean's whole being tight and vibrating. Inside he was on fire while cold thrills rippled over his skin. It took tremendous effort of will to hold himself back another instant to listen, to look, to feel, to make sure. And that instant charged him with a mighty current of hot blood, straining, throbbing, damming.

When Jean leaped this current burst. In a few swift bounds he gained his point halfway between door and window. He leaned his rifle against the stone wall. Then he swung the ax. Crash! The window shutter split and rattled to the floor inside. The silence then broke with a hoarse, "What's thet?"

With all his might Jean swung the heavy ax on the door. Smash! The lower half caved in and banged to the floor. Bright light flared out the hole.

"Look out!" yelled a man, in loud alarm. "They're batterin' the back door!"

Jean swung again, high on the splintered door. Crash! Pieces flew inside.

"They've got axes," hoarsely shouted another voice. "Shove the counter ag'in' the door."

"No!" thundered a voice of authority that denoted terror as well. "Let them come in. Pull your guns an' take to cover!"

"They ain't comin' in," was the hoarse reply. "They'll shoot in on us from the dark."

"Put out the lamp!" yelled another.

Jean's third heavy swing caved in part of the upper half of the door. Shouts and curses intermingled with the sliding of benches across the floor and the hard shuffle of boots. This confusion seemed to be split and silenced by a piercing yell, of different caliber, of terrible meaning. It stayed Jean's swing—caused him to drop the ax and snatch up his rifle.

"Don't anybody move!"

Like a steel whip this voice cut the silence. It belonged to Blue. Jean swiftly bent to put his eye to a crack in the door. Most of those visible seemed to have been frozen into unnatural positions. Jorth stood rather in front of his men, hatless and coatless, one arm outstretched, and his dark profile set toward a little man just inside the door. This man was Blue. Jean needed only one flashing look at Blue's face, at his leveled, quivering guns, to understand why he had chosen this trick.

"Who 're—you?" demanded Jorth, in husky pants.

"Reckon I'm Isbel's right-hand man," came the biting reply. "Once tolerable well known in Texas. . . . *King Fisher!*"

The name must have been a guarantee of death. Jorth recognized this outlaw and realized his own fate. In the lamplight his face turned a pale greenish white. His outstretched hand began to quiver down.

Blue's left gun seemed to leap up and flash red and explode. Several heavy reports merged almost as one. Jorth's arm jerked limply, flinging his gun. And his body sagged in the middle. His hands fluttered like crippled wings and found their way to his abdomen. His death-pale face never changed its set look nor position toward Blue. But his gasping utterance was one of horrible mortal fury and terror. Then he began to sway, still with that strange, rigid set of his face toward his slayer, until he fell.

His fall broke the spell. Even Blue, like the gunman he was, had paused to watch Jorth in his last mortal action. Jorth's followers began to draw and shoot. Jean saw Blue's return fire bring down a huge man, who fell across Jorth's body. Then Jean, quick as the thought that actuated him, raised his rifle and shot at the big lamp. It burst in a flare. It crashed to the floor. Darkness followed—a blank, thick, enveloping mantle. Then red flashes of guns emphasized the blackness. Inside the store there broke loose a pandemonium of shots, yells, curses, and thudding boots. Jean shoved his rifle barrel inside the door and, holding it low down, he moved it to and fro while he worked lever and trigger until the magazine was empty. Then, drawing his six-shooter, he emptied that. A roar of rifles from the front of the store told Jean that his comrades had entered the fray. Bullets zipped through the door he had broken. Jean ran swiftly round the corner, taking care to sheer off a little to the left, and when he got clear of the building he saw a line of flashes in the middle of the road. Blaisdell and the others were firing into the door of the store. With nimble fingers Jean reloaded his rifle. Then swiftly he ran across the road and down to get behind his comrades. Their shooting had slackened. Jean saw dark forms coming his way.

"Hello, Blaisdell!" he called, warningly.

"That y'u, Jean?" returned the rancher, looming up. "Wal, we wasn't worried aboot y'u."

"Blue?" queried Jean, sharply.

A little, dark figure shuffled past Jean. "Howdy, Jean!"

said Blue, dryly. "Y'u shore did your part. Reckon I'll
need to be tied up, but I ain't hurt much."

"Colmor's hit," called the voice of Gordon, a few yards
distant. "Help me, somebody!"

Jean ran to help Gordon uphold the swaying Colmor.
"Are you hurt—bad?" asked Jean, anxiously. The young
man's head rolled and hung. He was breathing hard and
did not reply. They had almost to carry him.

"Come on, men!" called Blaisdell, turning back toward
the others who were still firing. "We'll let well enough
alone. . . . Fredericks, y'u an' Bill help me find the body
of the old man. It's heah somewhere."

Farther on down the road the searchers stumbled over
Gaston Isbel. They picked him up and followed Jean and
Gordon, who were supporting the wounded Colmor. Jean
looked back to see Blue dragging himself along in the
rear. It was too dark to see distinctly; nevertheless, Jean
got the impression that Blue was more severely wounded
than he had claimed to be. The distance to Meeker's cabin
was not far, but it took what Jean felt to be a long and anxious time to get there. Colmor apparently rallied somewhat. When this procession entered Meeker's yard, Blue
was lagging behind.

"Blue, how air y'u?" called Blaisdell, with concern.

"Wal, I got—my boots—on—anyhow," replied Blue,
huskily.

He lurched into the yard and slid down on the grass and
stretched out.

"Man! Y'u're hurt bad!" exclaimed Blaisdell. The others halted in their slow march and, as if by tacit, unspoken word, lowered the body of Isbel to the ground. Then
Blaisdell knelt beside Blue. Jean left Colmor to Gordon
and hurried to peer down into Blue's dim face.

"No, I ain't—hurt," said Blue, in a much weaker voice.

"I'm—jest killed! . . . It was Queen! . . . Y'u all heerd me—Queen was—only bad man in that lot. I knowed it. . . . I could—hev killed him. . . . But I was—after Lee Jorth—an' his brothers. . . ."

Blue's voice failed there.

"Wal!" ejaculated Blaisdell.

"Shore was funny—Jorth's face—when I said—King Fisher," whispered Blue. "Funnier—when I bored—him through. . . . But it—was—Queen—"

His whisper died away.

"Blue!" called Blaisdell, sharply. Receiving no answer, he bent lower in the starlight and placed a hand upon the man's breast.

"Wal, he's gone. . . . I wonder if he really was the old Texas King Fisher. No one would ever believe it. . . . But if he killed the Jorths, I'll shore believe him."

CHAPTER 10

Two weeks of lonely solitude in the forest had worked incalculable change in Ellen Jorth.

Late in June her father and her two uncles had packed and ridden off with Daggs, Colter, and six other men, all heavily armed, some somber with drink, others hard and grim with a foretaste of fight. Ellen had not been given any orders. Her father had forgotten to bid her good-by or had avoided it. Their dark mission was stamped on their faces.

They had gone and, keen as had been Ellen's pang, nevertheless, their departure was a relief. She had heard them bluster and brag so often that she had her doubts of any great Jorth-Isbel war. Barking dogs did not bite. Somebody, perhaps on each side, would be badly wounded, possibly killed, and then the feud would go on as before, mostly talk. Many of her former impressions had faded. Development had been so rapid and continuous in her that she could look back to a day-by-day transformation. At night she had hated the sight of herself and when the dawn came she would rise, singing.

Jorth had left Ellen at home with the Mexican woman and Antonio. Ellen saw them only at meal times, and often not then, for she frequently visited old John Sprague or came home late to do her own cooking.

It was but a short distance up to Sprague's cabin, and since she had stopped riding the black horse, Spades, she walked. Spades was accustomed to having grain, and in the mornings he would come down to the ranch and whistle. Ellen had vowed she would never feed the horse and bade Antonio do it. But one morning Antonio was absent. She fed Spades herself. When she laid a hand on him and when he rubbed his nose against her shoulder she was not quite so sure she hated him. "Why should I?" she queried. "A horse cain't help it if he belongs to—to—" Ellen was not sure of anything except that more and more it grew good to be alone.

A whole day in the lonely forest passed swiftly, yet it left a feeling of long time. She lived by her thoughts. Always the morning was bright, sunny, sweet and fragrant and colorful, and her mood was pensive, wistful, dreamy. And always, just as surely as the hours passed, thought intruded upon her happiness, and thought brought memory, and memory brought shame, and shame brought fight. Sunset after sunset she had dragged herself back to the ranch, sullen and sick and beaten. Yet she never ceased to struggle.

The July storms came, and the forest floor that had been so sear and brown and dry and dusty changed as if by magic. The green grass shot up, the flowers bloomed, and along the cañon beds of lacy ferns swayed in the wind and bent their graceful tips over the amber-colored water. Ellen haunted these cool dells, these pine-shaded, mossy-rocked ravines where the brooks tinkled and the deer came down to drink. She wandered alone. But there grew to be company in the aspens and the music of the little waterfalls. If she could have lived in that solitude always, never returning to the ranch home that reminded her of her name, she could have forgotten and have been happy.

She loved the storms. It was a dry country and she had learned through years to welcome the creamy clouds that rolled from the southwest. They came sailing and clustering and darkening at last to form a great, purple, angry mass that appeared to lodge against the mountain rim and burst into dazzling streaks of lightning and gray palls of rain. Lightning seldom struck near the ranch, but up on the Rim there was never a storm that did not splinter and crash some of the noble pines. During the storm season sheep herders and woodsmen generally did not camp under the pines. Fear of lightning was inborn in the natives, but for Ellen the dazzling white streaks or the tremendous splitting, crackling shock, or the thunderous boom and rumble along the battlements of the Rim had no terrors. A storm eased her breast. Deep in her heart was a hidden gathering storm. And somehow, to be out when the elements were warring, when the earth trembled and the heavens seemed to burst asunder, afforded her strange relief.

The summer days became weeks, and farther and farther they carried Ellen on the wings of solitude and loneliness until she seemed to look back years at the self she had hated. And always, when the dark memory impinged upon peace, she fought and fought until she seemed to be fighting hatred itself. Scorn of scorn and hate of hate! Yet even her battles grew to be dreams. For when the inevitable retrospect brought back Jean Isbel and his love and her cowardly falsehood she would shudder a little and put an unconscious hand to her breast and utterly fail in her fight and drift off down to vague and wistful dreams. The clean and healing forest, with its whispering wind and imperious solitude, had come between Ellen and the meaning of the squalid sheep ranch, with its travesty of home, its tragic owner. And it was coming between her two selves, the one that she had been forced to be and the other that she did not know—the thinker, the dreamer, the romancer, the one who lived in fancy the life she loved.

The summer morning dawned that brought Ellen strange tidings. They must have been created in her sleep, and now were realized in the glorious burst of golden sun, in the sweep of creamy clouds across the blue, in the solemn music of the wind in the pines, in the wild screech of the blue jays and the noble bugle of a stag. These heralded the day as no ordinary day. Something was going to happen to her. She divined it. She felt it. And she trembled. Nothing beautiful, hopeful, wonderful could ever happen to Ellen Jorth. She had been born to disaster, to suffer, to be forgotten, and die alone. Yet all nature about her seemed a magnificent rebuke to her morbidness. The same spirit that came out there with the thick, amber light was in her. She lived, and something in her was stronger than mind.

Ellen went to the door of her cabin, where she flung out her arms, driven to embrace this nameless purport of the morning. And a well-known voice broke in upon her rapture.

"Wal, lass, I like to see you happy an' I hate myself fer comin'. Because I've been to Grass Valley fer two days an' I've got news."

Old John Sprague stood there, with a smile that did not hide a troubled look.

"Oh! Uncle John! You startled me," exclaimed Ellen, shocked back to reality. And slowly she added: "Grass Valley! News?"

She put out an appealing hand, which Sprague quickly took in his own, as if to reassure her.

"Yes, an' not bad so far as you Jorths are concerned," he replied. "The first Jorth-Isbel fight has come off. . . . Reckon you remember makin' me promise to tell you if I heerd anythin'. Wal, I didn't wait fer you to come up."

"So," Ellen heard her voice calmly saying. What was this lying calm when there seemed to be a stone hammer at her heart? The first fight—not so bad for the Jorths! Then it had been bad for the Isbels. A sudden, cold still-ness fell upon her senses.

"Let's sit down—outdoors," Sprague was saying. "Nice an' sunny this—mornin'. I declare—I'm out of breath. Not used to walkin'. An' besides, I left Grass Valley in the night—an' I'm tired. But excoose me from hangin' round thet village last night! There was shore—"

"Who—who was killed?" interrupted Ellen, her voice breaking low and deep.

"Guy Isbel an' Bill Jacobs on the Isbel side, an' Daggs, Craig, an' Greaves on your father's side," stated Sprague, with something of awed haste.

"Ah!" breathed Ellen, and she relaxed to sink back against the cabin wall.

Sprague seated himself on the log beside her, turning to face her, and he seemed burdened with grave and important matters.

"I heerd a good many conflictin' stories," he said, ear-nestly. "The village folks is all skeered an' there's no be-lievin' their gossip. But I got what happened straight from Jake Evarts. The fight come off day before yestiddy. Your father's gang rode down to Isbel's ranch. Daggs was seen to be wantin' some of the Isbel hosses, so Evarts says. An' Guy Isbel an' Jacobs run out in the pasture. Daggs an' some others shot them down . . ."

"Killed them—that way?" put in Ellen, sharply.

"So Evarts says. He was on the ridge an' swears he seen it all. They killed Guy an' Jacobs in cold blood. No chance

fer their lives—not even to fight! . . . Wal, then they surrounded the Isbel cabin. The fight lasted all thet day an'
all night an' the next day. Evarts says Guy an' Jacobs laid
out thar all this time. An' a herd of hogs broke in the pasture an' was eatin' the dead bodies . . ."

"My God!" burst out Ellen. "Uncle John, y'u shore
cain't mean my father wouldn't stop fightin' long enough
to drive the hogs off an' bury those daid men?"

"Evarts says they stopped fightin', all right, but it was
to watch the hogs," declared Sprague. "An' then, what d'
ye think? The wimminfolks come out—the redheaded
one, Guy's wife, an' Jacobs's wife—they drove the hogs
away an' buried their husbands right there in the pasture.
Evarts says he seen the graves."

"It is the women who can teach these bloody Texans a
lesson," declared Ellen, forcibly.

"Wal, Daggs was drunk, an' he got up from behind
where the gang was hidin', an' dared the Isbels to come
out. They shot him to pieces. An' thet night some one of
the Isbels shot Craig, who was alone on guard. . . . An'
last—this here's what I come to tell you—Jean Isbel
slipped up in the dark on Greaves an' knifed him."

"Why did y'u want to tell me that particularly?" asked
Ellen, slowly.

"Because I reckon the facts in the case are queer—an'
because, Ellen, your name was mentioned," announced
Sprague, positively.

"My name—mentioned?" echoed Ellen. Her horror
and disgust gave way to a quickening process of thought,
a mounting astonishment. "By whom?"

"Jean Isbel," replied Sprague, as if the name and the
fact were momentous.

Ellen sat still as a stone, her hands between her knees.
Slowly she felt the blood recede from her face, prickling

her skin down below her neck. That name locked her thought.

"Ellen, it's a mighty queer story—too queer to be a lie," went on Sprague. "Now you listen! Evarts got this from Ted Meeker. An' Ted Meeker heerd it from Greaves, who didn't die till the next day after Jean Isbel knifed him. An' your dad shot Ted fer tellin' what he heerd. . . . No, Greaves wasn't killed outright. He was cut somethin' turrible—in two places. They wrapped him all up an' next day packed him in a wagon back to Grass Valley. Evarts says Ted Meeker was friendly with Greaves an' went to see him as he was layin' in his room next to the store. Wal, accordin' to Meeker's story, Greaves came to an' talked. He said he was sittin' there in the dark, shootin' occasionally at Isbel's cabin, when he heerd a rustle behind him in the grass. He knowed some one was crawlin' on him. But before he could get his gun around he was jumped by what he thought was a grizzly bear. But it was a man. He shut off Greaves's wind an' dragged him back in the ditch. An' he said: 'Greaves, it's the half-breed. An' he's goin' to cut you—*first for Ellen Jorth!* an' then for Gaston Isbel!' . . . Greaves said Jean ripped him with a bowie knife. . . . An' thet was all Greaves remembered. He died soon after tellin' this story. He must hev fought awful hard. Thet second cut Isbel gave him went clear through him. . . . Some of the gang was thar when Greaves talked, an' naturally they wondered why Jean Isbel had said 'first for Ellen Jorth.' . . . Somebody remembered thet Greaves had cast a slur on your good name, Ellen. An' then they had Jean Isbel's reason fer sayin' thet to Greaves. It caused a lot of talk. An' when Simm Bruce busted in some of the gang haw-hawed him an' said as how he'd get the third cut from Jean Isbel's bowie. Bruce was half drunk an' he began to cuss an'

rave about Jean Isbel bein' in love with his girl. . . . As
bad luck would have it, a couple of more fellars come in
an' asked Meeker questions. He jest got to thet part,
'Greaves, it's the half-breed, an' he's goin' to cut you—
first for Ellen Jorth,' when in walked your father! . . .
Then it all had to come out—what Jean Isbel had said an'
done—an' why. How Greaves had backed Simm Bruce
in slurrin' you!"

Sprague paused to look hard at Ellen.

"Oh! Then—what did dad do?" whispered Ellen.

"He said, 'By God! half-breed or not, there's one Isbel
who's a man!' An' he killed Bruce on the spot an' gave
Meeker a nasty wound. Somebody grabbed him before
he could shoot Meeker again. They threw Meeker out
an' he crawled to a neighbor's house, where he was when
Evarts seen him."

Ellen felt Sprague's rough but kindly hand shaking her.
"An' now what do you think of Jean Isbel?" he queried.

A great, unsurmountable wall seemed to obstruct Ellen's thought. It seemed gray in color. It moved toward her.
It was inside her brain.

"I tell you, Ellen Jorth," declared the old man, "thet
Jean Isbel loves you—loves you turribly—an' he believes
you're good."

"Oh no—he doesn't!" faltered Ellen.

"Wal, he jest does."

"Oh, Uncle John, he cain't believe that!" she cried.

"Of course he can. He does. You are good—good as
gold, Ellen, an' he knows it. . . . What a queer deal it all
is! Poor devil! To love you thet turribly an' hev to fight
your people! Ellen, your dad had it correct. Isbel or not
he's a man. . . . An' I say what a shame you two are divided by hate. Hate thet you hed nothin' to do with."
Sprague patted her head and rose to go. "Mebbe thet fight
will end the trouble. I reckon it will. Don't cross bridges

till you come to them, Ellen. . . . I must hurry back now. I didn't take time to unpack my burros. Come up soon. . . . An', say, Ellen, don't think hard any more of thet Jean Isbel."

Sprague strode away, and Ellen neither heard nor saw him go. She sat perfectly motionless, yet had a strange sensation of being lifted by invisible and mighty power. It was like movement felt in a dream. She was being impelled upward when her body seemed immovable as stone. When her blood beat down this deadlock of all her physical being and rushed on and on through her veins it gave her an irresistible impulse to fly, to sail through space, to run and run and run.

And on the moment the black horse, Spades, coming from the meadow, whinnied at sight of her. Ellen leaped up and ran swiftly, but her feet seemed to be stumbling. She hugged the horse and buried her hot face in his mane and clung to him. Then just as violently she rushed for her saddle and bridle and carried the heavy weight as easily as if it had been an empty sack. Throwing them upon him, she buckled and strapped with strong, eager hands. It never occurred to her that she was not dressed to ride. Up she flung herself. And the horse, sensing her spirit, plunged into strong, free gait down the cañon trail.

The ride, the action, the thrill, the sensations of violence were not all she needed. Solitude, the empty aisles of the forest, the far miles of lonely wilderness—were these the added all? Spades took a swinging, rhythmic lope up the winding trail. The wind fanned her hot face. The sting of whipping aspen branches was pleasant. A deep rumble of thunder shook the sultry air. Up beyond the green slope of the cañon massed the creamy clouds, shading darker and darker. Spades loped on the levels, leaped the washes, trotted over the rocky ground, and took to a walk up the long slope. Ellen dropped the reins over the pommel. Her hands could not stay set on anything. They pressed her breast and flew out to caress the white aspens and to tear at the maple leaves, and gather the lavender juniper berries, and came back again to her heart. Her heart that was going to burst or break! As it had swelled, so now it labored. It could not keep pace with her needs. All that was physical, all that was living in her had to be unleashed.

Spades gained the level forest. How the great, brown-green pines seemed to bend their lofty branches over her, protectively, understandingly. Patches of azure-blue sky flashed between the trees. The great white clouds sailed along with her, and shafts of golden sunlight, flecked with gleams of falling pine needles, shone down through the canopy overhead. Away in front of her, up the slow heave of forest land, boomed the heavy thunderbolts along the battlements of the Rim.

Was she riding to escape from herself? For no gait suited her until Spades was running hard and fast through the glades. Then the pressure of dry wind, the thick odor of pine, the flashes of brown and green and gold and blue, the soft, rhythmic thuds of hoofs, the feel of the powerful horse under her, the whip of spruce branches on her muscles contracting and expanding in hard action—all these sensations seemed to quell for the time the mounting cataclysm in her heart.

The oak swales, the maple thickets, the aspen groves; the pine-shaded aisles, and the miles of silver spruce all sped by her, as if she had ridden the wind; and through the forest ahead shone the vast open of the Basin, gloomed by purple and silver cloud, shadowed by gray storm, and in the west brightened by golden sky.

Straight to the Rim she had ridden, and to the point where she had watched Jean Isbel that unforgettable day. She rode to the promontory behind the pine thicket and beheld a scene which stayed her restless hands upon her heaving breast.

The world of sky and cloud and earthly abyss seemed one of storm-sundered grandeur. The air was sultry and still, and smelled of the peculiar burnt-wood odor caused by lightning striking trees. A few heavy drops of rain were pattering down from the thin, gray edge of clouds overhead. To the east hung the storm—a black cloud lodged against the Rim, from which long, misty veils of rain streamed down into the gulf. The roar of rain sounded like the steady roar of the rapids of a river. Then a blue-white, piercingly bright, ragged streak of lightning shot down out of the black cloud. It struck with a splitting report that shocked the very wall of rock under Ellen. Then the heavens seemed to burst open with thundering crash and close with mighty thundering boom. Long roar and longer rumble rolled away to the eastward. The rain poured down in roaring cataracts.

The south held a panorama of purple-shrouded range and cañon, cañon and range, on across the rolling leagues to the dim, lofty peaks, all canopied over with angry, dusky, low-drifting clouds, horizon-wide, smoky, and sulphurous. And as Ellen watched, hands pressed to her breast, feeling incalculable relief in sight of this tempest and gulf that resembled her soul, the sun burst out from behind the long bank of purple cloud in the west and flooded the world there with golden lightning.

"It is for me!" cried Ellen. "My mind—my heart—my very soul.... Oh, I know! I know now! ... I love him—love him—love him!"

She cried it out to the elements. "Oh, I love Jean Isbel—an' my heart will burst or break!"

The might of her passion was like the blaze of the sun. Before it all else retreated, diminished. The suddenness of the truth dimmed her sight. But she saw clearly enough to crawl into the pine thicket, through the clutching, dry twigs, over the mats of fragrant needles to the covert where she had once spied upon Jean Isbel. And here she lay face down for a while, hands clutching the needles, breast pressed hard upon the ground, stricken and spent. But vitality was exceeding strong in her. It passed, that weakness of realization, and she awakened to the consciousness of love.

But in the beginning it was not consciousness of the man. It was new, sensorial life, elemental, primitive, a liberation of a million inherited instincts, quivering and physical, over which Ellen had no more control than she had over the glory of the sun. If she thought at all it was of her need to be hidden, like an animal, low down near the earth, covered by green thicket, lost in the wildness of nature. She went to nature, unconsciously seeking a mother. And love was a birth from the depths of her, like a rushing spring of pure water, long underground, and at last propelled to the surface by a convulsion.

Ellen gradually lost her tense rigidity and relaxed. Her body softened. She rolled over until her face caught the lacy, golden shadows cast by sun and bough. Scattered drops of rain pattered around her. The air was hot, and its odor was that of dry pine and spruce fragrance penetrated by brimstone from the lightning. The nest where she lay was warm and sweet. No eye save that of nature saw her in her abandonment. An ineffable and exquisite smile wreathed her lips, dreamy, sad, sensuous, the supremy of unconscious happiness. Over her dark and eloquent eyes, as Ellen gazed upward, spread a luminous film, a veil. She was looking intensely, yet she did not see. The wilderness enveloped her with its secretive, elemental sheaths of rock, of tree, of cloud, of sunlight. Through her thrilling skin poured the multiple and nameless sensations of the living organism stirred to supreme sensitiveness. She could not lie still, but all her movements were gentle, involuntary. The slow reaching out of her hand, to grasp at nothing visible, was similar to the lazy stretching of her limbs, to the heave of her breast, to the ripple of muscle.

Ellen knew not what she felt. To live that sublime hour was beyond thought. Such happiness was like the first dawn of the world to the sight of man. It had to do with bygone ages. Her heart, her blood, her flesh, her very bones were filled with instincts and emotions common to the race before intellect developed, when the savage lived only with his sensorial perceptions. Of all happiness, joy, bliss, rapture to which man was heir, that of intense and exquisite preoccupation of the senses, unhindered and unburdened by thought, was the greatest. Ellen felt that which life meant with its inscrutable design. Love was only the realization of her mission on the earth.

The dark storm cloud with its white, ragged ropes of lightning and down-streaming gray veils of rain, the purple gulf rolling like a colored sea to the dim mountains, the glorious golden light of the sun—these had enchanted her eyes with the beauty of the universe. They had burst the windows of her blindness. When she crawled into the green-brown covert it was to escape too great perception. She needed to be encompassed by close tangible things. And there her body paid the tribute to the realization of life. Shock, convulsion, pain, relaxation, and then unutterable and insupportable sensing of her environment and the heart! In one way she was a wild animal alone in the woods, forced into the mating that meant reproduction of its kind. In another she was an infinitely higher being shot through and through with the most resistless and mysterious transport that life could give to flesh.

And when that spell slackened its hold there wedged into her mind a consciousness of the man she loved—Jean

Isbel. Then emotion and thought strove for mastery over her. It was not herself or love that she loved, but a living man. Suddenly he existed so clearly for her that she could see him, hear him, almost feel him. Her whole soul, her very life cried out to him for protection, for salvation, for love, for fulfillment. No denial, no doubt marred the white blaze of her realization. From the instant that she had looked up into Jean Isbel's dark face she had loved him. Only she had not known. She bowed now, and bent, and humbly quivered under the mastery of something beyond her ken. Thought clung to the beginnings of her romance—to the three times she had seen him. Every look, every word, every act of his returned to her now in the light of the truth. Love at first sight! He had sworn it, bitterly, eloquently, scornful of her doubts. And now a blind, sweet, shuddering ecstasy swayed her. How weak and frail seemed her body—too small, too slight for this monstrous and terrible engine of fire and lightning and fury and glory—her heart! It must burst or break. Relentlessly memory pursued Ellen, and her thoughts whirled and emotion conquered her. At last she quivered up to her knees as if lashed to action. It seemed that first kiss of Isbel's, cool and gentle and timid, was on her lips. And her eyes closed and hot tears welled from under her lids. Her groping hands found only the dead twigs and the pine boughs of the trees. Had she reached out to clasp him? Then hard and violent on her mouth and cheek and neck burned those other kisses of Isbel's, and with the flashing, stinging memory came the truth that now she would have bartered her soul for them. Utterly she surrendered to the resistlessness of this love. Her loss of mother and friends, her wandering from one wild place to another, her lonely life among bold and rough men, had developed her for violent love. It overthrew all pride, it engendered humility, it killed hate. Ellen wiped the tears from her eyes, and as she knelt there she swept to her breast a fragrant spreading bough of pine needles. "I'll go to him," she whispered. "I'll tell him of—of my—my love. I'll tell him to take me away—away to the end of the world—away from heah—before it's too late!"

It was a solemn, beautiful moment. But the last spoken words lingered hauntingly. "Too late?" she whispered.

And suddenly it seemed that death itself shuddered in her soul. Too late! It was too late. She had killed his love. That Jorth blood in her—that poisonous hate—had chosen the only way to strike this noble Isbel to the heart. Basely, with an abandonment of womanhood, she had mockingly perjured her soul with a vile lie. She writhed, she shook under the whip of this inconceivable fact. Lost! Lost! She wailed her misery. She might as well be what she had made Jean Isbel think she was. If she had been shamed before, she was now abased, degraded, lost in her own sight. And if she would have given her soul for his kisses, she now would have killed herself to earn back his respect. Jean Isbel had given her at sight the deference that she had unconsciously craved, and the love that would have been her salvation. What a horrible mistake she had made of her life! Not her mother's blood, but her father's—the Jorth blood—had been her ruin.

Again Ellen fell upon the soft pine-needle mat, face down, and she groveled and burrowed there, in an agony that could not bear the sense of light. All she had suffered was as nothing to this. To have awakened to a splendid and uplifting love for a man whom she had imagined she hated, who had fought for her name and had killed in revenge for the dishonor she had avowed—to have lost his love and what was infinitely more precious to her now in her ignominy—his faith in her purity—this broke her heart.

CHAPTER 11

When Ellen, utterly spent in body and mind, reached home that day a melancholy, sultry twilight was falling. Fitful flares of sheet lightning swept across the dark horizon to the east. The cabins were deserted. Antonio and the Mexican woman were gone. The circumstances made Ellen wonder, but she was too tired and too sunken in spirit to think long about it or to care. She fed and watered her horse and left him in the corral. Then, supperless and without removing her clothes, she threw herself upon the bed, and at once sank into heavy slumber.

Sometime during the night she awoke. Coyotes were yelping, and from that sound she concluded it was near dawn. Her body ached; her mind seemed dull. Drowsily she was sinking into slumber again when she heard the rapid clip-clop of trotting horses. Startled, she raised her head to listen. The men were coming back. Relief and dread seemed to clear her stupor.

The trotting horses stopped across the lane from her cabin, evidently at the corral where she had left Spades. She heard him whistle. From the sound of hoofs she judged the number of horses to be six or eight. Low voices of men mingled with thuds and cracking of straps and flopping of saddles on the ground. After that the heavy tread of boots sounded on the porch of the cabin opposite. A door creaked on its hinges. Next a slow footstep, accompanied by clinking of spurs, approached Ellen's door, and a heavy hand banged upon it. She knew this person could not be her father.

"Hullo, Ellen!"

She recognized the voice as belonging to Colter. Somehow its tone, or something about it, sent a little shiver down her spine. It acted like a revivifying current. Ellen lost her dragging lethargy.

"Hey, Ellen, are y'u there?" added Colter, in louder voice.

"Yes. Of course I'm heah," she replied. "What do y'u want?"

"Wal—I'm shore glad y'u're home," he replied. "Antonio's gone with his squaw. An' I was some worried aboot y'u."

"Who's with y'u, Colter?" queried Ellen, sitting up.

"Rock Wells an' Springer. Tad Jorth was with us, but we had to leave him over heah in a cabin."

"What's the matter with him?"

"Wal, he's hurt tolerable bad," was the slow reply.

Ellen heard Colter's spurs jangle, as if he had uneasily shifted his feet.

"Where's dad an' Uncle Jackson?" asked Ellen.

A silence pregnant enough to augment Ellen's dread finally broke to Colter's voice, somehow different. "Shore they're back on the trail. An' we're to meet them where we left Tad."

"Are y'u goin' away again?"

"I reckon. . . . An', Ellen, y'u're goin' with us."

"I am not," she retorted.

"Wal, y'u are, if I have to pack y'u," he replied, forcibly.

"It's not safe heah any more. That damned half-breed Isbel with his gang are on our trail."

That name seemed like a red-hot blade at Ellen's leaden heart. She wanted to fling a hundred queries on Colter, but she could not utter one.

"Ellen, we've got to hit the trail an' hide," continued Colter, anxiously. "Y'u mustn't stay heah alone. Suppose them Isbels would trap y'u! . . . They'd tear your clothes off an' rope y'u to a tree. Ellen, shore y'u're goin'. . . . Y'u heah me!"

"Yes—I'll go," she replied, as if forced.

"Wal—that's good," he said, quickly. "An' rustle tolerable lively. We've got to pack."

The slow jangle of Colter's spurs and his slow steps moved away out of Ellen's hearing. Throwing off the blankets, she put her feet to the floor and sat there a moment staring at the blank nothingness of the cabin interior in the obscure gray of dawn. Cold, gray, dreary, obscure—like her life, her future! And she was compelled to do what was hateful to her. As a Jorth she must take to the unfrequented trails and hide like a rabbit in the thickets. But the interest of the moment, a premonition of events to be, quickened her into action.

Ellen unbarred the door to let in the light. Day was breaking with an intense, clear, steely light in the east through which the morning star still shone white. A ruddy flare betokened the advent of the sun. Ellen unbraided her tangled hair and brushed and combed it. A queer, still pang came to her at sight of pine needles tangled in her brown locks. Then she washed her hands and face. Breakfast was a matter of considerable work and she was hungry.

The sun rose and changed the gray world of forest. For the first time in her life Ellen hated the golden brightness, the wonderful blue of sky, the scream of the eagle and the screech of the jay; and the squirrels she had always loved to feed were neglected that morning.

Colter came in. Either Ellen had never before looked attentively at him or else he had changed. Her scrutiny of his lean, hard features accorded him more Texan attributes than formerly. His gray eyes were as light, as clear, as fierce as those of an eagle. And the sand gray of his face, the long, drooping, fair mustache hid the secrets of his mind, but not its strength. The instant Ellen met his gaze she sensed a power in him that she instinctively opposed. Colter had not been so bold nor so rude as Daggs, but he was the same kind of man, perhaps the more dangerous for his secretiveness, his cool, waiting inscrutableness.

"Mawnin', Ellen!" he drawled. "Y'u shore look good for sore eyes."

"Don't pay me compliments, Colter," replied Ellen. "An' your eyes are not sore."

"Wal, I'm shore sore from fightin' an' ridin' an' layin' out," he said, bluntly.

"Tell me—what's happened," returned Ellen.

"Girl, it's a tolerable long story," replied Colter. "An' we've no time now. Wait till we get to camp."

"Am I to pack my belongin's or leave them heah?" asked Ellen.

"Reckon y'u'd better leave—them heah."

"But if we did not come back—"

"Wal, I reckon it's not likely we'll come—soon," he said, rather evasively.

"Colter, I'll not go off into the woods with just the clothes I have on my back."

"Ellen, we shore got to pack all the grub we can. This shore ain't goin' to be a visit to neighbors. We're shy pack hosses. But y'u make up a bundle of belongin's y'u care for, an' the things y'u'll need bad. We'll throw it on somewhere."

Colter stalked away across the lane, and Ellen found herself dubiously staring at his tall figure. Was it the situation that struck her with a foreboding perplexity or was her intuition steeling her against this man? Ellen could not decide. But she had to go with him. Her prejudice was unreasonable at this portentous moment. And she could not yet feel that she was solely responsible to herself.

When it came to making a small bundle of her belongings she was in a quandary. She discarded this and put in that, and then reversed the order. Next in preciousness to her mother's things were the long-hidden gifts of Jean Isbel. She could part with neither.

While she was selecting and packing this bundle Colter again entered and, without speaking, began to rummage in the corner where her father kept his possessions. This irritated Ellen.

"What do y'u want there?" she demanded.

"Wal, I reckon your dad wants his papers—an' the gold he left heah—an' a change of clothes. Now doesn't he?" returned Colter, coolly.

"Of course. But I supposed y'u would have me pack them."

Colter vouchsafed no reply to this, but deliberately went on rummaging, with little regard for how he scattered things. Ellen turned her back on him. At length, when he left, she went to her father's corner and found that, as far as she was able to see, Colter had taken neither papers nor clothes, but only the gold. Perhaps, however, she had been mistaken, for she had not observed Colter's departure closely enough to know whether or not he carried a package. She missed only the gold. Her father's papers, old and musty, were scattered about, and these she gathered up to slip in her own bundle.

Colter, or one of the men, had saddled Spades, and he was now tied to the corral fence, champing his bit and pounding the sand. Ellen wrapped bread and meat inside her coat, and after tying this behind her saddle she was ready to go. But evidently she would have to wait, and, preferring to remain outdoors, she stayed by her horse. Presently, while watching the men pack, she noticed that Springer wore a bandage round his head under the brim of his sombrero. His motions were slow and lacked energy. Shuddering at the sight, Ellen refused to conjecture. All too soon she would learn what had happened, and all too soon, perhaps, she herself would be in the midst of another fight. She watched the men. They were making a hurried slipshod job of packing food supplies from both cabins. More than once she caught Colter's gray gleam of gaze on her, and she did not like it.

"I'll ride up an' say good-by to Sprague," she called to Colter.

"Shore y'u won't do nothin' of the kind," he called back.

There was authority in his tone that angered Ellen, and something else which inhibited her anger. What was there about Colter with which she must reckon? The other two Texans laughed aloud, to be suddenly silenced by Colter's harsh and lowered curses. Ellen walked out of hearing and sat upon a log, where she remained until Colter hailed her.

"Get up an' ride," he called.

Ellen complied with this order and, riding up behind the three mounted men, she soon found herself leaving what for years had been her home. Not once did she look back. She hoped she would never see the squalid, bare pretension of a ranch again.

Colter and the other riders drove the pack horses across the meadow, off of the trails, and up the slope into the forest. Not very long did it take Ellen to see that Colter's object was to hide their tracks. He zigzagged through the forest, avoiding the bare spots of dust, the dry, sun-baked flats of clay where water lay in spring, and he chose the grassy, open glades, the long, pine-needle matted aisles. Ellen rode at their heels and it pleased her to watch for their tracks. Colter manifestly had been long practiced in this game of hiding his trail, and he showed the skill of a rustler. But Ellen was not convinced that he could ever elude a real woodsman. Not improbably, however, Colter was only aiming to leave a trail difficult to follow and which would allow him and his confederates ample time to forge ahead of pursuers. Ellen could not accept a certainty of pursuit. Yet Colter must have expected it, and Springer and Wells also, for they had a dark, sinister, furtive demeanor that strangely contrasted with the cool, easy manner habitual to them.

They were not seeking the level routes of the forestland, that was sure. They rode straight across the thick-timbered ridge down into another cañon, up out of that, and across rough, rocky bluffs, and down again. These riders headed a little to the northwest and every mile brought them into wilder, more rugged country, until Ellen, losing count of cañons and ridges, had no idea where she was. No stop was made at noon to rest the laboring, sweating pack animals.

Under circumstances where pleasure might have been possible Ellen would have reveled in this hard ride into a wonderful forest ever thickening and darkening. But the wild beauty of glade and the spruce slopes and the deep, bronze-walled cañons left her cold. She saw and felt, but had no thrill, except now and then a thrill of alarm when Spades slid to his haunches down some steep, damp, piny declivity.

All the woodland, up and down, appeared to be richer, greener as they traveled farther west. Grass grew thick and heavy. Water ran in all ravines. The rocks were bronze and copper and russet, and some had green patches of lichen.

Ellen felt the sun now on her left cheek and knew that the day was waning and that Colter was swinging farther to the northwest. She had never before ridden through such heavy forest and down and up such wild cañons. Toward sunset the deepest and ruggedest cañon halted their advance. Colter rode to the right, searching for a place to get down through a spruce thicket that stood on end. Presently he dismounted and the others followed suit. Ellen found she could not lead Spades because he slid down upon her heels, so she looped the end of her reins over the pommel and left him free. She herself managed to descend by holding to branches and sliding all the way down that slope. She heard the horses cracking the brush, snorting and heaving. One pack slipped and had to be removed from the horse, and rolled down. At the bottom of this deep, green-walled notch roared a stream of water. Shadowed, cool, mossy, damp, this narrow gulch seemed the wildest place Ellen had ever seen. She could just see the sunset-flushed, gold-tipped spruces far above her. The men repacked the horse that had slipped his burden, and once more resumed their progress ahead, now turning up this cañon. There was no horse trail, but deer and bear trails were numerous. The sun sank and the sky darkened, but still the men rode on; and the farther they traveled the wilder grew the aspect of the cañon.

At length Colter broke a way through a heavy thicket of willows and entered a side cañon, the mouth of which Ellen had not even descried. It turned and widened, and at length opened out into a round pocket, apparently inclosed, and as lonely and isolated a place as even pursued rustlers could desire. Hidden by jutting wall and thicket of spruce were two old log cabins joined together by roof and attic floor, the same as the double cabin at the Jorth ranch.

Ellen smelled wood smoke, and presently, on going round the cabins, saw a bright fire. One man stood beside it gazing at Colter's party, which evidently he had heard approaching.

"Hullo, Queen!" said Colter. "How's Tad?"

"He's holdin' on fine," replied Queen, bending over the fire, where he turned pieces of meat.

"Where's father?" suddenly asked Ellen, addressing Colter.

As if he had not heard her, he went on wearily loosening a pack.

Queen looked at her. The light of the fire only partially shone on his face. Ellen could not see its expression. But from the fact that Queen did not answer her question she got further intimation of an impending catastrophe. The long, wild ride had helped prepare her for the secrecy and taciturnity of men who had resorted to flight. Perhaps her father had been delayed or was still off on the deadly mission that had obsessed him; or there might, and probably was, darker reason for his absence. Ellen shut her teeth and turned to the needs of her horse. And presently, returning to the fire, she thought of her uncle.

"Queen, is my uncle Tad heah?" she asked.

"Shore. He's in there," replied Queen, pointing at the nearer cabin.

Ellen hurried toward the dark doorway. She could see how the logs of the cabin had moved awry and what a big, dilapidated hovel it was. As she looked in, Colter loomed over her—placed a familiar and somehow masterful hand upon her. Ellen let it rest on her shoulder a moment. Must she forever be repulsing these rude men among whom her lot was cast? Did Colter mean what Daggs had always meant? Ellen felt herself weary, weak in body, and her spent spirit had not rallied. Yet, whatever Colter meant by his familiarity, she could not bear it. So she slipped out from under his hand.

"Uncle Tad, are y'u heah?" she called into the blackness. She heard the mice scamper and rustle and she smelled the musty, old, woody odor of a long-unused cabin.

"Hello, Ellen!" came a voice she recognized as her uncle's, yet it was strange. "Yes. I'm heah—bad luck to me! . . . How 're y'u buckin' up, girl?"

"I'm all right, Uncle Tad—only tired an' worried. I—"

"Tad, how's your hurt?" interrupted Colter.

"Reckon I'm easier," replied Jorth, wearily, "but shore I'm in bad shape. I'm still spittin' blood. I keep tellin' Queen that bullet lodged in my lungs—but he says it went through."

"Wal, hang on, Tad!" replied Colter, with a cheerfulness Ellen sensed was really indifferent.

"Oh, what the hell's the use!" exclaimed Jorth. "It's all—up with us—Colter!"

"Wal, shut up, then," tersely returned Colter. "It ain't doin' y'u or us any good to holler."

Tad Jorth did not reply to this. Ellen heard his breathing and it did not seem natural. It rasped a little—came hurriedly—then caught in his throat. Then he spat. Ellen shrunk back against the door. He was breathing through blood.

"Uncle, are y'u in pain?" she asked.

"Yes, Ellen—it burns like hell," he said.

"Oh! I'm sorry. . . . Isn't there something I can do?"

"I reckon not. Queen did all anybody could do for me—now—unless it's pray."

Colter laughed at this—the slow, easy, drawling laugh

of a Texan. But Ellen felt pity for this wounded uncle. She had always hated him. He had been a drunkard, a gambler, a waster of her father's property; and now he was a rustler and a fugitive, lying in pain, perhaps mortally hurt.

"Yes, uncle—I will pray for y'u," she said, softly.

The change in his voice held a note of sadness that she had been quick to catch.

"Ellen, y'u're the only good Jorth—in the whole damned lot," he said. "God! I see it all now. . . . We've dragged y'u to hell!"

"Yes, Uncle Tad, I've shore been dragged some—but not yet—to hell," she responded, with a break in her voice.

"Y'u will be—Ellen—unless—"

"Aw, shut up that kind of gab, will y'u?" broke in Colter, harshly.

It amazed Ellen that Colter should dominate her uncle, even though he was wounded. Tad Jorth had been the last man to take orders from anyone, much less a rustler of the Hash Knife Gang. This Colter began to loom up in Ellen's estimate as he loomed physically over her, a lofty figure, dark, motionless, somehow menacing.

"Ellen, has Colter told y'u yet—aboot—aboot Lee an' Jackson?" inquired the wounded man.

The pitch-black darkness of the cabin seemed to help fortify Ellen to bear further trouble.

"Colter told me dad an' Uncle Jackson would meet us heah," she rejoined, hurriedly.

Jorth could be heard breathing in difficulty, and he coughed and spat again, and seemed to hiss.

"Ellen, he lied to y'u. They'll never meet us—heah!"

"Why not?" whispered Ellen.

"Because—Ellen—" he replied, in husky pants, "your dad an'—uncle Jackson—are daid—an' buried!"

If Ellen suffered a terrible shock it was a blankness, a deadness, and a slow, creeping failure of sense in her knees. They gave way under her and she sank on the grass against the cabin wall. She did not faint nor grow dizzy nor lose her sight, but for a while there was no process of thought in her mind. Suddenly then it was there—the quick, spiritual rending of her heart—followed by a profound emotion of intimate and irretrievable loss—and after that grief and bitter realization.

A n hour later Ellen found strength to go to the fire and partake of the food and drink her body sorely needed.

Colter and the men waited on her solicitously, and in silence, now and then stealing furtive glances at her from under the shadow of their black sombreros. The dark night settled down like a blanket. There were no stars. The wind moaned fitfully among the pines, and all about that lonely, hidden recess was in harmony with Ellen's thoughts.

"Girl, y'u're shore game," said Colter, admiringly. "An' I reckon y'u never got it from the Jorths."

"Tad in there—he's game," said Queen, in mild protest.

"Not to my notion," replied Colter. "Any man can be game when he's croakin', with somebody around. . . . But Lee Jorth an' Jackson—they always was yellow clear to their gizzards. They was born in Louisiana—not Texas. . . . Shore they're no more Texans than I am. Ellen heah, she must have got another strain in her blood."

To Ellen their words had no meaning. She rose and asked, "Where can I sleep?"

"I'll fetch a light presently an' y'u can make your bed in there by Tad," replied Colter.

"Yes, I'd like that."

"Wal, if y'u reckon y'u can coax him to talk you're shore wrong," declared Colter, with that cold timbre of voice that struck like steel on Ellen's nerves. "I cussed him good an' told him he'd keep his mouth shut. Talkin' makes him cough an' that fetches up the blood. . . . Besides, I reckon I'm the one to tell y'u how your dad an' uncle got killed. Tad didn't see it done, an' he was bad hurt when it happened. Shore all the fellars left have their idee aboot it. But I've got it straight."

"Colter—tell me now," cried Ellen.

"Wal, all right. Come over heah," he replied, and drew her away from the camp-fire, out in the shadow of gloom. "Poor kid! I shore feel bad aboot it." He put a long arm around her waist and drew her against him. Ellen felt it, yet did not offer any resistance. All her faculties seemed absorbed in a morbid and sad anticipation.

"Ellen, y'u shore know I always loved y'u—now don't y'u?" he asked, with suppressed breath.

"No, Colter. It's news to me—an' not what I want to heah."

"Wal, y'u may as well heah it right now," he said. "It's true. An' what's more—your dad gave y'u to me before he died."

"What! Colter, y'u must be a liar."

"Ellen, I swear I'm not lyin'," he returned, in eager passion. "I was with your dad last an' heard him last. He shore knew I'd loved y'u for years. An' he said he'd rather y'u be left in my care than anybody's."

"My father gave me to y'u in marriage!" ejaculated Ellen, in bewilderment.

Colter's ready assurance did not carry him over this point. It was evident that her words somewhat surprised and disconcerted him for the moment.

"To let me marry a rustler—one of the Hash Knife Gang!" exclaimed Ellen, with weary incredulity.

"Wal, your dad belonged to Daggs's gang, same as I do," replied Colter, recovering his cool ardor.

"No!" cried Ellen.

"Yes, he shore did, for years," declared Colter, positively. "Back in Texas. An' it was your dad that got Daggs to come to Arizona."

Ellen tried to fling herself away. But her strength and her spirit were ebbing, and Colter increased the pressure of his arm. All at once she sank limp. Could she escape her fate? Nothing seemed left to fight with or for.

"All right—don't hold me—so tight." she panted. "Now tell me how dad was killed . . . an' who—who—"

Colter bent over so he could peer into her face. In the darkness Ellen just caught the gleam of his eyes. She felt the virile force of the man in the strain of his body as he pressed her close. It all seemed unreal—a hideous dream—the gloom, the moan of the wind, the weird solitude, and this rustler with hand and will like cold steel.

"We'd come back to Greaves's store," Colter began. "An' as Greaves was daid we all got free with his liquor. Shore some of us got drunk. Bruce was drunk, an' Tad in there—he was drunk. Your dad put away more 'n I ever seen him. But shore he wasn't exactly drunk. He got one of them weak an' shaky spells. He cried an' he wanted some of us to get the Isbels to call off the fightin'. . . . He shore was ready to call it quits. I reckon the killin' of Daggs—an' then the awful way Greaves was cut up by Jean Isbel—took all the fight out of your dad. He said to me, 'Colter, we'll take Ellen an' leave this heah country—an' begin life all over again—where no one knows us.'"

"Oh, did he really say that? . . . Did he—really mean it?" murmured Ellen, with a sob.

"I'll swear it by the memory of my daid mother," protested Colter. "Wal, when night come the Isbels rode down on us in the dark an' began to shoot. They smashed in the door—tried to burn us out—an' hollered around for a while. Then they left an' we reckoned there'd be no more trouble that night. All the same we kept watch. I was the soberest one an' I bossed the gang. We had some quarrels aboot the drinkin'. Your dad said if we kept it up it 'd be the end of the Jorths. An' he planned to send word to the Isbels next mawnin' that he was ready for a truce. An' I was to go fix it up with Gaston Isbel. Wal, your dad went to bed in Greaves's room, an' a little while later your uncle Jackson went in there, too. Some of the men laid down in the store an' went to sleep. I kept guard till aboot three in the mawnin'. An' I got so sleepy I couldn't hold my eyes open. So I waked up Wells an' Slater an' set them on guard, one at each end of the store. Then I laid down on the counter to take a nap."

Colter's low voice, the strain and breathlessness of him, the agitation with which he appeared to be laboring, and especially the simple, matter-of-fact detail of his story, carried absolute conviction to Ellen Jorth. Her vague doubt of him had been created by his attitude toward her. Emotion dominated her intelligence. The images, the scenes called up by Colter's words, were as true as the gloom of the wild gulch and the loneliness of the night solitude—as true as the strange fact that she lay passive in the arm of a rustler.

"Wal, after a while I woke up," went on Colter, clearing his throat. "It was gray dawn. All was as still as death. . . . An' somethin' shore was wrong. Wells an' Slater had got to drinkin' again an' now laid daid drunk or asleep. Anyways, when I kicked them they never moved. Then I heard a moan. It came from the room where your dad an' uncle was. I went in. It was just light enough to see. Your uncle Jackson was layin' on the floor—cut half in two—daid as a door nail. . . . Your dad lay on the bed. He was alive, breathin' his last. . . . He says, 'That half-breed Isbel—knifed us—while we slept' . . . The winder shutter was open. I seen where Jean

Isbel had come in an' gone out. I seen his moccasin tracks in the dirt outside an' I seen where he'd stepped in Jackson's blood an' tracked it to the winder. Y'u shore can see them bloody tracks yourself, if y'u go back to Greaves's store. . . . Your dad was goin' fast. . . . He said, 'Colter—take care of Ellen,' an' I reckon he meant a lot by that. He kept sayin', 'My God! if I'd only seen Gaston Isbel before it was too late!' an' then he raved a little, whisperin' out of his haid. . . . An' after that he died. . . . I woke up the men, an' aboot sunup we carried your dad an' uncle out of town an' buried them. . . . An' them Isbels shot at us while we were buryin' our daid! That's where Tad got his hurt. . . . Then we hit the trail for Jorth's ranch. . . . An now, Ellen, that's all my story. Your dad was ready to bury the hatchet with his old enemy. An' that Nez Perce Jean Isbel, like the sneakin' savage he is, murdered your uncle an' your dad. . . . Cut him horrible—made him suffer tortures of hell—all for Isbel revenge!"

When Colter's husky voice ceased Ellen whispered through lips as cold and still as ice, "Let me go . . . leave me—heah—alone!"

"Why, shore! I reckon I understand," replied Colter. "I hated to tell y'u. But y'u had to heah the truth aboot that half-breed. . . . I'll carry your pack in the cabin an' unroll your blankets."

Releasing her, Colter strode off in the gloom. Like a dead weight, Ellen began to slide until she slipped down full length beside the log. And then she lay in the cool, damp shadow, inert and lifeless so far as outward physical movement was concerned. She saw nothing and felt nothing of the night, the wind, the cold, the falling dew. For the moment or hour she was crushed by despair, and seemed to see herself sinking down and down into a black, bottomless pit, into an abyss where murky tides of blood and furious gusts of passion contended between her body and her soul. Into the stormy blast of hell! In her despair she longed, she ached for death. Born of infidelity, cursed by a taint of evil blood, further cursed by higher instinct for good and happy life, dragged from one lonely and wild and sordid spot to another, never knowing love or peace or joy or home, left to the companionship of violent and vile men, driven by a strange fate to love with unquenchable and insupportable love a half-breed, a savage, an Isbel, the hereditary enemy of her people, and at last the ruthless murderer of her father—what in the name of God had she left to live for? Revenge! An eye for an eye! A life for a life! But she could not kill Jean Isbel. Woman's love could turn to hate, but not the love of Ellen Jorth. He could drag her by the hair in the dust, beat her, and make her a thing to loathe, and cut her mortally in his savage and implacable thirst for revenge—but with her last gasp she would whisper she loved him and that she had lied to him to kill his faith. It was that—his strange faith in her purity—which had won her love. Of all men, that he should be the one to recognize the truth of her, the womanhood yet unsullied—how strange, how terrible, how overpowering! False, indeed, was she to the Jorths! False as her mother had been to an Isbel! This agony and destruction of her soul was the bitter Dead Sea fruit— the sins of her parents visited upon her.

"I'll end it all," she whispered to the night shadows that hovered over her. No coward was she—no fear of pain or mangled flesh or death or the mysterious hereafter could ever stay her. It would be easy, it would be a last thrill, a transport of self-abasement and supreme self-proof of her love for Jean Isbel to kiss the Rim rock where his feet had trod and then fling herself down into the depths. She was the last Jorth. So the wronged Isbels would be avenged.

"But he would never know—never know—I lied to him!" she wailed to the night wind.

She was lost—lost on earth and to hope of heaven. She had right neither to live nor to die. She was nothing but a little weed along the trail of life, trampled upon, buried in the mud. She was nothing but a single rotten thread in a tangled web of love and hate and revenge. And she had broken.

Lower and lower she seemed to sink. Was there no end to this gulf of despair? If Colter had returned he would have found her a rag and a toy—a creature degraded, fit for his vile embrace. To be thrust deeper into the mire—to be punished fittingly for her betrayal of a man's noble love and her own womanhood—to be made an end of, body, mind, and soul.

But Colter did not return.

The wind mourned, the owls hooted, the leaves rustled, the insects whispered their melancholy night song, the camp-fire flickered and faded. Then the wild forestland seemed to close imponderably over Ellen. All that she wailed in her despair, all that she confessed in her abasement, was true, and hard as life could be—but she belonged to nature. If nature had not failed her, had God failed her? It was there—the lonely land of tree and fern and flower and brook, full of wild birds and beasts, where the mossy rocks could speak and the solitude had ears, where she had always felt herself unutterably a part of creation. Thus a wavering spark of hope quivered through the blackness of her soul and gathered light.

The gloom of the sky, the shifting clouds of dull shade, split asunder to show a glimpse of a radiant star, piercingly white, cold, pure, a steadfast eye of the universe, beyond all understanding and illimitable with its meaning of the past and the present and the future. Ellen watched it until the drifting clouds once more hid it from her strained sight.

What had that star to do with hell? She might be

crushed and destroyed by life, but was there not something beyond? Just to be born, just to suffer, just to die—
could that be all? Despair did not loose its hold on Ellen,
the strife and pang of her breast did not subside. But with
the long hours and the strange closing in of the forest
around her and the fleeting glimpse of that wonderful star,
with a subtle divination of the meaning of her beating
heart and throbbing mind, and, lastly, with a voice thundering at her conscience that a man's faith in a woman
must not be greater, nobler, than her faith in God and
eternity—with these she checked the dark flight of her
soul toward destruction.

CHAPTER 12

A chill, gray, somber dawn was breaking when Ellen dragged herself into the cabin and crept under her blankets, there to sleep the sleep of exhaustion.

When she awoke the hour appeared to be late afternoon. Sun and sky shone through the sunken and decayed roof of the old cabin. Her uncle, Tad Jorth, lay upon a blanket bed upheld by a crude couch of boughs. The light fell upon his face, pale, lined, cast in a still mold of suffering. He was not dead, for she heard his respiration.

The floor underneath Ellen's blankets was bare clay. She and Jorth were alone in this cabin. It contained nothing besides their beds and a rank growth of weeds along the decayed lower logs. Half of the cabin had a rude ceiling of rough-hewn boards which formed a kind of loft. This attic extended through to the adjoining cabin, forming the ceiling of the porch-like space between the two structures. There was no partition. A ladder of two aspen saplings, pegged to the logs, and with braces between for steps, led up to the attic.

Ellen smelled wood smoke and the odor of frying meat, and she heard the voices of men. She looked out to see that Slater and Somers had joined their party—an addition that might have strengthened it for defense, but did not lend her own situation anything favorable. Somers had always appeared the one best to avoid.

Colter espied her and called her to "Come an' feed your pale face." His comrades laughed, not loudly, but guardedly, as if noise was something to avoid. Nevertheless, they awoke Tad Jorth, who began to toss and moan on the bed.

Ellen hurried to his side and at once ascertained that he had a high fever and was in a critical condition. Every time he tossed he opened a wound in his right breast, rather high up. For all she could see, nothing had been done for him except the binding of a scarf round his neck and under his arm. This scant bandage had worked loose. Going to the door, she called out:

"Fetch me some water." When Colter brought it, Ellen was rummaging in her pack for some clothing or towel that she could use for bandages.

"Weren't any of y'u decent enough to look after my uncle?" she queried.

"Huh! Wal, what the hell!" rejoined Colter. "We shore did all we could. I reckon y'u think it wasn't a tough job to pack him up the Rim. He was done for then an' I said so."

"I'll do all I can for him," said Ellen.

"Shore. Go ahaid. When I get plugged or knifed by that half-breed I shore hope y'u'll be round to nurse me."

"Y'u seem to be pretty shore of your fate, Colter."

"Shore as hell!" he bit out, darkly. "Somers saw Isbel an' his gang trailin' us to the Jorth ranch."

"Are y'u goin' to stay heah—an' wait for them?"

"Shore I've been quarrelin' with the fellars out there over that very question. I'm for leavin' the country. But Queen, the damn gun fighter, is daid set to kill that cowman, Blue, who swore he was King Fisher, the old Texas outlaw. None but Queen are spoilin' for another fight. All the same they won't leave Tad Jorth heah alone."

Then Colter leaned in at the door and whispered: "Ellen, I can't boss this outfit. So let's y'u an' me shake 'em. I've got your dad's gold. Let's ride off to-night an' shake this country."

Colter, muttering under his breath, left the door and returned to his comrades. Ellen had received her first intimation of his cowardice; and his mention of her father's gold started a train of thought that persisted in spite of her efforts to put all her mind to attending her uncle. He grew conscious enough to recognize her working over him, and thanked her with a look that touched Ellen deeply. It changed the direction of her mind. His suffering and imminent death, which she was able to alleviate and retard somewhat, worked upon her pity and compassion so that she forgot her own plight. Half the night she was tending him, cooling his fever, holding him quiet. Well she realized that but for her ministrations he would have died. At length he went to sleep.

And Ellen, sitting beside him in the lonely, silent darkness of that late hour, received again the intimation of nature, those vague and nameless stirrings of her innermost being, those whisperings out of the night and the forest and the sky. Something great would not let go of her soul. She pondered.

Attention to the wounded man occupied Ellen; and soon she redoubled her activities in this regard, finding in them something of protection against Colter.

He had waylaid her as she went to a spring for water, and with a lunge like that of a bear he had tried to embrace her. But Ellen had been too quick.

"Wal, are y'u goin' away with me?" he demanded.

"No. I'll stick by my uncle," she replied.

That motive of hers seemed to obstruct his will. Ellen was keen to see that Colter and his comrades were at a last stand and disintegrating under a severe strain. Nerve and courage of the open and the wild they possessed, but only in a limited degree. Colter seemed obsessed by his passion for her, and though Ellen in her stubborn pride did not yet fear him, she realized she ought to. After that incident she watched closely, never leaving her uncle's bedside except when Colter was absent. One or more of the men kept constant lookout somewhere down the cañon.

Day after day passed on the wings of suspense, of watching, of ministering to her uncle, of waiting for some hour that seemed fixed.

Colter was like a hound upon her trail. At every turn he was there to importune her to run off with him, to frighten her with the menace of the Isbels, to beg her to give herself to him. It came to pass that the only relief she had was when she ate with the men or barred the cabin door at night. Not much relief, however, was there in the shut and barred door. With one thrust of his powerful arm Colter could have caved it in. He knew this as well as Ellen. Still she did not have the fear she should have had. There was her rifle beside her, and though she did not allow her mind to run darkly on its possible use, still the fact of its being there at hand somehow strengthened her. Colter was a cat playing with a mouse, but not yet sure of his quarry.

Ellen came to know hours when she was weak—weak physically, mentally, spiritually, morally—when under the sheer weight of this frightful and growing burden of suspense she was not capable of fighting her misery, her abasement, her low ebb of vitality, and at the same time wholly withstanding Colter's advances.

He would come into the cabin and, utterly indifferent to Tad Jorth, he would try to make bold and unrestrained love to Ellen. When he caught her in one of her unresisting moments and was able to hold her in his arms and kiss her he seemed to be beside himself with the wonder of her. At such moments, if he had any softness or gentleness in him, they expressed themselves in his sooner or later letting her go, when apparently she was about to faint. So it must have become fascinatingly fixed in Colter's mind that at times Ellen repulsed him with scorn and at others could not resist him.

Ellen had escaped two crises in her relation with this man, and as a morbid doubt, like a poisonous fungus, began to strangle her mind, she instinctively divined that there was an approaching and final crisis. No uplift of her spirit came this time—no intimations—no whisperings. How horrible it all was! To long to be good and noble—to realize that she was neither—to sink lower day by day! Must she decay there like one of these rotting logs? Worst of all, then, was the insinuating and ever-growing hopelessness. What was the use? What did it matter? Who would ever think of Ellen Jorth? "O God!" she whispered in her distraction, "is there nothing left—nothing at all?"

A period of several days of less torment to Ellen followed. Her uncle apparently took a turn for the better and Colter let her alone. This last circumstance nonplussed Ellen. She was at a loss to understand it unless the Isbel menace now encroached upon Colter so formidably that he had forgotten her for the present.

Then one bright August morning, when she had just began to relax her eternal vigilance and breathe without oppression, Colter encountered her and, darkly silent and fierce, he grasped her and drew her off her feet. Ellen struggled violently, but the total surprise had deprived her of strength. And that paralyzing weakness assailed her as never before. Without apparent effort Colter carried her, striding rapidly away from the cabins into the border of spruce trees at the foot of the cañon wall.

"Colter—where—oh, where are y'u takin' me?" she found voice to cry out.

"By God! I don't know," he replied, with strong, vibrant passion. "I was a fool not to carry y'u off long ago. But I waited. I was hopin' y'u'd love me! . . . An' now that Isbel gang has corralled us. Somers seen the half-breed up on the rocks. An' Springer seen the rest of them sneakin' around. I run back after my horse an' y'u."

"But Uncle Tad! . . . We mustn't leave him alone," cried Ellen.

"We've got to," replied Colter, grimly. "Tad shore won't worry y'u no more—soon as Jean Isbel gets to him."

"Oh, let me stay," implored Ellen. "I will save him."

Colter laughed at the utter absurdity of her appeal and claim. Suddenly he set her down upon her feet. "Stand still," he ordered. Ellen saw his big bay horse, saddled, with pack and blanket, tied there in the shade of a spruce. With swift hands Colter untied him and mounted him, scarcely moving his piercing gaze from Ellen. He reached to grasp her. "Up with y'u! . . . Put your foot in the stirrup!" His will, like his powerful arm, was irresistible for Ellen at that moment. She found herself swung up behind him. Then the horse plunged away. What with the hard motion and Colter's iron grasp on her Ellen was in a painful position. Her knees and feet came into violent contact with branches and snags. He galloped the horse, tearing through the dense thicket of willows that served to hide the entrance to the side cañon, and when out in the larger and more open cañon he urged him to a run. Presently when Colter put the horse to a slow rise of ground, thereby bringing him to a walk, it was just in time to save Ellen a serious bruising. Again the sunlight appeared to shade over. They were in the pines. Suddenly with backward lunge Colter halted the horse. Ellen heard a yell. She recognized Queen's voice.

"Turn back, Colter! Turn back!"

With an oath Colter wheeled his mount. "If I didn't run plump into them," he ejaculated, harshly. And scarcely had the goaded horse gotten a start when a shot rang out. Ellen felt a violent shock, as if her momentum had suddenly met with a check, and then she felt herself wrenched from Colter, from the saddle, and propelled into the air. She alighted on soft ground and thick grass, and was unhurt save for the violent wrench and shaking that had rendered her breathless. Before she could rise Colter was pulling at her, lifting her to her feet. She saw the horse lying with bloody head. Tall pines loomed all around. Another rifle cracked. "Run!" hissed Colter, and he bounded off, dragging her by the hand. Another yell pealed out. "Here we are, Colter!" Again it was Queen's shrill voice. Ellen ran with all her might, her heart in her throat, her sight failing to record more than a blur of passing pines and a blank green wall of spruce. Then she lost her balance, was falling, yet could not fall because of that steel grip on her hand, and was dragged, and finally carried, into a dense shade. She was blinded. The trees whirled and faded. Voices and shots sounded far away. Then something black seemed to be wiped across her feeling.

It turned to gray, to moving blankness, to dim, hazy objects, spectral and tall, like blanketed trees, and when Ellen fully recovered consciousness she was being carried through the forest.

"Wal, little one, that was a close shave for y'u," said Colter's hard voice, growing clearer. "Reckon your keelin' over was natural enough."

He held her lightly in both arms, her head resting above

his left elbow. Ellen saw his face as a gray blur, then taking sharper outline, until it stood out distinctly, pale and clammy, with eyes cold and wonderful in their intense flare. As she gazed upward Colter turned his head to look back through the woods, and his motion betrayed a keen, wild vigilance. The veins of his lean, brown neck stood out like whipcords. Two comrades were stalking beside him. Ellen heard their stealthy steps, and she felt Colter sheer from one side or the other. They were proceeding cautiously, fearful of the rear, but not wholly trusting to the fore.

"Reckon we'd better go slow an' look before we leap," said one whose voice Ellen recognized as Springer's.

"Shore. That open slope ain't to my likin', with our Nez Perce friend prowlin' round," drawled Colter, as he set Ellen down on her feet.

Another of the rustlers laughed. "Say, can't he twinkle through the forest? I had four shots at him. Harder to hit than a turkey runnin' crossways."

This facetious speaker was the evil-visaged, sardonic Somers. He carried two rifles and wore two belts of cartridges.

"Ellen, shore y'u ain't so daid white as y'u was," observed Colter, and he chucked her under the chin with familiar hand. "Set down heah. I don't want y'u stoppin' any bullets. An' there's no tellin'."

Ellen was glad to comply with his wish. She had begun to recover wits and strength, yet she still felt shaky. She observed that their position then was on the edge of a well-wooded slope from which she could see the grassy cañon floor below. They were on a level bench, projecting out from the main cañon wall that loomed gray and rugged and pine fringed. Somers and Colter and Springer gave careful attention to all points of the compass, especially in the direction from which they had come. They evidently anticipated being trailed or circled or headed off, but did not manifest much concern. Somers lit a cigarette; Springer wiped his face with a grimy hand and counted the shells in his belt, which appeared to be half empty. Colter stretched his long neck like a vulture and peered down the slope and through the aisles of the forest up toward the cañon rim.

"Listen!" he said, tersely, and bent his head a little to one side, ear to the slight breeze.

They all listened. Ellen heard the beating of her heart, the rustle of leaves, the tapping of a woodpecker, and faint, remote sounds that she could not name.

"Deer, I reckon," spoke up Somers.

"Ahuh! Wal, I reckon they ain't trailin' us yet," replied Colter. "We gave them a shade better 'n they sent us."

"Short an' sweet!" ejaculated Springer, and he removed his black sombrero to poke a dirty forefinger through a bullet hole in the crown. "Thet's how close I come to cashin'. I was lyin' behind a log, listenin' an' watchin', an' when I stuck my head up a little—zam! Somebody made my bonnet leak."

"Where's Queen?" asked Colter.

"He was with me fust off," replied Somers. "An' then when the shootin' slacked—after I'd plugged thet big, red-faced, white-haired pal of Isbel's—"

"Reckon thet was Blaisdell," interrupted Springer.

"Queen—he got tired layin' low," went on Somers. "He wanted action. I heerd him chewin' to himself, an' when I asked him what was eatin' him he up an' growled he was goin' to quit this Injun fightin'. An' he slipped off in the woods."

"Wal, that's the gun fighter of it," declared Colter, wagging his head. "Ever since that cowman, Blue, braced us an' said he was King Fisher, why Queen has been sulkier an' sulkier. He cain't help it. He'll do the same trick as

Blue tried. An' shore he'll get his everlastin'. But he's the Texas breed all right."

"Say, do you reckon Blue really is King Fisher?" queried Somers.

"Naw!" ejaculated Colter, with downward sweep of his hand. "Many a would-be gun slinger has borrowed Fisher's name. But Fisher is daid these many years."

"Ahuh! Wal, mebbe, but don't you fergit it—thet Blue was no would-be," declared Somers. "He was the genuine article."

"I should smile!" affirmed Springer.

The subject irritated Colter, and he dismissed it with another forcible gesture and a counter question.

"How many left in that Isbel outfit?"

"No tellin'. There shore was enough of them," replied Somers. "Anyhow, the woods was full of flyin' bullets. . . . Springer, did you account for any of them?"

"Nope—not thet I noticed," responded Springer, dryly. "I had my chance at the half-breed. . . . Reckon I was nervous."

"Was Slater near you when he yelled out?"

"No. He was lyin' beside Somers."

"Wasn't thet a queer way fer a man to act?" broke in Somers. "A bullet hit Slater, cut him down the back as he was lyin' flat. Reckon it wasn't bad. But it hurt him so thet he jumped right up an' staggered around. He made a target big as a tree. An' mebbe them Isbels didn't riddle him!"

"That was when I got my crack at Bill Isbel," declared Colter, with grim satisfaction. "When they shot my horse out from under me I had Ellen to think of an' couldn't get my rifle. Shore had to run, as y'u seen. Wal, as I only had my six-shooter, there was nothin' for me to do but lay low an' listen to the sping of lead. Wells was standin' up behind a tree aboot thirty yards off. He got plugged, an' fallin' over he began to crawl my way, still holdin' to his rifle. I crawled along the log to meet him. But he dropped aboot half-way. I went on an' took his rifle an' belt. When I peeped out from behind a spruce bush then I seen Bill Isbel. He was shootin' fast, an' all of them was shootin' fast. That was when they had the open shot at Slater. . . . Wal, I bored Bill Isbel right through his middle. He dropped his rifle an', all bent double, he fooled around in a circle till he flopped over the Rim. I reckon he's layin' right up there somewhere below that daid spruce. I'd shore like to see him."

"Wal, you'd be as crazy as Queen if you tried thet," declared Somers. "We're not out of the woods yet."

"I reckon not," replied Colter. "An' I've lost my horse. Where'd y'u leave yours?"

"They're down the cañon, below thet willow brake. An' saddled an' none of them tied. Reckon we'll have to look them up before dark."

"Colter, what 're we goin' to do?" demanded Springer.

"Wait heah a while—then cross the cañon an' work round up under the bluff, back to the cabin."

"An' then what?" queried Somers, doubtfully eying Colter.

"We've got to eat—we've got to have blankets," rejoined Colter, testily. "An' I reckon we can hide there an' stand a better show in a fight than runnin' for it in the woods."

"Wal, I'm givin' you a hunch thet it looked like you was runnin' fer it," retorted Somers.

"Yes, an' packin' the girl," added Springer. "Looks funny to me."

Both rustlers eyed Colter with dark and distrustful glances. What he might have replied never transpired, for the reason that his gaze, always shifting around, had suddenly fixed on something.

"Is that a wolf?" he asked, pointing to the Rim.

Both his comrades moved to get in line with his finger. Ellen could not see from her position.

"Shore thet's a big lofer," declared Somers. "Reckon he scented us."

"There he goes along the Rim," observed Colter. "He doesn't act leary. Looks like a good sign to me. Mebbe the Isbels have gone the other way."

"Looks bad to me," rejoined Springer, gloomily.

"An' why?" demanded Colter.

"I seen thet animal. Fust time I reckoned it was a lofer. Second time it was right near them Isbels. An' I'm damned now if I don't believe it's thet half-lofer sheep dog of Gass Isbel's."

"Wal, what if it is?"

"Ha! . . . Shore we needn't worry about hidin' out," replied Springer, sententiously. "With thet dog Jean Isbel could trail a grasshopper."

"The hell y'u say!" muttered Colter. Manifestly such a possibility put a different light upon the present situation. The men grew silent and watchful, occupied by brooding thoughts and vigilant surveillance of all points. Somers slipped off into the brush, soon to return, with intent look of importance.

"I heerd somethin'," he whispered, jerking his thumb backward. "Rollin' gravel—crackin' of twigs. No deer! . . . Reckon it 'd be a good idee for us to slip round acrost this bench."

"Wal, y'u fellers go, an' I'll watch heah," returned Colter.

"Not much," said Somers, while Springer leered knowingly.

Colter became incensed, but he did not give way to it. Pondering a moment, he finally turned to Ellen. "Y'u wait heah till I come back. An' if I don't come in reasonable time y'u slip across the cañon an' through the willows to the cabins. Wait till aboot dark." With that he possessed himself of one of the extra rifles and belts and silently joined his comrades. Together they noiselessly stole into the brush.

Ellen had no other thought than to comply with Colter's wishes. There was her wounded uncle who had been left unattended, and she was anxious to get back to him. Besides, if she had wanted to run off from Colter, where could she go? Alone in the woods, she would get lost and die of starvation. Her lot must be cast with the Jorth faction until the end. That did not seem far away.

Her strained attention and suspense made the moments fly. By and by several shots pealed out far across the side cañon on her right, and they were answered by reports sounding closer to her. The fight was on again. But these shots were not repeated. The flies buzzed, the hot sun beat down and sloped to the west, the soft, warm breeze stirred the aspens, the ravens croaked, the red squirrels and blue jays chattered.

Suddenly a quick, short, yelp electrified Ellen, brought her upright with sharp, listening rigidity. Surely it was not a wolf and hardly could it be a coyote. Again she heard it. The yelp of a sheep dog! She had heard that often enough to know. And she rose to change her position so she could command a view of the rocky bluff above. Presently she espied what really appeared to be a big timber wolf. But another yelp satisfied her that it really was a dog. She watched him. Soon it became evident that he wanted to get down over the bluff. He ran to and fro, and then out of sight. In a few moments his yelp sounded from lower down, at the base of the bluff, and it was now the cry of an intelligent dog that was trying to call some one to his aid. Ellen grew convinced that the dog was near where Colter had said Bill Isbel had plunged over the declivity. Would the dog yelp that way if the man was dead? Ellen thought not.

No one came, and the continuous yelping of the dog got on Ellen's nerves. It was a call for help. And finally she surrendered to it. Since her natural terror when Colter's horse was shot from under her and she had been dragged away, she had not recovered from fear of the Isbels. But calm consideration now convinced her that she could hardly be in a worse plight in their hands than if she remained in Colter's. So she started out to find the dog.

The wooded bench was level for a few hundred yards, and then it began to heave in rugged, rocky bulges up toward the Rim. It did not appear far to where the dog was barking, but the latter part of the distance proved to be a hard climb over jumbled rocks and through thick brush. Panting and hot, she at length reached the base of the bluff, to find that it was not very high.

The dog espied her before she saw him, for he was coming toward her when she discovered him. Big, shaggy, grayish white and black, with wild, keen face and eyes he assuredly looked the reputation Springer had accorded him. But sagacious, guarded as was his approach, he appeared friendly.

"Hello—doggie!" panted Ellen. "What's—wrong—up heah?"

He yelped, his ears lost their stiffness, his body sank a little, and his bushy tail wagged to and fro. What a gray, clear, intelligent look he gave her! Then he trotted back.

Ellen followed him around a corner of bluff to see the body of a man lying on his back. Fresh earth and gravel lay about him, attesting to his fall from above. He had on neither coat nor hat, and the position of his body and limbs suggested broken bones. As Ellen hurried to his side she saw that the front of his shirt, low down, was a bloody blotch. But he could lift his head; his eyes were open; he was perfectly conscious. Ellen did not recognize the dusty, skinned face, yet the mold of features, the look of the eyes, seemed strangely familiar.

"You're—Jorth's—girl," he said, in faint voice of surprise.

"Yes, I'm Ellen Jorth," she replied. "An' are y'u Bill Isbel?"

"All thet's left of me. But I'm thankin' God somebody come—even a Jorth."

Ellen knelt beside him and examined the wound in his abdomen. A heavy bullet had indeed, as Colter had avowed, torn clear through his middle. Even if he had not sustained other serious injury from the fall over the cliff, that terrible bullet wound meant death very shortly. Ellen shuddered. How inexplicable were men! How cruel, bloody, mindless!

"Isbel, I'm sorry—there's no hope," she said, low voiced. "Y'u've not long to live. . . . I cain't help y'u. God knows I'd do so if I could."

"All over!" he sighed, with his eyes looking beyond her. "I reckon—I'm glad. . . . But y'u can—do somethin' for me. Will y'u?"

"Indeed, yes. Tell me," she replied, lifting his dusty head on her knee. Her hands trembled as she brushed his wet hair back from his clammy brow.

"I've somethin'—on my conscience," he whispered.

The woman, the sensitive in Ellen, understood and pitied him then.

"Yes," she encouraged him.

"I stole cattle—my dad's an' Blaisdell's—an' made deals—with Daggs. . . . All the crookedness—wasn't on—Jorth's side. . . . I want—my brother Jean—to know."

"I'll try—to tell him," whispered Ellen, out of her great amaze.

"We were all—a bad lot—except Jean," went on Isbel.

"Dad wasn't fair. . . . God! how he hated Jorth! Jorth, yes, who was—your father. . . . Wal, they're even now."

"How—so?" faltered Ellen.

"Your father killed dad. . . . At the last—dad wanted to—save us. He sent word—he'd meet him—face to face—an' let thet end the feud. They met out in the road. . . . But some one shot dad down—with a rifle—an' then your father finished him."

"An' then, Isbel," added Ellen, with unconscious mocking bitterness, "your brother murdered my dad!"

"What!" whispered Bill Isbel. "Shore y'u've got—it wrong. I reckon Jean—could have killed—your father. . . . But he didn't. Queer, we all thought."

"Ah! . . . Who did kill my father?" burst out Ellen, and her voice rang like great hammers at her ears.

"It was Blue. He went in the store—alone—faced the whole gang alone. Bluffed them—taunted them—told them he was King Fisher. . . . Then he killed—your dad—an' Jackson Jorth. . . . Jean was out—back of the store. We were out—front. There was shootin'. Colmor was hit. Then Blue ran out—bad hurt. . . . Both of them—died in Meeker's yard."

"An' so Jean Isbel has not killed a Jorth!" said Ellen, in strange, deep voice.

"No," replied Isbel, earnestly, "I reckon this feud—was hardest on Jean. He never lived heah. . . . An' my sister Ann said—he got sweet on y'u. . . . Now did he?"

Slow, stinging tears filled Ellen's eyes, and her head sank low and lower.

"Yes—he did," she murmured, tremulously.

"Ahuh! Wal, thet accounts," replied Isbel, wonderingly. "Too bad! . . . It might have been. . . . A man always sees—different when—he's dyin'. . . . If I had—my life—to live over again! . . . My poor kids—deserted in their babyhood—ruined for life! All for nothin'. . . . May God forgive—"

Then he choked and whispered for water.

Ellen laid his head back and, rising, she took his sombrero and started hurriedly down the slope, making dust fly and rocks roll. Her mind was a seething ferment. Leaping, bounding, sliding down the weathered slope, she gained the bench, to run across that, and so on down into the open cañon to the willow-bordered brook. Here she filled the sombrero with water and started back, forced now to walk slowly and carefully. It was then, with the violence and fury of intense muscular activity denied her, that the tremendous import of Bill Isbel's revelation burst upon her very flesh and blood and transfiguring the very world of golden light and azure sky and speaking forestland that encompassed her.

Not a drop of the precious water did she spill. Not a misstep did she make. Yet so great was the spell upon her that she was not aware she had climbed the steep slope until the dog yelped his welcome. Then with all the flood of her emotion surging and resurging she knelt to allay the parching thirst of this dying enemy whose words had changed frailty to strength, hate to love, and the gloomy hell of despair to something unutterable. But she had returned too late. Bill Isbel was dead.

CHAPTER 13

Jean Isbel, holding the wolf-dog Shepp in leash, was on the trail of the most dangerous of Jorth's gang, the gunman Queen. Dark drops of blood on the stones and plain tracks of a rider's sharp-heeled boots behind coverts indicated the trail of a wounded, slow-traveling fugitive. Therefore, Jean Isbel held in the dog and proceeded with the wary eye and watchful caution of an Indian.

Queen, true to his class, and emulating Blue with the same magnificent effrontery and with the same paralyzing suddenness of surprise, had appeared as if by magic at the last night camp of the Isbel faction. Jean had seen him first, in time to leap like a panther into the shadow. But he carried in his shoulder Queen's first bullet of that terrible encounter. Upon Gordon and Fredericks fell the brunt of Queen's fusillade. And they, shot to pieces, staggering and falling, held passionate grip on life long enough to draw and still Queen's guns and send him reeling off into the darkness of the forest.

Unarmed, and hindered by a painful wound, Jean had kept a vigil near camp all that silent and menacing night. Morning disclosed Gordon and Fredericks stark and ghastly beside the burned-out camp-fire, their guns clutched immovably in stiffened hands. Jean buried them as best he could, and when they were under ground with flat stones on their graves he knew himself to be indeed the last of the Isbel clan. And all that was wild and savage in his blood and desperate in his spirit rose to make him more than man and less than human. Then for the third time during these tragic last days the wolf-dog Shepp came to him.

Jean washed the wound Queen had given him and bound it tightly. The keen pang and burn of the lead was a constant and all-powerful reminder of the grim work left for him to do. The whole world was no longer large enough for him and whoever was left of the Jorths. The heritage of blood his father had bequeathed him, the unshakable love for a worthless girl who had so dwarfed and obstructed his will and so bitterly defeated and reviled his poor, romantic, boyish faith, the killing of hostile men, so strange in its after effects, the pursuits and fights, and loss of one by one of his confederates—these had finally engendered in Jean Isbel a wild, unslakable thirst, these had been the cause of his retrogression, these had unalterably and ruthlessly fixed in his darkened mind one fierce passion—to live and die the last man of that Jorth-Isbel feud.

At sunrise Jean left this camp, taking with him only a small knapsack of meat and bread, and with the eager, wild Shepp in leash he set out on Queen's bloody trail.

Black drops of blood on the stones and an irregular trail of footprints proved to Jean that the gunman was hard hit. Here he had fallen, or knelt, or sat down, evidently to bind his wounds. Jean found strips of scarf, red and discarded. And the blood drops failed to show on more rocks. In a deep forest of spruce, under silver-tipped spreading branches, Queen had rested, perhaps slept. Then laboring with dragging steps, not improbably with a lame leg, he had gone on, up out of the dark-green ravine to the open, dry, pine-tipped ridge. Here he had rested, perhaps waited to see if he were pursued. From that point his trail spoke an easy language for Jean's keen eye. The gunman knew he was pursued. He had seen his enemy. Therefore Jean proceeded with a slow caution, never getting within revolver range of ambush, using all his woodcraft to trail this man and yet save himself. Queen traveled slowly, either because he was wounded or else because he tried to ambush his pursuer, and Jean accommodated his pace to that of Queen. From noon of that day they were never far apart, never out of hearing of a rifle shot.

The contrast of the beauty and peace and loneliness of the surroundings to the nature of Queen's flight often obtruded its strange truth into the somber turbulence of Jean's mind, into that fixed columnar idea around which fleeting thoughts hovered and gathered like shadows.

Early frost had touched the heights with its magic wand. And the forest seemed a temple in which man might worship nature and life rather than steal through the dells and under the arched aisles like a beast of prey. The green-and-gold leaves of aspens quivered in the glades; maples in the ravines fluttered their red-and-purple leaves. The needle-matted carpet under the pines vied with the long lanes of silvery grass, alike enticing to the eye of man and beast. Sunny rays of light, flecked with dust and flying insects, slanted down from the overhanging brown-limbed, green-massed foliage. Roar of wind in the distant forest alternated with soft breeze close at hand. Small dove-gray squirrels ran all over the woodland, very curious about Jean and his dog, rustling the twigs, scratching the bark of trees, chattering and barking, frisky, saucy, and bright-eyed. A plaintive twitter of wild canaries came from the region above the treetops—first voices of birds in their pilgrimage toward the south. Pine cones dropped with soft thuds. The blue jays followed these intruders in the forest, screeching their displeasure. Like rain pattered the dropping seeds from the spruces. A woody, earthy, leafy fragrance, damp with the current of life, mingled with a cool, dry, sweet smell of withered grass and rotting pines.

Solitude and lonesomeness, peace and rest, wild life and nature, reigned there. It was a golden-green region, enchanting to the gaze of man. An Indian would have walked there with his spirits.

And even as Jean felt all this elevating beauty and inscrutable spirit his keen eye once more fastened upon the blood-red drops Queen had again left on the gray moss and rock. His wound had reopened. Jean felt the thrill of the scenting panther.

The sun set, twilight gathered, night fell. Jean crawled under a dense, low-spreading spruce, ate some bread and meat, fed the dog, and lay down to rest and sleep. His thoughts burdened him, heavy and black as the mantle of night. A wolf mourned a hungry cry for a mate. Shepp quivered under Jean's hand. That was the call which had lured him from the ranch. The wolf blood in him yearned for the wild. Jean tied the cowhide leash to his wrist. When this dark business was at an end Shepp could be free to join the lonely mate mourning out there in the forest. Then Jean slept.

Dawn broke cold, clear, frosty, with silvered grass sparkling, with a soft, faint rustling of falling aspen leaves. When the sun rose red Jean was again on the trail of Queen. By a frosty-ferned brook, where water tinkled and ran clear as air and cold as ice, Jean quenched his thirst, leaning on a stone that showed drops of blood. Queen, too, had to quench his thirst. What good, what help, Jean wondered, could the cold, sweet, granite water, so dear to woodsmen and wild creatures, do this wounded, hunted rustler? Why did he not wait in the open to fight and face the death he had meted? Where was that splendid and terrible daring of the gunman? Queen's love of life dragged him on and on, hour by hour, through the pine groves and spruce woods, through the oak swales and aspen glades, up and down the rocky gorges, around the windfalls and over the rotting logs.

The time came when Queen tried no more ambush. He gave up trying to trap his pursuer by lying in wait. He gave up trying to conceal his tracks. He grew stronger or, in desperation, increased his energy, so that he redoubled his progress through the wilderness. That, at best, would count only a few miles a day. And he began to circle to the northwest, back toward the deep cañon where Blaisdell and Bill Isbel had reached the end of their trails. Queen had evidently left his comrades, had lone-handed it in his last fight, but was now trying to get back to them. Somewhere in these wild, deep forest brakes the rest of the Jorth faction had found a hiding place. Jean let Queen lead him there.

Ellen Jorth would be with them. Jean had seen her. It had been his shot that killed Colter's horse. And he had withheld further fire because Colter had dragged the girl behind him, protecting his body with hers. Sooner or later Jean would come upon their camp. She would be there. The thought of her dark beauty, wasted in wantonness upon these rustlers, added a deadly rage to the blood lust and righteous wrath of his vengeance. Let her again flaunt her degradation in his face and, by the God she had forsaken, he would kill her, and so end the race of Jorths!

Another night fell, dark and cold, without starlight. The wind moaned in the forest. Shepp was restless. He sniffed the air. There was a step on his trail. Again a mournful, eager, wild, and hungry wolf cry broke the silence. It was deep and low, like that of a baying hound, but infinitely wilder. Shepp strained to get away. During the night, while Jean slept, he managed to chew the cowhide leash apart and run off.

Next day no dog was needed to trail Queen. Fog and low-drifting clouds in the forest and a misty rain had put the rustler off his bearings. He was lost, and showed that he realized it. Strange how a matured man, fighter of a hundred battles, steeped in bloodshed, and on his last stand, should grow panic-stricken upon being lost! So Jean Isbel read the signs of the trail.

Queen circled and wandered through the foggy, dripping forest until he headed down into a cañon. It was one that notched the Rim and led down and down, mile after mile into the Basin. Not soon had Queen discovered his mistake. When he did do so, night overtook him.

The weather cleared before morning. Red and bright the sun burst out of the east to flood that low basin land with light. Jean found that Queen had traveled on and on, hoping, no doubt, to regain what he had lost. But in the darkness he had climbed to the manzanita slopes instead of back up the cañon. And here he had fought the hold of that strange brush of Spanish name until he fell exhausted.

Surely Queen would make his stand and wait somewhere in this devilish thicket for Jean to catch up with him. Many and many a place Jean would have chosen had he been in Queen's place. Many a rock and dense thicket Jean circled or approached with extreme care. Manzanita grew in patches that were impenetrable except for a small animal. The brush was a few feet high, seldom so high that Jean could not look over it, and of a beautiful appearance, having glossy, small leaves, a golden berry, and branches of dark-red color. These branches were tough and unbendable. Every bush, almost, had low branches that were dead, hard as steel, sharp as thorns, as clutching as cactus. Progress was possible only by endless detours to find the half-closed aisles between patches, or else by crashing through with main strength or walking right over the tops. Jean preferred this last method, not because it was the easiest, but for the reason that he could see ahead so much farther. So he literally walked across the tips of the manzanita brush. Often he fell through and had to step up again; many a branch broke with him, letting him down; but for the most part he stepped from fork to fork, on branch after branch, with balance of an Indian and the patience of a man whose purpose was sustaining and immutable.

On that south slope under the Rim the sun beat down hot. There was no breeze to temper the dry air. And before midday Jean was laboring, wet with sweat, parching with thirst, dusty and hot and tiring. It amazed him, the doggedness and tenacity of life shown by this wounded rustler. The time came when under the burning rays of the sun he was compelled to abandon the walk across the tips of the manzanita bushes and take to the winding, open threads that ran between. It would have been poor sight indeed that could not have followed Queen's labyrinthine and broken passage through the brush. Then the time came when Jean espied Queen, far ahead and above, crawling like a black bug along the bright-green slope. Sight then acted upon Jean as upon a hound in the chase. But he governed his actions if he could not govern his instincts. Slowly but surely he followed the dusty, hot trail, and never a patch of blood failed to send a thrill along his veins.

Queen, headed up toward the Rim, finally vanished from sight. Had he fallen? Was he hiding? But the hour disclosed that he was crawling. Jean's keen eye caught the slow moving of the brush and enabled him to keep just so close to the rustler, out of range of the six-shooters he carried. And so all the interminable hours of the hot afternoon that snail-pace flight and pursuit kept on.

Half-way up the Rim the growth of manzanita gave place to open, yellow, rocky slope dotted with cedars. Queen took to a slow-ascending ridge and left his bloody tracks all the way to the top, where in the gathering darkness the weary pursuer lost them.

Another night passed. Daylight was relentless to the rustler. He could not hide his trail. But somehow in a desperate last rally of strength he reached a point on the heavily timbered ridge that Jean recognized as being near the scene of the fight in the cañon. Queen was nearing the rendezvous of the rustlers. Jean crossed tracks of horses, and then more tracks that he was certain had been made days past by his own party. To the left of this ridge must be the deep cañon that had frustrated his efforts to catch up with the rustlers on the day Blaisdell lost his life, and probably Bill Isbel, too. Something warned Jean that he was nearing the end of the trail, and an unaccountable sense of imminent catastrophe seemed foreshadowed by vague dreads and doubts in his gloomy mind. Jean felt the need of rest, of food, of ease from the strain of the last weeks. But his spirit drove him implacably.

Queen's rally of strength ended at the edge of an open, bald ridge that was bare of brush or grass and was surrounded by a line of forest on three sides, and on the fourth by a low bluff which raised its gray head above the pines. Across this dusty open Queen had crawled, leaving unmistakable signs of his condition. Jean took long survey of the circle of trees and of the low, rocky eminence, neither of which he liked. It might be wiser to keep to cover, Jean thought, and work around to where Queen's trail entered the forest again. But he was tired, gloomy, and his eternal vigilance was failing. Nevertheless, he stilled for the thousandth time that bold prompting of his vengeance and, taking to the edge of the forest, he went to considerable pains to circle the open ground. And suddenly sight of a man sitting back against a tree halted Jean.

He stared to make sure his eyes did not deceive him. Many times stumps and snags and rocks had taken on strange resemblance to a standing or crouching man. This was only another suggestive blunder of the mind behind his eyes—what he wanted to see he imagined he saw. Jean glided on from tree to tree until he made sure that this sitting image indeed was that of a man. He sat bolt upright, facing back across the open, hands resting on his knees—and closer scrutiny showed Jean that he held a gun in each hand.

Queen! At the last his nerve had revived. He could not crawl any farther, he could never escape, so with the courage of fatality he chose the open, to face his foe and die. Jean had a thrill of admiration for the rustler. Then he stalked out from under the pines and strode forward with his rifle ready.

A watching man could not have failed to espy Jean. But Queen never made the slightest move. Moreover, his stiff, unnatural position struck Jean so singularly that he halted with a muttered exclamation. He was now about fifty paces from Queen, within range of those small guns. Jean called, sharply, *"Queen!"* Still the figure never relaxed in the slightest.

Jean advanced a few more paces, rifle up, ready to fire the instant Queen lifted a gun. The man's immobility brought the cold sweat to Jean's brow. He stopped to bend the full intense power of his gaze upon this inert figure. Suddenly over Jean flashed its meaning. Queen was dead. He had backed up against the pine, ready to face his foe, and he had died there. Not a shadow of a doubt entered Jean's mind as he started forward again. He knew. After all, Queen's blood would not be on his hands. Gordon and Fredericks in their death throes had given the rustler mortal wounds. Jean kept on, marveling the while. How ghastly thin and hard! Those four days of flight had been hell for Queen.

Jean reached him—looked down with staring eyes. The guns were tied to his hands. Jean started violently as the whole direction of his mind shifted. A lightning glance showed that Queen had been propped against the tree— another showed boot tracks in the dust.

"By Heaven, they've fooled me!" hissed Jean, and quickly as he leaped behind the pine he was not quick enough to escape the cunning rustlers who had waylaid him thus. He felt the shock, the bite and burn of lead before he heard a rifle crack. A bullet had ripped through his left forearm. From behind the tree he saw a puff of white smoke along the face of the bluff—the very spot his keen and gloomy vigilance had descried as one of menace. Then several puffs of white smoke and ringing reports betrayed the ambush of the tricksters. Bullets barked the pine and whistled by. Jean saw a man dart from behind a rock and, leaning over, run for another. Jean's swift shot stopped him midway. He fell, got up, and floundered behind a bush scarcely large enough to conceal him. Into that bush Jean shot again and again. He had no pain in his wounded arm, but the sense of the shock clung in his consciousness, and this, with the tremendous surprise of the deceit, and sudden release of long-dammed overmastering passion, caused him to empty the magazine of his Winchester in a terrible haste to kill the man he had hit.

These were all the loads he had for his rifle. Blood passion had made him blunder. Jean cursed himself, and his hand moved to his belt. His six-shooter was gone. The sheath had been loose. He had tied the gun fast. But the strings had been torn apart. The rustlers were shooting again. Bullets thudded into the pine and whistled by. Bending carefully, Jean reached one of Queen's guns and jerked it from his hand. The weapon was empty. Both of his guns were empty. Jean peeped out again to get the line in which the bullets were coming and, marking a course from his position to the cover of the forest, he ran with all his might. He gained the shelter. Shrill yells behind warned him that he had been seen, that his reason for flight had been guessed. Looking back, he saw two or three men scrambling down the bluff. Then the loud neigh of a frightened horse pealed out.

Jean discarded his useless rifle, and headed down the ridge slope, keeping to the thickest line of pines and sheering around the clumps of spruce. As he ran, his mind whirled with grim thoughts of escape, of his necessity to find the camp where Gordon and Fredericks were buried, there to procure another rifle and ammunition. He felt the wet blood dripping down his arm, yet no pain. The forest was too open for good cover. He dared not run uphill. His only course was ahead, and that soon ended in an abrupt declivity too precipitous to descend. As he halted, panting for breath, he heard the ring of hoofs on stone, then the thudding beat of running horses on soft ground. The rustlers had sighted the direction he had taken. Jean did not waste time to look. Indeed, there was no need, for as he bounded along the cliff to the right a rifle cracked and a bullet whizzed over his head. It lent wings to his feet. Like a deer he sped along, leaping cracks and logs and rocks, his ears filled by the rush of wind, until his quick eye caught sight of thick-growing spruce foliage close to the precipice. He sprang down into the green mass. His weight precipitated him through the upper branches. But lower down his spread arms broke his fall, then retarded it until he caught. A long, swaying limb let him down and down, where he grasped another and a stiffer one that held his weight. Hand over hand he worked toward the trunk of this spruce and, gaining it, he found other

branches close together down which he hastened, hold
by hold and step by step, until all above him was black,
dense foliage, and beneath him the brown, shady slope.
Sure of being unseen from above, he glided noiselessly
down under the trees, slowly regaining freedom from
that constriction of his breast.

Passing on to a gray-lichened cliff, overhanging and
gloomy, he paused there to rest and to listen. A faint crack
of hoof on stone came to him from above, apparently farther on to the right. Eventually his pursuers would discover that he had taken to the cañon. But for the moment
he felt safe. The wound in his forearm drew his attention.
The bullet had gone clear through without breaking either
bone. His shirt sleeve was soaked with blood. Jean rolled
it back and tightly wrapped his scarf around the wound,
yet still the dark-red blood oozed out and dripped down
into his hand. He became aware of a dull, throbbing pain.

Not much time did Jean waste in arriving at what was
best to do. For the time being he had escaped, and whatever had been his peril, it was past. In dense, rugged country like this he could not be caught by rustlers. But he
had only a knife left for a weapon, and there was very little meat in the pocket of his coat. Salt and matches he
possessed. Therefore the imperative need was for him to
find the last camp, where he could get rifle and ammunition, bake bread, and rest up before taking again the trail
of the rustlers. He had reason to believe that this cañon
was the one where the fight on the Rim, and later, on a
bench of woodland below, had taken place.

Thereupon he arose and glided down under the spruces
toward the level, grassy open he could see between
the trees. And as he proceeded, with the slow step and
wary eye of an Indian, his mind was busy.

Queen had in his flight unerringly worked in the direction of this cañon until he became lost in the fog; and

upon regaining his bearings he had made a wonderful and heroic effort to surmount the manzanita slope and the Rim and find the rendezvous of his comrades. But he had failed up there on the ridge. In thinking it over Jean arrived at a conclusion that Queen, finding he could go no farther, had waited, guns in hands, for his pursuer. And he had died in this position. Then by strange coincidence his comrades had happened to come across him and, recognizing the situation, they had taken the shells from his guns and propped him up with the idea of luring Jean on. They had arranged a cunning trick and ambush, which had all but snuffed out the last of the Isbels. Colter probably had been at the bottom of this crafty plan. Since the fight at the Isbel ranch, now seemingly far back in the past, this man Colter had loomed up more and more as a stronger and more dangerous antagonist then either Jorth or Daggs. Before that he had been little known to any of the Isbel faction. And it was Colter now who controlled the remnant of the gang and who had Ellen Jorth in his possession.

The cañon wall above Jean, on the right, grew more rugged and loftier, and the one on the left began to show wooded slopes and brakes, and at last a wide expanse with a winding, willow border on the west and long, low, pine-dotted bench on the east. It took several moments of study for Jean to recognize the rugged bluff above this bench. On up that cañon several miles was the site where Queen had surprised Jean and his comrades at their campfire. Somewhere in this vicinity was the hiding place of the rustlers.

Thereupon Jean proceeded with the utmost stealth, absolutely certain that he would miss no sound, movement, sign, or anything unnatural to the wild peace of the cañon. And his first sense to register something was his keen smell. Sheep! He was amazed to smell sheep.

There must be a flock not far away. Then from where he glided along under the trees he saw down to open places in the willow brake and noticed sheep tracks in the dark, muddy bank of the brook. Next he heard faint tinkle of bells, and at length, when he could see farther into the open enlargement of the cañon, his surprised gaze fell upon an immense gray, woolly patch that blotted out acres and acres of grass. Thousands of sheep were grazing there. Jean knew there were several flocks of Jorth's sheep on the mountain in the care of herders, but he had never thought of them being so far west, more than twenty miles from Chevelon Cañon. His roving eyes could not descry any herders or dogs. But he knew there must be dogs close to that immense flock. And, whatever his cunning, he could not hope to elude the scent and sight of shepherd dogs. It would be best to go back the way he had come, wait for darkness, then cross the cañon and climb out, and work around to his objective point. Turning at once, he started to glide back. But almost immediately he was brought stock-still and thrilling by the sound of hoofs.

Horses were coming in the direction he wished to take. They were close. His swift conclusion was that the men who had pursued him up on the Rim had worked down into the cañon. One circling glance showed him that he had no sure covert near at hand. It would not do to risk their passing him there. The border of woodland was narrow and not dense enough for close inspection. He was forced to turn back up the cañon, in the hope of soon finding a hiding place or a break in the wall where he could climb up.

Hugging the base of the wall, he slipped on, passing the point where he had espied the sheep, and gliding on until he was stopped by a bend in the dense line of willows. It sheered to the west there and ran close to the high wall. Jean kept on until he was stooping under a curling border of willow thicket, with branches slim and yellow and masses of green foliage that brushed against the wall. Suddenly he encountered an abrupt corner of rock. He rounded it, to discover that it ran at right angles with the one he had just passed. Peering up through the willows, he ascertained that there was a narrow crack in the main wall of the cañon. It had been concealed by willows low down and leaning spruces above. A wild, hidden retreat! Along the base of the wall there were tracks of small animals. The place was odorous like all dense thickets, but it was not dry. Water ran through there somewhere. Jean drew easier breath. All sounds except the rustling of birds or mice in the willows had ceased. The brake was pervaded by a dreamy emptiness. Jean decided to steal on a little farther, then wait till he felt he might safely dare go back.

The golden-green gloom suddenly brightened. Light showed ahead, and parting the willows, he looked out into a narrow, winding cañon, with an open, grassy, willow-streaked lane in the center and on each side a thin strip of woodland.

His surprise was short lived. A crashing of horses back of him in the willows gave him a shock. He ran out along the base of the wall, back of the trees. Like the strip of woodland in the main cañon, this one was scant and had but little underbrush. There were young spruces growing with thick branches clear to the grass, and under these he could have concealed himself. But, with a certainty of sheep dogs in the vicinity, he would not think of hiding except as a last resource. These horsemen, whoever they were, were as likely to be sheep herders as not. Jean slackened his pace to look back. He could not see any moving objects, but he still heard horses, though not so close now. Ahead of him this narrow gorge opened out like the neck of a bottle. He would run on to the head of it and find a place to climb to the top.

Hurried and anxious as Jean was, he yet received an impression of singular, wild nature of this side gorge. It was a hidden, pine-fringed crack in the rock-ribbed and cañon-cut tableland. Above him the sky seemed a winding stream of blue. The walls were red and bulged out in spruce-greened shelves. From wall to wall was scarcely a distance of a hundred feet. Jumbles of rock obstructed his close holding to the wall. He had to walk at the edge of the timber. As he progressed, the gorge widened into wilder, ruggeder aspect. Through the trees ahead he saw where the wall circled to meet the cliff on the left, forming an oval depression, the nature of which he could not ascertain. But it appeared to be a small opening surrounded by dense thickets and the overhanging walls. Anxiety augmented to alarm. He might not be able to find a place to scale those rough cliffs. Breathing hard, Jean halted again. The situation was growing critical again. His physical condition was worse. Loss of sleep and rest, lack of food, the long pursuit of Queen, the wound in his arm, and the desperate run for his life—these had weakened him to the extent that if he undertook any strenuous effort he would fail. His cunning weighed all chances.

The shade of wall and foliage above, and another jumble of ruined cliff, hindered his survey of the ground ahead, and he almost stumbled upon a cabin, hidden on three sides, with a small, bare clearing in front. It was an old, ramshackle structure like others he had run across in the cañons. Cautiously he approached and peeped around the corner. At first swift glance it had all the appearance of long disuse. But Jean had no time for another look. A clip-clop of trotting horses on hard ground brought the same pell-mell rush of sensations that had driven him to wild flight scarcely an hour past. His body jerked with its instinctive impulse, then quivered with his restraint. To turn back would be risky, to run ahead would be fatal, to hide was his one hope. No covert behind! And the clip-clop of hoofs sounded closer. One moment longer Jean held mastery over his instincts of self-preservation. To keep from running was almost impossible. It was the sheer primitive animal sense to escape. He drove it back and glided along the front of the cabin.

Here he saw that the cabin adjoined another. Reaching the door, he was about to peep in when the thud of hoofs and voices close at hand transfixed him with a grim certainty that he had not an instant to lose. Through the thin, black-streaked line of trees he saw moving red objects. Horses! He must run. Passing the door, his keen nose caught a musty, woody odor and the tail of his eye saw bare dirt floor. This cabin was unused. He halted— gave a quick look back. And the first thing his eye fell upon was a ladder, right inside the door, against the wall. He looked up. It led to a loft that, dark and gloomy, stretched halfway across the cabin. An irresistible impulse drove Jean. Slipping inside, he climbed up the ladder to the loft. It was like night up there. But he crawled on the rough-hewn rafters and, turning with his head toward the opening, he stretched out and lay still.

What seemed an interminable moment ended with a trample of hoofs outside the cabin. It ceased. Jean's vibrating ears caught the jingle of spurs and a thud of boots striking the ground.

"Wal, sweetheart, heah we are home again," drawled a slow, cool, mocking Texas voice.

"Home! I wonder, Colter—did y'u ever have a home—a mother—a sister—much less a sweetheart?" was the reply, bitter and caustic.

Jean's palpitating, hot body suddenly stretched still and

cold with intensity of shock. His very bones seemed to quiver and stiffen into ice. During the instant of realization his heart stopped. And a slow, contracting pressure enveloped his breast and moved up to constrict his throat. That woman's voice belonged to Ellen Jorth. The sound of it had lingered in his dreams. He had stumbled upon the rendezvous of the Jorth faction. Hard indeed had been the fates meted out to those of the Isbels and Jorths who had passed to their deaths. But no ordeal, not even Queen's, could compare with this desperate one Jean must endure. He had loved Ellen Jorth, strangely, wonderfully, and he had scorned evil repute to believe her good. He had spared her father and her uncle. He had weakened or lost the cause of the Isbels. He loved her now, desperately, deathlessly, knowing from her own lips that she was worthless—loved her the more because he had felt her terrible shame. And to him—the last of the Isbels—had come the cruelest of dooms—to be caught like a crippled rat in a trap; to be compelled to lie helpless, wounded, without a gun; to listen, and perhaps to see Ellen Jorth enact the very truth of her mocking insinuation. His will, his promise, his creed, his blood must hold him to the stern decree that he should be the last man of the Jorth-Isbel war. But could he lie there to hear—to see—when he had a knife and an arm?

CHAPTER 14

Then followed the leathery flop of saddles to the soft turf and the stamp of loosened horses.

Jean heard a noise at the cabin door, a rustle, and then a knock of something hard against wood. Silently he moved his head to look down through a crack between the rafters. He saw the glint of a rifle leaning against the sill. Then the doorstep was darkened. Ellen Jorth sat down with a long, tired sigh. She took off her sombrero and the light shone on the rippling, dark-brown hair, hanging in a tangled braid. The curved nape of her neck showed a warm tint of golden tan. She wore a gray blouse, soiled and torn, that clung to her lissome shoulders.

"Colter, what are y'u goin' to do?" she asked, suddenly. Her voice carried something Jean did not remember. It thrilled into the icy fixity of his senses.

"We'll stay heah," was the response, and it was followed by a clinking step of spurred boot.

"Shore I won't stay heah," declared Ellen. "It makes me sick when I think of how Uncle Tad died in there alone—helpless—sufferin'. The place seems haunted."

"Wal, I'll agree that it's tough on y'u. . . . But what the hell *can* we do?"

A long silence ensued which Ellen did not break.

"Somethin' has come off round heah since early mawnin'," declared Colter. "Somers an' Springer haven't got back. An' Antonio's gone. . . . Now, honest, Ellen, didn't y'u heah rifle shots off somewhere?"

"I reckon I did," she responded, gloomily.

"An' which way?"

"Sounded to me up on the bluff, back pretty far."

"Wal, shore that's my idee. An' it makes me think hard. Y'u know Somers come across the last camp of the Isbels. An' he dug into a grave to find the bodies of Jim Gordon an' another man he didn't know. Queen kept good his brag. He braced that Isbel gang an' killed those fellars. But either him or Jean Isbel went off leavin' bloody tracks. If it was Queen's y'u can bet Isbel was after him. An' if it was Isbel's tracks, why shore Queen would stick to them. Somers an' Springer couldn't follow the trail. They're shore not much good at trackin'. But for days they've been ridin' the woods, hopin' to run across Queen. . . . Wal now, mebbe they run across Isbel instead. An' if they did an' got away from him they'll be heah sooner or later. If Isbel was too many for them he'd hunt for my trail. I'm gamblin' that either Queen or Jean Isbel is daid. I'm hopin' it's Isbel. Because if he ain't daid he's the last of the Isbels, an' mebbe I'm the last of Jorth's gang. . . . Shore I'm not hankerin' to meet the half-breed. That's why I say we'll stay heah. This is as good a hidin' place as there is in the country. We've grub. There's water an' grass."

"Me—stay heah with y'u—alone!"

The tone seemed a contradiction to the apparently accepted sense of her words. Jean held his breath. But he could not still the slowly mounting and accelerating faculties within that were involuntarily rising to meet some strange, nameless import. He felt it. He imagined it would be the catastrophe of Ellen Jorth's calm acceptance of Colter's proposition. But down in Jean's miserable heart lived something that would not die. No mere words could kill it. How poignant that moment of her silence! How terribly he realized that if his intelligence and his emotion had believed her betraying words, his soul had not!

But Ellen Jorth did not speak. Her brown head hung thoughtfully. Her supple shoulders sagged a little.

"Ellen, what's happened to y'u?" went on Colter.

"All the misery possible to a woman," she replied, dejectedly.

"Shore I don't mean that way," he continued, persuasively. "I ain't gainsayin' the hard facts of your life. It's been bad. Your dad was no good. . . . But I mean I can't figger the change in y'u."

"No, I reckon y'u cain't," she said. "Whoever was responsible for your make-up left out a mind—not to say feeling."

Colter drawled a low laugh.

"Wal, have that your own way. But how much longer are y'u goin' to be like this heah?"

"Like what?" she rejoined, sharply.

"Wal, this stand-offishness of yours?"

"Colter, I told y'u to let me alone," she said, sullenly.

"Shore. An' y'u did that before. But this time y'u're different. . . . An' wal, I'm gettin' tired of it."

Here the cool, slow voice of the Texan sounded an inflexibility before absent, a timber that hinted of illimitable power.

Ellen Jorth shrugged her lithe shoulders and, slowly rising, she picked up the little rifle and turned to step into the cabin.

"Colter," she said, "fetch my pack an' my blankets in heah."

"Shore," he returned, with good nature.

Jean saw Ellen Jorth lay the rifle lengthwise in a chink between two logs and then slowly turn, back to the wall. Jean knew her then, yet did not know her. The brown flash of her face seemed that of an older, graver woman. His strained gaze, like his waiting mind, had expected something, he knew not what—a hardened face, a ghost of beauty, a recklessness, a distorted, bitter, lost expression in keeping with her fortunes. But he had reckoned falsely. She did not look like that. There was incalculable change, but the beauty remained, somehow different. Her red lips were parted. Her brooding eyes, looking out straight from under the level, dark brows, seemed sloe black and wonderful with their steady, passionate light.

Jean, in his eager, hungry devouring of the beloved face, did not on the first instant grasp the significance of its expression. He was seeing the features that had haunted him. But quickly he interpreted her expression as the somber, hunted look of a woman who would bear no more. Under the torn blouse her full breast heaved. She held her hands clenched at her sides. She was listening, waiting for that jangling, slow step. It came, and with the sound she subtly changed. She was a woman hiding her true feelings. She relaxed, and that strong, dark look of fury seemed to fade back into her eyes.

Colter appeared at the door, carrying a roll of blankets and a pack.

"Throw them heah," she said. "I reckon y'u needn't bother coming in."

That angered the man. With one long stride he stepped over the doorsill, down into the cabin, and flung the blankets at her feet and then the pack after it. Whereupon he deliberately sat down in the door, facing her. With one hand he slid off his sombrero, which fell outside, and with the other he reached in his upper vest pocket for the little bag of tobacco that showed there. All the time he looked

at her. By the light now unobstructed Jean descried Colter's face; and sight of it then sounded the roll and drum
of his passions.

"Wal, Ellen, I reckon we'll have it out right now an'
heah," he said, and with tobacco in one hand, paper in the
other he began the operations of making a cigarette. However, he scarcely removed his glance from her.

"Yes?" queried Ellen Jorth.

"I'm goin' to have things the way they were before—an'
more," he declared. The cigarette paper shook in his fingers.

"What do y'u mean?" she demanded.

"Y'u know what I mean," he retorted. Voice and action
were subtly unhinging this man's control over himself.

"Maybe I don't. I reckon y'u'd better talk plain."

The rustler had clear gray-yellow eyes, flawless, like
crystal, and suddenly they danced with little fiery flecks.

"The last time I laid my hand on y'u I got hit for my
pains. An' shore that's been ranklin'."

"Colter, y'u'll get hit again if y'u put your hands on
me," she said, dark, straight glance on him. A frown wrinkled the level brows.

"Y'u mean that?" he asked, thickly.

"I shore do."

Manifestly he accepted her assertion. Something of incredulity and bewilderment, that had vied with his resentment, utterly disappeared from his face.

"Heah I've been waitin' for y'u to love me," he declared,
with a gesture not without dignified emotion. "Your givin'
in without that wasn't so much to me."

And at these words of the rustler's Jean Isbel felt an icy,
sickening shudder creep into his soul. He shut his eyes.
The end of his dream had been long in coming, but at last
it had arrived. A mocking voice, like a hollow wind,

echoed through that region—that lonely and ghost-like hall of his heart which had harbored faith.

She burst into speech, louder and sharper, the first words of which Jean's strangely throbbing ears did not distinguish.

"———— ———— you! . . . I never gave in to y'u an' I never will."

"But, girl—I kissed y'u—hugged y'u—handled y'u—" he expostulated, and the making of the cigarette ceased.

"Yes, y'u did—y'u brute—when I was so downhearted and weak I couldn't lift my hand," she flashed.

"Ahuh! Y'u mean I couldn't do that now?"

"I should smile I do, Jim Colter!" she replied.

"Wal, mebbe—I'll see—presently," he went on, straining with words. "But I'm shore curious. . . . Daggs, then—he was nothin' to y'u?"

"No more than y'u," she said, morbidly. "He used to run after me—long ago, it seems. . . . I was only a girl then—innocent—an' I'd not known any but rough men. I couldn't all the time—every day, every hour—keep him at arm's length. Sometimes before I knew—I didn't care. I was a child. A kiss meant nothing to me. But after I knew—"

Ellen dropped her head in brooding silence.

"Say, do y'u expect me to believe that?" he queried with a derisive leer.

"Bah! What do I care what y'u believe?" she cried, with lifting head.

"How aboot Simm Bruce?"

"That coyote! . . . He lied aboot me, Jim Colter. And any man half a man would have known he lied."

"Wal, Simm always bragged aboot y'u bein' his girl," asserted Colter. "An' he wasn't over-particular aboot details of your love-makin'."

Ellen gazed out of the door, over Colter's head, as if the forest out there was a refuge. She evidently sensed more about the man than appeared in his slow talk, in his slouching position. Her lips shut in a firm line, as if to hide their trembling and to still her passionate tongue. Jean, in his absorption, magnified his perceptions. Not yet was Ellen Jorth afraid of this man, but she feared the situation. Jean's heart was at bursting pitch. All within him seemed chaos—a wreck of beliefs and convictions. Nothing was true. He would wake presently out of a nightmare. Yet, as surely as he quivered there, he felt the imminence of a great moment—a lightning flash—a thunderbolt—a balance struck.

Colter attended to the forgotten cigarette. He rolled it, lighted it, all the time with lowered, pondering head, and when he had puffed a cloud of smoke he suddenly looked up with face as hard as flint, eyes as fiery as molten steel.

"Wal, Ellen—how aboot Jean Isbel—our half-breed Nez Perce friend—who was shore seen handlin' y'u familiar?" he drawled.

Ellen Jorth quivered as under a lash, and her brown face turned a dusty scarlet, that slowly receding left her pale.

"Damn y'u, Jim Colter!" she burst out, furiously. "I wish Jean Isbel would jump in that door—or down out of that loft! . . . He killed Greaves for defiling my name! . . . He'd kill *y'u* for your dirty insult. . . . And I'd like to watch him do it. . . . Y'u cold-blooded Texan! Y'u thieving rustler! Y'u liar! . . . Y'u lied aboot my father's death. And I know why. Y'u stole my father's gold. . . . An' now y'u want me—y'u expect me to fall into your arms. . . . My Heaven! cain't y'u tell a decent woman? Was your mother decent? Was your sister decent? . . . Bah! I'm appealing to deafness. But y'u'll *heah* this, Jim Colter! . . . I'm not what y'u think I am! I'm not the—the damned hussy y'u liars have made me out. . . . I'm a Jorth, alas! I've no home, no relatives, no friends! I've been forced to live my life with rustlers—vile men like y'u an' Daggs an' the rest of your like. . . . But I've been good! Do y'u heah that? . . . I *am* good—an', so help me God, y'u an' all your rottenness cain't make me bad!"

Colter lounged to his tall height and the laxity of the man vanished.

Vanished also was Jean Isbel's suspended icy dread, the cold clogging of his fevered mind—vanished in a white, living, leaping flame.

Silently he drew his knife and lay there watching with the eyes of a wildcat. The instant Colter stepped far enough over toward the edge of the loft Jean meant to bound erect and plunge down upon him. But Jean could wait now. Colter had a gun at his hip. He must never have a chance to draw it.

"Ahuh! So y'u wish Jean Isbel would hop in heah, do y'u?" queried Colter. "Wal, if I had any pity on y'u, that's done for it."

A sweep of his long arm, so swift Ellen had no time to move, brought his hand in clutching contact with her. And the force of it flung her half across the cabin room, leaving the sleeve of her blouse in his grasp. Pantingly she put out that bared arm and her other to ward him off as he took long, slow strides toward her.

Jean rose half to his feet, dragged by almost ungovernable passion to risk all on one leap. But the distance was too great. Colter, blind as he was to all outward things, would hear, would see in time to make Jean's effort futile. Shaking like a leaf, Jean sank back, eye again to the crack between the rafters.

Ellen did not retreat, nor scream, nor move. Every line of her body was instinct with fight, and the magnificent blaze of her eyes would have checked a less callous brute.

Colter's big hand darted between Ellen's arms and

fastened in the front of her blouse. He did not try to hold her or draw her close. The unleashed passion of the man required violence. In one savage pull he tore off her blouse, exposing her white, rounded shoulders and heaving bosom, where instantly a wave of red burned upward.

Overcome by the tremendous violence and spirit of the rustler, Ellen sank to her knees, with blanched face and dilating eyes, trying with folded arms and trembling hand to hide her nudity.

At that moment the rapid beat of hoofs on the hard trail outside halted Colter in his tracks.

"Hell!" he exclaimed. "An' who's that?" With a fierce action he flung the remnants of Ellen's blouse in her face and turned to leap out the door.

Jean saw Ellen catch the blouse and try to wrap it around her, while she sagged against the wall and stared at the door. The hoof beats pounded to a solid thumping halt just outside.

"Jim—thar's hell to pay!" rasped out a panting voice.

"Wal, Springer, I reckon I wished y'u'd paid it without spoilin' my deals," retorted Colter, cool and sharp.

"Deals? Ha! Y'u'll be forgettin'—your lady love—in a minnit," replied Springer. "When I catch—my breath."

"Where's Somers?" demanded Colter.

"I reckon he's all shot up—if my eyes didn't fool me."

"Where is he?" yelled Colter.

"Jim—he's layin' up in the bushes round thet bluff. I didn't wait to see how he was hurt. But he shore stopped some lead. An' he flopped like a chicken with its—haid cut off."

"Where's Antonio?"

"He run like the greaser he is," declared Springer, disgustedly.

"Ahuh! An' where's Queen?" queried Colter, after a significant pause.

"Dead!"

The silence ensuing was fraught with a suspense that held Jean in cold bonds. He saw the girl below rise from her knees, one hand holding the blouse to her breast, the other extended, and with strange, repressed, almost frantic look she swayed toward the door.

"Wal, talk," ordered Colter, harshly.

"Jim, there ain't a hell of a lot," replied Springer, drawing a deep breath, "but what there is is shore interestin'. . . . Me an' Somers took Antonio with us. He left his woman with the sheep. An' we rode up the cañon, clumb out on top, an' made a circle back on the ridge. That's the way we've been huntin' fer tracks. Up thar in a bare spot we run plump into Queen sittin' against a tree, right out in the open. Queerest sight y'u ever seen! The damn gun fighter had set down to wait for Isbel, who was trailin' him, as we suspected—an' he died thar. He wasn't cold when we found him. . . . Somers was quick to see a trick. So he propped Queen up an' tied the guns to his hands—an', Jim, the queerest thing aboot that deal was this—Queen's guns was empty! Not a shell left! It beat us holler. . . . We left him thar, an' hid up high on the bluff, mebbe a hundred yards off. The hosses we left back of a thicket. An' we waited thar a long time. But, sure enough, the half-breed come. He was too smart. Too much Injun! He would not cross the open, but went around. An' then he seen Queen. It was great to watch him. After a little he shoved his rifle out an' went right fer Queen. This is when I wanted to shoot. I could have plugged him. But Somers says wait an' make it sure. When Isbel got up to Queen he was sort of half hid by the tree. An' I couldn't wait no longer, so I shot. I hit him, too. We all begun to shoot. Somers showed himself, an' that's when Isbel opened up. He used up a whole magazine on Somers an' then, suddenlike, he quit. It didn't take me long to figger mebbe he was out of shells. When I seen him run I was certain of it. Then we made for the hosses an' rode after Isbel. Pretty soon I seen him runnin' like a deer down the ridge. I yelled an' spurred after him. There is where Antonio quit me. But I kept on. An' I got a shot at Isbel. He ran out of sight. I follered him by spots of blood on the stones an' grass until I couldn't trail him no more. He must have gone down over the cliffs. He couldn't have done nothin' else without me seein' him. I found his rifle, an' here it is to prove what I say. I had to go back to climb down off the Rim, an' I rode fast down the cañon. He's somewhere along that west wall, hidin' in the brush, hard hit if I know anythin' aboot the color of blood."

"Wal! . . . that beats me holler, too," ejaculated Colter.

"Jim, what's to be done?" inquired Springer, eagerly. "If we're sharp we can corral that half-breed. He's the last of the Isbels."

"More, pard. He's the last of the Isbel outfit," declared Colter. "If y'u can show me blood in his tracks I'll trail him."

"Y'u can bet I'll show y'u," rejoined the other rustler. "But listen! Wouldn't it be better for us first to see if he crossed the cañon? I reckon he didn't. But let's make sure. An' if he didn't we'll have him somewhar along that west cañon wall. He's not got no gun. He'd never run thet way if he had. . . . Jim, he's our meat!"

"Shore, he'll have that knife," pondered Colter.

"We needn't worry about thet," said the other, positively. "He's hard hit, I tell y'u. All we got to do is find thet bloody trail again an' stick to it—goin' careful. He's layin' low like a crippled wolf."

"Springer, I want the job of finishin' that half-breed," hissed Colter. "I'd give ten years of my life to stick a gun down his throat an' shoot it off."

"All right. Let's rustle. Mebbe y'u'll not have to give

much more 'n ten minnits. Because I tell y'u I can find him. It'd been easy—but, Jim, I reckon I was afraid."

"Leave your hoss for me an' go ahaid," the rustler then said, brusquely. "I've a job in the cabin heah."

"Haw-haw! . . . Wal, Jim, I'll rustle a bit down the trail an' wait. No huntin' Jean Isbel alone—-not fer me. I've had a queer feelin' about thet knife he used on Greaves. An' I reckon y'u'd oughter let thet Jorth hussy alone long enough to—"

"Springer, I reckon I've got to hawg-tie her—" His voice became indistinguishable, and footfalls attested to a slow moving away of the men.

Jean had listened with ears acutely strung to catch every syllable while his gaze rested upon Ellen who stood beside the door. Every line of her body denoted a listening intensity. Her back was toward Jean, so that he could not see her face. And he did not want to see, but could not help seeing her naked shoulders. She put her head out of the door. Suddenly she drew it in quickly and half turned her face, slowly raising her white arm. This was the left one and bore the marks of Colter's hard fingers.

She gave a little gasp. Her eyes became large and staring. They were bent on the hand that she had removed from a step on the ladder. On hand and wrist showed a bright-red smear of blood.

Jean, with a convulsive leap of his heart, realized that he had left his bloody tracks on the ladder as he had climbed. That moment seemed the supremely terrible one of his life.

Ellen Jorth's face blanched and her eyes darkened and dilated with exceeding amaze and flashing thought to become fixed with horror. That instant was the one in which her reason connected the blood on the ladder with the escape of Jean Isbel.

One moment she leaned there, still as a stone except

for her heaving breast, and then her fixed gaze changed to a swift, dark blaze, comprehending, yet inscrutable, as she flashed it up the ladder to the loft. She could see nothing, yet she knew and Jean knew that she knew he was there. A marvelous transformation passed over her features and even over her form. Jean choked with the ache in his throat. Slowly she put the bloody hand behind her while with the other she still held the torn blouse to her breast.

Colter's slouching, musical step sounded outside. And it might have been a strange breath of infinitely vitalizing and passionate life blown into the well-springs of Ellen Jorth's being. Isbel had no name for her then. The spirit of a woman had been to him a thing unknown.

She swayed back from the door against the wall in singular, softened poise, as if all the steel had melted out of her body. And as Colter's tall shadow fell across the threshold Jean Isbel felt himself staring with eyeballs that ached—straining incredulous sight at this woman who in a few seconds had bewildered his senses with her transfiguration. He saw but could not comprehend.

"Jim—I heard—all Springer told y'u," she said. The look of her dumfounded Colter and her voice seemed to shake him visibly.

"Suppose y'u did. What then?" he demanded, harshly, as he halted with one booted foot over the threshold. Malignant and forceful, he eyed her darkly, doubtfully.

"I'm afraid," she whispered.

"What of? Me?"

"No. Of—of Jean Isbel. He might kill y'u and—then where would I be?"

"Wal, I'm damned!" ejaculated the rustler. "What's got into y'u?" He moved to enter, but a sort of fascination bound him.

"Jim, I hated y'u a moment ago," she burst out. "But

now—with that Jean Isbel somewhere near—hidin'—watchin' to kill y'u—an' maybe me, too—I—I don't hate y'u any more. . . . Take me away."

"Girl, have y'u lost your nerve?" he demanded.

"My God! Colter—cain't y'u see?" she implored. "Won't y'u take me away?"

"I shore will—presently," he replied, grimly. "But y'u'll wait till I've shot the lights out of this Isbel."

"No!" she cried. "Take me away now. . . . An' I'll give in—I'll be what y'u—want. . . . Y'u can do with me—as y'u like."

Colter's lofty frame leaped as if at the release of bursting blood. With a lunge he cleared the threshold to loom over her.

"Am I out of my haid, or are y'u?" he asked, in low, hoarse voice. His darkly corded face expressed extremest amaze.

"Jim, I mean it," she whispered, edging an inch nearer him, her white face uplifted, her dark eyes unreadable in their eloquence and mystery. "I've no friend but y'u. . . . I'll be—yours. . . . I'm lost. . . . What does it matter? . . . If y'u want me—take me *now*—before I kill myself."

"Ellen Jorth, there's somethin' wrong aboot y'u," he responded. "Did y'u tell the truth—when y'u denied ever bein' a sweetheart of Simm Bruce?"

"Yes, I told y'u the truth."

"Ahuh! An' how do y'u account for layin' me out with every dirty name y'u could give tongue to?"

"Oh, it was temper. I wanted to be let alone."

"Temper! Wal, I reckon y'u've got one," he retorted, grimly. An' I'm not shore y'u're not crazy or lyin'. An hour ago I couldn't touch y'u."

"Y'u may now—if y'u promise to take me away—at once. This place has got on my nerves. I couldn't sleep heah with that Isbel hidin' around. Could y'u?"

"Wal, I reckon I'd not sleep very deep."

"Then let us go."

He shook his lean, eagle-like head in slow, doubtful vehemence, and his piercing gaze studied her distrustfully.
Yet all the while there was manifest in his strung frame
an almost irrepressible violence, held in abeyance to his
will.

"That aboot your bein' so good?" he inquired, with a
return of the mocking drawl.

"Never mind what's past," she flashed, with passion
dark as his. "I've made my offer."

"Shore there's a lie aboot y'u somewhere," he muttered,
thickly.

"Man, could I do more?" she demanded, in scorn.

"No. But it's a lie," he returned. "Y'u'll get me to take
y'u away an' then fool me—run off—God knows what.
Women are all liars."

Manifestly he could not believe in her strange transformation. Memory of her wild and passionate denunciation
of him and his kind must have seared even his calloused
soul. But the ruthless nature of him had not weakened nor
softened in the least as to his intentions. This weather-
vane veering of hers bewildered him, obsessed him with
its possibilities. He had the look of a man who was divided
between love of her and hate, whose love demanded a
return, but whose hate required a proof of her abasement. Not proof of surrender, but proof of her shame!
The ignominy of him thirsted for its like. He could
grind her beauty under his heel, but he could not soften
to this feminine inscrutableness.

And whatever was the truth of Ellen Jorth in this moment, beyond Colter's gloomy and stunted intelligence,
beyond even the love of Jean Isbel, it was something that
held the balance of mastery. She read Colter's mind. She
dropped the torn blouse from her hand and stood there,

unashamed, with the wave of her white breast pulsing, eyes black as night and full of hell, her face white, tragic, terrible, yet strangely lovely.

"Take me away," she whispered, stretching one white arm toward him, then the other.

Colter, even as she moved, had leaped with inarticulate cry and radiant face to meet her embrace. But it seemed, just as her left arm flashed up toward his neck, that he saw her bloody hand and wrist. Strange how that checked his ardor—threw up his lean head like that of a striking bird of prey.

"Blood! What the hell!" he ejaculated, and in one sweep he grasped her. "How'd y'u do that? Are y'u cut? . . . Hold still."

Ellen could not release her hand.

"I scratched myself," she said.

"Where? . . . All that blood!" And suddenly he flung her hand back with fierce gesture, and the gleams of his yellow eyes were like the points of leaping flames. They pierced her—read the secret falsity of her. Slowly he stepped backward, guardedly his hand moved to his gun, and his glance circled and swept the interior of the cabin. As if he had the nose of a hound and sight to follow scent, his eyes bent to the dust of the ground before the door. He quivered, grew rigid as stone, and then moved his head with exceeding slowness as if searching through a microscope in the dust—farther to the left—to the foot of the ladder—and up one step—another—a third—all the way up to the loft. Then he whipped out his gun and wheeled to face the girl.

"Ellen, y'u've got your half-breed heah!" he said, with a terrible smile.

She neither moved nor spoke. There was a suggestion of collapse, but it was only a change where the alluring softness of her hardened into a strange, rapt glow. And in it seemed the same mastery that had characterized her former aspect. Herein the treachery of her was revealed. She had known what she meant to do in any case.

Colter, standing at the door, reached a long arm toward the ladder, where he laid his hand on a rung. Taking it away he held it palm outward for her to see the dark splotch of blood.

"See?"

"Yes, I see," she said, ringingly.

Passion wrenched him, transformed him. "All that—aboot leavin' heah—with me—aboot givin' in—was a lie!"

"No, Colter. It was the truth. I'll go—yet—now—if y'u'll spare—*him!*" She whispered the last word and made a slight movement of her hand toward the loft.

"Girl!" he exploded, incredulously. "Y'u love this half-breed—this *Isbel?* . . . Y'u *love* him!"

"With all my heart! . . . Thank God! It has been my glory. . . . It might have been my salvation. . . . But now I'll go to hell with y'u—if y'u'll spare him."

"Damn my soul!" rasped out the rustler, as if something of respect was wrung from that sordid deep of him. "Y'u—y'u woman! . . . Jorth will turn over in his grave. He'd rise out of his grave if this Isbel got y'u,"

"Hurry! Hurry!" implored Ellen. "Springer may come back. I think I heard a call."

"Wal, Ellen Jorth, I'll not spare Isbel—nor y'u," he returned, with dark and meaning leer, as he turned to ascend the ladder.

Jean Isbel, too, had reached the climax of his suspense. Gathering all his muscles in a knot he prepared to leap upon Colter as he mounted the ladder. But Ellen Jorth screamed piercingly and snatched her rifle from its resting place and, cocking it, she held it forward and low.

"Colter!"

Her scream and his uttered name stiffened him.

"Y'u will spare Jean Isbel!" she rang out. "Drop that gun—drop it!"

"Shore, Ellen. . . . Easy now. Remember your temper. . . . I'll let Isbel off," he panted, huskily, and all his body sank quiveringly to a crouch.

"Drop your gun! Don't turn round. . . . Colter!—*I'll kill y'u!*"

But even then he failed to divine the meaning and the spirit of her.

"Aw, now, Ellen," he entreated, in louder, huskier tones, and as if dragged by fatal doubt of her still, he began to turn.

Crash! The rifle emptied its contents in Colter's breast. All his body sprang up. He dropped the gun. Both hands fluttered toward her. And an awful surprise flashed over his face.

"So—help—me—God!" he whispered, with blood thick in his voice. Then darkly, as one groping, he reached for her with shaking hands. "Y'u—y'u white-throated hussy! . . . I'll . . ."

He grasped the quivering rifle barrel. Crash! She shot him again. As he swayed over her and fell she had to leap aside, and his clutching hand tore the rifle from her grasp. Then in convulsion he writhed, to heave on his back, and stretch out—a ghastly spectacle. Ellen backed away from it, her white arms wide, a slow horror blotting out the passion of her face.

Then from without came a shrill call and the sound of rapid footsteps. Ellen leaned against the wall, staring still at Colter. "Hey, Jim—what's the shootin'?" called Springer, breathlessly.

As his form darkened the doorway Jean once again gathered all his muscular force for a tremendous spring.

Springer saw the girl first and he appeared thunder-struck. His jaw dropped. He needed not the white gleam of her person to transfix him. Her eyes did that and they were riveted in unutterable horror upon something on the ground. Thus instinctively directed, Springer espied Colter.

"Y'u—y'u shot him!" he shrieked. "What for—y'u hussy? . . . Ellen Jorth, if y'u've killed him, I'll . . ."

He strode toward where Colter lay.

Then Jean, rising silently, took a step and like a tiger he launched himself into the air, down upon the rustler. Even as he leaped Springer gave a quick, upward look. And he cried out. Jean's moccasined feet struck him squarely and sent him staggering into the wall, where his head hit hard. Jean fell, but bounded up as the half-stunned Springer drew his gun. Then Jean lunged forward with a single sweep of his arm—and looked no more.

Ellen ran swaying out of the door, and, once clear of the threshold, she tottered out on the grass, to sink to her knees. The bright, golden sunlight gleamed upon her white shoulders and arms. Jean had one foot out of the door when he saw her and he whirled back to get her blouse. But Springer had fallen upon it. Snatching up a blanket, Jean ran out.

"Ellen! Ellen! Ellen!" he cried. "It's over!" And reaching her, he tried to wrap her in the blanket.

She wildly clutched his knees. Jean was conscious only of her white, agonized face and the dark eyes with their look of terrible strain.

"Did y'u—did y'u . . ." she whispered.

"Yes—it's over," he said, gravely. "Ellen, the Isbel-Jorth feud is ended."

"Oh, thank—God!" she cried, in breaking voice. "Jean—y'u are wounded . . . the blood on the step!"

"My arm. See. It's not bad. . . . Ellen, let me wrap this

round you." Folding the blanket around her shoulders, he
held it there and entreated her to get up. But she only clung
the closer. She hid her face on his knees. Long shudders
rippled over her, shaking the blanket, shaking Jean's
hands. Distraught, he did not know what to do. And
his own heart was bursting.

"Ellen, you must not kneel—there—that way," he implored.

"Jean! Jean!" she moaned, and clung the tighter.

He tried to lift her up, but she was a dead weight, and
with that hold on him seemed anchored at his feet.

"I killed Colter," she gasped. "I *had* to—kill him! . . .
I offered—to fling myself away. . . ."

"For me!" he cried, poignantly. "Oh, Ellen! Ellen!
the world has come to an end! . . . Hush! don't keep sayin' that. Of course you killed him. You saved my life.
For I'd never have let you go off with him. . . . Yes,
you killed him. . . . You're a Jorth an' I'm an Isbel . . .
We've blood on our hands—both of us—I for you an'
you for me!"

His voice of entreaty and sadness strengthened her and
she raised her white face, loosening her clasp to lean back
and look up. Tragic, sweet, despairing, the loveliness of
her—the significance of her there on her knees—thrilled
him to his soul.

"Blood on my hands!" she whispered. "Yes. It was
awful—killing him. . . . But—all I care for in this world
is for your forgiveness—and your faith that saved my
soul!"

"Child, there's nothin' to forgive," he responded.
"Nothin' . . . Please, Ellen . . ."

"I lied to y'u!" she cried. "I lied to y'u!"

"Ellen, listen—darlin'." And the tender epithet brought
her head and arms back close-pressed to him. "I know—
now," he faltered on. "I found out to-day what I believed.

An' I swear to God—by the memory of my dead mother—down in my heart I never, never, never believed what they—what y'u tried to make me believe. *Never!*"

"Jean—I love y'u—love y'u—love y'u!" she breathed with exquisite, passionate sweetness. Her dark eyes burned up into his.

"Ellen, I can't lift you up," he said, in trembling eagerness, signifying his crippled arm. "But I can kneel with you! . . ."

Forge

Award-winning authors
Compelling stories

. . . .

Please join us at the website
below for more information
about this author and other great
Forge selections, and to sign up for
our monthly newsletter!

. . . . FORGE www.tor-forge.com . . . .